A SEARED SKY

An adult epic fantasy trilogy

Book 2

PARTINGS

by

STUART AKEN

First Published 2014 by Fantastic Books Publishing

Cover design by Heather Murphy

ISBN: 978-1-909163-48-5

DEDICATION

This trilogy is dedicated to Kenneth Burden, who died before I was born: the father I never knew.

Book two is dedicated to my talented and wonderful daughter, Kate Elizabeth Allison.

ACKNOWLEDGEMENTS

Books are never the work of the author alone. Fantasy trilogies make special demands on their creators. Although I wrote this book, without the help of the following people, it would never have achieved publication.

I give a great 'thank you' to Dan Grubb and his editorial team locked in his cellars. In spite of their imprisonment, they made the final edit of this book, removing those errors that elude even the most careful author.

Many thanks to cover designer, Heather Murphy, for her imaginative and stylish evocation of the book.

My thanks to Hornsea Writers, a supportive group of professional authors who provided constant encouragement, contributed ideas and acted as beta readers for parts of the text.

I could attempt to list all authors who've influenced me during my life, but I've read and absorbed so much wonder and creativity during those centuries, that I'd be bound to forget someone. I'll simply thank all the authors I've read and enjoyed.

Finally, and most importantly, I thank Valerie, my wonderful wife, for her constant support with food and other domestic necessities. But, much more than this, she employed her excellent memory, sound grounding in English language, and ability to spot clichés, inconsistencies, repetitions, and anachronisms at seven leagues to coax me into vital changes. She made the antepenultimate edit, before I read aloud the printed text. I then felt confident enough to rip the MS from my computer and send it to the publishers. For her attention to detail and her dedication in reading this tome, I thank her most warmly.

CONTENTS

Chapter 1

A DIFFERENCE OF OPINION

*C*halamamnon hid in darkness as Aklon-Dji entered its streets. Slipping from shadow to shadow, he considered Ivdulon's description of the illuminated night streets of Litkala and thanked fate that his own island had yet to discover such sophistication. Darkness allowed him to steal a bed cover draped over a line to dry. Without a sound, his knife reduced it to strips, which he tucked into his belt in readiness.

He approached his father's house with caution but Aklon-Dji's prolonged absence had lulled the authorities into a false sense of security. No one stood guard. Candles burning within showed the stand-in High Priest abusing a woman, in Jodisa-Li's bedroom, and a couple of female house slaves, arguing in the kitchen.

He hated harming victims of injustice. His first task, therefore, was to disable the slaves without injuring them. Both were young women; the priest's predilection for readily available female flesh governing his choice. Through gaps in the woven window blinds, he could see them, clearing up after the evening meal. The aroma of food wafted through and Aklon smiled grimly as the tang of scorching indicated the slaves had been selected for appearance and lubricity rather than their culinary skills. Idling and disorganised, they squabbled over who should do which job, making little progress. The blonde girl flounced, pouting as she lost the tussle and was left to clean one of the cooking pots. The dark girl opted to dispose of the waste.

Aklon waited by the door and put a hand over her mouth as she stepped outside. He pushed the door shut behind her and swiftly forced her to the ground on her front. 'Make a sound and I'll slit your throat.'

She stopped struggling at once. He gagged her with a band of linen from his belt. A second band secured her wrists behind her back. A third tied her ankles together. He whispered to her to be quiet and still, threatening swift death if she disobeyed, and left her on the ground as he picked up the waste bucket and returned to the kitchen.

The blonde girl, back to the door, concentrated on trying to shift a sticky black mess from the cooking pot. Aklon was behind her in three silent strides and gagged her with his hand. 'One sound and you're dead.'

She went limp and waited, terrified by the tone of his voice. Once he'd tied and gagged her, he placed her face down on the floor, extinguished the candle, and carried her companion in from outside. Placing them back to back, on their sides, he used touch to tie the two girls together at their wrists, inadvertently stroking smooth skin and apologising for the unintended intimacy. Finally, he tied their ankles together, so they

1

couldn't shuffle across the floor.

'Sorry, girls. I do this for your own good, so you remain free of suspicion. I suggest you lie still and await my return and explanation. I will not harm you.'

He left them and moved silently along the narrow corridor to Jodisa-Li's room, extinguishing candles on the way, so that his actions were less likely to be seen from outside. He could hear Wesdan taking perfunctory pleasure with the free woman he'd taken as consort. The priest had her draped uncomfortably over a chair and was mechanically thrusting from behind. Aklon dragged him out of her and struck him hard in the face with his elbow.

'Stay quiet, Diryss, and I will not hurt you.'

The strip of cloth ready in his hand, he tied swiftly and tightly around the man's mouth before pushing him to the floor. A swift kick to the head disabled the priest for long enough. The woman, surprised by his sudden intervention, simply stared with her mouth open.

Quickly, he gagged and bound her. By the time he'd finished, the priest was regaining consciousness. He pulled him sharply to his feet with a hand in his hair.

'Before I kill you, Kaz-Ca-Wesdan, I want you to be aware that I am Aklon-Dji. I know enough about your evil practices to be certain that Ytraa will not have you in the Garden of Delights. You will spend eternity, according to your own beliefs, in the maws and bowels of Mhortag.' He wasted no further time but drew his long knife and plunged it through the man's chest, killing him instantly.

The deed complete, he took the lighted candle and led Diryss to the kitchen to sit her with the slaves as he set about making the women as comfortable as he could whilst keeping them secure.

'They will question you, Diryss, but they will neither torture nor hurt you, as long as you tell them exactly what happened. And I do mean exactly; including the humiliating way I found you with the priest. Then you can go back home to Morstahn. Yes, I know where you are from. I know many things.'

He released the slaves at their ankles and removed the tie that bound them at their wrists. 'The priest is dead. When they find him, they will be rather upset. They will probably accuse you of murder. I do not want you to suffer for what I have done, which is why I offer you a choice. Understand that you must make your choice now and there is no going back once you have decided. I stay alive by being ruthless but fair.'

The terrified women merely looked at him and waited.

'Diryss, as High Priest's consort, you have some standing, and I suggest I leave you bound and gagged so that no blame can attach to you. You two young slaves, however, are not so fortunate. I do not expect you will be killed. But the Holy Ones who interrogate you will not be gentle. They will undoubtedly rape, beat and torture you. Again, I will leave you bound and gagged, if you wish. But, as slaves, you fall for suspicion regardless of your innocence. What I offer you is this: either stay here, as I have described, and face the possible consequences, or come with me. I will lead you on a dangerous and difficult journey to a place where you will be free. However, the sanctuary is not a place of luxury but a hard place to live. I am sorry to offer you this most unpleasant set of alternatives but I feel you ought to know exactly what you face. Choose now.'

The dark girl nodded and he removed her gag, after warning her to make no noise.

'I'll risk it with you, Aklon-Dji, Paltrohn. I'm sick of bein' a slave.'

'You are absolutely positive? I shall kill you if you endanger me on the journey.'

'I'll take that risk, rather than stay a slave for the rest for my life, Paltrohn.'

'Good girl.' He turned to the blonde. 'And you?'

Released from her gag, she trembled and looked at the girl she'd served with in the house. 'I...I'm scared. I think I'll take my chances here with Paltra, Diryss.'

'So be it.' He turned to the dark girl, released her bindings and helped her to her feet. 'What is your name?'

'Cymlihter, Paltrohn.'

'I am always Aklon and never Paltrohn. And you are now a free woman. Find something to wear, not Diryss's, mind. You may find a tabard left behind by my sister and you are welcome to it, as she is unlikely to return. When you are dressed, collect food for us. I will deal with these two and string up the body. Be quick and be silent, Cymlihter.

'I must tie you securely and gag you again, young lady. I am sure Diryss will explain you were left with no choice and that, like her, you were innocent of the killing.'

Diryss nodded; fear still bright in her eyes.

'Now, I have tied you together in relative comfort but you will be unable to escape. I am sorry; you must remain gagged. It is most important that you tell them the absolute truth. That means you must explain about your squabbling over who did what tonight, young lady and why Cymlihter went out with the rubbish. It is really important that you hide none of the truth. If you try to make things sound better than they really were you will both suffer. They will question you separately and compare your stories. It is essential for your mutual wellbeing that you both tell the truth. Do you understand?'

They nodded; eyes wide with fear and uncertainty.

Cymlihter returned, dressed in one of Jodisa-Li's slightly less revealing tabards, and collected food whilst he dealt with the priest's body. He returned to discover the freed slave waiting, a bag ready on the table.

'In the morning, they will find you. I shall leave the window shutters open, so you can be seen from the street. I have hung the priest's body upside down from the rafters, so he can also be seen from outside. I do not expect you to be left like this for long. But at least they cannot sensibly accuse you of helping or having anything to do with his murder. Now. We must be away to Krohtl. Mhortag's balls! Do not tell them, will you?'

He checked their bindings once more to make sure they were secure but not too tight, and blew out the candle. 'So sorry you had to be involved.'

Moments later, he was on his way toward The Point with Cymlihter in tow; food and goods stuffed in his pack and weapons on his belt.

'You're very trusting, Aklon-Dji.'

'Silence; until we are out of town, Cymlihter.'

They travelled quietly, the girl quickly mimicking his way of moving and keeping up with him as he wound his way through sleeping streets and out to open countryside.

'Trusting, Cymlihter?'

'I might've run off after you freed me; gone to warn the authorities that the Prime Renegade was at the High Priest's house.'

'You might. If so, I would have killed you before you had gone ten paces, and then escaped without finishing my task. I have excellent hearing and know the house well enough to detect exactly where everybody is.'

'Still, it's a risk, isn't it?'

'My whole existence is risk, Cymlihter. But necessity has made me a reasonable judge of character. I was sure I could trust you, as soon as you asked to be freed.'

'I suppose you'll want to join with me now.'

'Not now, pretty one. I think we should get well away first, do you agree?'

'Silly. I didn't mean right now! Oh, Aklon-Dji, you are funny.'

'I look forward to discovering the pleasures of your unfettered self when we are in a safe place and at the time you wish to share, if you ever do. Remember, you are free now. You no longer have to do anything you have no wish to. Come; shall we concentrate on our escape? We have a good way to travel before it grows light.'

'Unfettered. Am I really, really free?'

'As the untamed birds.'

'You're wonderful. Thank you. I never believed you could be as bad as they say you are, you know.'

'Oh, save your thanks for when I deliver you to my friends. You may not be so grateful when I leave you in the only place of safety I know. But enough.'

'I thought you said we were going to Krohtl, Paltrohn... sorry, Aklon-Dji?'

'Aklon. Ah. A little none-too-subtle subterfuge. When they get it out of the captives, overcoming the little difficulty their gratitude and mingled fear will cause, the authorities will be tempted to seek us in that direction.'

4

'You're ever so clever, Aklon. Not at all the demon they make you out to be.'

'You do not know me well enough, Cymlihter. Time may disclose a real fiend.'

'I think you're kind, gentle and wonderful, so there!'

'There goes my reputation again.'

'But you talk ever so nice, don't you?'

'I treat language as the precious device it is, that is all.'

They travelled quickly through the dark hours and, by dawn, were in the hills leading to the Scar, at the south-western end of the island. When Cymlihter saw the place they were to descend, she trembled with fear. 'This is the Death Drop.'

'Only when Holy Ones use it. With me, you are perfectly safe, if you do as I say.'

He took a fine rope from his pack and looped it under her arms, took her to the edge of the sheer cliff and explained how to help him lower her in safety. She was white with fear but followed his instructions and, before the sun was fully up, they were both at the base of the Scar, resting and eating in preparation for the last leg of their escape to the settlement.

'You had best remove that now, Cymlihter. No one wears clothes on The Point and you will be less welcome if….'

'Oh yes, I'm sure. It's all right; I don't mind taking it off if you want to join with me. I'd like to, in fact.'

'It is well that you use your mind, Cymlihter, but I was simply speaking the truth. As you will see when we arrive.'

'You're still clothed.'

'I do not live here. I am a visitor; you are about to become a resident. And any woman who claims more status than the leader here had better beware. The One is not a force to challenge lightly. Though Chellyth might accept your tabard as a gift.'

Two days of early starts and long easy marches, with nights spent in song, dance and tale-telling, saw the party of travelling pilgrims approach the eastern fringe of the Greenreald towards evening. The city of Litkala was now far behind them. They decided to spend that night sheltered by trees before venturing onto the more open landscape of the plains.

Aglydron took advantage of a quiet spell to speak to their guide, Sondukal. 'How long will you stay with us?'

'Feldrark says I've to stay till you don't need me no more.'

'Are you being paid, your family bein' looked after while you're away?'

'Feldrark'll see them right. The Wharhll's a great man.'

'How well d'you know the route we're taking?'

'Better'n most. Been as far as Lake Mhistahn, in the north, wi' Feldrark.'

Satisfied, he sat back against the tree, as Sondukal checked the horse was content and well. Aglydron watched Okkyntalah in conversation with the girls. They were too far away to hear but the young man was amusing them with some tale that had them both laughing. Closer, Myllthlan, the amazing healer who'd rescued them so long ago on the small island, tended to herbs and roots she'd picked up as they walked through the lush vegetation of the forest. She was sorting them; tying some into small bunches to hang from the panniers and dry in the sun. He considered her and found his attraction to her physical qualities enhanced by her natural grace and quiet, unassuming manner. He knew she was devoted to him for giving her a name and an identity, after she'd helped them escape fire and death, knew she'd risk her life for him if necessary.

She turned suddenly, as if aware of his eyes on her, and smiled back. He nodded at her and she approached to sit beside him so he could feel the warmth of her skin, smell the woman in her. They said nothing, content simply to be together.

Aglydron was pleased she found as much pleasure in their coupling as she gave, and made their joining more than simply the act of worship that was required. He found, as so often these days, a picture of another lover in his mind and, as always, tried to dismiss it.

Through his meanderings, seemingly unbidden, there came the image of Shoarhn and he felt sudden guilt for his neglect, his lack of thought about his wife, so far away now on his home island of Muhnilahm. She'd never displayed the delight that Myllthlan showed so openly. Was it his fault? Had he failed to give her time and the attention she needed to build real pleasure during an act he'd always made primarily one of worship? From Chislanda, Myllthlan and that mysterious erotic woman who'd visited him in the city, he'd learned a great deal about giving as much pleasure as he received. Why hadn't that wanton returned, as she'd promised, once he'd agreed with the dubious choice of Linlyss as Virgin Gift?

He looked across at the three youngsters, still laughing and indulging now in horseplay amongst and around the trees. Why had Linlyss agreed to be substitute for Jodisa? She'd made it plain she wanted Okkyntalah to take her virginity, yet she'd agreed to come with them on this journey in the certain knowledge he'd never penetrate her.

'Dorltah for them, Aglydron?'

He smiled at Myllthlan. 'Women. Never understand them.'

'The mistake is in trying. Women, Aglydron, are for accepting, not understanding.' She laughed at her own silliness and glanced across at the object of his speculation. 'My guess is she either expects he'll give in and let her have her way or hopes something will happen to make the journey pointless.'

'That's a forlorn 'ope, either way, from my point of view.'

6

'But not hers. I truly can't see any other reason why she'd come. By being with us, she has the object of her desire close and constantly in view. Come the chance, she'll take it, I'm sure.'

'Not if I've a say in the matter.'

'What of Okkyntalah? Do you think he'll be tempted?'

'Oh, he's got Stellanyl so he's no need of Linlyss. And he wants Tumalind back. That'll stop 'im prodding the virgin's fern, no matter how hot and willin' she is.'

'How do you feel about him frowking so openly and willingly with these others when he's your daughter's betrothed?'

'He's a young man, with a young'un's appetites. Ytraa, as you're learning, says we must join when and as we can. He's doin' the will of Ytraa, that's all. Tumalind, as a Virgin Gift, isn't available and may never be his but these others are, and all too willing. What else would he do? He's not about to refuse such pleasures, is he?'

'And you? What about your wife, waiting patiently at home for you?'

'I was thinking about her when you came over. I'm fond of her, of course. But I've been a poor lover. Too worried about doing right by Ytraa. That's what she always said. But you've taught me joinin' can be more'n worship; we can share joy and pleasure without lessenin' the celebration of Ytraa's gift. I've been so full o' the letter of the law, Myllthlan, that I've forgot its spirit. When I go back to Shoarhn, I hope she'll find me a better lover than she lost.'

'Will she be with other men whilst you're away?'

'I hope so, for her sake and Ytraa's. She's a very attractive woman still, though she's borne four children. And we're faithful to one only at need, y'know. At celebrations or during forced separation, it's common for married couples to indulge in joining elsewhere.'

'So, there's no difference for men or women?'

'Ylcrat was different. You were a toy, Myllthlan, maybe even a slave to the men.'

'Slave.'

'Exactly. Your pleasure didn't matter. You had to do what they wanted but you weren't free to do as you wished. We hold men and women, as equal parts of the beings Ytraa created, of equal value with equal dues.'

'And if I decided to try Sondukal tonight in your place?'

'I'd be disappointed. But it's your body and you must share it as you will.'

'You don't feel any claim on me, because you saved me and gave me a name and identity?'

'I gave you nothing you didn't already 'ave, Myllthlan. You left a way of life on Ylcrat but brought yourself with you. If anything, you saved my life and I should be beholden to

7

you.'

'You're very honest, Aglydron.'

'Followers believe in truth.'

'I was only curious, anyway. Sondukal's made it plain he wants none of our pleasures and will wait for his return to the city and his wife before he makes love again, as he puts it.'

'You asked 'im?'

'He gathered us together and warned us not to try! Says he'll square his debt to Ytraa when he returns to his wife.'

Aglydron laughed. 'An unusual man, then.'

'In his way. But no more than you, or Okkyntalah, or Feldrark. You each have your peculiarities and odd ways. I like that; it makes life more interesting. But it does show how different are the Followers in Litkala from those on your island.'

A sudden scream of real terror came from Stellanyl. Sondukal was running toward her before Aglydron got to his feet. The girl continued to scream, though the volume and intensity reduced. Okkyntalah tried to discover the reason for her fear but she was incoherent, merely pointing to a space in the vegetation near her legs.

'What's up?'

She continued to cry out, apparently oblivious of Sondukal's question. He followed her pointing finger and laughed raucously as he bent and plucked a very large black and yellow spider from beneath a broad-leafed wood athlott. It struggled to free itself from his fingers but he was unconcerned and held it for them to examine.

'Nowt to be scared of. 'Armless. Lives on yellowflies. You'll 'ave to get used to such things, lass. There'll be worse afore we're through wi' this trip.' He tousled her hair with his free hand and tossed the spider lightly into the trees at the edge of the clearing.

Okkyntalah embraced the girl and held her close until she stopped trembling.

'Get some supper on, eh? Give you summat to teck your mind off it, lass.' Sondukal nodded at the campfire.

Linlyss and Okkyntalah brought more wood, and Stellanyl, settling down after Okkyntalah's attentions, began to prepare food for their evening meal.

Aglydron, with nothing to do, called Shaulah over and took the hunting dog with him for a short stroll away from the company, curious to discover the reason for an odd feature he'd noticed on the road ahead. He walked two hundred or so paces and found the road took a sudden sweep to the south where it had clearly at one time continued more or less due east. He began to follow the old way, wondering at its complete lack of vegetation in spite of the fact that it was plainly no longer used. Shaulah refused to follow him, hanging back and staring after him into the relative gloom, the whites of her eyes showing. After a few paces, he stopped and turned back for the camp, feeling a growing sense of unease, sensations of threat, fear and revulsion for no discernible reason. He was still glancing over his shoulder as he returned to the campsite.

'Aye, 'appen you'll none of you want to be straying that way.' Sondukal gestured to catch the attention of the rest of the party. 'Just up yonder there's a parting of the road under the trees. Old road goes on east. Don't tread on it less you want to be killed or go mad.'

'Mhortag's Dread?'

'Feldrark told you, then, Okkyntalah? He did right. There's those as don't believe in it but they've never been this way. I've known grown men fall hysterical just walkin' alongside it. An' others go mad after crossing it. Leave the dead alone, I say, an' they'll like as not leave you alone. Onny reason you got away wi' it, Aglydron, is 'cos you just got on the start. Any further and you'd have been in real trouble.'

All stared in the direction Sondukal indicated and, glancing at Aglydron, nodded in agreement.

'Feldrark told us, when we were all captive in that turd hole, Mipahnhil, that he'd stayed into Mhortag's Dread and nearly lost his mind. What happened there? Why is it so haunted?'

Sondukal looked from Okkyntalah to the girls. 'You know the story?'

They both nodded.

'Reckon they'll tell you better'n what I could, young'un.'

'After supper, I think. Don't you?'

'And after prayers!' Aglydron's reminder made them all suddenly aware. The sun was gone from sight and the colour of the sky outlining the gaps in the canopy above suggested it was as near to sundown as they could tell in the trees. They made their prayers, Linlyss, Stellanyl and Sondukal adopting the Litkala posture, upright and facing the setting sun and the other three keeping to the Muhnilahm tradition.

'I think I might start doing it the way they do, Aglydron, if you don't mind. It's more dignified and I'd feel less vulnerable.'

'Up to you, Myllthlan. I understand. Whether Ytraa will, I don't know. The easy way's not always best, I believe.'

'You're right, of course. I'll stick to what you taught me.'

Aglydron touched her shoulder in a gesture of gratitude and affection.

'Aye, appen that were just one o' the reasons for yon.' Sondukal nodded at Mhortag's Dread. 'Mebbie a bit o' common sense and less stiff necks might've stopped it.'

Aglydron wondered at this but the food was ready and they ate at once.

Flames flickered round the larger logs and resin sizzled, flaring blue, green and gold amongst the red and orange of the fire. They sat around, full and satisfied after their evening meal.

'That were right good, lass. Thank you.'

Stellanyl nodded her acknowledgement and the others murmured their appreciation. The horse grazed just within the circle of light and Shaulah lay with her head in Okkyntalah's lap, dozing after the day's walk.

'So. Which of you young ladies will tell us the tale?'

Linlyss took up her lyre and strummed a few bars to check it was in tune before she began a soft, slow melody, which she clearly intended as background to the words she expected Stellanyl to say.

'You all know the Epic of Gadhallah, of course?'

All nodded except Myllthlan. 'I know only parts, but don't worry. I'm still learning.'

'So, you know about the first Great Division at Kah-Labaz?'

'What we call the Lake of the Lost, yes.'

'Yes, Aglydron, Lake Mhistahn that lies under Mount O'bo, the mountain of smoke and fire.'

'Oh! Like Krakgragog? There's another who breathes fire?'

Sondukal smiled at the healer. 'Yes. But it's not a 'who', Myllthlan, it's just a mountain as breathes fire. Some say it's dragons, but Ivdulon holds that the whole world's full o' fire under the rocks an' such an' that it 'as to come out somewhere. Mount O'bo's one of them places. I go with the wise woman; Ivdulon knows everything.'

'I used to think Yatukon knew everything, Sondukal.'

'Who's this Yatukon, then?'

'He was...on Ylcrat, where I was born, he was a magical...'

'Yatukon's just a clever charlatan.'

Myllthlan frowned at Okkyntalah.

'I've met Ivdulon and she's the wisest and most knowledgeable person I've ever seen, Myllthlan. Believe me, Yatukon might be a clever man, maybe even a magician, but he's not a patch on Ivdulon when it comes to knowledge and figuring things out.'

'Ay, 'appen there's a woman wi' knowledge from the Gods themselves.'

There was a brief pause, full of unasked questions that Aglydron didn't want raised just then. 'Shall we let Stellanyl tell her tale?'

Silent nods and murmurs of agreement let her go on.

'After that time, when the true Followers travelled on, they reached Shorrannon on the Sure. The city, even then, was a wonder and seduced some Followers to stay. It was here that Gadhallah was tempted by Mhortag and lost his way....'

'What are you saying, Stellanyl? Are you accusing Gadhallah of...?'

'The lass is tellin' the tale, Aglydron. 'Appen she ought to do it wi'out you chewin' 'er 'ead off. She's onny tellin' it the way it's allus told in Litkala.'

'I'll not listen to blasphemy!'

'Then lass'd best not say no more. From what I've 'ad from Feldrark, there's a deal we don't agree on wi' you lot from Muhnilahm.'

Chapter 2

REVELATIONS AND THREATS

'I'd like to hear it, Stellanyl.'

'You would! Your head's so full o' fern you've lost sight of Ytraa and the truth.'

Okkyntalah turned deliberately to Aglydron, the young man's anger held barely in check, making him flinch. 'I heard and saw what Ivdulon had to teach us. There was truth in that. I've seen at first hand the falsehood given out by our own High Priest, Dagla Kaz, and the Holy Ones about the people of The Point. I've seen that Ylcrat, corrupt and vile though it may be, isn't the home of cannibals, as we were warned. I've met the people of Litkala and found nothing but good, honesty and tolerance, in spite of the foul lies we were told. I've heard and seen new things all through this journey, Aglydron, and I'm now certain that what we've been taught isn't the truth. I'd rather make judgements on facts than on the word of those who may have their own reasons for keeping us misinformed.'

His reasoned and mature assessment startled Aglydron. 'Quite a speech for a lad of eighteen cycles.'

'I've not seen anything yet that makes me feel age brings wisdom or makes judgement more reliable. But I've seen experience makes for better understanding of the world, especially if we have the humility to understand its lessons.'

'You're suddenly very wise, Okkyntalah.'

'Tired of being thought young and foolish. I've gone through more in these last sixdays than most folk on our island see in a lifetime. Is it any wonder I've changed?'

'You think I'm stuck in my ways, don't you?'

'Aren't you?'

He could see truth in what the boy said but it was hard to admit he might've been wrong all his life. 'I've been around longer, that's all. I'll hold my tongue and hear the tale and see what I think in my own time. Sorry for my outburst, Stellanyl; it's because I'm uncertain and maybe even afraid. Tell your story and ignore my huffing and puffing.'

Myllthlan leant across and kissed him. 'That's brave and honest, Aglydron.'

Stellanyl looked around the circle and all nodded.

'As I was saying, Gadhallah was tempted by Mhortag. No one knows what that vile being said, though it's believed the great liar told him the road to the One True Home would be easier and shorter if he followed his advice. No one knew, not even Gadhallah, at this time, exactly where it might lie. In fact, the land Ytraa promised to the Followers was unknown back then. Mhortag made Gadhallah believe he should travel down the Sure and out to sea but others were positive they should turn west, across the plain, where a faint road seemed to make a way across the grassy plain. A great dispute divided the Followers but those who wished to go west prevailed and so they went that way.'

Aglydron grunted.

'For many days and nights they travelled, stopping each day after only a few leagues as the animals and carts made progress in a long file along the old roadway. But, at last, they came to the borders of the forest we call the Greenreald. The road continued through the trees, becoming more plainly a way where there should be none, for all who knew that land said the forest was impenetrable and that nothing lay beyond it but sea. But true Followers knew the road to be a sign.'

Aglydron huffed but waved her on.

'Gadhallah was persuaded by Mhortag that all would perish if they went into the trees. And some thought the road, so clear and straight, must be an evil thing. A great dispute began on that day and the people argued amongst themselves about many things they'd done in acceptance of Gadhallah's rules and laws. Then it was that some said the prayer positions were the fruits of men and women with twisted minds and those who disagreed with what Gadhallah said began to stand for prayer, even as true Followers stand today.'

Aglydron was minded to comment but made do with snorting and grinding his teeth. He nodded at her to continue.

'Many of those who took the standing position, also believed the punishments for disobedience were harsh and cruel. These people came together and made their own rules and devised their own punishments under the guidance of a man called Wharhll. This group of true Followers discarded many things and the gap between them and those who followed Gadhallah grew wide. Small acts of violence broke out, and then some were stoned and others burned by Gadhallah's militia. One day Wharhll declared his intention to lead his own Followers along the road through the forest.'

'Fool!' Aglydron signalled that his growl hadn't been meant for their ears and nodded for her to continue. He clenched his fists in rage. It was hard, listening to such insults, but he'd said he would hear the tale, and hear it he would.

'Then... then it was that fighting broke out amongst the two factions. Even families had disputes within them. Son fought father, daughter attacked mother, sister struggled against brother. And then Mhortag came amongst them and caused them to perform the Unforgivable Acts. As the last of Wharhll's Followers moved along the road under the trees, so did those who followed Gadhallah come after them and do unspeakable things. Son raped and despoiled mother, sister robbed brother of manhood, father raped and murdered son, mother tore the living heart from daughter. Such was the brutality that happened on that evening as the sun went down that none dare return to the place when all was done.

'By morning the remaining Followers of Wharhll had departed through the trees. Many sixdays later, a party set out to bury the dead at last. They found no bodies on the road, only the dry and broken bones of those who'd been murdered and tortured. But the space held the ghosts and spirits of the dead. So fearful and terrible was the place that the party could go no further and fled, leaving the bones undisturbed and unburied. They made a short new way through the trees and, when they reached the plain to re-join the old road, they found all trace of Gadhallah and his Followers gone.

'Since then, that part of the old road has been called Mhortag's Dread and no man or woman may walk it unscathed. No animal or bird will cross the track and nothing grows there. Those who've been within its borders, and returned with some part of their mind intact, tell of fearful acts, cries of pain and terror, blood and gore and vile betrayal and corruption. They say spirits haunt the place, forever locked in what they did as they killed or were killed and that they know they'll find no peace and must remain that way forever. And it's said that any who go there and don't escape will become as one of them and spend eternity in anguish, pain and suffering beneath the trees.'

Stellanyl looked about, uncertain. Linlyss ceased playing.

'So much for stories told by those from Litkala. I've never heard such lies! I know nothing of any division amongst Followers. Seems to me, you make up your own tales.'

Stellanyl was unabashed. 'What's your lot say, then, Aglydron? How do your priests explain what happened?'

'There's no mention of any division at Shorrannon. But we all know of the split at Kah-Labaz, don't we? Seems to me there's some explanation needed as to why you lot have this tale and we don't.'

'So, what happened at Shorrannon according to your stories?'

'I'll tell you, Stellanyl. Some Followers stayed, of course. But most went down river till they reached the sea. It was then Ytraa told Gadhallah and his heir, Sonclusipah, where the One True Home was. That's how they knew they must cross to the island.

'The Chronicler tells us they stayed on the shore of Rophan-Ra for many years, preparing, and then sailed the Shylnah Sea. They learned of the evil ways of those on the Island of Fire and knew they'd be devoured by the cannibals if they landed there. So the Followers kept to the open sea. They found many small islands but Gadhallah wouldn't land at any except to take on fresh water and food. None were populated but all were too small for the Followers to make their home. At last, Gadhallah sent Yldohn and Zerryth, his deputies, ahead and they discovered Muhnilahm and returned to guide the rest to the

15

One True Home.'

"Cept everyone knows Litkala's the One True 'ome, o' course.'

Aglydron refused to rise to Sondukal's assertion. 'Gadhallah landed first and declared it the One True Home for Followers. He set off, alone, unarmed and naked, as Ytraa decreed, to discover where the Godwood must be carved and set up. He returned after two Moontimes and took Sonclusipah, Yldohn, Zerryth, the Godwood and some Holy Ones to the site he'd found. There, as the chisels made the first cuts, to form the Godwood into the likeness of Ytraa, Gadhallah breathed his last, being a hundred and fifty-seven summers. They put him in a small pit on the Plain in sight of Ytraa and there, to this day, all Followers go when they pass from this life to the next.

'Your tale's false, you see, Stellanyl. True Followers went with Gadhallah and found Muhnilahm, the One True Home.'

'Horseshit! Mhortag led Gadhallah from the true road. We don't honour the renegade. Anyone wi' eyes to see must know Litkala's the One True 'ome.' Sondukal's voice surged with anger.

'Only a fool would believe such a story. No one who knows the truth could…'

'The Great Division 'appened, Aglydron of Muhnilahm. It 'appened. That's the proof of our truth. Where's yours?'

'Just because you say it happened, doesn't make it so. Our tales don't mention it. They tell of Kah-Labaz, so why not Litkala? No. Your story has no truth in…'

'It's 'cos your tales meck no mention of the Great Division that they must be false! Any fool can see we're Followers; we know of Gadhallah an' follow Ytraa. If we didn't come by such knowledge from our tales, 'ow did we get to be Followers living in Litkala?'

'It's obvious! Some of… no, no, that won't do. Maybe some who stayed in Shorrannon came to Litkala afterwards. Yes, that must be it! And they made up the story of this so-called Great Division so Gadhallah's name would be ruined and this Wharhll character would be thought a hero.'

'If that were true, what 'appened 'ere to cause Mhortag's Dread?'

'I don't know. Maybe…maybe there's no such thing. Yes, of course, it's just to back up the other lie. There's no such thing as Mhortag's Dread.'

'You was squittin' in the shadows when you come back just now, Aglydron. Why might that've been then, if not for Mhortag's Dread?'

'I don't know! Maybe there's some other… it doesn't matter anyway. I know Gadhallah was the chosen of Ytraa and I know Muhnilahm's the One True Home for Followers and I'll challenge anyone who says otherwise!'

'Ay, an' I know it were Wharhll as led true Followers an' found the One True 'ome in Litkala; that there wondrous city just beyond the trees. An' I'll do anyone as says it's not!'

16

They both rose quickly and went for their weapons; Aglydron's sword drawn and Sondukal's double-headed axe in his hand. They glared at each other, ready to strike.

'Stop!' Myllthlan placed herself between the two of them. 'Stop this madness, unless you want a new Mhortag's Dread right here. I've heard both stories and I'm new to all this thinking. Sit down and I'll tell you what I think happened.'

Aglydron glanced at Myllthlan and then glared back at Sondukal, reluctant to stand down. Okkyntalah grasped the wrist that held the sword. Aglydron shook himself free but the young man persisted.

'This isn't the way, Aglydron. We don't spill the blood of Followers.'

Stellanyl moved to stay Sondukal's hand. He lowered his weapon and Aglydron did the same, though they continued to glower at each other. The tension slowly ebbed to leave a background of unease and mutual suspicion but all sat down again in the circle.

'Will you hear me?'

Aglydron nodded and, as Myllthlan turned, Sondukal grunted agreement.

'This Great Division, and I think it really happened if Mhortag's Dread is anything to go by, was a thing of great shame to those who went with Gadhallah. It's clear Mhortag influenced those involved, trying to cause maximum trouble; trying, in fact, to end the journey itself. No, hear me out, Aglydron, please. It's understandable that Gadhallah's Followers wouldn't want to recall such an event. Though, had they looked at it more closely, they'd have seen that their completion of the journey and their discovery of Muhnilahm showed that they'd eventually defeated Mhortag and therefore were the better for their lapse.'

She held up her hand to silence Aglydron again. 'As for those who followed Wharhll; they'd keep the memory alive, since they saw themselves as victims of treachery. In fact, of course, both groups were probably equally to blame for what happened. If they'd both been more tolerant of each other, they'd never have allowed the fighting and bloodshed.

'Ytraa wanted groups of Followers spread over the world: you told me it was part of the mission we're on, Aglydron, not only to keep ties between Choshinahm and Muhnilahm but to widen the area of worship of Ytraa. What better way to start that than by having groups of Followers in four different locations?'

Sondukal nodded appreciatively at her. 'For a new Follower, lass, you've a right grand grasp on it. I can see your argument an' I'm willin' to leave it at that.'

'Myllthlan might have a point. I don't know. It needs thinking about. But I'll let it go till I've decided.'

'We're on the road together for a long time. Will you two show there's no bad blood between you?' Myllthlan, seated between the two men, pulled back to make space for them to give their assurance.

Aglydron and Sondukal eyed each other suspiciously.

'If not, you might as well go home and admit defeat to Feldrark, Sondukal. I wonder how he'll react? And you, Aglydron, will have to lead us over dangerous and unknown lands without a guide. Are you willing to risk the mission?'

He had to admit she had something. They both nodded and each clenched their fists and pushed them toward each other so their knuckles touched briefly in a gesture of peace. Myllthlan moved back in again, relieved.

'Something light to sleep on, I think, don't you?'

Stellanyl smiled at Okkyntalah's suggestion and raised an eyebrow at Linlyss. As the young man leant over and kissed Myllthlan in a gesture of gratitude, the girls took out their instruments and began a gentle song on the joys of motherhood and childhood and the pride a father found in family. It was a fitting choice and the party went to their sleepsacks in less sombre mood, to prepare themselves for the first stage of their journey through the dangerous open country of the plain. Myllthlan came to Aglydron, intent on showing she remained loyal. But it was late into the night before he found the peace to sleep, and the story he'd heard left him deeply troubled.

They'd walked since sun up, under a cloudless sky, and reached the point where the road crossed a small river on a stout wooden bridge. At the far side, a small area of scrub and low trees promised shelter for the night and they decided to stop even though it was short of sunset.

Sondukal informed them. 'Ain't no more shelter, nor surface water for a couple o' leagues an' we'd not do that afore sun goes down.'

They set up camp beside the river with a small stand of trees and scrub hiding them from the grassy plain ahead. The three women immediately went a short distance downstream to bathe, away from the view from the bridge. Okkyntalah sat with his legs crossed beneath him, watching the clear swift water, no longer muddied by the recent rains but still deeper and faster than normal, and tried fishing. Aglydron took Shaulah for a short examination of the scrub and trees, looking for signs of danger from wild animals or other sources. Sondukal hobbled the horse and built a fire for supper before taking his bow and going in search of game to supplement their diminishing supplies.

Okkyntalah quickly caught two largish red-bellied trout and a smaller flatfish with green upper scales and a pale blue underside; it was a variety he hadn't seen before. He knocked their heads on the wooden boards of the bridge and strung them by their tails from a small branch near the fire. Gutting them took no time at all and he tossed their entrails onto the ground close to the silvery trunk of the tree for Shaulah to eat on her return.

18

Alone, he returned to the river and plunged in, finding the water pleasantly cool and the current not too strong. He swam across and back a few times before gathering sweet-smelling flame iris blooms from a still stretch of water. Crouching in shallow water under the bank, he crushed the petals between two stones from the riverbed and used the juice to wash his hair and skin. On the bank, he used two of the sharp edged leaves, shaped like long spearheads, to scrape water from his skin.

Returning to the camp, to dry himself beside the fire, he noticed a small plume of blue grey smoke rising some distance away, just south of east. It was clearly a campfire. He found this discovery slightly disturbing but reasoned his fears away: it must simply mark the place where some merchants had stopped for the night.

He was still drying himself when Sondukal returned with a pair of conies. The women quickly followed, running back full of laughter and giggles at something one of them had said. They giggled more when they caught him by the fire and didn't turn away as he replaced his tabard. Their hair was wet and they sat by the fire to dry it, helping one another with bone combs to untangle their locks. A bit of friendly rivalry ended with Linlyss doing the same for Okkyntalah, as he sat between her thighs, his back to her. When Aglydron returned a short time later, he reported nothing untoward from his survey.

'What about the fire?'

'Fire?'

Okkyntalah pointed at the faint wavering line in the sky. Aglydron shook his head and Sondukal frowned. None of the others could see it, though Stellanyl claimed she could make out a slight change in the colour of the sky.

'Wouldn't have known it was a fire, though.'

'That's Okkyntalah for you. Eyes that can see what others miss. Beautiful eyes, so full of passion, don't you think?'

'Ay, well, Linlyss, beautiful or no, eyes like that are worth a deal. I'll be askin' you to keep 'em skinned, lad, now we're out in t'open.'

Linlyss's warm praise of Okkyntalah made Aglydron look anxious, but he merely shrugged when Okkyntalah glanced at him.

'I'm going to find a better vantage point. I'd like to see whose fire it is.'

'Not too far, Okkyntalah. I don't want you in no trouble.'

'Nor me, Linlyss.'

He grinned at her concern and left the campsite to make for a low ridge to the east, some thousand or so paces off. Shaulah ran beside him as he covered the ground in long, loping strides, making easy going across rough grass that reached his knees. There was no sign of human life elsewhere but he noted a large herd of the cattle like creatures they'd

19

seen on their earlier trek with Feldrark; mostly black, though some dark brown, with bulky shoulders and short, vicious horns. They were tempting to hunt.

'Very dangerous if cornered.' Feldrark had warned him, as they'd made their escape to the city.

Nevertheless, he thought the meat would reward the effort and it could be worth taking the risk when they ventured further onto the plain.

As he approached the summit of the ridge, he made for cover in some small bushes clustered about an outcrop of red rock to the east. The colour of raw flesh and much cracked, the rock stuck out of the hilltop like some giant weathered thumb tip. Odd marks, carved into the west-facing surface, coloured with some substance pressed into the indents, made him curious. But he could make no sense of them. He crouched low, to avoid being seen and finally went on all fours, keeping Shaulah behind him.

From his vantage point, he peered across the undulating country below. Further to the east and marked by a dark line of tall trees, the Sure ran in its bed, no doubt much less treacherous since the rains had stopped. Seeking the point where smoke met land, he gazed intently. The fire was a bright spark in the growing gloom of early evening, close to the edge of a small open copse of tall trees and less than half a league from the line of the road. He shaded his eyes and concentrated. He made out twelve figures, though gender was uncertain from this distance. No pack animals or carts visible, just people.

They seemed to be doing nothing more threatening than setting up camp along the same lines as the one he'd just left. For a while, he studied them but learnt no more. Something about them troubled him but he could find no reason for his disquiet until he recalled that the only other people on the plain should be Bruxa or, perhaps, a group of merchants. Bruxa were reputed to be small and these folk were normal size. Merchants would have packhorses and wagons but there were none. So, who might they be?

He slipped quietly and cautiously back below the summit of the ridge, wondering at his concern not to be seen, and began his easy trot back; his companions' campfire a ready beacon in the sudden dusk. He paused to pray, strangely at one with Ytraa in the open with no one to distract him. By the time he got back, it was growing dark and the smell of cooking reminded him of his hunger.

'What's the story, lad?'

'I wish you'd call me by my name, Sondukal. It's a party of twelve. Men and women, I'd guess. No packhorses, no carts. And they're too big for Bruxa.'

'How far off, Okkyntalah?' Their guide held his clenched fists out to be touched by Okkyntalah's in recognition of mutual dependence and respect. He grinned as they made contact.

'About a league.'

20

'So much detail at that distance?'

'Should've seen 'im on the way to the city. 'E were telling me 'ow many men was walking the walls afore most of us could even see the walls!'

'Canny gift for 'unter.'

'What do you make of it, Sondukal?'

'Don't want to meck the lasses fret but I can't think of no-one as'd be out on t' plain at this time. No. Can't meck nowt on it.'

Myllthlan looked up from the cony leg she was stripping with her teeth. 'Malarhah told us they'd never stop until they'd killed us all.'

Aglydron glanced sharply at her but then relented. 'Perhaps.'

'What's this, then?'

'Did you hear of our escape from Mipahnhil, Sondukal?'

'I 'eard you killed some o' them 'eathen swine to get free an' killed a few more on the way back. What of it?'

Okkyntalah described how they'd let one of them, a woman called Chislanda, go to warn her people to send no more killers.

'An' now she's back wi' more on 'em to finish off the job by the looks on it.'

'Could be, I suppose. But mightn't it just be a party out hunting, maybe even someone from the other city?'

'Too far out for folk from Shorrannon, Okkyntalah. No one's out from Litkala or I'd a' known. Us guides keep well in touch; else we might end up huntin' each other, like. No. Can't think of nowt but these assassins o' yours. Reckon we'd best meck it back to the forest an' lose the beggars. We're no match for 'em in a group like this. Not agin a dozen.'

'Will we be safe for tonight, do you think?'

'What was our smoke like, from yon ridge?'

'Barely visible. You light a good fire Sondukal. Unless they've got a hunter with even better eyes than me, I doubt they know we're here. And, even if they saw the fire, they've no reason to think it's us. They've no clue where to even start looking. Last they knew, we were heading for the city.'

'They know you was on this mission, like?'

'Chislanda knew. I told her, when I was trying to get her pregnant so we could leave the godforsaken place. She probably knows where we're headed.'

'Let's look at the odds, then. They know you was mekkin' for Litkala with Feldrark. Where do you go from there to get back to your mission? Ain't no choice but the route we're takin'. Makes no sense to go no other way. My guess is they'll wait where t' road leaves t' forest. Send one on 'em to the city to meck enquiries and then leg it after us as fast as they can. Our best hope's to get back to Litkala, capture their scout as he arrives and get the soldiers to kill the rest on 'em, includin' the frowkin' woman this time!'

'She's carrying my child, Sondukal.'

'She'll be carryin' your 'ead an' all if she gets a chance from what I've 'eard. It's either 'er an' the unborn kid, Aglydron, or you an' the rest of the party.'

'She's a beautiful, passionate woman.'

'She's after your frowkin' blood. Wake up, man.'

Aglydron nodded, but without conviction.

There seemed to be little they could or need do just then. Sondukal paired them off for watches in the night, just in case, and he doused the fire with water, leaving them in darkness relieved only by a low crescent moon and a myriad stars in the black sky.

Okkyntalah looked up and around the horizon. 'Skyfire's not changed much.'

'Seems Ivdulon was right. Wonder what Dagla Kaz will make of it now?'

'Like Jodisa said, he'll probably continue, take a break in one of the cities somewhere on his route and arrive in Choshinahm under the real Skyfire with a bit more time to make the return journey with the new Godwood.'

Stellanyl moved close to Okkyntalah and whispered. 'Okkyntalah, I'm frightened.'

Sondukal, seeing how it was with them, kept Linlyss with him to share the first watch. 'You two get some sleep, when you're done. I'll wake you after midnight. Aglydron can take last watch wi' Myllthlan. We all need to keep alert.'

Chapter 3

MEETINGS AND INJURIES

Aglydron was unsure whether birdsong or daylight had woken him. Everyone else, including Myllthlan, whose head relaxed on his shoulder, was asleep. Disorientated for a moment, he couldn't understand why they were propped against the uncomfortable bole of a small tree. Then he remembered why they weren't lying on the soft down of their sleepsacks.

'Ytraa's balls! Myllthlan, wake up!' He shook her and began to stand.

'Take me back to… Aglydron? What…? How long have we been asleep?'

'I don't know. But it's past sun up.'

They roused the others quietly, listening and looking for signs of the hunters. As Aglydron prepared for prayers, Sondukal stopped him with a curse and a quiet but dire warning that they'd be his last.

'Knew I should've taken last watch. Mhortag's frowkin' squitter! Can't I trust you?'

'Impiety and irreverence may do in Litkala, but on Muhnilahm we pride ourselves…'

'You can pride your frowkin' self 'ow you like! I've orders from Feldrark to see you all safe an' I'm frowked if I'll let you get us all killed wi' your righteousness. Now, shift!'

They packed quickly, in silence. No breakfast. Within a few moments of waking, they were ready to cross the bridge. But Okkyntalah stopped them where they stood and pointed, as they emerged from the scrub onto grassland. Nine men and three women faced them from the far end. Three had bows already strung with arrows and the others bore swords, spears and shields as they had on the previous occasion, when he, Feldrark and the others had fought them off. The hunters must have passed by as they slept and had only become aware of them when they spoke on waking.

'We might've been murdered in our sleep.'

Aglydron felt the bite in Stellanyl's accusation but said nothing.

'We can't make a stand and we can't win the crossin'. We'd best leg it an' 'ope they're not so fleet o' foot as us.'

As Sondukal spoke, an arrow shot between Aglydron and Okkyntalah. They moved off at once, Okkyntalah stopping to retrieve the arrow and stringing it as he ran. A second missile lodged in the pannier on the horse, near Aglydron. Okkyntalah turned, took careful aim, and felled a bowman, his arrow striking just below his ribs. Dodging another, Okkyntalah ran a few more paces as he strung a second arrow. Again, he turned. Aimed at the other male archer. His shot grazed the man's arm causing the returning arrow to fly wild. Retreating a few more steps, Okkyntalah strung another and faced his enemy. The woman, waiting her time, let fly as he turned and pierced his thigh to the bone. He gritted his teeth and sent his own missile into the eye of the other bowman. He fell without a sound. The female archer knocked another as Okkyntalah wrenched the arrow from his leg, grimacing with pain. The point was no more than fire-hardened wood and he thanked Ytraa that these hunters lacked skill with metal barbed arrowheads of the type he used. Sondukal arrived beside him and took aim with his own bow.

The other hunters grouped round their remaining archer. Unconcerned, Sondukal let the arrow fly and a swordsman by the archer fell, pierced through the throat, choking on his own blood. Aglydron, to his shame, silently prayed they wouldn't hit Chislanda, though she stood with the rest, her sword and spear ready to kill. The assassins halted, unsure of their next move. Sondukal helped Okkyntalah limp back to the others.

'Let me mend your wound, Okkyntalah.'

'No time, Myllthlan. Save your healing until we've dealt with this brood of Mhortag.'

'Again? Let me bind it, or you'll bleed to death.'

Recalling the last time she'd used these words, he acquiesced, reluctantly, and she cut two wide strips from her short robe. One she made into a pad to staunch the pulsing flow of blood and the other she used to secure it.

Then began a dog and rhaat chase with the hunters from Mipahnhil keeping just out of range of the Followers' arrows. They retrieved the bows from their fallen colleagues but it seemed none matched the skill of the archers they'd lost.

As the companions slowed after their initial rapid flight, Okkyntalah and Sondukal aimed at their pursuers but had no need to release any more precious arrows. They moved across the plain, keeping the small river on their western flank as they made for its source, north of their position. Sondukal would guide them through the bog surrounding the lake that fed the river and then turn west to lose themselves in the forest. But the dogged hunters remained close.

They'd covered a little over two leagues, without loss or further engagement with their enemy, when Sondukal found the place he sought. Okkyntalah again took the rear as defender now that progress was slowed over spongy ground around the wide shallow lake. The land gradually rose in a horseshoe about the lake and was rock strewn and dotted with low thorny bushes affording little cover but causing considerable obstruction. Okkyntalah threatened with his bow, dissuading the hunters from coming too close. Continually turning to avoid falling or becoming entangled in the bushes, his progress slowed and the assassins closed in. He let fly with an arrow at the foremost, hitting him just below his knee. The man cried out but broke off the shaft a handbreadth from the

24

flesh and continued the chase, slowed only a little by his injury. But the hit made them wary again.

He glanced back and realized he was becoming isolated as his companions kept pace with Sondukal. He tried to speed up by facing forward for longer periods but this allowed the hunters to gain on him. He put on a burst of speed, misjudged the ground and the effect of his injury, and fell his length, jarring his arm against a rock. He was on his feet at once, ready with another arrow. As he rose, one pursuer let fly with her spear. The point stuck in the ground between his feet. At the same time, an arrow shot past him from behind and found its target in her chest. She fell where she stood. Okkyntalah turned to see Sondukal, grim faced, paces away, beckoning him urgently.

They'd reduced their assassins to seven able-bodied and one injured. But the odds were still stacked against them, especially as the girls were untrained in fighting. Okkyntalah made firm land alongside Sondukal and the party moved more rapidly across the springy turf of the ridge. Still their hunters came on, relentless and determined.

The forest came in sight as they crested the ridge, little more than a league distant. But, closer by far, a dozen or so men and women gathered to the north. Less than five hundred paces away, they'd been hidden by the low hill. Shaulah, running with Linlyss and Stellanyl, suddenly stopped and turned to the new group. The dog nosed the air and then set off, at speed, toward them. Okkyntalah's calls and Aglydron's yells had no effect on her. She bounded up to the group and began jumping at one of the figures.

Okkyntalah shaded his eyes and spoke in disbelief. 'That's Tumalind! It's Dagla Kaz and his party!'

Aglydron thought him mad. Sondukal glared at the assassins ranked close behind them, waiting to attack.

'It is! It's Tumalind!' Okkyntalah turned and followed the line taken by his dog, running with long limping strides, heedless of his injury, toward the other group. The rest followed more slowly, Sondukal firing another arrow at the hunters to dissuade them from coming too close. Myllthlan coaxing the horse at a trot at the rear.

The larger group remained still, looking across the plain.

Tumalind couldn't believe her eyes, as Shaulah bounded over the grass toward her. But, as the dog grew closer, she was in no doubt. Tryonta fed an arrow and made ready to strike the dog.

'No! Don't, Tryonta. It's Okkyntalah's dog! But what's she doing here?'

Shaulah reached her and stood on her hind legs to greet her with an enthusiastic lick. 'What, indeed?'

Tumalind stroked and patted her like the long lost friend she was and looked up to

25

see one of the group running in their direction. She knew at once it was Okkyntalah, and told her companions. Before he reached her, the rest of the small party began to run in their direction, pursued by another group.

They embraced as lovers, forcibly parted, will; holding each other close, determined never to let go.

Corphanda touched her shoulder. 'What's this? Who's this young buck and what's he doing here?'

Tumalind gave no response, lost in Okkyntalah, living the dream that had sustained her for so long. The rest of them caught up and stood close, the chasing party halting a little distance off, aggressive but uncertain now the group was so enlarged.

'Father! You, as well?'

Aglydron at once bent his knee and bowed his head before the High Priest. He took no notice of her and remained with head bowed before Dagla Kaz. The High Priest seemed bemused and hostile.

'Beggin' your pardon, Paltrohn, but you seem to be in charge 'ere. Greetin's from the Kiral an' Kirallah of Litkala an' welcome, I'm sure. I'm Sondukal, a guide an' 'unter from the city. The folk yonder are after killing these 'ere an' might I beg your 'elp to see 'em off as I'm charged wi' keeping 'em alive, like?'

Dagla Kaz looked from the top of Aglydron's head to the man called Sondukal and then to the party of hunters eyeing them from a safe distance. 'I've no idea what any of this is about or what it has to do with us. It seems the young man, incredibly, knows Tumalind and that this fellow, equally unlikely, is her father. Since the youth is too besotted with the girl to make any sense and this man is too overawed by my rank to speak, perhaps you'll explain?'

'I guess you're the 'igh Priest these two 'ave spoken of? I'm escorting them on a mission to…why, come to think on it, if you're the man I believe, my mission's done. We was trying to find you, Paltrohn.'

Dagla Kaz seemed even more disturbed by this than by the sudden appearance of the two islanders. 'And what's the meaning of consorting with a naked woman in public? Are you not Followers? Do you not know…?'

'The woman used her garment to bind lad's wound or he'd 'ave bled to death. What's it matter she's naked? More important things, ain't there…?'

Dagla Kaz, discomforted by this assessment, clearly decided it wasn't the time to dwell on it. He poked her father. 'Get up, man, and explain yourself!'

Aglydron stood but seemed unable to meet the eyes of the High Priest. 'I beg your forgiveness, Dagla Kaz. I seek forgiveness before Ytraa and your own high office for any offence. Okkyntalah and me are plain men. We were at the Choosing and we saw a

26

mistake in Tumalind being chosen.' He spoke very fast as if afraid a pause might hamper him but softly so that others nearby might not hear, though Tumalind heard well enough.

'You did? And what, exactly do you mean by…?'

'Beggin' your pardon, Paltrohn, but them there's assassins an' may attack any time. They'll not give in till these two and this woman's dead an' any others they believe are friendly to 'em. Can we deal wi' them first an' explain after, Paltrohn?'

'They're no friends of mine, Sondukal. Let them be assassinated. I've nothing to do with them.'

Tumalind stepped forward. 'If you abandon Okkyntalah and my father, Dagla Kaz, I will stay with them. Do you want them to assassinate me as well?' She stepped quickly between the two men.

Dagla Kaz frowned at her. 'I must know more of the circumstances before I sanction action of this sort in a foreign land. Tell me, quickly, what you know.'

'These 'ere are after more'n just these three. They'll try to kill my Wharhll and his new bride, Jodisa, if they get the…'

'Jodisa-Li?'

Okkyntalah nodded.

'How's my daughter implicated in all this?'

'Dagla Kaz, may I speak plainly?'

The High Priest nodded at Okkyntalah.

'How we came to this, I'll tell you later in great detail. If I say that those hunters are from the cesspit of Mipahnhil and that they'll stop at nothing until they've killed us and your daughter, is that enough to make you act? The Wharhll is spiritual leader in this land and he's also under threat. I've fought and lived beside him and know he'd be grateful if these hunters are driven from his land; killed if possible.'

As they were speaking, all engaged in the talk, one of the women hunters approached and flung her spear at Aglydron.

Tumalind caught the movement. 'Look out, Father!'

He moved and Dagla Kaz, turning too late, was hit high on his thigh. He cried out in pain. Okkyntalah loosed off an arrow but the woman, already retreating, skipped and ducked and he missed.

Without further delay, Dagla Kaz called the men of his party. 'Deal with the killers. Go with these others and, if you can't capture them, drive them off or kill them.' He turned to Sondukal. 'You seem to have some sense, in spite of your rough ways. Leave your women and your packhorse with us and do what must be done. But do it quickly.'

Tumalind was reluctant to lose Okkyntalah so soon, especially as he was injured, but she couldn't prevent him. 'Take care, my love. I can't lose you again.' She watched them approach the hunters and then pursue them as they fled. Soon, the hill took them out of sight.

The naked woman approached and examined the High Priest's leg, lifting his tabard to see it properly. It was a deep wound and she bid him sit. 'I'm a healer, Paltrohn. I can repair this.'

He frowned at her. 'I doubt a heathen knows about such things. We have our own healer. Corphanda?'

She bustled over and examined the wound. 'Best lie down, Dagla Kaz. You hold his leg up to help stop the bleeding, while I get me 'erbs and some linen to bind it.'

The other woman did as she was asked. 'I can repair it without bindings.'

'Yes, dear, of course. Now, just keep his leg up for me, and I'll see to it.' She took the things she needed from her pack and used some of the water with a mixture of her herbs to wash the wound before binding it tightly with a length of the cloth from Xythonl.

'Will someone please clothe this woman? I won't have such blasphemy continue without good cause.'

The other healer seemed unconcerned by her exposure but watched Corphanda with interest and made no further comment. Wendarah placed a tabard over her head but she seemed oblivious, merely accepting the item as if it were of no importance. She helped Corphanda get Dagla Kaz back to his feet. He grimaced slightly as he put weight on the injured leg. The bleeding, however, seemed stemmed for the moment.

'Thank you, Corphanda.' He looked askance at the other woman who simply nodded.

They set off down the slope and up the small hill to see what they might from there.

'Well, this is a right turn up. How comes your young man to be 'ere, Tumalind? How did he know where to find you? You been sendin' messages? Come on, young lady, out with it. I'll not 'ave my charges making a fool of me so easily.'

'Corphanda, I know as much as you do. I'm amazed to find Okkyntalah and my father here. I can only guess they also felt I was wrongly Chosen and have been trying to do something about it. It's the sort of thing Father would do. And Okkyntalah would do anything to have me back.'

'I hope, for your sake, that's all there is to it. If I find you've been secretly meeting him, you'll have more'n a smack or two to contend with, I can tell you.'

'How could I, Corphanda? And how could I send messages? I'm as amazed as you.'

'Ay, but a lot more pleased.'

'Wouldn't you be?'

When they topped the hill, the men were already amongst the rocks and scrub of a lakeside in pairs or alone, engaged with the enemy. Dagla Kaz halted the party of women, and Jhonaht, on the brow. Some sat on the ground, watching the fighting with varying degrees of interest. Tumalind couldn't decide if she could bear to watch but, when she closed her eyes, found she had to open them again.

The High Priest spoke to the three new women and found, to his evident surprise and displeasure, that the healer, the one called Myllthlan, was the most forthcoming. He nevertheless began to question her about what had befallen her and the other men and how they came to be on the plain, pursued by such determined killers. Myllthlan, undaunted by his rank, gave what information she had, freely and without concern. Tumalind listened in awe to the account and couldn't help thinking that this strange and beautiful woman made the best of Okkyntalah and, especially, Aglydron in telling her amazing tale.

⁂

Aglydron watched Chislanda circle him, as her female colleague targeted a man he'd heard named as Tryonta with her arrow and missed. Tryonta ran at her before she could string another, tackling and bringing her down with his superior speed and strength. He took no further part in the fighting. But stripped her of her two bands of cover and held her prisoner with his sword at her breast as she lay at his feet.

Caarl, a soldier he recognised as the husband of his wife's friend, had been cornered by two men and was tackling them hand to hand. Okkyntalah, on the edge of the area of the fight with his bow already strung, let fly and pierced one attacker in the back, felling him, as he was about to strike Caarl with his spear.

Aglydron dodged the spear Chislanda flung at him and retrieved it. He must run her down before she could try to kill him. She now had only her sword and he ran at her with his own blade raised, the spear a further weapon. She stood her ground until, seeming to realize her danger, she turned and ran. He chased, gaining and finally catching her by shoving her in the back with the blunt end of the spear so she stumbled, fell and rolled along the ground, losing her sword in the process. He leapt on top of her before she could turn and attack him. Striking her hard across her face, he straddled her and pointed his blade at her throat, standing abruptly as the memory of her flesh on his threatened softer treatment.

'On your front.'

She hesitated and he kicked her over. Dropping, he pressed her to the ground with his knee in her back, looking about him to make sure none of her companions was a danger. He dragged her hands up behind her. Ripping off her loincloth, he bound her wrists behind her back before he left her, face down on the ground.

A cry for help came from Caarl, fending off three men with only his sword. The giant called Tarruss decapitated the man wounded earlier by Okkyntalah. He'd tried to skewer

29

the huge man on his spear, missed and been unable to escape on his injured leg. Tarruss tried to capture him but he fought fiercely and the big man killed him and went to help a nondescript man who bore a great scar on his thigh.

As Aglydron ran to aid Caarl, he saw Sondukal making for Chislanda. He turned back at once, fearing the guide would kill her. 'Leave her. She's no threat now.'

'Aye, you say. But for 'er, this lot would never've come for us.' But Sondukal let him have his way and set off to help Caarl instead.

Okkyntalah let fly an arrow and brought down another of Caarl's attackers without killing him, the dart piercing his shoulder. Caarl, taking advantage of the brief hiatus, bested the man to his left, sweeping the sword from his hand with one blow and killing him as he brought the blade back again and sliced through muscle and bone, belly and chest. Okkyntalah ran to help Caarl as the injured attacker brought his blade round to strike the soldier. The young man leapt forward, yelling to distract the attacker. The man turned at the threat and pointed his sword at Okkyntalah's charging form. Stumbling as he landed on his injured leg, he fell onto the sword. Tarruss, having helped the other man kill his foe, charged up to the fray. He and Caarl slashed at the man and he fell, dead.

Caarl, badly wounded himself, bent over Okkyntalah, motionless, blood flowing freely from the new wound to his stomach. The soldier dropped to one knee beside him. At that moment, one of the wounded attackers regained his feet and bore down on Tarruss, spear in hand. Okkyntalah cried out a warning and Tarruss turned in time to ward off the blow with his sword, gaining a cut to his hand. He plunged his blade into the man's belly, withdrew it and hacked him across the neck. The hunter fell, twitching in death, as blood gushed from his throat.

They'd been unable to capture a single male enemy and all lay dead.

Aglydron forced Chislanda back to her feet and prodded her toward the group on the hill. Tryonta hauled his female captive to her feet with her hair and jabbed her forward, his sword point at her back.

Tarruss and the unknown man carried Okkyntalah back up the hill where the rest waited. On the ridge, Chislanda and the other woman were bound hand and foot and left on the ground.

⁂

Tumalind sat, resting Okkyntalah's head in her lap. Myllthlan left Dagla Kaz and dashed over to tend to his wounds, removing his tabard.

'No! You mustn't. Not here.'

She looked at Tumalind with tenderness. 'I understand your concern but is it better he stays covered and dies or is exposed and lives?'

Tumalind sensed the healer knew more than most. 'Do what you must.'

30

She helped her undress her man and watched her examine his injuries.

'This one's easy. But this other is bad. I can stop the bleeding but it's a deep wound and he'll need much rest and care to recover.'

Tumalind forced her gaze away from the man she loved and watched in amazement as Myllthlan made herself naked again and performed a short dance, gesturing to the air and singing a short song in a language she couldn't identify. She knelt and applied her fingers and mouth to the wounds, bringing the edges of the gashes together and seeming to knit the gash whole with her fingertips, blowing on the wounds and leaving the skin intact. She laid her ear and then her forehead against the larger wound, closed now and no longer pulsing blood. Unwrapping the bloodied strip from his thigh, she then healed that wound in the same way. Concentration and will closed her eyes and formed her face into a mask of supplication as she covered both wounds with her palms and called out in the strange language. At last, her eyes opened, staring but unseeing and rolled in her head as she collapsed backwards, away from her patient. She lay prostrate, her skin grey, and seemed insensible.

Aglydron came over. 'She's healed before but I've never seen her give so much of herself.' He seemed unsurprised at the actual healing however.

Tumalind touched the edges of the skin where it had knit together again, leaving only red scars on the surface, unable to believe what she'd witnessed.

Dilanthas bent over the healer, placed the discarded tabard over her and stroked her forehead. 'Are you all right?'

Myllthlan opened her eyes and sat. She seemed concerned only for Okkyntalah. She examined the scars and again placed her ear over the larger wound. 'The bleeding will stop, but the internal wound will take longer to heal. Don't let him move at all, for the moment. Keep him still and calm.' Her voice shook and she sounded exhausted but, inexplicably, she bent and kissed his mouth.

Tumalind let that pass. 'Thank you, oh, thank you…'

Myllthlan smiled at her. Slowly, the colour returned, but she looked weary. She became aware of herself again and, without embarrassment, rose to her feet and, with help from Dilanthas, replaced the borrowed tabard.

Corphanda, who'd been watching, stood with her mouth open. 'However did you do that? I've never seen nothing like that in all me life and I've used healing 'erbs for years. Is it magic? You a magician?'

'I'm a humble healer whose skills were enhanced by the power of…something I… can't quite recall. But I know there was…no. Memory fails me.'

'Simple in the 'ead, but I can't question your healing powers.'

'That she's not. I've travelled long leagues with her and she can't speak of her powers because of the way she came by them.'

Corphanda gave Aglydron a knowing look that said a man would be ignorant of such things and turned to the healer. 'Whatever the case, I've never come across the like before. Do you know 'erbs and the like?'

Myllthlan nodded and the two set about dealing with the wounds suffered by Aglydron, Caarl, Phildrad and Tarruss. Myllthlan, aware her special skills were needed again, made herself ready and sealed the skin on each wound.

Her healing complete, she rested for a while. Corphanda, impressed, covered her and then sat with the healer's head in her lap and waited for her to recover fully.

Dagla Kaz approached Tumalind's father, the priest's face troubled after witnessing the woman about her healing acts. 'Now the emergency's over and we have some peace, perhaps I can discover more of what brings us together on a hilltop in the heathen land of Litkala, so many leagues from our island home. I've some understanding of the situation from your healer friend; a remarkable heathen. But, more to the point, what part does my daughter play in this and how did she come to be with you? And, more importantly, where is she now?'

Once content that Okkyntalah was no longer in immediate danger, he begged the High Priest to walk with him. 'I think it might be best if we talked where we can't be overheard, Paltrohn.'

Tumalind was close enough to hear her father's whisper and the High Priest's indignant response. 'Oh, do you?'

'There are things I've to tell you that, well, I think others might not understand.'

Dagla Kaz glared at him and winced as he moved on his injured leg. 'Very well, if we must.' And he set off along the ridge with Aglydron.

Tumalind feared for her father and, now she had time to consider the implications of the two of them here, and some of what Myllthlan had said, she began to fear for Okkyntalah. And that fear had nothing to do with his wounds.

Chapter 4

CONSEQUENCES AND MOVES

Dagla Kaz summoned Jhonaht. 'This man has been in the city of Litkala and met there an astronomer who convinced him that the Skyfire's a false sighting. What do you say?'

Jhonaht grasped eagerly at this lifeline. 'That I said more or less the same only last night but you seemed unwilling to accept it.'

Dagla Kaz nodded and turned to the man. 'Litkala Followers are anathema to us; sworn to kill us on sight. How did you escape?'

'Litkala; a city ripe for commercial advantage. A wise man might make a proper killin' there.'

The High Priest had grown so used to the intruding voices that he rarely even acknowledged them now. The man before him described experiences in the city, mentioning glass working and something called an observerscope. 'It's complicated, Paltrohn. I've never seen nothing like it. There's glass things she calls lenses and mirrors, and metal tubes and wheels with teeth and a sort of three-legged thing to support it all. I can't really tell you because I don't have the words, but I looked through it and saw the Moon and it had mountains and valleys and was a ball…'

'Enough!'

Dagla Kaz and Jhonaht had long known this truth but it was disturbing to have a common man declare it so confidently. 'Leave me to think. There's much new here; much that denies truths I've been given and passed on. I must have peace to consider all I've been told. You, Aglydron, are under sentence of death for your acts.' He turned to Jhonaht. 'Tell Caarl to bind him. He can be executed later, at my pleasure.'

Dagla Kaz wandered a short way along the ridge to stand alone, his gaze fixed on the distant trees of the great forest they'd skirted. Jhonaht took Aglydron back to the rest of the group, where Dagla Kaz watched Caarl put him in shackles.

The High Priest spent enough time alone to give the impression he'd been thinking deeply before he strode back to where Jhonaht stood a little apart.

'What do you think, then, Dagla Kaz?'

'I was inclined at first to hang both those bowelcreeps upside down and whip their hides off with tnetsi thorns. But I can wait. They may be more use alive, for the moment.'

'I agree. What of this business with Jodisa-Li and Tumalind?'

'That's what troubles me most, Jhonaht. I was about to seek your counsel. I can't deny it's true, of course. I hadn't expected anyone to notice or, if they did, I certainly didn't think they'd have the temerity to actually say or do anything about it. Aglydron's clearly a zealot of the worst kind. There's nothing worse than a believer who truly believes in ceremony and rite. Okkyntalah's motives were entirely passionate and I've some sympathy with that. Now I find myself in the position of the accused in a strange land where these fellows obviously have friends, as well as enemies…and that's something else I must discover more about. These hunters wanted to kill them, and Jodisa-Li by all accounts; what's behind it? But that can wait. What am I do with these two for the moment? What am I to do about this unholy, frowking mess?

'Will you hear me, Dagla Kaz?'

'Have your say. You can't make things more confused than they are already.'

'My advice is that we return, all of us, to the city. Wait! Hear me, Dagla Kaz. It's clear that the passage of so many cycles has mellowed their hostility toward us and these two and Jodisa-Li were made very welcome. Indeed, if Jodisa-Li is now married to this spiritual leader, this Wharhll of theirs, I doubt we've anything to fear. We might even find some credit by turning this sorry sequence of events to our advantage: suppose Ytraa decided, without our knowledge of course, that the time had come for Followers of Muhnilahm to be reunited with Followers of Litkala. What better way than to make the Choosing appear to be in error? These two, clearly smiled upon by Ytraa, were guided to take Jodisa-Li and, in so doing, have fulfilled the will of Ytraa.'

'Not only do they get off without punishment, but they seem rewarded into the bargain. I don't like…'

'You evade suspicion, Dagla Kaz. And, as for their punishment; if that's so important to you, why, what's to prevent us taking them with us the rest of the way?'

'We could hardly let them go home on their own anyway. I don't know. Your scheme has merit. I need to consider the implications. For the moment, I believe you're right about Litkala. To be honest, I doubt I can travel far on this leg. In any case, we have to stay some place until the real Skyfire appears. The city they describe sounds civilised and comfortable. And I'm well aware the lies told us by Gadhallah about the Followers there are likely to be even more evil than his others. Besides, I could do with a soft bed and privacy to entertain our priestess in the manner we both prefer.'

'This Ivdulon sounds interesting. I'd like to meet her. A female astronomer; amazing.'

'There are still many things undecided, Jhonaht. Don't get too enthusiastic. I feel the need to revenge myself on someone for being made to look a fool. And don't tell me it's my own fault.'

'I wasn't about to. But, with careful thought and silent consideration, communing with Ytraa, as only you know how, you could come out of this very well indeed. The people like a man with a streak of mercy and they respect a man who's spoken with Ytraa and discovered secrets known to no other. Gadhallah worked wonders with such, er, deception.'

'Take care, Jhonaht, lest those who shouldn't hear…But I take your point. We'll be silent on most things for the moment. You'll agree with whatever I decide should and should not be done and said, of course.'

'Naturally.'

Dagla Kaz nodded and Jhonaht strode back along the ridge to where the party waited, talking and comparing the trials and excitements of their journeys.

The High Priest stood alone for a little longer. He returned to the gathering and held up a hand for silence. 'I've thought long and hard and it's clear to me that there is more behind what's happened here today than can be seen by mere mortal eyes. It is my belief that Ytraa works here to an end we have yet to discover. In view of all I've heard and some of what I already suspect of Ytraa's intentions, I declare that Aglydron may be released but must remain a member of our pilgrimage. Okkyntalah is similarly subject to the pilgrimage. What punishment is decreed for their forcible removal of my daughter from Muhnilahm will be made clear as time progresses. As for Tumalind and her situation, I haven't yet reached a conclusion and I warn all of you that she remains, for the moment, a Virgin Gift.

'There are strangers and even non-Followers in our party; what I say applies to them also. I understand Aglydron has done his best to instruct Myllthlan, the heathen healer, in our ways and I commend him for that attempt, limited as it has clearly been.

'As to what we do now and where we go, I've given serious thought to information Aglydron has passed to me from a learned source. It's just possible that this early spark is not the true Skyfire.'

There was much disquiet at this news but he held up his hand again, commanding silence as he continued.

'At present I have no way of knowing whether this is the case or not, but the question has been raised and Jhonaht believes it worthy of consideration. For this reason, I'm prepared to interrupt our pilgrimage for a few days. In any case, it's clear that the brave young man who fought so courageously and saved Caarl's life is himself in danger of death if we try to continue through rough country before he's properly healed. I am also wounded and will need to rest my leg if it's not to give me trouble for the rest of our pilgrimage. Taking all these factors into account, together with the experiences of Aglydron and Okkyntalah in Litkala, and the fact that my daughter is now married to the son of the Kiral and Kirallah of this country, I'm inclined to risk a visit to the city to see if more can be discovered.'

As expected, his party expressed concern at this, though Tumalind seemed pleased at the proposal and he wondered what she knew that she hadn't disclosed to him. And how she knew.

'For those who believe we'll be in danger at the hands of Followers of Litkala, let me remind you that Stellanyl and Linlyss are both from that city. Linlyss has been provided as a Virgin Gift, voluntarily, by their High Priest. And this man, Sondukal, also from the city, has just helped save us all from the murderous intentions of those evil creatures from Mipahnhil. On that point, the captives will remain bound for the journey. Their nakedness, uncouth and offensive as it is in the eyes of Ytraa, will remain a token of their heathen ways and their vulgarity; not sacrilege, as they're not Followers. I remind you that, whilst these women are available for joining and instruction in the error of their ways, they must not be taken against their will. I will punish such violation in the same way as if they were Followers. I won't have it said that we treat those not of the faith in a less than human manner.

'I hope and expect to gain guidance from Ytraa, along the way, regarding our immediate future, as well as answers to some of the questions raised by our peculiar situation. For now, I suggest we eat and then find a way to carry Okkyntalah at least as far as the road, which I understand is a little over two leagues distant. Sondukal tells me that trade is quite frequent along the road and it's possible we may meet a merchant who will aid us with transport to get us to the city in more comfort, for a price, no doubt.'

Aklon-Dji, with Por-Kildu and Mkolo-ti, scaled the Scar with the agility and confidence only practice brings. They checked no spies followed them and began their trek southeast, along the edge of the hostile precipice that separated the rest of the island from The Point.

Chellyth had been reluctant to let all three go but agreed after Aklon-Dji explained.

'I think it very likely the Holy Ones and priests will want vengeance for my killing of their temporary leader. And I am certain that revenge will be visited on your people, Chellyth. It is suspected that we are in league, after all. That is why we must now select a suitable alternative place for you to live.'

Over the past few years, Aklon-Dji had searched for safe sites for his friends and supporters in the event of such need. He'd identified three locations on the peninsula south of Pampahn and east of The Point. A triangular spit of land, mountainous and covered in rain forest, haunt of numerous wild beasts, it had never been inhabited by the island's natives or by Followers, who considered it inhospitable.

The three places he'd discovered were valleys with watercourses, meadows free of forest, and small lakes. He was now taking the others to select the most suitable site.

They climbed the slope ahead, entering the trees after a trek of a couple of leagues over rough grassland and under constant cloud.

Once within the trees, they were soon soaked by the humid and dank interior. Aklon led his friends with confidence to the nearest site. Within a day they'd decided it was suitable only as a last resort. The lakes were full of crocodiles, the valley slopes home to a large pride of tawny manecats, the river a haunt of venomous water snakes and the grass home to flying insects that seemed intent on devouring them. They were glad to be back in the trees for the night.

The second site was further inland, no more than a league from the first but separated from it by steep, rocky hills, which more or less surrounded it. They spent two days there and it never stopped raining, though the other side of the mountains to the south were cloudless. Again, they decided the place would do as a refuge only in desperate circumstances.

Finally, he led them south toward the coast and his preferred location.

'This is more like it!' Por-Kildu sounded as though he immediately felt at home and Mkolo-ti, beside him on the ridge, looked down at the wide valley, a broad smile on her dark face.

'It is my favourite spot. The only disadvantage is its isolation. You could not find a more remote place on the island, apart from The Point, of course.'

'But, in present circumstances, Aklon, that's surely a significant advantage?'

Aklon nodded absently at Mkolo-ti and then brightened. 'Of course it is!'

They set about exploring. There were signs that a stripecat had an occasional lair on the western slope of one mountain, and a modest collection of the smaller breed of crocodiles occupied the shallow lake at the head of the valley. The river, however, teemed with fish and was free of venomous snakes. Smaller streams tumbled down the slopes, providing crystal clear drinking water, and the three lakes were also full of fish. A good-sized herd of four-horned antelope grazed on the grass of the lowlands. They hunted one down with relative ease and ate well that night for the first time on the trip.

Aklon took them to his favourite feature the next morning.

'Take the river around that bend and you arrive at the coast in less than half a league. The outlet is hidden from the sea, unless you know exactly where to look. You would be able to fish and maybe even travel without too much danger of detection.'

They spent three days in the place and decided it was the best they were likely to find.

'Beats The Point, by a long way.'

Mkolo-ti nodded her agreement with Por-Kildu's assessment. Their journey back was slow and careful, marking the way secretly so that they could retrace their steps when they led their people to their new home.

＋ ←—

Tumalind kissed Okkyntalah gently on his lips and then fed him with her fingers, breaking the food into small pieces for him. 'You're so pale, my love.'

'Blood loss, that's all. It's so good to be with you again.'

She told him of her journey and all that had occurred; how she'd never given up hope that he'd somehow find a way to restore her to her previous condition. The story of her kidnap in Rhonholoah had him asking many questions and, in telling him the tale, she came to understand more fully how close she'd come to being made a sex slave to earn coin for that vile old crone.

'Dagla Kaz says I'm still a Virgin Gift but I don't see how he can hold to that after what you and Aglydron told him. I tried to make him see the error but no one would believe me. Now there are three witnesses, I don't see how he can ignore it.'

'But will he accept Linlyss as the substitute, now Jodisa's married? If he does, we should be safe and we can marry as soon as I'm recovered.'

'Linlyss and Stellanyl both look at you with hunger, Okkyntalah. Have you joined with them?'

'Not Linlyss, obviously; she wants to, though. With Stellanyl and Myllthlan, who healed me once before.' He showed her the faint scars. 'There were others, in Mipahnhil, when we were captive, but it's you I love, Tumalind. When we're married, I want to be only with you for the rest of our lives.'

'And if I decide to take another at some time?'

'I'd not blame or judge you, Tumalind; after all, it's what we're supposed to do, isn't it? I just hope I'll be enough for you.'

'I was teasing. I've never felt that way for anyone but you. Porryh thinks I'm foolish and Dilanthas thinks I'm lucky. I think I'm in love with you and always will be.'

'And I with you.'

She watched them construct a litter from spare clothing and belts, with spear shafts as a frame.

'What of the dead, Dagla Kaz?'

The High Priest frowned at Caarl. 'Heathens. Let the wild beasts take them. They're nothing to Ytraa.'

'Forgive me, Dagla Kaz, but shouldn't we show mercy in victory?'

'A woman who goes willingly naked. You should take her, like a man!'

He glanced at Myllthlan with distaste and shrugged. 'Ask their women what they would have us do with the carrion. But waste no time.'

The healer approached Chislanda. 'How should we deal with your fallen comrades?'

38

'I told you last time we met. Let them lie. They've failed and found death as their reward. They're of no value. I live on in hope of fulfilling my purpose.'

'To kill the man who filled you with another life? As you wish.'

Tumalind took Okkyntalah's hand, as they lifted him carefully onto the stretcher. She walked beside him, as Tarruss, Sondukal, Phildrad and Tryonta took a corner each. Caarl urged the captives forward, a sword at their backs. Tumalind noticed that the woman called Chislanda glanced frequently at her father with a strange mix of hatred and desire. What had the healer meant about him filling her with life and wanting to kill him?

They covered the ground quite quickly, the other men completely healed by Myllthlan and able to take turns to carry the litter or guard the female captives. Only Dagla Kaz delayed them, limping on his damaged leg. But by mid-afternoon, they reached the paved road where it emerged from the forest.

Linlyss walked between Porryh and Dilanthas asking questions about the pilgrimage and the likely outcome at its end. Corphanda seemed to have taken a liking to the packhorse and it to her as she led it at the rear of the party, talking with Myllthlan.

The road was deserted and they met no other travellers. But at dusk they sought a place to camp for the night and Sondukal spotted flames in a clearing in the trees. He scouted ahead, fearing no danger but determined to ensure the safety of his charges.

He returned and spoke to Dagla Kaz. 'Small group o' merchants, some wi' wagons, on their way out of Litkala.'

They decided to camp with the merchants and learn what they might. There were a dozen wagons, most with two drivers. Just three merchants were travelling together to Shorrannon. One was Ven-Gadla, who'd finished his business in Litkala and was now on his way to the other city with his secret cargo. As soon as he saw Tumalind, he greeted her like a long lost lover, hugging her and making her blush with his attentions. Spotting an opportunity to help Okkyntalah, she tried to persuade him to take them back to Litkala. He wavered, uncertain of his likely reward. Stellanyl wandered past, on her way to see how Okkyntalah was feeling.

'Who's that beauty?'

'She's from Litkala. She's a friend of one of the Virgin Gifts, why?'

'Not virgin, is she?'

'I don't know.' Tumalind understood him straight away. 'I'll make enquiries.'

She'd spoken just a little to Stellanyl and thought her removal from the company could only be good for her, and Okkyntalah. The young beauty had joined with her lover whereas Tumalind had yet to have that pleasure. And, whilst she was sure Okkyntalah's intentions were exactly as he'd declared, she'd feel happier in this uncertain climate if Stellanyl were otherwise occupied. She found the young woman bending over

Okkyntalah, talking, and drew her to one side.

'Ven-Gadla, who's very wealthy, wants to know if you're a virgin, Stellanyl.'

'Does he? Rich, you say?'

'Very. And looking for a travelling companion.'

'Travelling where?'

'All over the world.'

'Companion or wife?'

'You'd have to ask him. He's travelled a great deal and been to many strange and exotic lands. I sat beside him for a few days and he was entertaining, courteous and generous, even though I'd nothing to give him.'

'Such a recommendation. And you think I might be interested in him? You don't think him a little old for me? And you've no wish simply to separate me from your handsome and rather gifted man, who you've yet to sample, of course.'

'He's not old. Experienced. I felt there was something of the adventurer about you, Stellanyl. One or two things Okkyntalah said me made me think you might have a taste for travel. Such a man as Ven-Gadla would certainly provide excitement. Perhaps even more than a poor young hunter destined to go on a mission for Ytraa.'

'Possibly. Worth a little exploration, anyway.' Stellanyl grinned at her and wandered back with Tumalind and appraised the merchant frankly. 'Such a shame you're going the wrong way, Ven-Gadla. From what Tumalind tells me, I'd enjoy the chance to get to know you better.'

Tumalind smiled as the merchant assessed the girl.

He was smitten. 'So you shall, my dear. But our roads are the same. Didn't Tumalind say? I'm taking you all back to Litkala, to ease the young man's injury and that of poor old Dagla Kaz, of course. Perhaps you'd ride with me, if you're free? There's much I could show you.'

'Oh, I'm free to do as I please. There's a bit I could show you, as well, I imagine.'

'I'll look forward to that.'

'Should I tell Dagla Kaz, Ven-Gadla?'

'What? Oh, Tumalind, my dear. Yes, yes, please do.'

The High Priest was organising their campsite with Sondukal's help and the guide seemed relieved when she intervened.

'Excuse me, Dagla Kaz; Ven-Gadla's offered to take us to Litkala. He made no mention of a charge but, perhaps you might want to speak with him?'

He shook his head at her. 'You've proved your worth on this trip, Tumalind. I've been impressed with your abilities and contributions. I hope you gain the reward you deserve. But, we'll have to see what comes of my attempts to speak with Ytraa. Here, in the trees, I feel Ytraa is likely to be found. Ytraa loves the trees, of course.' He turned to Sondukal. 'You'll forgive my leaving you to it, I hope?'

'Happen I'll manage, Paltrohn.' Sondukal winked at Tumalind.

Dagla Kaz wandered over to the merchant and coin was transferred.

Tumalind relaxed now that Okkyntalah would be carried in greater comfort and speed to a place where she could take better care of him. She went in search of her father and found him talking with Myllthlan at the eastern edge of the clearing.

'Have I offended you, Father?'

'What makes you think that?'

'You've not said a word to me since we met, not even greeted me.'

'I've been busy. I came on this journey and risked a great deal to save you from…'

'Father, please. You came because you wanted to right a wrong. You thought only of Ytraa. Had it been any other girl, you would've done the same.'

He looked at her solemnly and then hung his head. 'You're right, of course. I'm sorry, Tumalind. I was ashamed of my motives when I saw you and realised how much I love you. That's why I didn't greet you. It seemed hypocritical. Forgive me?'

'Nothing to forgive, Father. You're always more pious than Mother or I and you always do what you consider to be right, regardless of personal feelings. I may not like being a secondary concern but I understand how it's the case.'

He took her in his arms then and hugged her close. 'I hope to…to, yes, put right the wrong and let you be united with Okkyntalah, if he lives.'

'If he lives? The healing woman said nothing to suggest he might be in danger.'

'Myllthlan's gifted, but the wound's deep and in an awkward place. Okkyntalah's strong but he's only a man.'

Myllthlan nodded when Tumalind looked at her for confirmation.

'Okkyntalah will be well. I know it. I'm going back to him, will you come and talk?'

Her father crossed the camp with her and they sat on the ground either side of Okkyntalah, now sleeping on the litter, which lay on a pillow of dry vegetation.

'What did Mother think of your plan?'

'Plan? We'd no plan. We saw what happened and set out to put it right. Shoarhn has no idea where we are. I couldn't tell her or send a message.'

'Father, I love you but you're a fool! She'll be frantic with worry. What's she supposed to do, not knowing whether you're dead or alive?'

'I hadn't thought. Ytraa's will 'ad been denied. My only thought was, is, to put it right. Shoarhn'll be fine. She's strong and there's other men who'll be happy to join with her in my absence.'

'Do you love Mother?'

'What a strange question.'

'What a strange reply. Do you?'

'I…I believe I love your mother as much as she loves me, Tumalind.'

'Love isn't just about joining, though, is it?'

'No…it's not. But, well, we're older and less…things change as you age, you know.'

'I'll always love Okkyntalah, and he'll love me forever.'

'I do and I will.'

She looked down into his face and kissed him softly. 'I thought you were sleeping.'

'I was.'

'How are you?'

'The pain is less. Weak, of course.'

'Myllthlan says you'll grow stronger as long as you rest.'

'She's a very great healer, you know. In Mipahnhil, we came across a slave called Malarhah, who'd been damaged as a child. Myllthlan made her whole again after we…Well, there was this sort of…it's no good, I can't bring it to mind now.'

'Something happened to you, didn't it? To all of you, as you were travelling.'

'It was after we escaped from Mipahnhil. We were at sea and we came to this…it was there we were…I can't recall.'

'You, Myllthlan and Father. Was there anyone else with you?'

'Feldrark and Jodisa, why?'

'Just curious. Perhaps I can ask them and see what they recall.'

'None of us can remember. Malarhah could remember but she couldn't tell us. Then she died on the road. But the thing that happened to us; it was a good experience.'

Phildrad rattled his cooking pot.

'Food's ready. I'll help you eat.'

'I'm thirsty.'

She nodded and found herself wondering how long it would be before he'd be able to join with her. Smiling at the prospect, she went for food and drink, forgetting her father in the delight of being with Okkyntalah again.

Chapter 5

A TIME OF LEARNING

Feldrark, a huge man who made even Tarruss appear of near normal stature, greeted Tumalind's father and Okkyntalah like friends, but joked that they'd returned rather sooner than expected. Jodisa-Li stood with him, her eyes on her own father, hiding whatever emotions she felt. The rest of the group, nervous and restless, awaited the outcome of this meeting. Sondukal had already left after giving his report.

Tumalind watched the faces about her; anxiety, curiosity, masks on some. She felt uncertain of the outcome and still concerned about Okkyntalah. Dagla Kaz was stern and dignified as he waited in the palace reception hall of this wondrous city. If he was overawed by the size, splendour or magnificence of the place, he didn't show it. He glanced from time to time at Jodisa-Li and her partner as they asked questions of Aglydron, Stellanyl and Linlyss but what he was thinking was impossible to determine.

'The prisoners first. What would you have us do with them?'

'You know how stubborn they are, Feldrark. They'll have to be kept safe; locked up. Chislanda carries my child, but they can't be trusted. Is there somewhere you can keep them till they come to their senses?'

'I doubt they'll ever do that in a way you or I would deem fit, Aglydron. We've a prison, little used, but I'd rather not incarcerate them in there. I'll put them in a secure house on the level below the palace and have them instructed in our ways. Must they be naked?'

'Let them stay exposed, so the people can see them for the heathens they are.'

'Ah, Dagla Kaz; I hadn't thought to involve you in such a small matter, but if you deem it important enough for your consideration, perhaps we might discuss it?'

Tumalind thought Feldrark's comment very astute and noted how the High Priest's face darkened at the subtle insult.

'It's nothing to me. Let it be as you decree, Feldrark. They're less to me than dust. But if you would be hospitable to such brutal savages, so be it. You rule here, after all.'

'I'd not shed even their blood lightly, Dagla Kaz, and if I'm to keep them alive, I'll not see them harmed or made to suffer unnecessarily.'

'Mercy wasn't a quality I expected from the ruler of this city.'

One of the palace guards came at a signal from Feldrark and led the captives away. Tumalind saw her father's eyes follow Chislanda, and the woman turned to stare at him. She wondered how much more than mere joining had been, and remained, between

43

them.

'Now, to the injured parties. Okkyntalah must go to the palace infirmary and space made available for his lovely nurse, Tumalind, to be on hand.'

'They're not yet joined before Ytraa, Feldrark. Tumalind remains virgin and I'd not have them placed where temptation might destroy them.'

'I see there are differences between us, Dagla Kaz. Let's get Okkyntalah comfortable at any rate. We can discuss further needs and wants at leisure. I trust you've no objection to Tumalind accompanying him, with my house staff, to the infirmary?'

Dagla Kaz nodded his assent. Tumalind wondered that he didn't react to the sarcastic tone. Two young women and men, clad in blue tunics trimmed and belted with gold, came from an antechamber and took up the stretcher.

'Myllthlan, perhaps you'd discuss his wound and its treatment with our healers?'

Myllthlan nodded. Beside the stretcher, her hand holding Okkyntalah's, Tumalind heard Feldrark address Dagla Kaz as they left.

'I'm sorry, Dagla Kaz, I see you're also injured. What would you have us...?'

But whatever the High Priest replied was lost in the calm silence of the corridors. They climbed three flights of steps, the stretcher-bearers keeping the litter level, and arrived in a room at the front of the palace, overlooking the city below through a great window. It was the first time Tumalind could look down from on high and she stared with wonder at the sight. She hit her head and pulled away, stretching out a hand to touch the unseen thing that had attacked her.

'It is rather amazing, isn't it?'

She turned to find Okkyntalah smiling at her. Reaching out again, she felt the invisible object she'd collided with, wondering if it was real. As the palace servants removed his torn tabard and settled him in a soft white bed with a light sheet to cover him, she returned to his side. Myllthlan was in a small room off the chamber discussing the patient with other women. One of the young serving women remained but the other left with the men.

'You needn't stay, Horsylth. I'm fine with Tumalind. And Myllthlan's close by.'

The young woman bowed her head. 'I must stay, Okkyntalah, until your chosen is ready to return. She may get lost if left to wander the palace alone.'

'You and Tumalind go back down and find out what's planned.' He spoke as though still in pain but his face displayed nothing of that as he smiled at them. 'I'll sleep, I think. The journey's made me weary and it's cool and quiet in here. I'm in good hands.'

Tumalind stayed to hear what the healers had to say, however. Myllthlan returned with the woman in charge of the infirmary and they pulled back the cover and quickly examined Okkyntalah. Unsure how she felt about his exposure and their indifference to it, Tumalind turned away. It was clear that Followers in the city had different attitudes from those of her island home. Then she recalled how Myllthlan had so casually removed Okkyntalah's tabard and her own as she drew her astonishing power from the sky. At the time, her mind had been all on Okkyntalah and his injury and only now did she recall how shocking those acts should have been to her. On reflection, however, the whole thing seemed natural and right in a way she couldn't quite put into words.

Tumalind looked out over the city. 'It's incredible.'

Horsylth stood beside her. 'I suppose it is. I'm used to it, of course, but it's still pretty wonderful.'

The other healer called Tumalind across after her examination. 'Myllthlan's done right well to 'eal skin an' muscle. But we both feel there's internal injury, which'll take time an' care an' skill to get better. It'll be a while before your young fellah's back on 'is feet but I've no doubt 'e'll recover. If Myllthlan hadn't sealed the wound at once, it might've been different. 'E was fortunate to 'ave 'er close. She's skilled and gifted an' 'as left me with nought to do but act as nursemaid. Now, off you go an' rest an' eat with your companions. You'll be better for it and Okkyntalah'll gain from you bein' refreshed. I'll 'ave a bed made up in 'ere so you can sleep together. 'E's to 'ave no excitement, mind. So, no joinin' if you don't mind, for the moment.'

Tumalind was about to raise Dagla Kaz's objections but she caught Myllthlan's eye and thought better of it. It would be good to spend time alone with him.

Horsylth led them from the infirmary to the main dining hall where Feldrark was pointing at Dagla Kaz's leg, a frown of concern on his face. He beckoned Myllthlan over.

'Perhaps you'd have a look at this wound, if Dagla Kaz will permit?'

The High Priest stepped back. 'She's heathen. I've seen her healing. I'll have no such blasphemy done for my sake.'

'As you will, Dagla Kaz. But I recommend you visit the infirmary. I see signs of infection and the wound needs treating.'

Caarl came over, frowning. 'What's wrong with Myllthlan, Dagla Kaz? See how she's mended me?' He showed the faint scars that remained.

'Her results I challenge not. It's her methods. She makes herself naked and calls to some foreign power. I'll not have such barbaric devotions made on my behalf.'

'Is it the nakedness or the unknown power to which you object, Dagla Kaz?'

'Both, Feldrark. The power may be demonic for all I know. And naked is sacred.'

'Do demons generally give aid to the wounded? I know well that naked is sacred. Why, then, object to her being naked as she makes supplication to this power? Might it not even be the same power that's invested in Ytraa but known by another name?'

Dagla Kaz evidently had no reply to this but he stuck out his chin and refused her help, going instead to sit by the table in silence.

'So be it, Dagla Kaz. But remember the hospitality of my house is open when you need it. Now, shall we eat? You've all travelled far and we've much to discuss and learn from each other. Please take your ease and let my people help you to food and drink.'

Tumalind, beside Aglydron on one of the upholstered chairs, watched Jodisa-Li walk across to her father and bow her knee before him. He spoke softly and touched her shoulder so she rose and sat beside him.

'What d'you think of the city, Tumalind?'

She turned to find her own father smiling at her. 'It's a wonderful place. I never imagined such a place could be, even though I've now seen others. None has matched this for elegance, cleanliness or beauty. It's cool within and light and full of soft, sweet air.'

They'd spoken on the journey through the Greenreald. But they'd been separated much of the time, as she'd chosen to shade Okkyntalah from the sun as best she could, keeping flies off as he lay in fitful sleep, or talking with him of their dreams whilst he smiled at her awake.

'And what do you think of our host and his people?'

Tumalind looked at Feldrark and found his eyes on her. He smiled and bowed slightly before continuing his conversation with Jhonaht. 'Feldrark's a strange man. I can't make up my mind about him. He's polite, courteous and seemingly wise. But there's something hidden and I don't know yet whether I like him as much as I feel I should.'

'Just like your mother. Shoarhn won't judge on sight. Feldrark's a great man and a fine leader. Some of his ways are strange and some of the beliefs of Followers here are close to blasphemy. He's a good man at heart and he's taught me a lot about the difference between true devotion and simply sticking to rite and ceremony.'

'If he's taught you that, Father, he's more remarkable than I'd thought.' She laughed as she saw anger cloud his face. 'I was teasing, Father. Don't be angry with me.'

Aglydron nodded and smoothed away his frown. 'How is it now with you and Okkyntalah? I thought Dagla Kaz said you might be allowed to wed after all.'

'He told me he was visited by Ytraa in the trees. It seems Ytraa planned all that's happened so Followers in Muhnilahm and Litkala would be united again. He's replaced me as Virgin Gift with Linlyss. She'll go to Choshinahm as soon as the real Skyfire's sighted.'

'The real Skyfire? Has Dagla Kaz decided it's false?'

'I don't think he's admitted it to himself, yet, but I'm sure he will. Certainly Jhonaht's convinced and, since he's the astronomer, I can't see Dagla Kaz deciding otherwise.'

'You've grown, Tumalind; become a woman. I left a child behind me and I meet you after these few days to find an adult.'

'Fifty-two days since we were together on the island, Father. And I'm no woman but a maiden, until Okkyntalah joins with me before Ytraa. Soon, I hope. As soon as he's well.'

'There's no Ytraa here. Will Dagla Kaz allow it?'

'No monument. But Ytraa's everywhere, surely, Father? I asked Stellanyl what they do here and I'm content all will be as it should be in the eyes of Ytraa, though it may be daunting for Okkyntalah and me unless others are ready for the first joining.'

'You've talked to Dagla Kaz about it?'

'He wants to consult Feldrark and the High Priests here. But, he can't expect us to go to Choshinahm and remain chaste. I think he'll let us wed and join as they do here.'

'I hope you're right. He still hasn't made up his mind about our punishment, you know. How do you feel about going to Choshinahm?'

'I'd rather go home, Father. But if I have to go to more foreign lands so I can be with Okkyntalah, I will.'

'He's not been alone, you know, like you.'

'He's not virgin. I am. In any case, have you remained alone, Father?'

'We must join when we may.'

'Exactly. So why this strange attitude to Okkyntalah?'

'He enjoys it too much.'

'He's a young man. Don't you remember your first days with Mother?'

'We were one. Such coupling is supposed to give as much joy as devotion.'

'Had you been in Okkyntalah's tabard, you'd have been just as keen.'

'Shoarhn wouldn't agree with you.'

'Mother would welcome more joy from you, Father. She told me so.' She regretted her words at once. 'I'm sorry. I didn't mean to…'

To her surprise, he didn't strike her or even threaten to do so. 'Your mother's been good to me, Tumalind. I don't deserve her loyalty or the pleasure she's shared with me. When we go back, I hope to show her what I've learned on my wanderings, what others have taught me. I've no real complaint against Okkyntalah, only jealousy that he's so admired by all the women, I suppose.'

His frankness astounded her but she had no chance to comment or act on it, as Feldrark came over with Jhonaht. Tumalind stood and bowed to him. 'Sire, thank you for your hospitality. I haven't had the opportunity until now to express my gratitude for the way you've welcomed us all into your home and offered care to Okkyntalah.'

Feldrark glanced at Jhonaht in approval and then bowed to her. 'You're the subject of much talk, Tumalind, did you know?'

'Me? Why?'

'A number of reasons. Have you noted your similarity to Jodisa?

'Jodisa-Li's far more beautiful than me; in any case, I…'

'Jodisa; now she's married to me. Her title no longer applies. Your modesty does you credit, young lady, but it's not true. I love Jodisa more dearly than life itself but there's no difference in the degree of beauty, only in its nature. That, however, wasn't my reason for wanting to talk with you, though, I admit, it makes the whole thing more enjoyable. See? I'll have to take care, my wife's watching closely.'

'She's no need to be concerned. I'm virgin still and will remain so until Dagla Kaz gives permission for me to wed Okkyntalah, after which he and I will be one. And Jodisa's clearly more suited to you, Feldrark than I could ever be, since it's plain she loves you and the two of you are one.'

'Well spoken, Tumalind. Aglydron, why didn't you tell me your daughter was clever, beautiful, and talented?'

'Because he doesn't think I am.'

'Fathers rarely appreciate the real worth of their daughters. Here, Aglydron, you have a gem. Jhonaht was telling me of your interest in all things. He's meeting our astronomer tomorrow. Would you like to come with us?'

'You do me great honour, Sire. I'd delight in such a meeting.'

'Feldrark, please. I count you a friend, as Okkyntalah's consort. But I must be truthful. There's a reason, other than your gratification, for my suggestion.'

Tumalind put a question on her face though not her lips.

'Ivdulon believes most women are generally inferior in intellect to men. She's already having doubts since she spoke with Jodisa. I believe if she speaks with you, it might just do the trick and change her mind completely.'

'I'll willingly visit her, Feldrark. Though, I've no hope of fulfilling your expectations. From what father's told me, Ivdulon sounds a fascinating character of great knowledge and learning.'

'Oh, she's that all right. Tomorrow, then. In the meantime, I think I'd better have a rather more detailed discussion with Dagla Kaz about the future.'

'You'll find him less rigid than my father, especially in matters of rite and ceremony, but more fixed and limited in his ideas of what's right and wrong than you, Feldrark.'

'Tumalind! You mustn't speak disrespectfully of the High Priest.'

'Not disrespect, father. Truth.'

Feldrark laughed delightedly and, bending, kissed her forehead before leaving to speak with Dagla Kaz.

A palace servant approached and asked what they wished to eat and drink. Aglydron gave his requirements and Tumalind followed his example. She was pleased and surprised when she was served with as much ceremony and politeness as the rest of the guests.

Later, after she'd checked on Okkyntalah and found him asleep, the sweat of the journey no longer on his brow, she went with Horsylth to the pool. Lying in cool, clear water, she reflected on what had passed during their journey.

They'd travelled at a slow pace to ease discomfort for Okkyntalah. During their second night under the trees, the High Priest had wandered off by himself and not returned until dark. He said he'd communed with Ytraa in a quiet glade and been told that the will of Ytraa had guided Aglydron and Okkyntalah to steal away his daughter from the island. It was also Ytraa's will that the Choosing be perceived as in error by these two and Tumalind but by no one else. Ytraa wished for peace between Followers in Muhnilahm and Litkala and the marriage of Feldrark to Jodisa was a first step in that process. Ytraa hadn't, however, yet explained everything about this sequence of events but had made it clear more would be revealed, once the party arrived in the city and spent time with leaders and citizens.

Tumalind listened and, schooled to believe the High Priest's every word, nevertheless felt the pronouncement was rather convenient in light of events. It was as if events had determined the announcement rather than the other way round. That she could come to that conclusion, against all her schooling and training, alarmed her a little.

They travelled for most of the next day and arrived at a wayside inn where Aglydron and Okkyntalah had stayed previously. They all bathed and she enjoyed this experience, though she was shocked to discover they were expected to do so as a group. Dagla Kaz, however, sought out the landlord and arranged for the men and women to bathe separately.

After they'd eaten, Dilanthas and Porryh played some airs and Linlyss, strumming her lyre, sang along with Tumalind to entertain the company. Others in the inn persuaded Linlyss to play The Lay of Malarhah, which made Tumalind cry. Though, when she learned that Okkyntalah had composed the piece, she asked to hear it again.

They arrived in the city just before noon and took a frightening journey, on specially designed carts, up the steep incline. Feldrark and Jodisa greeted them but they hadn't yet met the Kiral and Kirallah.

Now, lying back in the comfort of the great pool, she felt more relaxed and certain of her future than she had for a long time. Dagla Kaz had spent time with the High Priests of the city. Afterwards, he'd let her know he was satisfied that the absence of a monument to Ytraa would be no bar to any ceremony they might decide to perform. Apparently, the Staff of Ytraa, which Feldrark had shown the company, would serve the purpose instead.

Corphanda was at the opposite side of the wide circle of water, with Dilanthas, Porryh and Linlyss. She seemed to have taken her new charge under her wing and had more or less ignored Tumalind since. Corphanda cared only that she had the right number of Virgin Gifts to supervise and didn't worry who they were. Tumalind smiled; her small experience of Linlyss suggested that the girl would need little, if any, discipline, apart from her infatuation with Okkyntalah, and he was unlikely to indulge her. Porryh was, again, the only one in real danger of feeling the guardian's stinging hand.

Wendarah and Netrodyl were lounging on platforms, the priestess luxuriating in a massage from a tall thin man and the strange tribeswoman enjoying an oiling from one of the palace girls. Stellanyl, with Ven-Gadla, had already left the palace. She'd decided to make her life with him and they'd gone to Rrildyss Kaz for a quiet form of wedding, which didn't involve joining before Ytraa, as Ven-Gadla wasn't a Follower. She hoped the girl hadn't acted precipitously but thought, on balance, she and the merchant would do well together.

Tumalind was idling, half asleep, when a figure slipped into the water beside her. Jodisa surveyed her rather speculatively. They hadn't spoken much but she wasn't in awe of the High Priest's daughter, their swim together before the pilgrimage having formed a basis for some form of friendship.

'My father tells me you're a clever girl, Tumalind. Says he took a liking to you because you remind him of me. Was particularly struck by your eyes.'

'I don't know why, I'm nothing like as…'

'Oh, it's all right. I'm neither jealous nor annoyed. In fact, I'm rather touched. You have a simple, natural beauty I don't possess and I suspect your intelligence is more to do with natural ability than learning. Come from Morstahn, if I remember rightly?'

Tumalind nodded, wondering where this conversation was leading.

'Okkyntalah's a brave and handsome young man. I owe my life and some of my skin to him. Your father would've beaten me more if Okkyntalah hadn't stuck up for me. I've a good deal to be grateful to him for and I've told my father I felt safe with your young man and was never in danger of violation whilst he was around. I gave him a hard time, you know. Tried to seduce him so they couldn't treat me as a virgin. Tried to escape. Even tried to kill him once. But he was always fair with me. Your father was brutally correct, of course. So, I've told my father I think Okkyntalah deserves you and I've reason to believe he'll let you marry as soon as he's recovered enough.'

'Thank you. But why would you do this for me, for us?'

'It's the truth.'

'I expect it is. But why tell your father?'

'You are bright, aren't you? Well, I'd like a favour in return.'

'Go on.'

'My father's going to find out some difficult things soon. His whole belief system will come into doubt. I know, because it's happened to me since I came to Litkala and learned things from Feldrark and Ivdulon. Rrildyss Kaz and Patradko Kaz have given me more food for thought. I was never like you, Tumalind; never had a real deep faith. I know too much of the truth to give our beliefs much credence. But I've learned things that make even me have doubts about so much that I'm certain Father will have difficulty coming to terms with them. What I'd like you to do is to act as an ear for him, a way of channelling and defusing his doubts, a mind he can discuss things with on the road to Choshinahm. Because he's still going, no matter what he learns here, and you're still going with him. Will you do that?'

'You make it sound as though I'll learn things to damage or harm my own faith....

'You will. You're going to meet Ivdulon. You'll learn things from her that'll set your world upside-down.'

'If all this is true, why are you all still Followers in Litkala?'

'An astute question. You can't change ordinary folk overnight. But they have some different beliefs here in Litkala, anyway. In any case, much of what Ivdulon has discovered only became known recently. It'll take time to understand exactly what it all means. If you take away the faith of people, they'll feel lost and afraid. So, until we've something to replace it, we have to keep the old faith going, changing it subtly as we go along. Feldrark's already started that. One of the reasons he took me as his wife was so we could start the process of uniting Followers in Litkala and Muhnilahm before too many changes take place. You see, Feldrark wants to change the world, not just Litkala. And it'll be so much easier if he has a foot in more than one country.'

'Much of what you've said to me could be considered blasphemy.'

'I know.'

'You don't believe in Gadhallah's word?'

'I never did. Oh, don't look so shocked; I have my reasons. But it's deeper than that. It's partly to do with Gadhallah but more to do with Ytraa and certain aspects of the faith that you're meeting Ivdulon tomorrow.'

'Suppose I don't want to?'

'You will.'

'You're very sure.'

'You're full of curiosity and want to know what Ivdulon has to show you. And, you want to marry Okkyntalah.'

'That sounds like a threat.'

'I suppose it might. Now, shall we go for a massage? The Spiritman is a master, you know. He leaves you feeling like new.'

'I'll do as you ask, Jodisa. Not because of your threat or your promise, but because I

51

want to know.'

'I know. I'll show you something quite interesting now, just as a taster of the sort of information you'll soon discover. Ask me for something. Anything at all.'

'Well, if we're going for a massage, I think I'd like a long cool drink of that wine we had at lunch. The pale green one, I don't know what it's called, I'm afraid.'

'Then you shall have one. And, so will I. No. I think I'd prefer the deep red. The drinks will be here in a few minutes. Do you have a particular vessel you would drink from?'

'Those glass goblets are as fascinating as they are elegant.'

'Fine. I'll have a silver one, though.'

Tumalind looked into Jodisa's face, as odd words seemed to come softly to her mind. The experience was so unexpected, so strange, that she dismissed it as something imagined. Jodisa smiled secretively.

Serving girls towelled them dry and they took their places on two of the tables. The masseur had finished with Wendarah and came over at a signal from Jodisa. One of the girls prepared Tumalind, oiling her with aromatic oils and tending to her nails as she lay waiting for the Spiritman to finish with Jodisa.

Another girl came in, carrying a tray with wine. She placed the pale green on the table beside Tumalind, the red near Jodisa and then left again without a word.

'Interesting. I like the Pastroahn Pale. I take it the Yilluk Deep is your favourite?'

'One of them. I'm glad you like the Pale; it's refreshing and clean, don't you think? *For now, just relax and enjoy. You'll learn how, and a lot more, tomorrow.*'

She was startled by this more definite intrusion but determined not to let it show and, if she could, to play the game herself. She wasn't sure how, but imagined simply thinking her words might do the trick.

'*Will I? I wonder, Jodisa, will I also learn, who?*'

'*Excellent! Keep it secret, Tumalind, though. Yes, you'll learn, who as well. Though I can tell you about Feldrark, Rrildyss Kaz, Patradko Kaz and Ivdulon.*'

'*Do you suppose I can reach them?*'

'*You'll only know if you try. But, remember; only a few of us are gifted. We may not reveal the gift to those who don't possess it and there are rules; we don't, for example, intrude on private moments.*'

'*I should hope not. Is it possible Okkyntalah might…?*'

'*No. There's a mark we all bear.*'

'*Eyes, of course. But that means Dagla Kaz should be…*'

'*Yes. But, for reasons I'm not at liberty to explain, it's absolutely vital you don't try to contact him. You're quick and you're bright, Tumalind. Please don't say anything to my*' *father, or try to mindtalk with him. Promise?'*

'Promise. But, oh, what a wonderful thing it is, Jodisa!'

'Yes. You see, you are special. Now, we must talk in our voices or the others will grow suspicious.'

'Jodisa? When that man's finished with you, do you think I might have a go, if he's willing? It looks so relaxing.'

Jodisa grinned at her and nodded. 'But only when he's done with me. I hate to have him leave me half way through.'

Tumalind watched the man at work on her companions' supple body, kneading pummelling and, eventually feathering her flesh so that she looked utterly relaxed. It seemed almost indecent to feel such delight at the hands of a man who would not join with her, yet she looked forward to the same experience with hopes and expectations that Okkyntalah would do this for her when they were one.

Chapter 6

OF JUSTICE AND COMPROMISE

The High Priest watched with distaste, as his opposite numbers replaced their tunics after prayers. He'd seen Stellanyl, Linlyss and Sondukal use this comfortable, less vulnerable, prayer position and was concerned it might spread to the rest of his party, further eroding his authority and opportunity for advantage. He rose to his feet, ignoring the mild amusement playing on their faces, and sat with them on the terrace.

'Take them when you can, and when you can't, use them in private. You're the man; use your power and strength.'

There was much he admired and envied about the city and he'd quickly accepted that the tales he'd read of its inhabitants were lies. Gadhallah's confessions, known only to him and his children, had always implied that the rumours about Litkala were doubtful. Its clean, elegant lines, atmosphere of calm prevailing in spite of the huge number of people, cool interiors and presence of clean running water for drinking, washing and to dispose of waste, all made it undeniably civilized.

Some ideas held by its leaders, were close to blasphemy, but that didn't concern him. His few real beliefs related to his certainty that a power for good and another for evil must exist in the world. He called these Ytraa and Mhortag out of laziness and convenience and, had they different names, it wouldn't unduly upset him. He was, however, deeply concerned about the common folk being given ideas that would diminish his role, his power and his wealth. He enjoyed his position as High Priest and had no wish to relinquish such privilege or even to have it reduced.

'Join us. We're creating a society in which the strong male will be king for all time.'

Some concepts hinted at by leaders in the city struck him as dangerous and radical. If adopted, they would irrevocably alter the entire structure of society and make his place in the new order less comfortable. Yet, there was no denying their strength of feeling. That Jodisa seemed content, even enthusiastic, about the new ideas was more disturbing.

'It's time to meet the Kiral and Kirallah, Dagla Kaz, will you attend them?'

'By all means. But explain, if you will, their function. I understood Feldrark was leader and you two, the High Priests. What role do these others play?'

'Rrildyss Kaz and I perform rites and ceremonies. We oversee life joinings, naming days, death rites and the like and ensure all is taught according to the traditions and beliefs of Followers. Feldrark's role is as moral and intellectual head of our society. He introduces new ideas. He has the hearts of the people in his keeping as well as their minds. It's a most difficult role; combining leadership with spiritual integrity and high honour. He must be seen to be pure in his dealings with the people. Therefore, he will make no pronouncements that do not accord with what is considered right both morally and ritualistically. This enables him to introduce new practices and beliefs when they come to him. The people trust him and are therefore more accepting of changes he proposes. His entire life is conducted under a shield of moral truth that allows for political duplicity where such is necessary.'

'That's what I do all the time in Muhnilahm.'

'I think not, Dagla Kaz. You're motivated by individual desire and personal power. Feldrark's entire life is a devotion to his people.'

'So that's why he married Jodisa. And there's me thinking it was her beauty and....'

'He married because the people require him to produce heirs. He married the beautiful and accomplished Jodisa because she embodies qualities we need to take our development forward and because, like him, she's intelligent and open to change.'

'You're saying he wouldn't have married her if he hadn't considered her to be...?'

'He was fortunate. The woman he's found as ideal for the role is also the woman he loves. But Feldrark loves easily and overlooks her many faults as only a generous spirit can.'

'Faults? My daughter is....'

Rrildyss Kaz touched his arm. 'Your daughter, like mine, Dagla Kaz, has faults. I overlook those in Pharah-Li and you overlook those in Jodisa. They have them, nevertheless. In fact, considering her predilections, you may find Pharah-Li closer to your own fancies than many other women; I'll introduce you....'

Patradko Kaz interrupted, urgency in his tone. 'As to the roles of the Kiral and Kirallah, who we're about to meet; they are secular and civil leaders. In their hands lie the many tasks needed to make a city state like Litkala work smoothly and efficiently. They're political heads of our society, separate from spiritual leadership, though connected through the ancestry of the Kiral. The Kirallah is from a foreign land; the country of your guest, Netrodyl, and held the same beliefs as that young woman when she arrived here. What her beliefs are now is neither known nor relevant to anyone but her and the Kiral.'

Dagla Kaz had no time or opportunity to pursue this further. They'd arrived in the presence of the Kiral and Kirallah and others of his party who were attending.

Okkyntalah was awake when Tumalind returned, and seemed much improved. He'd eaten and been bathed by careful hands. Content beneath the coverlet, he was ready to talk and learn what she'd discovered. She sat on the edge of his bed and held his hand as she bent to kiss his mouth.

'Get well, Okkyntalah. My impatience for you grows each time I see you, especially when you're so available.' Glancing round to ensure no one overlooked them, she pulled back the cover. She gazed at him, stroking the length of his body from shoulder to knee. The wound wasn't dressed, because of Myllthlan's healing, but it was swollen. He flinched as her fingers lightly kissed the surface. She took her hand away and pulled the cover back over him. 'Is that all right, or does it need treating?'

'It's fine. I'm fine. I just want to be well so we can be one. What have you been doing? You've been gone so long I was beginning to think you'd found someone else.'

She smiled at his teasing. 'I've been busy. I have met someone else, but not a partner. Dagla Kaz and I met Ivdulon. She's amazing. You know how dark Netrodyl is? Well, Ivdulon's even darker and her hair's black and very curly. She has a deformed foot but no one refers to it at all because she's very sensitive....'

'You've forgotten; I've met this wonder.'

'Of course. But her eyes, Okkyntalah, her eyes are the same as mine, and Jodisa's.'

'And Dagla Kaz, Rrildyss Kaz, Patradko Kaz and Feldrark. Is there some sort of conspiracy between you? You all have exactly the same colour eyes. It's very odd.'

Tumalind nodded. 'There's something. I'm not sure what I can say about it, but there's definitely something. Anyway, it's not important.' She was fairly certain she could mindtalk with all of them but hadn't yet tried. 'What did you think of her tower?'

'Impressive, isn't it? See the observerscope?'

She nodded. 'I'm going back, to look at the stars and the false Skyfire. It's definitely false, by the way. Even Dagla Kaz admitted that after talking with Ivdulon. Jhonaht stayed up there with her, to discuss various things. We're all staying in the city until the real Skyfire's confirmed. Feldrark's going to send a few of his own people with us, perhaps even more virgins. But he wants to exchange boys as well as girls and he'll only send volunteers. You never said how clever he was.

'Ivdulon says the world goes round the sun, the moon round the world. She showed me diagrams and figures. The drawings were wonderful but I'd need more help to understand the numbers. I understand what she meant, though and how she'd worked it out. But it goes against what we've always believed, doesn't it? I'm a bit uncertain how I should feel about it all, to tell the truth. Father's always been so certain and I tried to follow his example.'

'But you're cleverer than us, Tumalind. You always understand stuff I can't grasp. You'll soon accept what Ivdulon's told you. Are we still going on the new pilgrimage?'

'Yes. It's your punishment for kidnapping Jodisa. I'll come as well. Dagla Kaz says it's up to me; he won't force me now Ytraa's told him I wasn't really Chosen. Father's got to be punished more than you, though. He's to be stripped and whipped in the same way he beat Jodisa, even though it's not normally allowed. Feldrark was angry when Dagla Kaz said it but he's going to let him do it anyway. They've been discussing all sorts of things and I think Feldrark's willing to put up with a bit of pain and humiliation for Father in exchange for something Dagla Kaz has promised for him and Followers in Muhnilahm. I'm not sure what it is, but it might have something to do with the prayer posture. Anyway, Father's to be beaten tomorrow and I've got to witness it. They're not doing it in public; just those from the party and a few from the city. I hope they don't hurt him too much.'

'Not tnetsi thorns?'

'Oh, no! Only what he did to her. Used his belt, didn't he?'

'On her bare skin. I had to grab hold of him more than once or he'd have made her bleed. Mind you, she was a lot of trouble to begin with.'

'What did you expect? You couldn't expect her to thank you, now, could you?'

'Tell the truth, I thought she coped really well. She's a lot like you, to be honest, Tumalind. Only not so wonderful.'

She bent and kissed him, untied her waistrope, pulled her tabard over her head and stood for him, before dousing the lamp and slipping into her own bed. 'Good night, my love. Soon; as soon as you've recovered, we'll join and I'll take you inside me. Sleep well.'

'And I'm supposed to just go to sleep now?'

She grinned under cover of the darkness, but allowed the teasing to filter into her voice for him. 'Of course. Why not?'

Dagla Kaz had learned a great deal from Ivdulon. When associated with knowledge from secret texts in his cell, it made devastating change inevitable. He wondered how Feldrark maintained his air of equilibrium. Dagla Kaz found Ivdulon's theories easy to grasp and it concerned him that Jhonaht found them so hard to understand. The attractive young virgin, Tumalind, had not only understood but asked questions that had surprised both himself and Ivdulon, showing remarkable insight for one so young and unschooled. She'd impressed them with her astute powers of reasoning and her directed curiosity.

The girl was clever, but also undeniably sensual and inviting, especially now she was no longer a sacred virgin. Blue eyes, like his. He considered her approximate age and origins and tried to work out if there might be a link between them. He had offspring all over the island, after all. Morstahn, seventeen or eighteen years ago. No. Not Morstahn, but the Plains of Ytraa. A lovely young woman, recently wed to a dull and hidebound commoner. It had been at the new cycle hallowday when the Morstahn contingent had attended the celebrations.

At the time, the woman he was frowking had had the temerity to suggest that he was a less than perfect lover. She'd even dared laugh at him. But he'd dealt with her disrespect and found a reason to have her hung in a beating bag, her cries of pain lessening the sting of her mockery. The hidebound commoner had taken part in the beating, with gusto. He'd seen him with his beautiful wife and determined he'd have her; it was unjust she should be saddled with such an oaf. He'd blessed her, taking her as she prayed, and filled her with his seed in the name of Ytraa. Even now, after so many years and so many women, he could recall the mingling of his lust and revenge as he used the space she offered to her God in worship. He'd felt like Ytraa then, her body surrendering utterly as she knelt with her face in the grass and gave herself to her God and welcomed his seed.

So, Tumalind may be his daughter. Else, how did she come by those eyes? And the oaf, who'd beaten his former consort with such enthusiasm, the oaf whose wife he'd taken so deliciously, was Aglydron. Dagla Kaz laughed. Tomorrow he'd have that poor fool at his mercy, naked and bowed as he strapped him for beating Jodisa.

Such delicious vengeance that he should have made this discovery before the punishment. He could give Aglydron a taste of what the fool had given the mocking woman who had, after all, done nothing against the laws of Ytraa. And, as he lashed his naked buttocks with the man's own belt, he could picture his beautiful wife giving herself to Ytraa and receiving the seed that had probably become Tumalind. He must ensure there was a willing woman ready for him afterwards, to release the lust and desire the beating would engender. Even as he thought of this, he felt want grow and demand satisfaction. But he was alone. He must have a woman.

'Where's Pharah-Li, daughter of Rrildyss Kaz? I have need of her.'

He had no hope that any answer would come but he must have satisfaction, some outlet for the urgent need he felt. He paced the chamber, his tabard cast off and revealing his desire, his feet slapping the floor. The lamplight shadowed the far corners and revealed his lonely bed, mocking in its emptiness. Would no one come to him?

The door opened without the customary knock and a lovely young woman entered, peeling off her tunic as she closed the door behind her. Without a word, she shoved him onto the bed. He gazed on her and knew he'd be in her hands completely and he felt, again, as with that unnamed beauty in a distant land, the fear and thrill of absolute dependency.

Tumalind responded to the summons after breakfast, following Horsylth to a terrace at the eastern end of the palace grounds. The towering cliffs of Mount Vaherht loomed sheer on one side and the palace walls rose four storeys on the other. The terrace was

59

backed by a low open wall of stone pillars, each carved in the likeness of a different animal standing on its hind legs. A balustrade of curved stone topped the columns. Two storeys below, the main courtyard of the palace swept to the rear. In front, the city lay in splendour, tier upon tier falling away to the flat plain of the lower half and beyond to the shining sea. In the morning sunlight, all shone white and clean, the shadows pale beneath the west-facing cliff.

The rest of the party was already assembled when Tumalind arrived: all who'd been with her or her father. Dagla Kaz, resplendent in ceremonial gold and red tabard, stood before the group, his face displaying barely concealed anticipation. With those that she recognised, stood a young woman she'd seen about the palace but didn't know. Stunningly beautiful with pale golden hair falling in shining waves below her waist, she wore a tunic in white and gold, parted over her full breasts and covering barely enough of her legs to make her decent. Her narrow waist was circled by a fine cord of woven gold thread and her lapis lazuli eyes were fixed on Dagla Kaz in a manner that left no doubt about her feelings.

Aglydron stood alone at the front of the terrace, gazing over the city. Feldrark walked over and spoke softly, patting his shoulder in token of friendship. She couldn't hear what the Wharhll said but it seemed to give her father some comfort and she was grateful for that.

It was hard; this punishment of her father. He'd always been first to strike a blow at public beatings and done so with enthusiasm born of zeal. Now he stood before this assembly to be scourged for...for what, she wondered. Had he been more merciful, she thought, Ytraa might have shown him more mercy. But he'd always encouraged others to beat the victim savagely to press home the message.

She could imagine Jodisa's pain and humiliation as she bent to his belt and felt the leather bite into her unprotected skin. Tumalind had suffered the same fate at his hands more than once. But Jodisa, alone, frightened, captive and without hope of aid, must have grown to hate Aglydron, and to feel more than mere gratitude for Okkyntalah's timely interventions. So, it was more difficult for her to feel real sympathy for her father now. She felt for him but he'd brought her up to believe that sympathy for a wrongdoer was irreverent. Nevertheless, this was one beating she'd have preferred not to witness. She only hoped this wasn't to be one of the occasions her father supported so enthusiastically, when witnesses were exhorted to take part in the beating.

Dagla Kaz stepped forward and asked Aglydron to approach. As he stepped closer to the High Priest, all fell still and quiet.

'You are wearing the belt that you used to beat Jodisa?'

Aglydron nodded. 'As you commanded, Dagla Kaz.'

'Remove it.'

He handed it to Dagla Kaz who swished the air with it and then allowed it to drop in a line from his hand.

'Aglydron of Morstahn, on the island of Muhnilahm, you have been brought to this place to face the charge that you kidnapped the virgin then known as Jodisa-Li of Chalamamnon. What have you to say?'

'I had to take Jodisa. I saw a mistake in the Choosing and had to put it right or all Followers would suffer. I didn't know how else to do it. I knew Jodisa wouldn't go freely, so I had to take her by force. I tried not to harm her and I didn't violate her or let any man join with her.'

'Hear, all who stand here present, that I have communed with Ytraa on this matter. Ytraa has let it be known that the Choosing was indeed conducted in error. It was Ytraa's will that Aglydron, Okkyntalah and Tumalind alone be aware of this. It is Ytraa's will that the Followers of Muhnilahm and those of Litkala be reunited. This has now been achieved by the marriage of Jodisa-Li to Feldrark, according to the will of Ytraa, and by the bringing of myself and my pilgrims into this fair city.

'We know that Ytraa works in mysterious ways. Even I, High Priest and father of Jodisa, was ignorant in this matter until all had been concluded according to the will of Ytraa. That Aglydron and Okkyntalah acted as they did is testament to their faith and courage and I applaud their act on those points. It is not for us to question the will of Ytraa and I do not do so. Ytraa willed a certain thing done and Aglydron and Okkyntalah were instruments of Ytraa, of that there can be no doubt. For their action in that regard, neither is to be punished. In fact, they are respected and praised for their brave and reverent act.'

There was general agreement at this, though the unknown blonde girl seemed less impressed.

'However, there are other matters to be considered.' He turned to Aglydron and indicated he should remove the tabard. Aglydron did so with what dignity he could and lay the garment over the balustrade behind him. 'All know that it is not usual to beat the naked. In this case, there are reasons why matters must be dealt with differently. But I move ahead of myself. There is another issue I must address first.'

Tumalind was sure he'd made her father naked at this stage to humiliate him further and she was disappointed that the High Priest should stoop to such a level for personal revenge.

'The men stole a fishing boat in order to escape the island. They deprived the owner of his means of making a living and will have caused him significant problems. Theft is not usual on our island and I cannot permit it to go unpunished. What have you to say on

61

this matter, Aglydron? Remember that you must also speak for Okkyntalah, who is recovering from his injuries.'

Aglydron stood upright and tall, his hands by his side and his head up. 'I admit the theft and I've asked Ytraa to forgive it. We couldn't think of any other way to do it. We had to be quick and secret and get Jodisa off the island. We had no choice. Stealing seemed better than denying the will of Ytraa. But we knew we were breaking the law and expected to be punished.'

'An honest statement, which does justice to the guilty parties. Ytraa has let it be known that these two acted as the servants of Ytraa. Nevertheless, a sin was committed and may not go unpunished. The two will complete the pilgrimage to Choshinahm as bearers, hunters and general aids to the party. No further restitution will be sought from them for this matter and the authorities will recompense the fisherman for his losses.'

A little muttering, approval and some mild dissent followed this but Tumalind was resigned to continuing the journey. At least she'd be with Okkyntalah. It occurred to her, however, that the theft had the same cause as the kidnapping and she wondered why they should be treated differently.

'There is a further issue which needs resolving and, though this may not be the perfect forum, I feel it best to have it out of the way at this stage. Clearly, Tumalind was never intended as a Virgin Gift. She is now, therefore, free to continue her life as she will. If, as I believe is her wish, she intends to marry Okkyntalah, then she may do so and either accompany him on the pilgrimage or else return to Muhnilahm with those I intend to send back soon with messages. Have you decided, Tumalind?'

'I want to marry Okkyntalah and go with him wherever he goes, if I may.'

Dagla Kaz nodded, evidently pleased with her decision. 'There remains a final consideration, the main reason for our assembly here. As I have already stated, the beating of the unclothed is not usual. However, Aglydron has been accused of beating Jodisa whilst she remained naked and, in some cases, bound. What have you to say to this?'

'I admit it. I'm sorry for it. She risked all our lives. I had to make her do as I told her. I think she hoped I wouldn't punish her if she was naked, so she misbehaved at the time for prayers. I never stripped her. I just beat her there and then.'

'How many times did you beat her? How many strokes?'

'I don't know.'

'Jodisa tells me you beat her on three occasions and that Okkyntalah stopped you after ten blows on two of these and that on the other you struck her six times. Do you agree?'

'Sounds right. Okkyntalah was right to interfere. I hit him but he still tried to protect her from my anger. That's what it was. I was angry and afraid and she suffered because of it. I apologise to Jodisa and ask her forgiveness. If she wants revenge, I don't blame her. Go ahead, Jodisa.'

She stepped forward, took the belt from her father and swished the air with it. 'I accept your apology, Aglydron. One stroke only, in repayment for the fear and pain you inflicted, and to demonstrate to you some of what you put me through. I believe you've earned a reprieve from the remainder through your sacrifice, bravery and devotion during our journey together. What Ytraa and the law may demand in addition isn't for me to decide.'

Aglydron turned, bent forward and placed his hands on the low balustrade. Jodisa lashed the leather belt swiftly and hard against his skin and handed it back to her father.

'Jodisa is more merciful than many. I, however, do not have the luxury of personal lenience and must administer according to law and precedent. I must therefore personally give another twenty-five, asking only that those present witness this punishment.'

Dagla Kaz moved so that he could administer the blows with ease and then lashed Aglydron's naked buttocks with measured, deliberate, harsh stripes. The beating left him cut, bleeding and bruised. Dagla Kaz limped off at once with the blonde stranger. Tumalind wondered at the expression of relish on the young woman's face as she'd watched the beating.

Wiping tears from her eyes, she followed her father to the infirmary, carrying his tabard and belt, stained with his own blood. He'd made no sound during the beating and walked with dignity in spite of his shame and pain. She hoped Myllthlan would heal his injuries immediately but, whether because of Dagla Kaz's obvious distrust of her or for some other reason, she wasn't present.

Tumalind made her father as comfortable as possible and left him lying on his front in his room. Then she dashed next door to tell Okkyntalah they could now definitely be married as soon as he was well.

Chapter 7

JOININGS AND PARTINGS

Dagla Kaz woke alone. He tried to raise himself to find Pharah-Li but failed. Paralysed, he saw only blinding light that pained him. What had happened to him? Violent pain seared his head as fever soaked his brow.

He heard laughter and female voices in conversation; sounds and tones distorted, maybe hostile, certainly mocking, so that he tried to twist round to identify their source. Movement increased the pain in his head so that he cried out.

'Dagla Kaz?'

The voice sounded as though it should be familiar. He knew it, without being able to identify it. He half opened his eyes and a shape, monstrous and dark, loomed over him, threatening to suffocate him as it fell toward his face. He cried out again but couldn't shift. Someone or something had taken all life from his limbs and muscles so he could no longer shift or lift any part of himself. Everything was hot. Too hot. Suffocating.

'Dagla Kaz, can you hear me?'

The question sounded concerned, but he wasn't so easily fooled. He knew he had enemies. Enemies who wished him dead. What had they done to him? Why was he helpless? He could feel no bonds, nothing tying him, only the huge weight of a cover stifling him with its heat.

'The women want you defeated.'

He must remove it. But the shape hovered over him, moving; a darker cave opening and closing somewhere in its shifting outline of haloed shadow. His hands couldn't lift the weight from him.

'Rise above them, show the women you're superior.'

He was drowning; falling into blank black nothing where his existence would cease and all would be pain forever.

He opened his eyes. Had time passed? Bright light. And a brilliance that was edged. Too bright; he closed his eyes again. Sounds: unidentifiable. Scent: something sweet and sharp. Air flowing across his skin. Cool softness at his forehead. Damp fabric beneath him and a soft surface.

'I think he's waking.'

Words that made sense yet meant nothing.

'Through it, at last. Fool, should've let Myllthlan treat 'im straight away. Just as well young Pharah-Li warned us when she did else 'e'd be good an' dead now, that's for sure.'

65

'What was she doing with him, though?'

'Pharah-Li? What else?'

Ribald laughter.

Memory began to return in pieces that lacked cohesion so that he recalled softness of female skin against his own, pain felt by another, a sensation of power, a surge of release into darkness and warmth, a bed, a lash without screams of pain, a gathering.

"Ow long's it been?'

'Three days. Should we send young Horsylth to fetch Jodisa?'

'She asked to be told when 'e started comin' round.'

These voices were unknown. Who was Horsylth? What did they need with Jodisa-Li? He moved and found he could. He opened his eyes again and the brightness that was light hurt only a little and was sunlight through a window. The brightness that was edged resolved into the white walls of a room. Two women, matronly, stood at his feet. One watched him move and signalled to the other who had her back to him.

'Awake, at last? How're you feeling, dear?'

He opened his mouth but words fell silent at his lips.

'Drink? Get 'im some water, will you? Touch an' go it's been. Hadn't been for Myllthlan, you'd be a goner, dear'

Soft strong arms slid beneath his shoulders and lifted him. 'Up you come. Have a drop of water.'

He tasted the lightness of it on his tongue, felt it drain into the cavities of his mouth, cooling. Felt it trickle down his throat. He managed to nod his thanks and tried to sit unaided, only to fall back again.

'Not yet, dear. You'll be too weak. Just lie still, now. You're lucky to be with us. Don't try anything ambitious yet. It's enough you're drawing breath.'

Suddenly Jodisa-Li was there, standing at the head of the bed, dropping to kiss his forehead, tears in her eyes. 'Oh, Father, I thought we'd lost you. How do you feel?'

He let her pull away and look at him, a smile of warmth and welcome on her lips.

'I...' His mouth could make sounds of speech. 'I feel so weak. What happened?'

'Your wound turned septic, poisoned you. You almost lost your leg, almost lost your life, but Myllthlan saved it and you, brought you back from the very doors of death. It's taken her nearly two days to recover.'

'Myllthlan? Did she....?'

'When you're better, Father. She did what she had to and made you well. Be content.'

'When is it? How long have I...?'

'It's the twenty-fourth of the twelfth portion, Father. You've been in here for three days and the evening of another. It's approaching noon. They'll feed you in a little. I must go back to Feldrark and let everyone know you're recovering now. Get some rest. They say you'll be in bed for a few days yet.'

'Myllthlan, you say? I owe her thanks, and an apology, don't I?'

'They'll wait until you're in a better state.'

She left as suddenly as she'd arrived and the two matronly women remained. Another woman moved close; at first, he thought Jodisa had come back but it was Tumalind and he realized he shared a room with Okkyntalah. He turned his head and watched her help her man sit up, carefully clothe him in a tunic and slowly draw him to his feet. They approached, hand in hand, and looked down at him.

'I'm glad to see you awake again, Dagla Kaz. For a while it seemed you might not return to us, you know.' She bent and kissed his forehead. 'Welcome back.'

'Okkyntalah, this gem is bright and warm and precious. See that you deserve her. She's...she's been like a daughter to me on this trip into the unknown.'

'I'll do all I can for her, Dagla Kaz. I love her and I think that's a good start.'

'Love. Yes, I've wondered about that. I hear of it and some say it exists. In you two, I begin to see what it might be. I've never known it. Perhaps I'm too...too selfish. Perhaps.'

'Rest, Dagla Kaz. The women here know what's needed to restore the body to full health. See; Okkyntalah was very ill and he's now on his feet. If all goes well, the day after tomorrow he and I will join and wed.'

'I wish to be there when you do.'

'If you're well enough, we'd welcome you.'

'But you won't delay if I'm not.'

Tumalind and Okkyntalah looked at each other.

'We've delayed enough, haven't we?'

Dagla Kaz nodded. He knew he might obstruct them if he wished but they deserved no such delay. They'd waited long enough because of his interference already. He would let them be what they wished to become. At least that would be one act of goodness he could claim when the time came for him to face the higher being he still called Ytraa.

'You join and wed as you've planned. It will please me to know, Tumalind, that you're happy and fulfilled as a woman. Go, with my blessing and the full blessing of Ytraa on your joining.'

Okkyntalah curled his fist and touched his knuckles to the back of Dagla Kaz's hand. Tumalind bent and kissed his forehead once more. He watched them leave his field of view and heard them depart the chamber, leaving him alone with the two matrons.

'You'll take some nourishment?'

He turned and found one of the women staring at him, a bowl and spoon in hand. 'Please. But I can't sit by myself...'

They helped, resting his back on a mound of pillows, and he saw his was one of four beds in the room. Okkyntalah's remained unmade after his departure.

'Who else sleeps here?'

'Aglydron spent a couple of nights 'ere, flat on 'is belly and bare-arsed to let the air an' ointment 'eal 'is skin. 'E's well enough to go about normally, now Myllthlan's mended them stripes you gave 'im. Not completely at ease yet when 'e sits down but Myllthlan was already weak from healin' you. Anyroad, it's no more'n 'e deserves for what 'e did to our Jodisa.'

'Your Jodisa-Li?'

'Is now. Not yours no more, is she? No more Jodisa-Li now she's married to our Wharhll. Our Jodisa's set to make 'im the 'appiest man that ever lived, I'd say.'

'And the other bed?'

'Why, Tumalind, o' course! Can't 'ave the young 'uns kept apart when they both 'ave so much need o' one another.'

'I made it clear they were not to…'

'Not up to you, though, is it? An' keep yoursen still or you'll do yoursen a damage.'

'Suppose they…they joined before…'

'With Okkyntalah so close death's door he almost fell through it? Use your 'ead, man. Anyroad, that Tumalind's a grand lass. She knows what's right, does that 'un. Wish there were more like 'er. She'd not let 'im, even if 'e'd tried.'

'You're very sure.'

'See that there window? Behind it's where I sleep. I'd 'ave known if they'd been up to more'n a harmless bit of comfort. I'm lookin' forward to their joinin'. They'll make Ytraa right proud, they will. An', in case you're plannin' otherwise than I say, fellah-me-lad, you'll do well to remember I've eyes on you at all times while you're in 'ere.'

'You forget to whom you speak, woman.'

'No. But you forget who's in charge in 'ere, fellah-me-lad. It's me. Not you. Nor all your titles nor your fancy dress'll 'ave no effect on me. In 'ere what I says, goes. You'll do well to remember that. I tell you to bare your skinny squitter for me, you does it, understand?'

'Nobody's ever spoken to me…'

'More's the pity. If they 'ad, you'd not 'ave such a grand opinion o' yourself. Right. That's all gone. I'll get you a drink. Drop o' pale or some o' the deep; which is it to be?'

'I have a choice?'

She actually stroked his head as if he were a child and smiled at him like an indulgent mother. He knew he was in safe, if insolent, hands and managed a smile in return.

'Aye, in this, if nowt else.'

'The deep, then, please, mother. And I'd thank you for a shoulder to lean on so I might relieve myself in the meantime.'

'You might but you'll not get it. Use this.' She handed him a glass container and left him to it.

He shook his head. Denying Myllthlan and refusing her healing had nearly cost his life, reduced him to this absurd, humiliating state and left him helpless in the hands of these old women who considered themselves more important than him. And, in the end, Myllthlan had healed him anyway. He made use of the vessel, shook his head, and wondered how many more lessons he had yet to learn. Humility seemed a high priority.

It was only as he placed the vessel on the floor beside his bed that he recognised it for what it was and marvelled at the skill and craftsmanship that could produce such an item. And to put such skill and artistry to this mundane use; what sort of society had he entered? It put to shame so much he'd praised in Muhnilahm. There was a great deal yet to be done before he set out on the proper pilgrimage to Choshinahm, but he knew that the man who led that mission would be very different from the one who'd taken them from the island.

'Don't go soft on us. We're relying on you.'

⁂

Jodisa, relaxed and utterly fulfilled, lay staring at the space in the blackness where the starlight showed her the open window. A breeze carried the smell of surf and sounds of breaking waves from far below. Beside her, Feldrark breathed shallow draughts in serene sleep, his body touching hers as night air drifted warm and soft over skin unhindered by covers. She stretched out and stroked him, for the simple enjoyment of touching him. He paused briefly, then resumed the sleeping rhythm of his breathing.

The day had been full and exciting. Tumalind and Okkyntalah had joined before Ytraa and wed in front of a group of witnesses including the Kiral and Kirallah as well as her father, seated for those parts of the ceremony not requiring his active participation. Pharah-Li had been remarkably considerate in her joining with him for the ceremony and he'd been able to make his own way back to the infirmary, with help, afterwards. She and Feldrark, reliving their own wedding, had engaged with more enthusiasm than some might deem proper for the event but no one had complained. The small feast that had followed had been occasion for congratulations and fun, with even the three Virgin Gifts seeming to enjoy themselves; eating, drinking, dancing and singing.

All present felt the couple were right for each other and fully deserving of the good wishes everyone expressed. To the astonishment of all, Ivdulon had attended the ceremony. The talk was that Tumalind had persuaded her to leave her tower and spend some time with the citizens so she might better understand them. It was something

69

Ivdulon hadn't done even for Jodisa's wedding to Feldrark. Forced to join, as she was attending the ceremony, she'd accepted a young buck from the upper city. Clearly unimpressed with his attentions, she'd disengaged as soon as possible and been first to rise to her feet.

Later, she'd spoken with the pretty woman Father had brought with him from Kabalyt. Netrodyl was much like the Kirallah to look at; younger, of course, but very similar in appearance and style. Perhaps that had made her interesting to the woman of knowledge, since she certainly didn't seem to be very bright.

'You all equate ignorance with stupidity. Intelligence and knowledge aren't the same. This young woman's been isolated from knowledge but that doesn't mean she has no intelligence. Give me a year with her and then see what you think.'

Ivdulon had invited her to her tower and Netrodyl had agreed, apparently content to live up there.

Corphanda, fussing round her charges like a mother hen, had made sure they weren't in any danger from the men. The tubby lady clearly revelled in her task and she hadn't even had to smack Porryh during the evening; the troublesome virgin apparently no longer trying to deny the reality of her situation.

Though she felt wonderfully relaxed, sleep evaded Jodisa. She and Feldrark continued to espouse Myllthlan's advice, wanting a period together before she began to nurture his seed and bring forth their first child. Jodisa hadn't told him about the procedure she'd endured at the hands of the Holy Ones. The reversal was something she could achieve by herself but it wasn't yet time. Though, if they continued to join as completely and frequently as they had since their first coupling, she felt sure Feldrark might soon question why she wasn't bursting with child.

She turned to look at him in the faint starlight, the shimmer giving form to his shape in the general blackness of the night. The landscape of his body still fascinated her.

A vague movement near the door caught her eye and she sat up. 'Who's there?'

At once, she was aware of the door closing, perhaps a figure disappearing from view. She slipped from the bed and stepped round to look into the corridor but could see and hear nothing. Maybe it had been imagination. Who would creep into their room in the middle of the night? She stood in the open doorway, staring into darkness beyond, where only faint edges of corners gave any clue to direction and distance. But she was certain no one moved, no one even breathed out there. Behind her, she could hear Feldrark's soft sleeping. She shrugged and returned to bed, closing the door behind her and, for reasons she couldn't quite determine, placed an empty chair against it.

Almost certain it must have been her imagination, perhaps the result of sleepiness she hadn't recognized, she lay down quietly, so she wouldn't disturb her husband, and listened to the night. Somewhere in a neighbouring room, someone moaned briefly in slumber and a question, wordless but full of doubt, was raised in a dream. Nothing moved beyond the breeze and the distant sea on the shore. All was at peace. Slowly, sleep drifted over her.

⁕

Aklon had spent late evening mindtalking with Ivdulon. Now he had to persuade Chellyth she must remove her people from The Point. Early morning sunshine drew sharp shadows over sand and stone as he took her hand and led her from the village so they could talk in private.

'I have sound reasons to believe you are no longer safe, Chellyth. I think that they will very soon send an army and wipe out your settlement. My advice is to go at once. I recommend the place I showed Por-Kildu and Mkolo-ti. It is surrounded by terrain difficult for any army to pass through.'

'This because you killed that no good priest?'

'In part. They are frightened, now, and you are not supposed to exist. They tell the population nobody can live here and they tolerate your presence only because it is a useful prison for dissenters and a convenient haven for parents to leave those infants who were born incomplete. They did not believe it was worth their while to do anything about The Point as long as the populace remained ignorant of your numbers. With the death of Wesdan Kaz, and a few others I have in mind, together with the imminent return of certain individuals from travels overseas, they will be forced to take action. That is why you should relocate before they send an armed force to patrol the Scar. The priest's death has stirred them into thinking for a change. I am disappointed to admit there is someone amongst the Holy Ones with a brain. Shame; I had so looked forward to their panic and the ensuing chaos. I think we need to move you before it is too late.'

'Will you lead us?'

'No. You have no need of me. I have other things I must do. News has reached me of changes that I need to deal with at once.'

'But you've been here or in the jungle for days, Aklon. How can you receive news?'

'I have ways of collecting information even you would not understand, Chellyth. But, believe me when I say that things are now moving, both on the island and off it. We are at the beginning of great change and I would prefer it if you could manage to live through the turmoil and share in the better times to come.'

'What ways?'

'You would not believe me if I told you. Worse, you would think me mad.'

'I think you're mad already. Try me.'

He stared at her for a long time but she didn't look away. He nodded and explained,

71

using the same words that had succeeded with Shoarhn and was delighted to find she responded positively. She was more interested and surprised than sceptical.

'I believe you, Aklon-Dji. I don't pretend to understand how such a thing could be but I believe you can do it. I wouldn't tell Por-Kildu, though. He's too much in need of proof to believe in something like that. But, if that's how you get your information, I'm willing to accept what you say and take my people on this dangerous journey. You've never let us down before. If we're to escape before you set your other wheels in motion, I'd better announce it now.'

He watched her walk across the dead dry earth to the shabby little hut to discuss plans with Por-Kildu. Her loveliness had always moved him and he saw, with regret, how the hardness of her life was beginning to age her. She was beautiful still but her youth was gone and she would never again have that bearing and vitality she had possessed when he'd first met her.

His latest contact with Ivdulon and Jodisa warned him that Dagla Kaz would soon send a party back to the island. They both seemed concerned that the High Priest would begin concerted action to destroy the inhabitants of The Point and to hunt him down and execute him. Ivdulon's concern was understandable but his sister's, and her repetition of Ivdulon's insistence that he mustn't contact Dagla Kaz by mindtalk, surprised him. It seemed Feldrark and Ivdulon between them had persuaded her that his way was better than her father's.

He scouted around the edge of the settlement and found Chellyth with Por-Kildu standing beside her, facing the assembled community and describing their imminent flight from The Point. He knew they'd go willingly and regardless of fear and difficulty. She'd earned their respect and won their love and they would go where she led, even to death if that was what she chose.

Without ceremony, he set off for the Scar at a comfortable lope that would take him to the foot of the cliff before mid-afternoon. Behind him, the murmuring of voices, raised in question and agreement, slowly faded and he wondered when he would again meet these most wronged victims of his father's reign.

⁂

The scrape of wood over polished stone broke into her dream and she emerged from enveloping sleep only reluctantly into wakefulness. Feldrark, raised up on an arm, gazed down at her with love and a question on his face as, beyond him, seen through the gap under his raised torso, a girl from the palace entered the room carrying a tray.

'Sorry, Sire. The chair....'

'It's all right. I placed it there myself, in the night. I thought someone had come into our room.'

72

The girl nodded gratefully and placed the tray of buttered fresh bread, red and green grapes and cool merphlion juice on the bedside locker. She took Feldrark's chamber wrap and held it for him to put on and then helped Jodisa into hers.

'Someone came in, you say?'

'I thought they did. It was probably just a dream. You know what it's like when you're half asleep...'

A horrified shriek shattered the peace, bursting through the quiet morning to tighten relaxed nerves into strings of tension. Jodisa and Feldrark stared at each other and the girl took a step toward the door. Footsteps populated the corridor, joined by the sound of concerned voices in a tumult of sudden confusion.

The door to their chamber burst wide. A palace guard crashed through, her face ashen with shock. 'Sire, I...I'm sorry, Sire. I do not mean to intrude but...Sire, the Kiral and Kirallah...they're...Oh, Ytraa have mercy!'

Chapter 8

PROMISES OF DEATH

Feldrark leapt from the bed and questioned the soldier. 'What? What's happened, woman?'

'They're dead. Murdered, Sire. Stabbed. In their bed. There's blood…'

He and Jodisa rushed next door, the soldier close behind. Feldrark hurried to the bed, his fists clenched so tightly the knuckles shone white, but blood alone told the story. It soaked the mattress and the room stank of gore and death. The Kiral and Kirallah lay uncovered, side by side. He, almost decapitated; she, stabbed through the heart. Other gashes and wounds punctured their bodies, arms and legs as if the killing had been frenzied. Blood splattered the walls, deepening in colour where it dried. Splashes of dark red marred even the pristine white stone of the high ceiling. There was no sign of intruders or a weapon.

'Call Myllthlan.' His voice struggled to escape gritted teeth.

Jodisa crossed her arms before her, clutching at her shoulders in an attempt to hold herself together. She knew the pair were beyond even the healer's help. Taking the soldier to one side, she spoke quietly to her. 'You can redeem yourself for your poor behaviour by organising a search of the city. Whoever did this will be covered in blood. If we act quickly, we may find them.'

The soldier hesitated only long enough to glance again at the carnage before she came smartly to full alertness, nodded her thanks to Jodisa, and left on her mission.

Feldrark took his mother's hand and clasped it between his own as he knelt beside the bed. Jodisa drew the sheet up from the end of the bed and covered them before taking the cold, lifeless hand of the Kiral between hers, holding back nausea and conscious of her need to be strong for Feldrark.

It was madness. There was no possible reason for this. Who would wish harm to the Kiral and Kirallah? The city was peaceful, civilized, calm. The people loved their leaders. No one wanted the deaths of these two beloved people. Yet, someone had murdered them. It made no sense. She gazed at Feldrark and saw him in need of what little comfort she might bring. Deserting the dead, she took the living flesh, holding his shoulders and feeling tension, grief, anger, shock and disbelief flowing through his very being. Her mind reeled in turmoil as he projected his feelings to her without control.

Myllthlan rushed in, still fastening her robe. She glanced at the scene and closed her eyes. 'I can do nothing here; I'm sorry. I've no power to raise the dead.'

Rrildyss Kaz and Patradko Kaz arrived together, as though answering a summons, and stood aghast. They pleaded with Myllthlan and the healer took pity, prepared herself and gathered her powers. For a brief time, she placed her hands on the bodies, her own form paling as the energy drained from her until she collapsed from the effort.

Others came; male and female guards, servants, officials and some of the guests; amongst them, Aglydron and Wendarah, who'd occupied a room further down the corridor. He went straight to the healer and raised her from the pooled blood she lay in, holding her as she slowly recovered consciousness. Last came Tumalind with Okkyntalah, hand in hand, faces still full of their night of joy. Along with all present, they were shocked into silence. The only word; 'why?'

'And who?' Ivdulon arrived from her high tower, Netrodyl trailing in her wake. 'Has anyone checked the prison, and the house where the captives are kept?'

Jodisa, grateful for her practical action, sent soldiers to find answers.

'I suggest we clear the room. I wish to see what may be discovered here.'

Ivdulon waited for all to leave, bloody footprints trailing through the exit. Netrodyl remained, ready to do the bidding of the wise woman. Jodisa led Feldrark away, giving what small succour she might.

The soldier escorting Aglydron to the meeting carried her sword unsheathed. He followed her along corridors scented with Threlepsis flowers crushed in hot water to cover the smell of slaughter. The woman hurried, and dashed away as soon as she'd shown Aglydron the open door to the chamber.

Feldrark, draped in the grey of death and mourning, leaned on one end of the huge oval table. Others he knew; Caarl, Tryonta, Dagla Kaz still recovering, the two High Priests of Litkala, Myllthlan and Okkyntalah, were already present. Ivdulon, deep in conversation with Feldrark and two senior soldiers, a man and a woman, spoke too softly to be heard beyond their closed circle. Looking for a place to sit, Aglydron spotted Jodisa, also draped in mourning grey, alone at one side of the table.

'May I sit here?'

She nodded, face solemn, lively eyes glistening.

Another three soldiers entered, the last two holding Chislanda firmly between them. A bruised eye was closed, her bottom lip split and bleeding, and her torn tunic exposing a gashed breast. Through her mask of feigned indifference, Aglydron saw very real fear. The soldiers goaded her to the top end of the table where they bound her with leather straps round her wrists to two rings in the wall above her head. She set her jaw and stared with affected defiance across the room.

Ivdulon nodded to Feldrark who looked up and around the room before striking the table three times with his fist. Silence came on the last beat and he stepped a little away from the table and closer to Chislanda.

'You all know why we're here. I'll not waste time with unnecessary talk. We know enough to be certain that the Kiral and Kirallah were murdered by the other woman from Mipahnhil who we spared with this whore after the fighting on the plain.'

He turned and swiped the back of his hand across Chislanda's face, making her nose bleed to drip more red onto her damaged body.

'She's escaped the palace, perhaps even the city, but she'll be caught and brought back. This woman has told us nothing of value, yet. She will.' He struck her again, closing her eye. 'Mhortag's whore!'

Ivdulon rose and touched his shoulder and, for a moment, the two stood in front of the captive, unspeaking but seeming locked in silent battle. At last, Feldrark nodded once and sat down.

'Ivdulon has examined the facts, such as they are. It's clear the woman acted alone except that, with the help of this...,' He gestured at Chislanda. 'She seduced their guards into carelessness. Well, her own victim died on his sword, the same blade she used to murder my mother and father. This whore used her body alone to ensnare the unfortunate man. He's already paid dearly for his stupidity and lives to regret his fall onto a hook that will never again lure him. How the murderer found the chamber of my mother and father and why she killed them we don't yet know. But this vile creature will tell all before she dies.

'I've called you all here today because these murders constitute nothing less than an act of war.'

Aglydron saw Chislanda start at this statement: such an outcome had never occurred to her. It was difficult to believe she could be so naïve but he was convinced her reaction was genuine.

'We have long felt the enmity of Mipahnhil and their false claims. We go, now, to end this fight in their own stinking cesspool. If we must, we'll kill every heathen soul. I've already called a muster and set in motion the means to invade the place by land and sea. In six days, on the third of the first portion of the New Cycle, we march. That the army and militia will go is beyond question. Some amongst our guests may wish to accompany us.'

'I'll go. I have a personal interest.'

'Thank you, Okkyntalah, your skill with bow, sword and spear will be valued.'

'I too, with my High Priest's permission, will come with you. We are indebted to your people in many ways, Feldrark, and I would repay some of that debt.' Caarl looked to Dagla Kaz who nodded his approval.

'I, of course, must go.'

'I wish you to stay, Jodisa. Who will govern, otherwise?'

'I go, my lord, nevertheless. Like Okkyntalah, I have a personal interest in this fight. I was there at the start and I'll be there at its end. There are many women in the army and militia of Litkala and the women of Mipahnhil fight alongside their men. Let Ivdulon and the High Priests control the city during our absence.'

'So be it, my lady. Though I would shield you from this danger. And, as I'll explain later, you weren't in at the beginning: this began many hundreds of cycles ago. Rrildyss Kaz will come with us to lead our prayers. Patradko Kaz and Ivdulon can keep the citizens safe until we return.'

'I, though I won't fight unless I must, will come. You'll have need of a healer before the battle is done.'

'Thank you, Myllthlan, yours is a welcome contribution and you shall have help.'

'I have to come, Feldrark. Maybe more than any other, I was in at the start of this thing that now seems to be a war. But, let me question the prisoner before you torture her. I know her well and might find out what you want without burning flesh or breaking bones.'

'For your companionship in battle, I thank you, Aglydron. As to the woman, she's but a midden witch and a whore of Tryhnn and less than dust to me. I'd have her questioned by those who know how to wring information from the unwilling.'

Aglydron tensed and breathed deep. 'Do you want information, Feldrark, or, forgive me; do you want her to pay in pain for what the other did to your parents?'

Everyone looked at him, shock or curiosity on their faces, and then back at Feldrark, who, in turn, gazed at Jodisa, as if seeking confirmation.

'You may have the woman to yourself for a day and a night, Aglydron. She'll be bound and naked so she can conceal no weapons, and a guard will stand at the door to the chamber. Do with her what you will; I care not if she lives or dies. But find answers. If she fails to give the information I require, I'll put her to blade and fire, hammer and chain until she tells all or perishes.'

Aglydron nodded and looked across at Chislanda who stared back at him; defiance modified only by the puzzled question in her eyes.

※ ✥ ※

The chamber was small and bare but for the stone bench on which Aglydron sat. Chislanda, wrists no longer bound behind her, huddled in the corner where an iron ring chained her ankle to the floor. She'd refused to look at him during the hours he'd spent trying to persuade her to give him what Feldrark sought. He'd tried threats, pleas, entreaty, logic, reason; all without response. Now the time was coming to a close and soon men would come with blades to cut her skin, irons to burn her, hammers to break her bones.

The thought of her under such torment was too much. He left the bench and knelt beside her, put his hand on her shoulder and felt her flesh tremble under his touch. 'If you'd just talk to me, Chislanda, I might save you...and our child.'

She looked at him, at last, unspoken questions still veiled by disbelieving eyes.

'It's possible. But you've got to tell me what I need to know.'

She seemed to consider but remained silent.

'I might even make Feldrark believe you're more use to us alive than dead. You could act as go-between when we get to Mipahnhil. But I can't do anything if you won't speak. Let me help you, Chislanda. Please. I love you.' The truth spilled from his lips, words in the open before he'd considered them or their effect.

His sincerity, at least, seemed to have penetrated her distrust. She ceased trembling and swallowed. 'The other woman, my brave companion; I won't name her and have you or your kind defile her memory, acted alone and unaided. My task was to keep the guard distracted. She was more courageous. She found her way into the palace without help. The guard she pleasured told her all she needed to know. The Kiral and Kirallah weren't who she meant to kill, though they deserved death as surely as anyone here. She hunted Okkyntalah, Feldrark and Jodisa. As long as I live, I'm permitted the honour of ending your life.'

'You can't do that if you're dead, Chislanda. If we go to Mipahnhil with a force of soldiers, what will happen?'

'You'll all be killed. For each of my people who dies, we'll destroy one of yours. We'll fight to every last man, woman and child, if we have to.'

'Why?'

'A life must be spent for a life taken, even if that life has been remade by the killer.'

'It's madness.'

'It's the way. The way. Honour, tradition, everything we believe demands this of us.'

'Even if you're all wiped out?'

'If that's our fate, so be it.'

'Pointless waste.'

'Life without honour is futile.'

'Honour. You talk of honour; you, who cheat and lie and make free men prisoners for your own ends? You, who steal men's lives to make your women pregnant because your own men are infertile. I tell you, honour without life isn't honour if no one's left to know of it.'

'We will prevail. You'll all die.'

'Chislanda, a hundred thousand people live here. How many in Mipahnhil? Twelve, fifteen thousand?'

'There's no other way.'

'I replaced the life, one I didn't take, in you. Why can't we do that?'

'Feldrark will avenge the death of his parents. We will end the lives of those who kill our people. You've taken our Galhta and the lives of those who hunted you.'

'We didn't take yours, or the other woman's.'

'Eighteen lives have ended now and, even if they replace them, those who killed shall die. You must die. And those who came to your aid in the field. Will Feldrark allow men to be taken to Mipahnhil to bring new life before they're eliminated?'

'Feldrark's given you more infants than that already. Why should he do more?'

'Feldrark's seed was a tithe. His was a small part of the price for the past. We'd have him father children till he died of old age. Litkala has long robbed Mipahnhil. It's just and proper that Litkala should repay some of its debt in seed.'

'How has Litkala robbed Mipahnhil?'

'They haven't told you?'

'You tell me.'

'Who do you think built this wondrous place? This brood of thieves has no skill to make a thing. We built Litkala. My ancestors.'

For a brief spell, Aglydron crouched, mouth open but silent. 'But why are you...?'

'Why do we live at the edge of the sea in a wooden town built on stilts? Many ages ago, those who now live here drove my ancestors out with trickery and fair words. They made us believe they were our friends, our brethren. Then, when we gave them access to the city, they drove us out with fire and blade.'

'Feldrark says Litkala was deserted when his ancestors arrived.'

'Feldrark lies. The city was occupied. It was home to my forebears who had skill with stone and metal. We were disinherited. That's why we kept Feldrark captive when he drifted into our land by the grace of Tryhnn. But there are too few of us to retake our true home and the seed of our men is poor and failing. There's some wasting force in the swamps and we diminish. That's why we made you lie with me, to replace the life of my beloved son. And was that such a trial? Did I not give pleasure in return for your seed? Each death is a loss we can't replace ourselves. We are forced to take seed from those outside or perish into nothingness. And now we come to avenge our people and find nothing here in return.'

'You'll find only death if revenge is what you're after, Chislanda. Revenge just makes more destruction, fear and loss. Revenge is the refuge of the spiritually corrupt.' He was so pleased he'd remembered Ivdulon's words and could now repeat them. They had an effect on Chislanda. She looked at him with a question in her eyes, as if doubt crept into her mind.

'Nobody gains anything. Everyone loses something. We could end the round of revenge and envy and destruction, Chislanda. Make your people see they can't win, and maybe we can find some way to reunite your people with their lost home.'

'You're a dreamer, Aglydron. You deal in pleasure and the softness of the body; talk of love and care. We're not interested in such things. Give us what's ours or give us death in the attempt. Tryhnn will take us gladly to her bosom; bring us joy in parting such as we never knew in life. The realm of Tryhnn is perfection, bliss and harmony, where joy and pleasure mingle through eternity. What is it to lose this life if we gain such rewards with its end?'

How could she put her faith in such as Tryhnn? 'What if Tryhnn doesn't exist? What if Tryhnn's false?'

She turned on him, hands outstretched to throttle. But beating, captivity and despair had weakened her. And she struggled with herself as much as with him. 'You'll die for that. Die for blasphemy. Die for the death you brought. Die for those you killed in the field.'

Aglydron took her hands in his and forced them from his throat. He saw confusion, fear and something deeper, remembered from their earlier contact. Holding her wrists, he pulled her toward him, driven by a want he'd never felt before. She resisted, struggled, but didn't lash out with her feet or spit at him as she might have. The fight was more within herself than with him. He watched her resistance break and her remembered passion with him boil to the surface, overwhelming her. She gave and he received her, took her, gave back. They joined, there, on the hard floor of her cell, her ankle still chained to iron and her face and body bruised and damaged by her captors.

Together on hard, ungiving stone, they lay entwined and spent. He kissed her swollen mouth, her closed and blackened eye, the gouges on her breast. She wept, silently, her tears salting skin until he dried them with the hem of his discarded tabard.

'What shall we do?'

'I'm required to destroy you for killing those who…'

'They were trying to end my life. You were trying to kill me. What am I meant to do, Chislanda? Offer my throat to slit and ask you to forgive me as you slay me?'

'What you're supposed to do is provide life in my belly and then die.' But there was no conviction left in her voice.

'Like the blackback spider? She takes a mate to fill her full of life and then eats him. Is that what you, proud builders of this fair city, have become, Chislanda? Are you just selfish destroyers, hungry for life only if it's of your choosing? Do you feed off death and call it living?'

'I've no more to say. What have you done to me? Am I to be shamed because I can't do what I must? You've made me fail, Aglydron. I'm nothing, now. You've destroyed me. Go! You have the information that thief Feldrark wants. Go, tell him your tale and let them do with me as they will. I'll speak to you no more. I'll pleasure you no more. I have your seed within me and, when he grows to be a man, I'll teach him how to hate and annihilate my enemies and he'll be my reward.'

She broke into sobs at this, trembling now her conviction had vanished along with her hatred. She'd shown him her love and, though she wasn't ready to admit it, Aglydron could see it written on her face, feel it in the way she held him, stark and real as life itself as she clung to him and sobbed.

'You've got to live to give birth, Chislanda. Remember that. And as for pleasure; I could 'ave none with you if that's what you are. I could pity you. If you're what you say, you're less than human and worse than the lowest beast. You say nothing's of value unless you wish it to be. It seems right to me that we should march on Mipahnhil and destroy it utterly if such is the spawn of its belly. I couldn't love you, Chislanda, if I believed you're what you pretend to be. But, if you're what you were just now in my arms…'

He broke from her with difficulty, feeling he must leave her now or lose himself in the care her love gifted him. He closed the door behind him and told the guard he'd finished for now but to feed her and leave her unharmed.

'Feldrark'll want to talk to her. And we might need her to lead us to the cesspit she comes from, so keep her safe. But beware; she'll try to seduce you. If you let her, she'll have you and use your own sword on you.'

In the palace, he found Feldrark and told him what he'd learned. 'Is it true? Did your ancestors drive hers out?'

Feldrark shook his head. 'If they did, they never let us know. The story I told you, that this place was empty when we arrived, is the only one I know. And there are texts, written on velum by those who were here at the time, to say only that. There's no hint of a people displaced and dispersed. But, if Chislanda and her people truly believe what she's told you, perhaps it goes some way to explain their attitude to us.'

'Does it make war less needed?'

'My parents remain dead, Aglydron. That they died through opportunism rather than design doesn't make them less so. Though, it does make parley less impossible, I suppose.

'So, what'll you do?'

'What they have forced me to do. End it. What other course do I have? It's plain they'll never rest until they've killed all of us and captured more of my men to act as fathers they will then dispose of. I have no choice, unless I'm to send escorts of armed men with every person, party or group that leaves the city from now until the end of time. It's clear that none will be safe in my realm until I've defeated Mipahnhil. And, it seems, the defeat of that foul midden means its total destruction, the annihilation of the population. I hesitate to put to death women and children but what else am I to do?'

'There might be a way. Maybe, once they've tasted real battle, they'll surrender to terms and live in peace.'

'The one point where I agree with Chislanda, Aglydron. You're a dreamer. But we'll see. I make no promises but I'll try to parley with them and if there's a way to keep alive even a few, I'll do it. Though I fear we may have to utterly destroy the place and its people.'

'And Chislanda?'

'I've no need to torture her. You found the information I required. She can be executed now.'

'Take 'er with us. She can be a go-between. And, if they decide to fight, she can die with them.'

'Can we trust her?'

'No. But can we simply execute her? Don't we have to try, at least?'

'Aglydron, you amaze me. I never saw you as mediator. Never saw you as a man of vision and judgement, reason and imagination. You're a plodder, a follower of rules and doctrines. What made you see? What happened to make you think and dream?'

'I spent many nights in Chislanda's bed. She was warm and kind. She gave me all of herself. She surrendered to me and blessed me with everything she had to give. I came to love her. She may despise and hate me now, Feldrark, but she loved me when I lay with her. I know she did. I felt it.'

'Perhaps; a man may be lured into thoughts of love by a woman who pleases him. In any case. You're right. I'll keep the bitch alive for now. Let her take our terms to the bowelcreeps of Mipahnhil. At least I'll not have to risk a soldier. But watch her, Aglydron. And, since you seem to care for her, you'll have charge of her on the march. But let her betray us and you're dead. If not by her hand, Aglydron, then by mine.'

Chapter 9

PREPARATIONS FOR WAR

*T*wo days after the war conference, Dagla Kaz had recovered enough to call his own meeting. Tryonta and Kaz-Ca-Wendarah would return to Muhnilahm with Phildrad, going back after his near-fatal injury in Kabalyt. With them would be unmarried volunteers from Litkala, willing to try a new life on the island and hoping to find suitable mates. Three girls and two boys would go; some virgin. Feldrark had provided a boat, with master and crew, and they'd take artefacts, selected by Dagla Kaz and Feldrark, as samples of what they might trade.

Ultimately, Tryonta would return with a number of young unmarried volunteers from the island prepared to live in the city. Feldrark didn't hold with selection of such and would only countenance volunteers. In this way, they'd begin the exchange of blood and culture between the two sets of Followers.

Feldrark, immersed in preparations for war, left Dagla Kaz to get on with the task, which suited him very well. Tryonta and Phildrad were charged with passing messages to the families of all those engaged in the pilgrimage, including those of Aglydron and Okkyntalah. Wendarah would ensure the right message was spread regarding the Skyfire. In addition, Tryonta would organise compensation for the fisherman whose boat Aglydron and Okkyntalah had stolen.

His brush with death had introduced a spell of uncharacteristic compassion regarding those two, but Dagla Kaz still felt bitter about their escape from justice and hoped to take revenge later that might be attributed to fate or chance. Many leagues separated Litkala from Kah-Labaz and opportunities to do either or both of them damage were likely on such a journey. He'd settled things with others by fabricating his story of the will of Ytraa and had come out of that well enough. But the two men who'd stolen his heir and forced him to change his plans couldn't be let off so lightly. Aglydron was a dull fanatic who might cause trouble on the road. And removing Okkyntalah from the scene would leave Tumalind free for his use on the journey. Tryonta would perform the necessary riddance of nuisance.

Fully recovered from the softness that had assailed him whilst ill, he now readily dismissed the possibility of her being his daughter. Such inconvenient conjecture failed to fit in with his plans and wishes for that attractive young woman.

'Dagla Kaz? You were saying?'

He looked up to see them staring at him and wondered how much of what he planned had shown on his face. Waving a hand in dismissal, he signalled that the meeting was over.

'But you were about to mention my situation on my return to the island, Dagla Kaz.'

'Ah. Yes. My apologies, my mind was engaged on spiritual matters. Yes, Wendarah, you must take over the High Priest's mantle from that fool, Wesdan. As Wendarah Kaz you'll reside in my house with my household and keep it in trust for me until my return. Wesdan can return to his village.'

He turned to the rest of the assembly. 'Ensure you're ready to set out for the island tomorrow and make sure the volunteers are ready to depart with you.'

It was rather sooner than they'd anticipated but it suited Dagla Kaz to keep them on their toes with unexpected announcements.

Sweat trickled along his arms and legs. Where his hands and feet found holds in the hot rock face, they left damp patches, which evaporated quickly, leaving no visible trace of his passage. Aklon recalled, as he laboured under the heat of the sun, why he'd always made this ascent either early morning or late evening. He looked up to check his progress and stared directly into the sun. For a moment, he was blinded and had to remain flat against the cliff face until he regained his sight.

Had that been movement above him? He stayed still and listened. Nothing but the distant whisper of surf breaking against the cliffs, a league or more away. Closer, the ubiquitous cicadas clicked, chattered and scratched their monotonous melody of heat. A hawk, he couldn't see its flight to identify it, screeched its cruel dry call to signal it had found carrion. There was no breeze, no soft wind soughing through dry grass. Everything spoke of heat and desert drought. Even the rocks seemed to cry out for shade and the cooling kiss of rain.

He moved, handhold to handhold, foothold to foothold, creeping up the near vertical face like an insect. A dislodged stone, small and irregular, skittered down to his left, a tell-tale trail of fine dust following it. He didn't look up, knowing it would alert the spy, but climbed as if unaware; vigilant, eyes scanning for moving shadows.

So proud, the Holy One stood with his arms folded across his naked body, the sun glinting from his polished scalp as he looked down with distain. Aklon said nothing. He reached a hand up over the edge and grasped an ankle, tugging it to show him how unstable was his stance. The Holy One at once tried to move back from the edge. Aklon's grip was tenacious and the Holy One tried to kick him free but stopped as he became aware of the risk to his own safety. He had to pull Aklon with him. Once above the edge, the renegade rolled and stood upright in one easy move.

There were three of them; a woman and two men. The man he'd grabbed still edged away from the drop as if fearful it would collapse and send him plunging to certain death.

'Come with us.' She belatedly drew a long sword from the scabbard that hung from the belt at her hips, the only thing she wore. The plaited tonsure sprouting from the centre of her otherwise bald scalp, curled down and round her neck to rest, black and snakelike, with its beaded end between her breasts.

Aklon thrust a hand out at the Holy One he'd used to climb up and sent him too easily to the death he'd feared on the rocks below. The woman bore down on him and the other man prepared his weapon for attack. Aklon drew his blade and swept it upward to catch her sword close to the hilt. He carried the move up with strength and speed to disarm her in a single sweep, the weapon following her colleague down the cliff. The man lunged at him but Aklon sidestepped, stuck out a foot and used the flat of his blade to strike him down to his knees before kicking him over the edge. The female Holy One stood before him, very much afraid.

'Too easy. Send fools to capture me? Are you blind to your frailty? On your knees.'

She knelt and looked up at him, hoping for mercy but expecting none from this feared and skilled opponent.

'Remove the belt.'

She was reluctant but the point of his sword encouraged her.

'Is that it? Just the three of you?'

She nodded but glanced over her shoulder. He followed her involuntary signal and spotted one of each sex waiting some distance away along the top of the Scar, with a packhorse. They clearly wondered how they should now act. He gave them no time to consider but tugged the kneeling woman to her feet with her plait. His sword in her back, he forced her to run ahead of him to her colleagues.

'Disarm or I shall slice her into minute pieces.'

They hesitated, the man making to draw his weapon. Aklon swept his blade in a quick arc that took the plait off her head without removing any skin. She shrieked with terror and dropped to her knees again. The male Holy One thought better of it and dropped his sword.

The other sneered. 'Slice her; she'll reach the Garden of Delights all the sooner.'

He pushed the supplicant onto her face, strode over her and kicked the man hard, disabling him, before engaging the reluctant woman. She was better than the average Holy One but not as skilled as most junior soldiers. After he had cut her arm and thigh, she dropped her weapon and swiftly removed the belt. Recovering slowly from the attack on his most vulnerable area, the man also removed his belt.

'Throw the swords down there. The weapons only, not the belts, in case you are uncertain.'

They did as they were told and he signalled them to the ground, on their faces, with their less reluctant colleague.

'Your usual practice is to rape the unfortunates you bring here. There is only me and three of you and I have no time, spare energy or inclination for such treats. And buggery is not to my taste. My difficulty is whether to kill or spare you. What do you say?'

'Ytraa will defend us. Ytraa is our strength.'

Aklon kicked the enemy's legs apart and placed the point of his sword against his scrotum. 'Ytraa seems not to be about at the moment. Should I wait, do you think, for your saviour? No. I have no time to wait for what will not be. Turn onto your back.'

The man turned gingerly, avoiding the blade that remained a threat.

'Should I unman you first, do you think, as you so frequently do your victims? Or would you rather I left that to the people of The Point?'

'You'll suffer eternal torment in the bowels of Mhortag. I've no fear of you.'

'Sounds absolutely dreadful. The idea of spending time in anyone's bowels lacks that certain attraction I always find appealing in anticipating events. Shall we look at yours?'

'Do as you will, Renegade. Ytraa is my guide and my saviour.'

'So, no guide, no saviour. You will have to rely on my mercy. Onto your face again.'

He used their discarded belts to bind their hands behind them and then searched their packs. As expected, he found a length of fine but strong rope, already noosed. He told the women to stand one at a time, adjusted their bindings in front of them and tied their ankles loosely to each other, so they could hold the cord but couldn't easily escape. Placing the noose around the man's ankles, Aklon stood him on the edge.

'Carry on, then. Let him down, the way you normally lower your prisoners. I hope he is not too heavy for you.'

Releasing the belt from his wrists, he gave the man a gentle push so that he slowly tipped over the edge of the cliff. The line tightened and then began to slip through the women's hands. They lost interest in saving him at the cost of rope burns. Aklon stopped the end of the line going over the edge. He urged the women forward to see the results of their failure. The broken body twisted between sharp rocks; a dark stain spreading from his head.

'Very careless. I hope you will be a little more careful with each other. Unless you care to curse Gadhallah the Gruesome and declare Followers irreverent and blasphemous and swear complete loyalty to me, on pain of certain death should you try to deceive me?'

The victim he'd originally used to bait the other two dropped once more to her knees. 'Please. I never intended for anyone to be hurt. I only wanted an easy life in the service of Ytraa. I don't want to…'

The other woman pushed and sent her sprawling onto her face on the very edge of the precipice. She would've forced her over it, in spite of their connection, had Aklon not intervened.

The upright one turned to Aklon with a sneer. 'Filth. Death rewards those without faith.'

Aklon nodded. 'Do you wish to follow your colleague in like manner or shall I help your more circumspect colleague here to let you down more gently?'

She glanced at her fallen comrade and seemed about to jump. But fear, or hope of some chance at life stopped her. 'Do what you will. I might serve your purposes better alive. My body's yours to do with as you please.'

'That is hardly relevant. You are bound and naked. I could use you repeatedly and in any fashion I choose, should I wish to soil myself. But do you renounce, openly and aloud, adherence to Ytraa and all the ways of Followers, as your companion is considering?'

She opened her mouth to speak but couldn't utter words she believed would banish her to Mhortag's bowels for eternity.

'Your unfortunate lapse with your colleague has rendered him incapable of releasing the rope from his ankles. I fear you will have to recover him in order to have the benefit of the line for your own descent. Unless, of course, you prefer to descend without its aid?'

With help from Aklon and the horse, they hauled the body back up, released the noose and let the man's ruined shell fall back to the rocks.

'You next, dear. But we will attempt a little more sophistication this time. I will not hang you by your ankles, but allow you to grip the cord with your hands, thereby giving you the use of your feet to aid your descent.

Aklon handed her the noose and gave the free end to the other woman. He released her arms from the belt, steadied himself, and persuaded her to the edge. 'Help me, my dear.' He passed the rope around the pommel on the horse's saddle and to her to take some of the strain. They lowered the prisoner until she lost interest or strength. The sudden change in weight made them fall back and his captive made a grab at his sword. Aklon merely grasped her reaching wrist and twisted it behind her back so she was forced onto her face.

'Just you and I. Having recently ascended, I am disinclined to return to the place below. Perhaps you would like to make that journey?'

'I'll die whatever happens. Why not just kill me here?'

'I hate to kill in cold blood. No, the worthy people of The Point might let you live, if you manage to get as far as their settlement. Or they might mutilate and kill you. It rather depends on the impression you make on arrival. Whether you live or die, like all those you sent before you, depends on you reaching your former victims. There is no food, no water to be had, except where they eke out their miserable lives. I leave you to their mercy. You may find the rope and discarded weapons useful in bargaining for your worthless skin.'

He opened the noose and fed it round her chest, above her breasts and under her arms, leaving her hands and feet free to aid her descent.

'Why didn't you use this way to help the others?'

'They had faith in their somewhat useless god. You have seen and shown that you lack that futile dependency. It seems only just that I help you so that you have a chance to live and gain the rewards of your late realisation of the truth.'

'I don't know whether you're cruel or good.'

'Only time will determine that.'

Tying the other end to the horse again, he eased her down. It was a slow and exhausting process ending only when the slackness of the line indicated she'd touched ground. He released the cord from the saddle and tossed it after her. In the unlikely event she should attempt to climb back up, it would be no use to her. On the other hand, if she died or left it there, it might be of great help to Chellyth and her people in their escape.

He peered down and watched her gather the weapons and attach them to one of the belts he'd tossed after her.

'Take them with you. In that direction. If you move quickly and are not bitten by a snake, you may reach them before morning. I strongly advise that you do exactly as you are told when you arrive. And tell them the truth about how you come to be there. They will know if you lie.

She collected the pack he dropped her and then examined the climb. Although it was clearly beyond her ability, he tossed a couple of small stones close to her, to encourage her away. She moved and he continued to persuade her with more well-aimed stones until she was out of range.

He watched her coil the trailing rope around her body and turn again. From a distance, she shouted something unintelligible, though the accompanying gesture made plain her meaning. Once certain she was too far away to return before dark, he dropped the other packs. Chellyth's people could collect these also on their journey.

He set up camp for the night. The horse would be useful for part of his journey, though he'd have to abandon it when he drew close to habitation. Only the Holy Ones used such large horses and his appearance with the animal would be a clear sign of the fate of its original owner.

Great change was taking place in the city and, once the militia had left, the level of civil protection would be considerably reduced. Concerned about the safety of the Virgin

Gifts, Dagla Kaz arranged for Corphanda and the girls to be housed together on the top floor of the palace. Jodisa made a room available and, at his insistence, organised a guard to protect them, though she deemed this unnecessary. For the duration of the war, the girls would stay in the room, with its private terrace, so they could have fresh air and sunlight. Female servants would provide all services they needed. Horsylth would be their personal maid. They weren't happy as prisoners. Dagla Kaz explained that their safety and continued virginity were his prime concerns.

'Others, you must remember, go to a situation from which they might not return. Yours is a small sacrifice by comparison.'

Dagla Kaz saw them safely housed and then travelled down to the harbour to wish farewell to Wendarah, and the rest as they set sail with the tide. Much to his pleasure, Tumalind, with little to do during the preparations for war, accompanied him. She had a special message for her mother, which she gave Wendarah, saying it was the sort of thing only a woman could properly convey. Rather annoyingly, she'd made it clear that she had no trust in Tryonta.

They watched those who'd be sailing to battle in Mipahnhil loading a fleet of five ships with stores and weapons. Commandeered, or hired for the purpose, they would enter one of the mouths of the Sure to act as ferries for the rest of the army. Once they'd transported the troops, the ships would anchor outside Mipahnhil to prevent its citizens attacking the army by sea. They were due to set out later, since the sea voyage would take significantly less time than the march that would take the bulk of the army to battle.

Dagla Kaz and Jhonaht, neither good with weapons, decided to remain in Litkala for the duration of the fighting. Tarruss, however, had volunteered to fight, once he'd learned that Jodisa was in danger from the people of Mipahnhil.

With little to occupy him, and no real contribution to make, Dagla Kaz spent his time getting to know Pharah-Li better. Having lost his heir to Feldrark, he'd told her that he was looking for a mate to bear him a child who could take her place. Pharah-Li, attracted by the power of his office and intrigued by his sexual proclivities, willingly agreed to be the receptacle of both his lust and his seed. She took to her role with an enthusiasm that startled even Dagla Kaz, and provided a worthy distraction.

Guessing that Feldrark planned to make extensive changes to the way Followers conducted their religion, he was determined to have his own power base secure. Accordingly, he'd instructed Wendarah and Tryonta to make the death of Aklon-Dji a matter of utmost urgency when they arrived back on the island.

'I want that reprobate dead and out of the way, as soon as possible.'

✦

'So, Delbon, did the New Cycle celebrations go well in Krohtl?'

'Why did I fall for a soldier, Aklon? Choryssa's perfect for me but I can't share our secret with her.'

'Does she still call you a scoundrel and wastrel?'

'Yes; I tell her she fell for my charm, good looks and, of course, great intelligence.

'I believe you missed out one quality.'

He looked at Aklon and cocked his head on one side. 'I did?'

'Modesty!'

They laughed and embraced in greeting.

Delbon told Aklon how he'd been back in Krohtl when Choryssa had returned after a tour of the island with her troop. That she was back in time for the New Cycle celebrations was a bonus and an indication of her troop leader's desire to be with his family for the Hallowday. Delbon hadn't seen her for a good many portions and they had much catching up to do. She refused to marry him because of her life as a soldier. He couldn't marry her because he was of the Few, though he used the same excuse she gave. The conflicting loyalties that knowledge of his connection with Aklon-Dji would bring might destroy her.

'I long for a normal life with Choryssa. But it's impossible as long as you're renegade, Aklon.'

'True. But things will change, and soon. That is why I have summoned you for instructions on the next phase of the Cause. But before we start the serious business, tell me, was Kaz-Ca-Charrohn present?'

'She was intent on visiting every group and demanded to join at each. No group could finish their celebrations until she'd visited.'

'And woe betide the group if her selected man was too tired to perform, if I know anything about that rampant whore.'

'She was bad enough before, but ever since that young Okkyntalah escaped her after the Choosing, she's been impossible. One after another, she's taken, and cursed them all for their lack of potency.'

'Even you, Delbon?'

'That young hunter gave her such a good time that anyone who fails to live up to his example gets twenty lashes in a beating bag. There's hardly a man in Krohtl who hasn't suffered. Even me. She deliberately aimed six blows, right there, finding it on four. Couldn't join for a sixday.'

'So, did you escape her for the Hallowday?'

'Choryssa protected me. Soon as the bitch appeared, she sat on me as if we were joining.'

'Okkyntalah is a concern. I have fears he may cause me, and others, more grief in

92

different ways before this business is concluded. Come; let us prepare for the freedom so many desire, before danger catches up with me and puts an end to me.'

Chapter 10

OF LOVE AND DREAD

*O*kkyntalah spent his days, before the coming battle, helping Feldrark with preparations; his nights, alone with Tumalind.

'Everything before was false, shadows, echoes. I didn't know joining, loving could be this way. Being one with you, Tumalind, is wonder beyond understanding.'

Her touch, smile and kiss of response said more than words. They both dreaded the coming morning with its parting and the danger he must face. But Tumalind was wise enough to know he had to go on this mission, and that she shouldn't go with him.

'What's happened to Aglydron? He spends too much time with that woman from Mipahnhil. It's not healthy.'

'As healthy as you and me. But it holds the seeds of tragedy. He can't have her as well as Mother. And, if things go badly in battle, he'll lose more than most.'

'You think he loves her, Tumalind?'

'In love with her. The way I am with you; you with me.'

'But she's…she's a killer and…'

'I don't think love notices such things. In Chislanda, Father's found something he never had with Mother. If it's anything like what we have for each other, can you blame him? I can't.'

'But what about Shoarhn?'

'I don't know, Okkyntalah. Theirs, like so many on the island, is a partnership of convenience and coincidence as much as anything else. They respect and care for each other but there's no real passion, none of what we share. If he saves Chislanda, Mother won't see him again. I'm certain of that. How she'll go on, I can't tell. We'll be with her eventually, of course, but that's hardly the same, is it? Perhaps there's someone else for her. Perhaps not. She's still young enough, and beautiful. But I don't know.'

Okkyntalah traced her outline with a fingertip as he rested on one elbow beside her. 'I love your honesty, Tumalind, love the way you say what you mean and mean what you say. I don't have to worry that I'll misunderstand you. You're much cleverer than me and I don't mind that because your honesty never lets you use your intelligence to trap or hurt me. I can trust you.'

Tumalind drew the tip of her finger down from his throat and across his chest. 'I'm only *thinking* clever. You're *doing* clever. You can make things; use those beautiful, wonderful eyes to see clearly where others see through a mist or not at all. You can shoot straight and true. You're brave and resourceful. Being clever's only one thing. And, anyway, you're not only all those things, you're beautiful and wonderful and oh so potent!'

Conversation ceased with that and it was only later, as they dressed for the evening feast to celebrate the march to war, that they allowed themselves to talk of the coming day; the day of departure and parting.

'You'll be gone for some time, Okkyntalah. I want you to know that my love will grow in your absence. When you join with another, let it be devotional only...'

'I'll join with no other after you, Tumalind. It'd be like...well, I just don't want to.'

'No more do I. But Ytraa requires it. We can't refuse if reasonably asked. Apart, there'll be no reason for refusing, should anyone wish it of us. Like you, I hope not to have to pleasure anyone else but it may happen and if it's the will of Ytraa, so be it. My love I save for you, even if I must share my body for a time with some other.'

He took her in his arms and held her close. 'I never thought to question what we do for Ytraa but I wonder why we must do this the way we do. I love you, Tumalind. I've no more wish to share you than I want to be shared. I know that's wrong but it feels right, somehow.'

She kissed him and moved him to arm's length to fasten the bone toggles through the loops of his tabard. 'I wonder as well. But scholars and the learned lead us in this. We Follow, Okkyntalah. We can't do as we like. But we can avoid taking another by choice.'

'That much, at least, we'll do. If others claim us, so be it; it's the will of Ytraa, as you say. But my love is yours and yours alone.'

'You see, I think that's how Father thinks of Chislanda. Things will be difficult for him. Help him if you can.'

'I will. For your sake.'

Aglydron spent much of the evening of the battle feast in turmoil. He'd gone twice to Chislanda's cell since he'd first questioned her, to comfort and share love with her, and she'd welcomed him each time more warmly than the last, in spite of her parting words. But he was conscious that more frequent visits might expose them both to danger. Feldrark hadn't forgiven her for her part in the murder of his parents and she was alive only because Aglydron's suggestion of her usefulness in the coming war had struck him as sensible.

When the feasting was done, the drink drunk and the dancing and singing over, Aglydron stole a last visit to her cell and found her weeping. 'What is it, Chislanda?'

'Before, when I first took you into myself and accepted your seed in my belly, I felt little more for you than I might for any man passing in the street. Then, I could've faced the morning, with its shame and danger and exposure as if it were nothing. Now, I love you Aglydron, with all that that means. I thought I was strong and invincible. Thought I could do my duty by my people and my past. Thought I was right to hate and kill. Now you've become more precious to me than life itself and I don't want my life, or that of our baby, to end. Or yours to be endangered. Yet every step we take tomorrow will bring us all closer to death.

'I can live with the shame of being led naked in chains to battle, as long as I know you're with me. But how can I face my people at the end of that journey? You've undone me, Aglydron. You've discovered my heart and taken it and now I've no strength to kill, only a wish to hide from danger and keep you close with me. I don't want to fight. I don't want anyone to fight. I want to live. I want you to live. I want us to be always together. I'm dishonoured, and I'm frightened. I was never frightened before you made me love you. I should hate you for what you've made me. But I don't. I can't. Hold me, Aglydron, hold me.'

Her concern about honour raised a protest in his mind, which he refused to allow to pass his lips. Instead, he held her. He was still holding her when the sun announced morning. He stood beside her as they locked the metal collar round her neck and handed him the chain to link her to his wrist before they struck the manacle from her ankle, the locksmith presenting him with the key to allow him some freedom when necessary. Against all sense and reason, he led her not into the open streets to show her as a trophy and have her mocked and spat upon, but took her instead to the palace and his room. He changed and packed his belongings as she rested on his bed. He summoned a palace servant girl and asked her to bring him two tunics for Chislanda.

She objected but went anyway, out of respect for his status in the home of her master. She returned with two that had been thrown out because of their worn and torn state. 'Please don't ask for more. A guest you may be, Paltrohn, but she helped murder our Kiral and Kirallah. I shouldn't give her even these rags.'

Aglydron shrugged. 'Thank you for your service and sacrifice.' He examined the reluctant gifts. One was less worn and tattered than the other. He helped Chislanda put it on and placed the other in his pack.

'Thank you, Aglydron. I'll repay your trust. I promise you.'

The journey to the inner gate was bearable only because they shared a wagon with Okkyntalah, Tumalind, Feldrark, Jodisa and the High Priests. Feldrark scowled at her but was too absorbed with the coming days and his last moments with Jodisa to say anything. No one dare throw anything objectionable at Chislanda, for fear of hitting the others.

'I thought you were coming along, Jodisa?'

She looked at Feldrark, her face an inscrutable mask. 'I was, Okkyntalah. But I've

97

been persuaded by powerful voices that I can do more good here. I'm learning that leading doesn't always give you the choice you might expect it to.'

Aglydron watched Feldrark take her hand and gentle it in his own. More passed through that touch than words could ever convey.

Once in the lower city, however, Aglydron's mind was taken off the problems of others as he was forced to shelter Chislanda within the ranks of the nearest company of foot soldiers. They accepted him with mixed feelings; not wishing a fighting companion to be abused but reluctant to protect a despised enemy. Both had been spat on and pelted with rotting fruit and excrement from the more extreme elements of the crowd as they crossed the open space to the muster. Within the rows of soldiers, however, they were safe from further missiles and had only shouts and taunts to bear as they waited.

It seemed a long time before the assembly was ready to move off.

For the army, the parade from the lower city to the eaves of the forest was a march of triumph and splendour with cries of praise and encouragement mingled with fond and tearful farewells. For Chislanda and Aglydron, it was a nightmare of abuse, hate and further defilement. At least this first day was the only one involving the crowd.

Once in the forest, they marched without spectators from city or countryside. From the camp, Aglydron led her beneath trees to the brook running a little way from the road. He released her and they washed filth from each other's skins and clothes and returned to camp wet but clean and sweeter smelling.

This first swift march had ended at a camp set up by those who'd gone before. Food was ready for the soldiers; tents had been erected in between the trees for officers. For the rest of the march, they'd break and set camp themselves but this first stopping place had been prepared so that they might leave the crowds and well-wishers behind in a single day.

Aglydron took Chislanda to the tables and unbound her again so she could carry her food back with her. The metal collar had rubbed a sore patch on her shoulder and, in spite of Chislanda's protests, he sought out Myllthlan to do her healing. She acted with the same concern for the captive as she would for any wounded person.

'If the collar's unnecessary, I think she should be spared it. Constant rubbing will make her skin bleed every day.'

'Would you intercede with Feldrark? I'd try but he thinks my judgement's awry. You might do better, as the healer.'

Myllthlan wandered off to tend blisters, cuts and aches gained from the long day's unaccustomed march. Aglydron and Chislanda sat with their backs to a tree and ate, the heavy chain rattling as they moved.

It was growing dark when Feldrark, escorted by three officers and two soldiers carrying torches, found them. Aglydron stood at once and Chislanda rose to her knees, her head hung in supplication.

'Myllthlan tells me the prisoner's complaining of the collar wounding her. She should be glad she's got wounds to cause her...'

'She didn't complain, Feldrark. She hasn't grumbled at all, in spite of the filth thrown at her, and the foul abuse. It was me who spoke with Myllthlan.'

'Let me see.'

'Myllthlan's healed the wound but you can see where it was. We'll be on the march for days, Feldrark, and if you want her in a fit state as our emissary, she'll do better freed of this collar.'

'She'll...'

'Sire, may I speak? Please?'

Feldrark stared down at her. 'Stand and speak.'

She remained on her knees and put her hands above her head, palms open and outward facing, her head up so she could look into his eyes. 'Sire, I was wrong. What I did was wrong. I acted as I did because that was what I was raised to do. I know now that I was at fault. I wish for no more death, either of your people or mine. I beg your forgiveness and place my life in your service to do with as you will. I cannot bring back the lives of your mother and father, for whom I weep with great sorrow, but I can lay down my own, if that's what you would have me do.'

Feldrark was clearly astounded by this change in his captive. He took her hands and raised her to her feet. 'I can't tell what's brought about this transformation but I hear truth in your words and I'll give you the chance to prove it. The collar will be removed and you'll march free of chains. For the moment, your wrists must be bound on the march and you'll remain in Aglydron's custody. If you attempt escape, I'll have you, and Aglydron, flogged. And the collar and chain will be replaced. Do you understand?'

'Thank you, Sire. I shan't try to escape. I've no wish to be apart from Aglydron and certainly no desire to see him harmed. The man I was to kill has stolen my heart and I'm entirely his now. I understand such change must be difficult for you to believe. It's the truth, though. I would've risked my own life to end Aglydron's only days ago; now I'd lay down my life to save his.'

'You're not pardoned for your act of war. But you may walk free as I've described. What becomes of you, when the war is over, will depend on your actions and those of your people.' Feldrark turned to Aglydron. 'Did you clothe her?'

'I've earned her trust, Feldrark. I wouldn't lose it for the sake of a rag.'

'So be it. She remains your responsibility, with all that entails. If she lets me down, she lets you down and you suffer with her. Understood?'

Aglydron nodded. Feldrark left to continue his inspection of the troops.

When the smith came to take off her collar and Aglydron's wristband, he gave him a pair of manacles to lock around her wrists. They were made of light, bright metal and lined with soft leather. A rigid bar held her hands apart and a simple key locked the device in place. The smith advised Aglydron to wear it on a cord around his neck.

Again, Aklon arrived in the depths of the night and, as always, held Shoarhn in silence for the time it took to be certain he had not been followed, before he spoke or allowed her to greet him.

'Things have moved, Shoarhn. You know that Morstahn is now patrolled, in common with all towns. No one must even suspect I am here. Should they guess at this stage, they are quite likely to set the whole place alight simply to catch me. Though why I should merit such inordinate effort, I find hard to imagine.'

'You shouldn't joke, Aklon. Was it you who killed Wesdan Kaz?'

'An unfortunate but necessary stage in the development of events. I take no life without need. His, miserable as it was, was forfeit. He had corrupted his office and was abusing the power loaned him by my father. An unworthy deputy chosen specifically because he was unlikely to try to usurp the power of the High Priest in his absence.'

'I'm glad it was you. A'ahl would like to demonstrate her gratitude, so I don't think I'll let you see her.'

'You have nothing to fear from A'ahl. Against all my plans and my determination never to allow myself to become attached to an individual woman, I appear to have fallen rather exclusively and entirely for you. It makes life a little more hazardous for both of us but A'ahl is not one of the hazards. Now, time is short, as ever with me. You and I have unfinished business from my last visit, I think. If I recall, last time we occupied this space, I discovered there was….'

She gave herself blissfully to their mutual passion.

In the early hours, he told her what he'd learned from Ivdulon, Feldrark and Jodisa. She listened with growing wonder and interest as he detailed the wedding of Feldrark to Jodisa, Aglydron's acceptance of Linlyss as substitute Virgin Gift and his liaisons with Myllthlan and Pharah-Li.

'You're just making that up so I won't feel bad about enjoying having you in my bed whilst he's far away.'

'Do you feel bad about our love, Shoarhn?'

'I never felt so good about anything in my life.'

'Apparently, Myllthlan worships your husband because he gave her a name; a concept I confess to understanding not at all. And Pharah-Li, an exceptionally beautiful and sexually adept creature, simply did Feldrark a favour by using her charms to help persuade Aglydron to accept the substitute for my sister. Jodisa confirms that, by the way.'

'All right. I believe you. I did anyway. What else have you found out?'

He explained how the two parties had met up, and how Dagla-Kaz had flogged Aglydron publicly.

'Your husband is now apparently rather taken with the hostage woman from Mipahnhil who originally tried to kill him. Tumalind is married to Okkyntalah, at last, and he and Aglydron are due to go off to war with Mipahnhil.'

'You are very quiet, Shoarhn.'

'I'm puzzled by Aglydron's exploits with other women but I'm more curious than anxious. Tumalind's wedding makes me very happy. I'm glad she's finally joined with the man she loves so deeply. Okkyntalah's a charming and pleasant young man, and they seem to have found real love. Have you tried to contact Tumalind? She's got lapis lazuli eyes, you know.'

'She may not be able to communicate at such a distance. Would you like me to try?'

'Yes. But not just now. She'll be asleep.'

'Probably.'

'We ought to sleep as well; especially you. You must be worn out.'

'Happily exhausted, after our mutual ministering of worldly delights and spiritual refreshment.'

'You do have a funny way of talking, Aklon, but I enjoy it. Now, look, if you start that again, we'll never get to sleep.'

But darkness eventually took them, until daylight brought the boys into her room where they woke to find them staring down at her and Aklon with slightly puzzled expressions on their identical faces.

'Phildrad arrived in the dark, after he got lost. He might be here for a few days this time, I don't know yet. But don't talk about him to anyone. He's supposed to be doing a job somewhere else and he'll get into real trouble with the man he works for.'

She left the comfort of his side and made breakfast.

The boys reminded them they hadn't said morning prayers and Aklon acted out his part with her so the children wouldn't be suspicious. She sent them on an errand to buy fresh fish from Okkyntalah's father whilst she and Aklon talked.

'I am unable to stay, Shoarhn. What I failed to tell you last night was that Kaz-Ca-Wendarah, Tryonta and an individual called Phildrad, would you believe, are on their way back to the island even as we speak. I hope to question the priestess and my father's right hand man sometime in the future but I need to find this Phildrad and discover what

I may from him as soon as possible. It requires my presence in Chalamamnon.'

'Can't you use mindtalk to find out what you need to know?'

'There are aspects of the journey, things about my father, I can best obtain from someone who travelled with him. Phildrad cannot mindtalk; I must speak with him face to face.'

'But you'll spend the night with me again, before you go?'

'You learn so quickly. I admire your strength and resolve. You make parting less painful than it might be, when you comply without questions or attempts to make me stay. I love you, Shoarhn. And, yes, I will be here for the night, or at least, the first part of it.'

As she lay in deserted darkness, the warmth of him still next to her, the scent of his love on her skin, she thought of all he'd told her about the reality of Gadhallah and Ytraa and the cruelty, betrayal and deception the priests and Holy Ones used in order to maintain their hold over the population. That her life's faith was built on such lies and perversions made her feel physically sick. Feldrark and Ivdulon were trying to make changes slowly on the mainland to protect their own people from the despair that sudden change would inevitably bring. But, here, on the island, the grip of the High Priest and the Holy Ones was too strong to allow such a transition and it seemed increasingly likely that violence would have to be the instrument of change.

Whether she and Aklon would emerge from the turbulence unscathed was a question she asked again and again, without hope of answer. It prevented sleep from rescuing her from doubt and anxiety, so she turned instead to the short conversation she'd had with Tumalind; Aklon acting as interpreter. Her daughter, unsurprised at the contact, sounded so happy with Okkyntalah and very anxious about his coming fight at Mipahnhil. Shoarhn smiled wryly; it seemed she couldn't escape thoughts of death and battle no matter which way she turned. Only time would heal the wound caused by that worry. Only the intersession of some force for good could bring about the ending she hoped for, the conclusion she desired. But the spectre of possible violence to all those she loved, lurked and taunted her awake and in dreams.

Chapter 11

RISKS

'Fool, Syylvah! You know the life I lead. You know you are only one of many. I do not choose to live this way.'

The girl looked up at Aklon with adoration but none of the fear he was hoping to instil.

'What you have done endangers the lives of hundreds. I have a simple choice now. Either I kill you where you lie or I take you into a life of great danger and probable death where your every action must be instant obedience to my command. There is no middle road. Sending your worthless man to tell the authorities I am here has placed you in mortal danger. Which is it to be?'

'I never meant…I were jealous o' that bitch you're so taken with…I love you, Aklon. I thought you'd take me more seriously. See?'

'No excuses, Syylvah. Will you come with me, on my terms, now?'

'Course.'

'Then come. Before they arrive to torture and question us, and to kill us, whether we answer or not. But understand me; a false move, even hesitation, will mean instant death.'

He grabbed her hand, dragged her to her feet and from the house, collecting his pack from the floor and allowing her to gather no more than the tabard she'd discarded on his arrival. She pulled it on as they left.

The street was already emptying of folk as day drew to a close. Evening fell soft on the town, as he hurried her, not running, along back ways and narrow passages, always alert for pursuit. He saw none but heard a commotion as sounds of the hunt escaped the house they'd left only moments before.

A lone Holy One moved softly up the narrow ways behind them; Aklon catching an impression of him as they angled into a narrow, deserted passage. He forced Syylvah behind him with a silent gesture and signed for quiet. The Holy One moved with cautious speed up the alley and turned the corner to come face to face with Aklon. In a single swift move, he killed the man before he could raise a cry. He fell, bleeding, at the girl's feet and she cried out in alarm and distress.

'You did this, Syylvah. Remember it when next you feel jealous.' He dragged her from the gore and made for a place where he could watch the harbour.

'Don't we 'ave to escape, Aklon?'

'That is what they expect. All roads out will be watched. In any case, I need information. It is why I came.'

He increased speed through twisting, many-branching, back ways of the upper town to arrive at his chosen spot sooner. There was no further evidence of pursuit, his deviations enough to fool most hunters.

The ship was already visible on the horizon and would enter harbour soon. By then, night would have fallen. He wondered whether the passengers would disembark at once or spend the night on board. He hoped for the former. He'd no wish to spend the night in this small cave.

'Would you really kill me?'

'Only your past service and devotion spared you at the house. You have been valuable to me and the Cause, Syylvah. Understand; much more hangs on this enterprise than the life of a jealous woman. I am sorry if you love me, though I do not believe you do. We have shared pleasure and I have no more than that for you. I have found love, against all hope and expectation and I can truly love only one. If you cannot accept that I am not yours, if I cannot trust you, then I will dispose of you. Do you understand?'

'It's not really love, Aklon. But I need you. Can't bear never 'aving you again. You give me summat I don't get with no other man.'

'And you have had plenty.'

'Jealous?'

'Why would I be? I was stating a fact. You, my dear, are ruled by a fern that would burst into fire with passion if left unattended. And that makes you dangerous. I really should get rid of you.'

'Frowk me instead. You don't 'ave to be wi' me all the time. Just once in a while. You're the only man who tecks away the 'unger for a while. Everyone else leaves me wantin'. Well, 'cept that Okkyntalah; he'd do as well. I can't 'elp how I am. Please?'

'You, young lady, are a hopeless case.' He checked the progress of the ship and scanned the area below for signs of pursuit. 'You are in luck. There will be time enough before the ship docks.'

She took what she desired and lay on hard ground in darkness, breathing deeply as she recovered. Aklon, back on watch at the narrow mouth of the small cave, heard her behind him and turned briefly as the ship sailed through the narrow gap into the harbour. Eyes wide and reflecting the dim light from behind him, she was exactly as he'd left her.

'Wanton.'

'I am, aren't I? Wonderful, isn't it? Am I wicked?'

'A child of the faith. Exemplar of all the priesthood hope for from their people. You know nothing of love, devotion, affection. All is lust, want and carnal desire with you. You excel at the act and bathe in sensation, give back the pleasure you receive. But you have no understanding of spiritual togetherness, of minds and souls intertwined with bodies so inextricably that there is no seam, no boundary. You give great pleasure, Syylvah, for my hands, my eyes and my prod. But you do not satisfy my heart and soul. No. You are not wicked, merely wanton.'

He turned back to find the ship approaching the wharf as darkness turned colours into shadow and tones of soft blue brown without contour. She knelt beside him, her head against his leg so that her hair brushed his thigh.

'Who you lookin' for?'

'Never you mind.'

'Two pairs of eyes see more'n one.'

'I do not know who I seek. He will be with a woman; the priestess, Wendarah, and that slug, Tryonta. But which of the number is the man I need, I cannot tell. He is called Phildrad. Not the alias I use, simply a man of the same name.'

'Let me go find out. They won't worry 'bout me; I'm well known on the docks.'

'You are wanted, Syylvah. Do you not understand? By sending your man for the authorities, you have named yourself, and him, accomplices of mine. If they catch you, they will torture you until you tell them all you know.'

'I wouldn't tell 'em nothin'. No matter what they did to me.'

'You would tell at the first touch of the red hot blade. Not because you are a coward but because you have no moral sense and you are a creature of sensation. You would not resist even mild torture, which is why I shall not let them take you alive.'

'You're frightenin' me.'

'Good. You should be frightened. This is no game. Many lives depend on what I do. I will not risk all I have done for the sake of a woman with a fern too hot to control. I care for you. But I will sacrifice you without a thought if I must. Do you finally understand me?'

'But you just frowked me…frowked me so well. You gotta feel somethin' for me, surely?'

'Let me make myself clear to you, Syylvah. I will end your life as suddenly as I did Wesdan's, or the Holy One I just killed. How I feel about you is immaterial. I owe more to the Cause and the people I lead. I will end your life, if necessary.'

'You mean it.'

'At last.'

'You really, really would.'

'Yes.'

She was silent a while, pondering this news. She shed no tears, made no entreaty as she assimilated his threat and seemed to understand it at last.

'I promise I'll be good. I won't never let you down again, Aklon.'

'You will. Not deliberately and not yet. You are a dangerous woman for a man like me. I should never have recruited you to the Cause but I was unaware of your unquenchable desire then. I do not blame you, Syylvah but you are a constant source of danger to yourself, to me and the Cause. For the moment, however, you remain safe as long as you do exactly as I say.'

Even under this threat, after learning he would end her life, she was incapable of ignoring her desire and handled him as she looked out from beside his legs.

He turned to the ship, now settled against the harbour wall, ropes tied to capstans, gangplank already lowered. A small party left the ship, with a couple of crew members, carrying extra packs. At their head, Aklon recognized Kaz-Ca-Wendarah with Tryonta. He assumed Phildrad was one of the other men in the party. A well-built woman, dressed outlandishly in a jacket, laced across the open front and barely long enough to conceal her considerable breasts, walked beside the priestess. A strange garment covered her from hip to ankle, clothing each leg separately, and an odd, flat, circular object balanced on her head with a tall feather sticking out of it. Aklon was intrigued and Syylvah had to cover her mouth to prevent laughter bubbling out.

The group walked into the town. Aklon didn't want to lose them and pulled Syylvah after him from their hiding place. They descended the short cliff face and then walked through deserted darkness, down the steep hill, dodging night patrols and arriving in time to see the small procession approach the High Priest's house. The group entered and, after a while, it was clear they'd spend the night there.

Aklon-Dji considered for a moment. 'Awkward. I was rather hoping to discover the identity of the man straight away. I am afraid, my dear, you are in for some discomfort. We must go out of town to a place of relative safety.'

'Thought you said they'd be watching all roads out of town?'

'We will go by other ways.'

'You goin' to frowk me again, when we get where we're goin'?'

'Is that the entirety of your hope?'

'That an' food.'

'A simple and delightful, if dangerous creature. Perhaps bestowing a mind on it might have been an unkindness. Come along. The sooner we arrive at our destination, the sooner you may have your desire.'

He shoved her very quickly behind him, so she tumbled over the low wall. Before she could recover, he was on top of her, his hand covering her mouth. He shuffled them both close under the low wall and remained, holding her down with his weight and his legs over hers. She tried to speak but he placed his mouth close to her ear. 'Quiet.'

They remained in their uncomfortable embrace for a long time whilst Aklon listened to movement about him. He neither moved nor allowed her more movement than breathing required.

At last, satisfied the activity had passed by, he whispered. 'I am going to take my hand away. If you utter a sound I will slit your throat. Lie still and quiet.'

He released her mouth and levered his body up to look over the wall. All was deserted. The patrolling group of militia with their attendant Holy One had passed to another part of the town. He rose to his knees and helped Syylvah to stand.

'Total silence. No footsteps, no words. If you sneeze, cough or even breathe loudly I will pierce your heart with this knife. Nod if you understand.'

She nodded and took the hand he gave her. She trotted beside him, as he strode quickly out of town. A few hundred paces before the last house on this track that led nowhere, he stopped her in the darkness. They had met no one.

'Stay here and make no noise.'

She lay where he placed her and he made a quick but thorough sortie into the nearby countryside, returning so quietly that she almost cried out when he knelt beside her again.

'Sorry; this is necessary. I cannot allow you to see where I am taking you.'

He untied her waistrope, lifted her tabard to cover her face and wound the rope about it to blindfold her. 'Hold onto me and you should be able to walk without falling over. Quiet, now.'

At several points, he stopped and turned her round a few times so she would have no idea of the direction she was walking. On one occasion, he walked her a hundred paces, spun her a few times and then took her back the way they had come. Once at the place, he urged her onto all fours and guided her ahead of him through the low opening. Only when they were inside did he remove the tie and allow the tabard to drop back into place.

'You may talk now, in a low voice.'

She looked about and then at Aklon. 'Where are we?'

He smiled in the light from the lamp he'd lit before undoing her blindfold. She watched him put a spark to a small fire, already prepared in the centre of the floor, and then sit on the rough wooden bed that rested against a wall.

The place was man-made; an abortive mining attempt. More than two hundred cycles previously, a merchant, convinced there was gold in the hillside above Chalamamnon, had set slaves to bore into the rock. It had become clear that what was in the hillside was rock and more rock, fissured in several places. After digging a tunnel some fifty paces long with a couple of short wide chambers, he had stopped the work. A few people had heard of the mine but not its whereabouts. Aklon had discovered it by accident when seeking a hiding place some years earlier, crawling under a bush and discovering the opening.

'We are underground. Safe. Out of sight.'

Over the years, he'd crafted the bed and installed lamps. He ensured a fire was laid ready when he left, so that he could be comfortable as soon as he arrived each time he had need. The smoke escaped through the natural fissures in the rock above the chamber to emerge high above, amongst a dense thicket, where it dispersed without giving any sign of its source.

He prepared a meal for them and they sat side by side, eating dried meat and stale bread and drinking wine from a flagon. Flickering firelight served them as he dowsed the lamp as soon as the fire grew bright enough, to preserve oil.

'But where, Aklon?'

'It is better you are ignorant. Should you be caught, you can tell them nothing. We shall be safe here for the night but we must remain relatively quiet. I am afraid there is only this bed and the service from the slaves leaves much to be desired.'

She looked around and he laughed, tousled her hair and pulled her close. 'There are no slaves, Syylvah. You will, however, find a spot round that corner where you may relieve yourself. The hole there is very deep, so be careful, unless you want to spend a brief but painful period in the bowels of the world before you die.'

'What you goin' to do with me?'

'Well, for tonight, I thought we should perhaps sleep?'

'After that?'

'That, my dear, depends on you. Fear not. I have no plans to end your life at present. Nor in the future, if you prove yourself more sensible and faithful than your uncharacteristic outburst suggested.'

'I promise I won't do it again.'

'The promise is unnecessary, Syylvah. You will not do it again.'

'No. I see.'

'Have I ever lied to you? Have I ever betrayed you or done anything to harm or alarm you, apart from the unfortunate incident earlier today?'

'You've always been a gentleman, Aklon. I'm really sorry.'

'Good. Make yourself comfortable and we will sleep, I think. Yes?'

'Well, eventually.'

And, eventually, they did.

In the faint light entering the cave from outside, he ensured her wrists and ankles were securely bound without being too tight. The gag was a necessary precaution he loathed, conscious that his untimely capture would inevitably mean a long and painful death in the dark for her.

'You leave me no alternative. I really cannot allow you to shout and alert someone passing. If only I trusted you, I could leave you here unbound and without the gag and be sure you would do as I ask. But you have to earn my trust again, my dear. I shall try not to be too long and will, whatever happens, return before the end of the day. You would do best to lie still. You will be thirsty and hungry when I return and I shall endeavour to bring you something pleasant to eat and drink. Until later, then.'

She looked at him imploringly and he almost set her free. But he couldn't risk it.

The sun was up but the day still young as he crawled carefully into the light. Nobody was near and he quickly scaled the steep rise above the mouth of the mine to emerge onto the main slope of the hillside.

Years as a fugitive had given him the skill to merge with the background so that, in spite of his great height and muscular frame, people rarely noticed him. He took a stance where he could watch his father's house.

Before long, Tryonta emerged. He was very tempted to follow this man who'd killed and tortured for his father on many occasions, probably including the torture of his childhood friend, Por-Kildu. But his present concern lay with Phildrad. Shortly after Tryonta left, Kaz-Ca-Wendarah came to the door with a man and the woman in the unusual clothes. Her short jacket now visibly even more scandalous than it had been in darkness, and her lower garment displaying a diaphanous quality in the sunlight, she kissed the priestess on the mouth and stroked her breasts. Placing the flat circle of green fabric on her head, its feather wafting, she turned for the harbour.

'Back in three days, you lubricious hussy. Be ready for me.'

Kaz-Ca-Wendarah viewed her until she was out of sight. She turned then to the man who stood beside her, prepared for travel.

'Well, Phildrad, we part at last. Sure you don't mind returning alone to Pampahn?'

'I found me way 'ere, Kaz-Ca-Wendarah. I'll find my 'ome all right. Will you be along later with Tryonta to give out the news?'

'I'm not sure, to be honest. One or both of us will certainly have to come soon. Thank you for your contribution to the journey and for the wonderful food. Do you know, you and I never got to join? Never mind, perhaps some other time.'

'For me, I'll be pleased to be back with Lasdilyss, my wife. Fare you well, Kaz-Ca-Wendarah.'

She returned indoors and Aklon gave the man a short start before following him through streets beginning to fill with early morning workers. His timing had been good. At present, it seemed, good fortune was his.

The patrols of soldiers and Holy Ones had been withdrawn too soon. They were so slow to learn, these religious fools. But a man stood in the shadows of an olive grove as they approached and Aklon made a short, quick detour to avoid the need to murder the spy. He allowed Phildrad to walk free of the outskirts before he made his approach.

'You will know of me rather than know me, Phildrad of Pampahn, so I will declare myself at once. You have returned from a futile journey led by Dagla Kaz. I am his son, Aklon-Dji.' He studied the man's face closely.

Phildrad took an involuntary step backwards but appeared unlikely to flee. 'What d'you want with me?'

'Information.'

'Why should I help you?'

'Two reasons. I will present that most advantageous to you first and hope it will suffice. You should help me because I can do great good amongst the people of this island and remove suffering and death, which currently occur with such unnecessary frequency.'

'I've only your word for that. What's t'other reason?'

'I will kill you if you refuse.'

Phildrad took another step back and grabbed the hilt of his sword. Aklon laughed, drew his own weapon, and swept the sword from his opponent's hand as soon it cleared the scabbard.

'What d'you want to know?'

'Everything you can tell me. Would you mind too much if we were to move away from the road? Interruptions are tedious and I would so like to get this interview over and allow you on your journey to that lovely wife of yours. Lasdilyss will be so pleased to see you.' Aklon motioned him off the road toward a grove of granota trees some five or six hundred paces away. He stooped to retrieve Phildrad's fallen blade and passed it to him.

Phildrad frowned and resheathed it but continued in the direction he indicated.

They settled a short way inside the copse, out of the sun and with their backs against the trunks of opposing trees. Phildrad was a few paces from Aklon but made no attempt to run off and simply sat, watching him with suspicion, as he ate one of the fruits.

'I will endeavour to keep you from your mission for as little time as possible but there are things I believe you know that will be of use to me.'

'Ask what you like. I've nowt to hide and nowt to be ashamed of.'

'No. I commend your bravery in tackling the terzet-horn, rescuing Netrodyl and saving Tumalind's life by sucking out the snake venom. And your skills as a cook in the field are admirable. Certainly, you managed to satisfy the culinary needs and wants of my father and he has a demanding palate.'

'You know a lot for a man asking questions.'

'I have sources. Now, to the information I seek.'

Aklon questioned him exhaustively, listening to all he had to relate. Some of his enquiries were aimed at discovering his honesty and he found Phildrad prone to tell the truth, if occasionally from a slightly odd perspective.

'Thank you, Phildrad. You have told me more than I expected and given me much food for thought. I will delay you no longer. But, before you go, let me plant a couple of truths that may make you see me in a different light. I am renegade only because I wish the people to learn truths I have had from my father. Dagla Kaz, however, wishes the people to remain ignorant because he may control them more easily that way.

'The other information concerns Gadhallah himself. When he was in the Groves of Ytraa, a place he named himself, ostensibly communing with Ytraa, he was actually raping a girl of thirteen cycles. He kept her bound and raped her repeatedly. When he had defiled her to the extent that she begged for mercy, he killed her in a manner I prefer not to describe. When he woke the following day and saw her poor, mutilated body, he decided to tell the story all Followers believe as the reason for the founding of the religion of Ytraa. What I say is true. It is recorded, in his own words, on texts and stone tablets stored in my father's house.'

Phildrad spat at him. 'Foul bowelcreeps. Only a sick mind could make up something like that.'

Aklon wiped spittle from his face. 'Or, perhaps, a truthful mind reveal it as the truth. I bid you farewell, Phildrad. Speak to your clever and lovely wife about what I have said, she will discuss it and give you further information, which may persuade you to a different point of view. And thank you for your information, it has been most useful.'

He turned and, without looking back, walked a short distance into the trees where he stood concealed until he was certain that Phildrad was on his way home. He sighed wearily and returned to the town for food and wine, which he obtained through another of the Few and took to the mine. Syylvah cried quietly as he massaged life back into her hands and feet but soon recovered enough to demand her price for her continued good behaviour.

'You are a problem, Syylvah. What am I to do with you?'

'What else?'

'I will take you where you can live in relative safety. Tomorrow, very early, we go to my friends. I hope you will not be adversely affected by a journey over the waves. I was rather hoping to visit another but she must wait until I have dealt with you.'

'Over the waves?'

'Yes. I believe my friends could make use of a boat and I know now where I may obtain one that will no longer be needed. I trust you have no objection to pointing out and helping to steal your former husband's boat? He will undoubtedly be dead or in permanent captivity by now. They will not take kindly to his claim to have me ready to deliver to them only to discover I have escaped them once again. They do not deal with such matters in the most just manner.'

'You think he's dead?'

'Almost certainly. He promised them me and, in the absence of my death, they will need to torture and, eventually, execute someone else. He seems the most likely candidate.'

'Oh, I never thought....'

'So many people never think, Syylvah. The burial grounds are full of those who failed to think.'

He blindfolded her again and took her from the mine at dead of night.

Chapter 12

WAR

After fourteen days on the march, Feldrark's army was leaner, fitter but a lot less clean and tidy than when it had set out. But the troops remained in good spirits, driven by the need to avenge their leaders and buoyed up by Feldrark's personal mix of discipline and good humour. The last ford proved muddy and unpleasant; stinging flies and gnats plaguing them as they struggled through deep silt; the oxen having to be reharnessed as fours and even eights to drag carts across. Everyone was heartily pleased to be on the far side with only one further stretch of water between them and their objective. This was the main stream of the delta that fanned out as the River Sure met the sea. Deep and strong running, they would cross that in the ships he'd sent ahead.

They'd met no resistance and seen no sign of their enemy. Feldrark wondered how the people of Mipahnhil could remain unaware of their danger.

A captain of the guard approached. 'All present an' fit, Sire. No illness nor injury to report. Had to put that slacker, Bisfollehn, on fatigues, again. Lost his frowkin' spear this time. I'm thinkin' he'd benefit from a public flogging, Sire?'

'Do as you think fit, Phrodil. But nothing that'll cause loss of morale. Perhaps embarrass him: have that small woman; you know, the soldier who throws any man she chooses, best him in unarmed combat?'

'Great idea, Sire. Make him think about his fighting skills as well; much better. I'll do that.'

'Any sighting of spies or lookouts…?'

'None, Sire. Still no sign of that murderous whore, neither.'

'Perhaps she died on the journey. We'll probably never find out. But the lack of scouts from the town suggests she never reached home.'

'Mebbie they just don't expect an attack, Sire.'

Feldrark considered. That might explain the lack of harassment. It seemed unlikely they'd leave themselves so open to assault if she'd returned and told them of her triumph. He dismissed Phrodil to get on with shaming Bisfollehn, expecting his suggestion would sit better with the troops than the simple brutality of a flogging. Morale was important far from home on a battle mission, especially with troops used to nothing more demanding than guarding the city from an attack that had never seemed likely.

Unsettled, he sought out Chislanda for her opinion, though, now he considered it, she'd already hinted at why they might not expect opposition at this stage.

The woman, proving her worth and loyalty repeatedly on the march, was no longer manacled. She'd acted as guide and advisor about route, food and safe drinking water. On one occasion, she'd physically prevented a soldier from drinking from a pool; come to think of it, that had been Bisfollehn. The man was a menace. Chislanda had risked her life to save his; he'd been about to skewer her on his spear, before he'd lost that, of course.

'Drink it if you must. It's full of bleedworms. They'll breed inside you and suck your blood until you die. They say it's very painful. But go ahead.'

The troops within earshot had all laughed at his discomfort and Chislanda had gone up another notch in their estimation. Another time she'd advised against bathing in a certain area because of alligators. The loss of a heedless soldier, amid screams and frothing blood, had proved her right again.

Feldrark's attitude to her softened with each show of loyalty. He'd already sought her advice about the best place to cross by boat and remain out of sight of the city.

'Once we reach the place, they'll already have been seen. Fishermen and reed gatherers travel widely. The main stream provides drinking water so they keep regular watch to protect against poisoning. Any case, there's always work needed on the waterways after the rains and there'll be plenty of townsfolk about at this time of the year. We can't hope to cross unseen.'

'Why didn't you let me know earlier, woman?'

'You didn't tell me what you had in mind, my Lord Feldrark.'

'What'll they do?'

'We've never been invaded. One reason the town's built there is to make it difficult to invade by land. They'll try to stop you landing troops, though.'

'How?'

'I don't know. We're not warriors but hunters. We've no tradition of soldiering. We hunt and kill only those we must.'

He glanced at her sternly, the memory of those bloodied bodies he'd loved so dearly, surging up into his mind.

'I'm sorry, my Lord Feldrark, forgive me.' She bowed her head.

'Continue.'

'Most have never raised anything more deadly than a reedpole, to beat the backside of some wrongdoer. But they'll fight. They won't accept defeat. They'll give their lives if the Galhta demands it. I hope to persuade him to some agreement with you, if you'll allow it. But, if they won't talk or make peace, you'll have to take them on hand-to-hand. Unless you burn them out. Fire's the biggest fear in a town of wood and reed.'

This earlier advice had allowed Feldrark to send a scouting party down river to divert the ships via a backwater Chislanda described. And, of course, it explained the lack of opposition so far.

They made most of the crossings without interference before the townsfolk became aware of them. By then it was too late for the population to do more than disrupt the last few ferryings with skirmishes in small boats, in which they were defeated. The townsfolk fought bravely but with little skill and no tactics and were mostly killed. Feldrark lost a handful of soldiers but over two hundred of the enemy died.

Seventeen days after they'd left Litkala, the army drew up in battle lines some three hundred paces from the edge of the town, just beyond bowshot.

Chislanda approached Feldrark. Behind a tent erected for eating, and out of sight of the tower, she stripped. 'Beat my back till it bleeds.' She turned, waiting.

Aglydron was with her. 'There's got to be another way.'

'Would I do this if there was?'

Feldrark turned her to face him. 'Why naked and why hurt?'

'If I approach unhurt and wearing the dress of a mother, to which I'm no longer entitled, they'll kill me on sight. If I'm to get within hailing distance, I must be naked and marked with cuts and stripes, as if I've been beaten into doing this duty.'

'I can't harm you in cold blood, Chislanda.'

'You were ready to torture me to death. Remember? I could've saved your mother and father, but I didn't. Are you too small a man to avenge them?' Her voice was full of scorn and contempt.

Feldrark struck her hard across her face, twice. Her nose was bloodied, her lips split.

'Enough, Feldrark! She's just trying to make you lose your temper.'

Feldrark stopped the third blow and gazed at her with amazement.

'Quickly! Before I lose my courage.'

Still feeling tension and wildness after her comments, he used Aglydron's belt to whip her until blood oozed from three stripes. She cried out only once.

'If you come from this alive, Chislanda, you are pardoned and set free.'

She nodded, wiped a hand across her eyes to clear the tears and, as arranged, strode through jeering and mocking soldiers towards the town.

Feldrark had explained that he knew nothing of her people's claims to Litkala. But she'd told him all that mattered to her was Aglydron. That he should live and, if there was a way, that she should live with him. How had Aglydron, of all men, made her his to love and be loved? He pictured himself with Jodisa and knew that love was glue that held the most unlikely couples together, that fed sacrifice and compassion and deeds of great bravery.

From the first line of his troops, he watched her climb the wooden steps and meet the challenge of the guard.

115

'Nobody lives this end. Where you taking me?'

Aklon and Syylvah sailed close under the cliffs of The Point.

'Somewhere you can be safe and I can be sure you will not betray me again. A word of warning; you can join with any man but one where we are bound. When first you see him, he may cause you to feel physically sick. Display your revulsion and you may find yourself similarly scarred, though not by him. He will tolerate the love of no woman but she who has loved him always. He fears all others pity him. And he is a very proud man. Remember this, Syylvah. Por-Kildu's woman is not to be crossed. Chellyth is stern, proud, brave and beautiful but she has no love for any who threaten the precarious balance of a world she struggles daily to maintain. Control your urge to sample every man; Chellyth will put you to painful death if you try to join with Por-Kildu.'

'Doesn't sound like my sort.'

'Once you accept the damage my father did to him, you will want him, Syylvah. Chellyth rules criminals, deviants, natives and outcasts. Do not cross her.'

'I thought the wicked ones lived on The Point. Why aren't we landing?'

'They did, but we have found a new home. It will not be as much to your liking as it is to theirs but you will live there until the Cause is well under way. Remember, these are a mixed group and get on well together because they have an important quality in common. They are tolerant. None care about hair or skin colour, height, strength, cleverness or any other attributes. All go naked, since they lack the means to weave cloth and consider constant exposure a gesture of defiance to the god who abandoned them. Join with any, but only by consent. Nobody will force themselves on you and you must not force yourself on anyone. They do not permit joining with those not initiated into adulthood.'

'No one joins with children. That's a terrible thing to do.'

'Terrible, cruel, deviant, iniquitous. Call it what you will, Syylvah, it happens on the island. The Holy Ones take advantage of their position. Many temple slaves are violated long before they are ready.'

Syylvah vomited over the side of the boat. Aklon comforted her. 'Such is the beast we destroy with the Cause. Remember it and, when that hot fern of yours tempts you to indulge where you should not, bring to mind what I have told you and ensure you remain alive to help eliminate such vile beasts.'

'I will. I'll be good, Aklon. Only, come to me when you can and cool my unquenched heat, please.'

'When I may.'

'Will the boat sail without your 'elp, for a bit?'

116

He shook his head. 'Incorrigible.'

'We've waited long enough. It's past midday.' Feldrark gathered messengers and prepared to advance.

'Let me go, Feldrark. See if they've an answer. The Galhta might not take Chislanda seriously; you know what strange views he has.'

Feldrark stayed the messengers. 'I'll send these men to all our fronts to prepare the troops. They'll light fires for flaming arrows. But I'll give you until noon to signal their acceptance of our terms. If we hear nothing from you in that time, Aglydron, I signal for war. Whether you return or not. Understand?'

'I understand. My thanks for the chance, Feldrark.'

Aglydron left the lines to follow Chislanda's route into the town. Had she done as she'd promised? Had she tried to talk them into accepting peace for the sake of both peoples? Or was his trust in her misplaced? He'd grown to care for her from the earliest days of their togetherness and had saved her life because his feelings for her grew with each contact. Even as she'd attempted to end his life, he'd tried to prolong hers. Was her declaration of love for him genuine? Even as he framed the question in his mind, he knew the answer. She'd been slow to recognise it and even slower to admit it but she loved him and he loved her. He was convinced that her only concern now was for his life as his was for hers.

He quickened his pace, knowing he might die before he even had a chance to find out why she hadn't returned. The guard at the entrance barred his way. Aglydron placed his spear on the ground, his sword beside it, in token of good faith.

'I come to speak with the Galhta and learn the fate of our prisoner.'

The guard spat at him but gave him access. An escort took him to the foot of the tower where the new Galhta waited. Aglydron glanced at Chislanda but gave no sign of concern at her condition; any sign of mutual love might bring death to both of them.

'Has she spoken with you?'

The Galhta struck him across the face and two of the others forced him to his knees. 'I question here.'

Aglydron fought his urge to struggle, and kept his head dropped and his gaze to the ground. How quickly he'd forgotten the rules of this place and how quickly violence returned the memory. 'I'll answer what you will.'

'How many are you?'

'Ten thousand on land. A hundred and eighty at sea.'

'How are you armed?'

'Bows, spears, swords and fire.'

'She gave no time for our reply. You have a time?'

'If we don't return by noon, battle will start.'

'On what terms?'

'Peace. The city offers trade and friendship, marriage even, should you want it. Feldrark will open his land to you. We only want a pledge that you'll stop seeking the death of those you imprisoned here and forced to kill in their attempts to escape or in defending their own lives against your assassins.'

'You ask much.'

'We offer more.'

'Put him with her. We'll see if their deeds match their words.'

Aglydron made no struggle as they stripped him and bound his wrists above his head to the poles of the platform. 'If you let the fighting start, it won't end until you're all dead.'

'Then you two will die also.'

'We don't matter. They'll fight whether we die or not. Neither of us is from Litkala.'

'You're that one who lay with her. You planted seed in her belly. Is that why you came? To save her because you have some foolish notion of caring for her?'

'I came because I know this place and some of its ways. What's between Chislanda and me is for us.'

The Galhta punched him between the legs. 'I know all.'

Aglydron controlled his breathing and ignored the pain. 'You'll destroy your people. If we don't return, everyone here will die.'

A woman in the escort party watched him with fear and concern. The Galhta, however, smashed his fist into Aglydron's belly. 'You know nothing. We are in the right. Tryhnn is on our side. We shall prevail.'

He returned to his tower, where he began calling to all four quarters, urging his people to fight the invaders.

The escort party melted away and he and Chislanda were left dangling side by side.

'Why did you risk your life, Aglydron?'

'Same reason you risked yours.'

'Are you in pain, my love?'

'No more than you. Will he really sacrifice his people?'

'For him it isn't like that. He believes Tryhnn will save them. He's proud. The people are proud. They'll fight, but they'll die, and so will we.'

Their feet were free and they stretched out a foot each just to be in contact. For a while, they waited, undisturbed and alone, as the pressure of their weight on their wrists numbed their hands, the pressure on their chests threatened to slowly suffocate them.

People passed, armed and ready for the fight. He and Chislanda faced north. The

118

main assault would be from the east. It was not long before smoke and flame rose from that side. Aglydron tried raising his legs to take the weight off his arms but there was nowhere to rest. Behind them was empty space. There was no way they could release themselves. They would die when fire reached them. Perhaps smoke would spare them the pain of slow roasting.

The sky grew dark; the air, thick with cries, screams and shouts of pain and hatred. Burning flesh stunk on the growing wind. Above, the Galhta drove his people on.

At first, in ones and twos, and then in larger groups, they fell back, running from flames that now began surrounding the tower. Some were blackened with smoke, some bore burns, others were wounded by blade or spear.

'Help us!' Chislanda pleaded with her people.

They gazed at them in fear and ran by.

'Cut us down!'

Fire consumed streets to north and east. Houses burned like hayricks, sending sparks and red-hot brands into the air to carry on the wind and spread more fire. Men, women and children screamed. And still the Galhta called above, his voice all but drowned by the surging roar of flame, his figure blanketed by smoke.

The woman from the escort party ran past them, escaping.

'Help us!'

She looked at Chislanda, and at Aglydron.

He pleaded, 'Please.'

She glanced up toward the Galhta, hesitated, saw the fire approaching. Then she was gone to safety.

Aglydron gazed at Chislanda. She looked back with love and sorrow on her damaged face. 'I'm sorry, my love. I might've spared you this.'

'Better like this, than you die alone, my love.'

And then the woman returned with a blade, climbing his suspended body and cutting him free, so she fell in a heap with him. She ran away, fearful. Aglydron's hands were so numb he couldn't grasp the knife she left him. Heat increased as fire approached; reeds and wood about them smoking. He took the handle in his mouth, rubbed life into aching hands, heedless of the pain.

'Run before you burn!'

He climbed her body, as there was no other way to reach her in time. Coughing, retching, struggling to bring strength to his blood-starved hands. He found her bonds and stretched up with the knife to free her. All about them buildings burned and burst into flame, exploding with heat. The screams and cries came now from behind them.

He cut one arm free and nearly fell as their angle tilted. He lashed the other bond,

119

cutting her skin. They fell. She cried out, her shoulder taking the weight of them both as they hit the ground. He began to pull her to where the fire was least.

'We'll never make it. Cut the bonds of the planks. We'll go underneath.'

Quickly, working on hands and knees as flame, heat, and smoke roared and swirled about them, he cut bonds holding planks to bearers. He freed the first, lifted it. They gained air free from smoke but tainted with the cesspit smell. They breathed again. He cut a second plank, a third. It was enough.

He helped her through, holding her by her good arm until she was at the full extent before letting her go. Just as he was about to drop down after her, the Galhta crashed to the ground beside him. His garment blazed, his hair flamed. But he leapt at Aglydron, intent on killing him. Aglydron moved sharply sideways and turned the knife into the Galhta's unarmed flesh. The leader screamed and fell. Aglydron slipped between the boards and fell beside Chislanda, in the filth and mud. She was on her knees, trying to stand.

He got to his feet and pulled her up. The Galhta, bleeding, dropped and landed close beside them. Before he could rise to his feet, Aglydron was on him with his knife again. They struggled as burning timbers showered around them. The Galhta turned the blade and stabbed Aglydron's arm. He pulled away and twisted the knife back from the wound and into the Galhta's heart. Blood coated him as ruined life spurted out.

Chislanda helped him to his feet and they looked about, terrified now they had a chance at life. Flaming timbers and falling burning wood closed off escape north and east. West, others struggled to the cooling quenching river. South, they saw ships with men still firing flaming arrows at the town.

Above, the tower blazed; a torch. They must move; to the river, west and south. Others ran, crawled and waded beside them. Intent on saving their lives and those of their children, nobody noticed Aglydron or Chislanda.

At last, they reached water, the city above, burning. All around, people cried in pain and terror. Panic drove some to swim from beneath the city floor. Death found them as arrows drove them underwater.

Aglydron and Chislanda knelt together in the muddy shallows watching fire sweep nearer, overhead.

'Will they kill us all?'

'We might escape. Pray we're known before we're shot.'

Chislanda looked into his face and he saw her disbelief that anyone would recognise them. He held her at arm's length, studied her smeared and sooted face and laughed at his naive assumption.

A sudden wind swept through the underground space, bringing flame, smoke and ash on its breath. They ducked under water and moved toward the deeper part of the river. When they surfaced, still clinging to each other, they were out of her depth. Aglydron barely touched bottom; stretched with water flowing over his shoulders, under her chin, as he held her.

The remaining pillars creaked and groaned as the weight of unburned buildings above bore down on them. They began to lean. North and east, the town burnt to ground level, the pillars on fire. Even as they watched, flames spread through the underside of the town.

The remains of the tower broke through the floor and sent fresh destruction roaring across a great part of the under-floor area. They had no choice now. It was burn, be crushed, or risk the arrows. At least, in the latter, they had a small chance.

They embraced, Chislanda clumsy with her useless left arm. Aglydron turned on his back and took her over his belly, kicked out and swam toward the danger of arrows.

The floor above cracked, creaked and strained. They emerged into sunlight dimmed by smoke, and watched the ruined town sink into water and mud, hissing and steaming. Around them, others splashed and swam and waited for the arrows.

But no more missiles flew; now the town was utterly destroyed. Boats collected them in twos and threes. Smoke and steam replaced flames. At last, a boat found them and rough hands hauled them from the water, ignoring Aglydron's pleas.

'Take care; she's hurt her shoulder.'

They lay exhausted in the bottom of the boat; the sailors seeking others in need of rescue. Once laden with the sorry rescued, they rowed for the shore, where other troops waited.

Those still clothed were roughly stripped and searched for hidden weapons. All were bound with leather ties at wrist and hobbled at the ankles.

'I'm Aglydron, friend of Feldrark. And this is Chislanda, who helped us.'

'Get in line. No talking.'

They took their place in the long line. No time was wasted on their fate. Thirty or so were ahead of them. There, a fire made iron glow.

They approached slowly, watching others questioned.

'Slave or death?'

Death came swift, on a blade. Few chose it. Slavery brought hot iron, smoking with charred flesh and forcing screams from the bravest, as soldiers held them and seared the tops of arms.

Their turn came.

'I'm a friend of Feldrark and this is the woman he pardoned.'

'Death or slavery?'

'It won't hurt you to check my story. If you brand us you might regret it later.'

'Make your choice, or I'll do it for you.'

A giant of a man, vaguely familiar to Aglydron, moved forward. 'Leave them be. They're friends of mine, and of Feldrark's.'

The soldier looked them up and down, hesitated at the stranger's confident tone. A soldier doing the job he'd been detailed to do.

'Stand aside. Next. Death or slavery?'

Aglydron and Chislanda stepped aside for the next unfortunate. Tarruss led them from the scene, soldiers watching them warily.

Some three hundred people made their choice, most accepting slavery. Two thirds were women, many pregnant. They were all that remained of the adult population. Children, fewer than fifty in total, were left free and unbranded.

'Aglydron! Chislanda! You survived!' Feldrark appeared and embraced them in spite of the filth and ash coating their bodies. 'Welcome back, welcome. But you're hurt. Come, let me take you to Myllthlan and have you healed.'

The soldiers visibly relaxed and nodded.

'Bring the children, Tarruss, and follow us.'

He led the children, mute, filthy and exhausted, in a long line from the chain of adults.

Climbing toward the reservoir, they saw the true scale of the devastation. Mipahnhil was gone. A smouldering wreck of charred wood and ruined, blackened bodies remained. Of the Galhta's tower, there was no trace, but his burnt body lay surrounded by destruction. Pride had cost him and his people dear but he would learn nothing from the lesson.

Aglydron turned to Chislanda and watched the emotions gather and cross her damaged face. Would she ever forgive him for his part in this? Would she ever love him again?

Chapter 13

OLD FRIENDS AND NEW

Aklon left Syylvah standing on the ridge of the hill, waving. She'd been as good as was possible for her, and Chellyth and Por-Kildu had accepted her.

Already, the settlement was taking shape. Chellyth had greeted him with such appreciation that both Por-Kildu and Syylvah had been jealous. But the moment passed with the end of their embrace. The female Holy One he'd lowered down the Scar was marked by vines of captivity at ankles, wrists and waist, restricting her movement. But her hair was beginning to grow, a dark fuzz covering her scalp. Cymlihter, the freed slave, welcomed by the community and enjoying her liberty, had insisted on demonstrating her gratitude.

He'd stayed longer than intended, helping with construction and organisation. Now, on his way to visit Shoarhn, he turned for a last wave at Syylvah, who'd accompanied him as far as he would allow. At his signal, she disappeared behind the far side of the ridge. She'd taken to her new home with enthusiasm, giving herself freely and receiving almost as much from the men as she desired. He was confident she'd find some contentment since the population was weighted in favour of men.

Chellyth and Por-Kildu had managed the journey from The Point with a loss of only two of their number, both older men. One had fallen into a deep gorge, drowning in the raging torrent, the other had been gored by a manecat disturbed whilst hunting.

The people were delighted with the place, for all its surrounding dangers. They'd lived with danger and need for so long that to live with danger but without need was a luxury. His gift of the boat had already produced a good catch of sea fish to add to that from the river and lake. Already they were healthier and fitter than they'd ever been in the dry heat of The Point.

Dense forest soon hid the more open country behind him. Steep hills crossed his route in parallel rows with almost vertical climbs and precipitous cliffs covered in dense bush. Running water, in swift, deep streams, divided all routes from the main part of the island to the small triangular peninsular. Crossing from the settlement was tedious, hard and dangerous. Most of the island's big cats lurked in these forests, as did the remaining terzet horns.

He fought his way down the steep slope of a ridge and then scaled the escarpment to the next. By the end of the first day, he'd covered only a little over three leagues but was ready to rest. He was making for Pampahn; the nearest town and the place where a road might take him on at least part of his journey to Morstahn. He wondered how Kaz-Ca-Porlesah fared these days. Many sixdays had passed since he'd seen her, avoiding her because of her strange hold over him and the great danger his presence brought her. He even avoided mindtalk with her, in case he caught her at an awkward moment. The village priest hadn't been in touch with him.

When he and she joined, the added dimension, a secondary pleasure that resulted from their minds meeting, made the act unique. It was different from what he experienced with Shoarhn. Deeper in some ways, yet oddly lacking the closeness he felt with Shoarhn. The blending of their minds, whilst forming an additional bond, caused a barrier to the true merging of their souls. Perhaps each felt too much of what the other experienced; too aware to really lose themselves in each other.

With Shoarhn, he was part of her and she part of him, so that they were a single being with no beginning or end. Her love left him feeling so whole and complete that he understood the hold the doctrine of joining had over Followers. Anyone experiencing such unity couldn't deny its rightness. It had to be the proper thing to do; maybe even the best reason for existence. By turning the sex act into worship for his god, Gadhallah had pulled off a masterstroke that gave his religion enormous attraction. It couldn't fail, even though it was grounded in Gadhallah's hideous crimes and motives. But Aklon's experience with Shoarhn was far removed from anything that abusing charlatan could have envisaged.

Reaching yet another ridge, toward the end of his second day, he looked out in the general direction of Pampahn. Standing in open space atop the rocky outcrop, with the roof of the forest below him, he could see for many leagues. Far away, the shimmer of late evening sun described the shapes of small lakes to the north-west of the town and, beyond them, the shaded slopes of bare mountains. Well past those and out of sight, lay the far end of the island, Morstahn and the object of his journey.

He was suddenly invaded by external thought and he recognized Kaz-Ca-Porlesah as she found him.

'You're elusive even when I seek you in my mind, Aklon. Do I find you well?'

'You do. To what do I owe this unexpected and unusual pleasure? And how are you now able to project over distance?'

'Don't tease. You've been avoiding me. I've news and I'd rather give it face to face than with this skill, which still troubles and disturbs me. Will you come to Pampahn? As to how; Ivdulon asked me to try something she called an experiment. I had to allow myself to be hypnotised; don't ask me what that means, or how she did it. Afterwards, I could project much further and no longer have to rely on line of sight.'

'Ivdulon continues to surprise us all. And, you discover me already on the road. I am

124

no more than three leagues distant and expect to be in the town this time tomorrow.'

'Then you'll arrive first. I'm still on the road from Chalamamnon, where I met with Kaz-Ca-Wendarah and other village priests. I've a lot to tell you and warn you about. If I give you news do you promise not to act on it until I've seen you?'

'As to that, I cannot say, Porlesah. Until I know your news I cannot judge the importance of responding to it.'

'You're always so... so careful!'

'That, my dear, is why I am also still alive.'

'Very well. The meeting decided that you've become the priority. Your death now brings a greater reward to the killer than your capture would've previously. And the people of The Point are to be eliminated. You'll have to go and warn them now, of course. Don't worry. I'll wait to give you the rest of my news. Go and do what you must.'

'I shall, as I said, be in Pampahn tomorrow night. I have no reason to go to The Point. Such a journey would be a fool's errand for me and will prove so for those who seek to kill my friends.'

'You've already moved them? How did you know?'

'I have many sources of information. When will you be in Pampahn?'

'The day after tomorrow, I hope. Take care, Aklon. They really do mean to kill you as soon as they catch you.'

'I look forward to seeing you then, Porlesah. In the meantime, I shall stay with a friend. Until the day after tomorrow.'

He waited to see whether she had more to say but found only silence. Just below the summit of the ridge, he came on a small hollow in the rock, too shallow for a cave but deep enough to provide cover from the frequent warm rains, and a flat space on which he could lie down. His fire gave little smoke and there was nobody near to see it. The smell of roasting meat as the snake turned on the makeshift spit flooded his mouth with saliva. In his bag, a small corked phial held the contents of the poison sacks that had fed the serpent's fangs. Applied to an arrowhead or the blade of a knife, it would disable a foe in moments. He'd been fortunate not to step on the creature as it lay basking and a swift stroke with his sword had parted head from body before it could strike.

The meal relaxed him and he slept free from interruption, so that he was well on his way by the middle of the next day. Porlesah's news, however, made him even more cautious than usual.

At the edge of Pampahn, he watched the sunset, midges from nearby swamps biting mercilessly at his exposed skin. When darkness was as complete as it would be on this moonlit night, he left the trees and stole down narrow streets between low houses of mud and thatched reed. Somewhere a hound howled its longing for a mate it couldn't reach and, closer, a man scolded his wife for burning the supper again; the acrid scent assaulting his nostrils. Some distance off, a child sobbed with pain and shame after a harsh beating.

Smoked fish scented the air until a pile of rubbish covered it with the sweet pungent smell of rotting fruit. Underlying all was the smell of the marsh, foetid and heavy with putrefaction.

He skirted the house of a suspected informer, slipped silently along a narrow alley between two older houses and emerged into the main square. Moonlight cast hard shadows into the spaces beneath houses built on short stilts to escape the occasional flooding of the lake. It shone brightly on the soft pale dust of the square. He paused; examined, listened, sniffed. Nothing unexpected. Across the far side of the square, he flitted into the narrow black space separating two dwellings and opened the gate into the rear of the one on the left. For a while, he stood in silence, his breathing settling to a stillness that revealed the smallest sound. He listened again, sniffed, scanned the area with keen eyes.

He ascended the short ladder noiselessly and stood for a moment on the wooden platform surrounding the walls. The blind was across the bedroom window and when he listened, he could hear only the soft breathing of sleep. But one or two? He opened the door carefully, knowing it scraped over an irregularity on the floor. He tested for the obstruction and discovered it gone. The door swung open without resistance. He closed it silently behind him and stood in the deep darkness of silence within. Perhaps, then, his earlier suspicions were well founded and she was not alone.

Touching the woven wattle of the internal wall, he felt his way until the space he sought was at hand. His feet told him the floor was clean. Another sign her man had returned. He stood listening to the breathing in the bed. Two occupants, breathing almost in unison. That was now expected if irritating; the husband was who he'd believed and had returned. He stood for a moment, considering. For her, it would be better if he left and kept a watch to see what happened come daylight. It meant a night in the trees on the edge of town but that was safer than disturbing her when it was still unknown whether her husband was yet a friend.

He escaped as carefully as he'd entered, leaving no trace. The return journey to the trees passed without incident and he settled uncomfortably in the crook of a thick branch, a few manheights above the ground.

Morning found him stiff, aching and wet, though the rain had been mercifully brief. He listened, dropped to the ground and edged toward the town again. It was early. Few were about the muddy streets. He dodged around the perimeter in the direction of the lake and approached the house he'd entered earlier. There was no sign of activity. He found a place to wait, inconspicuous and almost out of sight.

At length, a man emerged from the house and wandered toward the lake. He recognized Phildrad at once, confirming what he'd expected. He slipped from his hiding place into the house.

'Phildrad! I wasn't expectin' you.'

'Will Phildrad be back soon or is he…?'

'He's gone fishing. He's only just back from the trip with…'

'Dagla Kaz. I spoke with him. Does he know?'

'About you? Yes.'

'And?'

'It's all right. He's changed since he's been away. I think 'e might even be for us now. Not agin us, anyway. Summat to do with things what 'appened when he was away and 'is meetin' with you. But he doesn't say much; never did. Taciturn, he calls himself. I just say he's quiet. But he's a good man.'

'When will he be back?'

'Soon. Will you think I'm terrible if, well, I want to, but we don't join?'

'It is what I would expect. I need a place to stay though. Will he be all right?'

'I'd best talk to 'im first.'

'I shall find a place to wait and…'

'Oh, that's all right. Wait in the bedchamber, Phildrad. Lie down if you want. He won't make no fuss.'

Aklon nodded. 'But you had better use my own name. Otherwise, it might become a little confusing.'

She nodded at him. He kissed her. After his night in the tree, and confident he could trust her, he fell asleep on her bed, only to wake what seemed moments later.

'Not so clever now.'

He opened an eye and saw instantly the threat both real and implied. Phildrad stood over him with Aklon's sword pointed at his throat. He opened both eyes and swept aside the blade with a hand as he sat up.

'Phildrad, you are not and never will be a killer. You have too kind a heart and too much respect for your superiors. I apologize for my intrusion into your home but your wife has no doubt explained?'

'Lasdilyss told me.'

'It was she who confirmed my suspicion of my father's intentions to follow the false Skyfire. You will no doubt have noticed it has now disappeared.'

'Dagla Kaz knows it's false, now. Ivdulon told him. He didn't believe it at first, even though it was frowkin' obvious. He's going to wait till the real one comes and then go on. Good luck to him. Everything I've learnt tells me it's a fool's errand. Any case, whole frowkin' thing's a sham, isn't it?'

'I am pleased you feel so strongly about it, Phildrad but I would advise caution. Not everybody knows what you know and not many would agree with us.'

'Just tell me, Aklon-Dji; if you're so sure Gadhallah was a vile bowelcreep and everything Followers stand for is evil and corrupt, how come you spent so many nights frowkin' my Lasdilyss?'

'Jealousy; or something else?'

'Call it what you like.'

'I was brought up in the faith. My attitude to joining is born of the doctrines of that faith. I can no more change that background and upbringing than I can change my height, Phildrad. Your wife, Lasdilyss, is a very lovely woman with a special sensuality that makes joining wonderful. I make no apologies for enjoying the customs of Followers in the absence of a different code of behaviour or a different set of values and ethics. When we finally decide on how we should properly worship, I will adhere to whatever new rules and traditions come along.

'In the meantime, I am a child of Followers and son of the High Priest. How else should I behave? Become celibate, perhaps? Should I take a partner and remain true to only her for the rest of our lives? Should I have a dozen wives, a hundred, and frowk my life away with them? Should I copulate with goats or bears or mhun-muhns? We are guided in habit and behaviour by the rules of the society we grow up in. I am no more capable of devising rules in the absence of spiritual guidance than anybody else. However, Phildrad, I have not joined with Lasdilyss today and will not do so again, because she has expressed a wish not to and you have now expressed a clear desire that you would rather I did not. Does that answer your question?'

'Sometimes a man wishes he'd not asked. You give more frowkin' words than I need. Have you eaten, Aklon-Dji? I've been down the lake and fetched back a couple of decent tonyina. You're welcome to join us. In a meal, that is.'

Aklon laughed at the little joke and stood. 'I would be delighted to sit at your table, Phildrad, gaze on the beauty of your wife, and share the meal you offer. Lasdilyss tells me you are singularly gifted with food. Perhaps we may learn more from each other, to our mutual benefit. Tell, me, did you actually meet Ivdulon?'

'Strange woman. Cleverest I've met. Funny about men. Like she thinks they're a bit simple.'

'What does she look like?'

Phildrad gave Aklon-Dji a full physical description, including Ivdulon's deformed foot. He looked forward to surprising and teasing the astronomer with that knowledge the next time they communicated.

Tumalind, standing on the quayside with the others, heard roars of greeting as the ship passed into the outer harbour. Soon she'd see Okkyntalah again; be in his arms. She'd greet her father and the woman who'd now supplanted her mother in his eyes. Feldrark would be there, on that first of the six returning ships. They would restock and return to the encamped army so that the rest of the troops could start the long march back to Litkala, supplied with fresh stores. When the ships returned the second time, Myllthlan would be with them, her healing work done, as the rest of the injured and hurt came with her.

Rrildyss Kaz had told her all this by mindtalk. On the second night of the march, the High Priestess had joined with Okkyntalah and sent her emotions and experience to Tumalind, believing she was doing the newly married girl a favour. Tumalind had quickly told her she considered it no kindness at all.

'I'm sorry for the misunderstanding, Tumalind. I hadn't realized you and he were actually in love. It's something we in the priesthood don't allow ourselves and I really did think I was doing you a favour; letting you feel as I felt when I joined with him. Amazing!'

Amazing was right. She recalled vividly her first private joining with Okkyntalah; an experience her public joining had only partly presaged. He'd shown her delights she hadn't known were possible. And now he was returning and they'd share their ardour, gaze again at each other in delight, touch and receive touch and find their joining truly made them one.

Rrildyss Kaz had promised to leave her man alone after her mistake and instead had sent daily bulletins from the field, up to and including the battle and all that had transpired since.

'Your father was hurt in the fire but is now recovering. The woman was pregnant with your father's child. I hadn't realized. Anyway, after what they did to her in the city and with the fire and fighting, she lost the infant; nearly bled to death, poor dear. That marvellous healer friend of yours, Myllthlan, brought her back from the very edge of death. She's with us on the ship, even as I speak to you.'

'How's Okkyntalah?'

'Some man, your husband. He fought bravely and managed not to be wounded. Feldrark's made him an honorary Captain. He's fine and asked me to let you know he's missing you and wants you very much. I didn't realize he didn't know about this. I just sort of assumed he must. Anyway, I've explained about the secrecy and he seems more intrigued about mindtalk than jealous or put out. Actually, Tumalind, I've probably done you a favour by letting him in on it. It's often difficult to explain it to a partner who can't do it. I've had all sorts of problems with Pharah-Li because she can do it only in a very limited

129

form and has little control; her emotions and passions get in the way, it seems.'

'Is Chislanda alright now?'

'Chislanda? Oh, the woman captive. Yes. Take her a while to be back on her feet, of course. All that blood loss. But she's out of danger. That Myllthlan's quite remarkable, isn't she?'

'From what I've seen and heard. Okkyntalah says she's healed him three times. She comes from Ylcrat, you know.'

'Ylcrat? I thought they were cannibals, with bones through their noses and human teeth on strings round their necks.'

So it had gone on. The High Priestess's tendency to chat and gossip in mindtalk, treating it as something everyday and common, she found disturbing. Tumalind used it only sparingly and selectively. But she'd confirmed, by her experience with Rrildyss Kaz, that distance was no object for her and it made no difference who she contacted. Her chat with Shoarhn, through Aklon-Dji, had shown her what was possible.

Chapter 14

UNKNOWN DANGERS

They'd been apart for too long and her want of him was undiminished. She seemed lost in him for a time.

'I've missed you, Aklon.'

'Yes. With you there is always something more than with others, Porlesah.'

'Except for the one you truly love.'

'I thought I had that hidden.'

'Some things no man can hide from a woman. Being in love with another is one.'

'I see.'

'I doubt it. I'll tell you my news whilst we eat and you may do as you wish after that. You will anyway.' She moved into the kitchen.

She'd released her slaves, to gain privacy. Together, they prepared a simple meal, peeling fruits and skinning fresh, gutted fish she'd been given as she returned home through the town. One of her flock had brought her a flagon of sweet yellow wine and she'd left the fish lying in a dish of this. They each drank more from stone goblets as they went about their various tasks.

'Does it worry you that you do not catch or reap your own harvest but rely on the generosity of others?'

'Does it worry you?'

'A valid response; though I often subsist on what I find along the way. But I am outside society because of my stance and beliefs. You, on the other hand, contribute to society only inasmuch as you purvey the untruths of a religion you no longer follow, and regulate worship of a deity in a manner in which you no longer believe.'

'You do what you can to further the Cause, Aklon. I do what I can. At present it's better I stay a priestess. I learn more and have more influence like that. When the time comes, I'll be beside you, drawing a sword for freedom.'

'You are right, of course. I wonder that you remain so loyal, under the circumstances. What news, then?'

'Loyalty, Aklon, isn't always the personal thing you assume it to be; some of us see the need for change even without your persuasive powers.'

'My apologies, I can no more help how I fall in love, or with whom, than I can exist without breathing.'

She smiled her wounded smile and reached up to kiss him. 'Jealousy isn't pretty, any

131

more than it's easily avoided. But I forgive you.' She wiped a tear with a finger and turned away to her task. 'We no longer have to place ourselves in those ridiculous and, for women, vulnerable, positions for prayer. In future we'll stand, like this.' She turned to show him and he circled her appreciatively. 'Men and women.'

'How will priests take on their role as Ytraa to abuse their subjects and frowk with such erect members of their gatherings?'

'Simple. If you were at prayer and I decided to join with you as Ytraa, I'd signal you like this; producing the erect member thus.' He responded to her demonstration. 'Guided by me, you must then take up the required position and allow me to do as I wish, with your eyes closed, of course, to avoid blindness.'

'Of course. And male priests?'

She took his hand and demonstrated the signalling method on herself, leaving him in no doubt of her own desires. He stroked her and completed the invited act.

After they'd finished on the narrow table, they sat and ate fruit followed by marinated fish.

'What of your other news?'

'Wendarah plans to go on the raid to The Point with the army, so she can, as she put it, indulge in a little sport. Where have they gone, your brigands and renegades?'

'It is safer you remain ignorant.'

'And if you're killed? Who'll tell them what they need to know?'

'It is a risk I have to take. They are safe and that is what is most important.'

'You don't trust me, Aklon.'

'Trust has nothing to do with it. I live by such secrecy and circumspection that it is second nature. The people are on a remote peninsula east of The Point. When is this raid intended?'

'She needs time to gather her forces. I think she's hoping to set out in about two sixdays. Why?'

'I thought I might see what sort of order they are in. Always a good idea to know your enemy's disposition. Is that from today or from the day of the meeting?'

'The meeting; but take care, Aklon. They'll be well guided on the march and I don't want to witness your public execution.'

'No. I prefer to avoid such spectacle myself. But you have to confess there is great temptation there.'

'Will you stay here until then?'

'Would that I could, my lovely priestess. I have business in the north.'

'Business? Is that her name?'

'Jealousy is a sad and sorry state and does not become you.'

'I just wonder what she's got that I haven't, what draws you to her for a lifelong partner, rather than me.'

'You are both beautiful, embodying perfection as sensual and visually stimulating women. Can I define love? With you, Porlesah, I feel delicious and acute physical sensations, I hear with your ears, feel with your fingers, see through your eyes as well as my own. With this other, I am part of her as she is part of me so that there is no me and her, only us. That is as much as I can describe of the physical. As for the spiritual, I can say only that her ceasing to be would end my being, that I care more for her than for anything or anyone else and that she is everything and all to me. Does that help you understand?'

'As usual, you give more information than I ask. Will you, at least, spend tonight with me?'

'It would give me great pleasure.'

'Undoubtedly. Though not, it seems, enough. No matter. I too will be pleasured, by you, I suspect for the last time.'

Tumalind had sought clarification of the battle and of Okkyntalah and her father's roles from Feldrark. He was more reliable and less chatty than Rrildyss-Kaz, simply answering her questions and maintaining a quiet dignity in his responses. He'd shown her the dreadful violence and death, the stench of charred flesh and the awful destruction of an entire town and most of its citizens.

She'd expected him to be full of joy at his victory, but he'd been overwhelmed by grief at the necessity of such devastation. She saw the smoking remains through his eyes and felt his grief and anger at the intransigence of the town's leader and his blindly loyal people. Her surprise at this ability to view through the eyes of another was diminished by what she saw.

Few of the troops from Litkala had been injured or killed. Only nineteen had been lost in battle and another thirty-seven injured. But they estimated around fourteen thousand people of Mipahnhil had perished in fighting, flames, or under the hail of arrows: men women and children. Such loss and waste clearly affected Feldrark deeply and he wondered what to do with the captives, branded as slaves. Litkala had no recent tradition of slavery and he was at a loss how he should treat them now they were his responsibility. The branding had marked them as different; something he now thought a mistake.

I've no experience in such things, Feldrark. But, trying to see things from their point of view, would it help if they could be treated with dignity, now they've surrendered? Maybe give them a choice of how they live, separating them to dwell amongst the main community

133

in Litkala, so they can't cause trouble as a group? I don't know. I'm just trying to think what might be best. Over time, they may even integrate with the citizens and no longer pose a threat to the city with their need for revenge. Perhaps your most trusted officers could speak to them and find out what they want and expect. If you go as far as you can to satisfy their needs, you'll be seen as magnanimous and they'll have less reason for acts of retribution. I'm sorry, I'm rambling on and I don't mean to. I just hate the idea of all those dispossessed people suffering even more.'

'Tumalind, you're a remarkable young woman. You've given me food for thought and helped clear my mind. There's something I could do in celebration of our coronation when we return. The ceremony usually involves an act of mercy, a gesture of kindness and goodwill to the unfortunate. This may be the solution. Thank you, my dear. You and Okkyntalah have proved yourselves of real value. I hope I might do something for you in return.'

'Avoiding the long trek to Choshinahm would be our best reward, if we deserve one. But Dagla Kaz is determined. I suppose we have no choice.'

'That's one area where I have no say. In fact, it's my own and Ivdulon's impression that you're fated to go on that pilgrimage, for reasons we can't quite foresee. We suspect you both have some important part to play in the unfolding of our hopes for a better future for all. If there's anything else I can do for you, however...?'

'I'd like Okkyntalah back as soon as possible...'

'Now, that is within my power. He'll accompany me on the first ship home.'

Three days had passed slowly and she now waited impatiently for the first ship to appear through the narrow opening in the outer city walls.

It came, at last, emerging through the high walled tunnel and sailing the narrow canal, toward the inner harbour and the quay. In the bows stood Feldrark with Jodisa, who had been taken out in a small boat, waving to the citizens lining the canal sides and docks. Okkyntalah stood near her father with Rrildyss Kaz between them. She waved and his keen eyes found her and she felt the passion in his welcoming salute. Aglydron waved at her; a gesture he wouldn't have made before he found love with Chislanda.

Time seemed to stop as the craft slowly approached. Seemeeuws squabbled, soft surf kissed the beach beyond the walls, the thin hum of the breeze touched her ears. The people nearby embraced her in perfumes and sweat, mingling with the scents of seaweed, fish and wet hemp. Bright sunlight shattered where it struck the small sharp waves before the bows and cast deep shadows under sail and mast. But sudden cheering from the gathered citizens drove away all other sound.

And then Okkyntalah was close enough for her to see his smile and read the love in his eyes and she knew that here was all she needed and wanted from life, and that everything in between there and here was interruption. All around her vanished into an awareness that resided only in her love and she reached out to him and drew him close, long before his feet stepped on the gangplank. When, at last, his arms encircled her and his mouth kissed hers, they were as one in joy.

Hand in hand, they walked clean smooth flags of stone through cheering crowds, and boarded the cart to the palace. Feldrark, Jodisa, her father and others, including Chislanda on a litter, were as fragments of a dream as she reclaimed her love. It was evening before they left their room in search of food and found themselves the source of warm, if ribald, comment and amusement.

They smiled at the mirth, knowing those who joked held them in high regard. Soon enough they'd be gone from this fair city with its sophisticated people and its civilised ways. They would tread ground unknown and uncertain on their way to different customs and traditions, moving into danger and doubt. The false Skyfire had set them on this road and soon the true Skyfire would dim the stars and threaten all with angry conflagration. Then they would be tested with all Followers. For now, they had each other and a chance of happiness. They ate quickly with their friends and new acquaintances and made no excuses when they went to be alone again.

He had gone to her, as always, in the depths of night. Weary and tense, he'd taken time to recover his normal composure and steadiness.

'Are we in danger of discovery, Aklon?'

'I would not be here if that were the case, Shoarhn. It is only that I hurried to be with you and have travelled further and faster than perhaps I should, risking much in my rush to be here. Even so, my stay will be brief. I must away tomorrow night to take the first steps in the beginning of our fight for freedom.'

She stopped his mouth with her own and would hear no more until morning woke them with brightness and hope.

'Did you speak with Tumalind, again, in your mind?'

'Not yet. I wanted you to be with me. In any case, after my experience with Jodisa, I thought we should take breakfast and give her a chance to be out of her bed.'

Shoarhn laughed and called the boys to her room. They came and looked solemnly on their mother.

'Phildrad makes you smile so much, Mother, why does Father only make you sad?'

Aklon raised his eyebrows at the youngster. 'You are very perceptive, young man. However, only age and experience will permit you to understand the union between a man and a woman.'

'He talks funny, doesn't he, Mother?'

Shoarhn shook her head at her son, frowning at his frankness. 'You shouldn't be rude to a guest. Now, off to your grandmother's, boys. Phildrad has news I need to hear and we have a lot of talking to do.'

'Frowking, you mean. We heard you. It's fun, isn't it?'

She ruffled his hair and that of his taciturn brother. 'When you're older, you'll understand. Go to Grandmother's. I'll collect you tomorrow. Be good.'

They kissed her forehead, respectful and loving. To Aklon, they bowed in unison before they left.

'They are good, obedient boys, Shoarhn.'

'Too like their father in some ways. I'd rather they had more of Tumalind's spirit. Mind you, she only got away with arguing with him because she's so beautiful. Even Aglydron couldn't always ignore that. He was harsh with her, as he was with me and the boys, but she seemed to soften his edges somehow.'

'Breakfast, then.'

'In a little while. We should give Tumalind and Okkyntalah plenty of time; they're newlyweds, don't forget.'

Later, he sat at the table, as the noonday sun dazzled from whitened walls of nearby houses and cast black, impenetrable shadows under trees and walls, and concentrated his mind by closing his eyes. It was impossible to concentrate with Shoarhn in sight. For a while, he sought. He discovered Ivdulon and teased her about her attitude to men.

'*You should try again, Ivdulon, court astronomer and wise woman. A woman should not be afraid of men. A woman without a man is incomplete and barely alive.*'

'*You escape the swift smack of my palm on your buttocks only by distance, Aklon. Even Feldrark would hesitate to say such a thing to me. However, you're right and you're wrong. I agree that sensual delight is a very human need. But, had I been besotted, as so many are, I wouldn't have discovered all those fascinating facts I now know.*'

'*You are, indeed, unusual. Until next time, Ivdulon.*'

Aklon closed his mind to her and searched instead for a less familiar contact.

'*Tumalind?*'

'*Oh! Aklon-Dji. Why have you called me?*'

'*Shoarhn wonders if you and Okkyntalah are as happy as she hopes you are.*'

'*Happier than anyone can imagine. Who else have you mindtalked with lately?*'

'*I have just spoken to Ivdulon. Phildrad told me she has a deformed foot and is rather peculiar in her attitude to men. I teased her over that and then she told me about Netrodyl. I am pleased she...*'

'*You didn't mention her deformity?*'

'*No. I thought I might save that as a...*'

136

'Please don't. Not if you value your contact. She's very, very sensitive about it and I think it may hurt her too much.'

'Thank you for the warning, Tumalind. You have probably stopped me causing pain and distress to someone I hold in high esteem. I spoke to her first in minds, long before I was aware there were others who could mindtalk. She sent me packing today as she was teaching her new companion; it seems Netrodyl has made quite an impression on her. An odd relationship, but one apparently founded on some sort of mutual love.'

'Most folk here don't understand. They think it's sexual, but it isn't: more like mother and daughter. But love is love, isn't it? And you love my mother, do you?'

'With every aspect of my being.'

'And she?'

'Shoarhn loves me, yes. Do you approve?'

'You ask me? Does it matter?'

'I would lie easier with her if I knew I caused you no offence or anxiety.'

'I'm delighted. Father's so taken with Chislanda that I doubt he'll ever return to mother. I'm pleased she's found love with you. Though, to be honest, I could've wished for a less controversial and dangerous partner for her.'

'She, at least, will be safe. Soon things will change here, Tumalind. Forces are in motion that I cannot let you know of at present but Ivdulon has a hand in what is happening, and my father's reign will end soon. Along with it will come the end of much cruelty and injustice. The new age will dawn with freedoms, justice and a chance of happiness for all.'

'I hope you're right, Aklon-Dji.'

'Tell me a little of Netrodyl. Anyone who impresses Ivdulon must be unusual indeed.'

'She's very lovely; dark, like Ivdulon and the late Kirallah. But she has no learning to speak of and can't understand Ivdulon's reasoning and ideas. But the wise woman's convinced she can teach her what she knows. She says ignorance and stupidity are not the same things.'

She went on to tell him of the battle for Mipahnhil and asked him to explain to Shoarhn about Chislanda.

'Tumalind can tell Aglydron he has my blessing. If he's found someone he can truly love, I welcome it and make no blame for his deserting me. Ask her to explain about you and me, Aklon.'

Tumalind and Aklon agreed on the necessary deception to keep Shoarhn happy, since they couldn't inform Aglydron without breaking the secret of mindtalk to him; something generally reserved only for the partners of those with the gift. Aklon recalled his exposure of the secret to Chellyth and wondered how that would be viewed by the rest of the community.

Aklon questioned her about those who'd accompanied her on the first part of the pilgrimage and, in particular, about Phildrad and his role and actions. What he learned gave him hope for an enterprise he had planned for the near future and when he left Tumalind, he felt happier about the days to come than he had before speaking with her.

'A truly delightful young woman. Mature, clever, gifted and wise beyond her years. Clearly more the child of her mother than of her father.'

'She has Aglydron's stubbornness, though they'd both call it determination.'

'I meant; Dagla Kaz. It is from him that she gained the ability to mindtalk, though he is unaware of the gift. I suspect he will have destroyed much of the potential by his prolonged use of a potency stimulant he uses.'

'You're not your father's son, Aklon. He left me feeling used and discarded, a thing to be had because he could have it and tossed aside without further thought. The gap between his joining and yours is a chasm so wide it could never be crossed.'

'The High Priest is what his position has made him. He dwells in a realm of power where he may act more or less as he wishes. Those who defy him die or disappear. It is hardly any wonder that such power over others should influence his attitude to what seem like lesser mortals to him. He must, indeed he does, see himself as a superior creation; almost a god. We are direct descendants of Gadhallah. And Gadhallah was descended from Vaarkil and Mythanpho. Mythanpho was a demigoddess and Vaarkil an offspring of Tryhnn and some mortal. So, there is, in the lineage, the blood of gods. Father is sure of his descent and feels the power of his antecedents without the respect and responsibility I feel should go with it.'

'So, you do believe in Vaarkil and Mythanpho, Ulkhon, Tryhnn?'

'One has to believe in something. Gadhallah promoted Ytraa from a lesser place in the ranks of the gods to the highest by his corruption of history. I believe there are good reasons why our forebears worshipped Tryhnn and Ulkhon. And the story of Mythanpho and Vaarkil is so well documented and told from so many different points of view, even in the secret texts, that I believe it to be based on fact. There are many things in the world that we do not understand and it is right that we respect those things that we can believe in.'

'What does your friend, Ivdulon, have to say about it?'

'We have never discussed it. I will, when next I speak with her.'

Their meal finished, Shoarhn persuaded him, in spite of the danger, to help her tend the animals; so they would have more time together. They were in the fields behind the house, when A'ahl approached. She waddled across the cropped grass, her pregnancy very clear.

'Aklon. I've not seen you for so long, I believed you've taken a dislike to me.'

'You know better than that, A'ahl. Aklon's been here only for brief periods. He must go again tomorrow.'

'And will you be with me, Aklon, before you leave?'

'Are you sure it would be wise, A'ahl? Wesdan lies dead and unmanned in the bowels of Mhortag, whilst his child swells your pretty belly. Should I enter that space he or she will shortly use to exit into the world?'

'She's in need, Aklon. Give her what she wishes but come back to me. We're friends and she deserves some pleasure. I can bear to share you whilst I must.'

'Thank you both. But I only came to warn Aklon about Kaz-Ca-Uldrad. He joined with me a few days ago, but I suspect he prefers small boys, judging by the style of the brief relief he took. I think he knows more about you than he should. He's gathering soldiers for something and I can't help feeling it's to do with you.'

'Thank you for your concern, A'ahl, and your bravery in coming to warn me.'

A'ahl left at once but turned her brief and telling gaze on Aklon as she crossed the fields to the house.

He helped with the chores on the small farm, spending the precious daylight hours in her company and disregarding danger for that short while. But the duties done, they returned to the house. 'I am sorry, Shoarhn. I can remain but a few hours more and will leave before morning.'

She took him and held him as if she believed he wouldn't be coming back.

In the darkness of night, he went. 'I will return; I promise you, though great changes are about to happen. When next we meet, our whole world may be different. I hope and pray we both live through the coming turmoil and find a way to be together for the rest of our lives, Shoarhn. Be brave, be careful, be true to the Cause. You are one of the Few and great deeds may be needed before we are together again.'

He tasted the salt of her tears, kissed her and left without another word, his mind already filling with actions he must set in motion if his dreams of justice were to be fulfilled. Come the real Skyfire, he should have most of his plans in place. If he hadn't begun the Cause by then, he might find it impossible beneath a sky ablaze with flames that would ignite righteous superstition in all those he wished to convert to peace and justice. If he timed his action well, however, the true Skyfire could be used to signal that the Cause was right and just. Much of what he hoped for and believed in depended on factors beyond his control. So, he must ensure that those he did control were carried out to maximum effect.

Chapter 15

DUTIES OF OFFICE

Close on the heels of victory, whilst elation and the heady emotions of success still enthused the people, Feldrark arranged the coronation. Spending her time in joy with Okkyntalah, Tumalind was occasionally interrupted by silent communication with Feldrark as he tried to work out what to do with his captives. Because of this, she almost regretted her earlier suggestions but hoped she'd made some difference to the way the captives would be dealt with.

The city seemed to hold its collective breath, as all assembled for a solemn ceremony which, by its very nature, would signal an end to the period of official mourning following the murders of the Kiral and Kirallah. Tumalind, hand in hand with Okkyntalah, sat on the specially constructed platform under the inner wall, with the flat meadow, packed with the citizens of the upper and lower city, spread in front. Beside them, Aglydron and Chislanda, now fully recovered physically, sat along with Myllthlan, Caarl, Tarruss, Corphanda and her Virgin Gifts, and Ivdulon and Netrodyl.

Under cloudless blue, all calmed and quieted as the royal party threaded through the respectful crowd to reach the dais. Rrildyss Kaz and Patradko Kaz led, with Dagla Kaz, as honoured guest, between them. Palace servants walked in attendance either side of Feldrark and Jodisa, all clad in simple white tunics devoid of decoration. Behind, marched the high rank soldiers, resplendent in their military tunics. And last, playing gentle music, came the musicians and choir, Linlyss plucking the strings of her lyre and staring straight into the eyes of Okkyntalah as she approached.

'Still wants you, I see.'

'I haven't seen her since we returned from battle. I'll have to tell her I'm no longer available.'

'It'll make no difference, Okkyntalah. I've seen that look before. In fact, truth be told, I had it myself. Still do.'

He stroked her leg in token of his love and she leant across to kiss his cheek before paying attention to the solemn occasion unfolding before them.

As they reached the platform, the high priests climbed three steps onto the level base and spread out with the men either side of the woman. The soldiers took their places as a formal guard of honour, facing the crowd, on the ground at the foot of the dais. Two by two, their various burdens held before them, the servants lined up behind the priests. As musicians and choir took their places on the smaller, lower platform to the southern side of the main dais, Feldrark and Jodisa slowly climbed the steps together and bowed, first to the waiting guests seated there and then to the assembled population.

Rrildyss Kaz signalled for quiet, which was almost complete anyway. Tumalind heard the sea behind the wall, kissing the shingle, the colourful birds in the ornamental trees as they flitted in pursuit of insects, but no other sound. She held Okkyntalah's hand and feeling slight tension there, turned and saw his eyes fixed on Feldrark and Jodisa and knew she, visible to the masses, should do the same.

Quiet music rose and the choir sang a lament for the Kiral and Kirallah, bringing tears to many. As the rounds repeated and the crowd joined in, so the palace servants surrounded the royal pair. Swift movements, performed with precision, soon exchanged their white tunics for multi-coloured garments. And, as the servants parted, to sit at the feet of the guests, Feldrark and Jodisa were revealed in their royal ceremonial clothes.

Matching tunics of deep orange fell from throat to ankle, unbelted and edged with a dark green band that circled the necks and ran down to their feet on each sleeveless side. They were fastened with three ties. Jodisa and Feldrark knelt to face each other and the three high priests moved to stand between them and the seated guests, briefly obscuring Tumalind's view.

Dagla Kaz seemed an appendage, taking no real part in the actual crowning. Rrildyss Kaz and Patradko Kaz accepted the matching crowns from servants who held them in readiness. She placed one on Feldrark's head as he placed the other on Jodisa's. Made of filigree myllth studded with precious gems, they shone with a strange gaudiness as they spiralled from the royal heads to raise their height by more than an arm's length. Once placed, the musicians stopped their music and singing.

Tumalind waited; the air tense with anticipation; even the birds and sea seemed to join in the moment of silence. After a brief spell and without any apparent signal, the entire population raised their arms high and cried out in acclaim.

'Hail the Kiral! Hail the Kirallah!'

Both phrases were called in unison, the women shouting out the Kiral's name and then the Kirallah's and the men performing the opposite call.

The crowned royals rose together and approached the front of the platform, accepting the acclamation of the crowd and waiting for silence to descend again.

'I hereby pledge my life to the people, lands and city of Litkala in service, love and absolute loyalty until the end of life releases me. This I do not as duty but from love, respect and joy. Know that I stand here your servant and remain at your disposal from this day until I breathe no more. Know that all are welcome at the palace and all will be heard. Justice, fairness and firm control will be my watchwords. None shall go hungry, none shall want, none shall be neglected, for as long as my rule lasts. I give you my pledge on this day and ask in return only your complete loyalty to the city, lands and citizens of Litkala. Do I have such a pledge?'

The people, as one, answered Feldrark and Jodisa's united question with an almighty, 'You do, most worthy ones; for all time.'

And that was it, it seemed. Feldrark and Jodisa signalled the populace to be seated and there was much shuffling and some merriment as all tried to sit on the grass, making room for one another. The musicians played merry music the while. At length, all was settled and Jodisa and Feldrark signalled for quiet.

'First, let it be known that today is a day of celebration and, as a consequence of the food, dancing, joining and drink, tomorrow will be a day of rest in the whole of Litkala.'

There was great cheering at Jodisa's announcement.

'Let me announce that all will be paid for by the palace for these two days. Enjoy and celebrate with us.'

Feldrark's announcement brought even louder cheering.

When all was silent again, Feldrark and Jodisa made a signal to a group at the very rear of the large open space and all watched as this small group moved forward. Tumalind saw four uniformed guards and half a dozen rather sorry looking people wearing rags.

'Who are they?'

She smiled at Okkyntalah. 'Prisoners, I think.'

In turn, Jodisa and Feldrark asked them what crime they had committed. As they confessed and made sincere apologies, each was pardoned, pledging service in exchange for their freedom. The final prisoner, however, was a man from another land. He was in chains and naked.

'You have committed the most unforgivable crime. The child you violated cannot be brought back to life. What have you to say?'

The man spat and snarled. 'I piss on your city. I curse you till the end of time. I...'

Even as the man spoke, Feldrark signalled to the guards. They forced him to his knees and, with a single blow, sliced his head from his body. Tumalind had to look away but she turned back as she heard those around her mutter their approval. The body was dragged away as two volunteers washed away the blood to leave the site of execution cleansed. But nobody moved close to the spot.

The musicians struck up a merry tune until the cleansing was complete and then Feldrark and Jodisa again signalled for quiet. From the back of the crowd a procession of men, women and children, all dressed in short black tunics and with their ankles hobbled and their hands bound before them, was led through to face the platform.

'Citizens of Mipahnhil, you've been brought here after the utter destruction of your

143

home, brought about by the intransigence of your leader and your culture of revenge. We now put before you a stark choice. We would have you live among us, free. But you will have to swear fealty to Litkala and abandon your belief that the deaths of your friends, families and other citizens must be avenged in blood. The alternative is exile to a small uninhabited island lying between Niphralon and Muhnilahm.'

The citizens of Litkala murmured doubt over Feldrark's announcement and the sorry lot from the defeated place stood amidst this, wavering and wondering what they should do.

Jodisa spoke with compassion. 'You've been taught that Followers stole this city from your ancestors many cycles ago. It isn't true. In the palace are ancient scrolls and parchments telling how this whole land was found deserted. It may be that those who occupied this place before the Followers came were those who took it from your nation. We'll never be sure. But be assured, as an outsider, I am certain that Followers did not force any living soul from this place. It was deserted when they came upon it.'

The people of Litkala murmured approval and those from the city on stilts glanced at one another, uncertain.

'This is what you must decide: to live here with us and adopt our ways. Or to go into exile. Those who wish to stay; approach and swear fealty to Litkala.'

To Tumalind's surprise, Chislanda rose from her place beside Aglydron and stepped quickly to the front of the platform. She descended the steps and faced what was left of her folk.

'I'm one of you. And I've chosen my way. This sorry mess began when my child was brought, dead from a snakebite, in the arms that now embrace and comfort me. He filled my belly with life, a life ended by the Galhta with his cruelty. Aglydron strives daily to replace that lost life again. I'll spend my remaining years with this man, who once I swore to kill. If I can forgive and accept a new partner from amongst those we saw as enemies, why shouldn't you do the same?

'One more fact might help you understand the truth about Litkala. You know I was one of the hunting party our Galhta sent to destroy those we saw as enemies of Mipahnhil. After that first fight, I was spared by those I tried to kill.'

There was some murmuring at this but Chislanda held up her hand and waited for silence to fall again.

'On my way back, I came on a ruined stone temple. Inside, I saw, with my own eyes, a carving of the face of Tryhnn as we know her. Our traditions say we were driven out of our stone home and we've always accused the present population of this fair city. But I ask you to think about what then occurred to me; that that ancient stone temple might be the site of our original home and that Litkala never was ours. Look at this place and ask

144

yourselves whether our ancestors could've built such a wonder. Even those who live here now admit they lack the skills. We can't ever really know, but I'm ready to believe Litkala wasn't ours, but that the more ancient place out on those plains so far from here and so much closer to our ruined home was where we came from.'

Chislanda mounted the steps and knelt before Jodisa and Feldrark. She took the hands they offered, kissed them and raised her voice so that all could hear. 'I swear before all the Gods, that I give my loyalty and service to the land, the city and the people of Litkala. May Tryhnn destroy me if I fail in that promise.'

The crowd cried out their approval.

Feldrark and Jodisa raised Chislanda to her feet, embraced her and gestured that she should re-join Aglydron. 'That was well done, Chislanda. We thank you.'

One by one, with varying degrees of reluctance, and led by mothers who still had children, those from Mipahnhil stepped up and declared loyalty to Litkala. As they did so, the palace servants released their bonds, removed their black tunics and dressed them in the blue and white of the common folk.

In the end, only three men refused citizenship and they were led away to a fate to be decided. But Feldrark had sworn there would be no more killing and the likelihood seemed that, too few to form a colony, they would go into exile to a place of their choosing.

Tumalind travelled back with the royal party for the rest of the celebrations, Okkyntalah ever at her side.

'Happy, my love?'

'With you, I'll be happy wherever I am, Okkyntalah. But I do love this fabulous city.'

'We won't be here for long. We'll soon be off on the pilgrimage again.'

'Yes; to an uncertain future in strange lands. Let's make the best of the time we have.'

The false Skyfire had died and the real hadn't yet made an appearance, though Ivdulon knew precisely where and when it would. Dagla Kaz was impatient to be on his way. Many leagues lay ahead before his mission was complete and he could relax again on Muhnilahm. Discussions with Ivdulon and Patradko Kaz had broadened his horizons and he was now aware of more secrets. The faith he led was founded in even more corruption and falsehood than he'd known; in particular, the history of Gadhallah.

Contact with Feldrark, Ivdulon and the two High Priests of Litkala had opened up new areas of thought and changed his perspectives on some fundamental issues.

'You know, Jhonaht, now we understand what caused the split amongst Followers, I can't help feeling our branch of the faith doesn't emerge well.'

'No matter how you examine that incident and its consequences, I can't help but feel

145

shame, Dagla Kaz.'

'You and I never had faith or belief in Gadhallah, of course. But I've always believed strongly in forces for good and evil. Ivdulon and Feldrark say Gadhallah was not just a thoroughly unpleasant human being, but say his unchallenged misuse of Ytraa leaves real doubt as to the nature of that god.'

Gadhallah, godlike and true to destiny. Now, there was a real man.'

'You didn't have a problem before with Ytraa as God.'

'No, Jhonaht. I dealt only with mild misgivings about usurping the beliefs of our people as a means of retaining power.'

'They get the leaders they deserve. If they're stupid enough to believe the ludicrous hocus-pocus and spurious ritual that form the faith of Followers, they deserve to be fooled.'

'Perhaps.'

'For all his ethical and moral faults, Dagla Kaz, Gadhallah understood us very well. To take a basic human appetite and invest it with religious imperative was pure genius.'

'And to make it all into a watcher's charter for the priests and Holy Ones, shows extraordinary insight into the minds of the common masses. I've no problem with perpetuating that myth, of course.'

Jhonaht rested his elbows on the stone ledge of the window of his room and looked out across the city. 'It makes for a stable society and brings almost as much happiness as grief. It's attractive for the majority, who don't think too deeply about what they're actually required to do and believe in. It rewards them with as much sex as they want.'

'Indeed it does, Jhonaht. And popularity and conformity are important qualities to common folk. No. Overall, I'm inclined to implement few changes in the structure of our faith, in spite of all we've learned from those with deeper concerns.'

'We'll have to make some changes, I suppose, to help unify the two groups.'

'The female vulnerability of the prayer posture is an unfortunate loss. I so enjoyed taking them when they were helpless. Wendarah will have her work cut out persuading the priesthood and Holy Ones of the prurient opportunities the upright stance provides; being able to view the whole body is a definite advantage, though. And, with the new refinements of the invitation by Ytraa, it doesn't actually reduce the ready availability of targets.'

'And Feldrark and his ilk aren't advocating that anyone should actually dress for prayer, Dagla Kaz.'

'I should hope not! Reducing violent punishment and torture will cause trouble. The Holy Ones enjoy the mutilation, flailing, burning, rape and buggery. But that's a minor concern. In the longer term I intend to reduce their power and numbers until they eventually disappear.'

'They've always been a thorn in your side; disputing with you over interpretations of texts and law. It'll be useful to get rid of them altogether. Maybe blame them for the changes we'll have to bring in; let them become even more unpopular with the people.'

'You know, Jhonaht, on balance, the wider opportunities for mixing with other Followers and the commercial advantages of putting some of Ivdulon's brilliant schemes into practice will probably outweigh any losses.'

'I agree. But Feldrark clearly wants to destroy the whole basis for Following and to replace it with a more spiritual faith. Doesn't that worry you?'

Dagla Kaz shrugged and turned his back to the city, staring into the quiet brightness of the chamber. 'I'm likely to be in office no more than another thirty or forty cycles and such change will take so long it won't be my problem. I'll raise my new heir alongside the new ideas and help him or her adapt to the new religion.'

'Is Pharah-Li with your child, Dagla Kaz?'

'Not yet. At least, I don't think so. But time's running short when I'll be able to frowk that delightful woman and have her indulge my favourite games. Soon I'll have to lead the pilgrims to Choshinahm on a journey with even fewer incentives than when we started. And now, of course, the whole sham's increasingly unpalatable.'

'Why bother?'

'Oh, Jhonaht; if I'm to continue in office and enjoy its luxury and advantage, I can't abandon the mission. The Holy Ones would flail my hide with tnetsi thorns, tear the love fruits from my shredded scrotum and roast them whilst they remained attached to me. And then they'd begin their torture.'

The thought made him shudder.

'And, if we're to go, it will be soon, I suppose?'

'We have to set out before the true Skyfire appears. The false one brought us here and to new problems; will the real Skyfire serve us better?'

'Only if we succeed, Dagla Kaz.'

'Nobody's failed the pilgrimage for the new Godwood, so far. I daren't be the first.'

'Unless, of course, it simply hasn't been recorded.'

'Use your sense, man. There are five Godwoods. There have been five visits of the Skyfire. No one's failed. And neither can I. We must go to Choshinahm. If I succeed, my life as High Priest will be secured. If we fail…But we can't fail, Jhonaht, my old friend, can we?'

'We won't fail, Dagla Kaz. And just think, even as we speak, Aklon-Dji will have been hunted down and destroyed, hopefully in agony.'

'You're a good friend; know just the right thing to say. The thought of his torture and death excites me. I'll leave you now.'

He went at once in search of Pharah-Li and her unique brand of entertainment and stimulation. He'd miss her comforts on the road. She'd made it clear that, whilst she was willing to be his consort and bear him an heir, even to return with him to his island, she wasn't willing to go into wild lands with him. He reminded himself that Tumalind was no longer virgin, so he could sport with that tender young woman on the journey, teach her some of his ways and alleviate the tedium.

The door of his room stood ajar and there, eager, lay Pharah-Li. She welcomed him, as only she knew how, and took away his troubles, at least until he was alone again.

⁕─⁕─⁕

Up the slope, Por-Kildu, Mkolo-ti and Delbon walked with other fit and willing volunteers in single file. They stopped at the fringe of the trees and turned to wait. Aklon stood with Chellyth at the foot of that faint track. He knew it would be long before they returned and, by that time, much would have already happened.

Delbon had arrived in the settlement two days previously with messages of the troop movements and they'd devised a risky plan to help defeat the army or, at least, cause it major embarrassment.

Delbon and some others, guided by Mkolo-ti, would return to the old settlement on The Point to make it seem still inhabited. They'd have to keep up this appearance for a few days, until the army arrived at the Scar and began their march over The Point to destroy the settlement and its inhabitants. They would then return to the Scar by night and re-join Aklon. After that, there were no real plans but he expected a large part of the army to be disabled or stranded on The Point, since the returning settlers intended to destroy the foot and handholds up the cliff as they climbed it. If all worked out, the coming battle to set the Cause in motion would be much less bloody in the absence of a large part of the island's fighting force.

Chellyth looked at the trees that would swallow her man and then turned back to Aklon. 'We're as ready as we can be, Aklon. When you've gone, I'll gather my people together and prepare them for justice and freedom at last.'

In the distance, the sea called on the hidden shore. And, closer, a new born cried into the night.

Aklon smiled at the sound. 'Food and plenty for all. No need now to sacrifice the male children.'

Chellyth was thoughtful. 'You remind me of that boy, Okkyntalah, who stole my authority and dragged me across the desert, humiliated me in front of those I lead, and escaped. When he returns, I'll teach him what it means to shame The One. He'll regret his defiance and disobedience, whatever you might think. I'll show him the lessons of blade

148

and fire before he begs me to relieve him of a life too agonising to continue.'

'Decide as you will, Chellyth. I have never pressed my hopes or wishes on you. But I say this of Okkyntalah. That young man did what he had to in circumstances over which he had little control. Had he not acted as he did, the Cause would not now be moving towards its conclusion and you would still be living that half life, that existence on The Point. He is a brave and daring soldier in our cause. Do not let tradition put death in his way.'

'It may be mere tradition to you, Aklon-Dji, son of High Priest and privilege. I've had to lead where most would've perished. I've had to create a land where there was only dust and death. I've spoken the words, Aklon. The actions must follow.'

'I say again, before I leave you for what may be the last time, words can be reversed though deeds may not, and forgiveness is a higher honour by far than vengeance.'

'Sometimes, honour is all, Aklon. Sometimes honour and respect are all a woman has to keep her in position as leader of rebels.'

He bent to kiss her and, in spite of the surrender and promise in her embrace, he knew she was a woman he would never share. He was half minded to explain that she would cease to be a leader, once the Cause had been completed, but it was better that she remained motivated for the moment. Letting her go, he turned and walked up the slope to join her man and the others, bent on the mission he'd dreamed of for so long.

The evening sky grew dark and they turned west, knowing the sign that had set their Cause in motion was already gone. It would be a few sixdays before the true Skyfire appeared and grew to trouble the general population. He must have the first part of his work complete by then.

He looked up through trees to the Eyes of Ytraa blinking faintly down and wondered what that falsely elevated god would think of all they did. He had had the thought before, but that did not make it less the case. Would Ytraa let them change the way they worshipped? Or would the real Skyfire, as the priests and Holy Ones predicted, burn up all who failed to travel in the ways dictated by that foul disciple, Gadhallah?

Now, though, was not the time for such doubts. He shrugged and turned to start the battle that would begin the war for freedom. The Skyfire was gone. But the Skyfire was yet to come.

Chapter 16

A TIME OF WAITING

Aklon touched Phildrad's knuckles with his own and, without a word, led him from the trees under a spangled sky onto the plain. For hours, they travelled silently, their passing noted only by night creatures whose paths they crossed. As dawn paled the eastern sky above the mountains, Aklon slowed his pace and melted into low bush under the foothills.

'Have you eaten?'

''Ad supper, if that's what you mean.'

'Good. We will rest during daylight; take turns on watch. No fire. We stay too close to the enemy to risk flame or smoke. Tonight, we finish the journey to arrive at the Scar before them and see them move into the trap.'

'We gonna eat before that?'

'We eat before we set off this evening. Cold and raw; for we have no way to cook.'

'What you got in mind?'

'There are grubs in bark, eggs in nests.'

'Maggots an' raw eggs. If I'd known I were goin' to be dinin' in luxury I'd 'ave brought me special knife.'

Aklon's laugh was soft but appreciative. 'You will feed well tomorrow or, at latest the night following. Be patient, Phildrad. We do dangerous work and the outliers of those we follow walk no more than three hundred paces from here. It is best we are silent. If you are able to watch now, I will sleep. Wake me at noon.'

He stretched out beneath the branches of the low bush that concealed them. Beetles and flies scurried but he took no notice. Phildrad settled into a sitting position that rested his legs whilst ensuring he was unlikely to fall asleep.

Waking before midday, without being roused, Aklon was alert at once. 'Your turn, Phildrad; I will wake you late afternoon.'

But it was growing dark when he nudged the man awake. Aklon had a freshly caught red-bellied trout already filleted, gutted and split. He handed Phildrad half and began to eat the other. Raw, it had been marinated in wine. He offered the flagon to his friend.

'Where 'n 'ow did you…?'

'The sentries are dreadfully slack. I could have slit three throats and still not been noticed. One of them will be whipped for allowing his officer to be deprived of this rather excellent Krohtl gold and his fish supper. And, hopefully, a little dissent will be caused when they accuse each other of my petty thefts.'

'Lasdilyss allus said you was a clever 'un, Aklon. I'm startin' to see what she meant.'

'A rare woman, your wife. I shall miss our joining.'

'Happen you've a way with women. She says you're never without a partner, even livin' the life you do.'

Aklon only nodded; his habit of joining with every woman he knew was no longer the unreserved joy it had been before he met and fell for Shoarhn. For a moment, he wondered in silence about what she might be doing now, away in the north-east of the island in her lonely village house. But he was confident her life remained as safe as it could be as a member of the Few and he knew that dwelling on her potential danger would only hinder his mission.

They ate in relative silence, ears alert for signs of searchers. But their enemies gave no indication they even suspected they were about. After burying the remains of Aklon's theft, they set off into darkness.

Night hid them for another four leagues of almost constant movement. Phildrad expressed relief on learning they'd reached their destination a short time before the stars were due to surrender to dawn.

'They have about a thousand soldiers at arms, a couple of hundred Holy Ones and a handful of kitchen slaves to do the field cooking. They will assemble on the flat space down there and we will begin to harry them once we have a better idea of exactly what they are about.'

'You an' me agin more'n a thousand?'

'Hardly more than five hundred apiece.'

'You're mad! Ravin'!'

'Sorry. My little joke, Phildrad. They will almost all go down the Scar to the plain below. We will then deal with those who stay behind and ensure the rest are unable to return to the main part of the island without a good deal of loss and effort. I expect to escape before we face real danger, and I have a route and destination planned. Have no fear. I wish to live every bit as much as you do. Now, I suggest you rest. There is a small cave a little further up the slope, invisible from the plain and, I believe, unknown to our enemy. We will spend the day there and then see what we may do to spoil their plans.'

'How d'you do it?'

'Do what?'

'Everything.'

'I am at a loss to understand you. Now, to the cave as quick as we may. I have a further task to complete before daylight comes.'

Aklon returned, under a brightened sky, and unslung his bow and quiver before he took his place in the entrance beside Phildrad, already awake again.

'You saw my signal?'

'Won't it let our enemies know we're 'ere?'

'They will not know its meaning or origin. But if there are no fires burning on The Point, they might believe all those they abandoned there have died and may not bother to go on their killing spree. My accomplices are even now setting a few smoky fires in the deserted village. You would not see their signal of reply from here but I did. With luck, they will return to the foot of the scar under cover of darkness tonight and we will help them ascend. Sleep again now, I will take the first watch. Oh, if you hunger, there is food in the back if you clamber up the rock fall and reach inside the dark space there. And there remains a drop of wine in the flagon.'

Phildrad returned a short while later, eating dried fruit. He passed some to Aklon. They drank from the refilled flagon and his new convert stretched out on the dry floor.

'Still don't see 'ow just two on us can make a difference to an army of over a thousand.'

'Come morning, you will understand.'

'If you say so, Aklon, if you say so.'

He rested his head on his pack and let tiredness take him. Aklon sat in silence, watching the sky darken, his thoughts on the carnage he must hasten come dawn.

⁂

Shoarhn felt need without understanding the call. Arriving at A'ahl's house in the darkness of early morning, she knew why she'd been called. The keening from within was a clear cry for help and she entered quickly. She found and lit a lamp, the thin trail of smoke rising and curling as she disturbed air around the flame. A'ahl lay on her sleep mat, uncovered and spread, her head thrown back in pain and her face drained of all colour.

'It's early, Shoarhn. And the pain is so strong.'

Her words came soft and full of despair, gasped out of her pain with only the effort she could spare.

Shoarhn knelt at the foot of the mat and examined her. The signs were what she expected from late stage labour but A'ahl was right about the early start to the birth. It was a whole portion before the due time.

'This is more than I know, A'ahl. I need help. Lie still and I'll bring Tasallyss.'

'Not Tasallyss.'

She said no more, but the tone and evident fear made Shoarhn hesitate.

'Why?'

'Too loyal.'

153

Shoarhn considered. The risk was minimal and A'ahl might die in childbirth without aid from an expert. 'We can worry about that later. For now, you need the best in the village.'

A'ahl, too weary to argue, nodded, but her eyes were full of concern as Shoarhn left the room.

The streets were still sleeping, the air a little fresher than daylight would permit. She trod silent steps quickly to the house of the acclaimed midwife, praying she was home and not attending some other woman in need. At the door, she paused and listened. There was nothing to disturb the silence beyond the distant lapping of waves on the shore and cries of circling sea birds as they woke to their dawn hunt for food.

A short, sharp rap brought a quick response and Tasallyss opened the door as she was donning her tabard. Shoarhn glimpsed flesh and wondered if A'ahl's concerns were founded in more than undeserved rumour. The woman smiled and posed a question with her face.

Shoarhn explained and the woman bent to pick up her pack from its place beside the door and followed her to A'ahl's house. She asked questions on the walk and Shoarhn realised she could give only basic answers. The woman seemed content enough with what she heard.

A'ahl was exactly as Shoarhn had left her and the midwife knelt between her legs and felt over her distended stomach with practiced hands, listening, concentrating, feeling for signs she would understand.

'The child is in the wrong position. I must try to turn it, or both you and it will die in the attempt to give birth. I will try not to hurt you but I must use enough force to make the turn. Are you ready?'

A'ahl nodded and gritted her teeth, waiting for the expected pain. But, ready as she was, the cry escaped her as Tasallyss pressed on her belly and urged the infant into a better position. She tried seven times before she was satisfied she'd done all she could.

'Shoarhn, help her stand and hold her in a crouched position. She needs the weight of the child to deliver it to the world.'

The women did as they were bid, Shoarhn holding her friend's hands or shoulders by turn as she pushed to let the baby leave her.

She screamed. The woman brought her water in a beaker, made her drink. 'You've been without liquid too long. You need to drink. It will help.'

A'ahl drank and pushed and screamed again. Shoarhn watched as blood slowly pooled around her knees between her friend's legs. Tasallyss nodded and sighed her concern.

'That damned priest! I'm glad he's dead!'

Shoarhn exchanged an anxious glance with the midwife but she merely nodded.

'It's common for women to say things they don't mean when giving birth. Don't worry. The tales you've heard of my zealous nature are no more true than those of your alliance to the heretic.'

Shoarhn tried to make her face neutral, to make no response at all to the implied threat. She urged A'ahl to push. Push. Push!

The blood increased. The infant slowly emerged, floppy and lifeless it seemed. But Tasallyss grasped the half born child and pulled him from her friend with one swift movement. A'ahl collapsed and the midwife examined the infant rapidly before she handed the bundle of flesh to Shoarhn.

'Dispose of this. I have more to do to keep the mother alive now.'

Shoarhn looked at the poor deformed thing in her hands, blood coating the flesh and bones of something that seemed never to have been a human child. There was no proper head, only a raised portion of the shoulders that protruded as an ugly mound of flesh. An arm and the legs joined along their length. No sign of life; a blessing in the circumstances. She lay the creature outside for dogs and beasts to take if they would.

Inside, Tasallyss ripped up bedding and used the strips to fold into a pad and to form a wrapping to keep it in place.

'I can do no more. She must lie still for as long as it takes for the flow to stop. At least there is nothing left inside that should be removed. But she's torn with the effort and unlikely to bear further fruit. I hope her man is forgiving.'

Shoarhn placed seven gold quounds into her outstretched hand and let her leave alone. She sat at the top of the blood soaked sleep mat and rested A'ahl's head in her lap, praying her friend would recover from a pregnancy she'd never desired and the birth of an infant that could bring only shame.

'A dorltah for them, Tumalind?'

She turned to Tarruss and looked up. He made even Okkyntalah appear short, but then he towered above everyone except Feldrark. She smiled and told him she'd been thinking about the poor dispossessed souls from Mipahnhil.

He turned to Okkyntalah, eating on the bench beside her. 'She's a soft heart this one, young 'un. I hope you'll not break it.'

The implied threat was plain and her man simply nodded at the giant before helping himself to more of the savoury meat from the platter.

'Needn't worry about Okkyntalah on my behalf, Tarruss. He's already shown himself more than worthy and I know in my heart, soft or no, that he'll always be by me. It won't be Okkyntalah who'll break my heart, though I might find grief from others.' Her eyes strayed to the High Priest, seated across the great hall, his paramour beside him displaying more than she concealed, as usual.

'You surely don't think he'll try, Tumalind? I thought you'd decided he's probably your father?'

'He as good as told me, and Jodisa more or less confirmed it. I've other information that makes it almost certain.' She glanced secretly at her lover and he nodded his acknowledgement of her mindtalk with Aklon that had linked her to her mother on the island. 'But he still looks at me the way men do when they want to join.'

'Aye, but you're a beautiful young woman, Tumalind. I've treated you as a daughter whilst you remained virgin but I've to confess I'd join with you in a trice now you're an adult Follower.'

She saw the twinkle in his eye and knew the jest was only half meant. If Tarruss, her guardian and long-term friend could feel like that about her then it was no surprise that Dagla Kaz should feel the same. It gave her some comfort, though only a little. If the High Priest wanted her to join with him, she could do nothing to prevent it. He could, if he desired, have her as his consort for the forthcoming pilgrimage. She hoped he'd be too concerned with leadership to be bothered with her. The forced separation from Okkyntalah had been hard on both of them; to have it prolonged now they were married and would be together on the road for many portions, would be intolerable. She wondered if she might use mindtalk to persuade Dagla Kaz she wasn't the woman he desired. It was something she'd discuss later with the wise woman, Ivdulon.

'How long before we set off, Tumalind? Do you know?'

She turned to Tarruss and nodded. 'Dagla Kaz wants to be on his way around the time the real Skyfire's observed. Ivdulon says she'll see it about three nights from now.'

'She can really be that sure?'

'She knows every date when the wanderers roam and where they'll be in the sky. She predicted the end of the false Skyfire absolutely to the day. She knows much does that woman. I wish I had her mind. To understand so many things.'

'And then we start on the road to Choshinahm. I wish we didn't have to go.'

'Me too, Okkyntalah.'

'Your punishment for kidnapping Jodisa-Li, isn't it, young 'un?'

'My name's Okkyntalah, Tarruss. I had enough disrespect from Aglydron to last me a lifetime. I'm a married man now, with a score of deaths to my name. But you're right. Dagla Kaz says we've to pay the price for capturing his daughter, even though he agrees we were acting as agents of Ytraa. Seems unfair to me, to be honest. Especially on Tumalind.'

'Aye, Okkyntalah, but happen she's the real reason you're going along, mebbie?'

156

Tumalind frowned at Tarruss. His throw away remark had just undone the good he'd done with his assurance that all men desired her and that Dagla Kaz was no more lustful for her than any other. The thought of his hard thin body pressed into hers was almost unbearable, particularly now she'd experienced the deep and passionate love of Okkyntalah. And especially now she was sure he was her father. It was insupportable.

⁕

Aklon looked down on the mustered troops and Holy Ones and saw his estimate had been accurate. The only unknown, now, was how many they would send onto The Point itself and how many would stay behind. He had only Phildrad, and Delbon, who would hopefully return early from the abandoned settlement to help them. A dozen soldiers and the odd Holy One would not be a problem but if they decided to leave a sizable force above, he may have to abandon his idea of marooning the troops and soldiers on The Point and, with them, Kaz-Ca-Wendarah.

Beside him, Phildrad remained silent, staring with terror at the force he intended to tackle. Aklon-Dji pointed at various parts of the gathering, identifying weaknesses, vulnerabilities and targets. Phildrad was not convinced and sighed almost audibly when they retreated to their hideout.

'They will do nothing tonight, other than light fires, cook, frowk and eat. I intend to make a slight nuisance of myself in the darkness, sowing seeds of dissention and causing arguments and some injustice to cultivate bad feeling. I would prefer if you could sleep, however, as we need to be fresh tomorrow and I will want you to keep watch for the first hours of daylight. Are you happy to do that?'

'Be 'appier on a full stomach. No, just jestin' Aklon. 'Course I'll do that.'

'Right. Make yourself comfortable toward the back. I will rig my standard defence against the intrusion of wild beasts and uninvited guests on two legs. Be careful if you decide to leave here after I have departed, Phildrad, or you may find yourself suspended rather uncomfortably from the ceiling by your ankles.'

Phildrad left him to it and went deeper in whilst Aklon-Dji set up his trap using ropes and the iron ring he'd fixed in the roof cycles before. Satisfied his companion was safe, he set off for the outer edge of the camp below.

Activity was dying down after the evening meal. The troop commander clearly believed they'd nothing to fear from outside their camp and set only two sentries at each compass point. The Holy Ones had made their camp, as expected, in the very centre of the gathering, though some had ventured out into the ranks to recruit partners for their peculiarly perfunctory form of joining.

Aklon-Dji looked long at the camp and the waning activity before deciding on action. He'd stripped off his tabard in the cave and was clad only in the dark leather belt

157

that held his sword and long knife. In his hand, he carried a small glazed earthenware bottle, stoppered with wax. He split the plug with the point of his knife and poured a dribble of the liquid from the bottle down between his shoulder blades. Using the broad, downy leaves of the plentiful but otherwise nondescript arthrarhta orchid, he spread the liquid over his back. Using his palms, he then covered every part of his skin, including his face, with liquid from the bottle. It coated him in a thin layer of dark blue-black pigment that had no gloss and that neutralized his body scents. He tossed the bottle down behind the rock he'd used for cover.

All but invisible, he crept up to the nearest edge of the camp and took stock. Almost everyone was now settling for sleep. A few more energetic souls were still engaged in joining here and there but he felt as little concern about them as they would about him. The sentries on this side were sitting at the edge of the light from their campfire and talking as they looked out into the darkness of the night. The bearded man with red hair looked directly at him but failed to see anything unusual.

He entered the area and began his campaign of disruption and petty theft, minor destruction and irritation. Come the morning, there'd be argument, bad feeling, a few fights and some need for discipline amongst the troops but there'd be little to suggest the cause was anything more than carelessness, jealousy or simple stupidity in the ranks. Removing fastenings, snagging stitching, attaching hair to a sword hilt, placing a blade to cut an unwary walker, holing a drinking cup, piercing a water bottle or polluting it with dust or ash, taking a bite from a piece of fruit and many similar acts of minor vandalism would provoke enough bad feeling to get the day off to a poor start tomorrow.

As he left, laden with food stolen from various parts of the camp, he placed a few discarded tabards just close enough to the various dying fires to be scorched or, with luck, catch fire later, so that the night might be disturbed by those careless soldiers who'd discarded their clothes so close to the flames.

He escaped as unmarked as he'd entered the camp and collected his earthenware bottle. Before he returned to Phildrad, he took a short detour into the hills and found the spring, which formed the water source for the soldiers. Here, he first scrubbed his skin as free of the dye he'd applied earlier as possible, then used the stream as a latrine. From the crag above, he removed an ancient nest that had once housed a pair of hawks and still held the bones and detritus of their various broods and the food they'd brought. He broke it up into the water and then, purely by good fortune, discovered the stinking corpse of a highland fox and dropped that into the stream as well. Washing his hands once more, above the pollution, he surveyed his handiwork under the moonlight and, satisfied he'd left no obvious trail, returned to eat and sleep.

Phildrad grumbled on being woken but was pacified by the offer of food and more wine. ''Ow do you do it?'

'Good fortune, mostly.' He couldn't see Phildrad's expression in the total blackness of the cave but knew the man would not believe him. 'As soon as it is light, we need to creep back to where we were today and view their activity. I would like a spell of rest. Will you watch until just before dawn and wake me then, Phildrad?'

Phildrad said he would. Aklon lay down in the full knowledge that the coming morning might be his last.

Chapter 17

THE NEW SKYFIRE

Tumalind took the riser with Jodisa, revelling in the sensation of the rapid climb beside the Red Rill and, with her friend, leaning out of the box-like lift to watch the water rush past as they ascended.

'Ivdulon says she's almost certain the vague brightness she saw first thing before dawn is the Skyfire.'

'So I gather. She does mindtalk with me as well, Tumalind.'

'I know. It's just still quite new to me and I forget we're linked sometimes.'

'Just as well. Aklon interrupted us again this morning. You'd think he'd appreciate Feldrark and I are newlyweds, wouldn't you?'

'I'll have to contact your brother again; see if he knows how mother is.'

'For the moment, I think you'll find him engaged in a rather dangerous game. You're aware he's started the rising; the thing he calls the Cause?'

'Sometimes, Jodisa, you amaze me. You're a ruler now. Surely you recognise Aklon's difficult position. You know how far in the past Muhnilahm lives. It's hardly any wonder he wants to bring the island up to date, is it?'

The woman who ruled the city of Litkala beside her husband, Feldrark, gazed at her as the riser came to a smooth halt. 'You've grown, Tumalind. I recall our short swim together on the beach of my hometown. You were a naive village girl then. You've learnt a lot on your voyage with my father.'

'Not only with Dagla Kaz, though he's given me a certain education it's true. But exposure to other societies, different lands, dangers and wonders is bound to open your mind, isn't it?'

'Not everybody's. Aglydron still seems set in his ways and beliefs. In spite of the terrors and dangers we faced together on our journey.'

'Father was always very conservative in his views. Some call him a zealot. I suppose he is, really. But it's harder for him to change. He has, though. Look at the way he is with Chislanda. He never showed affection in public for my mother, of course.'

'Your poor mother; Shoarhn, isn't it? Left alone with two children to bring up. How will she manage?'

'She's got Aklon, of course, when he's there. But the farm will keep her busy and well fed. I just hope she doesn't find love with your brother only to have it snatched away by his untimely death in the Cause.'

161

Jodisa nodded thoughtfully but they'd reached the door of Ivdulon's tower and their conversation must wait until she'd finished her business with them.

'Up so early? I thought the pair of you would still be frowking with those energetic husbands of yours. Newlyweds!' Her snort of derision brought neither complaint nor correction from her guests.

'So, Ivdulon, what brings us up here when you could've done your nagging with mindtalk?'

'Don't think that bangle of office will spare you a sound slap on your perfectly formed posterior, young lady. I wouldn't waste my talk calling for your presence if I could merely connect through our minds, would I?'

Neither replied; it was unnecessary.

'What I want to show you requires your presence and your absolute secrecy. You can share this knowledge with no-one. Not even Feldrark, Jodisa. Are you prepared to make that pledge?'

'Without knowing what you're going to tell me, I don't see how I can promise, Ivdulon.'

The wise woman turned to Tumalind. 'Are you prepared to make the pledge?'

'I don't have Jodisa's responsibilities, Ivdulon. Only Okkyntalah shares my secrets and even he doesn't understand all, yet. I'll promise, if you deem it necessary.'

'Good. Jodisa?'

'You place me in an impossible position, you wicked woman. At least give me a clue.'

Ivdulon ruminated and clicked her fingers a few times. Netrodyl appeared abruptly, yawning and apparently fresh from sleep.

'Did you want something, Ivvy? Oh. Sorry. Didn't know we had guests. I'll put something on.'

'If you must. Please prepare some refreshments for these two. I wasn't actually signalling you, my dear. Merely trying to make a difficult decision.'

Netrodyl wandered off and could be heard in the other room, clinking crockery and cutlery as she prepared food and drink.

'Ivvy? You let her call you Ivvy?'

'Say a word to another soul and I'll torment you with interruptions every time you join with that husband of yours.'

Jodisa grinned but turned to Tumalind. 'And she would. Doesn't do to get on the wrong side of Ivvy. Sorry, I mean, Ivdulon, of course.' Jodisa's smirk earned her a glare from the wise woman.

'You still haven't answered my question.'

'And you still fail to give me a clue to help me decide.'

'Very well. It has to do with the Skyfire, if that's any help to you.'

Jodisa stood in silent consideration for a moment. 'I think I can probably risk keeping that sort of thing from Feldrark, for the moment anyway.'

'Oh, it will be for a few sixdays, no more.'

'Very well. I promise to keep what you're about to tell me secret until you release me from the pledge.'

The wise woman turned to Tumalind, her expression one of expectation.

'Oh. I also promise to keep the information secret 'til you tell me otherwise.'

Ivdulon relaxed and lost the tension that had surrounded her since their arrival. She led them to the upper chamber and opened the observation slit so she could point the observerscope at a specific point in the sky. Once found, she invited the two young women to peer through the finder in turn.

'So, what do you think?'

Jodisa shook her head. 'A smudge, that's all; a slight brightness that has no meaning to me. What do you.?'

'Sorry, Jodisa. This is the true Skyfire, Ivdulon?'

The wise woman nodded at Tumalind.

'And we can see it a day early and during daylight. I think you're predicting that this Skyfire will be very strong indeed once it fully forms?'

Ivdulon actually gathered Tumalind in her strong arms and hugged her. 'I knew you'd understand. I shall be sorry to lose you to that damned stupid pilgrimage the old fool High Priest is so set on taking. What I could do...'

'Ivdulon, you forget that old fool is my father!'

'Forget? I simply ignore the unfortunate fact. In any case, he's also Tumalind's father and she seems unconcerned by my opinion of him.'

'That's because he doesn't publicly acknowledge her as his daughter. I was his heir, don't forget.'

'Not now. Pharah-Li bears the growing spawn and she'll be ripe for bursting if the old fool manages to get back here with his Godwood and exchanged virgins at the appointed time.'

'But, Ivdulon, if this is to be a truly awesome Skyfire, won't it create so many more difficulties?'

'Oh, Tumalind, that you had been my daughter instead of that dullard's...'

'You can't have children if you don't join with men.'

'I'm not a fool, Jodisa, and I'll...Oh. Of course. Play your games. I'm not in the mood for jests at present. Don't you realise the significance of this event? Tumalind obviously does.'

163

'Well, she'd best explain it to me, then.'

Jodisa turned to Tumalind as Netrodyl ascended the stairs carrying a flat metal platter bearing four slender glasses of merphlion juice and a small assortment of exquisitely prepared dainties.

'Thank you, my dear. Now, do put a garment over your loveliness, have some breakfast, and then engage yourself in those duties you perform so well.'

Netrodyl gave a little bow and returned downstairs. The other three raised their glasses in mutual respect and drank the cool fresh liquid.

'She's a treasure. Panders to my every whim. If I'm not careful, she'll ruin me. However, to more important matters. Do you want to explain to Jodisa, or shall I?'

⸜⸻✦⸻⸝

The mouth of the cave was clear as the sky beyond paled toward dawn when Phildrad woke him. They ate what was left of the stolen rations, drank fresh water from their flasks and set off to the crags to watch the soldiers rise.

It was almost noon before they were able to plan any action. By then, the bulk of the soldiers and Holy Ones had descended to the Point using the score of rope ladders they'd brought with them. These were now drawn back up to the top of the Scar, rolled in readiness for their return. A group of fourteen soldiers, men and women, and two Holy Ones, one of each sex, had been left behind with the slaves.

Aklon waited until the marching army of destruction was visible well out on the plain below before he instructed Phildrad about reducing their enemies by at least half before moving closer. Aklon was expert with a bow and Phildrad had learned some skill whilst on the road with Dagla Kaz.

'Target the men first. They are likely to be stronger and therefore more difficult to fight hand to hand in any number. We must work silently and secretly. Take your time, Phildrad. Pick off your targets as they go about their tasks and try to wait until they are out of sight of their companions.'

'Easier said than done. But I'll do me best.'

'The camp is all but deserted. If we act with patience, we should be able to reduce the opponents to manageable numbers before we need make ourselves known.'

There'd been some strong disagreements due to Aklon's night manoeuvres and a regular had been given a thorough beating for having in his possession the choice piece of cheese from his officer's pack. He'd been left behind, stretched naked over the beating frame as additional punishment, as he was in no state to march. Another had fought so fiercely with one of his fellows, over a dispute about damage to his kit, that he'd killed him. He, in turn, had been executed and both bodies tossed over the Scar.

Aklon picked out the man detailed to tidy and store the rope ladders ready for use on the return of the army. Waiting until he was at the very edge, he put an arrow through his chest. He fell down the Scar without a sound. His next victim was also alone; tending the dozen or so oxen tethered close to the edge of the small copse at the eastern edge of the camp. Once the soldier was amongst the beasts, he pierced him with an arrow through his throat. He fell silent under the hoofs of the oxen.

Phildrad was able to follow a man who left the camp in search of unpolluted water. Once he was alone, he put an arrow in his back. He fell but tried to struggle to his feet and Phildrad fired a second missile, which penetrated the man's neck and laid him quietly to rest.

The female Holy One made for the oxen, as Aklon was about to find a new target. He preferred to take the men first but she would soon discover the fallen soldier. He watched her out of sight of the rest of the camp and then felled her with an arrow through her chest.

Patience now became the watchword as they awaited opportunities to reduce the numbers further. By mid-afternoon, they'd despatched enough of the enemy to ensure only six female and two male soldiers remained alive; slaves were not considered either enemies or friends at this stage. As the survivors began to grow anxious and search for their missing colleagues, Aklon and Phildrad dealt with another three, leaving just four women and one man alive.

Bows strung and aimed at the small group, they strode boldly into camp toward the remainder, who gathered together as they approached.

'Would you mind disposing of your weapons, please?'

They looked at the pair of hunters and one of the women plucked a spear that was standing in the ground beside her.

'Please, I would prefer that do not threaten us.'

She pulled her arm back to throw the spear but was dead before she could let fly. Aklon had a new arrow strung and waiting.

'I would rather not kill you where you stand but I am not inclined to warn you again.'

The remaining guards did as they were told.

'Would you all move away from the discarded ironmongery? A few steps to your left should suffice.'

They did so.

'My apologies, but I must ask you to remove your clothing.'

The man hesitated but two of the women obeyed at once. Phildrad pointed his bow at the man and he and other woman reluctantly obeyed.

'I wonder if you would lie down on the ground, face down, and place your arms behind your backs?'

They did as he said, without demur this time. Aklon and Phildrad approached within a few paces. 'Tie their wrists together, if you would.'

Phildrad took his long knife from his belt and held the blade between his teeth as a ready defence against trickery and went to the man first. He tied his wrists using the belt from a tabard and then did the same with the women.

'You may make yourselves as comfortable as circumstances permit.' Aklon nodded to Phildrad and indicated he should help the soldier to his feet.

They took him a little way from the group and Aklon questioned him. He was short and swarthy with dangerous eyes and a sneering mouth and refused to answer the questions Aklon posed.

'It is so distressing. I do so regret having to take life but at every turn I find myself obstructed by stubborn and ill-educated people. Your leaders have no use for you. They consider you an expendable item. Your god is false and will not aid you.'

The soldier lunged forward, desperate to attack Aklon who stepped sideways and helped him fall on his face.

'You will damage yourself if you behave in that manner. Your hero, Gadhallah, was a rapist and torturer and declared himself thus. I speak the truth: I have read the texts he left behind. The High Priest, my father, is a charlatan who keeps you under his protection and his rules merely because it allows him to continue to lead a life of luxury and advantage.'

'Renegade! Bowelcreep!'

'Do I take it you are unwilling to aid me in my attempts to free the people from the slavery the faith encourages?'

'May Mhortag shit in your mouth forever!'

'That has a distinctly unpleasant and boring ring to it. No. I think I shall endeavour to do without that particular fate. Will you help me, at all?'

'Go suck Mhortag's arse!'

'Very well.' He turned to Phildrad. 'Take him to the scar. Put him on the edge and allow him the opportunity to publicly retract his faith. Otherwise, he may jump if he will. Push him down to join his fellows if he would rather not volunteer the act. But bring me one of the others first, please.'

Phildrad hauled the nearest of the female soldiers to her feet and shoved her toward Aklon. He prodded the man in the back with his sword and urged him toward the edge of the scar.

'Your unfortunate companion seems to feel that death is a better option than the choice of life I offer. Shall we see how you fare in the choosing? I believe, no, I know, that Ytraa is a false god. How do you react to that?'

166

'Believe what you like, it's no matter to me.'

He told her the truth about Gadhallah. 'What do you say?'

The woman had not moved her eyes from his face as he spoke. 'If what you say is true, then everything I've ever believed is false and vile and foul and I'd want to put right some of that wrong. But how can I tell whether you speak the truth?'

'You are on the way by simply allowing the question. There may be some hope for you, after all. I may be able to spare you. You will appreciate that time is short and I have few resources and must therefore act very quickly. Would you be willing to take action to prove your willingness to serve the Cause?'

'I never said I'd serve you.'

'You are in a position where two alternatives face you. You may continue to serve those who have been your masters, in which case I will, regrettably, be obliged to kill you. Or you may accept that I have a valid alternative to offer, that I must decide what is done for the sake of that alternative and that I am to be obeyed, without question, until a proper freedom can be allowed to develop on this island, at which time I shall willingly place myself in the hands of the new authorities for judgement. If you accept the latter, you will be my prisoner and will do as I require, without question or demur.'

'I need to be sure. I've no idea who you are or what you stand for.'

'As to who I am, I am Aklon-Dji the son of the High Priest. As for what I stand for; I hope and expect to gain freedom for all those who remain alive at the conclusion of the conflict that is now beginning. In order to gain that freedom, you will have to be willing to fight, kill, steal, lie, cheat and obey. I will not promise you glory or honour or greatness or peace. I will promise you hard work, danger, injustice at the hands of those we fight, a cruel death if you are caught, an even more cruel death if you betray me and the possibility of a good and rewarding life if we win through.'

'I'm still not certain. But I'm willing to try your way until I find out more. Will you give me the chance?'

'How well do you know your colleagues?' He nodded at those who remained seated on the ground some paces away.

'A little. We marched here together from Chalamamnon but I come from the Krohtl defence and they hail from Pampahn and Morstahn.'

'Are they honest? Do they tell the truth?'

'As far as I can tell.'

'Do you tell the truth?'

'Mostly. That is, I'd lie to save my skin. Oh, and I sometimes don't tell the truth if I think it might hurt someone I love.'

'Who do you love?'

'My parents, a brother and a younger sister. There was a young buck once but… he decided on another.'

'Do I tell the truth?'

'I hope you do. I fear you do. You don't seem like a liar for all that your words seem so unlikely.'

'Go and fetch one of your colleagues to me.'

She turned and spoke to the women, helped one as best she could to get to her feet. They returned together, the first soldier looking at him with curiosity and her colleague showing very real fear. He nodded to the woman he had already interviewed and indicated she should move away. She did so.

'Are you a liar?'

'Are you?'

'If I told you that Ytraa was a false god, how would you respond?'

'I fight in an army dedicated to the defence of Ytraa and the ways of Ytraa. If I were free, I'd place you in captivity to be dealt with by the priests or the Holy Ones for your blasphemy.'

'Do you accept it is possible that all you have been told about Ytraa and Gadhallah is false?'

She considered him seriously before replying. 'I see you believe it. But you're wrong, Aklon-Dji. You're a renegade because of your foul beliefs and ways and you'll be caught and punished.'

'I am renegade, not simply because I have different beliefs from you and my father but because I wish all to know the truth. I think everyone should have the opportunity to make up their own mind. I believe that everybody should learn the secrets I have learnt at my father's house. My father made me renegade only because he wishes to maintain a life style that suits him.'

'You'd turn us all into blasphemers and send us to Mhortag's bowels for eternity.'

'No. I would have you all free to decide for yourselves. I would have you all given the information to allow you to decide for yourselves what and whether you believe. Now, however, I have little time to spare. Your male colleague has paid the ultimate price for his beliefs and now lies ruined at the foot of the scar. Your female colleague is deciding on her fate even as we speak but shows an inclination to give me a chance to prove my truths to her. I offer you the same choice.'

He gave her the options he had offered the others.

'Swap my stripes for spots? I can't; any more'n I can change the colour of my eyes.'

'I ask you to consider that your stripes may only be a coat of dye and that spots might suit you better.'

168

'It comes to this, Aklon-Dji. Either I die and go to the Garden of Delights or I listen to you and your beliefs and spend eternity drowning in Mhortag's shit.'

'No. It is a choice between what you choose to believe and what you have been taught you should believe. You must decide now whether you die here or whether you live as my captive and obey my every command until I release you from such service. I cannot spare further debate with you but I will make a final plea to you. It costs me nothing to kill you now. It costs me trust and effort and continued fear of betrayal to offer you life, yet I offer it nevertheless. Which will you take?'

Chapter 18

ALLIES AND ENEMIES

Shoarhn had dealt with infant deaths before. Twice, she'd lost her own. One, a stillborn baby, perfectly formed and perhaps too beautiful to inhabit this world, and another, normal infant, who'd lived only moments. She recalled the look in those new eyes as they saw her for the first time, and the way that the life had drained from them even as she stared back with love. What had extinguished it and why, she would never know. But such loss was common, and she'd buried her grief along with the children.

Maybe she should rescue the thing that A'ahl had birthed, and allow her the chance to bury her grief? But, no, that wasn't a child. It was a bundle of flesh and bones with no human features worthy of the name. It was the priest's abomination and A'ahl was better protected from such dishonour.

Her friend lay silent and unmoving. Her usual honey colour had drained with the blood and left her pale as sand on the shore. Her breathing was shallow and fluttering, so that she seemed only barely alive. As she watched, a brief flash of pain crossed the still face but her eyes remained closed.

'Can you hear me, A'ahl?'

She opened her eyes with an effort that spoke of great labour. It was clear that her sight was unfocussed, but her lips tried to smile as she recognised her friend.

'Rest. We'll get you through this. I'll bring you some water.'

But her hand moved to grasp Shoarhn's arm and prevent her leaving, though the strength was not enough to stop a butterfly rising. Shoarhn remained.

'Is it a boy or a girl?'

What to tell her? She searched her friend's face and knew, without knowing how it could be, that she would not live out the day.

'A beautiful, healthy boy, A'ahl. I'll bring him to you when you have the strength to hold him. For the moment he's sleeping peacefully.'

The lie, an unnatural response, came more easily than it would have before she'd met Aklon, with his revelations about the faith she'd followed so properly for years. Knowing that the priests and Holy Ones lied constantly to fool the populace, made it easier to lie in order to spare the feelings of her friend.

'Will you stay with me?'

Shoarhn had asked Tasallyss to alert her parents that her boys were alone in the house. They would be safe and she had no reason to go home until A'ahl ceased to need her. Aklon wouldn't return yet. He'd made it clear he was now involved in the active part of his campaign, her campaign, A'ahl's campaign, to free the people. He was unlikely to visit until many changes had been made.

'I'll stay.'

A'ahl relaxed again. Shoarhn took the opportunity to visit the other room and pour each of them water from the pitcher. Tepid and stale, it at least provided moisture. She drained her own cup but fed the liquid in small sips to her friend. After only three, she turned her head away as if the effort was too much.

Dawn became day, silence merged into sounds of everyday life as the town awoke to begin another round of living. Shadows moved across the room, the bright trapezoid of sunshine glared through the window and dropped from the wall to crawl across the floor until it reached Shoarhn's feet. A'ahl made no sound or movement in all this silent time.

The light rode along her feet and pooled around her ankles, heating her and reminding her of the movement and energy that passed outside as she sat waiting. The cattle would need her attention, the fowls want feeding, but the goats could fend for themselves and her parents would nurture her children. Unbidden, the thought of Aglydron came to her and she wondered what he was doing, how he fared in that city of white stone that Aklon had shown her in his careful, vivid words. What would it be like to visit such a place?

'Shoarhn?'

A'ahl's voice was so soft she would've missed it had there been any other sound at that moment. She bent close to hear more, and the world itself seemed to slow.

'Thank you for being my friend.'

The pause was long and filled with breathing that sounded hard and demanding of her frail body.

'Tell Caarl I love him. Tell him…I'm sorry.'

Shoarhn moved to look into the face of her friend, intent on rousing her from this self-pity. But, in that instant between those words of regret and the movement it took to focus on her face, A'ahl had passed into eternal sleep and taken her place in the Garden of Delights.

Shoarhn bent and kissed the warm forehead, shuttered the bright topaz eyes and raised the cover to hide the now dead face. For a moment, she wondered what she should do. Habit and tradition had her prepare herself and make the prayers she'd said too often for those who had departed. As she rose to her knees again and glanced at the still figure of her friend, she fell forward over the body and allowed herself the tears at last.

Naked, bound and helpless, she considered the choices he'd given her. 'I'll live a little longer, Aklon-Dji. Prove that you're as good and honest, as truthful and caring as you'd like me to believe and I might fight for you. But if I see a sign of the evil you're supposed to be, I'll try and kill you. Will that do?'

For reply, he unbound her wrists and retied them at her front. He called the first woman to him and unbound her hands. 'There is a soldier lashed to the beating frame over there. Should I spare him or put him out of his misery?'

'He's a thief. Stole cheese from his commanding officer.'

'That tells me your beliefs regarding his guilt but it informs me neither of the facts relating to his case nor of your judgment in the matter I requested.'

'He was caught with the cheese in his pack. What more proof do you need? If he should live or die isn't my decision.'

'And you, trooper from Pampahn?'

'I go along with my friend.'

'Friend. That is a much abused term.'

'It's right though, Aklon-Dji. I'm in the hands of a known killer and hater of authority. Choryssa's known to me; she's willing to fight beside me. I call her a friend.'

'And you, Choryssa, you consider her your friend?'

'Patrilha's trustworthy and dependable. A soldier can't ask for more from a comrade.'

Phildrad approached, alone.

'Silly sagger wouldn't give up. 'Ad to shove 'im over the cliff. Don't like killin' an 'elpless man, Aklon.'

'He would have killed you in your sleep had he known you were with me. Those are your orders, are they not, Choryssa?'

'Anyone with you's to be killed on sight. You, though, are to be caught alive, if possible and brought captive to the acting High Priest.'

'And what does that official intend for me on behalf of my beloved father when I am caught?'

The women looked at each other. Patrilha spoke. 'You're to be stripped, whipped and then unmanned by being dropped from the monument of Ytraa so a cord tied to your parts rips off your prod and love fruits. They'll hang you by your toes over a slow fire whilst Holy Ones pull out your finger and toe nails one at a time. Then they'll peel the skin off your arms and legs in thin strips. Your eyelids'll be cut off, oil poured on your eyes and set alight and your tongue split into four; hot peppers crushed into the cuts. Hooks'll be hung from your nostrils with weights attached and your ears'll be stopped with red hot stones.'

'So, a pretty merciful death, then. Just like my father to be so thorough in his

173

instructions for my demise. Phildrad, any sign of Delbon at the foot of the Scar?'

'Not yet.'

He indicated they should walk toward the man stretched over the beating frame. It was clear he was in pain and almost delirious because of his exposure under the sun with no protection and no water.

'Back to our whipped soldier. You are both convinced, because of the evidence, that he is guilty of the theft?'

They nodded.

'So he was rightly punished?'

'Can't have thieves in a camp.'

'We all depend on each other for our lives. Can't have comrades stealing. What happens to trust if you let that happen?'

'Very laudable sentiments, except that the man is innocent. He stole nothing.'

'The cheese was in his pack.'

'Someone else put it there.'

'Why would someone do that?'

'Why indeed? Perhaps to make him suffer? Perhaps a comrade was jealous of him? Perhaps he failed to pleasure a woman in the way she desired. Perhaps he made some remark that was taken as an insult by someone too timid or cowardly to face him with it.'

'Possible, I s'pose.'

'But you were both convinced of his guilt, both convinced the right thing had been done because of the evidence. I know the truth, you see. Because I stole the cheese from his officer and placed it into the soldier's pack. I did it precisely because I knew it would cause this sort of injustice.'

'You can't have. They were bang slap in the middle of the camp. You couldn't get past the sentries.'

'You think so, Patrilha? There was a certain amount of dispute and bad feeling this morning. Some tabards caught fire in the night. Some folk discovered bites had been taken out of fruit and hair had been caught in the hilts of swords so it pulled as they rose. Some cut their feet on colleagues' badly placed swords…need I go on?'

'You did all that? You an' this man?'

'Don't blame me, Choryssa. Aklon did it all 'isself. An' 'e pissed and shat in your water supply; dumped a dead fox in there an' all.'

'You a magician?'

'No. I have survived by using my brain and my limited skills for a good many years. Infiltrating a camp at night is not difficult, if you know how to do it. But, enough. This poor man is innocent of the crime for which he was beaten. What do you advise?'

'Free him, of course.'

'And you, Patrilha?'

'Yes. He's suffered a cruel wrong.'

'Very well.' He untied Choryssa's bonds. 'Set him free.'

She looked down at her freed limbs in surprise and rubbed at her wrists before helping Patrilha untie their colleague from the frame. He was unable to stand or speak. Aklon-Dji handed Choryssa his water bottle and she placed it close to the victim's lips so he could drink.

They tended to his needs and then approached the other female soldier, who had managed to release her bonds and armed herself with a sword. She lunged at Aklon as soon as he was within reach. Before he acted to defend himself, Choryssa disarmed her with a swift move that had the woman on her back at his feet.

'You'll die in fierce pain for that, traitor!' Still bound, the other captive glared at her erstwhile comrade with real hatred.

Aklon took her aside and questioned her as he had Patrilha and Choryssa. She proved as intransigent as the section leader had but he was reluctant to end her life. He released a rope ladder and sent Phildrad down to check the ground for spare weapons, which he brought back to the top. Only then did Aklon send the woman soldier to the foot of the Scar to await the return of her colleagues.

'Why didn't you kill her? You did the section leader.'

He stared at Patrilha and decided truth was the simplest answer. 'I hate loss of life, but killing beautiful, even ordinary, women, I suppose, has always been difficult for me. Call me an old softy, but I see your sex as carriers of life and it seems almost a double insult to existence to kill one unnecessarily.'

'You're not at all as you've been described, you know.'

He smiled at Choryssa. 'I suspect you are the partner of a member of my Few. A man called Delbon?'

She frowned. 'Delbon's one of your gang?'

'Of the Few, yes. Has been for a number of years. That is his reason for not taking you as his wife. He feels it would compromise your loyalty and place you in a difficult position. I feel free to tell you the truth now that the situation has altered.'

'Mhortag's balls! Delbon. He believes what you've told me, then?'

'That, and much, much more.'

'Well. I'm speechless. Lost for words.'

He smiled at her inaccuracy. 'It seems not, but shall we eat whilst we await the return of Delbon and the others who provided the impression of habitation on The Point?'

'You mean there's nobody down there?'

Aklon nodded. 'Just a few of my men. I am afraid your colleagues have undertaken a wasted journey.'

Though they pressed him, he would say no more on the matter.

They ate as a group, the women unclothed as a sign of their trial status. Aklon sent Choryssa to the edge of the Scar to look out for Delbon and the others returning from the abandoned settlement. Patrilha he nominated nurse and attendant to the whipped soldier until he was well enough to respond to interrogation.

Phildrad loosed the oxen from their tethers so they might wander free, keeping one tied to act as their own beast of burden when they were ready to set out. Then the two men gathered the bodies of those they had killed and tossed them over the cliff. The troops could give them proper funeral rites if they felt so inclined on their return.

Late in the afternoon, Choryssa ran to let them know there were men approaching the Scar. Aklon returned with her to find Delbon, Mkolo-ti, Por-Kildu and the other two companions at the bottom of the precipice, arguing with the female soldier. He let down a rope ladder and they shinned up, Delbon coming last and, threatening the captive as he climbed out of reach. Aklon pulled the ladder back up. Delbon glanced briefly at Choryssa with a mixture of surprise and relief as they returned to the fire where Patrilha was helping Phildrad prepare an evening meal.

Delbon gave Aklon his report. 'The invading army will reach the old settlement by nightfall. We'll have the night to sleep and prepare our next move.'

'Ah, our next moves. I fear our new recruits may feel reluctant to aid us in that enterprise, Delbon. They are new to the Cause and not yet committed, though both women have displayed a tendency toward obedience, so far.'

'You know this is Choryssa, my woman, Aklon?'

'I am please she acted in a way that allowed me to spare her, Delbon. I suspected she was your lover, but could only guess until I had confirmation from you. However, they are still earning the trust I have granted. Perhaps you might spend some time with them, explaining your reasons for connecting with the Few? A spell alone with Choryssa may strengthen her loyalty to the Cause. In any case, the night should give us a clearer indication of their true feelings.

'The whipped man has only just recovered enough to respond to my questions and shows greater ambivalence. Understandable, given that I am to blame for his lacerated skin. Nevertheless, he has displayed a willingness to at least consider our alternatives. Tomorrow, when he is better rested, he may show us his mettle in practical ways.'

He turned to the captive soldiers. 'I regret that we may be obliged to kill a number of your former colleagues in the coming days.'

They showed their immediate concern and he held up a hand to pacify and silence

176

them as he continued.

'I intend to give them all an opportunity to join the Cause but the pressure of their situation, involving them in making public declarations at odds with their beliefs, training and upbringing, may render many of them incapable of independent thought. You will know which of them may be more inclined to become members of the Few and which will most definitely be opposed. I am placing huge trust in you by telling you what we plan and yet allowing you to remain unbound. How you respond to my trust will determine what I do with you and what I ask of you in the coming days.'

'Have we got to be naked?'

'An aspect of our faith is that naked is sacred and you therefore feel, quite understandably, uncomfortable without clothes when you are neither at prayer nor indulging in the act of joining. I wish you to become acquainted with nakedness as a natural state, the state in which we are all born and in which we should all have a right to live if we choose. Therefore, you will remain without clothes for the moment.'

'Bit hypocritical, isn't it? You lot are dressed. What's so different about us?'

'A valid question, Patrilha. We are clothed because we are proven members of the opposition to the faith and need no further lessons in nakedness than those we have already experienced. Also, and more importantly, once we have completed the task here, we will lead you and any others who join the Cause, to a place of safety on the island where you will wait in readiness to fight the coming battles. I and my friends, however, must be part of normal society and we could hardly do that whilst naked, could we?'

'Are we never to wear clothes again, then?'

'The choice, Choryssa, will be yours, once we have completed our task in ridding the island of its current rulers and its current rules. That is a task we begin over the coming days. I suggest we sleep now. The following days will be taxing and difficult both physically and emotionally and rest is the best preparation for such exertion.

'Tomorrow we prepare, perhaps, to end many lives and begin freedom for many more. I need your help in this enterprise and I leave you free to make your own decisions. If you have questions to ask, the next three days and nights will provide answers. Delbon, Phildrad, and I are here for you to ask what you will and we will all answer only with truth, since truth is the foundation of the Cause in which we are united.

'One more thing. You may join, or not, according to your own desires and wishes. Nobody involved in the Cause would either demand that you join with them or demand that you remain celibate. Choice is yours as long as you wish to take the responsibility for what you choose to do.'

Tumalind responded eagerly to Ivdulon's call when it came. 'Come on, we can go up

177

and view the new Skyfire.'

'I love the way you're so interested in things, Tumalind. You're like a child waiting for a naming day gift. So excited.'

She gave him her smile and he enfolded her in his arms so that she wavered between surrender to her tactile and emotional responses and those more spiritual sensations awaiting her on the mountain. Okkyntalah recognised her dilemma and solved it for her.

'Come on. We'll indulge each other once we've seen the new sign. Our minds will be entirely on the important activity then.'

'You're so good for me, Okkyntalah. I love you.'

Hand in hand, they approached the Riser and found Feldrark and Jodisa waiting there along with a sullen faced Dagla Kaz and an expectant Jhonaht. The Riser seemed unaware of the load it carried and travelled at the normal speed, arriving just as the sun was setting on the far horizon, so that they were obliged to make their prayers before they entered the tower. Jodisa and Okkyntalah adopted the new posture and received a glare of disapproval from Dagla Kaz, even though he also now used the less demanding position for his prayers.

Ivdulon was, of course, nowhere to be seen. But Netrodyl, clothed, greeted them with small glasses of wine and a tray of savouries. She merely nodded at them and indicated that her mistress waited above, setting up the observerscope for their instruction.

'How do you like it up here, Netrodyl?'

'I understand more now, Tumalind. I was in awe of your accomplishments and status when we first met. Now I know a little more of the world and I see that you are not a common woman but someone with special qualities. Ivdulon believes you're destined for greatness.'

Tumalind smiled, assuming she was still too easily impressed by things she didn't understand, in spite of her statement. 'I'm pleased to see you happy.'

'Oh, Ivvy's a real eye opener for me. I think I'll be happy to live the rest of my life up here, serving her.'

'I'm just pleased she's found someone to reduce her loneliness.'

'Ivvy's never lonely. She's in contact with so many…'

Tumalind glanced at Dagla Kaz to see if he'd heard. But the High Priest made no sign he'd understood what the native woman meant. Netrodyl nevertheless bit her bottom lip in anxiety at her slip. She mouthed a silent 'sorry' and then indicated that they should all go up and attend Ivdulon.

The new Skyfire caused them to gasp with its brilliance, even though it was but a spark at this time. Tumalind gazed in rapture at the sign, dazzled by the luminous ball of light, which already trailed a fine tail visible only through the observerscope.

'Give it a few more days and it'll be visible as a true sign even with the naked eye. What then Dagla Kaz, for your islanders?'

The High Priest glared at the astronomer and shrugged. 'My messengers will have prepared the people for what is to come, have no fear on my behalf, Ivdulon.'

But Tumalind was sure he was deeply worried by what he'd seen and she wondered what truly caused him such anxiety.

⁂

By the second day, the whipped soldier had recovered enough to walk. The following morning, they found him gone, a rope ladder extended to the foot of the cliff and tethered there and a tabard missing from the small pile they'd made in readiness for their journey. The camp slaves, seven in number and in awe of their newly acquired freedom, continued their duties as if enslaved, in spite of Aklon's explanation that they were now able to do as they wished.

The two women, however, remained and Delbon had found reciprocated delight with Choryssa, once she'd done with castigating him for never telling her of his association with Aklon-Dji. Patrilha had shaken blonde locks at Aklon and received smiles and a gentle kiss but no more.

'Don't I please you?'

'Very much. You are lovely. I am devoted to the love of a particular woman, however, and I daily grow more convinced that I should be true to her. I do not understand this feeling, only that it seems right in spite of all we have been told about joining whenever we may. I would join with you readily and no doubt have pleasure as much as I gave, Patrilha, for you have the sort of charm that enchants men. But it would feel wrong for me. I can express it no more clearly than that.'

'Phildrad won't have me either. What's wrong with me?'

'I believe if you told Phildrad to join with you, rather than asked, he would do so and do so willingly. He loves his wife but is not in love with her as I am with my special partner. He requires a more determined need from you, that is all.'

The following day she came to him and put her arms about his neck, reached up and kissed his mouth. 'Thank you. You were right about Phildrad. In fact, I think you're probably right about a lot of things. I'm ready to be yours, Aklon, to command as you will.'

She stood a little away from him and took a stance, facing the others assembled for breakfast. 'I renounce Ytraa, I curse Gadhallah and I accept Aklon's ideas about freedom for all. I feel odd and strange and lost with no God to guide or protect me but I also feel free and alive in a way I've never known before. Frightened but excited.'

'Thank you, Patrilha; later you will have the opportunity to demonstrate your

179

dedication to the Cause. Today the troops and Holy Ones will come back, defeated by the desert and their lack of battle and angered by their fool's errand. We shall make sure that none but those we deem deserving will climb these heights. Those we leave behind will either die at our hands or return to the settlement to eke out what existence they may in the barren lands of The Point.'

'I'm ready to do your bidding.'

Choryssa, in spite of her clear devotion to Delbon, remained silent.

Late in the afternoon of the third day, the troops returned to the foot of the Scar and a captain called for the ladders to be lowered for their ascent. The ladder that the whipped soldier had left tethered, Aklon had severed a little distance from the top and allowed to fall to the ground. It seemed the beaten one had found his troop but they'd taken little note of his warnings or those of the woman who accompanied him. When Aklon poked his head over the edge and gazed down at them, they realized their mistake.

The only place where they could have climbed without artificial help was where they now stood. Aklon's party had made that route impassable by hacking off all remaining hand and foot holds four manheights below the edge. It remained just possible for a determined climber to reach that point but beyond it, he or she would need wings or the grip of a spider to ascend further.

Aklon allowed the troops and their commanders to absorb their situation. There was much calling of dire threats and urging of the converts to return to the proper path and dispose of the enemies of Ytraa. But to no avail. The time they'd spent with Aklon and his men had convinced them of the truth and good intent and they had all become converts to the Cause. Choryssa had been last to declare, even after all the freed slaves had taken up weapons to fight on the side of Aklon.

A lengthy dialogue, curt and terse because distance required raised voices, ended in a stalemate as the sun began to sink. The troops remained at the foot of the Scar and Aklon with his small band of rebels sat tight at the top, occupying the narrow shelf that gave access to the camp on the plateau. With willing help from the former slaves, they transferred weapons, gear and stores to the shelf and lit a watch fire. Taking turns on watch, and using flaming brands to examine activity below to ensure the troops found no way to surprise them in the dark, they awaited the coming morning to discover how many of those below would convert to the Cause.

Chapter 19

DEPARTURE

 Sun up found them all more or less as they had been, except that the troops were in more urgent need of water. There was dissent in the ranks and some outspoken grumbling that threatened to develop into rebellion until the commander made examples of the most strident. Spilt blood and the brutal silencing of voices of disagreement held the rest in check for a while but the feeling of burgeoning riot was palpable even at the top of the Scar. It was as Aklon had expected.

He called Kaz-Ca-Wendarah to step forward and speak. She moved, reluctantly, and looked up, squinting against the brightness of the sky. Aklon poured water into his mouth from his flask, splashed his face and then trickled water over the edge, causing some to surge forward in the futile hope of catching a drop.

'Wendarah, perhaps you would like to leave the common rabble so that you and I may converse in a civilized manner up here?'

'If I come up there, it'll be to put an end to your life, Aklon-Dji.'

'And if you do not, you and all those with you will perish. The sun grows hot. There is no water on the Point, other than in the settlement you so obligingly visited at my suggestion. I neglected to let you know that my friends had moved to a safer place and in that I was remiss. I should not have led you astray so. But, there it is. And there you are. And here am I. Now, for the second, and final, time I invite you to ascend and parley. There will not be another opportunity, I assure you.'

For a while, she was silent, taking council with the Holy Ones and commander. At length, she called up. 'I'll parley. Let down the ladder so I can climb up.'

'Ah. I am pleased you see reason. I am afraid, however, that I place conditions on your ascent to this higher plane. You will discard your weapons and clothing. Further, all others must retire to a distance of no closer than five hundred paces from the foot of the cliff.'

'I'll do no such thing! I'm the High Priest and I won't be humiliated in this way. Lower the ladder and I'll come up to you.'

'Oh dear. You do seem to have a false sense of security regarding your position, Wendarah. I have the means of your ascent. Of course, should you prefer to die of thirst and hunger, you are perfectly placed to do so exactly where you stand. I will ask you again when you have had time to consider. Until then, Wendarah.' He pulled away from the edge and sat on the top with the others.

Occasionally, one of them tossed a stone or the chavelled remains of a bone over the edge. Now and again, they poured a little water down; supplies now secure after they'd removed the soiling he had earlier used to pollute the source. And all the time, they kept an eye on their enemy to ensure that they were not making any potentially successful attempt to climb the precipice.

'There are friends of ours, down there, Aklon. Must we sit up here in comfort whilst they slowly die of thirst and starvation?'

Aklon stroked Choryssa's arm. 'Your solicitude does you credit, but we are few. If we allow unfettered numbers of those soldiers up here, how long do you suppose we will continue to live? You and Patrilha are already committed; your acts of obedience to my demands have made you enemies of those who remain loyal to the Follower's creed and you will be judged as harshly, perhaps more so, as me and Delbon when your former comrades ascend. Do you wish me to allow them up here?'

Choryssa nodded and sighed her agreement. She and Patrilha exchanged glances of resignation and distress, but it was clear they understood their new position.

The commanders had sent out scouting parties in both directions to discover other places where the cliff might be climbed. Aklon, however, knew the entire length of the Scar and had no fear of a surprise attack.

A little after his talk with Wendarah, a couple of arrows sailed up but they were at the limit of the archers' reach and fell harmlessly. Por-Kildu strung them to his own bow and, having the advantage of height on his side, demonstrated their superiority by returning the arrows with deadly accuracy to those who'd fired them. No further attempts of that sort were made.

Time passed and Aklon returned to the edge to speak to Wendarah. 'You are ready?'

She turned to those around her and waved them away. As they moved, she stripped and waited, her whole body shouting her humiliation and impotent rage. Once satisfied no one else was within reach, they lowered a ladder to her.

She began to ascend and some of the men moved closer, clearly intent on following her up the rope ladder. The rebels simply pulled up the ladder, with her clinging to it, until it was beyond the reach of the others. They then let her climb the rest of the distance and hauled up the empty ladder when she arrived at the top.

'Do sit. You will need to catch your breath after your exertions. Perhaps a drink of water?'

She took the proffered flask greedily, almost choking as she drained it into her throat.

'Do be careful, my dear. We do not wish to have you die. Well, not just yet, anyway. I wonder, did you perhaps notice in the night how there is a new spark in the west? I am certain that it is the real Skyfire, come as was appointed. Now, what do you make of that?'

'I'm not here to bandy words with you, Renegade! I'll have you killed as slowly and painfully as possible and your bunch of criminals and …'

'Ah, yes. My death. These young ladies have described its proposed manner in great detail to me. I find myself distinctly disinclined to accept the offer of my demise in such a sophisticated and civilized manner. I prefer to leave this life, as a very old man, during my sleep; it is such a comfortable way to end, do you not agree?'

'Tell me what you want and either set me free or kill me, Aklon-Dji. I've no patience with your silly games.'

'Games, my dear? I think you confuse manners and civility with playfulness. I assure you, my intentions are serious and deadly. As for what I want, it is but a trifle. I wish for nothing more, or less, than your complete and utter defeat.'

'Why have you brought me up here?'

'I was under the impression you rather wanted to ascend. We are willing to allow you to descend, should you so desire.'

'Then, let me go.'

'Ah. I may permit you your freedom in a little while. If you do as I require, you may leave this place unharmed.'

'What's your price, shitsucker?'

'My price includes civility, Wendarah. I find myself disinclined to respond favourably to those who are coarse and vulgar. Such behaviour offends my delicate preferences.'

'Tell me what you want!'

He arched an inquisitory eyebrow at her.

'Please.'

'Ah. Education; such a wonderful device. What I require, Wendarah, is your aid in persuading a male Holy One up here to accompany you on your mission.'

He told her what he wanted and, after much argument, she agreed to his terms. She stood on the edge, unbound and clothed, and addressed the Holy Ones below, explaining that she would be returning freely to Chalamamnon and that Aklon-Dji and his comrades could be trusted to do them no harm, as he had explained to her.

It took all her persuasive skills to tempt one of the male Holy Ones to climb the ladder. Once he was atop the cliff, they seized him and took him and Wendarah well away from the ledge and into the soldiers' camp. There, they drove them from the camp, attached to each other by leather collars fixed about their necks and fastened to either end of a rigid pole, fashioned from a spear shaft, that held them beyond the reach of each other's outstretched arms. It was secured so that they were incapable of releasing either themselves or each other. Their wrists, securely bound in front of them, retained enough movement to allow them to manipulate items. Around the neck of each, was hung a large water skin and, on a belt about their waists hung pre-cooked meats enough to last until they should reach civilisation.

Thus, they could return to Chalamamnon to do as he'd ordered but couldn't escape either alone or from one another. He made Wendarah naked to reduce her sense of power and clad the Holy One for the same reason. The chances that they would follow any of his demands were remote, and he knew this. But the humiliation of the priestly caste was a necessary step along the route to freedom.

Delbon escorted them for the first part of their journey and then watched them out of sight, delighted by their constant bickering and chiding of each other. By the time they reached Chalamamnon, he told Aklon later, they would be in a state fit to kill each other.

Aklon now turned his attention to the matter of the Holy Ones and others on the plain. He summoned the other Holy Ones in the same manner as he had Wendarah and, reluctantly, they ascended, one by one. By then, the troops below were becoming very restive and mutiny was looking increasingly likely.

He dealt with the Holy Ones as he had the soldiers who'd remained in the camp. That none of them was willing to renounce their ways and join his Cause came as no surprise, but it troubled him to end so many lives like this. The last two, a man and a woman, he hobbled in the same way as he had Wendarah and her companion and sent them off to spread his message to the Holy Ones on the plain. Again, he had no real hope of success in that quarter, but he felt he should at least make the attempt. Finally, with much difficulty, argument, and false bribery he persuaded the soldiers to release the remaining slaves and allowed them to ascend and gain their freedom. Only three remained loyal to their previous lords. Given the alternatives he offered, he was unsurprised that these few returned to the soldiers below.

The task to deal with that mass was one he dreaded but knew he must undertake very soon.

<hr />

Aglydron looked at Chislanda, sleeping, on top of the bed. The paleness had left her and she'd gained energy with the last few days of rest, good food and freedom from fear. Myllthlan had repaired the damage to her shoulder, her skin and internal wounds. She looked much as she had when he'd first met her, except that her face now bore the experience and wisdom that comes only with pain and grief. He loved her and now understood what that powerful word really meant.

He knew he'd never loved Shoarhn. For all his inability to pleasure her the way she deserved, he'd only ever lusted for her. Her body had attracted him; her mind and spirit had no meaning for him. And, since Tryonta's return with news that she was suspected of joining with Aklon-Dji, he'd dismissed her from his thoughts. Let her do as she would; if they killed her, his boys would be recruited to work for the Holy Ones and would therefore be safe. He no longer felt anxious or concerned for Shoarhn if she'd truly taken up with the Renegade.

With Chislanda, it was different. He was intrigued and fascinated by every aspect of her. That he loved her body as well was a huge bonus but he thought he would've loved her anyway. Tomorrow he was due to leave Litkala. The real Skyfire had appeared, as Ivdulon had predicted, low in the southwest on the night of the fifth of the second portion, six days ago. The transition from 1457 to 1458 had passed with minimal celebration due to preparations for the war. Now, however, the new cycle had begun and the true Skyfire was growing brighter by the night.

They would begin their pilgrimage in the morning and tonight would spend a final night of luxury and comfort after a feast with dance and song in the great hall. Feldrark had been crowned Kiral and Jodisa-Li was now Kirallah. The search for a Wharhll, to act as spiritual leader until their first child came and grew old enough to take on the duties, was still on, but that wouldn't involve Aglydron.

His real concern was Chislanda's insistence that she come on the pilgrimage. She was well enough to travel. But it would be a long, hard and dangerous mission and he wished to spare her that risk and hardship. He'd discussed it with Okkyntalah and agreed with him: their women were as hardy as they were themselves and, if they didn't volunteer to take them along, they'd follow them anyway. He'd given in and now she lay asleep, resting after sharing joy with him again.

He moved to the window and looked out through the wonder of the glazing at the city. The sun was going down and it would soon be time for prayer. He'd wake her then, so they might worship together. The journey ahead was a pilgrimage of great importance and moment. He still felt proud to have been the instrument of Ytraa, the means by which his God had wrought a miracle and brought two divided bands of Followers together. Soon, he'd take his place in that momentous march to find the other bands of Followers: those who dwelt in Kah-Labaz and those who lived in the blessed land where lay the Groves of Ytraa. Tonight would mark the end of what he'd begun when he left his island home. Tomorrow would begin a new phase of his life, as member of the pilgrimage to exchange the Virgin Gifts and return with the Godwood that would glorify Ytraa when they raised it on the Plain of Ytraa in Muhnilahm.

He sighed and turned back from the window into the room to find Chislanda sitting up and watching him through those startling eyes of deep viridian, her long, dark auburn hair drifting over soft shoulders and falling like a dark mist across her sweet breasts. She smiled and held her hand out to him. He pulled her to her feet and kissed her. Side by

185

side, they stood before the window, raised their hands over their heads, placed their feet apart and made obeisance to Ytraa, now their mutual God.

Aklon was now faced with the most difficult of his tasks. He had planned on what action he should take and decided he must be harsh and not allow himself to be swayed by the number of potential victims concerned. His cause was just and he'd moved so far along the road already that he could only continue forward. A backward step would spell certain death for him and his many adherents. He owed steadfastness to those he had recruited, those who gave him the trust of their lives.

He stepped forward for his last address from the Scar. The troops fell silent once it became clear he would speak with them again. 'You are presented with a stark choice. Already you suffer the effects of the bitter drought that exists always on The Point. You will be aware, from your marches, that there is little food or water on the barren peninsular you occupy. You are trapped. There is no descent from the cliffs into the sea unless you wish to drown. There is no way up here other than by means I control. Those that your commanders sent to scout the Scar will confirm that. I know, because I have travelled the entire length on numerous occasions. You ascend here or not at all.

'Your choice, then, is as follows. You may stay on The Point. It has, in the past, supported a small colony of those who your society rejected and outlawed. That settlement, which you cruelly destroyed, has never numbered more than a few hundred. There are around eleven hundred of you assembled here. Those of you who remain stand a good chance of dying, since you have now destroyed the only sources of cultivated food. Those who manage to survive will be few and will exist under extreme conditions. You have no means of producing fabric, no metal for new weapons or ploughshares, no way to obtain fish from the sea. You will live on snakes, reptiles, birds and their eggs. The only fruit is the bitter yurhtz, and that will cause you to vomit if you eat too much. The only vegetation lies within the flesh of the large cactus and you have to remove the poisonous spines to get at it. There are few trees on The Point and, should you be unwise enough to chop them down for fuel or building materials, you will lose the only source of broad leaves with which to roof your homes, such as they will be.

'I believe the picture I paint is accurate but you may wish to dispute it. Let me explain that those who do not hear me today will have no future opportunity to change their minds.

'If you take the other alternative, you must do so now, and publicly. It requires you to deny the existence of Ytraa…'

The general noise and consternation made it impossible for him to be heard and he awaited their silence before he continued.

'Hear me out, for I will not repeat myself. And you have witnessed the fate of the Holy Ones who failed to change their minds.'

He allowed the upsurge of outrage that followed to subside before he continued.

'You must, I repeat, publicly denounce Ytraa. You must curse Gadhallah for the charlatan and rapist I know him to have been. You will pledge yourselves, on pain of death, to overthrow the vile perversion that is the faith of the Followers.'

Again he allowed them to quieten after their expressions of outrage.

'Now, I will explain why I make these demands. How you hear me will determine how you live or die, so pay heed. My words are the absolute truth. I have nothing to gain by presenting you with facts you have been denied. It would be easier for me to simply leave you where you are. But I believe that amongst your ranks there are many who are good. Already, two of your number have converted to my Cause.'

He gestured Choryssa and Patrilha forward and they stood proud, on the edge of the Scar, and opened their arms to their former comrades below.

Great shouts of disapproval and jeers of 'shame!' rose up, but the young women only shook their heads and gestured for quiet. When it came, Aklon continued.

'I will now tell you what I know; not what I suspect or think or believe, but what I know of the history of this great religion into which we have all been tricked and deceived for so long.'

Some, the pious and the zealous, began to chant loudly, clearly intent on drowning out any words he may speak. For a while, he remained unmoved, silent and awaiting their silence. They kept up their chant for an hour or more and the sun was starting to lower in the sky before they grew silent again.

'Some do not want you to hear the truth. I leave it to you to decide whether or not you wish to hear me. But, I repeat, this is your final opportunity. I will speak no more after the sun goes down and those who have not replied in the manner I require, by the morning, will have no choice but to remain where they are now.'

He began to explain what he had learned from the texts under his father's cell. The zealots set up their chanting once more but other soldiers forced them into silence, having to kill two as examples. Aklon continued his explanation. He ended by requiring those who wished to be saved from a life on The Point to be ready for him in the morning in the manner he described. In spite of protest and disagreement, he then stood back from the edge and left them to make up their minds.

Choryssa, on first watch, was distressed to report the fighting between those who wished to stay on The Point and those who wanted to turn to the Cause.

'I share your concern, Choryssa. But, under the circumstances, we have no alternative. We have neither manpower nor time to interview each individual. We will

187

have to rely on passion and conviction to lead their choices. Those who now feel strongly about defeating the faith will find a way to fight the others. Innocents will perish with the guilty, as is always the case in war, but we will find two very different camps by morning. Those who wish to kill us and those who want to fight beside us.'

'What about the false ones? I wondered, when you set me and Patrilha free, how you knew we wouldn't betray you. How did you know we wouldn't try to kill you in the night?'

'Falsehood comes hard to Followers. I had a good idea that I was right about you but I did not know whether or not I was. I took a risk, aware that any attempt to kill me or the others would declare the truth about you. It was a risk I took with my eyes open, Choryssa. I have long been able to give the impression of sleep whilst awake and alert. Had you made any attempt on my life or that of the others, you would have died where you stood. With those below, I expect there to be too great a number to take such risks. We shall deal with them as captives and lead them bound and, for part of the journey, blindfold, to the place I have secured. To that end, we all need to cut the cord and rope we have into suitable lengths and any remaining tabards into blindfolds.'

❦

The High Priest sneered at the two Holy Ones swaggering along the swept, stone path to the outer gates of the city. He turned to look at Pharah-Li, her face bright with morning light, secret satisfaction still curling sensual lips until she faced him, puzzled.

'What displeases you so, Dagla Kaz?'

He nodded at the man and woman ahead. 'So pious. Their superiority revolts me. Can they really believe their display places them higher in the eyes of Ytraa?'

'I'd have thought you'd be used to it. You've lived with them always. Perhaps they simply enjoy the freedom; I know I would.'

'This one's as they should be. Strip and frowk her here and now. Frowk her hard and rough, man!'

'Exhibitionists, every one of them. Oh, they act out their role with enthusiasm, I'll grant you that, Pharah-Li. But, at heart, they love only themselves and want everyone to see and desire them. Hypocrites.'

She felt for his hand and squeezed it. 'You've all the days ahead on the road to concern yourself with them. Let our last moments together be ours, Dagla Kaz.'

'You're surely not pretending you'll be sorry to be free of my demands? You'll be back to your old life as soon as I'm out of sight.'

'I might. But I'm carrying precious fruit now and may make my worship less enthusiastic until your heir is born. And, by Ytraa's grace, you should be back for that event.'

188

'Will you return to the island with me?'

'Ask me when you come back. My life on Muhnilahm would be limited, and you're older than my father. Ask me then, Dagla Kaz.'

He squeezed her hand but resisted the strong urge to embrace and kiss her. Pharah-Li would scorn such a display of affection in public. She responded to his pressure with her own and he saw the promise in her eyes and on her lips and knew he must content himself with that for now and for the coming period without her.

'Why so glum?' She smiled her promise at him, rubbing salt into the wounds of parting. 'Not just because you're leaving me behind, surely?'

'That. And the privations, risks and labours ahead. I lead this rabble into the unknown and, for what? To maintain a position of power and control, no more.'

'Not enough for you?'

'Set against the alternatives, I suppose it must be, or I wouldn't be going. I just wish I had what little faith I started out with. Feldrark and Ivdulon have reduced that to nothing and now I journey with only my need for self-preservation and rank as motive. I wonder; will it do?'

'You have me, and our child, to hasten your return, Dagla Kaz. That should help you through.'

'Yes. But if I didn't have to go, I wouldn't need to return. I could be with you for all the time I'll be on the journey.'

'The choice is yours.'

'Choice is never so simple. I could, I suppose, stay in Litkala with you and start a new life entirely. But, incredible as it may seem, I accept my responsibility to the Followers of Muhnilahm; I'm their leader. I can't merely abandon them. And, if I'm to play my part in the changes Feldrark and Ivdulon have planned, I can do so only if my people hold me in high regard. No, I have no real alternative, Pharah-Li. Tempting and desirable as you are, I must abandon you and step toward the danger of the unknown.'

It both amused and startled him that he could lie so easily to her.

'I'd never seen you as noble or brave, Dagla Kaz. You grow in stature and worth even as you leave me. I look forward to rewarding you.'

At least his deception had produced the required effect. Would she remain as full of admiration when he returned? Be sufficiently impressed to accompany him to the island and abandon this wondrous city he'd grown to prize and desire as his own?

They reached the outer gates of Litkala and all gathered close as they bade farewells to loved ones and friends; some couples, heedless of convention, were open in their displays of love. Dagla Kaz surveyed the crowd and sighed; this party numbered more than twice those he'd brought from the island. Then, he'd been head of eleven and that

189

had been responsibility enough. Now he must lead over twenty across unknown lands and through dangers feared, though not defined.

As he counted heads, to ensure everyone was present, the hazy sunlight of the early morning broke into stark brightness. Looking up behind him, he saw Mount Vaherht was no longer capped with cloud, its lofty crown of snow and ice dazzling against a sky the colour of his daughter's eyes. He looked across to where Jodisa stood with Feldrark, now joint rulers of Litkala. Despite his help and advice, Dagla Kaz still felt wary of him; there was too much hidden behind that handsome face.

Jodisa saw him looking in her direction and wandered over. 'Well, Father, the day arrives. Our thoughts go with you and we hope you find what you seek. I look forward to your return in glory.' The sudden kiss and embrace, no scandal for their relationship, softened the formality of her speech. He felt her respect and affection, and was content.

'I leave you better than I could've hoped, Jodisa. And I'll keep my word regarding those two reprobates who brought you to this fate; they clearly had no wish to harm you and brought you to a happiness you'd not have found in Muhnilahm.'

'You've punished Aglydron for his cruelty to me, but watch him, Father; he's still fanatical and could cause trouble on the pilgrimage. He kept me chaste and safe for all the wrong reasons, but he risked everything for me and I can't forget that. Okkyntalah was always on my side and saved my hide, so I've a soft spot for him even though he did help kidnap me. Take care of him, Father; I owe my life to that young man.'

It was typical of the new Jodisa to be concerned for the wellbeing of others. He thought of the girl he'd left behind on the island; how selfish, headstrong, pragmatic and oddly naive she'd been. Marriage to Feldrark had changed her. But she'd journeyed from the island under protest and come through many dangers with her captors, as well. It was hardly surprising she should've emerged from that experience as a more mature young woman. Exposure to Ivdulon had further changed her and made her more tolerant; a quality he despised. The Jodisa he'd left on Muhnilahm would've demanded the most painful deaths for those who'd kidnapped her. Now she was asking him to care for them.

Pharah-Li stroked his arm 'I think they're waiting, Dagla Kaz.'

He nodded, took both her hands in his and stepped away to look her up and down, to fill his memory with her so he might carry her with him. She let him take in her voluptuous form, barely concealed by silk, her lovely face declaring her wanton nature. At length, he let her go and, without another word, moved to the open gateway to take his place beside their guide, Sondukal. Behind him, voices clamoured their goodbyes to loved ones and he waited till the party was well free of the city gate before he turned to make sure, again, that all were present.

He knew some of them well; those who'd accompanied him from Muhnilahm.

190

Others were from the island but had been strangers to him until recently and the rest were from the city state and known to him by name alone. They were a mixed group with diverse needs, wants, hopes and fears, united by the will to see the new pilgrimage through to the end. Though, Porryh and Dilanthas, the two remaining Virgin Gifts from the island, selected against their wills, might be less keen than the rest. The other Virgin Gifts, both male and female, were volunteers. He considered Feldrark's differing application of the various rules of the Followers and conceded that the Wharhll's approach was better in this instance. But it was too late now to change things for the island girls.

Chapter 20

NEW BEGINNINGS

The following morning brought the conclusion Aklon had expected. Most of those who would not believe the new information he'd given had already departed for the settlement and a chance of water. Others, and there were many, had fought and perished so that the ground was littered with bodies. About two hundred soldiers gathered at the foot of the cliff, naked and unarmed as directed. They looked up as he peered down at them.

'More than I could have hoped for but fewer than I might have wished. The mob at your back remains a threat. I advise that you form some sort of guard as you ascend or those beyond may try to kill you.'

A band of remaining uncertain soldiers stood a little way off, armed, dressed and seeming uncertain as to their actions. There were around a hundred of them and they were clearly desperate and thirsty. Aklon and the others fired a few rounds of arrows into their ranks and this had the desired effect of dispersing them after some of their number fell. A handful deserted their ranks, stripped, dropped their weapons, and ran toward those who'd decided to go with Aklon. Two were cut down by arrows from those who remained, but the group on the cliff again fired into the mob and they desisted and moved off, clearly determined now to follow the others who'd gone to the settlement in the night.

The party on the cliff lowered ropes and lifted the surrendered weapons and tabards to the top. They then lowered a single ladder and instructed those who would surrender to ascend singly. As each soldier arrived at the top of the cliff, he or she was bound and offered water. They were led to a prepared compound and bound together in small groups, back to back and seated on the ground around wooden posts set in the ground to prevent movement.

The process took time and, as the ascents continued, Aklon ordered those waiting below to strip their fallen comrades of undamaged tabards and weapons. These they collected at the top of the cliff, with the others. It was well past noon when the last of the captives was led from the cliff edge and the ladder withdrawn. Por-Kildu and Mkolo-Ti sliced the remaining ladders into short lengths and dropped a couple of these to the plain below to show that, in the unlikely event those who'd stayed behind should find a way to the top of the cliff, the ladders would be of no use to their comrades. The remaining lengths they burnt in the campsite.

They fed their captives, retying each individual's hands in front to allow them to eat. The freed slaves volunteered to cook and serve now they were able to be dressed and to choose their activities. The novelty of their freedom still surprised them and they seemed unsure how to react. Aklon assumed the familiarity of service helped them deal with their new status. At least they presented no danger to the Cause, as they were, without exception, grateful for their release, and, in a few cases, anxious to heap vengeance on their former captors.

Tumalind relinquished her husband's hand at last and whispered her intent to speak to Porryh and Dilanthas. 'I know how they must be feeling. Maybe I can help them.'

Okkyntalah smiled at her. 'They might resent that you were one of them and now you're married. Porryh strikes me as vindictive.'

'I'd like to try.'

'I don't want you hurt.'

She reached up and pecked his cheek. Convention was no matter to newlyweds and, in any case, Dagla Kaz was up ahead and couldn't see. 'You're so good to me.'

Picking her way through the travellers, she was apprehended by Corphanda, the very person she wished to avoid.

'Now, young 'un. How's married life suitin' you? Joining like newlyweds, they say. I can see it's doing you no harm. Bet your thighs are strangers, aren't they?' She laughed and tapped Tumalind's bottom. 'No more smacks for you, eh? You've a man to keep you in line now.'

She considered reminding the portly widow that she didn't need Okkyntalah to keep her in line and that she hadn't needed such supervision even as one of her virginal charges, but knew it would be a waste of time. 'No doubt Porryh will keep your hand in practice, Corphanda. I doubt the delay in Litkala has taught her any useful lessons.'

'You're right there. Only this morning I stuck a palm print on her bum. Making eyes at a palace guard, she was.'

'Hardly risking her virginity in that, was she?'

'It's what she were showing 'im as earned the slap.'

'I'm surprised you allow her to wear such short tabards. If she wore the knee length, like Dilanthas, she'd give less trouble.'

'Got to let her 'ave some of her own way. It's 'ard on these young girls, you know. All the needs and desires of women and no chance to indulge.'

'You're telling me? I spent all those sixdays, at sea and on the road, with my mind full of Okkyntalah and never knowing if I'd see him again.'

''Course. Still; got your reward, didn't you? And a fine young 'un he is. I'd not refuse the chance to join with him.'

'You leave him alone. The only joining he'll be doing is with me, as long as I'm around.'

'As if he'd bother with me when he's got a young beauty like you. No danger there, Tumalind. It's him what's got the challenge, not you. The way the men ogle you, he'll be hard pressed to keep you for himself alone.'

'Oh, Okkyntalah faces no challenge. He's all the man I want and, at least while we're together, I've no reason or desire to let another join with me.'

'Aye, 'cept the High Priest's got his eye on you. You can't refuse him, dear. Let's hope he doesn't let lust override his sense of fair play.'

'Dagla Kaz won't join with me; I'm sure of that. No, it's only Tryonta who worries me here. That man's a snake. He looks at me with heat in his eyes. I wouldn't trust him not to try and force me if we were alone.'

'Take care, Tumalind. That's a dreadful accusation.'

'You know as well as I do he'd have raped me when I was recovering from the snake bite, if you hadn't come along when you did.'

'True enough, Tumalind. You'll take care o' yourself, of course, but I'll need to keep an eye on him with the other girls.'

'Anyway, I was going to talk to Porryh and Dilanthas; give them a bit of moral support, sort of.'

'I'd not bother if I were you. Porryh's still mad at you for getting your own way and Dilanthas isn't sure what she feels. Both jealous. You'll need to step careful with 'em for a bit. Give 'em a few days. The journey might bring us all together. You've got to remember, this is the first time they've been out in public since before the battle with Mipahnhil. They've been cooped up wi' nowt but me and yon servant for company for more sixdays than you could wave a branch at.'

'I hadn't realized they blamed me for what happened. I thought they'd be glad for me, under the circumstances. I'd have been glad if they'd been allowed to marry.'

'Aye, but you're you and they're them, Tumalind.'

'Thanks Corphanda.' She returned to Okkyntalah to find him in conversation with Horsylth, who was in tears.

'What's the matter, Horsylth?'

The girl turned away from Okkyntalah and frowned at her. 'What d'you think? How would you like to be made to go away without your man, before you'd even had a chance to join with him?'

Tumalind didn't remind her that was precisely what had happened to her. 'I thought you'd volunteered?'

'She volunteered me.' Horsylth pointed at Corphanda.

'Did you tell Feldrark you didn't want to come along?'

'How could I? I'm just a serving girl. I can't complain to the Kiral. I must do what he requires of me.'

'Feldrark wouldn't have you come along against your will. I know he wouldn't. I'll see what I can do.'

'You can't do anything. I can't return on my own and, anyway, I'm needed to look after the Virgin Gifts.'

'Do you want to go home?'

'Of course I do. But I can't and there's an end to it!' She stamped off and went to join Dilanthas and Porryh.

'Poor soul.'

'Yes. I'll speak to Feldrark and see if I can put it right before we're too far away. Just hold my hand so I don't stumble whilst I'm concentrating.'

Okkyntalah shook his head at her in wonder but held her and watched as she prepared to communicate with Feldrark.

'*Can you speak, Feldrark? I hope I'm not interrupting.*'

'*You would've if you'd left it a little longer, Tumalind. How can I help?*'

She explained what had happened and was pleased to find Feldrark sympathetic.

'Well?' Okkyntalah looked at her, expectantly.

'Don't say anything just yet but I expect we'll sort it when we stop for the night at the Wanderer's Joy.'

'Amazing.'

'What?'

'The way you do that. If Rrildyss Kaz hadn't explained to me, I'd never have believed it. It's still hard to accept.'

'I suppose so. It's sort of second nature to me now. I know I can trust you to say nothing, Okkyntalah, but do you realize I probably got this from Dagla Kaz? Jodisa thinks he's probably my natural father. I've not said anything to him, of course, or to Aglydron. But I've reason to believe Mother knows already. It's the eyes.'

'All the same colour. Does it mean the High Priest can mindtalk as well?'

'He should be able to but, rather oddly, nobody seems to trust him enough to let him know and he's certainly never mindtalked with me or Jodisa, Feldrark or Ivdulon. We think he can receive but not send, like Gadhallah. He could hear a number at the same time but couldn't control his own sending. It was when a group of Followers picked up his thoughts that they found out…anyway, that's not for now. I'll explain as we travel the road.'

'Lovely as you are, Tumalind, you can be frustrating.'

'Me, frustrating?'

'Not like that! I mean…oh, you're wicked, you are.'

She grinned at him and slipped her hand very briefly underneath his tabard, hoping no one saw her covert sign. He laughed and shook his head at her.

'Wicked.'

'Anyway, you were going to tell me some more about your adventures with Aglydron and Jodisa. I still don't know what happened after she poured away your fresh water and you had to go to The Point in search of more.'

He was happy to relate the tale to her, how they'd beached the stolen boat at the foot of the cliffs. 'We were lucky to find a place to climb up. It's supposed to be inaccessible from the sea. Anyway, I climbed up and crossed the desert to a ridge where there were trees growing, expecting to get water there. The criminals and perverts who live there don't wear clothes. They captured me and took me to their leader, a beautiful woman, who rules with this man who's terribly disfigured. Like a monster from a nightmare. They say Dagla Kaz did it with hot knives. I tricked them, and got away with three full water skins. Just made it to the boat before they reached me. Fortunately, Aglydron had the boat already in the water and we escaped. Mind you, if I ever have to return to The Point, I'm a dead man. She promised she'd kill me.'

Tumalind knew he told her less than half the tale and missed out the dangers he'd faced and his bravery in overcoming them. She would ask Jodisa or her father. 'And then you all sailed off to Ylcrat?'

'It's a good job we had Jodisa with us. Aglydron and I are no sailors. She was brilliant. We'd have foundered or sunk without her along.'

'And that's where you found Myllthlan?' She looked ahead to where the healer was walking beside one of the packhorses, Aglydron and Chislanda at her other side.

'She didn't know she had such great healing powers then. She got us off that island whilst the fire mountain was vomiting fire and rock and ash and smoke. Talk about brave. She was amazing. She came away from there with nothing; said she couldn't take anything from the island with her, even her name. Jodisa gave her a spare tabard. Aglydron named her Myllthlan, but it was my suggestion, because of the colour of her hair. She's pledged to serve him for the rest of her life because he named her.'

'I don't suppose Chislanda's too impressed with that.'

'Oh, Aglydron's joined with Myllthlan, so have I, of course, but he's so besotted with Chislanda he doesn't know any other woman exists now. Bit like me with you.'

She squeezed his hand. She'd joined only with Okkyntalah and hoped to keep it that way. When he'd gone with Feldrark and the army to fight at Mipahnhil, she'd remained with Corphanda and the other Virgin Gifts. Since his return from the battle, she'd managed to refuse advances on the grounds that she was married and her husband was her first choice. Though she sometimes wondered what it would be like to join with another, she had no real wish or intention to find out.

◦ ⸻

The Wanderer's Joy welcomed them like long lost friends, the patron as full of himself as usual and eager to have the trade of more than twenty to fill his hostelry. He invited them to bathe in groups and Dagla Kaz used his position as leader to split the sexes. Corphanda was a capable guardian but she was only one woman and she now had charge of eleven virgin boys and girls. Although most of these were volunteers, the opportunities for misbehaviour were many and he wanted no more problems than he already had. He was happy for Corphanda to keep an eye on the girls but he needed a man to look after the lads. For the moment, Tarruss would have to do, since he couldn't trust Tryonta not to abuse such power.

Once they were all bathed and relaxed, he had the landlord arrange the tables to allow them to eat as a group, with himself at the head of the table and eleven pilgrim members down each side. He recalled the same situation as it had occurred in his own house on the island: the day before they had set sail, he'd brought them all together and introduced them to each other. It had worked well then. It seemed a sensible plan to do the same again and would act as a method to let everybody meet everyone else.

Prayers over and the meal already served and eaten, he called for a round of drinks and stood as they were handed round.

'I would've preferred to have let you all get to know each other before we set out. But time is short and we have many leagues to travel before our duty is done. Some of you here have already travelled with me across sea and land, facing danger and meeting new experiences along the way. Those who set off together from Muhnilahm need no introduction to one another but the newer members need to be aware of who we all are, our place in the scheme of things, and our hopes and intentions. Similarly, the newer members are strangers to us at present and it will help us all if we know more of these newcomers. So, I make no apology for asking you to stand in turn and tell us all a little about yourselves. I will start and then we shall move along the table from my left to the foot and back up the other side to my right.

'I am Dagla Kaz, the High Priest from the island of Muhnilahm or, as we call it, the Chosen Land.' He held up his hand at the signs of dissent. 'I understand that this is a matter of some dispute and I mention it only as a means of letting you all know that differences do exist in our party. There is danger of argument turning to fighting and I want everyone here to understand that such conflict will not be tolerated. Now, to more

198

important matters. I lead, since I initiated it and reside as a senior individual here with the possible exception of Rrildyss Kaz, my counterpart from Litkala. It is I who am bound by the rules, rites and traditions of my forebears to lead you all to the land of our forefathers in Choshinahm. It's true that some will be exchanged for others in Kah-Labaz, but, for the moment, let us assume we will travel the long road as one party, since it is not yet known who will leave the pilgrimage when we reach that fiery mountain.

'I will explain, for those who do not know, that I am charged with exchanging Virgin Gifts with similar individuals from our homeland. It has ever been the custom that we take three female virgins and return with three female virgins. However, Feldrark has pointed out that not only does this go against the express wishes of our founder, the Lord Gadhallah, in that the sexes...'

The uproar at the mention of Gadhallah's name took a little while to subside and Dagla Kaz decided not to use this meeting to open yet another debate, so he let it lie for now.

'The sexes, having equal status amongst the Followers of Ytraa, should be equally represented in any virgin exchange. I've ignored the traditions of more than fourteen hundred cycles in order to satisfy the wants of a brother from a foreign land and therefore decided to take along male virgins with the original three girls from the island. Which is why some of you are here, of course.'

'Equality for the women with men? Are you mad, man?'

The inn door burst open and a young man entered, followed by an older man. Dagla Kaz frowned at the interruption but, before he could continue, the young man strode to the table and took hold of the young servant from the palace who was accompanying them as a help to Corphanda. She rose and embraced him and the rest of the party watched as they kissed and held each other like parted lovers.

The older man approached Dagla Kaz and bowed. 'My apologies for the intrusion, Paltrohn, but the Lord Feldrark, Kiral of Litkala sends his compliments and begs that the palace servant, Horsylth be allowed to leave the pilgrimage, since she was not a volunteer, and be replaced by myself.'

Dagla Kaz was minded to reject the exchange but then recalled his earlier assessment that Corphanda could do with a male helper for the Virgin Gifts. This man seemed mature enough to take on such a role. If Feldrark considered him a suitable replacement, he felt confident the man would prove trustworthy.

'So be it.'

The girl, Horsylth, thanked him, left the room to gather her belongings, and departed at once with the young man. The sound of horses moving rapidly away from the inn at least explained how the pair had arrived. Though, why she hadn't let her situation be known before they reached this stage was a mystery to him. He noticed Tumalind smiling and wondered what she knew that he was as yet unaware of. No matter, it was a small issue and had been settled to his satisfaction. He turned back to the gathering, to continue his introductions.

⚬ ═━◈━═ ⚬

The journey from the campsite to the new settlement was difficult, long and tiresome for all but they managed it without loss. Aklon smiled at Chellyth's amazement as she watched the new recruits march into their new home. First came oxen, a male and three females to form breeding stock, burdened with weapons wrapped in tabards. Then followed separate lines of captives, strung together with each member bearing a pack but naked and blindfold; each line led by one of the Few. Once out of the trees, the blindfolds, used only at the beginning and end of the journey, were removed and the captives were unlinked. They sat on the ground and awaited their fate, not yet convinced they would not be tortured, beaten or killed by the reprobates they knew to inhabit this colony.

'Your new army, Chellyth. Weapons, trained soldiers, food and oxen. Do I repay you for the years of waiting and devotion?'

'As always, you exceed my hopes and expectations. You owe us nothing, Aklon-Dji. And I pledge again my life and those of my people to the Cause.'

He explained all that had happened and left it to her discretion as to when she should release the captives, how to determine who could be trusted and when.

'Tell me, why did you let that bowelcreep, Wendarah, go free?'

'Yes. Wendarah and the Holy Ones. Forgive my moment of pity. I believed, as I still do, that I must at least give them an opportunity to tell the truth to their respective groups. I have little hope that they will do so but I felt compelled to give them the chance. Also, by returning them in the manner I did, I hoped to reduce their status within their communities and shame them.'

'Won't they just stir up more hatred against us?'

'Almost certainly. But they have already made strident attempts to make the people hate and despise us. I suspect the fact that I have sent them back alive will make it more difficult for them to paint a picture of me as an indiscriminate murderer, at least.'

'What about the partners of the soldiers who died or stayed on The Point?'

'Most soldiers take partners from within the army and they would have been there as pairs. Many who have decided to take our side are partners. Of the others, some in the various towns will have lost loved ones and will be struck with their own grief, of course. But I cannot fight a war without killing, unfortunately. Your compassion does you credit, Chellyth.'

She laughed. 'I asked only for practical reasons, Aklon. I was never bothered by the sort of conscience that keeps you awake nights.'

He looked into her eyes and saw there the partial truth and the hidden reality that she cared deeply for all people but must reserve her concern and energy for those who loved her. His scrutiny disturbed her enough to make her almost brusque.

'So. When do we act, Aklon? When do we start fighting for our Cause and gaining the freedom of my people?'

'Soon, Chellyth. First, I must tour the island and test the water in each community. We will have to proceed town by town and I intend to start with the nearest first. But I need to ensure that all preparations are in place and I must sow seeds of doubt in the minds of the general populace before we begin our advance. For your part, you need time to raise the strength and training of your people and to determine the true level of trust amongst those I have brought to you. The two free women and the camp slaves are, I am convinced, completely with us. They had many opportunities to escape or to do damage on the road here but they have behaved better than I could have hoped. I think you may rely on them.'

'Aklon, Aklon! I didn't know you was comin'.' Syylvah ran up to him and threw her arms about him in joy.

'This the special woman you mentioned?'

'No, Patrilha, she is an early convert who has a very special need of me and a certain claim on me as well. Syylvah has risked her life and wellbeing for me and the Cause in numerous ways and on a multitude of occasions. She is the exception that proves the general rule. Here, in the settlement, you should find a partner to appreciate your beauty and your charms. There are men aplenty here.'

'Not like you.'

'Oh, I do not think I am so different. One man is much like the next.'

'No, Aklon-Dji, you're not like other men. You're different and you're better and I'll always be in love with you no matter what you say or do to me.'

'Patrilha, is it? We all feel like that about him. He used to be more willin' to join an' give us all his special pleasure. But he's found a mystery woman who's won 'is heart. I wish it'd been me, an' you wish it'd been you. But we'll 'ave to face it, it's not, an' make do with what we can get. Come wi' me, Patrilha, I've found a few men here who appreciate women and know what we need.'

He watched Syylvah lead his new admirer away and hoped he had escaped the need to satisfy the old.

Chellyth smiled at him and shook her head. 'Am I the only one, Aklon?'

'Oh, no. There are many. But those who want will always believe that others desire the same as they do. It is only those who have what you and I separately have who

201

understand that not all need and desire is the same.'

They ate and the captives were fed and taken off in groups to be cared for and guarded by sections of settlement folk until their true feelings and loyalties could be determined. But Syylvah returned after dark, demanding and receiving her due from him. In the morning, he, Phildrad and Delbon would leave the settlement to return to the main body of the island and preparations for the fight to come. Delbon suggested Choryssa should accompany them. But Phildrad thought she might be a dangerous distraction on this mission and he reluctantly agreed. Aklon, however, made no comment on the matter.

Chapter 21

PREDICTION

'I thought she seemed a bit ungrateful, Tumalind.'

'She was so pleased to see her man, she never gave a thought to anything else, Okkyntalah. Anyway, she can't know I had anything to do with it. I'm just pleased to see her happy and reunited. I wonder who the other man is, though.'

The newcomer conversed with the High Priest before taking his place at the opposite end of the table, though he seemed a little uncomfortable there.

'As I was saying, before we were interrupted, many of you are here because I've changed a tradition hundreds of cycles in age. I hope those from the city will be equally willing to accommodate any necessary change in your own schemes and plans. But, enough of that. I am, as you all know, Dagla Kaz, High Priest of Muhnilahm. It's my duty and privilege to lead this momentous pilgrimage to our homeland and gather a new Godwood to take back to our island, where it will be added to the five already standing as a monument and embodiment of the great and powerful Ytraa. We are a party now of twenty six and it's important that we all get on with each other. I don't demand that we all love or even like each other, but I do insist on cordial relations for all. No intolerance will be tolerated.'

His little joke was treated as such and there was little laughter. Tumalind gripped Okkyntalah's hand in agreement at the High Priest's lack of real humour but she dare not turn to face him in case she smiled too openly.

'On, then, with the introductions.'

Dagla Kaz sat and Tumalind's father rose.

'Aglydron, from Muhnilahm. I'm Tumalind's father and along on this trip as punishment for kidnapping the High Priest's daughter to replace Tumalind, who was Chosen by mistake. Chislanda is my woman and we are exclusive partners. I hope you will all respect that.'

Tumalind hadn't expected her father's declaration of exclusivity; a habit in Litkala though not on the island. But the lack of comment from Dagla Kaz gave her hope for her own future.

'Okkyntalah; like Aglydron, I'm here as a punishment. Tumalind is my wife and we're also an exclusive partnership.'

Dagla Kaz looked irritated by the comment but said nothing.

Tumalind rose and looked around at those assembled. She smoothed down the hem of her tabard and addressed the High Priest directly before speaking to the rest of the gathering.

'Tumalind, originally a Virgin Gift from Muhnilahm. The High Priest has very generously opened his heart to Ytraa and learned that my part in the Choosing was in error only in order that we would be brought together with the Followers of Litkala. For my part, I'm happy that we're now friends and united as Followers. I was given the option of returning to my island home but prefer to be with Okkyntalah, having been separated from him for so long. I would very much appreciate your respect for our wish, especially as newlyweds, to be an exclusive partnership.'

She sat and a young man dressed in a nondescript tunic rose. He wasn't much taller than her, of slight build and wore a sullen look.

'I'm Bardrohn, from Litkala. I've come along 'cos I want to. I hope to find a good woman, mebbie in Kah-Labaz, mebbie Choshinahm, it don't really matter. But that's why I'm 'ere. Oh, an' I'm a Virgin Gift, of course, and 'ave to stay that way till we get exchanged.'

His voice was a little high pitched and bore a slight moaning quality that Tumalind found unattractive. But she had no time to dwell on this young man as his neighbour, an entirely different type, who reminded her uncomfortably of Tryonta, rose to speak. He was blond, well-built and as tall as Okkyntalah. His tunic was flamboyant and his whole air was one of self-satisfaction.

'I'm Fehtohn of Litkala, another volunteer Virgin Gift, though why the girls in that great city have failed to appreciate my qualities is a mystery. I'm on this voyage of discovery to find a woman who'll treasure the gifts, skills and pleasures I can bestow. Whether that'll be at our first stopping place or our last is of no matter to me. But, I warn all you ladies that I am a Virgin Gift and will therefore have to deny you my accomplishments. You must find your pleasures elsewhere.'

His voice was rich and deep and he spoke with confidence. But his good looks and carriage were overwhelmed by his conceit and Tumalind knew she'd have as little to do with him as possible. Another young man stood. He hesitated before he spoke. Unremarkable, his face suggested a young man with little confidence.

'My name is Gidwallehn and I also come from Litkala. I'm looking for a wife who will be a friend and partner to someone happy to serve. I'm a Virgin Gift as well.'

He sat more quickly than he'd risen and seemed glad to be no longer prominent. Another young man rose to say his piece. Slightly shorter than the average height of the last speaker, he had a nose that was too big for his face but his mouth seemed made for smiling.

'Me? I'm Uhstyhll of Litkala and I want a woman who can cook. I'd have stayed in the city but my past makes me bad company. You'll all hear about it sooner or later so I might as well admit it right now. I once stole some food. I was hungry and it was the only way I could get to eat, but I was flogged for it and now everyone thinks I'm a thief. It was once. Once. But, there you are. I'm branded a thief in the city. Maybe I'll be judged more fairly where we're going. And, yes, I'm another sad Virgin Gift, but only 'cos all the girls in Litkala think I'm no good. One mistake and you're marked for life. Not fair, is it? But who said life was fair, eh?'

In spite of his words, his tone was one of lightness, as if his misfortune didn't really touch him. Tumalind rather liked him and thought he might be good company if he could get over his past. She was still considering his words when yet another young man rose to speak. He was almost as tall as Okkyntalah but quite slim. His tabard was plain and close fitting and his black hair was worn very short, making him look severe.

'Wakkyll from Muhnilahm, along for a woman who knows the man's in charge. Virgin Gift, so don't get your hopes up, ladies. But if you want summat carved in wood, I'm your man.'

His voice was harsh and his abrupt, slightly conceited manner left Tumalind with the impression that he wouldn't be good company. At last, another woman rose.

Okkyntalah was impressed by the girl who stood. Her auburn hair flowed like silk across her shoulders and down her back. The colourful tunic clung to her form almost as a second skin and her bright eyes of dark blue shone with confidence as she surveyed the whole table before speaking in a rich, sultry voice.

'I'm Zyreenha and, like the speakers before me, I'm a volunteer Virgin Gift. I could've stayed in Litkala and made my name as a maker of jewellery in silver and gold but I lost the only man I've ever loved. His death haunts the city for me and I'm escaping in the hope of finding some happiness away from the scene of my loss. I'll do as I'm told and cause no trouble if left alone. The only skill I have is likely to be of little use on our journey, but if I can help anyone, I'll gladly do so. I'm proud to represent my city in this venture.'

She sat again and lowered her face until the next speaker rose. This was Caarl, who Okkyntalah knew well from his time at his side, battling the enemies of Litkala in Mipahnhil. The soldier gave a brief account of himself and explained that he'd be the field commander and would punish any transgressions. He expected to be obeyed without question, and warned against misbehaviour.

The man who'd lately arrived was seated in the next spot and he got to his feet with quiet dignity. Tall and well made, he spoke softly with a deep bass tone and addressed his comments directly to Dagla Kaz.

'Rehthlynn, from the palace of Litkala, at your service. I have replaced the young girl, Horsylth, as palace representative. It will be my task to guide and mentor the male Virgin Gifts and keep them in line. I'm fair and just but firm at need, so I suggest you behave well. Although I represent the palace, I should tell you that I'm here entirely voluntarily. I've some skill in cooking, if that will be of use to the party.'

Corphanda stood next and made the company laugh with her account of herself. She looked at both Dagla Kaz and Caarl and then at the previous speaker before she addressed the Virgin Gifts. 'I might be fat but I'm fast on my feet, aren't I, Porryh?'

The tall virgin from the island nodded.

'I've a hand that'll mark any bum that makes trouble but I've skill with herbs an' the like to deal wi' anything what ails you. Come to me with any problems of the body or the heart and I'll do what I can. Course, should any on you suffer a proper wound, you'll need the skills of our wonderful healer: Myllthlan's a wonder with her hands and can heal almost any injury. One other thing: these men who lead are in charge of the party but I'm the one as is lookin' after the girl Virgin Gifts, so if anyone has anything to say about any of the lasses, it's me you tell. Right?'

There were murmurs of agreement which seemed to satisfy the portly lady and she sat again. A tall man with weathered face rose next.

'Sondukal, your guide from Litkala.'

He sat again and the giant next to him rose to his feet with a grace that seemed unlikely in one so huge.

'Tarruss, from Muhnilahm. I've accompanied the party from the beginning and act as guardian, hunter and companion. I welcome all the new faces here and wish you all well on the journey.'

Jhonaht, the astronomer from the island stood, introduced himself and sat again with no mention that he'd caused the party to set out early when he'd mistaken another heavenly body for the Skyfire.

Dilanthas explained her position as an original Virgin Gift from Muhnilahm. 'I didn't volunteer, but was Chosen by Ytraa an' though I'd sooner 'ave stayed home. I'm 'ere an' I'll not complain.'

Porryh spoke next, her short tabard drawing the gaze of all the men, including Okkyntalah, to her shapely legs. She thrust her chest out, exposing more cleavage than was generally expected, and spoke in the tones of a spoilt child as she declared herself a fellow sufferer with Dilanthas and let it be known she was unhappy with her status and would do her best to alter it if she could.

Dagla Kaz used her declaration to interrupt the flow of introductions around the table, standing as she sat.

'I will make something very clear, repeating a message I have given to Porryh previously. All the Virgin Gifts, including those who have volunteered for this pilgrimage, are sacrosanct and must not be penetrated or seduced. Whether male or female, Chosen or volunteer, all will be treated the same in respect of their virginity. It is an absolute condition of this pilgrimage that the young people we exchange with our brethren in Kah-Labaz or Choshinahm remain intact. Any Virgin Gift who places him or herself in danger of violation will be severely punished. Any person who actually violates any of the virgins will be executed in the most painful way I can devise. I hope you all understand this.'

He waited until all around the table had acknowledged his warning before he sat again.

Rrildyss Kaz stood and echoed his warning about violation of the Virgin Gifts, but without the dire warnings. She introduced herself as the High Priest from Litkala and offered her spiritual shoulder should anyone need such to lean or cry upon.

An olive skinned young woman rose to her feet, her tabard seemed to have been made for someone else but it clothed a body Okkyntalah could see would be prized by any partner. Her voice was rich and fruity but she spoke with a sad tone. 'I'm here as a volunteer from the island. I'm a Virgin Gift only 'cos my previous life isolated me and kept me away from potential partners. I'm glad to leave the island behind and hope for a chance to find love. Oh, my name is Yytlomohn.'

Okkyntalah wondered what made those big dark eyes so sad and felt sorry for this lovely girl. But his thoughts were interrupted as Myllthlan rose and smiled at the party. He knew her very well and didn't listen to her words as she introduced herself, instead recalling the times she'd joined with him and those times she'd healed his battle wounds. He knew her as a truly wonderful healer and a warm and generous lover. There was the merest regret that he wouldn't join with her again that vanished as soon as he turned to face Tumalind and found there the love he'd sought and regained.

After the healer, Linlyss and Chislanda introduced themselves. The young girl stared at him with hunger as she described her selection and her skills as a musician. Chislanda held Aglydron's hand throughout her short speech and seemed relieved when she'd said her few words.

Tumalind had described Tryonta as a mirror image of himself and Okkyntalah looked at this man, a few years his senior, who now stood tall and muscular as he addressed the party. His tone was oily and his words seemed insincere as he explained he was a guardian of the party and the right hand man of the High Priest.

'He might look like you, Okkyntalah, but he's as different from you as wine is from piss.'

207

Okkyntalah understood her mistrust of a man she'd described as loathsome.

Finally, a tall, slim girl with raven hair and grey eyes rose to her feet. The short tunic hugged her curves and revealed legs long and shapely. She seemed totally unaware of her effect on the men present as she spoke softly.

'I'm Xylthynn and along as a volunteer Virgin Gift from Litkala, where I was a worker in the glass making trade. I can blow an exquisite goblet or turn a beautiful bowl but I don't suppose my skills will be of use on our journey. But I can sing, and my needlework is much admired, if that'll help? I've yet to discover a man I could love but, in the hope there's one out in the world for me, I'm here for adventure along the road to discovering him.'

She sat again. The eyes of some of the men followed her graceful movements and suggested they wished they might become the man she'd discover along the way.

Introductions over, the meal was eaten with much conversation before Dagla Kaz ordered a final glass of wine all round and then sent the party to their beds in readiness for an early start in the morning. Okkyntalah was happy to go with Tumalind to their room to spend a last night in a comfortable bed before the rough road took them.

The action on the Point had seriously depleted the army, which had only ever been a peacekeeping force and never been needed to defend against attack from without. In fact, Aklon knew the soldiers played a largely ceremonial role and existed in the main to prop up the regime headed by Dagla Kaz. If the island people were left without the threat of punishment, backed-up by the fighting force, it was probable that many would have long ago rebelled against the priests and Holy Ones.

'So, what now, Aklon?'

He considered Delbon and Phildrad. Would they fare better alone or as a threesome on the road? At the back of his mind, he knew that his doubt was fired in part by his desire to be with Shoarhn, alone with her, as soon as possible. But he had lived for the Cause almost all his adult life. And things were reaching a point where his dream could become reality.

'I think we travel the island and alert the Few to the situation, prepare them in each town and the smaller settlements, for action.'

'You seem a little uncertain, Aklon. What's bothering you, if you don't mind me asking?'

He smiled at the honesty shown by his long-term companion. 'I will tell you, Delbon. I would dearly love to visit my new love in the north-east. But our need is for the action I have just described, so I do that duty with an element of reluctance, which you are perspicacious enough to notice. Nevertheless, it is the route we will take. Are you ready,

Delbon? Are you ready, Phildrad?'

'Yes.'

'Aye, 'appen I am. Where first?

'We are closest to Pampahn, it seems sensible to make that our first call.'

The companions agreed and set out in the direction of the town near the marsh; Phildrad's home and the place where Aklon's devoted priest dwelt. It would be good to see Porlesah again.

They made the edge of the rain forest just before dusk and found enough heat and light in the setting sun to dry them out before night fell. A small cave in the steep hillside served as shelter, should the night bring more of the rain they'd endured in the trees, but it remained dry.

Toward dawn, Aklon stepped out of their shelter and sought across the leagues for the mind of that remarkable woman. He found her, as ever, awake, about and full of purpose.

'To what do I owe this pleasure, after so long in silence, young man?'

'Ivdulon, I seek again your help and guidance.'

He told her of the events of the past few days and asked how things progressed on the mainland. She told him of the enlarged pilgrimage and that it had set off once more.'

'This time, the Skyfire they follow is at least the real thing. It'll grow, Aklon; it will be a fearsome sight on this occasion, dragging a fiery trail across the sky and visible in daylight at its height.'

'When will I first see it?'

'Why, tonight. A small bright smudge, visible in the evening sky immediately after sunset. Look to the north-east as the afterglow diminishes and you'll watch it rise between the forelegs of the Manecat. You know that formation of stars?'

'Every child is taught such things, and told the stories of the animals of light, Ivdulon. But your news is timely and gives me great hope. If I can get around the island quickly enough on this occasion and alert the population to the coming Skyfire, I can convince them of at least one truth from my lips. It may do something to dispel my reputation as a liar. I need the trust of the people if I am to succeed in our ambition to modify and eventually defeat the faith of Following.'

'You're wise to understand the significance and advantage of the new Skyfire, Aklon. I've no doubt you'll use the knowledge well. Take care how you rouse the people. They've been kept ignorant of so much and their faith is their foundation. Remove that, without something to replace it, and you create a void into which all manner of evil might so easily collect. Be prepared for acts of stupidity, expect vindictiveness and watch out for violence, for all these things will result from your fight. I wish you well, Aklon, and hope to see you

209

live through this time of turmoil. But, make no mistake, this is going to be the hardest thing you've ever done. Take care. I make that injunction in the full knowledge that you'll be reckless and headstrong, but, perhaps, you'll keep my wish somewhere at the back of your mind and it might save your life in days to come.'

He found he was incapable of denying her prediction of his action but resolved to keep her hope that he would see it through to the end and live.

Delbon and Phildrad woke easily on his return to the cave and they ate well on the remains of their previous day's hunting. Yet another snake from the trees, the lives of these creatures so infrequently threatened by any other animal that they'd grown lazy and almost arrogant in their habits. Almost too easy to catch, so that there was none of the usual challenge he found in hunting for meat. At this stage, however, such easy game was a blessing and he thanked his personal god for that.

'I have a prediction to make for you both.'

They were attentive, as they tidied up their camp prior to setting out for the town below.

'You know that the false Skyfire has now diminished and faded to nothing, of course. But you will be unaware that this evening we will see rise the new and real Skyfire. I shall predict it to the people and they will see I know things they do not. Will that bring me converts, do you think?'

Delbon shrugged. 'Only if you're right. I'd not risk telling folk there was a new Skyfire until I'd seen it meself. It'll make it even harder for folk to trust you if you turn out to be wrong, Aklon.'

'And you, Phildrad?'

'Don't ask me. I know nowt. Just tell me what you need and I'll do it.'

He sighed. One counsellor uncertain and another incapable of an opinion. 'Nevertheless, Delbon, if the evening looks to be fair, I shall announce my news in the centre of the town, before it comes to pass. Will you stand with me as I do this?'

'Course I will, Aklon. I were only sayin' what might 'appen if you're not right.'

'And if I am?'

'It'll be a brilliant start to the Cause in the town and word will spread to the other towns about 'ow you made the prediction, of course. But I still think it's risky when you can't possibly know it's going to 'appen.'

'Trust me, Delbon. I know it will.'

Delbon shrugged and the three set off down the steep hillside toward a town now visible by the early morning smoke of cooking fires. For all his declared certainty, he felt that stirring of doubt that he supposed all men must feel when dealing with a matter over which they lacked proof. But Ivdulon had never advised him badly. He could rely on her;

had always relied on her as long as he had known her. There was no reason why she should let him down now, not when so much hung on the truth of what she'd told him.

Chapter 22

ON THE ROAD

The first few days of the pilgrimage would be slow and steady, to help the newcomers adjust to life in the wild. City dwellers and children of relative ease on farms or from towns, the young people had much to learn of this life in the open and Dagla Kaz, no longer beset by the need for urgency, was minded to give them time to get used to their new lives. They'd left the inn mid-morning, giving everyone time to prepare for the first of many long days marching from known to unknown. He wanted no unnecessary tension, no dissent, no troublesome fears to deflect the purpose of the journey or impact on his personal comfort more than absolutely necessary.

'What is our purpose, Dagla Kaz?'

He saw the glint of confidence residing in the eye of the once-nervous astronomer and decided to restore him to that more malleable condition.

'You know our purpose, Jhonaht. Why would you ask such a question?'

'Merely trying to lighten the load of your concern.'

'Really? Sure you're not confusing my recent leniency for a softness that doesn't exist?'

'Dagla Kaz?'

'Some men are unequal. Some men deserve their fear. This is one such.'

'I take this trip to fulfil the needs of those who Follow, Astronomer. What's your purpose? And, before you answer, consider that I have yet to determine how I should reward you for your mistake in falsely identifying the event that began our errant start.'

That had the desired effect. Jhonaht twitched, paled, and assumed a thoughtful silence. It was how he preferred the man. He might be as frivolous as he wished with others, but Dagla Kaz wanted more than mere respect, he needed fear.

The silence that ensued allowed him to continue with his interrupted thoughts. But the question lingered; an irritation in the way of his contemplation of the enticing loins of that available young woman who preceded him. Hand in hand with her new husband, Tumalind was all a man could wish for in a woman. And, no longer virgin, no more a sacred sacrifice to a faith he'd endured rather than embraced, she could now be had. He could take her when and as he wished. But not just yet. The road was long, the journey just begun. He'd await a more propitious time and let the waiting increase his want of her. But those hips moved so tantalisingly, those legs invited without awareness.

Jhonaht must have noticed his preoccupation, for he had the temerity to speak again.

213

'A dorltah for them, Dagla Kaz?'

But the man's demeanour showed he knew exactly what the High Priest had been thinking. In fact, it was likely that the same thoughts had been surging through the mind of the astronomer.

'That one is not for you, Jhonaht. Any more than her physical double, my daughter, was for you. Remember it well.'

'Suppose she should ask me, Dagla Kaz?'

He stopped himself from laughing; such a reaction might not help his cause. 'She won't. She won't ask any man. Okkyntalah is all the man she sees, and always will be.'

'Except you'll take her, against her will, and frowk her till she begs, eh?'

The voices made sense, as they so frequently did. He was, after all, the superior man here. Why not?

'You intend to have her, even against her wish, then?'

'Rank, as always, Jhonaht, has its privileges. And I intend to use them. It's bad enough I have to lead this rabble over hundreds of leagues of strange lands, face dangers that might kill us all, keep this bunch of fools and knaves in order: if I can't indulge in some form of recreation on the road, what is there for me?'

'What indeed?'

And he was back to where the man had started, placing in his mind the question he would rather not face. Yet it must be done.

'We are here, Jhonaht, you and I alone of all who travel, because we have no choice.'

'You might say that of our own Virgin Gifts, and of Aglydron and Okkyntalah, who you forced along for no legitimate cause.'

'True enough. But they're mere servants. We lead. I lead and you hold a position of some consequence. In a just world, we would send others on this fools' pilgrimage and await the outcome in the comfort of our homes. We would enjoy the advantages of office, uncaring of the hardships and dangers they would face in our stead. But we cannot. And why? Because that fool and user, Gadhallah, set a precedent that means the people now expect their High Priest to lead the journey to the homeland on the coming of the Skyfire. Neglect that duty, Jhonaht, and the people, for all their foolishness and naivety, would put us to a most painful death. And that, Jhonaht, is the answer to your question. Now, are you satisfied?'

The astronomer nodded and bowed his apology for raising the matter, and Dagla Kaz knew he'd hear no more of it now.

'As to the Skyfire. When can we expect to see it without the aid of that extraordinary device owned by the strange woman in the tower?'

'Ivdulon is brilliant, Dagla Kaz. I never thought to hear myself describe a female astronomer in such terms, but she's incredible and gifted. Would that I had such a brain.'

'Now that's something on which both of us can firmly agree. When?'

'Ah. Three nights. It'll be visible from dusk till dawn.'

'I can only hope its sudden, unannounced appearance on the island will signal such panic that the Renegade will be found at last and killed for his heresy.'

Jhonaht seemed about to speak but saw he was glaring with open hostility at the figure to his left. When Tryonta had first announced that he'd been unsuccessful in capturing Aklon-Dji, there had been a moment when the astronomer believed the High Priest might actually kill his hired assassin.

'That man has much to do to prove his worth to me after failing such a mission. He'd better make his value understood, or he might yet discover what it means to cause me such displeasure.'

Jhonaht nodded, the fear he felt at such a threat for such as Tryonta, clearly infecting his own sense of danger. It was enough. To have the man exactly where he wanted him would do for now. Such compliance and obedience meant there was one less individual to worry about on this long road.

'Dagla Kaz, we goin' to walk all day wi' no break? These young women need to rest if we're to get 'em to that there place in good condition.'

The woman was a menace. But it had to be admitted she was perfect for her role. 'Very well, Corphanda. Ask Sondukal to select a suitable place for us to pause.'

She had the nerve to nod as though he did her bidding. But he'd let her have her head; she was no threat. The fat little guardian took away one aspect of his many worries as she guarded her charges with such ardour that no man would ever be a danger to them. His female Virgin Gifts were no worry under her supervision.

'I'm not convinced he won't demand me for his consort, Okkyntalah.'

'Neither am I, my love. But there's nothing we can do about it, except hope he stays satisfied to have one of the others.'

'I could always remind him he's probably my father, I suppose.'

'It might work. But, from what I've heard, even if it's true and he believes it, if he wants you, he'll take you anyway.'

'Maybe I should make it public, then?'

'That might work, Tumalind. But it could be dangerous.'

'You think so?'

'I wouldn't put it past him to have that snake, Tryonta, do you some harm if he thought you were denying him. I think we have to be very careful, Tumalind. I can't lose you again. And I can't allow you to be hurt in any way. You're far too precious.'

She felt his arms about him in the soft warmth of the night and allowed herself to be reassured enough for now. Joining on the journey was pleasant enough but she longed for the privacy and comfort of their own bed in their own room. Three nights in the open had already shown them that their love and desire were undiminished by hardship, but they both preferred their passion in private and without constraints.

They slept again, their long walks through the flat grass plain enough to tire them. Already they'd left the Greenreald far behind and had crossed the first of the tributaries of the Dash. The main river flowed fast and deep beside them and they would cross it in the morning. Soon, they'd reach the city of Shorrannon and find a boat to take them up the mighty River Sure and the big lake that lay beneath the fire mountain. Okkyntalah had described the fearful escape from the island of Ylcrat, where they'd met Myllthlan. The terror he'd described as they ran from that place made her anxious about what they'd face once they crossed Mhistahn, the Lake of the Lost. But that was many days away. For now it was enough to be with Okkyntalah and enjoy his love. That she must take the journey with him had never been in doubt. He rewarded her loyalty and love with his steadfast love and care for her, and that would be enough to sustain her on a journey she'd never wished to make.

In the meantime, she'd mindtalk with Ivdulon and see if there was any way she might deflect the sexual advances of the High Priest. The other men seemed content to leave her with her new husband. Except Tryonta, who had once been ready to rape her as she lay paralysed from a snakebite in what now seemed another life. She wondered why Corphanda hadn't told Dagla Kaz of the incident, but supposed she had her reasons. If Tryonta did attempt to take her, she'd threaten him with exposure to the High Priest. For some reason she didn't understand, this unpleasant man, who'd previously been held in high regard by Dagla Kaz, was no longer a favourite, so he was unable to rely on his position as he might otherwise have done. That, at least, was a relief. And she fell asleep at last.

Morning brought the penultimate day on the plain. Sondukal had risen early and recruited Okkyntalah to go with him. They returned with the sun, dragging behind them the carcass of a great plains bull on a wooden frame behind a pack horse. There would be meat enough for all for the rest of their walk to the city. It meant Okkyntalah wouldn't have to hunt again for the time being.

They prayed together, and she praised him for his expertise in hunting and killing such a beast.

'Sondukal's the one you should thank. I was just a decoy really.'

'I 'eard that, Okkyntalah. And that you weren't. It were a two man job an' you played your part right well. All on 'em 'ere should be grateful we're blessed wi' such an 'unter.'

It pleased Tumalind greatly that Okkyntalah's response was one of modesty. He never took advantage of his reputation with the women, most of whom would join with him eagerly. So far, they'd managed to keep to their decision to be exclusive partners, apart from the unfortunate occasion with Rrildyss Kaz. Now everyone seemed to respect their devotion to each other. Everyone except Dagla Kaz.

'If this goes wrong, Aklon, if your contact is wrong, I'm dead; you know that, don't you?'

'Porlesah, I would never place you in danger of that sort. Trust me. Trust me now as you have always trusted me. I promise you that what I say is the truth.'

And so he had left her to gather the people of the town together on grazing land to the east of the town. Here, the land rose steeply, so that there was a clear view of the sky over the rooftops and, as importantly, a rocky outcrop above, on which Aklon could remain hidden until ready to make his announcement.

The three travellers had moved swiftly over the grasslands and now waited as people collected below. They could hear voices of conjecture, wonder, concern and simple irritation that their day had been disrupted for some reason they couldn't understand. Aklon peeked between towers of rough rock and watched Porlesah make her way, as he had described, to the foot of the outcrop. It was essential all eyes be on him when he told them the facts.

'I still say it's risky, Aklon. Suppose it isn't there? They'll tear her limb from limb. We can escape from up here, but she's at their mercy down there.'

'I understand the risk; so does Porlesah. Quiet now, Delbon; the time comes.'

Porlesah had climbed the first few steps up the outcrop and was now visible to all the gathered townsfolk. She raised her arms in a signal that she would speak, and silence gradually fell on the crowd.

'First, my people, I have a short announcement to make. For some it will be good news, for others, perhaps, unwelcome. Nevertheless, it comes direct from Dagla Kaz, who sent his spokesman, Tryonta and…'

There was some muttering from those who'd heard rumours of this henchman, but they were silenced by neighbours.

'…and the newly appointed deputy High Priest, Wendarah Kaz, to spread this piece of news. It is but the first of a small series of changes that will occur over the next few portions. There's no choice in this, you understand; this first change is a decree that has been passed down to us by a higher authority. I, for one, welcome the alteration. Note, the sun is about to set and we are due to pray. It is about our prayers that I need to explain a change. Prepare, but remain standing.'

Aklon watched secretly as she removed her tabard, and the people, unsettled but obedient, followed her example.

'Now, we are to adopt a new prayer posture; both men and women. I'll demonstrate. Make your prayers in the fashion I now show you.'

Porlesah took up the upright prayer posture, closed her eyes, and made her silent prayer. This was the time she feared most; vulnerable and alone, she must rely on obedience from her congregation. Apart from some small muttering, and a few shouts of relief, there was silence as they followed her example. Once done, they made to cover themselves again but she stayed them with her raised hand.

'There is something more and it is fitting you should hear it in your most sacred state.'

This brought more muttering, some calls of outrage, some of anxiety.

'I'll be brief. But hear me well. And understand that all you hear is the truth.'

The tone of her voice, her choice of words, settled the people into a state of expectancy and concern.

'You'll have observed, as true Followers, that the Skyfire has been absent from our skies for some days.'

There were cries of assent and mutterings of 'shame', and 'why?' from them. Again she held up her hand for silence and again they obeyed.

'That signal in the sky was not the true Skyfire. That signal in the sky was a false trail, sent, we must believe, by Mhortag, to deceive us.'

This was the sign. Whilst the people absorbed this news, which was no real news to those more observant and thoughtful, Aklon-Dji made his presence above them known. Slowly he was seen, and recognised by some. The murmurs of warning quickly rose to a crescendo of fear and threat. But Porlesah stood her ground and signalled that she was aware of his appearance. It took some small time to settle the crowd back down, as they'd expected, but there was, at last, silence.

Aklon spoke. 'I come to announce the arrival of the true Skyfire.'

Calls of derision, catcalls and insults, even missiles and stones were hurled up at him by those closest. He moved only to ensure he wasn't hit by any of the objects that reached high enough. But he remained in sight and calm, awaiting the silence Porlesah demanded from her perch below. It took some time and when it fell the sky was already growing dark.

'As proof of my statement, I point you to the formation of the stars we call the Manecat. There, between its forelegs, you will see the first dim sign that the True Skyfire is arising.'

The crowd turned, though some were reluctant even to take this easy suggestion

218

from a renegade they'd been taught to hate and despise. But many turned and saw that what he said was true. There was a new and fuzzy blur of light exactly where he pointed. Those nearest the small number who wouldn't heed him, explained what they could see and these were then persuaded to look.

'I tell you, Followers of Ytraa, this is not only the True Skyfire, rising to be seen by all. But I predict that this particular appearance of the sign will be the brightest ever known. In the days to come, the Skyfire will outshine the stars, the Moon and, when it comes close to its fullness, will still be seen even in daylight, when the sun usually outshines all else.'

He had their full attention now. Fear and superstition governing them, as his father's regime had dictated. Now he had to try to win them over. And he knew he must do this thing slowly, a little at a time.

'I have only one more thing to tell you at this time. I ask only that you hear my words and reach your own conclusions after the truth I have revealed this night. I am, as you all know, considered Renegade.'

As expected there were calls echoing this description and many wanted him to come amongst them so they could deliver him for execution. Others threatened or shouted insults and yet others stood in silent rage, willing him to fall to his death so they might witness his demise. He waited and, again, Porlesah signalled silence. That they eventually obeyed her even though she appeared to call for this at his behest was a sign of the respect and fear the people felt for the office of their village priest.

'I am Renegade for one reason alone. Hear me. It can do you no harm to hear this one item of fact.'

The further eruption of noise was eventually quelled by those amongst the crowd who would hear what he had to say.

'I am Renegade only because I wish you all to know the truth; the truth you have been denied by my father, Dagla Kaz and by the Holy Ones who would keep you ignorant because it suits their purposes. I leave you with that fact. But I will return in days to come. I will come openly, now that there is no army to arrest me.'

He left them with that astounding news, knowing they would soon know it was also true. The Skyfire would grow more visible each night and there would be those who the Few would more easily convert to the Cause because of his announcement. He had no hope or expectation that the majority would be easily turned from their indoctrination, but he was confident that enough would voice and feel their doubts to make the Cause more readily achieved. If he could oversee the changes with as little loss of life as possible, it would be a great achievement.

'She's in league with him!'

This sudden insight came from a man right in the middle of the crowd and his finger pointed, with little need, at Porlesah. The sudden change in mood of the crowd was almost tangible and Aklon knew that what he did next would determine whether or not she lived. Yet, he also knew that any lie he might tell to save her life could destroy the good he had done to his reputation by his truth about the Skyfire. He called to the crowd in the hope he could bring their attention back to him.

'Your village priest is of the class I wish to defeat. She knows who I am. She knows my stated aim is to destroy the priesthood and the Holy Ones. She is amongst those I would see stripped of office. But I will see none harmed or reviled who do not deserve such action. I would have no one innocent suffer because of me and my beliefs. The words of that man, the one who, without reason or evidence, accuses your priest of association with me must be subject to doubt. Can you believe a man who I tell you, with no fear of contradiction, regularly beats his wife because she will not willingly engage in the sexual perversions he demands of her?'

He prayed that the woman, now her plight was made known, would have the courage to admit the truth. The light was now such that individuals were no longer discernible in the mass below but he heard sounds of movement and a woman's voice raised in surprise.

'How's the Renegade know this? 'Cos what he says about my husband is true. He takes me from behind, up the squitter.'

This perversion was so outrageous that the people turned on the man as one and the potential threat to Porlesah was diverted. The crowd focussed their anger and confusion against the man he knew had been a spy for Dagla Kaz. Let him face the wrath of the folk he'd tried to direct at Porlesah.

'It is vital you now return to your home, without interference in this marital dispute, Porlesah. I advise that you intervene only if requested. But keep an eye on that man; he is the one I warned you of many portions ago. Perhaps I should have killed him, but he is acting in this, at least, only out of a strong belief. I must go now. Do you feel safe?'

'I'll fare well enough, Aklon. Don't worry about me. I have authority here still. Be off, though I'd have welcomed you to stay had you been able.'

'Another time, perhaps. I will return later in the battle for freedom. Please let Lasdilyss know that Phildrad remains with me. It is unsafe for him to return home for the moment, now he has been seen with me. Farewell for now.'

'Take care, Aklon. I'll begin the slow changes we discussed and see you soon, I hope, in better circumstances.'

She cut the connection and he led his companions from the high point and on past the town towards the capital, where their task would not be so simple. There, Wendarah, experienced in politics, would make it very difficult to make an announcement such as he had delivered here in the most backward of the island's towns. There, in the place most closely ruled by his father, the place most under the High Priest's influence, it would be a difficult and dangerous business to persuade the people to his own beliefs and ideas. But it was a task that must be done, and done now.

Chapter 23

SEEKING A WAY FORWARD

*T*hey'd expected to see the city earlier, but an injury to Uhstyhll had slowed them down. The young man had been clowning to impress one of the new female Virgin Gifts and turned his ankle as he leapt from the bough of a tree onto the ground before her. It had rather spoilt his attempts to impress, leaving him looking a fool.

But the incident had delayed them and they now entered the sprawling city mid-morning instead of during the previous evening, as Dagla Kaz had intended.

Tumalind stared about her at this strange but beautiful place, with its thronging crowds of diverse peoples. That it was a port was clear from the mixture of races. So far inland, the harbour was no less important to the area than a coastal dock would be. Here, Dagla Kaz had told them, he hoped to engage a boat to take them upriver to the Lake of the Lost.

Another voyage aboard ship: neither she nor Okkyntalah were sure how they felt about such a prospect. Her encounter with the pirates and his with submerged rocks forming a lethal crescent about the isle of Ylcrat had left them both with some distaste for sailing.

But it was out of their hands and she took to examining her surroundings, as was her habit, hoping to learn as much as she could simply for the love of encountering and collecting new knowledge. Okkyntalah remained by her side, his hand gentling hers and reassuring her that she would be in no danger here as she had been in Rhonholoah, when that awful old crone had kidnapped her for purposes she would rather not contemplate.

Yet, here, in this wonderful city, with its wide, open ways and low houses surrounded by their walled and cultivated gardens, she understood the trade in women sold for sex was rife. Here, it seemed, they even had a name for the trade, calling women who peddled their bodies 'whores', their trade, 'whoring'. And, since it wasn't prevented by law, the women were happy to let men know of their wish to trade their favours for money.

Tumalind found their manner of dress disturbing, displaying nipples and female parts, though covering the rest of their bodies. Such costume drew the eyes of men to the wares on offer and even Okkyntalah found it hard not to look. She'd seen him stare openly at the first of these women they'd passed until Sondukal had explained what they were about. Although her husband had lost his initial curiosity as soon as he understood, he was still driven by male interest in their display. That the women of Shorrannon had a well-deserved reputation for beauty, made their exposure all the more difficult to ignore.

223

She wondered whether she'd be equally drawn to men who showed themselves off in that manner and was honest enough to believe that, though she'd try to resist, her natural curiosity would probably drive her to glance at least.

Other people were dressed in different styles, some of which she'd seen in the ocean port of Xythonl, though others were new to her. And it wasn't long before she was exposed to a test when a group of men, shoulders draped with short scarves that dropped to the centre of their backs but left their chests exposed, stopped a short distance from their party. They wore nothing other than this brief item and long boots that clothed their legs, from sole to mid-thigh, in soft leather.

'Not as easy as you thought to ignore them, is it, my love?'

She smiled at Okkyntalah. 'I didn't think it would be. But neither did I expect to find it engaging. Mind you, I'd still rather look at you.'

She knew he felt the same for her and was content to leave the strange men to whatever they were about.

A party of women, clothed entirely in black, their faces hidden behind windings that left only their eyes visible, passed, chatting and apparently unconcerned by the constricting nature of their clothes. She was reminded of the shrouds they'd had to wear in that heathen city in Niphralon and shuddered at the memory.

'How long we staying 'ere, Dagla Kaz? Onny I need to know how I'm supposed to keep these 'ere girls under control with so much male flesh on display.'

The High Priest, ahead of her, turned to face Corphanda. 'We shall remain only as long as it takes to find passage on a ship going up river, dear lady. As to how long that will take; I have no answer. But, if necessary, we will find appropriate lodgings until we can sail away. Does that satisfy you?'

'For now, I s'pose it'll 'ave to, won't it?'

She fussed about her charges like a mother hen. In contrast, Tumalind noticed that Rehthlynn controlled his male Virgin Gifts with as little fuss as possible; exercising a quiet but firm control. But, then, his charges were all volunteers; none had been coerced as had Dilanthas and Porryh.

Her two former companions had slowly reverted to their previous attitudes toward Tumalind as they'd travelled the road.

'Tain't your fault, is it Tumalind, if we're still Virgin Gifts an' you ain't? Anyroad, I allus liked you an' don't see why I should stop jus 'cos you're married to that 'ansome man.'

Dilanthas had been first to come back to her as a friend and Porryh had let it be known she was no longer bitter at Tumalind a short time afterwards.

The party walked slowly along the wide thoroughfare, led by Sondukal who'd visited this city previously, until they reached a huge open space. Here, large groups seemed to have gathered in certain places and there was much shouting and calling within the groups, but none between them, as if they conducted their activity in isolation from one another. It made the space both noisy and confusing for visitors but Sondukal seemed confident enough and led them to the fringe of a group of disparate men and women in the south-eastern quadrant.

'Please rest here. I shall be a short while finding a ship. We will then, depending on circumstances, either find a hostelry or make our way to the docks to board the ship.'

Dagla Kaz hadn't previously made such helpful announcements and Tumalind wondered if his contact with Feldrark had made him see things a little differently. It was certainly an improvement.

She watched him vanish into the crowd, accompanied by Sondukal and Tryonta, and took the time to look about whilst stationary for this time.

⋆

'How do you feel, Chislanda?'

Aglydron had been concerned at her presence on the pilgrimage, especially after her injuries and loss of the child in battle. But he was pleased to have her with him.

'I'm fine, Aglydron. Don't fuss. Do you know anything about this place or our journey? The High Priest talks of taking a ship. Do they sail so far up the river?'

'So they say. It must be a mighty river if it can take a ship as far as Lake Mhistahn.'

'Is that where this mountain is that breathes with the fire of dragons?'

'Jodisa says they're not dragons. She says the wise woman, Ivdulon, explained that the world's a ball of molten rock beneath the earth we walk on and that fire mountains are places where the hot rock escapes from time to time.'

'Sounds unlikely to me.'

'Me too, but that's what the wise woman believes. Me, I go for the dragons. At least everyone knows they exist, don't they?'

Chislanda stared wide-eyed. 'You've seen one?'

'Not personally. But I know people who've spoken to those who have.'

She was thoughtful. 'Funny, isn't it? We all believe in them but I bet no one here has actually seen one.'

'We don't have any on the island. But we know the stories.'

'I wouldn't want to meet one, from what I've heard.'

They looked about them, as if expecting to find one of the creatures in this civilised and open square and then both laughed at the same time as though they'd read one another's mind.

'What do you suppose that is, Aglydron?'

225

He followed the line of her pointing finger to a towering object that rose high into the sky some distance from them, toward the river. He could see what appeared to be lines of some sort attached to it at angles.

'No idea. Never seen anything like it.'

'The Galhta's tower was a bit like it, but that looks a lot stronger, and taller.'

'Can't see any stages on the way to the top either. It looks as though it just rises in one complete piece. Can't think what it's for, though.'

Unable to solve the mystery of the structure, they looked about the more immediate area and studied the people and buildings.

'There's a woman, look; leading a naked man on a rope about his neck. See?'

Aglydron watched as the tall, elderly woman, dressed in multi-coloured fabric that was draped over one shoulder and secured with a belt, use a switch to make the young man do as she wished. He was only marginally shorter than her and almost black in colour, his broad shoulders suggestive of strength and power. It seemed odd that this frail looking woman should be able to so easily control such a man. He heard her tell the man she was tired and, without any coercion, he lifted her off her feet and carried her, as though she were an infant. Aglydron gazed after them as they left the great square and puzzled over the strange relationship.

As he moved his gaze back toward Chislanda, his eye was caught by a large party of men. They were armed with spears and wore swords at their hips. Each wore a close-fitting headpiece that hid their hair and had plates of shiny metal protruding at each side, covering their faces and allowing only their eyes and noses to be seen. They walked in an organised group and Aglydron realised they were in rows of three, and walked in step, so that they seemed to move as one creature. He heard no words spoken and was amazed when they turned, as one, keeping formation, and walked away in a different direction.

'Soldiers, I expect. Would that I had them under my command. I could achieve much with such disciplined troops.' Caarl watched the men disappear from view, admiration written large on his face.

'It's a strange place, isn't it, Caarl?'

'Very civilised and orderly. I like it. But I came to inquire about the health of your partner. Are you well, Chislanda?'

'I wish everyone would stop treating me like an invalid. I'm fine.'

'You had serious injuries and lost much blood. It's my duty and concern that you remain fit for the journey ahead of us. At least aboard ship you'll have the chance to rest and rebuild your strength. I'm pleased to learn you are recovered, anyway. And you, Aglydron; you are well?'

'Better than I've been in many a cycle, Caarl. Chislanda gives me great joy and that does wonders for a man.'

'Indeed it does. I miss my A'ahl. I wonder how she fares. Tryonta says he never got to see her, though he reported on your wife, as I recall?'

'Yes. Yes, said she was well and the twins are growing into fine boys.' He decided against any mention of Shoarhn's alleged relationship with Aklon-Dji; it wouldn't give the right impression.

'Good. Good.'

The soldier moved off to interrogate the rest of his charges. But, before he could ask anything of the two young newcomers he approached, Dagla Kaz returned with Sondukal and a well-built woman dressed most outlandishly. Her jacket, laced across the open front, was barely enough to conceal her considerable breasts. Strange garments clothed each leg separately, overlapping across the front where each tube split and formed a triangle tied at the hip. The fabric was fine enough that her skin was just visible through it. On her head, an odd, flat, circular object balanced with a tall feather sticking out of it.

The High Priest made a sign to Caarl, who gathered the party around, making Dagla Kaz and the strange woman central, occupying a small space that allowed them to see her properly. She seemed delighted to be observed and actually turned and postured so that all could take in her strange manner of dress and her voluptuous form.

'This is Quyreena, who will be captaining her ship for us as we sail to the Lake of the Lost under Mount O'bo. She may be known to some of you, as she provided passage for Tryonta and Wendarah back to the island, and picked up our volunteer Virgin Gifts to bring them back.'

The woman surveyed the crowd around her until her gaze fell on Porryh. 'Now, you lubricious hussy, I think you and I might get along just fine.'

To Aglydron's amazement, the fiery young virgin blushed and turned her face away.

Dagla Kaz made no comment but gestured for their attention. 'We shall spend one night in a tavern down by the quay and board ship before noon tomorrow. I need time to organise supplies and Quyreena has to gather her crew together, since they were expecting a break before setting sail again. She may need your help, Caarl, in that task.'

Caarl nodded his compliance.

Dagla Kaz turned to the woman. 'Lead on, Quyreena. I'm sure everyone is looking forward to a refreshing bathe, good food and somewhere comfortable to spend the night.'

'Then you'd best avoid the place I'm staying. I'll take you somewhere more civilised. How many are we? Oh, twenty six. No problem for the landlord of the place I'm thinking on. Follow me. And don't dally. Get lost here and you'll spend the rest of your days wandering unfound.'

She set off at a brisk walk so that they all had to concentrate on merely striding after

227

her, with no time or spare energy to talk.

Okkyntalah looked around the place they'd entered. Cool stone beneath his feet soothed them after the speed of their march through the city. The interior was bright but calming, with large cushions scattered around the edge of the vast room. Dagla Kaz, accompanied by Quyreena, gestured them to take their rest as he arranged for lodgings for the night.

'She's a bit odd, isn't she?'

Yytlomohn, one of the volunteer virgins from the island, moved a cushion and sat opposite him and Tumalind. 'She's one of them women what likes other women, you know? She tried it on with me on the ship from Muhnilahm but I wouldn't let her, not like that. All her crew's women as well. Not Followers.'

Okkyntalah concentrated on her eyes as he spoke. 'Maybe if you sat in a slightly different way, Yytlomohn?'

'Am I showin'…? Oh, d'you think that's why she tried it with me? I always sit this way. I never thought. Thanks. I'll sit a bit more modest, like, in future.'

'Didn't your father ever mention anything about it to you?'

'Never spoke, most of the time, Tumalind. Never really looked at me. He thought it was my fault my ma died when she gave birth. Just the two of us most of me life. Onny time I saw other folk was when he let me go with him to carry our fruit to market. That's why I came on this trip. Wanted to get away. Wanted to be with other folk.'

'You're not too worried about what sort of husband you might get, then?'

'I'll not be lucky enough to get a man as fine as yours. But any will be better than none and, with the life I've had, a man who sees me as a woman will be a good thing.'

'Well, I must whisper so Okkyntalah doesn't get too swell-headed, but he really is a wonderful man and you're right; you won't find another like him. But you're a pretty woman and I'm sure there'll be plenty of very attractive, and good, men for you either at Kah-Labaz or in Choshinahm.'

'I hope so. I think Okkyntalah heard you, though.'

Tumalind laughed. 'He was meant to. I think you've a lot to learn about how men and women relate to one another, Yytlomohn. But you'll have plenty of opportunities to watch as we make our way up river. Oh, I'm so glad we won't have to walk all those leagues. I did enough walking in Kabalyt to last me a lifetime.'

'I thought you weren't too keen on sailing, my love?'

'Having seen the river, I'm sure it'll be less stormy than the sea, and there aren't likely to be pirates! Better than tramping dusty roads, isn't it?'

A young man, long apron hanging from his hips, bent to her with a thick wooden tray laden with metal cups of various drinks and waited for her to choose one.

'This dark purple one smells nice. What is it, please?'

The young man blushed at her question and bowed. 'That be the juice of the barmble fruit, miss. Barmbles is very prickly but the fruit be very tasty an' they say, very good for keeping away the sickness, like.'

She thanked him and took the goblet. It tasted as good as it smelt and was very refreshing. Yytlomohn and Okkyntalah asked for the same drink and he was obliged to return to the kitchen to collect more goblets.

The afternoon, and the shared evening meal in the restful atmosphere of the tavern, served to strengthen bonds of friendship between the newcomers and the more experienced party, so that they all knew each other better when they set off for the quay the following morning.

'I wish we could've spent more time here, Okkyntalah.'

'Me too. I'd like to explore this place. But Dagla Kaz is determined to get us on our way. Do you know how far we have to sail before we get to the lake?'

Tumalind nodded. 'I asked Jhonaht last night. He says it's more than sixty leagues. He thinks, as we'll be sailing against the current, the best we'll do is about ten leagues a day. We can't sail at night, so we'll anchor for the dark time. So, that's about six or seven days to reach the lake itself. He says it's another twenty five leagues through the lake before we reach Kah-Labaz, but thinks we'll be able to sail that none stop, as there won't be a current to slow us down.'

'He's always willin' to tell you things, Tumalind. When I ask 'im a question, 'e jus looks at me like I'm soft in the 'ead.'

Tumalind smiled at Dilanthas, who'd latched onto the couple as they set off from the tavern. 'I think it's because I remind him of Jodisa, and he just answers me before he's really thought about it.'

'That's not it. All the men think you're bright an' clever; and you are. An' they all think you're beautiful, too. And you're that as well. Seems 'ardly fair for one person to have so much good stuff in them. An' it's not even like you're ever nasty or unkind. I mean, Tumalind, who could ever do anythin' but like you?'

She turned to Porryh, who'd come up on the other side of Dilanthas, expecting laughter to follow this praise. But there was none. Porryh just nodded in agreement. Tumalind wondered what had happened to change her.

'Oh, it's not you, Tumalind. It's me. I've just been seeing the way you are with everybody and remembering how good you were with Dilanthas and me on the first pilgrimage. It was me that was bad. I even let you get lost in that horrible place where we had to wait for the ship to be repaired. You might've been sold into slavery because of me, but you never said anything against me, even then. No; I just have to admit that you're a clever, kind and beautiful woman after all. And, judging by Okkyntalah's constant expression of satisfaction, I bet you're a right good frowk as well.'

Tumalind blushed under this onslaught of praise and personal description but could think of no reply, so just shrugged.

'Modest as well. All the rest of us women should hate you, you know. But you're just too nice.'

Having said her piece, Porryh flounced off and squeezed herself between the two male virgins ahead, walking close enough to Fehtohn to touch his arm with her own.

'Well, that was a surprise. Not that it wasn't deserved, my love. Wonder what brought that on?'

'Am I a good frowk, Okkyntalah?' She was serious. It wasn't a way she'd ever considered herself. She knew she gave pleasure when they made love, but wondered whether she gave as much as he presented to her.

'The best. In fact, even if I didn't love you the way I do, I wouldn't want any other woman after you.'

'Is that really true?'

'Why the sudden doubt, Tumalind? Haven't I shown you how much I love and want you?'

'Oh, it's not you, Okkyntalah. I just find myself surprised at my good fortune and wonder how long it can last. I couldn't be happier; well, perhaps if we were at home instead of on the road, but I can't imagine being any more content and happy than when I'm with you. I just hope you feel the same.'

'Always. Without you, my life would have no meaning now. You're my life. I just want to get you back home to the island, fill you full of babies, and spend the rest of my days with you.'

She wondered if he knew that she took the herb to prevent unwanted pregnancy on the road and then relaxed again, smiling and wondering why she'd felt sudden doubt about her future happiness. It seemed silly to question something that seemed perfect. Better to accept that she and Okkyntalah had been blessed and that Ytraa clearly wished them to be together. Yes; that was the way to be.

But, as she squeezed Okkyntalah's hand in gratitude for his love and trust, she saw movement to the other side of her. Turning, she caught a look on Tryonta's face that had her anxious and fearful once again. That man was a snake, she knew. With Tryonta, it wasn't her beauty, her intelligence or even her sensuality that appealed. She knew his desire was power; he wanted control over her, wanted to conquer her and invade her simply so he could say he'd mastered her. Afterwards, he'd lose interest and be indifferent to her. But she knew he'd try every way he could to get her away from Okkyntalah and into his clutches. And, with Dagla Kaz wanting the same thing, she feared one of them might succeed.

Chapter 24

A REVELATION

'*Y*ou're quiet, Phildrad.'

'I were 'oping to see my Lasdilyss.'

Delbon turned to Aklon in the falling darkness. 'And I thought we were going to explain things to the Few before we left. So they'd know about the army and all that?'

Aklon stopped so suddenly that the other two, following, collided with him.

'Mhortag's balls! Am I such a fool to forget such things? Of course we must. I was so intent on humiliating Wendarah again, I allowed my loathing to overcome my common sense. Do not allow me to do anything so stupid again, please. You are my partners and advisors in this; keep me alert and on the right track.'

They retraced their steps toward the town and waited in the trees until the people were sleeping. The streets were silent, the night brighter than he would have liked, with the moon still almost full. Practice and experience kept Delbon to the shadows by instinct but Phildrad had to be guided yet, keeping close with Aklon.

They went first to see Lasdilyss. As always, the house was silent and dark. They stopped before the entrance and he told them to still their breathing, listening for the evidence of more than one. Though, later, when he thought about this, he wondered why he had made that cautious approach when the only person likely to be with her for the night was right behind him.

He motioned the two of them back, moved with them a little distance from the house before he whispered in tones too soft for anyone else to hear.

'Does Lasdilyss take other lovers, Phildrad?'

'Not as I know of, why?'

'I heard three people in the house, maybe four; one was muffled so well it was hard to detect. The question, now, is do we enter in the dark, with no guide about who is in there, or wait until we have some daylight to inform us?'

'She'd never take more'n one to her bed at night, Aklon. Never.'

'So, three indicates something unusual. A trap, perhaps. Someone, maybe father's informants, maybe some Holy Ones, lying in wait for you to return to your wife.'

'How'd they know, Aklon?'

'Wendarah. She would have recognised you at the Scar. And, of course, you were visible tonight when I made my announcement. I should have planned for this. I hope Lasdilyss is unharmed. I think we must risk entry in the dark, since we have no way of

233

knowing what they might do to her whilst we wait. No, Phildrad, wait! Any unplanned action could have her killed before we reach her. We must be careful.'

They circled the house three times, until they were as certain as they could be that no others waited outside to trap them once they entered. The most dangerous part would be their entry into darkness; they'd have nothing to guide them, but those inside would see them silhouetted in the doorway, with the stars and moon behind them.

Phildrad wanted to go first; citing his absolute familiarity with the house as his reason, when Aklon questioned the wisdom of this. It made sense. He was learning silence and caution, at last. It seemed he was swiftly learning common sense to go with these valuable traits.

The door made no sound as he pushed it open and slipped straight inside. The two outside listened for clues and heard only the increase in the sound of breathing, now the barrier of wood no longer muted it. Phildrad moved more silently than a cat hunting for rhaats. But waiting for his signal to advance was torture. A sudden sharp knock of flint brought a spark to a candle and, as the flame rose, so those waiting for them awoke.

One apiece.

Phildrad stabbed the Holy One straight through her heart, spilling her blood on his gagged and bound wife, lying terrified beside her. Aklon took the one who lay beneath the window. His short knife sent a shower of blood to splash him, as he slit the man's throat. Delbon attacked the man waking from behind the door, his knife silencing the rising cry of fear and warning, even as it rose.

He shut the door behind him and they surveyed the scene now that their hunters were all dead. Phildrad made a sign to Lasdilyss and waited for her to acknowledge the need for silence. He undid the gag first and then cut the bonds at her wrists and those at each foot so she could be released from her position of abuse and usage. He found her tabard and enclosed her in it before he took her in his arms and held her close. She was unmarked apart from her striped thighs and buttocks.

Aklon sent Delbon back outside to watch for any further enemies. He poured water from the pitcher into the wide bowl and helped Phildrad tend his wife with care and love. They worked in silence, needing no words to inform them what had happened, or why. When she was as comfortable and clean as they could make her, Aklon suggested Phildrad should lie with her for comfort in the privacy of their bedroom. He first made sure that space was also vacant.

First light brought the sounds of birds but nothing else. They woke Lasdilyss and spoke softly to her, asking if she'd been examined and interrogated.

'They raped me, after the whippin'. Nothin' else. Didn't want to know nothin'. Said they was waitin' for you an' Aklon an' would torture you in front of me before they killed me. That woman Holy One were the worst; licked my blood!'

She shuddered with revulsion and her face displayed disbelief still. But, pained as she was, she could walk and was content to leave the house with them.

'What about your parents, Phildrad?'

He looked at his wife and wondered aloud how he'd come by this gem of a woman. They travelled to the small house where the old man and woman lived. Inside, the evidence was clear. There was no doubt about who had been there or why. In spite of their habit of treating her like a slave, Lasdilyss wept at the brutal treatment that had been visited on the bedridden pair.

'They'll be in peace now, at least.' Phildrad tidied up the bodies and covered them with the rags that remained before they left the wrecked house.

Aklon led them away, seeking the house of one of the Few and discovering it both unguarded and welcoming. As the town woke up about them, the group of four were made comfortable by the two who lived in this bigger house, childless yet and newly married. They were willing to nurse Lasdilyss back to health and for her to stay with them until the situation was better known.

'You've other things to do, now the Cause has begun, Aklon. We'll pass word round. The groups overlap, so everyone'll get to know. And your announcement of the real Skyfire should make it easier to convince waverers of the truth and justice of our Cause.'

They spent the day with these safe friends; fed and rested. They made it clear they'd deal with the informer who'd led the rapists to Lasdilyss. But, come night, Delbon and Aklon made to leave without Phildrad.

'No. I've spoke with Lasdilyss an' she wants me to come with you. Says she'll be safe enough now she's with the Few. She's goin' to 'elp with spreadin' the word an' getting' rid o' them bodies.'

'Will you be content to let her do that, Phildrad? Will you be able to act as we must, knowing you may not see her again, knowing either one of you could die?'

Phildrad turned to the small group in the safe house. 'E's such a comfort, isn't he? Likes to make sure you know all the good stuff. Look, Akon, this thing's started an' we're all on us in it. We can 'ardly leave you now, when we're right at the edge of the action, can we?'

So it was that the three crept from the town, secure in the knowledge that the Few residing there would soon all know about the army. They would start their task of spreading the truths they'd learned from Aklon. And, soon, their ranks would swell with those who believed and cared enough to fight for freedom. But how many would be hurt or killed along the way? It wasn't a question Aklon could dwell on, as they moved toward the coast and the great danger of the capital.

'Did you hear that screaming in the night, Okkyntalah?'

'It woke me. I thought you were asleep, or I'd have comforted you.'

'Whoever was attacked is probably beyond comfort. Those screams; terrible.'

'I know, Tumalind. A fair city to look on but not as safe as Litkala, it seems. If that's a sample of the night here, I'll be glad to be aboard the boat and on our way.'

But their walk passed without further incident and no mention was made of the violence in the night by their host or others in the party. And their arrival at the quay took all conjecture from her mind as she examined the vessel they were to travel on. Smaller than Baklan's Nupraxyss, the Mekoque bore twin triangular sails and a prow that rose in a curve higher than the structure that straddled the space between the masts. The keel, a pronounced curve of solid wood that flowed from beneath the ship to the prow, was carved into the form of a naked woman with her arms stretched above her head, her hands gripping the bowsprit. A woman so voluptuous in life would've been unable to keep her balance and the figure made Tumalind smile at its unlikely form. But when Quyreena stopped before it and prostrated herself in what was plainly an act of worship, she was glad the ship's captain hadn't noticed her mockery.

The crew greeted their captain and then helped the party to move their belongings on board. All the sailors, mostly young women, with a few older ones, were clad in minimal dress that left little to the imagination. She watched Okkyntalah as he surveyed them and then observed the reactions of the other men in the party. Without exception, they were captivated by this display of female sexuality. It didn't bode well for the voyage, she thought.

Once aboard, they set sail without having to wait for the tide, as they had in the sea ports. Sailing upriver, the current and the winds would be the guiding factors to their progress. As they left the quay, a south-westerly breeze pushed them smoothly through the flowing waters of the river, trailing a wake that Tumalind watched as they moved away from the city.

At the stern, she stood with Okkyntalah beside her, and watched the city pass them. It was easier now to see how the main roads formed a star shape centring on the quay, where the wide river split the city in half, and the side roads all formed concentric circles with the same centre point. It had clearly been well-planned and gave the city an open and airy feel with its preponderance of large, detached dwellings. But the violence of the night still haunted her. Those screams of pain had been so terrible that the person involved must have suffered greatly. It had seemed an act of deliberate cruelty rather than an unplanned attack and she wondered at the cause and reason for it.

'I don't suppose we'll ever know, Tumalind. Another mystery; like the dead woman I found near Ylcrat, who turned out to be Feldrark's sister. We'll never know how or why she died.'

'No. I suppose not. But I can't get the sound of those screams out of my head.'

'Things'll happen on our journey to stop your worries over a stranger. I just hope we aren't involved in any trouble. I want to get back home without us suffering. Then we'll raise that family. You still taking something so you won't get with child whilst we're on the road?'

'Of course. I couldn't cope with giving birth on this sort of journey. Don't worry. I'm doing all mother taught me in that respect, even though it's supposed to be against the wishes of Ytraa. And I've passed the information and some of the powder on to Chislanda: she can't risk another pregnancy so soon after losing her baby in that way.'

'A sensible precaution, my dear. I would not wish to lose you in such a way.'

Dagla Kaz had approached so quietly that neither of them had heard him. It came as a shock that he approved of her methods. But his face bore a look that gave weight to his words so that it seemed he really did think she was doing the right thing.

'Thank you, Dagla Kaz. It helps to know that you feel it unwise to risk pregnancy on the pilgrimage.'

'Only a zealot would deny the sense of your actions. Such precautions are to the advantage of all on this pilgrimage. In fact, I shall make sure all the others who may be at risk share your methods. Perhaps you'll instruct those less knowledgeable, my dear? It will make joining so much more pleasurable for all of us, don't you think?'

She did, but the way he said it made her sure he was giving her a message about joining with her. She merely nodded and looked away; more than uncomfortable at the thought. Perhaps it was time to make it public knowledge that she thought he was her father. But she'd have to speak to Aglydron first, or he might feel slighted and insulted.

The High Priest touched her bare arm softly, stroking his fingers from shoulder to elbow, before he nodded at her, smiled, and walked off to talk to the High Priest from Litkala.

'Really worries you, doesn't he?'

'He wants to join with me, Okkyntalah. How can I prevent him? I must tell Aglydron, then I can let everyone know of our relationship. Once it's public knowledge, he's unlikely to join with me, as his daughter, don't you think?'

'I hope so. But he's determined when he wants something. Speak to Aglydron and tell him your worries. Even if he won't believe you're not his daughter, you might make him see that telling others would save you from being his consort.'

'Consort? That's too much to bear. I was expecting just a simple joining; an older man taking advantage of a younger woman, that's all. You think he really wants me for his consort?'

'Wouldn't surprise me. I hate the thought. But he's used to getting his own way, Tumalind. I think telling everyone he's your father is our best chance of stopping him taking you.'

Tumalind realised that Okkyntalah's earlier words had already come true: her concerns for the stranger who'd screamed in the night had already diminished under the anxiety about her own situation.

❖ ❖

'How in the world do you know, Irrildys?'

'I'm the link, Shoarhn, with another group. I was told by one of them. And she was told by a runner from Krohtl. Word's now out to all the Few. We're all ready to start on the Cause at last.'

Shoarhn glanced at this woman she knew from her group; a woman she'd known as a fellow trader all her adult life. They'd never been friends and had had little to do with each other. But, if she was the link, then she deserved at least the respect she'd never been given as a Follower. In a society where promiscuous behaviour was actively encouraged by priests and Holy Ones, Irrildys had always been an enthusiast. It was said she'd had more partners even than the village priest.

'You might as well put your tabard back on. There's no man here, you know.'

Irrildys shrugged, making her breasts bounce. 'I don't go naked in other's houses just for men to desire me, Shoarhn. It's how I'd like to be all the time. Come the Cause, I'll be without clothes for the rest of my life. Won't you?'

'I'd not really given it any thought, to be honest. There are far more important things I want from the Cause. Being constantly naked wasn't one of my hopes, but it wouldn't worry me either.'

'So, what are we going to do? Aklon has told the groups about the new Skyfire, the real one.'

'Yes. I've seen it. Wondered what it was, to tell the truth, Irrildys. It's already brighter than the other one was at its best. People are talking about a sign in the sky; perhaps we should tell them what we know and see if it helps us spread the cause.'

Irrildys sat, uninvited, and bit into a magrana from the table. 'It's not like there's an army to speak of, not now Aklon's isolated most of them on the Point. We shouldn't have any real fear about...'

'The army's on the point? Was that part of the message?'

'You got friends in the army, Shoarhn?'

'My late friend A'ahl's husband is a high ranking officer. But he's on the mainland with Dagla Kaz, so I'm not worried about him. I've other friends through Caarl, though. I

238

never thought we might lose friends in the Cause, I suppose.'

Irrildys was silent and thoughtful for a moment, before she resumed her attack on Shoarhn's fruit.

'Hungry, are you?'

She blushed, as if suddenly aware of what she was doing. Her hand covered her mouth and she gaped, allowing the part chewed flesh to show.

'Sorry, Shoarhn. I don't know what got into me. The danger, I suppose, now that things have really started. I'm anxious for the children and there's no way my useless man will become one of the Few. He thinks Ytraa and the priesthood are the only reason to be alive. What should we do?'

'Wasn't that part of Aklon's message?'

'He said to take care but make ourselves heard to those we think might welcome the news.'

'I think the first thing we should do is let everyone know about the new Skyfire. If we tell them and they see it grow, as Aklon says it will, quite quickly, they'll maybe be more willing to believe us when we start to spread the truth about Gadhallah and the Followers of Ytraa.'

Irrildys nodded. They decided which of the Few each of them should approach with the news. Irrildys had taken the message first to Shoarhn, as a near neighbour who she'd begun to know better after A'ahl's funeral.

'Will we start to spread the word yet?'

'I think it's got to be a personal decision how we let others know. I'm going to do it gradually. Just drop the odd bit into conversation here and there and see what sort of reaction I get. With your reputation, you might get quite a few men on our side by adding a few words to the joining, so you reach them at their most receptive.'

Irrildys smiled and brightened at this idea and Shoarhn could see her mind working, her hopes of new partners already coming to the fore. Irrildys went to the door to leave and opened it before Shoarhn reminded her. She giggled and returned to slip her tabard over her head before leaving the house still fastening the two side ties.

Shoarhn awoke the boys and pretended to pray with them. But her mind was on the coming tasks, the danger she might have to face, and the hope that Aklon would soon come to her.

Aglydron sat with his back against the bulwark, shade extending only as far as his knees and sun baking his lower legs against the dry wood deck. Beside him, Chislanda rested against his shoulder, her head touching his so he could feel the movement of her body as she breathed softly in sleep. They'd slept on deck, the cramped quarters no place

239

for rest on this small vessel. But, whilst he was used to the hardship a boat could bring, this was Chislanda's first real voyage by water; her first trip, on the way back from the burned city on stilts had no meaning for her, ill as she'd been. She was feeling the discomfort and the lack of sleep and he did what he could to help her cope with it.

Tumalind approached and crouched before him, squinting into the sun over his shoulder until he gestured her to sit at his other side. He knew she had something to say to him that he might not want to hear, something she'd been trying to tell him for the past two days, as they'd made a slow way upriver. He relented, aware that whatever it was would be best dealt with rather than avoided any longer.

'Out with it, girl.'

She raised her eyebrows and he recalled that, as a wife, she was no longer the girl he'd supervised in childhood. He nodded, acknowledging his mistake.

'I don't know how to say this, Father, without causing you distress. First of all, I need you to know why I'm going to tell you something you won't want to hear.'

He waited, silent and unwilling to encourage what appeared to be bad news.

'You love Chislanda, don't you?'

He nodded, puzzled by the direction of her talk.

'You'd prefer not to join with anyone else, and for her not to have to join with others, I think.'

'We must do as Ytraa decrees, Tumalind. Our desires and hopes are as nothing when set against the wishes of Ytraa.'

'I know, father. But I'm right in what I say, aren't I?'

'I'd prefer that, if it were possible. Yes.'

'So you understand the desire for a couple to be exclusive, the way that many are in Litkala, where they're also Followers?'

'I'm not blind, Tumalind. I know you and Okkyntalah only wish to join with each other, but if another wishes to join with you, you can't refuse. You can only tell them your worship's completed with your chosen partner. No one can take you against your will, so I think...'

'Except the High Priest.' Her words brought him to a halt.

'You think Dagla Kaz wants to join with you?'

'Not simply join, father. He wants me as his consort.'

He nodded. Such a situation would make life very hard for both of them. He understood about love now. His own rested her head on his shoulder and he knew it would break his heart to have to give her to another man, even for a single joining; how he'd cope if she were chosen as consort for a priest he didn't know. But that was the way. Followers of Ytraa did what was required of them. They always had and always would,

240

especially with the real Skyfire now so bright and promising to bring such glory to the faithful, such destruction to the sinners.

'I can't do anything for you in this, daughter. Though I feel for you. If that's what the High Priest decides, you've no choice but to obey him. As your father I can say no more than that.'

'What if you weren't my father? What if Dagla Kaz fathered me with mother on the Plains of Ytraa, on the day you so zealously beat a woman who'd been his consort and who'd upset him in some way you never knew?'

It was too much to take in. What was the girl saying?

'Mother told me she always thought my father was Dagla Kaz, because of the colour of my eyes. He took her, as Ytraa, whilst she prayed on the Plains of Ytraa. She said she'd been blessed by Ytraa but that, since the blessing wasn't as pleasant as it was with you, when she saw Dagla Kaz walking away, still unclothed, she believed it had been he who'd implanted seed within her.'

Too much. This was too much to take in. The accusation from his daughter and wife of the High Priest's actions. The blasphemy that put a human being in the place where only Ytraa should've been. The fact that Tumalind said such things out loud. It was rumoured, talked about behind closed doors by the irreligious; this idea that a Follower blessed by Ytraa during prayer might've actually been joined by a priest or Holy One acting on behalf of Ytraa. But no one would suggest such a thing openly. It wasn't what the priests and Holy Ones said. Such a joining was the blessing of Ytraa in human form, and that was different from what Tumalind suggested. What she said made it sound like the High Priest had taken advantage of his wife for his own pleasure.

'No. No, I won't believe it, Tumalind. I won't denounce you, to have you hung in a beating bag and whipped. But I won't believe it, either.'

Tumalind nodded, as if this was what she had expected.

'I ask you one thing only then, father. If you gave me life, why do my eyes exactly match those of the High Priest and not yours?'

She rose and smoothed down her tabard. He looked up and saw the beautiful woman who was his daughter and, even as she turned to leave, wondered if he could have fathered such a woman. Shoarhn was beautiful. But Tumalind was as startling as the High Priest's daughter, Jodisa. No. He wouldn't consider such a thing. It wasn't possible. He was her father, not the High Priest. He'd never admit to what she'd suggested.

Chapter 25

CONSULTATIONS

*T*hree days, travelling mostly by daylight, took Aklon and his companions to the capital. The other two stayed the night in his secret cave until he'd scouted the city and learned the news from members of the Few. The loss of the army and humiliation of Wendarah and the Holy One had made a profound impact on the general population. That his announcement at Pampahn reached the port shortly before he got there, delivered by one of the Few acting as a runner, made the city ripe for further activity from him.

But how best to capitalise on the mood of indecision and confusion? He needed to consult Ivdulon before he took any precipitous steps. His action in Pampahn had nearly turned into disaster and he could not afford another error like that. He recalled the wise woman's words about how easy it would be to cause a rebellion that might turn to violence and kill many people on both sides of the argument. He wondered if he should now seek material help from Litkala, in the form of an army contingent to help control forces of dissent that would inevitably accompany his moves to force change on the population. He had the people from the Point to turn to, but felt they'd already suffered more than their fair share and so wanted to spare them the risk of death and injury if possible.

No, he must consult with Ivdulon before he did anything further. He found one of his quiet places, where he could be sure he wouldn't be disturbed, and moved his thoughts into the void to find that fruitful and wise mind from the distant city.

'Aklon, to what do I owe this pleasure?'

Where to start? How to explain his doubts and his needs?

'I see you're alone and I feel you're troubled. If it's hard to know where to start, simply tell me of your worries.'

'You always know what to say, Ivdulon. Always manage to set my mind at rest. I am troubled. I am perplexed. I am full of doubt.'

He described what had happened at Pampahn, how he felt he'd placed Porlesah in serious danger because he hadn't thought through the consequences of his actions before he had made the announcement.

'This thing that we do was never going to be easy, Aklon. It was always fraught with danger, subject to the unexpected, full of threat. But that doesn't mean we should delay or put off the time when the moment arrives for action. It may be that your announcement at

Pampahn could've been handled slightly better, but it had the desired effect and resulted in a positive move forward. Your beautiful priestess remains in her post, as a figure of authority you can use to gently spread the changes we envisage, so no harm has come from your action. You worry too much and about the wrong things.

'You're now outside the capital city of your small island, wondering how to make the best of the developing situation there. If you seek my advice on how to move forward here, I'd say that your watchword is caution. Bold moves here will subject both you and your followers to unnecessary dangers. Subtlety is all in this phase of the action.'

'So, I do what, Ivdulon?'

'Use your stealth to visit and inspire all the members of the Few you're able to reach without placing yourself in danger. If an opportunity presents itself for you to do anything to undermine or, better still, ridicule the priests in this place, grasp it with both hands and make the most of it. But I advise against initiating anything precipitate. It's too soon for that. The remains of the army are now gathered in the town. The Holy Ones are alert for signs of dissent from the general population and will quickly quash any signs of uprising. You're not yet sufficient, nor organised enough to defeat the forces that face you for this next, most dangerous, part of the process. Don't overstretch yourself or your forces.'

'I have been cautious and careful for so long, Ivdulon. I long for real action. I long to do something to bring things to a head.'

'Yes, and if you do, you may destroy everything we've worked so hard to achieve, and die in the process. Patience is what I counsel; for a little while longer.'

'I wondered if you might persuade Feldrark to let me have a small fighting force; some troops to help me keep order whilst the changes take place?'

'That's something we may do in a short while. But not yet. For you to succeed in what we intend it's best you're seen by your people to have done the essential work yourself, without outside help. If we interfere now, the people may resent you for bringing in what they'll see as invading troops to support you. You'll lose any goodwill you might build and ruin any chance of a quick resolution into peace.'

'As ever, I come to you for answers and find the answers you provide simply raise more questions. Oh, I am not complaining, Ivdulon. What you say is full of merit. I have no argument against your counsel, but I would welcome a simple solution that I could follow with some certainty instead of this continued uncertainty.'

'We all look for settled and simple solutions, Aklon. They're rarely to be found, I'm afraid.'

'Do I interrupt, or may I join in whatever you two are up to?'

'Feldrark, welcome. Are you alone or is your paramour yet beside you?'

'I'm here as well, Ivdulon. Aklon, how are things on the island?'

'Jodisa, I have begun the Cause in earnest. Ivdulon's advice about the real Skyfire has provided me with a tool I can employ as a way of convincing the population that there are things I know that they do not. My prediction that the Skyfire will grow rapidly into a bright and terrifying omen is set to make the people see me in a different light, if you will forgive the pun. Feldrark, I was in the process of asking Ivdulon for her help in persuading you to send me some forces to aid me, but she has, as always, given advice against that I cannot ignore or deny. Perhaps, however, you will give some thought to such assistance for the future?'

'Bearing in mind the fact that what we do is going to damage Jodisa's father irreparably, I feel the need to consult her and ask for her consent in that, Aklon. To send troops against her own people is something I couldn't contemplate otherwise.'

'Consider the consultation over, Feldrark, my love. I've long known my father's way was wrong and Aklon's right. I simply didn't have the courage, or the wish, to see my own future damaged to let me publicly support my brother. I leave it to you and he to decide what you should do in this, and when.'

'Thank you, sister. I will do all I can to make the changes peaceful and with as little bloodshed as possible, though the army and Wendarah have already made that difficult, of course. Had father been a little less determined to have his own way, we might have been able to start this movement with less opposition.'

'Father's always been selfish and obsessive about his position on the island. It's why he's decided to continue the pilgrimage even when he knows Gadhallah's claims are false. He's not concerned about what's right or wrong, only about how he can gain personally from any situation. I'll tell you all here and now a secret I've held for too long...'

'Hello? Ivdulon? Are you there, please? I need some advice?'

'Tumalind. Welcome. You find me in conversation with Aklon, Feldrark and Jodisa. Are you in a position to wait until we've concluded, or is your need urgent?'

'Not urgent, Ivdulon.'

They all greeted one another.

'I can withdraw if what you wish to discuss doesn't concern me.'

'I can't tell, Tumalind. Jodisa was about to reveal a secret. It's probably best if she decides who should and shouldn't hear it.'

'Tumalind, you of all people, deserve to hear what I have to confess. Please be patient with me, for what I have to tell you is shameful and doesn't reflect well on me. I ask your understanding and forgiveness.'

'Sure you want to do this, Jodisa?'

'I must, Feldrark. And now. It's waited too long.'

Aklon felt he could almost hear her draw a deep breath in preparation.

'You all know that I was with child once and that the infant was dragged from me unformed, and the father tortured and killed.'

There was silence as they all acknowledged that tragedy.

'What none of you, what no one else knows, is that the father was not murdered. Because the father was Dagla Kaz.'

The silence that followed this announcement was tangible and prolonged. It was broken at last by Tumalind.

'I'm so sorry to hear that, Jodisa. But not as surprised as you might imagine. The way Dagla Kaz looks at me and the way I've feared he'll join with me even though he knows I'm also his daughter, was the reason for my connection today. Your revelation's made that enquiry pointless. I grieve for you, Jodisa, truly. But I now fear more for my own situation.'

'This is dreadful. I feel for you, my sister. I believe we all understand that in this you were not a willing partner. Your part in this was therefore not your fault. And I, for one, place no blame on you at all.'

'Is Aklon right, Jodisa?'

'Yes, Ivdulon. I had no choice.'

'Then I, also, attach no blame to you, Jodisa.'

'My love, you should've told me before the monster was allowed to leave the city in charge of so many innocents. I might then have spared Tumalind her fears, at least. We must let Rrildyss Kaz know; perhaps there's some way she can prevail on Dagla to stop him taking advantage of your availability, Tumalind. I'll do that presently.'

'A good move, Feldrark. I'll also prevail on her.'

'You can try. But I'll warn you, Tumalind, once my father has a desire, he's determined to satisfy it. You may not be able to prevent him forcing himself on you. Would that we could use mindtalk to somehow prevent him.'

'Absolutely not, Jodisa! I'm sorry, Tumalind, but more than your personal comfort and feelings rest on this. It's vital, crucial, that Dagla Kaz remain unaware of the existence of mindtalk, let alone his potential to use it. Any suggestion to him could place the lives of thousands in danger. I can't explain why at present, it's too soon. But please believe me when I say that his ignorance is pivotal to the future for countless people, perhaps the peace of our entire world. Can I have your word that none of you will tell him or attempt to use mindtalk in any way that involves Dagla Kaz?'

In their separate ways, they all agreed to Ivdulon's request. After Jodisa's revelation the conversation slowly died until Aklon withdrew to allow the wise woman to give comfort and advice to Jodisa on her own.

Aklon maintained contact with Tumalind for a while, initially giving her some comfort but eventually asking her for a report on the state of affairs on the pilgrimage. She explained their current situation and how they'd reached the stage they were at and he left her with an invitation to contact him whenever she wished so that he could, if possible, offer her any help he might.

His own problems were still unresolved, though Ivdulon's advice seemed sound in spite of its opposition to his own desires for immediate action. He returned to the cave to consult with Delbon and Phildrad on a way forward that would place them and the Few in the capital in as little danger as possible whilst they set about the tasks of both increasing numbers and finding ways to discredit the current authorities.

'Why did you choose now to announce this, Jodisa? What happened to make you need to bring potential shame on your head?'

She looked at her husband and gentled him into the seat in the corner of their room before kneeling at his feet so that she looked up into his face. He seemed stern in his confusion and she felt confident that he would understand, having already forgiven her, though it was a hard thing for him to know.

'I chose this time, Feldrark, because I'm once more with child.'

He stared at her without emotion, and she wondered if he'd heard her words.

'It's yours.'

That simple phrase seemed to unlock whatever held him in thrall and he took her hands and raised her to her feet, standing to hold her in an embrace so entire that she felt more secure than she had at any time in her entire life.

'Of course it is, my love. That was never in doubt.'

'I didn't consent.'

He seemed confused again, and then smiled, clearing the sudden anxiety and holding her out at arm's length at the same time.

'I didn't think you had, Jodisa. For me, the incident is done with. How do you now feel about it?

'It's over. Now I've told you all, I no longer want to think about it. I don't know why I protected him for so long, Feldrark. Why would I do that?'

'A parent's hold over a child is a strong thing. We must keep that in mind as ours grow and develop, remembering that a child may do things for a parent it may never even consider for anyone else. Our child, Jodisa. You carry our child.'

'An heir. Yes.'

'Are you past the danger period yet? Can we announce it?'

247

'Three portions is the safe time. I've failed to bleed only twice. Three more sixdays and we can tell the world, I think.'

'I must tell someone. Ivdulon.'

'She already knows. I didn't need to tell her.'

'Remarkable, that woman.'

'Tell Rrildyss Kaz. She can keep a secret, can't she?'

'She can.'

'And you can remind her about me and father whilst you're at it. She might be able to do something to help poor Tumalind.'

The ship, anchored mid-stream, bobbed gently on the current as night slowly enclosed them in its darkness. Tumalind stood alone at the prow, looking down at the slight disturbance as the water broke apart against the ship and gave off dim hints of light there. Her mind was on the news she'd shared with Jodisa. She'd yet to share the news with Okkyntalah and had left him on their shared sleepmat, asking to be left alone for a short while. His look of incomprehension had almost undone her but she'd walked away. She needed time to think and to work out what she would do now.

'Lover's tiff, Tumalind? Perhaps you'd like to make your worship to the great and good Ytraa in my arms tonight instead?'

How could this be? At the very time she was considering how to reject the advances of this vile man, he should turn up and attempt to use her the same way he had his other daughter. He even laid a hand on her bare arm, feeling the flesh and making her shrink away from him, the very idea of such intimacy making her body repulse him absolutely.

'No lover's tiff, Dagla Kaz. Sometimes I feel the need to be alone, that's all. I was hoping for some time on my own. Nothing more.'

'But you will join with me?'

'No, Dagla Kaz. I will not. And, if you make me, if you force me into such a vile coupling, I shall not only tell everybody here that you're my father. I'll tell the whole assembly how you fathered a child on Jodisa and then had the unformed infant dragged from her protesting body and had an innocent man tortured and exiled for your crime. Please leave me alone.'

In the darkness of the prow, where the ship's light cast only the flickering glow of distant candles and oil lamps, his face was hard to see. But she felt his body tense at her threat. To her amazement, he turned, without a word, and stalked away. She felt her fear at her rejection of him slowly fade. Would she have been so courageous had she seen him approaching her, had she had time to guess at his intentions? Was it just that he'd come upon her at precisely the time she was considering his vile behaviour that had given her

248

the courage to reject him so absolutely? And what would he do now?

'You think to insult the High Priest and get away with it, girl? Well, you won't find me so easy to turn away. On your hands and knees, now. Make ready. Or I'll cut off your breath and toss your worthless carcass in the river. You're not a Virgin Gift now, to be so precious. Take your tabard off and give yourself to me. Or I'll take you by whatever force I deem necessary.'

He'd approached so quickly. So quietly. And she knew this was revenge from Dagla Kaz; to send the only other man she feared in the party.

'You tried once before, Tryonta. When I lay paralyzed and helpless. But for Corphanda, you'd have raped me there and then. Don't use the High Priest as your excuse. You need none. You've wanted me since the day we met. I saw it in your eyes. But your want isn't wholesome; there's no worship of our God in it. You lust for me to use and overpower me, no more. Well, I won't give myself to you and you won't cow me into joining with you.'

She saw movement just in time to escape the blow to her face but his hand struck her head and she cried out. Her reaction was to strike him, catching his face with her nails. He enclosed her then, his strong arms holding hers close to her body so she could no longer fight him that way. She knew it was a matter of moments before he would have her at his mercy.

'Okkyntalah, come and look at this, my love.'

Tryonta was so taken aback by the calm of her request, and by the words she used, he actually released her. Okkyntalah had arrived silently, a moment before. She moved swiftly to her husband and took his hand.

'I'll show you later.'

And she went with him back into the lighted area of the ship, where others could be witness and where her danger from these two men was reduced at least.

'What was that about? I saw Dagla Kaz come from the prow whilst you were there. That's why I came.'

'I knew you'd be watching and alert for me.'

She told him, softly and without any drama, what had happened. And she held him close to stop him going to the High Priest or Tryonta. She told him, also, what Jodisa had explained about her unborn child. He was appalled and held her, comforting her as only he could. But silent and tense.

'Should we tell the others, do you think?' Her question seemed to break his need to consider.

'Yes. We should let as many know as we can. The more people who know the truth, the better. That way, they'll understand if either of them puts you in a position where you're forced to reject them publicly.'

'Thank you, Okkyntalah. I knew you'd agree with me. But I hadn't expected you to come to the same conclusion so quickly.'

'You think me too dull to realise that you…?'

'No. I thought your first reaction might be to fight. And that would never do; not here, not under these circumstances. Though, I wouldn't mind if you did Tryonta serious harm, I have to confess.'

He embraced her with his love. She knew he'd never allow her to come to any harm whilst he was in a position to defend her.

'We'll have to be on our guard, Okkyntalah. The High Priest isn't a man to cross. And Tryonta, from what I've heard from others, is used to making sure Dagla Kaz gets what he wants. I wouldn't put it past them to devise some sort of scheme to separate us just so he can have his way with me. And I don't think Tryonta could be stopped from having me afterwards, no matter how I felt. I need you to stay calm and alert around me, Okkyntalah, to protect me. But who's going to protect you, my love?'

'I'm big enough to take care of myself. Dagla Kaz is an old man and I've no fear of him in a physical sense. Tryonta may be hard and tough, but I've proved myself his equal in battle. I don't fear the man. Don't you worry, Tumalind.'

'I trust you and I know you're brave and able, but Tryonta isn't one to fight fair, you know. If he can find a way to wound you from behind, he will. I don't think he has any respect for Ytraa at all. You'll have to keep your wits about you. So will I.'

'We'll keep each other safe. I won't let you be harmed in any way.'

She knew he meant what he said, but she also knew he was just one common man against an enemy with power and resources, against two men who were unscrupulous and who would use whatever means they could to have their way. Okkyntalah's life would be no obstacle to them, and her own concerns would be of no matter at all. From now on, they must stay in each other's sight, or risk dishonour for one and death for the other.

Chapter 26

A THREAT MADE

Okkyntalah watched the High Priest approach Myllthlan and escort her to his private quarters. He hoped she wouldn't suffer the cruelty the High Priest was rumoured to inflict on unwilling partners. But there was nothing he could do to help her in this, and at least she seemed to go willingly. Perhaps her experience on Ylcrat, where she'd been a sex slave in all but name, would allow her to more easily perform whatever acts he required.

Tryonta gathered one of the crew members, who seemed bemused but compliant, and took her past them, to a private place. Okkyntalah had thought all the crew members were inclined toward their more heathen practice with other women, but she appeared content enough to be with the man. He couldn't concern himself with her.

All his attention was for his wife. No matter what might happen, he wouldn't allow Tumalind to be harmed in any way. If that meant killing Tryonta, or even the High Priest, then that's what he'd do.

He considered what Tumalind had told him about Jodisa and her father. Rape was an offence so dreadful that no proper Follower would ever contemplate it. For the High Priest to rape his own daughter and make her with child, and all that came after this perversion, was beyond comprehension. It placed Dagla Kaz in an entirely different light, of course. How could he respect such a criminal? The man who led them on a sacred mission had violated every law that mattered. And now he wanted to do the same to his other daughter, to Tumalind. Okkyntalah would stop him. But, if the High Priest made a public declaration that he was taking Tumalind as his consort, what could he really do, short of murdering the man?

And Tryonta? It was rumoured he'd killed for the High Priest, and Tumalind had said she was certain he would've raped her on two occasions now, but for the intervention of others. This was the High Priest's trusted henchman, and the worst sort of sinner.

Okkyntalah was desperate to keep Tumalind safe, but could think of nothing, apart from killing them. And that would make him a criminal. He'd lose Tumalind and she'd lose him, to torture and death for the crime.

Now that they'd made their intentions clear, it struck Okkyntalah they were likely to act on them sooner rather than later. It gave him little time to devise a plan, to form a scheme that might resolve this situation. He knew he must act, and act now, if they were to escape harm.

251

Escape.

That was the answer. The only answer. They must leave the pilgrimage and...go where? To Litkala. Of course. He could fend for them on the journey; his hunting skills would keep them fed and he knew how to live in the wild. It would be hard on Tumalind, but she'd prefer hardship with him to the fate awaiting her aboard this ship.

Would the High Priest send others after them? Possibly; but he could afford no more than two, and one would probably be Tryonta. He'd have no qualms about killing that snake in the wild. What would happen to them when they arrived back at the city? Tumalind had told him that Jodisa had informed Feldrark as well. So they were likely to be welcomed back with open arms. They might even stay there until the rest of the island party returned, and go back to...No, that wouldn't work. They'd have to avoid Dagla Kaz for the rest of their lives, or at least his.

Could they live in Litkala, perhaps? Should they try? Tumalind would miss her mother. They wouldn't enjoy the life they'd dreamed of; raising a family in their home next to Shoarhn. But, they could raise children in the city. He could find employment of some sort. Maybe he could continue to hunt, or learn to take on the same role as Sondukal. That would take him away from Tumalind more frequently than he wanted, but it was a possible answer to their problems.

What would happen when Dagla Kaz came back with the Godwood? Would he demand that Feldrark return the pair to the party for execution? Would Feldrark even consider such a thing?

And would Tumalind consider escaping? Could she bring herself to disobey in such an irredeemable way?

'Why not ask me, Okkyntalah?'

He sat up, surprised at her sudden question; as if she'd read his mind.

'It's obvious you're planning, and the trouble you feel is written plain on your beautiful face. Tell me.'

Of course. Better to ask her and discuss the options than to wallow in a mire of questions with no answers.

He whispered his idea to her and watched shock turn to mere surprise and then to consideration. That she didn't reject his plan out of hand was a good start. At least she was willing to consider the idea.

The night about them settled into silence, with only the soft slap of the river waves on the hull of the ship to compete with sounds of breathing on deck and the shrill of night insects on the distant shore. Tumalind took his hand and urged him from the crowded deck to the stern, where only a single member of the crew stood by the wheel, on lone watch for the night. The space beyond her was devoid of others and they easily found a place they could converse in tones a little louder than a whisper.

'I can find answers to the questions about Litkala. Mindtalk with Feldrark will uncover his feelings before we leave. But I'll have to wait for them to wake before I can do that. How soon do you think we should make our escape?'

'Now they've made their wishes clear, they'll act very soon. Maybe even tomorrow. If we're going to do this thing, we need to do it tonight. Now, in fact.'

'We'll have to swim the river in the dark. Are there dangers in the water?'

'The current's strong, but it'll take us down the way we want to go anyway. There might be crocodiles, but I haven't seen any sign of them whilst we've been sailing and I think I would've if they were present. The real danger is that we won't be able to see much and might get caught up in floating stuff as we swim toward the bank. And the bank itself might be difficult to climb in the dark.'

'But if we stay, Dagla Kaz will take me. You'll feel forced to take action to stop him. That means certain death for you, Okkyntalah. I can't stand the idea of that man penetrating me. He's evil. And Tryonta will do everything he can to have me once the High Priest's taken me from you. I know he will. So, I think you're right. We have to go tonight. We must gather what we can carry and slip into the water in the dark. I can't see any other way. Once we're away from the ship, I'll contact Feldrark and see what he feels about us returning to the city. If he isn't in favour, we'll just have to make our way to Shorrannon and find a new life there.'

'We'll do it. Let's go back and collect what we can carry.'

'What brings you two here so late? Hoping for a quiet place to join in private?'

He felt Tumalind jump with surprise but his hunter's instincts had taught him to show no reaction to such shocks and he turned to face the man who stood so near them in the darkness.

'Is that what brings you here, Aglydron? Chislanda with you?'

'She's sleeping. I noticed your sleepsacks were empty and came for you. The High Priest's on the prowl and seems to be looking for you, Tumalind. It's your duty to do his bidding, whether you wish it or not.'

'There's no way I'm letting that...'

'You're right, of course, Father. But, if I'm to be his consort, I think I've the right to spend this night with my husband, don't you? I'm sure you'd feel the same, if the High Priest wished to take Chislanda in my place, wouldn't you?'

'I might. But we've got no choice, have we? I'll go back but I won't tell him I found you. Make sure you're ready to submit to his demands come morning, Tumalind. I brought you up to know your duty and I won't be shamed by your disobedience or reluctance.'

Aklon made his way into the abandoned mine, knowing he must now declare his ability to mindtalk and risk ridicule from Delbon and Phildrad. But how else could he let them know what he had learned? Lying to the men now was out of the question.

But, in the end, it came easier than he'd expected. They expressed a little confusion, but there was no question about believing him, so it seemed. In fact, when he considered it, everyone he'd told about this skill had been full of admiration and wonder but none had expressed disbelief. Perhaps the faith itself predisposed Followers to believe the incredible.

They discussed options, worked out what was possible, what was desirable and what they could actually do. There were pockets of the Few in the capital. By now, if the runners the Pampahn Few had sent had done their job, they should all be aware of his announcement in the hill town. Their visit to the first contact would soon determine that, of course.

Before sunrise, they left the mine and travelled through silent streets to the nearest home of a supporter. The woman greeted them and woke her man, also a member. They were fed and offered shelter but warned against explicit action yet.

'We've no idea what Wendarah Kaz will do when she hears about your announcement, as she will very soon, believe me. News travels fast in this town. It might be best for you to lie low for a while, until we can gauge the mood of ordinary folk.'

'How big is the garrison here?'

'Usually four hundred troops. But Wendarah Kaz took at least three hundred with her to the Point. Everyone seems to know they're not coming back and there'll be some partners out for your blood, Aklon, just because of that.'

'We should spread word that most of them are with the lot from the Point. Tell the population they've joined the Cause since they saw how sensible it was.'

'An interesting idea, Delbon. But my whole reason for engaging in this task is my concern that people should learn the truth. I cannot teach them that if I start with a lie.'

'You mightn't, Aklon. But there's nowt to stop us feedin' them a little bit of truth instead of all on it. Tell 'em there were converts at the Point. Add to that that none of 'em 'ave come 'ome an' let them make up their own stories.'

'Phildrad, you're remarkable. When we have completed our task, I shall have to warn the people against electing you a spokesman; you have all the qualities my father would expect from one of his own.'

'It's a good idea, Aklon. You may need to remain true and fixed. But the rest of us have families and friends to consider. We can spread word without involving you. In fact, I think we have to.'

He stood in silent surprise as the woman sheltering them turned away and gave the names and addresses of contacts with two groups of the Few she knew. Delbon left without a word and Phildrad gave Aklon a look of mild regret before he went to find the other named contact.

So it began. Aklon had always known he would have to rely on others come the time for real action. Now it was here and events had governed that action. It was not the way he would have chosen, but it was begun and would undoubtedly progress the Cause. He must accept that they would have to employ some subterfuge in order to achieve their goal. But it sat unhappily with him and he made no secret it was not what he wanted.

'I say again, Aklon, you've no one to lose but the Few in this. We, though, have families and friends to think about. There are some things we'll have to do simply because you can't and won't do them yourself. Now, breakfast?'

He accepted her assessment and her offer, eating with her alone as her husband went off in search of other group members with the news. It alarmed him to learn how many other members these two knew between them. This was not the safe and secure system of isolated groups he had originally set up. How many other changes had been made without his consent or knowledge?

'We do what we must, Aklon. You make the rules, sort out strategy, lead the Cause and spread the word of truth. We live our everyday lives under the cloud of fear at being caught and tortured for our sympathy with you and your ideas. We allow you to stay pure so you can remain a figure of respect and trust amongst those who know the truth. You've got to let us do what we must in dangerous and difficult circumstances. Now, you've been on the road for some days, without female company. Would you join with me?'

He was staggered by her analysis of the real situation. She taught him much in her few words.

'I think, if you have no objection, I will spend a little time in quiet contemplation. I have much to think about at the moment.'

She slipped her tabard off and stood before him, enticing. 'That's not like you, Aklon. Or have I suddenly become an old and unattractive hag?'

He glanced up at her and shook his head. Then, catching her expression, studied her more fully. 'You remain a beautiful and desirable woman, Tasallyss.'

'Words, Aklon. Show me you still want me.'

'Do you love your husband?'

'That's an odd question at such a time.'

'And you do not think your response also a little odd?'

She shrugged invitingly. He was stirred. But the physical response, so deeply rooted

255

in habit, custom and necessity, was no longer enough.

'I am in love with a woman, Tasallyss. Against all the odds and in contradiction to my own imposed rules, I have lost my heart to a single woman. I could join with you, that is obvious enough. But I do not wish it. I wish only to join with her. Is that something you can understand?'

'Might be one day. But you're here and I have my needs. It's not all about you, Aklon. And we won't be alone for long, so let's stop the talk and satisfy our needs, eh?'

He knew further refusal would be both churlish and inadvisable. He was a guest, a dangerous guest, in this woman's house. He had enthusiastically joined with her on more than one occasion. To fail to please her now would not only be an insult to her but might even make her question her loyalty. He smiled and took her in his arms.

Afterwards, he lay in thought and, not for the first time, wondered what they were about here on this island. He knew in his heart that being one with Shoarhn was all he really wanted. That he was physically able to share lust with other women had never been a problem in the past. Now it seemed a betrayal, even though he knew that Shoarhn may well be joining with others in his absence. In fact, if he were considerate of her feelings, he should welcome her alternative activity. He should want her to join and satisfy her needs and wants.

But that, he understood now, was what the old faith was about. This casual joining, this promiscuity, so endorsed by Followers, signalled how superficial was their whole approach to one another as human beings. Based on the lies of a man he despised and loathed, it was an expression of the mind of that pervert and bully, that liar and cheat, Gadhallah. But, again, he was forced to admire the man's genius in taking this basic appetite and turning it into a required and central tenet of the religion, which must be obeyed by adherents if they were to express true loyalty to their god. It removed from their minds all doubt about whether such spreading of their sexual wants was right or wrong. It was enshrined in the very fabric of the creed.

Followers of Ytraa joined whenever the opportunity arose, and the partner was not a major concern. It was the act itself, the striving to recreate the oneness that Mhortag had divided. Oh, but it was clever. How absolutely seductive and enrapturing. And, now, he was about to change all that. He was about to tell them all that such behaviour was not right, or was at least questionable. How was he to even start with such conversion? How many were there in the land who felt as he felt for Shoarhn? How many were in love with those they had as partners?

He would soon find out. And then the real work would begin. He had feared the violence and disruption of the Cause. But, in reality, it would be the changes he envisaged to their basic philosophy, their basic way of life, that would be most difficult to achieve.

He turned and saw Tasallyss, raised up on one elbow, looking down into his face with a frown.

'Well, I thought it was good, Aklon. You did what you always do and made me whole again. So what's wrong with you?'

He smiled and, knowing words would not do what he needed them to in this situation, kissed her and showed her what he felt for her again. It was enough this time. But he knew he couldn't do this with all his women. The time was fast approaching when he would be exclusively for Shoarhn. What then for his Cause and the Few?

'Stay here, Tumalind. I'll collect Shaulah and whatever of our belongings we can carry with us.'

'Be quick.'

He kissed her and left. The ship slept. Only the woman at the wheel, on watch, was alert. He smiled at her face in the dim light that spread from the lantern positioned at her feet and she nodded as he passed.

The deck was a maze of bodies in or on top of sleep sacks, belongings piled in haphazard stacks next to those who slept. Aglydron, he noted, had returned to Chislanda and Dagla Kaz was nowhere to be seen; perhaps in his quarters. There was no sign of Tryonta, but that man could be anywhere. The thought had him hurrying to collect what he could as he gentled Shaulah from sleep.

He began to seek out and gather those items that were both portable and necessary, collecting them together into a small pile that would either fit into his pack or could be carried over a shoulder on straps and strings. His work was silent. A sound had him still and alert and he waited in the dark to discover the source. Footsteps approached and a figure moved against the background of the stars. He knew her at once and waited, puzzled.

'Why have you come, Tumalind?'

But she stilled his words with her mouth on his and began to unfasten his tabard as she slipped out of her own. In silence and without explanation, she urged him into their shared sleepsack and held him in a close embrace.

In the silence, her breathing was all he heard until another set of steps followed and he discerned, creeping through the thronged bodies, the shape of a man he recognised.

Tumalind's whispered explanation was only a confirmation of his suspicions.

'How soon after I left did he appear?'

'Very soon. Luckily, I saw movement and guessed it was Tryonta. So I just pretended to follow you back here in the hope he'd suspect nothing. I daren't stay there alone with him so close. Do you suppose he's been spying on us?'

257

'No doubt. You did well, Tumalind. We'll have to await another opportunity. But this places you in danger from the High Priest in the morning.

'I'll deal with that. Can you do something about Tryonta until we escape?'

The only thing he could think of was a direct approach. And he didn't hold out much hope for success in that.

Come morning, following prayers, he sought out Tryonta and engaged him in conversation as he leant against the rail on the larboard side of the boat. A number of the party stood on either side, looking out at the river and the land beyond.

'I can't think of any other way to say this, Tryonta, but you need to know. Tumalind doesn't want to join with you, or anyone else. We've decided to do things the Litkala way and become exclusive. I'd like you to respect that wish, especially Tumalind's. I know you'd never dream of taking any woman against her will, of course.'

The man glared at him, unable to quell the hatred and envy that lurked so close to the surface of his being. But Okkyntalah had placed him in a position where the only acceptable response, in public, was agreement. He nodded briefly and turned away, leaving Okkyntalah certain that his acquiescence was no more than token. It was clear he'd still have to ensure Tumalind was never alone with this man.

As he returned to her, she was also approached, by Dagla Kaz. He watched from a short distance as she greeted the High Priest warmly. Her manner seemed the absolute opposite of what she'd expressed and he was startled by her familiarity with the man.

'Father, good morning.'

Her voice was loud enough for all on deck to hear and it brought silence. Okkyntalah glanced at Aglydron and saw his face cloud with anger but he made no move to deny her claim on the High Priest.

'Father?'

'I'm sorry, Father. Did you wish that to remain secret?'

Dagla Kaz appeared lost for words. He clearly hadn't expected this from her and had nothing prepared to deal with it.

'I apologise if I've offended you by declaring my respect and admiration for the man who brought me life, the man who blessed my mother with his seed to make me the woman I've become. If you'd prefer me not to refer to it again, so be it.'

Okkyntalah was filled with admiration. She'd outwitted the man, placed him in an impossible position. If he denied her claim, he'd be calling her a liar and he must know that everyone in the party knew Tumalind to be absolutely truthful. If he accepted her claim he couldn't be seen to lust after her.

'My child, how could I be other than pleased to have you acknowledge our relationship? I'm merely surprised that you chose this particular moment to announce the fact and did so without warning me. I was caught unawares, that's all. I am, of course, happy to acknowledge you as a child of my loins. I have many, of course, but your close similarity to Jodisa, who was my heir, marks you as special. Certainly, it's unlikely you would gain your intelligence or beauty from the man who married your mother.'

So, that was how he would punish her; make Aglydron the object of ridicule and hope to place a wedge between them. By way of public demonstration of their bond, he took her in his arms and bent close, whispered something in her ear. Okkyntalah had little doubt that his words were far from affectionate.

Tumalind gave him a brief bow when he released her and came straight over to Okkyntalah, ignoring the hubbub her announcement had caused on deck. He embraced her and praised her bravery and cleverness.

'We have to escape, Okkyntalah. And soon. He's made it clear I've angered him very greatly and he isn't going to take it lightly. He and Tryonta will do whatever they can to make life very hard for both of us. We're now in danger of death at their hands. We've got to get away as soon as possible. And I've no doubt they'll be watching for us to do exactly that.'

Chapter 27

INTO THE WILD

The land had slowly risen in rounded hills to their west and the river now widened and opened up before them. This was the southern end of the Lake of the Lost. To the east, the land continued flat and grew marshy; tall stands of rushes waved in a gentle breeze from the north. The prevailing wind had slowed their progress and they were pleased to be out of the current at last and on the less difficult waters of the lake.

Dagla Kaz wandered the deck like a tethered stripecat. His face was dark with thunder after Tumalind's announcement and he spent many hours talking with Tryonta. She knew they must escape very soon or face the consequences. It had been necessary to stall Dagla Kaz and make his advances difficult. But his threat, whispered as he embraced her and allowed his fingers to probe her flesh in a most unfatherly way, had been as explicit as it could be.

'You'll bend to my will as and when I require and say nothing to anyone about what we will do together.'

Okkyntalah had been as concerned as she knew he must be when she told him. During the day they spent odd moments selecting items; always conscious of eyes on them and careful to avoid giving clues to their plans. But, out in the lake, they seemed far from the bank and the swim grew longer with each passing league.

Tumalind approached Corphanda and chatted to her, complementing her care for her charges.

'They're good lasses; even Porryh seems to 'ave come to 'er senses at last. You're enjoying your freedom with yon lad, I notice. And why shouldn't you?'

'I know. I've been very lucky, haven't I? I do feel sorry for the girls, though. I bet they must be sick of being on this ship, so confined after everything else they've sacrificed. Seems such a shame they can't have a bit of freedom to wander on land again for a while, take their minds off the coming ordeal they face in Kah-Labaz.'

Corphanda agreed and they spent a little time in continued chat until Tumalind noticed her father and mentioned she had some words she needed to share with him. The portly lady understood and happily released her.

Aglydron, as she expected, snubbed her as she approached him. But she forced her way into his attention by facing him and addressing him even though he turned his back.

'Would you have me permit the man who fathered me join with me? You don't see such a union as against your precious laws?'

261

That grabbed his attention. He turned on her and made to slap her for her insolence but she dodged back and her expression clearly made him think better of pursuing such a show of force in public.

'You've shamed me, girl. How can you be certain he fathered you and not I?'

She pointed to her eyes; her hair. 'In any case, mother told me.'

He clearly wanted to argue but her assertion was too much for him to deny. He was full of mixed emotions and embarrassed by his inability to accept the truth. She could see the emotions chase each other across his face and she felt pity for this man who'd raised and cared for her all her young life.

'I never wanted to hurt you, father. But I couldn't let the High Priest sin with me, could I?'

He stared at her as he might a stranger, but there was admiration in his eyes and his nod was more than mere agreement. She understood that she was, at least, no longer blamed. Forgiveness might take longer to achieve, however. It was enough for now.

As she returned to Okkyntalah for the evening meal, she watched Corphanda approach the High Priest. She gripped her husband's hand as the woman spoke, loudly, to the leader of the party, hoping her seed had been planted in fertile land. The portly lady did not disappoint her.

'Now then, Dagla Kaz, is it too much to ask that we spend the night on shore for once? My girls 'ave enough of a sacrifice to make without havin' to spend every night on a floating, bouncing deck.'

Tumalind saw the anger on the High Priest's face and wondered if her plan might go awry because of it. She was counting on going ashore so they could at least begin their escape without having to abandon most of their gear for a swim.

'Your complaint is heard, woman. I have no concern at present. See what the captain has to say, but leave me to silence.'

Corphanda, of course, was completely unfazed by his brusque manner and went straight off in search of Quyreena. Tumalind smiled at the contrast as the small portly woman stood looking up at the tall captain, like a child pleading with a parent, it seemed. She was too far away to catch all that was said but it seemed the captain had no argument against them finding a place close to shore for the night. But, to her dismay, the boat shifted to turn west.

'What is it, Tumalind? You seem worried.'

She bit her lower lip and took Okkyntalah by the hand so they could talk without being overheard. At the prow, they stood and watched as the coast slowly approached, the breeze making small waves for the boat to cut as it tacked toward the land.

'I was hoping we'd go east, Okkyntalah. That way, the land is flat and deserted.'

'How do you know?'

'Sondukal told me.'

'Full of surprises. So, what's wrong with the western shore? A few hills won't hurt us. In fact, they might help us make our escape more easily.'

'Oh, it's not the landscape or terrain, Okkyntalah. Sondukal says the Imalsu of Tohltaz sometimes send raiding parties into the hills there. They'd be an added danger, that's all.'

'Tohltaz; where's that?'

She pointed to the distant mountains, now growing clearer as they approached the land. Small, soft hills fed down to the coast ahead but they rose, tier on tier, until they became huge mountains, the like of which neither had seen before.

'They live in a dry region the other side of those mountains.'

'So why would they come all this way? What do they want?'

'Sondukal says they lust after pale skinned women for what they call the harem of their leader. A man called the Ul111bard rules the whole region and he has more wives than you could count. I don't understand it, but, according to Sondukal, the more wives he has the more powerful and manly his people believe him to be.'

'Sounds like a story for children.'

'I agree. But he was quite firm that we should avoid being alone on the western shore if we should land there.'

'When did you speak to him about this? You haven't mentioned anything about our plan…?'

'Do you think me a fool, Okkyntalah? I speak with everyone, as you know. I like to learn about the lands we're travelling. I spoke to him when we were walking the forest road, in the Greenreald, and asked him what he knew about the lands we were due to visit.'

'You're amazing, Tumalind. Truly amazing.'

'Interested, that's all. But Sondukal seemed quite concerned about these men from what he called the desert.'

'Yes, but he also warned us about the Bruxa and we never saw anything of them, did we? And I've been across that land twice now. No sign of them on either occasion. I think he just likes to make his position as guide more important by pretending he has to defend us from things that don't actually exist.'

'You might be right. But we'll have to be careful if we do go that way.'

'We'd better go back. Don't want people think we're plotting anything.'

They kissed for comfort and returned to the company on deck. Already, they could smell the land they approached. Faint traces of wood smoke reached them, along with the aromas of cooking food and animal smells. Okkyntalah shaded his eyes.

'There's a small village just to the north. But we don't seem to be making for it. Wonder why.'

'I'll tell you why, lad.' Quyreena placed her arm about his shoulders, tall as him and standing close enough that he could feel her warm skin against his own, smell the woman in her.

'They're an unfriendly lot around this lake, especially this end. Suspicious of strangers. But they'll leave us alone as long as we leave them alone. Funny folk. Keep their women almost locked up like prisoners, by all accounts.'

'Because of raids from Tohltaz?'

She laughed; loud and derisive. 'Tales told to make the children frightened. You don't want to pay no heed to such stories, lad. Too far from that sandy place and a great range of mountains in the way. No. Those are just rumours.'

And she wandered off to the place where the wheel was being turned by a crew woman.

Tumalind watched the woman with surprise. 'I hope she's right.'

'She seems quite certain, anyway.'

*

'I'll burst if I don't tell someone, Feldrark.'

'I thought you were going to tell Rrildyss Kaz?'

She gave him a look he'd started to understand. 'She's not someone I feel comfortable confiding in, to be honest.'

He nodded; the High Priest had a reputation for gossip, though he was fairly certain she wouldn't share a secret like this, until it was officially recognised.

'Too early to make an announcement here. Speak to your twin. She's far enough away to be of no concern and she'll be as pleased as anyone at your news.'

Jodisa nodded. It would do the job. In any case, it would be interesting to know how they all faired on their pointless pilgrimage. She sat in their bedchamber, Feldrark warm and relaxed beside her after their loving. At peace with the world and full of the excitement the coming event promised. It had been difficult to reverse the work the Holy Ones had performed to prevent unwanted pregnancy, but a little pain and determination had shifted the obstruction. Not that she'd destroyed it. The device would prove valuable in the future, when she'd borne enough heirs for both of them. It would be good to know that Feldrark could join with her as often as they wished and not make her with child again, until she was ready.

She concentrated her mind on Tumalind and found her distracted but accessible.

'Can you talk? Not joining with your delightful man, are you?'

264

'No, Jodisa. I'm free to talk for the moment. But not for long. What is it?'

'I was hoping for a bit more of a welcome, but I imagine things are not too easy on the road are they?'

'I'm sorry if I seem a bit distracted, Jodisa. Things have taken a worrying turn. But nothing you need be concerned about. I'll tell you about it later. You clearly have something you want to tell me.'

'You're good at this, Tumalind. I wish we could've spent more time together before you had to go on this fool's errand with my father. Still, we can't always have what we want, can we?'

'I think you've got more or less everything you want, haven't you? And I'm pleased for you. It's good to know that someone is at least having a good time and doing what they prefer. So, what's your news?'

'I'm pregnant.'

Tumalind was silent for a moment. This was unexpected news, since Jodisa had made it clear she wasn't prepared to have a child until she and Feldrark had had at least a year together.

'Accident, or was it deliberate, Jodisa?'

'Oh, you are clever. I confess, when I removed the barrier, I expected it to be a few months before anything actually happened; that's what those no good Holy Ones said would be the case. They were wrong. I fell pregnant almost at once.'

'And you're happy?'

'Delighted. So is Feldrark, of course. But I'm too early to make an official announcement. Feldrark won't have the people made excited only to risk them being disappointed if I don't come to full term. You know how easy it is to lose a baby in the early stages.'

'Wants you to wait until you've missed three bleeds, I suppose?'

'Exactly. I knew you'd understand. But it's so hard, carrying this new life and not being able to talk to anyone about it.'

'I envy you, Jodisa. I long to carry Okkyntalah's child. But I daren't let anything happen whilst we're on the journey. Imagine having to give birth out in the open, away from any proper help.'

'Doesn't bear thinking about. What are you using?'

'Something my mother taught me. I've enough to keep me safe for about a year. I don't know what I'll do if we're not back home by then.'

'Let me know before you run out. There are other ways. A little more dangerous than the methods we used on the island, but worth the small risk, I think.'

'Thank you, Jodisa. So, do you want a boy or a girl?'

'Oh, for Feldrark's sake, I think a boy first, don't you?'

'It's what he'd want. Any signs yet?'

'Well, the sickness has started and they do say that means a boy, don't they?'

'They do. I'll pray for you. But now I must go. There are things I need to do but I can't tell you about those just now. I'll talk with you later. I'm pleased for you, Jodisa. And tell Feldrark I'm happy for you both, won't you?'

'You could tell me yourself, Tumalind.'

'Feldrark. I'm so pleased for you. But I must go now, or people will wonder at my silence.'

'How long have you been listening in, you wicked man?'

'Just now. I spoke as soon as I connected. Why?'

'I was talking about you, Feldrark, not to you. Don't want you hearing things that might make you swell-headed.'

'Swell-headed, eh? This do instead?'

She smiled and replied with her body, letting sensation form her response and luxuriating in his passion and love for her.

Okkyntalah sat with his back to the tree on the edge of the small copse and kept his ears alert for possible dangers. So far, the night had been without incident but, in spite of the captain's laughter about raiding parties, there was an air of concern and anxiety in the camp behind them. Aglydron was silent and morose, just a few paces away, his back to another tree, deliberately ignoring him.

He wondered if Dagla Kaz had placed them on watch together because he suspected he and Tumalind might try to escape. Or whether they'd been removed so the High Priest might find Tumalind alone and unguarded. But Tarruss had been kind and friendly enough to act as her guardian for the dark hours and Okkyntalah was confident that neither Dagla Kaz nor Tryonta would try to take her whilst that giant was close. He wondered if she'd let him know their concerns; it would be like Tumalind. The new Tumalind, that is.

Since they'd married, or was it since she'd met that remarkable seer, Ivdulon, or maybe it was her experiences on the long road before they had come together again? But, whatever had caused the change, she was changed. For the better in so many ways. She was a woman; no longer the submissive child he'd seen fearfully following the others into those dark caves beneath Ytraa's Peak after the Choosing.

He knew she had her doubts about the claims Dagla Kaz had made over her false selection, doubts about his communication with Ytraa in the Greenreald. Until this last

266

incident, Okkyntalah had always been prepared to give the High Priest the benefit of the doubt. He'd been schooled all his life to respect and obey the priesthood. But the man's rape of Jodisa and all that followed, his insistence on threatening to take Tumalind and his refusal to do anything about Tryonta's rapacious intent had changed all that. The High Priest was really no more than another man placed in a position of authority for which he appeared to have little merit. He used his position to satisfy his own desires rather than to express his love and respect for their god. Dagla Kaz was not, after all, a good man. And that reflection influenced Okkyntalah's feelings about the whole religion now. He'd discussed it with Tumalind over the last few days, when they'd found space to be alone on the crowded ship and could talk in private.

'I don't see how Dagla Kaz can demand that Aglydron and I, and with us you and Chislanda, go on this pilgrimage when he's guilty of worse crimes than us. I mean, he raped Jodisa and killed her child. Anyone else would've been skinned and roasted by the Holy Ones for just one of those sins. How can he get away with it? It makes me question everything about him.'

'Good. You should question everything, Okkyntalah. And not just about him, but about this whole religion of ours. The more you actually think about it, the more you come to realise there's much that's wrong with it. I find myself questioning Ytraa when I'm at prayer, instead of praising Ytraa, as I should.'

And so it had gone on, with their doubts and questions feeding each other and the answers each provided to the other not the answers they would want true Followers to hear. That they'd been guilty of private blasphemy wasn't in doubt. But their conclusions seemed natural from the lessons they'd learned in life. It was difficult to learn these things, to understand in slow steps that everything you'd been taught to believe, to respect, to fear and to love was based on falsehood and lies.

It was Tumalind's revelations about the things she'd heard from that renegade, Aklon-Dji, that had really damaged their faith. Their initial response had been one of disbelief. But, as she learned more through her mindtalk, and discussed these things with Ivdulon and Feldrark, she came to believe that the High Priest's son must be right after all. It made the fact of Dagla Kaz's fatherhood of her even more difficult to take and hastened their reducing respect for this man with so much power but without the corresponding conscience or honour.

'You're quiet, boy.'

He turned to look across the darkness to Aglydron, visible by starlight under the tree. The man was looking at him, that much he could tell in the dim glow but his expression was hidden.

'I am not a boy, Aglydron. I'm stronger, faster, wiser and harder than you. Don't pick a fight that can only end in your defeat. I've no wish to humiliate the man Tumalind still thinks of as her father no matter that the High Priest's seed made her.'

'She still thinks of me as her father?'

'As you would know if you had the sense to let her speak with you instead of making her miserable with your stupid vanity.'

The man was silent for a while and Okkyntalah concentrated on the sounds of the night about him. Somewhere, too far to discern the details but near enough for him to be certain, a party of men rode horses across the plain from the west. They were approaching slowly, of that he was sure. Not many. Perhaps five or six. But far enough away for their actual destination to be unknown for now.

'I'm a simple man, Okkyntalah. I've my faith and the knowledge the Holy Ones gave me so I could pass on lessons to the children on the island. But my life, until this pilgrimage, has been with my beasts and my trees. I'm too old now to change my ways, even if I wanted.'

'If you're fixed in your ways, it's you who makes the fixing. Any man can change if he wishes to.'

'You're suddenly very wise.' There wasn't the usual sarcasm in that. He said it as if he meant it.

'Think about it, Aglydron. We've sailed together across seas we never knew existed. We've kidnapped a girl and taken her in a stolen boat away from all she loved and expected in her life. We've met magicians and healers who, according to all we've been led to believe, shouldn't exist. We've battled enemies we never even knew we'd made. And we've seen sights through the instruments of that wise woman, Ivdulon, that have proved we've been lied to all our lives. If we're not changed by such experiences, then nothing's going to change us.

'And it isn't true that you're unchanged. You were a pious, unthinking fool when we left the island, your only concern to do the will of Ytraa regardless of the consequences to you, me or Tumalind. But now you sit with me, guarding a camp of pilgrims not for the faith but because you love a woman and wish to ensure her safety. Yes, you've changed, Aglydron. You just don't want to admit it.'

'I've been very unfair to you. Unjust in my ways with Tumalind. I'll let her know I do understand, in the morning.'

'I'll let her know to expect your fatherly approach, then, shall I?'

'Thank you, Okkyntalah. And, I'm sorry. You make a fine daughter-son. I'm proud to have you as my daughter's husband.'

'That makes it easier to be proud of you as my wife-father, Aglydron. Thank you.'

They were silent for a while and Okkyntalah detected the horsemen moving closer.

The moon, waning to its last quarter, rose above the trees and gave more light as a noise from behind alerted them to their replacements on watch. Rehthlynn, the male virgin's keeper, and Wakkyll, the sneering volunteer Virgin Gift from Muhnilahm, came to relieve them. Okkyntalah was grateful for their arrival but not at all confident these two would know what to do if anyone should attempt to enter the camp.

'There's a party of half a dozen horsemen riding from the west. They're about two leagues distant and they're trotting in this general direction. They may not be coming here at all, of course, but you need to keep alert for them.'

'How do you know this?'

Okkyntalah swallowed his contempt for this city man's lack of essential knowledge. 'Listen with your feet. You can feel the steps of their horses in the ground. And, if you remain silent, make your breath silent, you'll hear them. Just be aware of them and let Sondukal know if they approach within half a league.'

He knew the city man and the boy from the island would be incapable of discerning such detail from the clues out there but he wanted to be back with Tumalind in time for them to make their escape before it grew light. He and Aglydron returned to their partners and their shared sleepsacks. Tarruss, ever the gentleman, patted his shoulder and rose to move a discreet distance away.

'Thank you, Tarruss.'

'Young love; wonderful.'

Okkyntalah snuggled close to Tumalind beneath the light cover and felt her response as their skin touched. She shaped herself to be in maximum contact in the dark and listened as he whispered softly to her. They'd planned their escape and this might be their last chance. It meant waiting until they were certain everyone else was sleeping soundly and then creeping from the camp via the shore to avoid the sentries. Though Okkyntalah was fairly certain the two who'd replaced Aglydron and him wouldn't notice if they passed within ten paces.

The sound of the horsemen continued to increase and he wondered how many others could hear them. If they came too close before he and Tumalind were ready, it might ruin their chances of escape.

'I can't hear anything, Okkyntalah. I think you forget we're not all hunters of your experience.'

'Sondukal is, though.' He hoped Dagla Kaz wouldn't send that man after them. He had no wish to kill a man he respected, a man who'd once saved his life. But he would do that if the man tried to prevent their escape. Escape.

He was leading Tumalind into a life that would be hard, lonely and difficult, at least until they reached Litkala. Then they'd have to decide where they would go and how

269

they'd live their lives together. Oh, why had all this happened to them, when all they wanted from life was the chance to be together, raise a family and live in peace in their own home?

Okkyntalah lay down, awake but pretending sleep until the night informed his sense it was safe for them to move. And still came the sounds of the moving horsemen. Now, he estimated, less than a league distant and still coming in their direction. It was enough. He sat and surveyed the camp. No movement, no sound but the breathing of sleepers and the soft natural noises of the night. They must move now or miss this one chance. For, very soon, the horsemen must be audible to even the most unwary amongst them.

He urged Tumalind into movement and she gathered those things they'd readied for this moment. Shaulah rose silently from her rest and the three of them threaded their way amongst the sleepers toward the shore and an unknown future.

Chapter 28

EVASION

*E*arly morning should have taken Aklon and his companions north-east along the road toward Krohtl, for the next phase of their difficult task. If the runners from Pampahn had done their job well, the task would be so much easier. This was so especially now the Skyfire was already bright enough to be causing consternation amongst the general population.

But one piece of information that had reached Aklon's ears was deeply disturbing. He knew he should have expected it, but he had not. Wendarah, it seemed, was not as inexperienced as he'd assumed. She'd sent a small, but capable, force of soldiers to the Point to rescue the rest of the army he'd stranded there.

'We'll do what we did before, Aklon. Go after them and cut them off. Can't be many of them.'

'Eighty, Delbon. And they will be alert to the danger now. We no longer have the advantage of surprise or of their ignorance of our intentions. No, we stand no chance of winning that type of battle. In any case, it appears they have two days start on us.'

'But if we leave them, they'll bring the rest of the army back onto the mainland and then we'll have an even bigger fight on our hands.'

'Can't we, at least' 'arry them a bit? Make the job 'arder for 'em, Aklon? I mean, it seems daft to let 'em just gather the rest of the army to fight agin us, don't it?'

He looked at his two companions with admiration. Their bravery and common sense impressed him. 'We will have to steal horses if we are to have any chance of catching them.'

'I can't ride, Aklon.'

'You can hang on behind me and we'll take three horses so I can swap to keep up our speed.' Delbon grinned at Phildrad's evident discomfort.

'Have it all planned, it seems. Very well. We must do what we must do. Killing and theft. I knew it would be difficult, but I wanted to do this with as little harm to the people as I might. I prefer not to make people suffer. But this is for the common good. Come; if we are to do this thing, we must do it now.'

Their chosen source was a large farm on the outskirts of the city. Before dawn few would be up and about and the three of them should be able to steal the creatures without too much resistance. But they had no time to plan properly or to reconnoitre before they set to work. The horses would be stabled in the low block just to the west of the house and barns. Aklon sent Delbon first to discover what he might before committing all three of them to action.

'There's a dozen horses, each in its own stall. The riding gear's stored with each horse, on a shelf and hooks. There's a dog tethered for warnings and I've seen to that. But we'll need to be quick. It's almost light now and, with livestock, they'll be up early to feed and milk.'

'Lead the way, Delbon.'

Silent as their training and experience had taught them, they entered the yard and crossed to the stable block. There were still no signs of life from the house and the dog Delbon had warned of was a sorry sight with its muzzle bound to prevent it barking and its legs tied to stop it moving to make a noise.

Some of the horses were skittish when they entered but they selected the three that appeared most calm. They were working beasts rather than hunter's horses; bred for plough and cart instead of speed and agility. But they'd take them to their destination faster than they could travel on foot. Aklon saddled a bay and helped prepare a black gelding as the spare, as Delbon readied a chestnut mare. They led the horses from the block and discovered three men standing near the dog, one releasing it. All hope of an undetected escape was lost.

'We must prevent them following us on horseback. Scatter the rest from their stalls.'

Aklon leapt on his chosen steed and took the attention of the three men in the yard, as Delbon held onto the other two horses and Phildrad returned to the stable to set free the loose animals. He'd little enough skill with the beasts, and some fear. But he'd be able to release and chase, shoo or slap them all from the building to run free. Delbon would wait for him and then get him to sit behind him on the chestnut.

Aklon drew no weapon but used his persuasive voice and charm to explain their need for horses, promising to return them as soon as they were able. The men seemed cowed in his presence and became more so as Delbon and Phildrad cantered over. The three galloped away from the farm, leaving hands and farmer dazed and confused by what had happened. Theft and raiding of farmsteads was so rare that they had no experience of it and seemed unable to take in what had happened. But it wouldn't be long before they caught the other horses and decided on whether to go after the robbers.

'We need to ride without a break for as long as the horses will carry us.'

As always, the element of surprise was their most potent weapon against superior numbers and the sooner they could engage the soldiers, the more likely they were to gain some advantage.

Aklon expected the small troop to take the road the whole way, travelling at little more than walking pace as they had wagons with them to carry any wounded and to cart necessary supplies. Wendarah had seen the Point first hand and knew its lack of food and water would render her trapped forces in need of considerable help before they'd form a capable fighting force again.

He took his men across country, cutting off a significant distance from their journey. By nightfall, they were within hearing distance of the place where the first soldiers had camped.

'Stay with the horses and keep them quiet, let them rest and feed; we'll need them again.'

Aklon set off on foot through the trees. If the gods were on their side, the soldiers would still be setting up camp and wouldn't yet have brought any of the troops up from the waste below the Scar. He moved silently through the wooded area, alert for soldiers on watch or patrol. They were unlikely to leave themselves as open to infiltration as the first lot had. Experience, learned from the fate of the others, would make them careful. The loss of the advantage of surprise and ill-prepared troops was a real problem, but he did not see it as an insurmountable barrier as much as an added challenge.

The first man he came upon was still in the trees, his back to a trunk and his mind on the baccy he was feeding into his pipe. Aklon caught the aroma of Eastleaf and knew this was a man of particular taste. It was the island's finest and must have cost the soldier the best part of a week's wages. But it was also known to relax the smoker, perhaps rather too much. He had the man disarmed and a hand around his mouth before the soldier even knew of his presence.

'I have no wish to spill your blood, friend. If I allow you to speak, you will do so only loudly enough to let me hear. Any sound greater than a whisper will bring you instant death. Nod if you understand and agree.'

The man nodded his head.

'Tell me your number and disposition.'

The soldier, the point of the sword at his throat, coughed and spat, missing his target and earning a slight nick that trickled blood down his neck.

'I prefer not to have to ask questions more than once. Time, you understand, is my enemy in this.'

The soldier took a deep breath and Aklon placed his hand over his mouth again.

'My warning threat was meant. You have a final opportunity to save your life. Understood?'

The soldier nodded.

'And agreed this time?'

The soldier nodded again.

'Good.' Aklon removed his hand.

'There are more on us than a rhaat like you can 'andle. We've already sent a party to the settlement to fetch the rest back. There'll be 'undreds on us by this time tomorrow. What you gonna do about that, Renegade?'

'In truth, I don't quite know at present. But I thank you for your information. Now, please kneel so that I may incapacitate you for the remainder of the night.'

'Gonna kill me?'

'Not if you do exactly as I say.'

'Yeah. I'm supposed to just let a 'eretic an' renegade like you truss me like a game bird an' then kill me wi'out a fight?'

'If I were intending to kill you, I would have no need of binding, would I?'

'They said you was a queer one. But I'll not meck it easy for you.'

The soldier moved. Before the man reached the point where he'd have enough force to drive his elbow into his ribs, Aklon sliced the blade across his neck and dropped him. He was dead as he fell. Aklon wiped the blood on the man's tabard and briefly shut his eyes against the despair he felt on killing an unarmed opponent.

He stepped warily through the remaining trees and stood on the edge of the small wood to survey the troops. Their camp was more or less complete and he counted around a dozen separate sentries on post around its perimeter. He would not move into this camp as easily as he had their first.

Informed and prepared, he returned to his companions and led them, and their horses, through the trees to a higher spot above the soldier's campsite and the cave he'd used previously with Phildrad. As before, it was unoccupied and unguarded. It seemed he had managed to keep the place secret. It would do as shelter and base for what they must now do. Though, what, exactly, they could do was unclear for the moment. It certainly wouldn't be as straightforward as his first engagement. This time he may need to kill a lot more before he could call the move a victory. And the risk to him and his companions would be far greater. He wished he had access to the men and women they'd rescued from the Point. But those soldiers dwelt in the safe place he'd led them and were too far off to be any help now.

Tumalind crept silently beside Okkyntalah as he led them from the clearing towards the shore, where small waves lapped the shingle. To the north, a gentle river ran into the lake, making the area boggy and difficult. It was the place he led her and she knew better than to question his decision, though they seemed to be travelling away from their destination. Okkyntalah, she knew, had good reason for his actions. Shaulah trotted beside her, silent and alert under the fading crescent moon.

They'd travelled no more than five hundred paces when a commotion from behind

274

reached her ears. Had they been missed already? Would they be pursued so soon after their escape? If they were caught now, Dagla Kaz would probably have them executed. He couldn't afford to allow his pilgrims to think they could do as they liked.

Okkyntalah grasped her hand and pulled her into the shadows of a small copse of low trees; so low, they were forced to crouch in silence with the dog lying between them.

From the camp the sounds of raised voices and some alarm came to them but there appeared to be no movement in their direction, at least, not yet.

'I don't think it's us. I heard horsemen approaching as we were leaving. I think they must've arrived in the camp.'

'Will the others be safe, Okkyntalah?'

'We can only hope so. We can't go back. Not now. We must save ourselves. We move on the route I've planned. Come. Silent and speedy.'

They moved out of the trees again onto the edge of the marshy area. Okkyntalah led them around reeds and pools of standing water, always moving west, away from the lake and following the line of the river towards the hills, north and west.

He stopped again, a couple of hundred paces further along and listened.

'The row's stopped. I think that means there's no danger. If there was, I'd expect sounds of fighting, and there are none.'

'Your hearing's as remarkable as your sight, Okkyntalah. Nearly as remarkable as your love-making.' She blushed as she realised she'd made that thought aloud. But he merely squeezed her hand and urged her on her way with him.

They travelled as quickly as the fading light from the setting moon would allow, stopping only when the crescent sank behind the mountains and left nothing but starlight and the increasing brightness of the Skyfire to guide them.

'We're distant enough to be safe until dawn, I think. But we must travel all of the coming day and not rest until nightfall. It'll be hard. Can you do that, Tumalind?'

'Of course. Can't we continue now?'

'Too dark. I don't know the land at all and we might come across all sorts of problems. There'll be wild beasts in this hill country and, once we reach the foothills of the mountains, other things might threaten us. No. It's best we rest as well as we may until it begins to grow light. There's a patch of dry ground on the rise here. We'll spread our sleep sacks and spend the time before dawn in rest.'

She was happy for him to lead in this. His experience and knowledge of such matters was far superior to hers. They kept on their tabards, however, as they snuggled together; at any time they may be forced to make a run for it.

Morning roused them with birdsong and they rose into a dawn pink and fresh. Okkyntalah asked her to make a light breakfast from the stores they'd stolen, whilst he surveyed the land ahead. She'd hardly finished her preparations of the cereal and fruit juice before he was back with Shaulah.

'No signs of pursuit. Whatever happened in the night must've hidden our escape I think; for now, at any rate. In any case, only Sondukal is experienced enough to follow and track us along the route I chose and he wouldn't consider setting out until light. We have to make the most of the time advantage we have, Tumalind. We eat and then set off into those mountains at a steady trot.'

'I thought we were going to Shorrannon and then Litkala?'

'So we are.'

'But you're taking us into the mountains; in the opposite direction.'

'I'm proud you noticed, especially under the circumstances, Tumalind. We're setting a false trail. They'll expect us to go south; it's the logical place for us to head. By going this way, we might just give ourselves a better chance of making it to Litkala. It'll take us longer, but at least we shouldn't have to worry about being chased, once we've had a couple of nights away from the main party.'

'Do you think Dagla Kaz will send anyone after us?'

'There's a chance. But he can only spare a couple of people. He won't want to lose Sondukal just now, although he might risk it, I suppose. He's no knowledge of the route beyond Kah-Labaz anyway. But I'm not worried about Sondukal finding us, to be honest. I think, once he knows why we're running away, he'll help rather than try to take us back. But Tryonta might be sent after us. And he's the one I don't want near us. He'll have orders to kill me and…well, what he'll do to you doesn't bear thinking about.'

'Let's eat and be on our way, then. I don't want that man anywhere near me.'

Their meal was swift but nutritious and they set off at a walk for the first league, Okkyntalah seeking out hard ground where he could and making her follow him across rocky outcrops and shale slopes on the steepening hillsides. At each high point, he paused and surveyed the land they'd crossed before turning to study the land ahead.

The river flowed behind them as they wandered steep hills and narrow valleys wooded with tall trees too dense to penetrate. They edged along the spaces where these forests bordered open grassland on the hillsides so that they were rarely on level ground. Around noon, Okkyntalah called a halt and they rested, in the welcome shade of tall trees, drinking tepid water from their carriers. Shaulah amused them, hunting in lush undergrowth between the trees. For a short while they were alone as she disappeared on her hunt. But she soon returned, a small rodent in her jaws. They allowed her time to devour the creature before setting off again.

Okkyntalah climbed ahead now, leading her ever upwards, taking them higher than she'd climbed before. In spite of the exertion, she felt a slight cooling of the air on her skin and recalled Dagla Kaz warning her about how cold it could be in the mountains. These were small in comparison with those they could see ahead to the south west and even more so when she climbed high enough to see the smoking cone of Mount O'bo, many leagues to the north. Beyond, they could see the first outliers of the huge mountain range that Okkyntalah told her was known as the 'Wings of the World'.

'It's an odd name for something as solid as a range of high mountains.'

'I asked Aglydron about it. He said it had puzzled him when the Holy Ones referred to "the distant Homeland, stretched out wide and fertile, between the Wings of the World", in their teachings. But he saw the maps in Dagla Kaz's pit and said there was a range of mountains on one of the maps that looked like the wings of a hawk and he thought those must be the ones they meant, especially as Lake Qonahn lay between them.'

'You never told me this before, Okkyntalah. In fact, you haven't really said a lot about your time with Aglydron and Jodisa and your voyage to Litkala.'

'Same for me, really. I don't know much about your journey to the city. We'll have plenty of time to tell our tales once we're safe. Come on, there's no sign of anyone following. I think we should make our way across the face of this mountain, travelling west and south until we come to the next valley. Then we'll follow that until we reach the plain again. We'll probably have to cross rivers along the way, but we'll find the main River Sure eventually and then keep to it until we reach Shorrannon. It's straightforward from there to Litkala.'

'You're a wonder, Okkyntalah. You make it all sound so simple.'

'No more of a wonder than you, my love. To follow me into an unknown land with no guide and no certainty of food or water. I take that as a great compliment.'

'I trust you, Okkyntalah. I know you'll never let me come to any harm. That, after all, is why we're running away. To keep me from harm. I love you.'

He smiled at her and stopped in his determined striding across the slope of the mountain to take her in his arms and hold her close for a spell. Together, they looked out over the land below. The mountainside sloped down to a small bright river flowing across a wider valley to the east. Above, beyond the immediate slope, the mountain rose higher, its head in a small clump of bright cloud. To the south, slowly emerging as they tacked their way in that direction, a range of low mountains spread before them, criss-crossed by many valleys. From this distance it was impossible to tell how many of those valleys were home to rivers where they could find water. Okkyntalah had warned her that water was their prime concern in the wild. Food he could always find. But water could sometimes be difficult. They must conserve their supplies until they came upon fresh sources.

He kissed her and then led onward, the slope of the mountain making speed difficult, but the grass more inviting than the patches of scree they'd crossed to keep trackers off their scent.

At least now they felt they were relatively safe from pursuit; they'd seen no sign of anyone following them and Okkyntalah, though still alert to such a possibility, seemed more relaxed.

'My guess is they didn't find our tracks where I doubled back in the swamp and made that false trail into the woods and onto the stony slopes. If they've sent out anyone at all, I think they've probably gone in the wrong direction. But we've been gone less than a day and we've travelled maybe four leagues. I won't really be happy until there's forty or more leagues between us.'

'Do we really have that far to travel, Okkyntalah?'

He nodded. 'The journey from here to Litkala must be at least a hundred leagues, maybe a little further.'

She did the simple sum in her head; Jhonaht's lessons on numbers proving she'd not wasted her time. 'So, we can expect to be on the journey for at least twenty five days?'

Okkyntalah frowned at her. 'How d'you work that out?'

She explained. But it was clear the calculation was beyond his comprehension. 'Of course, that's assuming we can travel at around four leagues every day: can we?'

'Not every day. I'll have to hunt, and that'll slow us down. Some days we'll have to rest as well. I'd be happy if we manage to cover three leagues a day.'

'Thirty three days, then, at best. Oh well, I'll be glad of a bed and a bath by then, I expect.'

He looked at her with deep admiration and then laughed at her comment, as she'd hoped he would. 'You're a marvel, Tumalind. No wonder I love you.'

'Do we have to travel further today?'

He shook his head in mock disapproval. 'Wanton.'

'I don't know what you mean.'

He lifted the hem of her tabard and gentled her with his fingers. 'Not now. We'll have time and opportunity when we find a place we can safely spend the dark time. But we must find that first. Sorry.'

She slipped her hand beneath his tabard and clasped him briefly. 'I hope we'll always be like this.'

'Me too. But we'll have to find a safe place before I show you just how much I love you.'

She released him and they set off again. 'I shall hold you to that promise, young man.'

'And I to yours, young and beautiful wanton.'

They managed to walk, scramble and trot hand in hand for another league, ever slowly descending and moving south. By dusk, they'd discovered a shallow vale at the foot of the slope and made their way down together. In all the time they'd travelled, they'd seen and heard no sign of any other human being. But, as they descended the slope, Okkyntalah halted their progress and stared out into the distance.

'What is it?'

'Dust rising. A troop of horsemen. About five or six; but from here I can't be sure. They're too far away. I doubt they're any danger to us. But we must stay alert.'

She could hear the concern in his voice, even if not in his words. Horsemen. More talk of horsemen, perhaps from the land of Tohltaz. For Tohltaz lay just beyond the mountains they were skirting.

Chapter 29

A DEAL IN THE NIGHT

Dagla Kaz awoke to the sound of voices calling, men shouting, women crying out in alarm and horses stamping the ground with impatience. In the darkness, it was at first difficult to follow what was going on but Tarruss took a burning brand from the central fire and used it as a torch to illuminate the scene. Five horsemen sat astride their mounts, outlandish wrappings spiralled into cones around their heads, and multi-coloured strips of fabric fastened to a wide collar to drape their bodies, cinched at the waist with a wide belt of woven leather. Each man bore a long sword hanging from the rear of the saddle and a long bow fastened at his back, a quiver of slender arrows hung from the shoulder.

'What brings you here, into our camp?' The High Priest slipped his tabard over his head as he approached the strangers.

They, in turn, seemed surprised to be upon the camp in the darkness, as if they'd expected this place to be deserted. One stepped out of his stirrups and glided gracefully to the ground, handing the reins to the man next to him.

'You are who?'

'I might ask the same question. We are Followers of Ytraa, travelling this land and resting on our way to Kah-Labaz. What brings you riding so suddenly into our camp at this hour?'

'Your name is what?'

'As to that, I am the High Priest, and leader of this party. Who are you and what do you want here?'

By this time, the rest of the camp, roused and dressed, were slowly gathering around the newcomers. Caarl and Bardrohn rushed up, weapons handy. Dagla Kaz signalled them to sheath their blades.

'I be at the head of these and am called K'ang Fi-Tozu. We expect to find none wander here in this deserted place. If Kah-Labaz is truly where you go, I pity you.' He spat at the High Priest's feet.

Dagla Kaz, uncertain of the import of this gesture, and aware that though they were only five, they were heavily armed, stood his ground but made no complaint. 'Did you intend to camp here? Is that the problem?'

'We travel by night. Fast. You have women, virgin women, we buy? Good prices for fair ones. Most for those with flaming locks.'

281

'We don't sell our women. And our virgins are sacred to our god, Ytraa. We would not have mere men defile them.'

'Women are no more than vessels for the pleasure of men. And virgins are the best for that. Yours will fetch a good price from these men.'

'I see. Less than men. Women are as horse, to trade and to riding. What other use are such creatures? That one, with golden hair; for her I pay you five gold quounds.'

Linlyss wrapped her arms protectively about her as the man pointed at her.

'They're not for sale. At any price.'

'You value too much the goods. They have no purpose but to lie with man and bear children, if they have such fortune. But we will not take them if they are not for sale at this time. We will camp for the last night hours by the lake. Water is scarce in our land and we watch it with hunger. The daylight will bring another offer, but we will not bargain more than their worth. The one with the reddish hair; for her, maybe eight gold quounds.'

'As I said, they are not for sale. None of them are for sale. We do not trade women.'

The man shrugged as though he didn't believe this and led his horse toward the unseen shore. His men followed, their eyes hungry for the young women.

'Well, I hope you'll have no more to do with those heathens, Dagla Kaz. The very idea that we'd sell our girls. Monsters, that's what they are.'

'They'll hear you, Corphanda, and I would rather not antagonise such men.'

'I 'ope they do hear me. Dreadful creatures. Thinking they can buy women like we were some sort of goods at market. Heathen rhaats, that's what they are.'

Dagla Kaz watched the men leave the circle of light and wondered at them. He'd heard of a culture of the dessert where women were used as slaves by the men and where the leader of the land had, it was said, very many wives. But until now he'd thought this a mere tale. He gathered the women into a group and set four men around them. The strangers didn't seem threatening, but he couldn't risk them returning in the night to steal one of the virgins.

Tryonta moved through the Followers and spoke softly to him. 'They've run off, Dagla Kaz. Shall I go after them?'

Dagla Kaz frowned and searched the group, confirming Tryonta's words. So, Tumalind and her husband had escaped under cover of darkness. Had they been gone long?

'You'll never find them in the dark, Tryonta. As soon as it's light, take a look around and see if you can determine which way they've gone.'

'They'll be out of reach if we don't go after them at once.'

'You know where they've gone, Tryonta?'

He shrugged. 'Shorrannon. Where else would they go?'

'Maybe, but by what route? You could pass them in the dark and have them after you. No; wait until morning.'

Tryonta was clearly disappointed but obeyed his wishes, as always. The girl's rejection of his advances had irked the man too much. He wanted nothing but revenge for her refusal. Dagla Kaz felt similarly affronted by her determination not to have him join with her, but it wasn't worth delaying their journey to find her and bring her back. True, it would give them an excuse to kill Okkyntalah and then they'd both force her to do their bidding. But it might take days of searching to discover them unless they'd been foolish enough to travel only a short distance in the dark. No. It was irritating that he wouldn't now have the chance to subject her to his ways, but she wasn't worth a hunting party. If she ever came into his sight again, however, he'd show her the price of her desertion.

There are many ways to punish disobedient women, are there not? Some of them delicious.

'Tryonta. Go to those strangers and describe Tumalind to them. Explain where she's bound and tell them she's virgin, but not likely to be so much longer. Tell them they can have her for nothing if they find her and kill the thief with her. With luck, they'll discover her with the advantage of their horses and she'll be sold as a sex slave to the desert dwellers.'

'Brilliant, Dagla Kaz. Perfect revenge on the girl and her worthless husband. I'll tell them at once.'

Tryonta left camp for the darkness that lay around the lake. Dagla Kaz could only hope his scheme would at least put the girl and her man at risk, and make them regret their disloyalty.

Within moments of Tryonta's disappearance into the darkness, he heard the sound of horses on the move again. It seemed the strangers were even more eager than he'd imagined.

Tryonta returned shortly, his face a picture of contentment. 'They'll hunt the land until they find them. It seems blue eyes and auburn hair are the favourite combination for their leader. If they take such a virgin to him, they'll be handsomely rewarded and given access to some of the wives he no longer wants. Strange culture, but it serves us well, eh?'

'Let's hope so, at any rate, Tryonta. What'll happen to the girl when their leader discovers she isn't virgin after all? With luck, they'll punish her as she deserves, maybe even torture her to death.'

'I hope so. I hope they cause her more pain than a body can stand. May she scream and beg for an end to her life at their hands.'

The High Priest nodded and returned to his sleepsack feeling more satisfied than he had for many days.

'Can't we risk a fire, Okkyntalah? There's been no sign of anyone after us.'

'We're still only just over a day away. But, yes. I suppose so. Gather wood and I'll hunt for a coney or gamebird to cook.'

He went at once, Shaulah following silently as though she were part of him. Alone, Tumalind searched the edge of the forest, collecting loose, dead branches. She arranged the smallest into a rough cone and began to pile some larger pieces around the structure. The sun, still in clear sight, would set in a little while but it remained strong enough for her purpose. Jodisa's burning glass, a gift on parting, slipped readily from the small leather bag that protected it from scratches and she soon had the point of light and heat on the centre of her kindling. It caught quickly, sending small sparks and a column of grey smoke into the sky.

The fire gave her comfort as she sat and awaited Okkyntalah's return. Out here in these wild valleys they'd seen no one. No habitations and no sign that anyone lived or farmed here. It had been both encouraging and unsettling to be the only people in the great landscape. Now, the silence of that solitary existence made her feel vulnerable to wild creatures that might be watching her, unseen, from the trees. She turned her back to the open landscape, resting against the trunk of one of the forest outriders and facing the bulk of the trees across her blazing fire. Okkyntalah would return soon. She pushed a longer length of wood into the flames to form a brand she might use as a weapon, and told herself she was safe out here; she was alone in this wilderness.

She would speak with Ivdulon, that contact would dispel her uncertainties and fears.

'My dear; how good to hear from you.'

The wise woman's presence in her head was comforting, making her forget her solitary condition, and soon they were catching up with each other.

'You know of Jodisa's good news, of course?'

'She told me a few days ago. Is she well, still?'

'The sickness has found her, but that's generally a good sign of course. Otherwise she's thriving. And you? I detect a slight anxiety in you and see you're alone before that fire. I can hear no sign of others around you. Tell me what's passed, Tumalind.'

She described the events that had forced them to escape.

'That's a real shame. I was relying on your cool head to keep me informed of events. Now I'll have to make do with Rrildyss and put up with her irrelevant chatter in order to get the facts I need.'

'I should've stayed?'

'Oh, no. You were right to get away from that evil man, Tumalind. And, from what I

know of Tryonta's activities, I know you were wise to escape his clutches as well. There's a man who seems to live for evil. How the pair of them have remained undiscovered in their wickedness is a bit of a mystery to me.'

'Does Feldrark know you feel this way, Ivdulon?'

'Of course. I know what you're thinking. But we had no choice but to allow him to lead the pilgrimage. In any case, I've a strong feeling Dagla Kaz is pivotal in events that are slowly unfolding. He has important things to do in our quest to defeat the evil of the Followers of Ytraa and other mistaken religions.'

'I still have difficulty accepting all I've learned from you and Aklon about Gadhallah. Oh, I know it's true, of course. Neither of you have ever said anything but the truth to me and Dagla Kaz has shown himself to be an evil man in so many ways that I can't doubt what you've told me. But it's hard, after a lifetime's belief, to discover your faith is built on lies and evil.'

'Not only the Followers, Tumalind. There are many religions that exist in this world simply to provide power for those who lead them. They attract both the good and the bad as secondary leaders, you know. Some of the priesthood here in Litkala and on your island are genuinely good people; most act in ignorance of the facts. Others, like the extraordinary woman, Porlesah who's one of Aklon's Few, understand they can achieve more good from within the organisation. The same is true of Rrildyss, though she, of course, doesn't face any real danger. She's merely helping Feldrark and me to slowly change things here in the city. Your own experience tells you what might result if we make changes too quickly for the ordinary folk. We'd cause panic and upheaval. So we have to work slowly.'

'You say there are other religions equally evil?'

'Not too far from where you sit, if your idea of your whereabouts is accurate, just beyond those mountains at your back, lies Tohltaz. There, they worship a male god who they won't name for fear of bringing his anger down on them. But they're made to believe that men are the chosen of god and women are mere chattels to be used for pleasure, work and breeding. They give women no rights whatever and treat them very badly. An example of a religion where the founder's original message has been distorted by evil men to serve their own ends. These men simply desire power over women and, unable to have their way by means of their own personalities, they've distorted the words of their founder to make the role of men seem more than it really is. Of course, it helps that this particular religion - they call themselves Disciples of Immallsu, but people usually call them Immalls - live in a land that was traditionally male dominated. The subjugation of women wasn't difficult for them. It's part of our plan to release the women there and have them treated as equals, which was the original idea held by their founder, a simple man of good heart but not much real *intelligence.'*

The merest suggestion of noise interrupted her concentration and she excused herself from Ivdulon's company as she sought the source. Shaulah appeared at a loping run from behind a rock outcrop on the ridge of the hill behind her. A short spell later, Okkyntalah appeared, a small deer across his shoulders and a brightly feathered gamebird in his free hand.

Tumalind rose to greet the dog with affection and relief. As soon as Okkyntalah dropped the carcass, she embraced him. They held each other as though they'd been parted for months.

Needing no words, she built up the fire as he butchered the carcase, tossing the entrails a little away from their camp for Shaulah to eat as she pleased.

As the meat roasted on their makeshift spit, making their mouths water from the hunger of a full day's walking without much food, they talked of their individual experiences.

'Good fire, Tumalind. I saw the first smoke, but you've made it well enough that there's almost no sign now it's really burning. Sondukal has taught you well.'

He'd seen no sign of anyone on his trip and the deer had been, for him, an easy catch. The meat would last them a few days. The gamebird had almost run into him as he emerged from a wide split in the face of one of the many rocky outcrops that seemed to litter this hillside.

The meal restored both their spirits and their energy and they used their isolation to express their mutual love under a sky bright with stars. The crescent of the moon lay hidden by the trees and the Skyfire was still below the rise of the hill. But the stars were bright and they lay back together, naming as many as they could. With the fire stacked with fuel to last the night, they fell into pleasant sleep, unmarred by fears of capture or discovery.

Aklon sat in the mouth of the cave, surveying the troops in their camp below. It would be a matter of half a day only before they started gathering the other soldiers from the old settlement and began to bring them up the Scar. The more there were, the harder would be the job of the Few. They'd have to kill a good number of these loyal troops; innocent men and women who merely served a faith they'd been brought up to respect and honour. Was he any better if he killed such folk in order to change the society he wished to lead to better things?

'No point philosophising about it, Aklon. It's a simple enough matter. Either we give ourselves up to be tortured to death, along with any of the Few who've exposed themselves in the action they've taken. Or we do what has to be done.'

286

'Thank you, Delbon. You put the matter into simple terms and I agree. Very well, we need a diversionary tactic serious enough to divide the camp below and send a number of them away from this place.'

'Fire the bushes near those 'orses an' carts. And meck another by the beck, so they can't use the water to put 'em out.'

'The conflagration might spread a little further than we would like, Phildrad. But you are right. It will create a diversion and split the soldiers into three parties. Easier to pick them off under those circumstances. If you would set the fire near the stream, then, and you do the other one, Delbon. I will place myself in a position where I can pick off those at the ladders and prevent new troops joining those already here.'

The sky was starting to brighten with coming day and the Skyfire, now the brightest point of light other than the moon, had set along with most of the stars. Delbon and Phildrad made their way to their different points of disruption and set about their tasks in silence. Aklon surveyed the troops below. If he moved along the ridge toward the face of the Scar, he would reach a small rise where trees would conceal him as he rained arrows onto the camp. And, from that vantage point, he could also watch the progress of soldiers returning from the old settlement.

The camp was slowly rousing as he found position. Near the beck, he could see flames begin to lick at the small bushes. It was a shame to damage the place this way; a place he'd always loved for its calm and tranquillity. He wondered how many other things he would have to do against his nature before the Cause was run.

Phildrad returned to the cave for his weapons. The extra stash of arrows they'd collected and made would be essential to the success of this particular raid. He signalled and caught his friend's eye and watched him make his way toward him, out of sight of those below. Delbon's fire suddenly burst into life and this had the desired effect that the fire by the stream had lacked. Nearer to the camp, and frightening the soldiers' horses, which Delbon now released so they could escape, it quickly brought both noise and action from the sentries.

The peace below was abruptly changed into partly organised action as the officers organised a party to make and use beaters against the quickly growing conflagration. Another batch of soldiers was sent off with canvass buckets to bring water.

Aklon watched Delbon position himself on the ridge to gain maximum advantage over those who would soon approach him. He would first deal with those fetching water, it being too dangerous to remain on the ground near the other fire.

In the ensuing chaos, Aklon picked off as many of the force as he could with the arrows he had with him, injuring rather than killing, where he could. Smoke reduced visibility, making it difficult for those in the camp to determine the direction of fire of the arrows that found their colleagues. Panic set in, as these soldiers, largely a ceremonial force, realised they were being picked off by unknown and unseen forces. When those who'd set out for the stream rushed back with tales of attacks there, the remaining soldiers realised this was an organised raid.

Of the eighty or so in the camp, the combined efforts of the Few had reduced the fighting force by half within those first chaotic moments. Aklon's arrows were accurate and swift, rarely failing to find a target. But he'd run out of missiles before Phildrad reached him with the new supply.

He used the brief pause to watch Delbon's progress, following the concealed route that Phildrad had taken, since he had no further targets down by the stream.

'Ere y'are, Aklon. I brought the lot, right?'

Aklon nodded and his helper passed arrows to him as he loaded his bow and continued with the assault. As a team, they were more efficient than he'd been alone and it wasn't long before the able-bodied soldiers below were reduced to a few more than twenty. All now moved out of accurate range, though some continued in their attempts to douse the fires, whilst others attempted to rescue their fallen and injured fellows.

One had worked out Aklon's location and was sneaking through the trees below, armed and ready. Phildrad spotted the woman and watched her climb toward them. Before he could act, however, Delbon reached a place on his route that made her attempt obvious and he easily despatched her. She fell, with a scream, down the four manheights she'd climbed.

Now they must act quickly to prevent those soldiers who were beginning to approach the foot of the Scar from ascending the rope ladders. There were six in all. Aklon detailed Phildrad, least skilled with the bow, to deal with them. No soldiers now guarded the ladders, so it was a matter of keeping out of trouble and cutting or raising the ropes.

Meanwhile, Aklon and Delbon must descend the rough rise quickly enough to reach the remaining troops, now forming barricades with the two carts that had escaped the flames. The fire near the stream followed the wind direction, away from the camp, leaving the trees bordering the small arena intact.

'If we use the trees as cover, we can keep our advantage, Aklon.'

Aklon assessed the situation as they scrambled down the slope between the sparse bushes growing on the stony ground there. 'Collect a few tabards from the dead as we go. I have an idea that might help us defeat the rest.'

Both men stripped a couple of corpses each, turning away from the desecrated bodies with distaste but recognising the necessity of their actions. Phildrad was working his way along the top of the Scar, and had the first of the ropes cut. From below they could hear the shouts of alarm from those approaching the ascent. How close they now were, Aklon could not tell, but he'd seen them slowly covering the dry ground of the Point and heading in their direction before he'd left his vantage point. It was certain that he and his companions had little time to do what was necessary to prevent them getting back onto the main part of the island.

As he and Delbon raced through the wooded edge, tearing the tabards into strips as they ran, he heard Phildrad cursing. Turning, he saw a soldier had gained on his fellows and managed to climb one of the ladders most distant from Phildrad. He'd seen the soldier and was running along the cliff to attack. Praying that this one man was a forerunner only, he urged Delbon on to the very edge of the fire with him. There, they must gather flames for their arrows and destroy the barricades with yet more fire. Time, however, wasn't on their side and, if they judged the situation wrongly, they'd soon be caught between those at the barricades and those ascending the Scar. That would be an impossible position and they might not even escape with their lives. The Cause hung in the balance as Aklon dipped his first arrow into the scorching embers at the edge of the forest fire. It seemed to take forever for the fabric to catch and, as he waited, he saw Phildrad engage in combat with the soldier on the very edge of the Scar, noise and movement from below suggesting others were now making their way up to the top.

Chapter 30

AN ATTACK IN THE NIGHT

Okkyntalah awoke at Shaulah's first growled warning. The fire had burned low and, with the moon hidden behind trees, the brightest light now came from the Skyfire. Surrounding their chosen shelter tree, he saw a ring of bright eyes. He gentled Tumalind awake. Drowsy, she was reluctant to leave her sleep and he had to shake her more than he wished.

'Tumalind! Wildhounds. Wake up!'

She woke at the name. Neither had encountered these notorious killers, though both knew of them. More dangerous even than manecats or stripecats, they roamed in packs and attacked anything that might provide a meal. Relentless in their hunting and fearless in attack, they were the most dangerous creatures living in the grasslands.

'Grab some branches and light them. Fire keeps them at bay.'

Okkyntalah gathered his bow and the quiver of arrows, knowing there was no hope of defeating this number. If Tumalind could coax the fire into life and wave a burning brand, it might give them time for the plan forming in his mind.

She was swift, and he felt proud of her courage and reliability, knowing many would have panicked under such a threat. Shaulah remained at his side, growling her threats. He kept her near; she'd quickly be killed should she venture too close.

Tumalind at last had a brand burning and placed others onto the embers, lighting the area with the blaze and making the pack retreat a little. She stood and brandished her torch, threatening the nearest and bravest of the pack to force them back. Okkyntalah used the opportunity to carry out his plan. He first cut down the gamebird from the bough where he'd hung it and tossed it toward the trees. A number of the pack ran after it, leaving a small gap in their ring.

The remains of the deer had attracted them. He cut it down and, swinging it high above his head, launched it in a great arc in the opposite direction. At once, the rest of the pack followed the meat, howling and yapping as they made for the food.

It would keep them away for only a short while.

'Climb the tree, Tumalind. No, leave our things. We'll worry about those later. Up. Now.'

She climbed into the branches. He lifted Shaulah and she took the dog from him and balanced her on the broad branch beside her.

'Come on, Okkyntalah. They'll be back soon.'

291

'In a moment.'

He replenished the flames with the remaining wood, making a real blaze and brightening a wide area that included the two parts of the pack devouring the meat he'd provided. In the flickering light, he fired off some arrows, killing and wounding a number of the pack. Instead of scaring them off, this made them turn and begin a slow return, again forming a circle around the tree.

Okkyntalah shinned up, with his bow and the quiver of remaining arrows, only just escaping the jaws of the leader of the pack. He counted his ammunition. One arrow more than the remaining wildhounds. Slowly, he picked them off, one by one. He'd expected they would run away as their number declined but they stayed, howling, trying to climb the tree, driven to destroy their killer.

Two hounds remained. Much larger than Shaulah, they bore vicious canine teeth capable of tearing flesh from any beast they caught. Powerful shoulders and haunches displayed their ability to run and jump. These last two moved swiftly about the base of the tree, making it difficult for Okkyntalah to hit them. Eventually he fired his penultimate arrow but missed completely. His final arrow must make its mark. One of the creatures he could tackle with his sword, but two would be very dangerous. He aimed, following the form of the larger beast in the unsteady firelight. Just as he let the arrow go, the branch on which he rested cracked. His projectile caught the rump of the creature. Okkyntalah lost his balance and fell to the ground. The animal that remained unhurt was on him at once.

'Shaulah!'

Tumalind released the dog and she leapt down to help her master. Tumalind watched in horror as he fought the creature. Shaulah took the attention of the wounded beast. But Okkyntalah's sword was still in its scabbard, lying with their packs. He couldn't reach the weapon and hold off the beast's teeth at the same time. Tumalind dropped to the ground and slipped the weapon from its sheath. She was no swordswoman, but she swept the blade in a wide arc and brought it down on the creatures back, frightened she might hit Okkyntalah if she went for its head. Her attack only wounded and angered the beast. It turned on her, releasing Okkyntalah. He grasped his hunting knife as it lunged at Tumalind. She held the blade in front of her and the animal caught the point in its chest, wrenching the weapon from her grasp. Okkyntalah fell on it with his knife, plunging the shorter blade deep into its eye socket, killing it at once.

Behind him, Shaulah yelped, as the other wounded beast gripped her shank in its teeth. He withdrew the blade from the dead hound and attacked the remaining animal. It released Shaulah and turned on him instead. As he wielded the small blade, the creature dodged to one side, its vicious jaws about to close on his other arm. From behind him, the sword blade flashed through the air and took the creature's head clean off. Tumalind let out a small cry of dismay and dropped the sword.

They dropped onto bloodied grass and held on to each other as their breathing slowly stilled. Only when they could breathe more easily, did Okkyntalah release Tumalind and examine her at arm's length. He bid her turn for him. Satisfied she was unhurt, he went to where Shaulah lay panting and bleeding. The wound in her side was ragged and deep.

He felt lost. Had no idea what to do to save his beloved dog. She'd rescued him from serious injury; may even have saved his life. He turned to Tumalind, seeking her advice and help. She nodded and moved to search their small stash of belongings. The fighting had disturbed the neat pile and their things were spread over a wide area, some beyond the firelight. But she found what she sought and returned to Okkyntalah.

'Hold her head in your lap. I can't do more than repair the wound with stitches. It'll hurt her, but it's the only thing we can do.'

He gentled the dog's head into his lap and stroked her, talking to her as Tumalind used her embroidery needle and thread to close the wound. She cleaned the sticky blood away as much as she could, using her tabard as the nearest thing to hand. Shaulah whined at the first piercing but seemed to sense they were trying to help her and lay still as Tumalind stitched together the ragged wound.

The bleeding stopped but the dog couldn't stand. Tumalind used some of their precious water to clean the blood from her hands and then washed more off the dog's side. Okkyntalah remained with her head in his lap as Tumalind gathered their scattered belongings. She dragged the nearest carcasses of the pack of beasts away from their immediate camp area and spread the crumpled sleep sack close to Okkyntalah. At last, she fed the remaining wood onto the fire and draped the edge of the sleepsack over Okkyntalah, using the rest to lie on.

The morning would be soon enough to search for what was missing. For the time being it was enough to simply rest after their victory. Okkyntalah felt his dog lick his fingers as he held her close and wondered would she live to see the daylight. And, if she did, how would they manage if she couldn't walk?

Three days had passed since Okkyntalah and Tumalind had sneaked from the camp. Three days in which Aglydron wondered what part he'd played in her secret departure. Had he openly confessed Dagla Kaz was her father, would that have prevented her foolish flight?

No one had gone to look for them. The High Priest had made it clear he had no time to waste on such things. The rumour was that the men on horses might want Tumalind as some sort of sex slave for their master in the desert land of Tohltaz, but Aglydron found that hard to believe. It seemed unlikely that men would travel so far on the off chance they might find a suitable captive in a land such as this. There were few farms, fewer villages and most of the land was wild and uncultivated. He'd examined the soil and found it fertile and full of those things that gave life to plants and animals. That it wasn't better husbanded seemed a waste and he wondered what kept people from taking advantage of the natural riches on their doorstep.

But the day's events took all considerations from his mind as they now approached the city of Kah-Labaz. The massive bulk of Mount O'bo frowned down over the habitation, dark clouds of smoke and ash weaving through the winds that swirled about its crown. He was reminded of their experience on Ylcrat and wandered over to Myllthlan who was staring at the fire mountain in awe.

'This is so much greater than Krakgragog, Aglydron. I wonder what the people here do to appease the fire god within the cone?'

'You should know better by now, Myllthlan. There's only one God. Ytraa is the only true god.'

'Still, it's a mighty mountain, and breathing fire and smoke. There must be something that causes such disturbance to the very ground. Can you hear it grumbling?'

'I can. But Ivdulon believes the world has burning rock at its centre and that the fire mountain is just a place where this comes out.'

'Burning rock, Aglydron? How could there be such a thing? What would make rock burn and melt and flow like thick honey? Surely no fire can be so hot as that?'

'In Litkala, I went to the glass works. There they have fires so hot that they turn sand into glass. If man can make such fires, perhaps Ytraa can make greater ones?'

'Well, I suppose that may be so. Or there may be dragons?'

'Maybe. I just hope it doesn't do what the one on your island did when we escaped.'

'Me too.'

They stood side by side and Chislanda came to take his hand and stare into the clouds with him. The wind that blew offshore was laden with the scent of the mountain, a strange acrid smell permeating the air around them. Small clouds of fine ash settled at their feet. The boat was only a short distance from the docks and they watched the city approach, wondering what they might find in this strange place.

A few ships lay at anchor in the centre of the harbour and a number of smaller vessels were tied up against the stone wall. Those smaller boats looked very much like fishing vessels. Aglydron knew the lake and river carried a stock of good fish for food, since they'd eaten it almost daily on their voyage. There was much activity on the wharf and a small party of officials had gathered to greet them. He wondered how strangers would be treated in this place, where the early Followers had first split into two factions so many cycles ago. As the boat closed on the land, he began to make out the individual people and noted their peculiar manner of dress. The men, mostly labourers by the look of them, wore bands wound about their foreheads with loose ends that trailed right down their backs as far as their waists. Their upper bodies bore dark tattoos on arms, chest and back. Around their waists they wore wide belts with simple triangles of the same material to partly conceal their manhood. The women, of whom there were few on the wharf, were also naked from the waist. They were without head covers and wore wide belts at their hips. A band of fabric dropped from the belt and passed loosely between their legs to be tucked into the belt at the back, providing more an appearance of cover than any real concealment.

'Primitives, by the look of it.'

'It might simply be the temperature that allows such freedom, Aglydron. I know I feel quite warm in my tabard.'

He glanced at Chislanda and nodded. It was true that the temperature here seemed higher than at home, though why he couldn't determine. As they sailed in and tied up, it became clear that there was no distinction between the groups of men and women. All seemed dressed more or less identically, with no indication of rank or position, unlike the Muhnilahm tabards. They allowed the powerful to demonstrate their status through richness of fabric or embroidery, like the Litkala tunics, which permitted distinction through different colours and trims.

Once the boat was secured, Quyreena donned her best headwear and, indicating that Dagla Kaz should remain aboard, left the vessel to converse with the small party awaiting her. The High Priest looked affronted but said nothing, merely pacing up and down the deck with impatience. It was only moments, however, before the ship's captain returned and spoke to all assembled.

'I've explained who you are and what you're about. They're happy for you to go ashore, but expect you to respect their customs and traditions. They may later insist on you reducing your bodily cover to meet their standards, but they'll discuss that with Dagla Kaz first. I'll be here for a few days until it's known what you'll be doing. But I'll wait no more than a sixday, during which I'll revittle the Mekoque. I've a living to earn and your commission is generous but not without limit.'

With that, she called her crew to her and gave them leave to take no more than three days of freedom on shore, once the cargo was unloaded and the pilgrim party had disembarked.

Aglydron and Chislanda collected their packs and, hand in hand, followed the High Priest off the boat. The small group of citizens who awaited them was made up of an equal number of men and women. They bowed low from the waist in greeting.

'Welcome to our city, Followers from afar. Know that we are glad to have you among us and that we will provide for you during your stay. Housing and food will be supplied by the Keepers of the Keys.' The speaker nodded to the man and woman standing next to her, and they, in turn, held out their arms in a sign of greeting.

'We recognise that you are attired according to your understanding of the word of the Lord Gadhallah but ask that you respect our tradition and adopt our manner of dress whilst you remain our guests. We will provide the means for you to display the gifts of Ytraa whilst allowing only a glimpse of the means of performing the great Joining. Such is the way here in the land gifted the Followers of Ytraa.'

Aglydron bristled and was gratified to see determination cross the face of the High Priest at this irreverence. He'd be reluctant to adopt their scandalous near-nakedness.

'I am gratified to accept your greetings and welcome and I convey my greetings from the island of Muhnilahm, the promised land of the Followers of Ytraa. And I...'

Rrildyss Kaz interrupted him. 'And I present the complements of the Kiral and Kirallah of the supreme city of Litkala, where Followers of Ytraa have long been settled, in the land chosen for them by Ytraa.'

The woman in the party held up her hand in a gesture of peace. 'It appears we have differences. Let us not allow these to impact on our greeting. Let us first grow to know one another, discuss our ideas and engage in conversation about our respective beliefs and traditions, for it is clear that we all, if nothing else, have in common our worship of Ytraa. Better to dwell on those things in which we are similar than to make paramount those things in which we differ.'

The High Priest from Litkala nodded her assent but Dagla Kaz appeared less open to such compromise. Aglydron nodded his approval of his leader's determination to remain true to the creed and wondered what might come of their differences, as the party left the wharf with the citizens of Kah-Labaz in the lead.

* ˙⸻·

'I sense you're in trouble, Aklon.'

'Not now, Ivdulon. I have no time for discussion. Action is what I need.'

'Show me the scene. I may be able to help.'

Aklon made a quick visual sweep of the area. *'What I cannot show you is the large group of soldiers prepared to ascend the Scar from below. Now, I must act, Ivdulon.'*

'Very well. May I keep visual contact?'

'Do what you must. But leave me free to concentrate.'

Aklon felt the odd sensation as Ivdulon kept herself in only part of his mind. He became unaware of her as his mind fully engaged on the conflict.

The flaming arrow had caught on the wood of the first cart and Delbon had followed

296

suit, setting the second alight. As expected, the soldiers behind their barricades were forced to either abandon the cover or burn with it.

Aklon glanced over to where Phildrad fought with the soldier who'd climbed the Scar, just in time to see his brave companion despatch the man and toss him over the cliff. He set to at once with his blade on the rope ladder.

From behind the burning barricades, two soldiers, one male and one female, strode out and faced their fellows. They were unarmed and therefore no threat. Delbon raised his bow, but Aklon signalled he was to leave them; they may well surrender.

'Lower your weapons, forces of Muhnilahm, and hear us speak.'

That the soldiers were addressing their colleagues became clear at once.

'We are the Speakers of Ytraa. Stay your slaughter!'

This announcement had the desired effect. The soldiers emerged from behind their now useless barricades and stood in orderly ranks a little distance from the flames. Aklon and Delbon remained under cover in the trees, but backed away from the fire, puzzled by this strange turn of events.

'We are the Speakers of Ytraa and will be obeyed! These who attack you are good people. These are my true Followers. These are those you should heed and obey, for they expose great corruption and evil on your island. Long have I sought for ways to convince your priesthood and the self-styled Holy Ones to abandon their wicked ways. But they have failed to heed my words. Now is the time to allow my true disciples to make the changes that must be made.'

'Get out there, Aklon, or you'll ruin my scheme here.'

Aklon had always known that Ivdulon was brilliant and talented. That she could do this thing was a wonder to him. At the back of his mind was the anxiety of those soldiers ready to climb the Scar. He emerged from the trees, persuading Delbon with him, and glanced across to where Phildrad stood. He seemed frozen with amazement, no longer hacking at the rope ladders, but transfixed by something occurring below.

'These three true Followers, led by the brave and true Aklon-Dji, son of your corrupt High Priest, are those you must allow to lead. Here begins a crusade to rid my island of those who would corrupt and distort my words and my commands. Elsewhere in your homeland dwell groups of devoted Followers who you must now support and help. This will be a time of trouble. This will be a time of upheaval. Already, Aklon-Dji has proved his worth to you in his prediction of the true Skyfire. You have seen it burning bright in the sky and you will see it grow in strength and power as the days progress toward the day when all will be placed under judgement. Let none say they were unaware of these my words when that day comes. For it is your sacred duty to spread to the people all my words of change. Hear what Aklon-Dji, my chosen emissary, has to tell you. Do his

297

bidding, which is my desire, and obey him without question. Or answer to my judgement and the flames of purification on the day the Skyfire outshines the noonday sun.'

The silence that followed the announcement saw a few hesitant movements from the soldiers in the camp. One took off his tabard and began to pray. The others swiftly took his lead until all were at prayer.

'Ivdulon, you are a miracle worker. I thought I had taken on more than I could manage here, but you have saved me. Thank you.'

'Do well with what I've started here, Aklon. Never falter. Never be other than yourself, and true. I rely on your honesty and sense of justice to do what now must be done. I can't easily interfere like this. But what I've started here should at least provide you with enough recruits to your Cause and the Few to ensure your success. There'll still be resistance, of course. But you no longer have to fight the remnants of the army.'

'There are still all those at the foot of the Scar to ...'

'I suggest you walk over to the Scar and look, Aklon. I hesitate to give you advice in the field, but, once you are done here, I think a trip to visit and collect your friends who once lived on the Point might serve you well. I'll leave you now, as I have other important things I must attend to, and speaking through the mouths of many is tiring for me.'

She was gone from his mind. He led Delbon, disbelieving and silent, through the praying soldiers to the Scar. There he stood beside Phildrad and gazed down on the mass of starving soldiers gathered there in hope of rescue and revenge on him. Every one of them was at prayer. Every one.

He turned to Phildrad with a question.

'Don't ask me, Aklon. About a dozen of 'em suddenly started talking like they was one person. Said the same words as them two. Ytraa's words. Right weird it was. But then this lot all just made their prayers like. Ytraa's words! I can't believe it. Thought we was done for, if I'm honest. Ytraa's words...'

Aklon felt, on this occasion it might be politic to omit that he had felt the same way. Instead, he stood tall and called to those still praying on the cliff top to gather near him. They seemed reluctant to leave their prayers, the words they had heard as Ytraa's causing them anxiety that was liable to turn to terror if left unexplained. But come they did, obeying the words of their God.

'You have heard what Ytraa has said. The Speakers of Ytraa shall be blessed and raised to suitable positions as the mouthpieces of Ytraa.'

Aklon examined the two who had spoken on the cliff top. It came as no surprise that their eyes were of lapis lazuli and flecked with gold. The dozen below the Scar would be similarly marked. There was a slight danger that their similarity might cause some comment and speculation, but, given the nature of mindtalk, Aklon felt there was little

298

real danger in this grouping and elevation of these who'd effectively saved not just his life but probably the Cause and the Few, even if was without their active consent. He must gather them and explore the possibilities here; a grouping of this type could make an enormous difference to his plans.

'Are there any now here who doubt that I have the blessing of Ytraa to make the changes necessary to restore our worship to what it should always have been?'

From the cliff top came no dissent. But from below, a few diehards remained unconvinced. The rest of the troops quickly silenced them.

'Stay your hands. Enough blood has been spilt in this already. Let us have no more violence, no more fighting amongst true Followers of Ytraa. Let us show those who do not yet believe that we are merciful and tolerant. They will learn by our example what they should become. We will not have it said that we new Followers, hereafter to be known as Adherents, are without respect or tolerance for the views of others.

'Now, it is time for you who gather below to ascend the Scar, so that we might feed you and give water to quench the thirst of your bodies. The thirst of your spirits will be quenched over the coming sixdays as we take our message to all the Followers on this wonderful island gifted us by Ytraa and convert them to Adherents.

'Understand that my father, Dagla Kaz, was corrupted by Mhortag into believing that all the lies we have been told are truths. What I must tell you all will be hard for many to believe and understand and now is not the time for such lessons. But let it be known by all assembled here that I serve God in the truth and that my wishes have always been that we should live in peace and harmony, free from the pain and terror that the High Priest and the Holy Ones would have us endure.

'First, however, we must make well those who have suffered the danger, hunger and privation of the Point and those here who have been injured in the conflict. Once all are able and strong, we shall make our first pilgrimage, as Adherents, with the great news to our long-suffering brethren who once dwelt on this barren strip of worthless land.

'Come; ascend and take food and water for your wellbeing.'

The soldiers, orderly and subdued by their experience of Ytraa's commands and words, heard at first hand, slowly climbed the remaining rope ladders, as Phildrad and Delbon, at Aklon's urging, led those already present in seeking what provisions they could find to feed the hungry.

Aklon watched with hidden amazement, as those he'd thought he must kill to succeed, gathered in ever-increasing numbers around him, offering no threat now. Ivdulon had proved herself not simply gifted but brilliant in her strategy. Now he had no further fear of imminent violence, he could concentrate on the difficult task of converting the rest of the island to the new ways of thinking. The Holy Ones and most of the priests

299

would resist most strongly. And he had no doubt that there would be pockets of resistance amongst the ordinary people, as those incapable of change tried to impose unrevised tradition on the rest of the population. But, with Ivdulon's timely interception, he'd avoided more bloodshed. For that, he would be eternally grateful.

Now began the real task. Changing minds and winning hearts would be challenging, difficult and dangerous. Not all would be as ready to obey as these trained soldiers who'd heard Ytraa's words in their own ears. And those with vested interests would reject change, whatever the evidence. He hoped he could take the rest of the island without further loss of life, but he doubted that would be the way of it.

Chapter 31

STOLEN

'We can't stay here, Tumalind. As soon as it's light, we'll move. The bodies will attract other animals from the forest. But, at least until we leave this Wildhound pack's territory, there won't be any more attacks and that'll make it safer for us.'

Come dawn, Tumalind gathered what she could of their plundered and spoiled supplies, whilst Okkyntalah took all his unbroken arrows from the corpses. They donned torn and bloodied tabards and set off for the southern slopes of the hill they'd camped on. Okkyntalah carried Shaulah across his shoulders and Tumalind carried his pack. But he kept his sword, quiver and longbow. They walked for a good part of the day but stopped long before dusk, the extra weight they both carried slowing their progress and making the shorter trek necessary.

'That tree should do for us. We'll set up camp here and I'll hunt again. Then we'll spend the remains of this day and another night resting here and see how Shaulah is by the morning.'

The tree, with wide branches spreading a manheight from the ground, gave them shade during the day and promised some safety from marauding animals during darkness. Tumalind, weary from the night's events and terrors, was glad of the promised rest, though it meant they remained relatively close to where they'd last camped with the pilgrims.

'You don't think we're likely to run into anyone from Dagla Kaz's group, do you?'

'I doubt it. If they haven't come looking for us by now, I don't think they're going to. No. I think he must've realised they wouldn't find us easily out here and they've sailed on up the lake. They might even be in Kah-Labaz by now, for all we know. But we'll need to remain watchful; you never know.'

Whilst Okkyntalah went hunting again, she gathered more wood and built a fire, ready to light and cook whatever he brought. She made her store of timber greater than the last one, recalling how the burning brands had saved them. Still nervous, and without Shaulah's company as she left the dog resting beneath the tree, Tumalind felt uncomfortable in the bloodied tabard. On her final trip into the trees, she'd come across a water source and filled both girbas ready for the next day. With no sign of Okkyntalah's return, she went back to the spring to wash herself and her tabard in the small pool of clear water. Refreshed and feeling cleaner and a little more relaxed, she returned to their camp and hung her tabard on one of the low branches before she took a sleepsack into the sun so she could dry her skin. Out here, in the middle of nowhere, with no sign of other human beings, the only eyes likely to see her were those she welcomed.

Shaulah was a cause of concern. The dog had woken only briefly, as Okkyntalah had lain her down. She'd yelped with pain and hadn't moved or woken since. Tumalind examined her for signs of fever but found only the wound she'd stitched. The dog's breathing seemed even, if shallow, and her body felt normal. Perhaps it was no more than fatigue after her exertions in the night. She'd also lost a lot of blood, of course.

Satisfied there was no more she could do for now, Tumalind lay down and let the sun lull her to rest. She recalled that they hadn't prayed the previous evening or at dawn this morning. Too tired to really care, she determined to make up for the lapse at dusk, the habit difficult to break even under the influence of her changing frame of mind.

The position of the sun suggested she'd been asleep only a short time when she felt an odd sensation in the ground beneath her. It felt as though the earth shook. She'd heard tales of such events happening around fire mountains. But, surely Mount O'bo was too distant to cause such disturbance here? As she awoke, she became aware of sounds, which at first she couldn't identify. Then she realised it was the hooves of horses as they covered the ground nearby. She sat and saw them. Five horses, all mounted, above her on the hillside and moving toward her at speed.

She rose quickly and dashed to her tabard to cover herself before they reached her. But they were on her as she was stretching for the garment. They stopped, surrounding her. One, a tall wiry man with pointed beard and eyes like coal, leapt from his horse and ran to grab her. She feared the strangers, and fought, but was quickly overmastered as another jumped down to help. They spoke to each other rapidly in what she recognised as the common tongue but spoken with an odd stress and speed that made it difficult to understand. They tied her hands behind her back with a leathern strap, gagged her with a dirty cloth pulled from one of their belts, and lifted her onto the horse to sit behind the man who'd first dismounted. They fed her tabard between her and the man, and wound a cord round both of them to prevent her falling or escaping.

Within moments, the five rode off the way they'd arrived, from the north-west. As they galloped away, Shaulah woke at last and barked. Her injury kept her where she lay helpless, her barks slowly fading as the men carried Tumalind away.

Aklon, Delbon and Phildrad allowed the troops to rest on the cliff top. Many were in a sorry state from their confinement on the Point. It was clear that the experience of hearing the combined voice of Ytraa speaking the words Ivdulon had provided, had made the soldiers deeply question their faith. Most were disturbed and contrite. Some expressed anger at the lies they'd been told by the priests, as Aklon dropped comments for them to hear. A few were indifferent, as though the whole matter was beyond their concern or comprehension. But a handful remained hostile, loyal to ideas and doctrines they'd known and served all their lives, in spite of the evidence of Ytraa's words spoken in their hearing. Outnumbered and kept under watch by the majority, they posed no real threat for the moment, but Aklon was aware of their potential for causing trouble in the future. Nevertheless, he could not bring himself to do away with them. There had been enough killing already: too much.

He gave the soldiers two days and nights of rest and food to recuperate. They'd quickly put out the fires and restored a route to the stream for fresh water. One or two of the heavier grazing animals had succumbed to the flames and these were carried into the camp for food. The oxen that had pulled their carts would be of no use where they were bound and, reluctantly, the remaining officers amongst the troops allowed their slaughter.

So, the party of around five hundred that Aklon led into the steaming jungle, was well fed and rested; a fighting force well equipped against any violence they might encounter. But it was slow work taking this many people through the confined trackways under the trees: slow and difficult. Inevitably, they lost some soldiers along the way and it came as no surprise when the officers he'd placed in charge reported that those who were dissatisfied had sneaked away.

'Do you want me to put together a small troop to follow the deserters? Bring them back, Paltrohn?'

'No. Leave them be. How many have gone? Do you know?'

The officer looked a little shame-faced. 'Sorry, Paltrohn. No count was made before we set off. But I estimate fifty to sixty have deserted.'

It was fewer than expected, though more than he had hoped. But it would take too large a party to follow and bring them back and more blood would undoubtedly be shed along the way. Let them be. He would deal with them when and if they caused problems.

'I hope they won't make trouble in their villages and towns, Paltrohn. I'm sorry they were allowed to escape like that.'

Aklon nodded his agreement. The thought of deserters spreading lies, rumours and ill feeling at this stage was worrying, but he had more pressing concerns. He moved the troop along, a laborious process in this unfriendly terrain, made a little easier as they carried the rest of the oxen meat with them. Water, at least, was no problem. The many streams were fast and sometimes deep, but the water was fresh and good.

At their rate of progress, he estimated it would take three days to travel the ten leagues to the new settlement. Three days he could use so well in other ways. But he had no choice. Events, and Ivdulon's timely interception, had set him on this course and he must follow it through. Once they reached Chellyth and her group, he would discuss with her the options. Though he suspected that she would want to free her people from their current way of life as soon as possible. And that would involve an even longer return journey with twice as many people to lead.

Life was not destined to improve for some time, it seemed. For the first time in many nights, he allowed himself to dwell on Shoarhn and wondered how she fared away up in the north of the island, alone and needing him as much as he needed her.

⁕ ⟶

Dagla Kaz surveyed the dark, deserted street outside his room with distaste. The citizens of this place were little more than savages. Their manner of dress, almost naked in reality, was offensive to Ytraa. Though he had to admit it was pleasing on the eye to have so many women displaying openly. But he'd yet to decide how to approach the coming discussions of exchange of virgins here. It seemed unlikely to him that any of his party would wish to remain. The rumble underfoot as the mountain grumbled and smoked, the fine ash that dusted all the surfaces, the low, squat buildings with their wooden doors and window covers, all combined with the oppressive heat of the region to make it most unpleasant to the islanders. And those from Litkala must see the settlement as primitive and savage after their lives of luxury in that great city.

He'd spent the night alone; Rrildyss having been inexplicably unavailable. She'd been so ever since the incident with those appalling tribesmen from the desert and he wondered, had Tryonta told her something of their exchange? Although it was unlike his henchman to betray him. Perhaps she'd overheard. She was no real loss; a conservative lover, unlike her splendid daughter, who knew exactly what excited him and found equal pleasure in the same activity. But the stimulant that nestled against his manhood had the unfortunate effect of exiting him regardless of the woman, and he was too well-steeped in the superstitions of tradition to relieve the urge alone. He knew, on a rational level, that such action would neither blind nor enfeeble him but his heart overruled his head on this and he wouldn't do it.

So, the night had been sleepless. That semi-heathen, Myllthlan had been claimed by Tryonta early on and Aglydron had taken his delicious creature from the swamp with him to his bed. The virgins were all sacrosanct and not to be trusted should he risk violating them. And Tumalind had escaped his intentions with her over-protective husband. Hopefully, that band of slave dealers had found them both and taken her as a sex slave to suffer in the desert. That left only Corphanda, and she'd spent the night with that gigantic oaf, Tarruss. An odd coupling, but one that had been more or less constant since the incident in that vile village where they'd rescued the woman from a terzet horn.

His ruminations and rememberings were disturbed by the opening of the door behind him. In darkness that had yet to break with dawn, he felt, rather than heard, another entering his room. Warm, soft hands explored his skin as he stood against the open window. Without words, but with gentle pressure on his skin, she moved him to the bed.

Darkness was receding like the tide when she finally released him in a pulse of such intense pleasure that he almost declared he loved her. And then she vanished, leaving him alone again, without revealing who she was or what had drawn her to his bed.

He slept, regardless of her desertion, her ministrations leaving him relaxed and satiated for the first time since he'd left the city and Pharah-Li. He wondered, briefly, was she well? Was his heir growing undisturbed in her belly, or was she pleasuring others as the infant made her swell?

Morning found him in a better mood for negotiation and bargaining. He fed alongside the others of the party and then, at his hosts' bidding, occupied a small room in the long low house and invited in the virgin gifts, one by one, to quiz them.

He had no interest in them as people and barely knew them as individuals. They were simply the means to an end that must be achieved if he were ever to return to the island and his position of wealth, power and privilege. And return he would. No matter what the cost. He had too much to lose to let the vagaries of fate undo him now. So, he called them to him in order of their names, knowing such behaviour would allow the party to imagine he was being objective and nonpartisan rather than employing methods that were simple for him.

Bardrohn, the pale skinned whining boy from Litkala, came first and sat across the wooden boards of the table in this dreadful place. A servant of the local High Priest, a pretty girl with coal black hair, eyes almost the same colour and the pert young breasts of maidenhood stood alert and attentive in the corner. He watched the boy examine her as he entered for his talk. Perhaps one of the young men might be persuaded by the open displays of womanhood here. It was a hope.

'So, Bardrohn, isn't it?'

The boy nodded and turned again to look at the girl, who smiled and tilted her head to one side as if in question. He forced himself to look again at Dagla Kaz.

'Have you thought on your options, lad?'

'Yes, Paltrohn. Easy. I want to stay 'ere. Take a buck from 'ere instead of me.'

Dagla Kaz nodded and dismissed him, marking his list as the boy left. 'I'll see what we can do.'

Dilanthas, one of the original Chosen, from the island, appeared before him next. She didn't sit but remained standing, her hands fiddling with the hem of her tabard in a manner he knew she didn't realise was tantalising. He tried to keep his eyes on hers as he asked her whether she'd made up her mind. This innovation, imposed on him by Feldrark as a condition for the inclusion of the city's virgin gifts, irritated him.

'Sell this one for a good sum. Virgin flesh and modest. Make a perfect submissive sex slave.'

'Decided what you wish for, Dilanthas?'

'I have, Paltrohn. I were Chosen by Ytraa to be swapped in Choshinahm. An' that's where I think I should go.'

'Very well. So be it.'

The marking on the list grew along with the tedium of the task until, at last, Zyreenha arrived, her sad eyes filling with laughter as she approached him. This was a young woman who was all generosity. Had she not been a Virgin Gift, he'd have had her on the trip. But Feldrark had made clear his rules and, even at this distance, Dagla Kaz felt unable to fall foul of that man's wishes. The leader was more powerful, more influential, younger and stronger and Dagla Kaz knew he'd come off worst in any form of dispute.

'So, my dear?'

'If it's all the same to you, Dagla Kaz, I'd prefer to stay with these folk. I'd feel more in touch with what I've left behind, if you see what I mean.'

'We shall have to see what we can do, my dear. Off you go, then. And tell their High Priest I'm ready to discuss the matter, will you?'

He marked his list to show that she would stay a member of the pilgrimage. Even if he couldn't have her, she was too much woman to be left behind in this backwater to display her breasts to all and sundry when he wouldn't be there to see.

He examined his findings. From the list he could select one of each sex to stay behind. Bardrohn was a whining child and would be no loss. He'd represent an exchange between Litkala and Kah-Labaz. Yytlomohn, the small, sweet-natured volunteer from the island, had expressed no preference, but she was the one he was least reluctant to lose. And she'd make no objection, since her whole life had been one of obedience and duty. She'd represent the exchange between Muhnilahm and Kah-Labaz.

Had it all been so simple after all? The High Priest from the city, if that was what this place preferred to style itself, entered and asked the young woman in the corner to turn her back. Her frontal view was a loss, but would allow him to concentrate on his duty more easily, especially since the High Priest here was, apparently by tradition, always male. The idea of sitting across the table facing a woman with her breasts displayed was fine for anything frivolous, but this was a serious issue and demanded his complete attention. He was just congratulating himself on his ability to concentrate when the female Keeper of the Keys, Nyaldi, a mature but stunning beauty with the full firm breasts of a mother, entered and took her place beside her High Priest. Now, how would he concentrate on what must be done?

Bohkrohn Kaz cupped her nearest breast in one hand, fondling her openly and making Dagla Kaz very uncomfortable with this public display.

'Nyaldi possesses that female charm that encapsulates all that Ytraa promises, don't you think, Dagla Kaz?'

'She is a fine woman, yes.'

'As Keeper of the Keys, she is for any visitor. Do you wish to join with her?'

'I'd prefer we spoke of the matter at hand for the moment. I will see to my pleasure once we've finished here, if you don't mind, Bohkrohn.'

'Pleasure? Is not worship foremost in your mind, as High Priest of your people?'

Dagla Kaz felt outmanoeuvred by one who seemed to understand him better than he understood the man. If he agreed, he might expose himself as a gullible simpleton, following the letter of the law. But if he denied the possibility he'd insult the woman and might find himself guilty of blasphemy in this strange place. How to answer?

'I am sorry, I hadn't realised that the two were distinguishable. For those of us who Follow on my island, pleasure and worship are so closely intertwined that they are inseparable, you see.'

The man actually smiled as though he'd made a joke and the woman held her hand to her mouth, clearly hiding an impulse to laugh.

'I see you have some skill as a diplomat, Dagla Kaz. Here, we may appear simpler than the reality of our situation suggests. Living with the perpetual danger of the fire mountain and so close to the borders of that heathen land, Tohltaz, we've adopted habits that might seem strange to a visitor. But I was playing with you and that was unworthy. Of course you would enjoy the sensual pleasures of joining with Nyaldi. I've done so often and never been other than delighted. She has, in fact borne me two heirs. One of them has volunteered to accompany you to Choshinahm and I've released him for that purpose.

'Now. As you say, to the matter in hand. You have volunteers who wish to be exchanged with virgins from our city?'

Dagla Kaz explained who'd volunteered and asked the young woman in the corner to bring the pair, naming them so she could find them in the party.

'Bring also Byfthlyn, Hephrastihn, Lethrymynyhl and, of course, Pedradol-Dji would you, my child?'

The girl nodded at her High Priest and left to collect the group.

'We are content that all these are doing this duty voluntarily?'

'Certainly, my two are happy with the idea and arrangements.'

Bohkrohn Kaz nodded and Nyaldi tilted her head to one side indicating her agreement.

'Do you intend to remain with us for long, once the exchange has taken place, Dagla Kaz?'

He stared at the woman, concentrating on her face. 'We've limited time available, but a short rest would benefit all of us, if you're able to accommodate us, of course.'

'Oh, I'm sure that will be accomplished with the minimum of effort and fuss, Dagla Kaz. I look forward to our joining; later today, perhaps?'

He swallowed, unused to such openness, and merely nodded his assent.

'If you're to remain any longer, however, we must insist that, even as guests, you adopt our manner of dress, since we find your excessive cover both insulting and blasphemous. We'll supply the necessary garments, of course.'

He bit his tongue at the superior tones of the other High Priest. Although everything in this city had been done with politeness and consideration, there lurked, beneath the surface, a hint of threat. He felt certain that, should any of the party fail to behave as expected, they could expect little mercy from these people.

'I understand your concerns, Bohkrohn Kaz and, whilst pointing out that we find your manner of dress both scandalous and blasphemous, as visitors to your realm, we are ready to conform to your wishes.'

'That is all as it should be. It is remarkable how differently the texts of Gadhallah may be interpreted, is it not? Especially when you bear in mind that ours must, by the very nature of the parting that happened here, be the most ancient of the texts in existence. Nevertheless, one understands that changes are bound to happen as parties move further from the source of inspiration. It's interesting that those from Litkala dress in a manner a little closer to our own, in that their fabric is less concealing than that which clothes your own people. But, of course, your own garb has the potential advantage that the hem may be easily disturbed by wind or hand to reveal the means of joining. I take it that you frown on the practice of joining whilst wearing any item at all?'

'Of course. Naked is sacred and joining is the most sacred expression of our worship; it is, therefore, essential that we conduct the matter unfettered.'

'Excellent. We're as one in the most important aspect of our faith, it seems. So, Dagla Kaz, you have heirs in plenty, I assume? I have two by this beauty and several others by other fine women in the city. In total, I can own to having sixteen daughters and fourteen sons. You?'

Dagla Kaz felt this was an intentional affront, as if the man knew that he had no way of counting his offspring. But he refused to allow his displeasure to show. His pilgrimage depended on so many factors and he wasn't about to damage his prospects of success by allowing unfounded suspicions to get the better of him.

'I have more than I can count. We do these things a little differently on the island.

But I have had to bend to the will of Ytraa concerning my two main heirs. The male turned out to be a great disappointment, incapable of understanding and accepting the reality of our faith when shown the secret texts. The young woman, though entirely suitable as a successor, fell by accident into the arms of the Wharhll of Litkala and is now Kirallah to his Kiral, following the unfortunate demise of his parents. But, no matter, I've already secured a new heir with the astounding daughter of Litkala's High Priest, Rrildyss Kaz, who accompanies me on this pilgrimage. Pharah-Li is both beautiful and accomplished and will serve well as the vessel to bear my seed and bring to life my new heir.'

'Which brings me to another matter. We have but one High Priest here, Dagla Kaz; another matter on which we are clearly in agreement. However, I feel it is important that one of our spiritual leaders should accompany you on this pilgrimage, if only to ensure that our volunteers have their spiritual needs fully satisfied. I shall, therefore, send a priestess with you. Again, as on your island, women are permitted the lower status role of priestess. Kaz-Ca-Valorysta, will, with your permission, go along with you.'

'I will, of course, have to meet her first.'

'You have done so. Last night, she pleasured you.'

Dagla Kaz nodded. If she was as visually pleasing as she was sensually, her company would solve a major problem for him.

The door to the room opened and a slender woman with pale skin for this city, small firm breasts, and the pale brown eyes of knowledge entered. She sat beside the Keeper of the Keys and brushed her long brown hair back over her shoulders as she leant forward, her face bearing an expression entirely carnal. Dagla Kaz nodded and knew he was captured. This was a woman who'd do for him what that unnamed beauty in Kabalyt had done, but without her particular price . A woman who might master him, control him, bend him to her will. Too dangerous to take on this pilgrimage. He opened his mouth to object but found his head overtaken by his loins.

'Wonderful. I'll be delighted to have Kaz-Ca-Valorysta along.' He said.

Chapter 32

THE HUNT BEGINS

Okkyntalah heard his dog barking, though the sound was muted by distance. But he recognised her distress. He dropped the deer he'd just draped on his shoulders, so he could run back more swiftly. He'd become conscious of horse riders somewhere in the area, but the lie of the land made their distance and direction uncertain. Was Tumalind in danger?

Approaching their camp, round the edge of the hill, he saw three horsemen disappear over the north-western ridge, above him. He saw only three but heard five. At the tree he was unsurprised to find Tumalind missing.

His immediate instinct was to run after them. But he reached only the crest of the hill before he stopped. It was enough to see Tumalind, naked and captive, on the second horse. No chance of rescuing her like this. For a brief moment, he watched them ride toward the distant valley, where he could see a river glinting in the afternoon sun. Tumalind turned and he waved, but whether she could see him from that distance was uncertain. He trotted back to the tree and the dog, still collapsed after her efforts to give warning.

'How could you let them, Shaulah? You've let me down. Bad dog!'

He collected the minimum he'd need for the journey. His sword, bow and arrows, one girba, refilled by Tumalind, the small cache of fruit she'd collected, and her burning glass in its pouch, and the small box that went with it. Surveying the scene, he realised all she had with her was her tabard. That she hadn't been wearing it was evident. But they'd taken it with them and they hadn't raped her at the campsite. That suggested they intended to keep her alive. It wasn't much, but it was hope enough to start him on a journey that might eventually prove pointless. One man on foot, following five men on horseback into unknown territory, with no idea of their eventual destination, was a fool's errand. But it was one he'd pursue until he had no hope of finding and rescuing his beloved Tumalind.

'I should leave you here to fend for yourself. Useless bag of bones. Up, dog!'

Shaulah struggled to rise but fell again. Her sorrow and shame were clear and she whined involuntarily as she tried, again, to get to her feet. Okkyntalah relented. Gently, he lifted her and draped her across shoulders already burdened with weapons and the girba. This would be hard. But he'd do it. He'd go wherever he must. He'd find and recover her, no matter what it took.

After her initial shock and the terror of being kidnapped for a second time, this time by men, Tumalind resolved to do whatever she must in order to remain alive. She couldn't be certain, but she believed she'd seen Okkyntalah waving from the hill. He had the skills to follow her and he'd already proved he would never abandon her until every last hope had gone.

What would these savage men require of her? That she'd be forced to join with each of them went without question. If she showed some willingness, would that make it easier, less brutal? Would they use her in ways she'd never known? There were tales on the island, and in other places she'd visited, of ways in which a man could use a woman. Brutal and offensive ways. Would they do these unknown things to her?

There was a tiny drop of comfort in the fact they'd brought her tabard with them. If they were intent on using her and then killing her, they wouldn't have bothered with her cover. Did they, then, intend to keep her as a plaything, a sex slave? Would that chance allow her to remain alive long enough for Okkyntalah to recover her?

The saddle underneath her bare skin was already chafing, making her sore. Sex would be bad enough, without the added pain of damaged skin. She must bear whatever she was sent. Must find a way to separate herself from the experience and not allow herself to be dominated by the bad things they'd do to her. How could she achieve this separation? How could she remain a woman with a heart yet let these savages abuse and use her?

Ivdulon would help. She would consult the wise woman and gain both succour in that secret connection and maybe even some advice on how to do what she must.

'I'm in trouble, Ivdulon. Help me if you can.'

There was a brief pause before her answer came and Tumalind became more fully aware of the movement of the speeding horse and found a way to move with it instead of fighting it. She grew more alert and aware, smelling the animal beneath her, the stale scent of the man she was tied against, feeling the strips of thin fabric against her skin, hearing the hooves and the sound of the wind they made in passing.

'You're headed north-west, alone with five horsemen. You're naked and afraid. I suspect you've been taken by a raiding party for the Uhmbard of Tohltaz.'

'As to who they are, I don't know, Ivdulon. They came on me after I'd washed out my tabard and was hanging it to dry...'

'Okkyntalah was out hunting; and the dog?'

'Shaulah's injured. What do I do? What do they want with me?'

'The obvious answer is what you fear but that fear may be unfounded, at least as far as they are concerned. If they believe you virgin, they'll not penetrate you, though you may

312

have to satisfy their lust in other ways; do you understand?'

Ivdulon explained what she might do to assuage their lust and yet remain unsullied in that place she wished Okkyntalah alone to inhabit. The ways seemed unpleasant when applied to strangers but she would do what she must.

'That's the way to treat the situation. Understand you've no choice, Tumalind. Begin by recognising you're largely helpless and must do their bidding, and that way you won't destroy yourself with thoughts of shame and wishful thinking that things were other than they are.

'Make them believe you're virgin. As such, your colouring and shape will make you far too valuable for them to harm. They'll want to sell you for the maximum price, so take advantage, and if anything they do or threaten to do will harm you physically, remind them. They're simple men, brought up in the belief that women are mere goods and chattels to be bartered, used and discarded. But remind them of your value to them as something to be sold and they'll take more care of you. Oh, they'll demand you satisfy their sexual needs, as I've explained, but they'll make you comfortable, guard you from harm and ensure your skin is free from damage. Tell your rider that your nakedness is making you sore below. He'll stop and they'll do something to make you more comfortable.

'Remember, to avoid punishment from these savages, you'll need to be obedient. Try to curb your natural tendency to independence. And, Tumalind, as long as you remain a captive, I'm here for you. I'll contact Feldrark; you need to keep your concentration on yourself. I'll get him to organise a party for your rescue. Keep me in your mind as much as you're able and I'll remain with you whenever I can.'

Tumalind felt the strength flow into her from Ivdulon's positive advice and actions. She would be rescued. Oh, it was true that Okkyntalah must chase after her on foot and that Feldrark's party must come perhaps two hundred leagues. But she hadn't been abandoned. She would be rescued. If only she could keep herself alive.

She tapped the man on his shoulder. 'I'm growing sore with my skin against the saddle. If you don't do something to relieve me soon, I'll be torn and bleeding.'

He yelled at the other men and they reined in their horses. One of them undid the belt that tied her to her rider and lifted her out of the saddle. The leader dismounted and walked around her, examining what he could see. Determined not to show her fear, she restrained herself from covering herself and allowed her hands to drop loosely by her sides.

'I'm a virgin, you know. I hope you'll remember that when you rape me.'

The leader slapped her rump hard enough to make her gasp.

'Talk only when told to, woman. Show me where you're sore.'

She pointed between her legs. Two of the men picked her up and turned her upside

313

down so that their leader could examine her without having to kneel or bend. She felt his fingers in her as he invaded that sacred place but she bit back her urge to scream or protest and let him do what he must. The men turned her upright and one flung her tabard at her. She dressed rapidly.

'Will that do it?'

'Not if I'm to ride your horse. I need something soft beneath me.'

He glared at her and raised his hand as if to strike her. She stared back, defiant, and this seemed to puzzle him. He lowered his hand, turned her round and, lifting the hem, smacked her bottom twice, just clipping the sore places. The strokes were hard and she had to grit her teeth to stop the cries of pain and humiliation escaping. The tears that started in the corners of her eyes she kept there. They would not see her weep.

The leader consulted with the others and one of them brought out a shape of soft woollen pelt, the hide of an ovellah, she thought. He gave it to the leader, who brought it close and, gesturing to her to spread her legs, rubbed it against her skin.

'Will that satisfy milady?'

His scorn was obvious, and the others laughed at her, but she merely nodded and continued to stare him in the eye. This seemed to unsettle him and she determined she would always look them all in the eye whenever she could. He placed the pelt on the saddle and lifted her back in place. Once she was strapped against the leader, they set off again. This time, their pace was more measured and the ride more bearable. She took the opportunity to look about her, to examine what she could of those who'd captured her and learn as much as she might from their mounts and the way they controlled these wondrous beasts.

Come evening, they'd camp under stars. Then she'd be required to do as Ivdulon had warned. It was a duty she faced with revulsion, but she'd do it to keep safe and alive until Okkyntalah could catch up with them. If there was any way she might delay them without causing them to hurt her too much, she'd do it. Anything to help her husband in his long and difficult attempt at her recovery. How she wished he had the gift of mindtalk. But, at least she had that with Ivdulon, and with any of the others she might contact. It would be a way of keeping her mind occupied when she was doing those other things. If her mind were engaged with another person, she might manage the unpleasantness without showing her revulsion and angering the men.

For the first part of the chase, the signs had been clear enough to follow. Okkyntalah had hardly needed tracking skills at all. The trail left by five horsemen was as clear as a road. Their tracks would stay that way for days. Only when they reach hard ground would it become a more exacting task to follow them. He trotted easily, engaging a speed and

314

gait that accommodated the extra weight of the water bag and the dog across his shoulders. That he'd be forced to spend some of his night in seeking food was obvious. His daylight hours would all be spent in following the chase. The men on horseback would gain on him each day; that was unavoidable. But he could slow their gain by using every last bit of light, tracking through dawn and dusk, when they, unconcerned about a single hunter after them, might allow themselves the luxury of early halts and late arising.

Tumalind would be raped, repeatedly. Of that he was in no doubt. Why else would they have taken her? He'd heard of the men of Tohltaz and their attitude to women, so he was sure that they'd use his wife to satisfy their lust. The thought of her helpless, invaded and despoiled that way, might send him mad. He must keep it from his mind and concentrate instead on her recovery.

The first night, he ran until it was almost dark and then lay Shaulah at the base of a tree, placed the pack with the other items next to her and prayed that Ytraa would protect them whilst he hunted. Dusk was an easy time for creatures of the night that came to drink at the watering places and he'd chosen to stop close to such a place, but far enough away to be safe from the more violent creatures. He moved silently toward the softly flowing water of the narrow river, stripped off his tabard, and slipped into the stream without a sound. His head just above the surface and the sun behind him, he moved slowly through the current until he reached a place where some of the grazing animals would take on water.

The fluid was cool and soothing after his long run, but he'd no wish to stay in it for long. His pressing needs were food, time, and fuel to make a cooking fire to prepare his meal and keep away night creatures, and sleep so he could set off in the morning refreshed and ready.

A small herd of the goats from the mountain slopes approached first. They were skinny creatures, with little flesh on their bones and he recalled that Sondukal had said that they tasted bitter because of their diet. They'd do if nothing else came his way. A solitary longneck came to the water's edge, splayed its long legs wide and dipped its mouth into the stream to drink. Such a vulnerable position it seemed, and he was reminded how Tumalind may be forced to shape herself to amuse those savages. His anger and distress almost made him miss the pair of wild ovellah that sauntered down to the bank to drink. He determined to cast such thoughts from his mind and concentrate on the job of finding her. He'd do more good by being fixed in purpose than by wallowing in pity for her or for himself.

The arrow he fired caught the nearest of the woolly creatures deep in its neck and it fell almost at once. He waded out, careless of his noise now he had his prey, and dragged the creature into the water, so that the liquid would support it for his trip back to his

315

camp site.

Shaulah rose as he approached and she actually wagged her tail. He fussed her and she stretched, but gave a sharp soft yelp of pain as the stitches pulled in her side. He told her to sit as he collected timber. The burning glass was no use, with the sun now gone and the stars beginning to show in fast falling darkness. He'd collected his own flints along with the glass and that small exquisite box Tumalind always carried with her. She'd never shown him it, but he'd seen her open it daily and take a tiny pinch of the grey powder it held. She always shuddered as she did this and she'd told him it was what stopped her from becoming pregnant. It was important to her, to them both, so he'd brought it on this hunt for her. He could only hope that none of the savages who'd stolen her would make her with child in the meantime.

The fire was soon roaring and he skinned and gutted the ovellah as flames created the heat he'd need for cooking. It seemed sensible to cook a small piece first, to eat now and then to spit the rest as he ate and rested, so that he'd have cooked meat to carry him through the next few days and nights. The extra weight would quickly be compensated for by the time saved. Shaulah hungrily consumed some of the entrails and he was pleased to see her walking, even if a little gingerly, once she'd eaten.

He piled the fire high with the remaining timber, made a quick obeisance to a god he found less and less credible, and settled for the night with his back to the tree and Shaulah between him and the fire. He'd brought no sleep sack but gathered leaves and dry grass to make the ground comfortable enough for his weary frame to sleep.

Dawn came with birdsong still strange to his ears and he woke to look around him in the growing light. All was as he'd left it and he thanked Ytraa for safeguarding him, feeling guilty at the previous night's lack of faith. He drank his fill and replenished his girba, urged Shaulah to drink and to relieve herself, and then collected all and set off again, the dog draped across his shoulders, the cooked meat now an added weight hanging from his pack. A steady trot took him back the short distance to the horsemen's trail and he followed it easily over the slopes of hills that diminished in height as he moved further west. He'd seen and heard nothing of other people. This land, fertile and green, seemed deserted and he knew Aglydron would wonder at the waste of such good pasture.

He followed the trail across the ridge of the third hill that day, early evening now approaching. His major need was fresh water and he sought the signs. Knowing he must stop in his chase soon, or lose the trail in the darkness of night, he rested for a moment and searched the horizon all round. There were two likely spots; one quite close, the other, though more likely, a little further and also in the wrong direction. As he picked out a route, making sure he'd be able to retrace his steps and regain the trail again come morning, he saw a thin plume of blue smoke rise from the trees he intended to approach.

For a moment he was unsure what to do. It wasn't the horsemen, of that he could be sure, since he'd followed their trail well away to the north and west and there was no deviation leading to the point he could see the fire. But, in the absence of other human beings, who could be lighting a fire out here?

'Only one way to find out. Come on, Shaulah.'

He set her on the ground and she now limped slowly after him as he crossed the grassland with stealth. It was important she exercise the wounded muscles of her flank so they might mend without tightening, leaving her able to move freely once fully healed. He entered the edge of the trees and stopped in his tracks. The smoke arose from a crude mud chimney at one end of a small shack made of tree trunks laid one atop the other and linked at the corners with grooves to make the whole thing stable. His ears sought signs of habitation and caught the sound of a woman's voice in soft song. From behind, unmistakable, came the sound of someone stalking him. He stepped aside and turned, his blade unsheathed even as he faced the man who emerged from the undergrowth.

For a moment, they stood and stared at each other, neither willing to make the first move. But, when it became clear the man was no threat; his size and age suggesting he was no match for Okkyntalah's youth and strength, he sheathed his sword and nodded his head. As the stranger in this place, he felt he should introduce himself.

'I am Okkyntalah, a Follower of Ytraa from the island of Muhnilahm. I seek water only and wish you no ill.'

The other man, utterly naked and carrying only a short hunting knife in one hand, nodded but said nothing. Instead, he jerked his head in the direction of the small house and walked toward it. Okkyntalah followed, wary but curious. A short distance from the opening, the man stopped and called out; a guttural sound that had no meaning or form, something between a grunt and a call of welcome it sounded. The signing stopped and the woman came to the entrance. Okkyntalah looked into her eyes and registered their colouring. She seemed more curious than afraid or unsure but there was no hostility in her.

'A visitor, my husband? We must invite this handsome stranger to dine with us.'

Okkyntalah again introduced himself. She smiled and nodded, gesturing him within the small house, but gave no name for herself or her husband. The interior of the house was warm, with a cooking fire at the end, under the makeshift chimney, and no windows. The only opening was that through which he'd entered, followed by the husband. A narrow bench, at waist height, clung to one side of the building. Opposite, a crude box contained a few pots and battered pans. Next to the fire, leaning against the wall, stood the frame of what he took to be some sort of bed, the bed linen draped carelessly across it.

That was it. Nothing else. The floor was bare earth, swept but uncovered. And a small quantity of meat hung from the rough wood rafters that stretched across the space above. From inside, the thatching of the roof seemed even cruder than it had externally.

There was no furniture on which to sit and the man indicated a space beside the fire. Okkyntalah sat with the man beside him, on the floor. They were close enough to the woman that her skin touched his as she bent and went about her cooking of the meal. The food, whatever it was, gave off an aroma that had his mouth watering. Shaulah moved awkwardly inside, having relieved herself before entering, and curled at his feet.

The woman glanced at the dog and frowned. 'I can help that.'

He watched as she gently parted the matted fur around the wound. She was a stranger; what might she do to the dog if she hadn't the skill she seemed to believe she possessed? He nodded but held out his hand, in a gesture intended to suggest that he'd no wish to argue with her on the point but that she should leave the dog alone. She either misunderstood or deliberately ignored him and turned to the small box of belongings. From within, she extracted a bundle of dried leaves and stalks bearing wilted flowers. When she approached Shaulah with the bundle, Okkyntalah reached out to stop her, but the husband, with surprising strength, prevented him with a hand on his arm.

Okkyntalah turned to frown at him and found the man smiling and nodding at his wife's activity. He turned again and discovered she was merely drawing the bunch of dead leaves across the wound, crossing it in all directions and sweeping the plants against the skin but causing the dog no discomfort. Since she seemed to be doing nothing to harm his dog, and clearly believed she was helping, he allowed her to continue. It was obvious she could do no real good with this treatment but it would do no harm to allow her to think she was helping.

When she'd finished her 'treatment', she returned the plants to their box and continued with the preparation of the meal.

'Your woman was still well and intact when they passed here last night. You need not fear that the slave takers will rape her. She has convinced them she is virgin and they will save her in that way for the Uhmbard of Tohltaz, who they, in their savage way, think of as a god in human form. He'll pay them a great sum of money for her as a virgin. But, once he discovers she's been deflowered he may allow the men to have her for their amusement. I must contact another and persuade her to use the trick with ovellah blood in a fragile skin to convince the man she is virgin. I think that will serve best.'

She related all this as if it was the most commonplace of information and then set about ladling the food into earthenware bowls, passing one to each of the men in turn before helping herself to what remained. The quantities suggested she'd made enough only to feed the two of them and Okkyntalah felt guilty at depriving them of their food.

But her announcements about Tumalind took that concern from his mind for the moment and he began to ask her how she knew and whether she had other information of use to him.

'Eat first, talk afterwards. It is best that way, I think.'

He opened his mouth to speak again, but she took a morsel from her own bowl and popped it into the open space, smiling in the most mischievous way. 'Eat first. It is good.'

And it was. But Okkyntalah had many questions and he ate the food more quickly than the taste would have dictated on a different occasion.

Chapter 33

INTO THE DESERT

'*U*ncover. You are off the horse.'

Tumalind obeyed.

'Gather wood for a fire. Cook the meat, woman.'

She wandered into the trees and gathered fallen branches, wondering if there was any point in trying to escape. But they never allowed her out of their sight and that hope was forlorn. She was bending to gather a large branch when she felt the intrusion. Her instinct, to turn and swipe his face, scream at him to leave her alone, lash out, she swallowed with difficulty. Fear mingled with the dread of violation, the disgust of defilement. She made her body rigid and waited. The man with the overdeveloped muscles lifted her and laid her on her back.

'I'm a virgin.'

He nodded, took her hand and placed it. She understood, completing the task as swiftly as she could. He grunted, stood again, and continued to watch as she gathered more wood, letting her carry it and offering no help; saying nothing to her.

The fire she laid quickly and with a skill that seemed to impress them. She had no means of lighting it however, and told them what she needed. The leader, who she'd heard the others address as K'ang Fi-Tozu when they were formal and simply as Tozu otherwise, threw a small pouch to her. She discovered a good quality burning glass within, smeared with dirty fingerprints. With the outside of the pouch, she polished it before directing the sun's rays at the sticks, to set them on fire.

The thin one, an older surly man the others titled K'ang Fah-Tesi, returned from the wooded area dragging a large snake. He tossed the carcase at her and squatted close as she began to prepare the meat for cooking. He watched her every movement with a sort of hunger that made her feel both vulnerable and unclean.

'*May we talk?*'

The strange voice came as such a surprise that she almost dropped a piece of the meat on the ground. Only her quick reactions prevented it falling.

'*Later. I'm not free.*'

She had no idea who the voice belonged to, but it sounded, even with those few words, a friendly presence and she wished to connect again as soon as possible. Tesi, however, had other ideas and, as soon as she'd finished spearing the meat onto a pointed stake and placed it to cook over the flames, he dragged her to her feet by her hair.

321

'The meat will burn if it isn't turned…'

He slapped her buttocks twice, hard enough to bring tears to her eyes. One of the other men walked over and began turning the spit as Tesi dragged her to the edge of the clearing. Still in sight of the others, he made it clear what he required and she did as bidden, turning to spit only when he'd left her, still on her knees.

'The meat, woman.'

She was given no chance to gather her thoughts or recover from the activity as she took over the turning of the spit. She'd cut the snake into six more or less even-sized pieces and handed one to each of the men and stood holding the last as she showed it to Tozu, who nodded his assent. She moved a little aside and ate, determined to keep up her strength.

Before she'd finished eating, K'ang Du-Saru, the one with the huge muscles, yelled at her and pointed to the water carriers hanging from the saddle of one of the horses. She stood at once and collected the opened carrier and passed it to him. He slapped her bottom and nodded at Tozu. She understood and passed the water to the leader first, waiting for him to finish before she passed it to each of the others in turn. Slaps or their absence indicated their order of importance and she memorised them so she'd avoid more punishment in future. She thought she had the measure of these men and could manage with the minimum of punishment if she only learnt quickly what they required of her. It came as no surprise when the other two men approached her at different points in the evening and made her satisfy their lust. The acts made her feel used and ashamed, but, as Ivdulon had predicted, they didn't attempt to penetrate her and that was some blessing.

Tozu alone made no sexual demands of her to begin with. He sent her for fresh water and she took the chance to bathe in the stream after filling the three containers. Saru watched and used her services. She returned to the camp and sat on her folded tabard, hoping they might allow her some rest and freedom from interference. Tozu drew a small windpipe from his sleeve and began to play the most beautiful melody, his back against the tree and his eyes closed. For a while, she sat entranced and able to take some pleasure, small though it might be. But he ended the music and gestured at her to rise.

'Dance.'

He started another tune; this, a sensuous piece clearly intended as a seductive accompaniment to the expected dancing. Should she perform well or badly? Would they know if she pretended to be a poor dancer, would they beat her again? Her bottom was still smarting from the last series of blows, given her by Saru after he'd caught her spitting out his essence.

'If you're able, dance the most provocative and sensuous movements you can produce, my dear. It may stand you in good stead when you arrive in Ov-Bebna. May even save you

further sexual exploitation. These men respect women who dance well. In fact, it's the only aspect of womanhood they have any respect for at all.'

The comforting voice of the stranger again; this time offering help. She knew she'd be a fool to ignore it. The tune was easy enough to follow and she set her mind to imagining she was dancing for Okkyntalah, weaving her weary body to the melody and picturing the look on his face as if he were there to witness her display. To her surprise, the men started tapping their hands on the ground in time with the beat and the other muscular one, whose name she hadn't yet learned, took up the tune with the words of a song. He sang of love and tenderness, sentiments so false from the mouth of this man who'd used her so selfishly. But her performance clearly engaged them and she moved as naturally and as sensuously as she dared.

When the music stopped, she was ready for rest and walked back to her tabard to lie down. Tozu made his way to her as dusk began to fall and led her, by her hand, to the shadows under the trees and out of sight of the other men.

'In a moment, you will pleasure me as you see fit. First I commend you for your dancing. You have the attributes a woman should possess and you use them well. If you're able to persuade me of your suitability for all the music I'll play on this journey, I'll express my respect for your movement to the Uhmbard when we arrive. If you then perform for the Blessed God Made Man, may his soul live for ever, as well as you have for me, you may find yourself esteemed and elevated to the rank of Dancer. Now, pleasure me. But take your time. I'm not one of those common men and would, if you were not virgin, show you delights you cannot imagine. For now, however, your dancing has aroused my lust and you must therefore satisfy it.'

She was tentative, unsure of his preferences and testing the strange techniques to discover which pleased him most. The methods were easy in a physical sense, though they left her feeling unclean and fouled. But she'd preserve her skin and her beauty, her body and her soul so that Okkyntalah could spend the rest of their lives together teaching her to forget this period of abuse. For she would be rescued. He'd found and rescued her once. He would do so again.

After she'd satisfied the leader, she was permitted to sleep. The bare ground seemed to be all they expected for themselves and she was obliged to spend the night in her skin on the dry grass of the clearing. So far, all had used her but none had attempted to penetrate her. Before she dropped off to sleep, she reached out to find the unknown woman for some comfort and found her waiting for the connection.

'I'm here. I'll be here for you whenever you need me. I'll not go from this place, which is my home now, until I die. I have with me Okkyntalah. His dog is now healed, though he doesn't believe it yet. He's a man and I forgive him his ignorance of such things. Continue as

323

you have so far, Tumalind. You're earning respect from these savages. Dance according to the music you hear from them. Sensuous when the melody winds and turns; provocative, saucy, crudely obvious at need. Succeed in this and you'll be free of invasion into your centre.

'*Learn to submit to their every demand and they'll no longer beat you. Learn to be their pleasure and they may be less harsh and give you treats. Whatever they give you, accept with grace, be it welcome or not. Only by being completely submissive will you gain ascendency. A Dancer is the highest rank a female can gain in their society. It doesn't confer freedom as you understand it, but it means you're not the plaything of every man, to be used, abused, beaten and kept naked as is the lot of the other women. Be humble before the men, make them believe you accept their superiority and you'll gain. Believe me, Tumalind, for I know of what I speak. I've been what you'll become and I escaped and live to tell the tale. Don't disappoint them, for they don't forgive. They don't forgive at all.*'

And, on this warning, the woman left her to try to sleep, though she wished to know so much more. The voice was gone from her head and wouldn't return, in spite of the earlier promise.

◦ ·≍•·≔·

'Please tell Tumalind I love her.'

The woman nodded. 'She already knows. But I'll explain your visit and reassure her that you'll follow her to Ov-Bebna, against my advice, and I'll always be here to support her when she needs me. Now, if you're to stand any chance of fulfilling your destiny, Okkyntalah, you need to leave us.'

He kissed her and she melted in his embrace again.

'Of this, I'll say nothing to Tumalind. You've paid well for what I might have done without cost to you, but I won't make her suffer for my price and pleasure. Now, go.'

He bent and retrieved his small cache of belongings from the floor, leaving the longbow to last. Shaulah rose from her place by the hearth and stretched, making no sound of pain as she flexed the flesh where her wound had been. She shook herself and he made to pick her up.

'The dog is well. She'll run beside you. You need carry her no further.'

As if to prove the point, Shaulah jumped up and placed her feet on the woman's shoulders and licked her ear. The woman stroked her and she dropped back to all fours, waiting.

Outside, the husband rose from the place where he'd spent the night and took Okkyntalah's hand between his rough small palms. He looked into his eyes, glanced at the woman and then squeezed with gratitude and nodded his thanks. The man handed Okkyntalah a small pack of fruits he'd collected and then stood beside his wife, holding

324

her hand.

The pair were still watching as he left the small clearing behind. He stopped at the edge to wave his thanks for their hospitality and then began his trot back to the trail of the horsemen, as the early light of the rising sun brought definition to the ground.

He ran all day, pausing only for occasional drinks and to check that Shaulah was still well. The woman's healing had done its job and the wound, though still marked by the scar beneath the fur, seemed fully healed. Her news of Tumalind's progress and condition, which she'd passed to him only when he'd satisfied her condition and paid the price demanded, had both encouraged and dismayed him. That she should be forced into such demeaning ways was distressing, but that she hadn't been penetrated or hurt, beyond the smacking, was some comfort.

The woman had explained that dance was a part of their religion and those who practiced it well and appropriately were honoured even as women. An ability to dance well ensured that she wouldn't be sought for sexual usage. In fact, she'd reside in the women's quarter as a guest, tended and waited on by the lesser women. Okkyntalah smiled, knowing she'd find such elevation difficult to cope with and wouldn't want such attention. He hoped she'd be able to adjust for the small time it would take him to find her and that she wouldn't insult the sensibilities of the other women by refusing their help and service.

The trail was still easy to follow as he left behind the hills and trod the grasslands in their shadows. But, as the day wore on, sweating under the relentless sun, he found the ground growing harder, the grass less lush, the trees disappearing completely. The woman had explained the direction of the city she'd escaped some years previously. She'd warned him of the lack of water in the sands and rocks that surrounded the small lakes beside which the city of Ov-Bebna was built. She'd given him directions on how to find the secret desert wells he would need to keep up his supplies of water, and she'd warned him not to cross the wandering tribes if he should be unfortunate enough to come in contact with them.

'Their hospitality is legend but their insistence that theirs is the only way in all things is even more well-founded. If you come to one of their camps, do exactly as they tell you. I've seen a man hamstrung and left naked in the sands for failing to eat food with the right hand. Remember, the left is for those things they consider unclean. The right is for all other things. And the right is used in greeting welcome strangers as well as friends. If a man reaches out to you with his left hand, refuse to take it. It's a test. And if you fail it, they'll strip you, allow the women to beat you, and peg you out to roast under the midday sun.'

She'd taught him much that he would need to survive in this hostile land. Each time he'd delighted her, she'd given him more information. At no point had the bargain been declared but he'd quickly realised that she gave only in response to his attentions and ability to please her needs and wants. From hints and things she explained to him he put together a picture of the woman as a dancer and later, through some event she hadn't described, as a sex slave in the harem of the Uhmbard. The man she now called husband had helped her escape before she was due to die as entertainment for the Uhmbard's birthday celebrations. Their journey to the shack where he'd found them had been hard and now they lived basic lives with small but simple pleasures.

He arrived in a place where the grassland ended in dunes with coarse sharp blades in clumps that held the small loose hills together. It would be a shelter for the first part of the night. He no longer needed the trail of the horses, which ran clear across the sands before him. By morning, the constant wind would have erased all sign. From now on he must navigate his way by stars and travel during darkness to avoid the searing heat of unshaded sun. And he must hunt the small venomous snakes that lived on the swift lizards inhabiting the sands. They were the only source of food.

He stood in the wide outstretched arms of the mountains failing limbs, in a place she'd referred to as the Mascuni Crannel. On the south-western edge of this place stood a small settlement, but he was far away from that place as he looked across the wilderness ahead. Thirty leagues of dry, empty sand and rock lay between him and the city where his beloved would soon reside, where, in fact she might already be in residence. He hoped the mindtalk of the woman would sustain and help Tumalind survive these first few days before he arrived to recover her and take her back to their intended home in Litkala.

It seemed only moments since she'd lain down to rest and they were waking her, making her rise and dress, lifting her onto the horse in the darkness. The last trees had disappeared behind her, the grassland vanished under the stars. Now she was in a world of trotting hooves that sounded soft upon the sands she knew passed underneath her. The stars, bright and clear in the utter blackness of the sky, except where they were so countless that they gave a milky look to the arcing void above, were her only guide to direction and speed. The Skyfire, unremarked as yet by her captors, rose and shone with a brilliance she found hard to ignore. How could they remain indifferent to such an obvious portent?

She wanted to ask them what they thought of it but had learned she must speak only when they required it. They'd given no explanation of their sudden rising in the night, no description of their intentions. None of them had referred to the Skyfire, though all had noted and avoided staring at it.

The woman who'd spoken in her mind wouldn't connect with her and she wondered why. She'd been so openly friendly and helpful to begin with but had left her without warning. With Okkyntalah in her house, was she demanding payment for her help? If so, it was a price Tumalind would pay for advice that had stopped her violation and spared her smarting skin more of the casual slaps she'd had for her unwitting disobedience.

The movement of the horse was different now, the length of the strides seemed greater, the ride a little smoother now they were on this endless stretch of sand. The man in front was one of those whose name she'd yet to hear; a younger man, with eyes that matched her own. He had the build and way of moving that reminded her of Okkyntalah, but his manner was so different. He was coarse and brutal. Demanding and selfish, looking on her with distain and planting a harsh slap on her buttocks for no apparent reason just before he required her to pleasure him. He smelled unwashed and it occurred to her that none of the men had used the streams they'd passed to bathe. But his eyes gave the possibility of mindtalk and she wondered; should she try it? How would he react if she invaded his mind? Was he a gifted, as she knew she must be to receive and connect so easily and over such long distances?

It was a risk, perhaps one she should avoid. But she might learn so much from him, if she could remain hidden. And he need never know it was she who intruded, as long as she remained silent, an observer only. Her life, she felt, depended on knowing what she could of these savage men.

She concentrated, trying to find a sign of him in that invisible but present world she'd discovered the first time she'd mindtalked. It was a world impossible to describe; there were no words to paint a picture of the intricacies and patterns that existed there. It was a world entirely separate from that she'd lived in all her life. And though it was a place of welcome for the most part, there were niches and crannies full of darkness, places she knew it was unwise to explore. Aklon had told her of the lies of Gadhallah, explained how he believed that their religious leader had been the victim of unscrupulous users of mindtalk. It was possible the man had been driven to his acts, at least in part, by the insistent voices of other evil men who could mindtalk.

Somewhere in that other place, it should be possible for her to find a link that would take her to this man in front of her. But every time she found a possibility it lurked close to the darkest places, those spots of activity that warned against intrusion. Was it worth the risk of the unknown danger and possible pollution of her mind simply to find out what this man was like? Would she learn more from his mind than she had already from his behaviour?

She risked a swift intrusion where she was sure his mind resided in the weave of mindtalk. At once, she plunged into a world of pleasure based on pain and power over others. He was unaware of her as she saw what he was seeing. A large room lit with many

327

candles. The spread of female flesh, exposed. Many women, more than she'd seen gathered in any one place before. She could feel the excitement in him as the mind he linked with scanned the many bodies, and sought out the women most on show. They were about their ablutions and, in one corner, several of them were doing something she couldn't comprehend to another woman spread-eagled on the ground. There was something odd about all the women that she couldn't, at first, identify. Something missing. It was only as the connection was ending that she realised none of the women had a trace of body hair.

As he broke the connection with the other mind in what she realised must be the harem, she felt his hand come round his back in search of hers. It wasn't easy, but she knew what he required and wasn't surprised, in light of what she'd witnessed. It was swiftly done and she wished the ride in darkness might soon end. Though she had no wish to be soon amongst that gathering of women knowing what awaited her.

The night seemed to never end and she dozed until dawn broke and sent light from the rising sun to warm her back. She looked out on long shadows leading them toward the unseen city. How long would they ride in daylight?

Long before the sun reached its zenith, they halted. Given quick instructions, she put up the folded shelter they carried with them on their separate horses. The men retired inside its shade at once but she must first erect another shelter for the horses. All the rods and pegs were shown her, the filmy rolls of black fabric. By the time she'd made the shelter for the horses, she found the men asleep with the only remaining space amongst them. It was suffer their stinking closeness or roast under the unforgiving sun. And she knew her skin was not prepared for such exposure. Curled into the small space, she tried to sleep, interrupted now and then by demands for attention.

Late afternoon, as the sun began its journey down to the horizon, she awoke and made the meal. They'd brought timber for a fire, and the last meat of their final hunt sufficed. Of water there was no sign but they carried some with them. She used it sparingly and passed the container to each man in turn before she took her own short swig.

For the first time since they'd captured her, she spent the time without a single smack and she hoped she had the measure of them now. Her anger and her fear, her disgust and loathing she bottled up inside and never let them see. There'd be time enough to pay these savages back for what they'd done to her. Already she'd imagined a fate for the most muscular of them. He'd been most brutal, most demanding, most humiliating. He'd regret his cruelty when she was done with him, if she ever got the chance to repay his abuse.

Chapter 34

ENDLESS SANDS

*O*kkyntalah was used to a landscape with markers. This endless, featureless sand was wearing on the spirit and gave no confidence in direction or territory covered. But he had the stars to keep him on track and the Skyfire, as it rose above and slowly descended toward the morning to remind him of the passage of the hours. The woman had warned him not to try to travel in the heat of midday. She'd gifted him a thin sheet of fine fabric and told him how to use it to protect his skin from the harshness of the desert. By dawn, he was growing weary from constant running but he would continue until the sun was higher and the heat too strong to bear.

In daylight, abandoned by the stars, he had no reference point beside the blazing sun to indicate direction. From time to time, he turned and looked behind him at his trail across the sand. The land was flat, and he could see only a league or so from where he stood to the horizon. But he could discern the curve of a track he'd imagined as a straight line. Adjusting direction for the deviation he knew was always likely in this terrain, he ran on, but stopped more often to check on the degree of his deviation from the straight line he required.

His supply of water was growing low and he knew it was vital out here where no clouds hid the glowing orb above, no trees provided shade. The woman had spoken of wells sunk in the desert over ages by the people who'd inhabited this land since the beginning of time, as she'd put it. They were not Followers of Ytraa. Their faith rested the sun god, Ulkhon. Those who lived in Ov-Bebna also worshiped Ulkhon, but via the words of an ignorant peasant who claimed the god had spoken to him during frequent sorties alone into the dunes to escape persecution by those who thought him mad. Later, following a series of miraculous events that Okkyntalah found unbelievable, the peasant's words had been written down and now formed the basis of the faith, called Immallsu. It seemed to him a lunatic foundation for a belief in any god, but that was what they believed here.

'And your god, this Ytraa, is his existence any less ridiculous, Okkyntalah?'

She'd asked him this during one of the breaks in a night of almost desperate passion, a night in which she'd urged their joining, wearying him at the very time he needed all the energy he could save for his hunt for Tumalind. But it had been clear that this was the price he must pay for her continued help for Tumalind. And, if he was completely honest, though he wouldn't have chosen such engagement with the woman, she gave pleasure as

329

though born to it. A result, she'd said, of being raised a woman by the Immalls. Sex was their only value to the men. A woman who could not or would not provide her body to be used to satisfy the lust of any man was worthless and wouldn't live long where she'd come from.

He looked up and realised he'd let his mind wander as he was running. A dangerous slip in this place. He turned and studied his tracks to find he'd deviated more than previously. Perhaps it was time to do as she'd suggested.

The roll of fabric seemed strangely rigid when he lifted it from the top of his pack. He untied the leather band that held it as a roll, and the whole thing unwrapped and leapt from his hands. He watched in silent amazement as the roll unfolded to become a form of shelter. The whole design and mechanism, using flexible rods of seasoned wood sewn into the material, was self-opening and formed a 'v' shaped shelter, open at one end. He turned it so that the apex was on top, and slipped inside. At once, the temperature seemed to drop to something much more bearable. He moved back out and oriented the shelter, had she called it a tent? Yes. He remembered that was her name for it. He lined the tent up with his direction of travel, gathered his other belongings and slid back inside. Before arranging his possessions to form a partial block to the open end, he invited Shaulah in to lie beside him. The pair had just enough space to stretch out. Once prone, he realised how exhausted he'd become and it was moments only before he was asleep.

'You're not simply besotted with the man, like the rest of us, are you, Shoarhn?'

She glanced at Irrildys and smiled a little wryly. 'I'm in love with Aklon. Have been since the day we met. And he loves me, too.'

'Well, he seems to love us all. I know A'ahl, in spite of her devotion to that soldier husband of hers, was completely taken with the man. And, to tell the truth, so am I. But, if he declares he wants to be with you exclusively, I can live with that. There'll be others, though, who won't be quite so generous.'

She didn't want to discuss an unknown future, not with all the rumours that were spreading through the town. 'Have you heard anything new, since the runner came with news of his announcement of the real Skyfire?'

Irrildys nodded. 'That's why I'm here. They say he and another man stole ten horses from a farm near Chalamamnon and killed the entire family there. He then rode overnight to the Scar and wiped out the entire army. Just him and this other man.'

'I don't believe any of that. Do you?'

'I believe he may have borrowed a horse. I believe he may have had some encounter with the army or what's left of them after the disastrous campaign that fool Wendarah sent them on…'

'How do you hear such things, Irrildys?'

The woman smiled and shifted on her stool to milk the next cow in line. 'You should employ a girl to help you, Shoarhn. Now Aglydron's gone, you can't hope to look after this lot on your own. You're becoming worn and weary and Aklon's not going to thank you for turning into an old hag before your time, is he?'

She'd given this matter some thought and concluded it was something she must do, and do soon. There was income enough to employ a couple of helpers and she must do that. Irrildys was right. She'd wear herself out this way. She'd find help today.

'You haven't answered my question.'

'I keep my ears and eyes open. In any case, you know my husband's brother is a town elder. That so-called priest has to tell him what he knows. And he says, putting two fish in the pond and making many, it's obvious that Aklon and some of the Few did somehow defeat most of the army at the Scar. That tale's not a rumour, apparently. Like you, Shoarhn, I'm eager to see Aklon again to find out what he's really doing. Things are starting to get difficult. They do say that the Few have already shown themselves in the capital and that cesspit of a place beside the marshes in the south.'

'Pampahn? Aklon visits it quite often. It's near enough the Point for him to get to see his precious rejects and convicts easily. I still don't quite understand how he's so devoted to such deviants, do you?'

Irrildys waited until Shoarhn had settled to her next cow before she spoke, making sure they were still alone before she did so. 'You're not thinking things through, are you? Why are you a member of the Few?'

Why was she? Was it because she was in love with Aklon? Was that the only reason? He'd told her things about the faith, explained some of the lies they'd been told, made it clear their religion was founded on a set of stories that were utterly false. The truths he'd told her had made her feel physically sick. And to think she'd worshipped as she had; had allowed that evil man, the High Priest, to invade her. She began to understand what Irrildys was getting at.

'You mean, because the rules and laws of the Followers are based on lies, those who break them aren't really as bad as we've always thought them?'

'More than that. If what we've believed has been untrue, then those who've done things against our beliefs might've been doing the right things all along, mightn't they?'

It made sense, uncomfortable as it was to contemplate the idea that she'd been wrong to Follow all her life. She wondered, briefly, whether she'd have been as willing to deny her faith if she hadn't been seduced by Aklon, if she hadn't fallen so far in love with him. 'Do you love Aklon? I mean, love him rather than just want him to frowk you?'

Irrildys laughed. 'No, I never loved him. I love my husband. But Aklon knows how to

331

please a woman better than any man I've ever had. And I've had a few, I can tell you. You know, it strikes me that young Okkyntalah's got the makings of a great lover. Your Tumalind would've been a lucky girl if they'd ever got to join. Wonder where she is now?'

'She's married to him, don't you know they..?' Of course she didn't know. How could she?

Irrildys looked at her strangely. 'Married? How could that be, Shoarhn? She's a Virgin Gift. Chosen at the ceremony. We all saw it.'

How could she explain? She knew she mustn't say a word about Aklon's wonderful gift of talking in minds to people far away. If such knowledge got out to the people they'd think him mad or cursed.

'I'm surprised your husband's brother hasn't said anything. Didn't Kaz-Ca-Uldrad pass on the message he was given by the one sent by Wendarah?' She was thinking on her feet, trying to imagine how she could have been given a message by those who'd returned from Litkala. There had been a man, someone no-one trusted. What was his name?

'I've heard nothing of Tumalind that way. What message is this?'

She stopped milking, gathering her thoughts so she could make a story that would convince her friend. It was so hard to do this thing, this thing they called lying. But honesty might harm not just Aklon but the entire Cause.

'I can't tell you the details. I don't know how it all works. But when the runner came from Wendarah, when she came back from the mainland to announce the change in prayer positions, you know? Well, he had a message for me about Aglydron and Okkyntalah and Tumalind.'

'But I thought Kaz-Ca-Uldrad went to Chalamamnon to meet with Wendarah? I didn't think they'd sent a runner for him here.'

Already this was getting harder than anything she'd ever tried before. 'I'm sorry, Irrildys. I wasn't supposed to say anything. I was supposed to keep it all secret. But he came to see me, not the priest.'

'A runner came to you? Just to you?'

She was in too deep now to retract it. 'Yes. I know it's almost unheard of. But, well because of the circumstances they felt they should let me know. And now I'll have to explain everything I know so you'll understand why they had to do it the way they did.'

She described the meeting of the two parties on the mainland, how Okkyntalah's bravery had impressed Dagla Kaz and how the spiritual leaders in Litkala had agreed that Tumalind must've been chosen in error so that Litkala and Muhnilahm could be re-united at last. She explained how Dagla Kaz had spoken to Ytraa and had decided Tumalind could be released and replaced by a virgin from the city so she could marry Okkyntalah.

Irrildys looked at her with renewed respect. 'And you've kept all that to yourself all this time? I'd have been bursting to let everyone know.'

'I've been desperate to tell folk, especially since a lot of them still say Aglydron and Okkyntalah were wrong to do what they did. Oh, things have quietened down a bit since Kaz-Ca-Uldrad passed on the news from Wendarah that the High Priest has forgiven them and that his daughter's now married to the most powerful leader on the mainland. But all the details about them weren't supposed to be passed on to the people. You can see why, can't you, Irrildys?'

'It wouldn't do for two of the common folk to have been right and the High Priest to be wrong. No. I can see that. Well, once Aklon arrives, I think we'll have to make this all public. It's just the sort of thing the Cause needs to persuade the people of the truth. What do you say?'

It hadn't occurred to Shoarhn that it might help the Cause in this way but her friend's suggestion made good sense, as long as they could make sure the news avoided any mention of the real way she'd heard about it. If people thought Aklon heard voices in his head, he might lose all credibility: she'd only believed him because her love told her he always dealt in truth. She could only hope that she'd get to see him before Irrildys so she could let him know what she'd said. If he told Irrildys the truth, as he was so likely to do, she knew that the woman, member of the Few or not, would think him mad.

Aglydron stood with Chislanda's hand in his as the whole company gathered in the large common room of the accommodation they'd been given. The room was abuzz with rumour and speculation and all the talk was of newcomers and of their intended short stay in this place for a rest and the replenishment of stores. It seemed Quyreena had been persuaded to remain on hand, and would sail the party up the river at least as far as Mehrrhyphrol. What would happen when they reached this outlying city wasn't yet known. But the thing that exercised most minds was the rumour that they were all to adopt the scandalous dress of the natives whilst they remained in Ov-Bebna.

'It can't be right to go about like that.'

'Does it worry you because other men will see my breasts, Aglydron? Or is there some other reason?'

She smiled as she asked her question and Aglydron was incapable of being as cross with Chislanda as he felt he should be.

'Of course I wish to keep you for my eyes and those of Ytraa. Why shouldn't I?'

'I thought we were all supposed to join freely with each other?'

'Yes. But joining is worship and naked is sacred. This is different. These people go around showing their upper bodies and wearing clothes that, instead of hiding their parts,

333

draw your eyes to them. It's blasphemy. And I'll tell that to the High Priest.'

'Looks like you'll get your chance, Aglydron.' Myllthlan nodded over to the entrance to the room, where Dagla Kaz, accompanied by the woman who was a Keeper of the Keys and a group of other people, entered. The people were carrying garments.

Dagla Kaz clapped his hands for silence. 'I understand your reservations. I sympathise with those of you who will find this uncomfortable, maybe even blasphemous. I agree with you. But if I've learned anything in my travels, it's that compromise is often the only way to satisfy the needs of this sacred mission we conduct. Nothing must prevent or interrupt our mission. With this in mind, I ask that, for as long as we remain the guests of these Followers in Ov-Bebna, you adopt their way of dress. I've consulted with their High Priest on the matter and, though I cannot quite agree with his interpretation of the texts, I can see how such an interpretation might be made. Since this is a matter of doctrinal interpretation, I've decided that, for the sake of peace and mutual understanding, we will subject ourselves to this sacrifice for the short time we remain here. And I'll have no argument on this matter. You will obey this command and dress as do our hosts.'

There was no room for doubt in the High Priest's tone or words and Aglydron reluctantly accepted the garment he was handed by one of the servants. He waited to see what exactly was required of them.

'You may change into these garments now. Your tabards and tunics will be collected and taken on board the ship to prevent any, er, forgetfulness for the duration of our stay here.'

This was intolerable. To strip in such conditions was unheard of. Aglydron stood firm.

'This can't be right, Dagla Kaz. Why can't we go to our rooms to change and bring our clothes back here?'

Dagla Kaz actually seemed relieved at this suggestion. 'You raise a good point, Aglydron. I've no doubt that you all have spare tabards and tunics anyway. So, do as Aglydron has said. I commend his wisdom. But I want all your other garments back here at once. Do not keep me waiting.'

He found it hard to look into the eyes of the women, once they'd re-assembled in the common area. Found it difficult to avoid those glances toward the region barely masked by those narrow strips of cloth. Yet, he had seen that the people who lived in this city looked each other in the eye without difficulty and avoided staring at the parts on show.

'It's just what you get used to, I suppose, Aglydron. I spent half my time naked on the island, as did many of the men. You stop looking after a while. It just becomes normal.'

He wondered if Myllthlan's words were true and whether their proposed stay of a few

334

days would be long enough to find out. For the meantime, there were many women on display and he was torn between his desire to appreciate their beauty and his wish to be seen as pious and devout. In the hope of at least assuaging the desire he felt, he persuaded Chislanda back to their room and joined with her.

'See, what they do here makes sense for Followers, Aglydron. The form of dress makes joining even more likely than your tabards or Litkala's tunics. And joining is worship, isn't it?'

He was unsure if Chislanda was mocking just a little, but he felt so relaxed and at peace after their love making that he had no heart to reprimand her. And, if her words were sincere, there was truth in what she said. He began to look forward to the delay in the city, to hope it might last longer than the few days Dagla Kaz had announced. A private room, a comfortable bed, and all the time they wished; what more could he ask? Comfort and contentment were his at last, for a while anyway.

'I wonder if Tumalind and Okkyntalah have reached safety yet.'

Chislanda's idle speculation, nothing more than simple curiosity, awoke his guilt at his denial of her wishes regarding the High Priest. He found his mind reviewing her reasons for escape and understood why she'd risked so much to avoid the possibility of joining with the man who must, after all, be her real father. He could've prevented her flight had he only had the humility to admit she wasn't his daughter. Pride alone had made him silent on the matter and now it had cost him the girl he'd brought up as his own, the girl he'd loved as his child for all of her life till now.

'Oh, Chislanda; what have I done?'

And he told her the whole sorry story, hoping she'd understand and not reject him when she learned of his selfishness.

They travelled mostly by night, resting during the day under the framed shelter they called a tent. The horses shaded by another of these devices that seemed magical to her. That such savage and brutal men could possess these wonders of design was amazing. Her curiosity was aroused and she yearned to ask how they made them, how they were designed. But any word spoken without a command from a man was rewarded with a slap to her bottom, still smarting from punishment for no more than her being there to punish, it seemed.

At dusk, with the desert city apparently only a little beyond the horizon, they stopped. She prepared everything, as expected, and two of the men challenged each other to a match. As she went about her tasks, she saw them draw a rough circle in the sand. Saru, the one with the huge muscles and the hands too ready to smack her, especially before he sought her service, stood at one side of the circle and removed his coat. It was the first time she'd seen any of the men naked. He was very muscular and stood proudly on display as the other men admired him. He caught her eye and she smiled and bowed her head, expecting she was supposed to be desirous of him in this state; though, in fact, she found his body rather repulsive and wouldn't have joined voluntarily with him even had she not been in love with Okkyntalah.

The other muscular man, the one whose name she'd only just learned was K'eng Hin-Seru, moved to the opposite edge of the circle and also stripped. He posed and postured, giving every impression that he was more in love with himself than any other being. He called to her. 'Stand in the centre of the circle, woman.'

She was preparing the evening meal, but she left it and did as she was commanded. Uncovered and on display between these two vain men. What was required of her?

'Choose.'

The command was aimed at her and she must obey. But there was no clue about what she must choose, or why. Neither did she know what her choice would result in. She made a play of staring at each of the naked men in turn and sought out the woman who had mindtalked with her earlier. To her relief, she discovered the woman unoccupied and willing to hear her.

'They will wrestle and the victor will have you to himself for the night. As a virgin, you'll still not be frowked, but you'll have to service him several times according to his whim.'

'And the one I don't choose?'

'If you select the one who wins, you'll be rewarded with a night free of your other duties and spend it with him, as I've described.'

'The loser will have to do my duties?'

'You catch on quickly, my dear.'

'And what will he do to me for having him act this way?'

'You do catch on quickly, don't you? He's not supposed to do anything. But, if he has the chance in private, he's likely to make demands on you, slap you a lot and make you wish you'd chosen him. It's a wonderfully fair and just system, isn't it?'

'Thank you. May I know your name, please?'

But the connection was broken and she had still to make her choice. Knowing that Saru, the over-muscled one, would smack her before, during and after she serviced him anyway, she selected the other one. Seru was a name too similar and she kept his other syllable in mind so she could more readily distinguish between them. Unsure what was required of her, she merely bowed her head at Hin-Seru and waited.

The man, preened and strutted and waved her toward him. He stroked her breasts and between her legs and pressed her to sit on the sand, a habit she'd avoided. But she had no choice and could only protect herself by curling her legs beneath her.

K'ang Fi-Tozu took his place in the centre of the empty circle. He gestured the two naked men to approach him until they stood within reach of his hands. He placed one on each of their shoulders. 'I expect a fair fight, without gouging, biting or nose poking. I wager three quounds on Seru for this match.'

The other men all made similar bets, and the coins were set in two separate piles, one on each of the men's discarded coats. Tozu approached Tumalind and pulled her to her feet with her hands. 'You have permission to call support for your champion and, if you dare, to insult Saru. Understand that the winner is the one you will pleasure all night.'

Was this his way of warning her not to be too vocal in her discouragement of either man, in case the one she insulted won? It was an act of almost kindness that surprised her.

The two men now performed identical sets of movements as they faced each other. This appeared to be some sort of preparation. Though its real purpose could only be the display of their muscles in an attempt to dominate the other man. Tozu called a command she didn't understand and it seemed that the match started at that word.

She watched the men close on each other, Saru's massive hands grasping Hin-Seru's great thighs and the other man matching the hold, so that they held each other in a grotesque embrace. Nothing appeared to happen for some time and Tumalind dared a short cry of encouragement, calling out the name of her champion. This seemed to galvanise him into action and, to her amazement, he lifted the huge bulk of the other man completely off the ground and tossed him onto his back. Saru moved quickly for one so thick-limbed and was back on his feet before Hin-Seru could take advantage of the throw. There followed a period of movement toward and away as the men seemed to size each other up but neither made any move to grasp his opponent.

'K'eng Hin-Seru!'

Her call again had the effect of making him act. He dived at his opponent's feet and upended him. But, still prone, from his dive, he was too slow, too involved in glorying in his victory, and Saru rolled over and placed his bulk on top of him. For a while, the slightly smaller man struggled.

'K'eng Hin-Seru, I await your victory!'

It was enough. Pride alone gave him the strength he needed. He reached up and found his opponent's throat, enclosed it with his hands, and stopped his breath. Saru, unable to disengage, tried to kick him, but Hin-Seru was too nimble and the kicks only met the sand, allowing Hin-Seru to move into the position of ascendency. Once on top of the man, he forced his face into the sand until Saru had to tap his hand in signal of submission. Hin-Seru at once released him and helped him to his feet. The men embraced and brushed sand off each other in token of their respect. As they left the circle, Saru made a point of glaring at Tumalind with such a look that she feared for her future safety if ever alone with him.

For the moment, however, Hin-Seru took her hand and led her a short way from the tent and instructed her to remove the sand from his parts before she pleasured him. He paid attention to her breasts, grating sand against the most sensitive parts as she brought the act to a conclusion.

Done, she awaited his command and wondered whether she'd live long enough to reach the city if Saru managed to take her alone before they reached that place.

Chapter 35

EXAMINED

*A*klon had decided it would be better to enter the new settlement in the early evening rather than during the day. That way, both sets of people would have a night's rest between introductions and the need to get along as one group. He stood at the head of the stretched column, overlooking the valley. Not so long ago, this had been a deserted place with only wild animals to disturb the tranquillity. Now, it was occupied by many small huts, thatched with broad leaves of trees that grew by the lake. There were people in quantity.

Behind him, a troop of over four hundred souls, mostly seasoned soldiers, lined up with a sprinkling of loyal slaves and camp followers. Below, Chellyth commanded a gathering swollen by the earlier crop of soldiers; a population of almost five hundred, including children and nursing infants. Many of her original people, from the Point, weren't fit enough to undertake the roles he had in mind. Perhaps it was time to take them into the open, to set up a new village on the main part of the island, whilst those who felt able and so inclined accompanied him on his quest to implement the Cause.

'Too many to take on the road, Aklon. We'd never feed them all. And the children…'

'Exactly what I was thinking, Delbon. We will consult with Chellyth and Por-Kildu and let them decide the move they wish to make.'

The woman greeted him, looking with wonder at the huge numbers he'd brought. She appeared briefly uncertain and cautious.

'You three captured all these?'

'We had help from a higher source.'

She'd hear soon enough about Ivdulon's intervention in the guise of Ytraa, without understanding the reality of it. For the moment, he wanted rest, food, and the peace to plan his next move. He'd expected violence, bloodshed and chaos when he started the Cause, but things hadn't happened that way. The army, always a huge worry for him, now stood beside him rather than facing him as an enemy and this altered much of what he'd planned during his years of waiting. He must review his ideas and adapt them to the new reality.

'Aklon, more men…and women, eh? You'll be free for me later?'

He nodded absently at Syylvah, noticing she was cleaner, and had put on a little weight, which suited her. In fact, was that small bump a sign of pregnancy?

'Yeah. I'm frowkin' full o' child. Don't know whose, mind. Mebbie yours.'

It was possible, of course. But she'd always taken care in the past to prevent pregnancy. What had changed, he wondered.

Por-Kildu arrived belatedly and grasped his arm. 'You need feeding, my friend. And a good long rest by the look of you.'

He was grateful for this practical help and service and happily fell in with his friend who led him to the central hut and sat him at a table where food was soon brought. More food than he'd ever seen at the colony. They made full use of their surroundings. No more starvation rations, no more plain food. This was feasting and seemed to be the rule for the day here. He was pleased he'd served their needs so well.

Chellyth allowed him to eat and gave him a place to sleep in a hut built for just that purpose. 'We never were able to treat our honoured guest as well as you deserved, Aklon. I was determined we'd do you proud for this visit.'

He was relieved to rest without need for constant vigilance. Being ever on guard exhausted him.

But he wasn't permitted to rest alone for long. Syylvah came and demanded her fill before she'd allow him to sleep. Once satisfied, she let him rest his head in her lap and stroked his brow as a mother might her child.

The morning brought the need for decisions before action could begin. He called a meeting with Chellyth, Por-Kildu, Delbon, Phildrad and three army officers who'd already proved their worth.

'I want all of you to have your say here. It is vital that we agree on the action we should now take. I want no dissent; only full agreement will do. First, let me set before you my vision of what we need and what I wish to achieve.

'I have explained to some of you how evil is the religion we were all made to believe was right for us. Some have had more information on that than others but all here are now agreed that we need to make changes, I think?'

There was general agreement amongst those assembled, but one of the officers looked unhappy.

'Tell me your doubts. But let me first know your name, please.'

'Yelbohn, Aklon-Dji, Paltrohn. I'm affeared some of the troops aren't sure about the changes you mean to make. Some 'ave lost partners in the fighting an' some just don't know whether they can face goin' back 'ome to towns where they'll mebbie be despised for getting in wi' you.'

'How dare you say such…?'

Aklon raised his hand to quell Chellyth's outrage. 'Thank you, Yelbohn, for your honest assessment. Try to remember, Chellyth, that not all assembled here have your advantage of knowledge and familiarity with the reality of the faith we have espoused for so long. I need openness and honesty here. It is vital that we start our campaign without secrets or bitterness. Yelbohn, do you know what, if anything, will help convince these doubters?'

'I reckon you're gonna tell us things here an' now what'll convince a good many of 'em. Let's see what your words do, eh? But I thought you should know; that's all, Paltrohn.'

'Thank you, again, Yelbohn. And, please call me Aklon. I have a deep dislike of titles.'

'Sorry, Aklon-Dji, but if the troops are to do your bidding, they'll need to know you by your title, or you'll not have their respect. They're soldiers, after all.' This from another officer.

Aklon shook his head, not in disagreement as much as in despair that such a need existed. 'Very well, for the moment, I will remain Aklon-Dji. Though that title is one of the things I would dispose of as early as possible in our campaign. I would thank any who can come up with some other title that conveys our new beliefs and concerns. For the moment, we need to discuss more important things than what I am to be called.'

<hr />

The wrestling done and her initial pleasuring of the champion complete, Tumalind and Hin-Seru returned to the encampment, where Saru had prepared the evening meal. As befitted his status as the loser, he served each of the men with their food and then, to his complete and utter shame, was forced to bring food for her. He approached her with a dish of gristle, fat and scrag ends of the meat, floating in a mess of pungent sauce. But he pretended to stumble on the featureless sand and spilled the contents of the pot all over her and on the sand between her feet.

He shrugged and walked away, leaving her to retrieve what she might for food.

'You are the woman in this, K'ang Du-Saru. Go to her and bare your arse so she can beat you for your clumsiness.' K'ang Fi-Tozu's tone of voice made it clear he'd brook no dissent, from either of them.

The defeated wrestler came her way, turned his back and parted the strips of linen covering his massive posterior. He bent a little forward, offering the target. Tumalind, given the opportunity to take revenge on this obnoxious man, instead showed mercy and merely tapped him lightly twice.

She went back to what she could retrieve of the food, amidst laughter from the others that may have been aimed at either her or Saru. Whatever the case, he clearly saw her mercy as an insult and glared at her with venom before he marched away again.

The food consumed, Hin-Seru took her to the place again and she did what was required, humiliated by the act. He left her to return to the camp and she followed only when she'd rid herself of his abuse.

K'ang Fi-Tozu took out his pipe and played. She knew she must dance for them, knew she must make her movements match the mood of his music, in spite of her tiredness, her anxiety, her hatred of them all. He began with the melody she'd first performed to and she recalled her movements, embellishing them where that seemed appropriate and refining them where she felt they lacked that certain finish. The music slowly wandered out of the purely sensual into the erotic. This was more difficult; she was forced to move in more suggestive ways to convince them of her skill and suitability for the role of dancer in the city. She swayed her torso, extended hands and feet at the end of each movement of her limbs, placed an expression of desire upon her face to mask her real emotions, drew attention to her breasts and her womanhood with her swaying and rocking.

He switched from the erotic to the vulgar in such a sudden move that she had to react quickly to keep their attention and respect. Understanding that her movements were required to illustrate the music as accurately as possible, she became a whore, a wanton, thrusting with her hips, widening the space between her thighs. She stuck out her chest, used her arms to press her breasts together and form more cleavage. Her success was evident by their expressions and physical reactions. She used their susceptibility, dancing before each in turn and thrusting herself as close to each as she dare without actually touching them. She was driving them wild and she went again to dance in front of the musician, seducing him with her body and the promise she wrote on her face, until he could no longer concentrate on piping and had to stop.

She had no idea what might happen now that she'd aroused all the men together to such a height of lust. But the choice wasn't hers to make and Hin-Seru grasped her and took her for the third time to his chosen place. He was undone in a trice and she returned to the brief applause of her captors and the reward of rest for the remainder of the night.

Approaching dusk held none of the clues that Okkyntalah knew from forest or grassland. Here, no night birds sang greetings, no insects chirruped, nothing changed the endless silence of the sands. He heard only the soft movement of the grains chafing each other in the ever-present soughing breeze, his own breathing, and the quiet panting of his dog beside him. Through the opening, he saw the sun was now low. He'd slept longer than intended and rose quickly, ate some of his shrinking hoard of meat, fed the dog, took a drink and swallowed what he would have normally spat out from swilling sleep out of his mouth. He poured a little of the precious fluid for Shaulah and she lapped up every drop. That was his greatest worry and his fear; the lack of water and no knowledge of when or where he might replenish his supplies. But he must move.

He recalled the way the tent had unfolded when released from its leather strap. He

342

recalled how it had looked when folded. Never having done this thing before, he had to try four times before he managed to achieve something resembling the original, but holding the sprung package together whilst capturing it within the restraining band of leather was more difficult. The tent unfolded once again and this time he held the leather strap in his teeth as he folded the fabric and bent the pliable supports. He finally had the knack and would remember it for next time. But, by now, it had grown almost dark and he must be on his way.

He ran, the dog trotting beside him. The stars allowed him some direction and the Skyfire gave a clue to the passage of time. Already the celestial portent was brighter than the waxing moon, now approaching its first quarter. He wondered, as his steps ate up the leagues of sand, how Tumalind was faring at the hands of those foul slavers. Were they, as the woman had suggested, treating her less roughly than they might if they'd known she was married? How was she responding to demands and orders so unfamiliar to her? Was she well? Was she hurting? Did she know he was running to be with her, moving fast to recover her and take her to safety?

Such questions didn't help. He must concentrate on the task in hand. His only object at the moment was to reach the city. Once there he'd have time enough for worry and anxiety. For the moment, simple survival dictated that he concentrate on direction and his speed. And that elusive, teasing water that he must soon find.

He'd drained the last, sharing it with Shaulah. Now they had to run with thirst their ever present companion. At least the desert night was cooler, the wind less drying and the sand less scorching on his feet. He must cover as much distance as he could until the daylight brought searing heat and the necessity for shelter.

He ran.

Ran.

Ran.

The sinking Skyfire signalled approaching daylight. But he moved forward, still checking direction by reference to stars. The moon slowly deserted him. The sky above brightened from its dense black into indigo. Deep blue arrived and he still moved north-west. Behind him, the first filaments of dawn brought colour to the sky at the horizon. On a different day, he would've rested and watched with awe and admiration as colours painted wonder in the sky. But now, hunger and thirst his ever faithful companions, he simply moved forward, following his shortening shadow until the day's heat forced a halt.

The tent unfolded and he slipped inside with Shaulah by his side. Sleep took him quickly as he shrugged off his growing disquiet in this foreign landscape. It was only when the tent moved above him that he understood the wind had grown in strength. He woke at the movement, looked out into the day and saw the thing he'd most feared. Far

343

on the eastern horizon the sky was no longer blue. There, the colour was as the ground beneath him. He'd heard about these storms. Terrifying winds that carried sand at great speed and could strip the skin off anyone exposed to them. The tent rocked in the wind and might be blown away. It was his only hope of surviving through the storm. There had to be some way to secure it to himself or the ground. There must be.

The rising after the night's dance was earlier than usual, so much so that it was still quite dark. But Tumalind carried out her duties as accustomed, in silence and with the expected respect and servitude. The food was finished with this breakfast and water supplies, replenished at the third well they'd visited a league or so before they'd stopped for the night, were also running out. After she'd satisfied the needs of the men and herself, she poured the remainder into the shallow trough for the horses.

K'ang Fi-Tozu signalled her as the others adjusted saddles and placed the heavier items on the packhorse. She approached and stood with her gaze averted downwards, as required. But he lifted her face gently with his fingertips under her chin and looked into her eyes with his of deep brown. For a moment he spoke no words as he explored her features with his stare and she wondered what passed through his mind as he scrutinised her so thoroughly. She hoped her face betrayed none of the hatred, rage and despair she felt in the hands of these savage men.

'We enter the city today before noon. As we approach, we'll reach two pools of water. In the first you'll bathe and take the stink and roughness of the desert from your skin to leave it fresh and sweet for your introduction to the Uhmbard. The second is the city's supply of drinking water. Anyone who pollutes that by entering is beheaded by a Guardian of the Source. Understand?'

She nodded.

'I will tell you what will happen, so that you do not shame us. Listen well and remember. Punishment will be swift and hard if you fail to do exactly as required.'

She nodded.

'Good.'

He explained how she must behave, what would be done to her and what she must do in response. The process sounded both daunting and humiliating but at least she wouldn't have to give herself to the Uhmbard at once.

The entrance to the city, after her passage through fields of cereal crops, groves of palms and scented bushes bearing strange fruits, surprised her with its sophisticated architecture. These men might be savages but the city had been built by men of culture. A different culture and belief system from her own, but one that respected line and form if this entrance was any guide. Tall towers of gleaming white held a perfect arch that rose to

344

a zenith some four manheights high. Solid wooden gates stood open and welcoming but were guarded by fierce men in short versions of the linen strip coats, these worn as skirts from the waist and leaving their upper torsos bare. The four guards were muscular and tall and showed no sign of fat on their bodies. They stared quite openly at her as she walked ahead of the horses, her tabard discarded in the sands and her hair flowing loose. She steeled herself to walk proud and straight, ignoring stares, pointing fingers, rude comments and ribald suggestions from men in the streets.

The sun was harsh on her skin and she feared she might suffer the burning that some had shown even on the island on occasions when they'd spent too long without cover under the sun at its highest. As if in answer to her unspoken concern, two women appeared, and opened a device above her, walking on either side of her so that she and they now walked in the shadow of a sheet of brightly figured fabric held in a frame aloft. The women, both young and proud, were also naked. Neither spoke and she knew better than to try to converse with them.

As they paraded through the dusty streets, she noted that all the men were clothed in either the coats of linen strips of her captors or the short skirts of the guards. She saw many women, all naked. The men idled and talked, pointed at her and spoke to each other. The women worked or hurried as if on important errands. Here and there, a sick dog lay panting in the shade of a palm, a mangy cat stalked pigeons that seemed to be everywhere. On one corner, as she passed through a crossroads, three disabled men sat on the ground, begging bowls before them, and cried out for alms. They were the only naked men she saw, and each had at least one limb missing.

The women either side of her, guided her now as they approached an imposing building. Long, low, built of some unseamed material she couldn't identify, and painted glaring white, with broad black borders around each opening, it stood behind a low wall of the same smooth, rounded substance. Between the wall and the building, lay beds of flowers in bright bloom; the only flowers she'd seen. From out of sight a brazen gong rang out three times. The central door to the building opened to reveal a dark entrance above the shallow steps she now crossed. As she entered, the two women dropped the shade canopy and stepped behind her.

A corridor ran ahead, long, dark and paved with burnished black stone that she didn't recognise, except that it had the same look as the white stone of Litkala. It felt cool beneath her feet and she remembered, as the sand under her soles made contact with the stone, that she must now dust off her feet as instructed. She lifted each foot in turn and used her hand to brush the sand into a small square tub that appeared to be for that purpose. The women, she realised, had now left her and she risked a turn to discover that the slavers had also vanished. As she glanced behind her into the street, she saw that people were rapidly making their way into the houses as a rising wind brought the first billows of the sand storm K'ang Fi-Tozu had warned her would start shortly after their arrival in the city.

Entirely alone, she walked the length of the corridor, trying to keep her gaze ahead but conscious of many rooms to both left and right, some occupied, others vacant. The air in the place was still and cooler than outside and her skin felt better for that. At the end of the corridor, that seemed to go on forever, a guard stood. He took his time to stare at her before he opened the door and indicated she should pass.

'Down.'

This was the signal and she dropped to her knees and then fell forward and shuffled her way across the floor on her belly, not daring to raise her eyes and feeling ahead with her fingertips for the ridge in the stone that would indicate it was time for her to stop. She found the place. Now she must do exactly as she'd been warned. Failure at this point would earn her a severe whipping and she'd be cast into the street to fend for herself; a fate she'd been warned would result in her being raped repeatedly and then beaten to death for sport by the city youths.

She lay, arms stretched in front of her head, legs placed so that her feet were the same distance apart as her shoulders. Face down on the hard stone, she awaited her fate.

The first movement came softly from bare feet on stone as he walked around her. His foot touched her shoulder, then her lower back. He stroked a sole across her buttocks and down her thigh. The foot moved up her body, touched her flank near her breast and she rolled away from it to lie on her back. Her eyes remained closed, as required.

For some time, he was silent and unmoving. At last, he knelt and moved her hair from where it had fallen to half cover her face. She resisted the urge to open her eyes, breathing slowly to calm her nerves and keep control of the fear and vulnerability she felt here alone with this man who was believed a god in this place.

He touched one breast, stroking the fingers across and then taking the nipple between two fingers and rolling it until her body responded naturally. He passed the hand down her stomach and pulled at the short hair, parting it and delving within before drawing the fingers free and testing the softness of the skin of her upper thighs.

He moved away again and she wondered what would happen next. The slaver had been unable to give her details of this part of the introduction as it was always conducted by the Uhmbard alone and the women would tell no one of their experience. She felt his flesh against her side, hard and curved; a knee, perhaps. His fingers were suddenly at her mouth and seemed to want to explore that orifice. She opened and felt his fingers on her teeth and gums. He traced her lips with the tips and then closed her mouth with her chin.

'Open your eyes.'

She did so. He still knelt beside her, his height diminished by his position but his decorated skin startling so close. His face was almost bland. The merest hint of desire in his eyes, black and deep and hard. He scanned her, seeking her reaction it seemed. She allowed her eyes to widen with what she hoped might convey admiration for this man who she knew must be utterly spoilt, a man for whom no command was ever denied.

He rose to his full height, almost as tall as Okkyntalah, but slimmer and entirely bald. And, she realised belatedly, he bore no hair at all on his body, just like the women. None of them had any body hair.

'Stand.'

She tried to rise gracefully and kept her face down as he walked around her again.

'My chosen.'

The command was soft, but clearly a summons. A woman appeared at once. Pale skinned, tall and slender but with full firm breasts, she entered the room on her feet, not her belly as was required of all other women. Tumalind noted her red hair as she came to stand behind her.

'Prepare her.'

The Uhmteld touched Tumalind's shoulder and she turned to face this powerful woman. As she lifted her face to read what might be written there, she was startled to discover that the woman observed her through eyes of Lapis Lazuli flecked with gold.

Chapter 36

STORM

Okkyntalah struggled with the tent as the wind grew in strength. If he lost this shelter, the sand would kill him; of that there was no doubt. There must, he was certain, be some way to keep the thing in place. He used his fingertips to examine the bottom of the frame, where the fabric was attached to the flexible rods, and found a short tag. Pulling this, he released a broad band of the fabric that stretched far enough to reach the other side. He searched for a corresponding tag, found and pulled this and discovered a slotted wooden tab, much like the belt fasteners used for some tabards. It took only a short while to discover seven such devices spread along the length of the tent. Once fastened, they formed a series of cross supports on which he and Shaulah could lay to hold the frame in place above them. The wind still buffeted them but, by lying at full stretch, he was able to keep the tent down with his weight. As the wind continued to blow sand against the tent, so it built up a drift, which helped keep the shelter in place.

The anxiety of losing the tent was gone, but he was now concerned that the sand storm might actually bury them alive. He must stay awake and alert to what happened in the blinding, cacophonous fury that now surrounded them. The day grew dark as clouds of dust obscured the sun, and the sand outside slowly built and covered the structure.

The noise, almost overpowering in its initial volume and tenor as the wind howled and screamed, slowly diminished. Sand dashed itself against this fine fabric that seemed too delicate to take such punishment. Inside, though the fury was lost from the driven sand, dust flowed like smoke from a poorly made fire. His nose and mouth seemed full of the dry powder and he coughed as his thirst increased. Shaulah lay still, breathing shallow breaths. He tried to settle with her, tried to stay calm under the assault on his senses. Day became night; the air so thick with dense clouds of sand that the sun no longer penetrated. Heat decreased; one small piece of comfort in a world of noise, chaos and dread.

It was impossible for Okkyntalah to judge the passage of time, but he noted a slowing of the wind, a reduction in the noise. He waited. Slowly, the fury subsided and, with an abruptness that seemed unnatural, the storm left him.

The mouth of the tent was blocked. He closed his eyes and pushed his way through and up. Clean air and bright sunlight greeted him just above the ridge of the tent. Where he'd crossed flat leagues of sand without ridges, mounds or features, he now stood surrounded by dunes. Some were high enough to cast shadows from the afternoon sun.

But, where his passage across the desert had been a matter of harsh but straight lines, he now perceived he must follow hills and vales. He must move on. Though the sun was still fierce, he dare not wait for better conditions. His water was gone, the food had all been eaten. With no idea how far he had yet to travel before he reached Ov-Bebna, he nevertheless knew that he must walk many leagues before he encountered the shade of trees and the welcoming reflection of sun on water.

He dragged the tent from the small dune that covered it. Shaulah sat and worried at her ears with her paws. Once packed and ready, he set off again, tackling the soft sand slope ahead and quickly tiring as he laboured up the steep rise. He reached the summit and surveyed the land as far as he could in all directions.

Back the way he'd come, the ground now undulated under soft, high-sided dunes where once it had been flat. To either side, the story was the same. Ahead, some dunes seemed even larger and more imposing. The climb was the hardest part. He resolved to follow the ridge of each dune as far as he could before tackling the next, making his journey longer but easier in terms of energy spent.

The afternoon wore on and his thirst grew until it was the only thing he could think of. Dry. Never had he known such dryness. His skin had ceased to sweat. His eyes no longer watered. His breath rattled in the dry cavities of his throat and mouth. Shaulah walked beside him, faithful, it seemed, to death.

Death that awaited his failure to find water.

He'd counted the dunes to begin with. Seventeen of varying lengths, all taking him more or less in the direction he needed to travel, but each a little at an angle to the optimum route.

Dry. So dry.

He hauled himself along the ridge of dune eighteen, weary beyond words.

Dry. Dry.

Something alien in the landscape.

There.

In the deep cleft between this dune and the one running almost parallel to the west, something.

Dry. So dry.

A stone slab.

Flat.

It meant something.

What?

Someone had said something important.

About such stones.

Who?

What?

He glanced at the stone.

It approached.

Soon to pass him by.

Should he go down?

Investigate?

Dry. So very dry.

Such effort.

Down.

Such effort.

Back up.

She'd said…

The woman. That woman.

In the leafy glade.

Where the small house stood.

'Look for stone slabs, built as a small raised block. Underneath lies sweet water.'

He looked down at the slab.

A flat smooth surface surrounded by sand.

No block.

Just flat.

But stone.

Stone.

Not sand.

He dropped pack and tent. Began to walk down. Fell to his knees. Rolled. Slithered. Fell down the slope. In the narrow space between dunes.

The sun was shaded.

Why?

Why was he here?

The slab.

Water.

He brushed away sand from the edge of the stone.

One edge.

His hands took sand away. Found another edge.

Hands scraped. Scrabbled with sand. So much sand.

Dry. So, so dry.

Move sand.

Large slab of stone.

Not natural rock or boulder.

Stone made by men.

He worked the sand.

Thick slab. Sat on four stone walls.

Must rest.

Weary.

Thirsty.

Dry.

Cool clear water. Under stone.

He pushed against the slab with his hands.

Nothing.

Tried again.

Nothing.

Heaved with all his might.

No movement.

Rested.

Thirst his only drive.

Torment.

So near. Under an impossible barrier.

He rested on the slab.

Drew breath for the last assault.

He moved. Placed his back against the dune. Feet on stone. Bent knees. Slowly stretched legs straight.

Sand behind gave.

But stone moved.

A little.

He tried again. Moved sideways for fresh purchase.

The slab moved. Showed inner edge of supporting wall.

Gap no wider than a finger.

But he could smell water.

Skinned fingers. Forced into gap. Pushed with all his might.

Slab moved. His hands in gap.

Exhausted by effort. Rested.

Body flopping onto stone. Hands in gap. See water below.

So close.

So, so far.

Shaulah barked. A warning. Mustn't ignore warning. Raised head. Looked around. Row of dark figures. Impossible creatures. On ridge above. In dark gowns. Looking down at him.

Army from nightmare. No strength. Raise hand.

Ward off danger.

Darkness.

Splash.

Nothing.

The meeting had been discussing possible action since breakfast. Nothing had yet been decided, but much that Aklon had said was at last finding comprehensive favour. He was conscious that he needed to follow up Ivdulon's impersonation of Ytraa as soon as he could, but he was also aware that any sudden move could well be considered unplanned and dangerous. It was vital that he carry the weight of the meeting with him. Perhaps it was time for a further demonstration, a further declaration of his reasons for making his proposed changes, for denying their life-long faith in the sect of Followers.

'I have things to tell that more than simply this meeting need to hear. I think, since these things may well alter the minds of those who still harbour doubts, that it would be wise for me to voice my knowledge before we consider further action. Therefore, I ask that all who reside here be gathered together in such a way that I may address them all at once.'

Chellyth immediately despatched members of her group to gather all together. A small tongue of high land protruded from the hillside that sheltered the north, overlooking the more or less flat plain where the river divided the valley. From that raised spot, Aklon would be seen by all and would see all as he spoke.

Whilst preparations were underway, the members of the meeting ate their midday meal. This was still something of a novelty for the members of the group who'd spent their lives on the Point: there, they'd eaten once or sometimes twice a day, depending on available food. Here they could eat as and when they wished, since food was plentiful.

All was prepared and Aklon made his way up the slope until he was high enough for all to see him but still close enough that he could make himself heard.

'Please, be seated. What I have to say will take a little while and I would have you comfortable. Some of what I am about to recount is already known by some of you. Some will be known by none of you, since I have not previously disclosed these secrets.

'You all know that I am, or was, the heir to the fortune and position of High Priest on this island. You all know that I was disinherited by my father. What only a handful of you know is why that is the case.

353

'I ask that you trust my words. Since I understand that many will question why I should make such a plea and expect it to be met, let me explain something that will be plain to many but may not have occurred to others. I am renegade. I could, now my father has left the island to follow the Skyfire, have been the man in charge of all. I could have gloried in that position and the wealth, power and privilege it brings. So, why did I not choose that way?'

He held up his hand in a gentle gesture, begging for silence. The small number who'd been tempted to cat-call were soon quiet again.

'I rejected that position of power and privilege because it is based on lies. I am renegade because, having been shown the reality, the truth, by Dagla Kaz, I rejected absolutely everything that the priesthood on this island stands for. Further, I reject all that the so-called Holy Ones consider normal and devout. Hear me out, please; before you pass judgement on me. First I must establish that I have nothing to gain personally by telling you the truth. I have already lost more than most of you will ever know in terms of riches, position and prestige, simply by rejecting the lies of the past and embracing the truth.'

He let that sink in, aware that there would remain many who would still doubt his every word. A reputation gained, however false it may be, is difficult to unseat in the minds of those without the means to think for themselves, as he knew only too well.

'So, I wish only to tell you the truth and to establish a system on this island of ours based on fairness, justice and honesty. Are there any among you who would reject such a proposal?'

''Ow do we know what's true?'

'A valid question and one I hope to explain. You all know, of course, that Dagla Kaz and the Holy Ones, alerted by the chief astronomer, Jhonaht, began the sacred pilgrimage to the homeland on sighting the Skyfire many sixdays past. There are those here, many in number, who also know that I spoke, at the time, of that event and declared that Skyfire false. Events have proved my words correct. You have all seen the true Skyfire now rising and growing brighter each day in the sky above us. I was correct about that, was I not?'

There were cries of agreement and some mutterings of doubt but the general sense was of acceptance.

'Many will know, either from their presence at the event or from reports by those who heard me speak at Pampahn, that I also predicted this true Skyfire and was accurate about its appearance and its likely growth, which continues to this day.'

Again there were calls that showed assent to this, and a few noises of uncertainty.

'Finally, there are very many here, lately arrived, who were present at the Scar when Ytraa spoke with the voice of The Speakers of Ytraa. There can be no doubt about what was then said by Ytraa. But for those who heard not those words, I will now repeat them. "We are the voice of Ytraa and will be obeyed! These who attack you are good people. These are my true Followers. These are the ones you should heed and obey, for they expose great corruption and evil on your island. Long have I sought to find ways to convince your priesthood and the self-styled Holy Ones to abandon their wicked ways. But they have failed to heed my words. Now is the time to allow my true disciples to make the changes that must be made." Those referred to by Ytraa as "These who attack you are good people." Comprise myself, Delbon, Phildrad, a few others and Por-Kildu.'

He pointed to his companions and urged them rise to be seen by the entire assembly. They were applauded by most, and sat again, most embarrassed by their sudden rise to fame.

'Now it can be seen, for those who have eyes to see and ears to hear, that I, with my companions, have been identified by no less than Ytraa as a True Follower. Does anyone here doubt that this can be the case?'

Only a handful of voices were raised in doubt and they were quickly silenced by those who'd heard The Speakers. Aklon silently thanked Ivdulon for her intervention. Though it would cause problems further down the line, at this crucial stage it had proved vital in establishing his reputation for truth: not an easy task after the years he'd been called the great liar and enemy of the people.

'What I now have to reveal to you will be difficult for many of you to even contemplate, let alone accept. But you need to know this fundamental truth in order to understand why I rejected the position of High Priest and why I was willing to forego a life of ease and privilege and live instead the dangerous life of a wanted, hunted criminal.'

He paused, seeking the words that would best express what he must tell them whilst allowing them the time to accept what they must all see as a great blasphemy.

'From what source comes the story of the Lord Gadhallah?'

No one spoke, as if this thought had not occurred to them.

'Very well, I will tell you. It is said to be recorded in tablets of stone, marked in letters at his direction when Followers first arrived here in Muhnilahm. Does that sound familiar?'

One or two agreed and others nodded but the remainder merely waited for his next words.

'I can tell you that such tablets, reported to be lost in the annals of time, exist. I can display them to you. Later, when we have established control, I will bring these tablets out for all to see. And I will also reveal the many rolls of ancient parchment, on which are written the very words of Lord Gadhallah himself; his own words written by his own hand, on the final leg of the voyage to Muhnilahm.'

355

This announcement did cause a stir. None of those present had known of such documents or records of the past. Those few individuals who'd progressed far enough along the paths of knowledge to have heard of the existence of such records, as taught by the Holy Ones, had been told the lie that they'd been lost.

'It was my sight of these tablets and manuscripts that turned me against the priesthood, the Holy Ones and much of what our faith is supposed to stand for. For the truths that are written in those documents and stone records are so terrible they will make grown men and women weep with shame and horror. Yes, and with despair that they have been so utterly abused and cheated all their lives. For the truth is this: the Lord Gadhallah, by his own admission, never heard the words of Ytraa in those holy glades so many years ago...'

There was uproar at this and Aklon allowed it to run its course as some, and then others, understood that he'd warned them they would not like what he had to say to them. Could he now expand on what he'd said? Was this the time to tell the whole truth of that appalling time Gadhallah had spent in the trees? Would the people accept such terrible and despicable truths? Were they ready? It was a risk he must take if he was to persuade them of his Cause and explain the presence of the Few before they set out on their tour of conversion of the island. He must have willing and believing disciples to spread the word. Now was the time, or never.

The murmuring quieted. The silence was enough for him to fill, whilst they yet remained attentive and receptive to his words.

'I ask you to remember now, before I tell you this one truth, that you have already accepted that I am an honest speaker and that Ytraa has already let it be known that I am a true Follower. Keep that in mind as I reveal the truth, the terrible and shameful truth, about our founder.'

He explained the history of Gadhallah, detailing his up-bringing, his sorry marriage and his failure to father children with his wife. He told them of the scorn and ridicule the man had suffered in his home. Many cried out at this unfair treatment of the man they'd always considered their true leader on Earth. To know that he was, like them, just a man, was news to all. They'd pictured Gadhallah as someone special and blessed by Ytraa, not as a pitiful failure nagged and scorned by his wife and the rest of the village.

'These are facts, facts disclosed by the writings of Gadhallah himself in an account he placed onto parchment towards the end of his days. This is no tale, but the truth. Though not, as yet, the whole truth. I have now to come to that part which will most distress you. Prepare now to hear what you would have not thought possible. But what I have to tell you is the absolute truth, as declared by Gadhallah himself in his own written words. This is no made up story. These are the facts.'

356

He allowed this to sink in and waited for silence to return.

'When Gadhallah spent those days away from his home village in the Groves of Ytraa, where he claimed to have been visited by Ytraa and to have received the first Commands of Ytraa, he was not alone.'

Aklon went on, with many pauses to allow for the exclamations of shock, the denials, the outraged threats, to describe the true events. He told them, in the man's own words, how he had repeatedly raped and despoiled the young girl who'd come to him alone and in a spirit of aid.

'In the end, he could not let the child live to tell the tale and he killed her and hid her damaged body in a swamp.'

Okkyntalah felt moisture touch his lips. Cool, fresh, life-giving water. He opened his mouth and felt liquid fill the cavity. It felt so good to wash away dust and dryness and he allowed the water to drain slowly down his throat. Fluid trickled across his face, pooling in the corners of his eyes and he luxuriated in the feeling. He was in the Garden of Delights and, when he opened his eyes, he would find himself surrounded by all those things he loved. But Tumalind would not be there.

He tried to raise himself.

'Stay. You are yet too weak. Save your energy, young hunter.'

The voice was soft, warm, gentle, caring and feminine. He blinked through the added tears to look out from wherever he had died.

Nothing had changed.

Except that his head was cradled by a woman in a black gown. A man held a bucket made of thick hide, water spilling from the edges as he dribbled it onto Okkyntalah's face.

Too many questions. Too much effort needed to do more than simply lie there and obey. He was not dead, then. And Shaulah lay close beside him, licking with her moistened tongue at his hand. It was enough. For now.

Time must have passed, though he was unaware of how much he'd lost. When he sought the sky to tell him, he found only the interior of some great room with ceilings made of fabric, blowing softly in a wind he couldn't see.

'He wakes.'

The voice attracted his eyes and he saw her, seated, cross-legged, on the floor, a woven mat beneath her. She smiled as he turned to face her. Bright eyes of the deepest green set in a face of pale honey skin enlivened by a mouth made for laughter and for love. She wore a simple shift in white that left arms and legs uncovered but concealed the woman.

'How do you feel now, young hunter?'

357

The other voice had him turn her way. She sat, dressed identically, with her knees beneath her as she stirred some aromatic mixture in a pot. He saw flames. He saw, beyond her, the opening, square and wide, exposing a night sky he'd come to know over the few nights of his desert trek. It was, by his estimation, only a short time after dusk.

'You must be hungry.'

He felt the gnawing of his empty stomach, tried to speak but found his mouth too dry. The woman he'd first seen rose and brought him a small vessel of water. Soft, strong hands helped him rise so he was sitting and she held the glazed pot to his lips to let him drink.

'Slowly, now. Too much will make you sick. You were almost too far gone for us to save. Had your dog not alerted us to your position, we would have passed on by. And we would also have missed the well. Your dog has saved us all, it seems. She is, of course, a much respected guest now.'

He followed her eyes to where Shaulah lay stretched and relaxed atop a mound of cushions. She looked entirely at ease.

Events returned to him then. He remembered most, though there were holes in his recalled story. Holes no one else could fill, since he'd travelled all alone. But he was safe, it seemed. Safe with strangers.

'Where am I?'

'We are the K'ahll. The people of the sands welcome you, stranger, and make no demands of you. Though, should you care to enlighten us about your past, your present or your future, we would receive such knowledge gratefully.'

He gave them his name. Their openness and kindness encouraged him to tell them why he was in their land and what he hoped to achieve.

The woman at the cooking pot shook her head in sadness and lowered her gaze from his. The woman with the water, closed her eyes as though his words had somehow wounded her.

'What is it? Have I insulted you in some way? I only told you what I'm doing here.'

'There is no insult, young hunter. And you may rest here on your way to death. But our ways prevent us actively helping anyone determined to destroy themselves. You may take from us anything you need. But we are not permitted to act as aids in the death you seek.'

'I seek life. I'm looking for my wife. I love her. How can I abandon her? Why is that such a bad thing to do? I don't understand.'

'You are a stranger here, so we will explain, though all who take to such a venture should be aware before they tread the road to certain death. You make for the abomination you call Ov-Bebna. It is known that all men who enter that great cesspit of

358

corruption either die there or are turned into the Immallsu and lost forever to the grace of life. That is all.'

'You're telling me that I'll be killed in the city?'

'Or, worse, you will become as they are; vile and lost from all salvation. Ov-Bebna is the very seat of evil and devours the souls of all men who reside there.'

'I'm not going to stay. I'm going to find Tumalind, rescue her and take her back home with me.'

'You speak with courage of things you do not understand, young hunter. It grieves me that you intend to end your life in this rash way. But you are clearly determined to make the sacrifice for this thing that you call love. We are your hosts and therefore all we have is yours. But we will see no more of you. Goodnight.'

She turned away and, no matter how he tried, neither woman would respond to him. Even when he touched one of them, she acted as though he no longer existed. He was lost as to what he should do. They'd rescued him from certain death and now would abandon him. How was he to carry on? He didn't even know where he was in relation to the well where they had found him. How could he find his way to the city if no one here would tell him where it lay?

Chapter 37

OV-BEBNA

Okkyntalah ate, alone, on food left in the pot. The women had gone to eat with the rest of the tribe. He'd been invited to take what he wanted. They'd saved his life and brought him back from the edge of death, only to abandon him to his fate. He could do no more than restore his strength and continue his mission to save Tumalind. A mission that now seemed even more dangerous than he'd first imagined.

By the mound of pillows where Shaulah lay, he found his belongings. His water carriers had been replenished, dried meat and some fruit now filled the space in his pack that his eating on the journey had emptied. Shaulah had been fed.

He took what was his and what they'd provided for him, urged Shaulah from her bed of luxury, and left the tent. Outside, the Skyfire declared approaching midnight and the stars gave him direction. But he had no way of knowing where he stood in relation to his destination. Without that knowledge he could wander for days and die of thirst in this vast ocean of sand.

The people of this tribe, the K'ahll, were gathered round a small fire in a circle, eating, talking, living lives with no connection to his. He approached, without hope of help.

'I thank you for your hospitality and your gifts of food and kindness. I understand you believe I go to certain death by visiting the city. Even so, I must do it. My wife, the only woman I love, was taken by slavers and I must get her back. If you think that's foolish, I can't help it. But if you let me leave here without knowing which way I need to travel, you send me to certain death in the sands. Does your way let you to do that to a guest?'

He heard the sharp intakes of breath and knew he'd judged them right. A man, dressed in the simple loincloth they all seemed to wear when not travelling, rose from the circle and gestured him. Okkyntalah, still weary and recovering from his collapse through lack of water, went after the man. Behind another of the tents, the man stopped and untied one of the creatures. He handed Okkyntalah the reins, helped him onto the animal's back, urged it back onto its feet from its kneeling posture, and pointed to a group of stars on the horizon.

'There is the death you seek. May the spirit of the sun defend you from the evil that dwells there. And may the spirit of the moon preserve your woman and release her from the slavery she faces.

'You are not familiar with the way of the camel. This creature can travel many days

361

without need of water or food. Treat it well and it will serve you better than your dearest friend. Treat it harshly and it will kick you to death as easily as you might squeeze life from a small serpent. When you reach the city, release the camel. It will return to us.' With that, the man turned and went back to the camp.

Okkyntalah urged the animal on, slowly, unused to riding, especially without a saddle. But the camel was well schooled and made the ride easy. Shaulah trotted to one side and they covered the ground faster than he could on foot.

Dawn painted the sky with pinks and browns, greens and yellows. And, on the horizon, small shapes came into view. At first, these were mere irregularities on the distant line that parted land from sky, but, as he moved closer, they displayed themselves as trees. And, closer to hand, the land slowly changed, with the endless sand finally growing stunted thorn bushes and occasional cactus plants. There followed fertile fields of various crops and then the trees and shrubs. As he closed on the these, their number and size increased, until he was weaving through the groves.

There was no sign of life as he reached the edge of the trees. The pool that first appeared he understood from the woman in the small house was used for washing. He allowed the camel and Shaulah to drink from this but quenched his own thirst from the full container he carried.

From here, the city was no more than a dark line of irregular roofs seen over the white wall that surrounded the place. The well-worn track that crossed the coarse grass between the first pool and the second, pointed the way to the city entrance.

He should free the camel, as directed, but it was his way of escape from this place with Tumalind. Better to be untrue to his unknown hosts than risk death for her. Taking the beast into the shadows of the more closely packed trees, he noted the tracks and forms of the plants so he could recover it later. He tied it with the reins, leaving as much length as he could. The man had said it would be fine without food or water for some days, but he was loath to leave it. No choice, of course. From here, he must move with stealth and care. The woman had warned him that strangers were unwelcome and that his mode of dress would mark him out for comment and maybe even capture, if they became suspicious of him.

The gate stood open, guarded only by two men who slept with their backs to the wall. It was simple to pass without waking them. He saw no one on the streets within the walls and he approached softly, warily, looking for signs of life in this strange and sprawling place. A woman slipped out of a doorway ahead of him, her movement and manner suggesting she was about something she should not be.

He called softly to her and she froze, standing still until he asked her to turn to face him. The bruised eye and swollen lips told him all he need know.

'Is there some place we can shelter you and help heal that mouth?'

She frowned at him, puzzled yet submissive. 'You wish sport with me, sire?'

'I wish to find a place where you might be safe from whoever's beaten you.'

She was surprised by this. He could see she was unwilling to believe him. He moved closer, expecting her to run. But she remained, head bowed and arms behind her back. He cut a small piece from the side of his tabard and soaked it with water from his girba. Gently, he wiped away the crusted blood from her mouth and then offered her a drink.

'From your vessel, sire?'

'Of course. I have no cup with me.'

She took the offered fluid and waited. 'You want sport with me, sire?'

As this seemed her only concern, he nodded. 'Show me where we may be undisturbed.'

She turned and he followed her. The streets began to waken, with women spilling from the houses and moving along the dusty ways. None wore clothing. Some were marked with bruises or stripes or redness to their seats, as though they'd been beaten or thoroughly chastised. All walked with their faces lowered and wouldn't meet his eyes. Such subjugation of women sickened him and he worried all the more for Tumalind in this place.

The woman turned down a small narrow alley and waited for him by a gap in the wall of a hut that stood at one side, close to the end of the passage. He understood she expected him to lead, and he entered. She followed into the dismal space. A low bed of reeds and dry grass occupied three quarters of the floor space. There was nothing else in the room, if room it could be called. She knelt at his feet and began to unfasten his tabard, fumbling with fastenings unfamiliar to her.

'Stay. Lie still and rest. I wish to talk with you.'

She obeyed at once, lying down, her legs parted and her arms flung over her head so that she was utterly exposed to him. It was only then that he realised her body was entirely devoid of hair. Fascinated, yet appalled by her display and her servitude, he sat beside her and rested her head in his lap. He took her hand and gentled her fingers, trying to convey comfort rather than lust and hoping to persuade her into trust instead of service.

'You wish for me to do a different thing, sire?'

'I wish you to talk with me. I wish you to tell me things I don't know. I am a stranger here. Will you do that?'

'I am yours to command, of course, sire. But your request is most unusual. I am clean and able and ready for your pleasure. I will do as you wish, of course.'

Okkyntalah had to look away from the body she offered and into her eyes.

'I've arrived here only today. I'm looking for someone, a woman who was stolen by slave traders and brought here. I want to know how I can find her. Will you help me, please?'

His request seemed to completely confuse her.

She moved and sat cross-legged, her hands rested on her knees. 'You find me undesirable, sire?'

'I find you very desirable. But I want information more than I want your services, if you don't mind.'

'I must serve you after we have spoken? Is that your meaning, sire?'

'If that's what you want of me.'

'My wants are of no matter, sire. I will do as you wish.'

'Then, please, answer my question.'

'The woman; what colour was her hair, and her eyes, please, sire?'

Okkyntalah described Tumalind fully and the woman nodded at each detail he gave.

'Is she a virgin, sire?'

'She's my wife.'

'I do not understand? You are not the Uhmbard, yet you have a wife, sire?'

'Where I come from, most mature men have a wife.'

'One wife only?'

'That's our custom. More than one seems a little unfair on the woman, doesn't it?'

She gave him an odd look, as if she thought him either mad or simple but she shrugged. 'If that's what you say, sire. If she's a virgin, or they think she might be, the Uhmbard will want her for a wife. It's his moonday at the first quarter and he'll be expecting a new wife for the occasion, of course. Perhaps your wife will perform this function?'

'If he's expecting a virgin and finds she is not, what then?'

'Oh, that's easy, sire. She'll be whipped, given to the lesser men and then banished to the sands.'

Okkyntalah tried to hide his concern at this. It would do no good to show weakness before this woman. From what little he'd been told and had learned, the men here were expected to be hard and unmoved by the plight of women. To be told such a thing and to experience it, however, he was discovering were two entirely different things.

'Where will she be held until the moon's first quarter?'

'In the harem, sire. With the other wives, of course. It's said that the Uhmteld instructs the new women in their duties and ensures they are properly prepared for the Uhmbard's wishes.'

'The harem? And where's that?'

'You make fun of me, sire. I am trying to help as you have requested but you make it hard if I'm not taken seriously in my words, sire. I'm sorry to seem to complain, sire. I will make it up when I serve you.'

'My question's perfectly reasonable. What's your name, by the way?'

Her eyes opened very wide and she shook her head as if trying to dislodge some unlikely invasion to her mind. 'Please, sire. Do not mock me for what I cannot be. I'm not of the palace, as you must know. Had I a name, would I not have announced it to begin with, so you'd understand my status and beat me as required before I serve you?'

Okkyntalah was equally flummoxed. 'Look, I'm a stranger here. Your ways are so different from what I'm used to that I make mistakes without meaning to. I don't understand. Surely everybody has a name? My question was normal, not an insult. I'd like to help you, if I can. I'm not used to seeing women treated as chattels, slaves by the look of it.'

'I'm no slave, sire! I'm a free woman.' She rose and stood, turned and showed her whole skin surface to him. 'Do you see the mark of the slave upon me, sire?'

'I wouldn't know what to look for.'

She stood still, her hips level with his face so that he had to stretch his neck up to look into her face again.

'Please sit again. It's very awkward staring up like this.'

'My womanhood offends you, sire?'

He felt obliged to gaze at her in admiration, simply to assure her she wasn't at fault in his eyes. 'You're a truly beautiful woman. No man would deny your attraction and desirability. Now, please sit.'

She did as she was told but her face continued to betray puzzlement.

'Now, please accept that what I say to you, what I ask, is all done at face value. I don't want to tease you, harm you, trick you or make you feel or look foolish. I simply want to know about this society so I can rescue my wife. Please will you just answer my questions, no matter how silly or surprising they seem?'

'I am your servant, sire. I will do as you wish, of course.'

It took many questions but he eventually learned that all women were treated as slaves, in spite of her assurance that she was a free woman, and had no power or rights at all. They were denied clothing and were ever ready for men to abuse and use, which was their daily experience of life. The men were brutal, unfeeling and uncaring and often treated the women cruelly. All work was done by women and men spent their time frowking, gambling in one way or another, sleeping, eating or playing games in which women weren't involved. The women put on shows each evening to entertain the men and it was as she explained this activity that he learned of the special status of the dancers.

'So, any woman who dances well is spared sexual duties?'

'Any woman who dances to the satisfaction of the men has no need to lie with them and may even keep a small portion of her body hair. It is an honour and a privilege to be allowed to dance until you are too old to be of delight. Then, of course, the dogs can have you for their supper.'

He questioned her more and discovered that Tumalind was likely to be in the palace, guarded by fierce warriors who lacked male parts, and who would give their lives in defence of the women in their charge. The woman was curious about him and offered to bring food as the day wore on. She asked that he give her the token so she wouldn't be claimed by another as she went to get food.

'Token? What do you mean?'

'I must bear a small item of yours to identify that I am taken, for the moment. Anything that you will entrust to me will do.'

He removed his belt and fastened it about her waist. She looked down at the item, touching it with wonder.

'No man has ever placed an item of clothing on my body. I thank you for the honour, sire. I shall return with the best I can find for you. And some meat for your dog?'

She went. No mention of money. He wondered how she'd pay for the food and hoped she wouldn't be required to serve some other man. Then he recalled that women did all the work here.

He'd learned much from the woman and had begun to understand her reticence and her peculiar mix of apparent reluctance and absolute submission. It was a society he must rescue Tumalind from as soon as he could. This nameless woman had been brought up in this way, with no other life to compare her fate with, but Tumalind was a free and free-spirited woman who'd never been anyone's servant and who'd escaped the Followers' camp in order to avoid becoming a sex slave to Dagla Kaz and Tryonta. There was grim irony in the fact that her escape had placed her into the hands of real sex slavers.

He awaited the woman's return, resting on the rough bed in the semi dark of the tiny shack. Was this her home? Did she live here when she wasn't in demand by one or other of the men? There was nothing to identify the place as belonging to anyone. Perhaps it was a place provided for sex. How would anyone know it was occupied? Would someone enter and eject him because he was alone?

The past few days had been so strange. Anxiety about Tumalind had receded for the short time he was dying of thirst and during his exposure to the sand from the storm. But it had returned in greater strength once he'd recovered. The people of this land were strange in ways he found difficult to deal with. Their dreadful treatment of women was the hardest thing to accept. He'd always loved and admired women, enjoying their softness, their love, their capacity for strength and wisdom and their sensual enjoyment in the act of joining. With Tumalind, the presence of their love made the act so much more than the physical pleasure it was with other women and he longed to be with her again.

This woman obviously expected him to join with her and he didn't want that. But, would she feel insulted if he rejected her?

As he contemplated these things, he heard voices approaching down the passage. One was definitely male. He rose to his feet and drew his sword in readiness for attack.

Tumalind, held tight by four other women, who spread-eagled her face down on the stone floor, felt each hair as it was plucked from her skin. They'd pounced on her as soon as she'd entered the women's quarters, giving her no time or opportunity to speak or look around. The torture felt as though it had gone on all day. But they suddenly released her as a gong sounded somewhere in the distance.

'You can stand up now.'

She did, turning to her torturers and finding two of them with faces lowered. One slipped behind her again with something scented, and washed her skin. The sensation of burning lasted only an instant to be replaced by a soothing balm and she felt normality returning to her body.

The woman with the sponge bowed to her. 'I'm Teh-blavv; I'm sorry we had to do that. We all go through it. The Uhmbard likes his women as naked as they can be. We'll finish off later on your back. Then we'll do your front. It'll never be as bad again; we keep each other plucked by taking out the hairs as they show. Now, it's time for food. Are you hungry?'

Tumalind studied the face before her, noticing at first the lapis lazuli eyes flecked with gold and wondering if Teh-blavv could mindtalk. It was too soon to try. She felt the woman was genuine in her concern for her, but it was too early to trust anyone in this strange place.

'Starving. We'd run out of food when we arrived. Those slavers aren't very bright, are they? No planning at all, it seemed to me. I'm Tumalind, by the way.'

'Nice name. Of course, you can't keep it. The Uhmteld will give you a wife label once you've been prepared and before you're given to the Uhmbard for his moonday.'

'Moon day?'

'He has a wife for every moon of his life. The Uhmteld keeps a tally. She'll tell you your number. I'm number three hundred and ninety six but it doesn't mean anything to me.'

'And how long have you been here, Teh-blavv? I'm guessing you weren't born here, not with that golden hair and pale skin.'

'Oh no. I was captured, like most of us here. I don't know how long ago, though. How would you keep tally of such a thing?'

Tumalind smiled; she'd keep a count, as she had all the time she'd been away from her home on the island. It wasn't hard to do, not if you started right at the beginning.

'The men said I must tell the Uhmteld I'm a dancer. Where will I find her?'

Teh-blavv shook her head. 'Everyone says that, once they know a dancer doesn't have to give her sex to anyone. But I bet they never told you the Uhmbard will still take away your virginity, even if he does let you become a dancer.'

'Supposing I'm not virgin?'

She smiled. 'That won't work either. You must be virgin for the Uhmbard. Any girl who's chosen for his moonday must be virgin. He must be the one to take away their girlhood and make them woman.'

'And if I wasn't virgin?'

'You don't want to make that claim. They'll whip you till you bleed, give you to the worst and lowest men of the city to use as they like, and then send you into the sands to die.'

'What if one of the slavers took me against my will? What if one of them had raped me?'

Teh-blavv looked shocked. 'They'd never do that. You're worth too much to them intact.'

'But if they did?'

'I don't know. It's never happened as far as I know. But...have they done it to you, Tumalind?'

Should she do this? What would be the outcome? Had she placed herself into danger with her attempt to preserve herself for Okkyntalah? She remained silent, hoping that would make the girl uncertain.

'If you have, the Uhmteld must know. She'll be furious with us if we don't inform her.' Teh-blavv gave her no chance to reply but walked quickly away through the throng of women.

Tumalind followed the girl, conscious of other women watching their behaviour as they threaded their way through the mass of female flesh. She glanced about her, noting the various shades of skin, the different figures, none overweight, and the length and colour of the hair on their heads. There was no doubt that she was amongst a collection of beautiful women. Not a face was plain, not a body unattractive. The Uhmbard clearly liked his women to be the best around. And she was now one of them. Or very soon would be. It was not a fate she relished.

She skirted a wide, circular pool, sunk into the floor and filled with still water. A second pool came into view between the gathering women and she passed two more before the girl reached her destination. The Uhmteld, seated on a chair of leather, her elbows resting on its gilded arms, watched Teh-blavv approach and fall to her knees before her. Tumalind moved close, to listen.

'Forgive me, Most Enlightened One, but I have a thing I must report to you.'

'Speak, child.'

'The new woman for the moonday has asked what would happen to her if she had been raped by the slavers. I did not know what to tell her.'

'Is her accusation true? Or did she merely ask what would be the outcome if it was?'

'She seemed only to ask but I believe she may be telling the truth, that she is no longer virgin.'

'You have done well, my child, to alert me to this matter. Tell her nothing in reply but send her to me after we have eaten.'

'Most Enlightened One, may I beg your indulgence? What would happen to such a woman?'

'She would be sent to the streets to do her duty with the other women of the city. If a true dancer, she would be spared, of course. Such talents cannot easily be dismissed.'

Tumalind walked away and mingled with the other women. She was confident the Uhmteld hadn't seen her listening and it seemed Teh-blavv was unaware that she'd been followed. She sighed with relief and went to seek food from the table at one end of the vast open space where the women were gathered.

'Do not look around to find me. Ivdulon has asked me to do what I might to protect you, Tumalind. Come to the far left end of the table, as if in search of some special morsel. I will greet you and introduce myself there.'

The intrusion was so unexpected that she stopped in her tracks. But she recovered quickly and followed the advice. At the end of the table, another girl, similar in many ways to Teh-blavv, but taller and with darker hair, approached her as she helped herself to food. She nodded at Tumalind and indicated she should follow her to a secluded place at the edge of the gathering. They sat together on cushions and ate their food in silence.

Ivdulon explained that I can mindtalk, then? How long have you been here?'

The girl looked around and then back at Tumalind.

'I didn't know others could do it. But we have to use it carefully here. They'll think it odd if we sit together and say nothing.'

Tumalind nodded her agreement. They introduced themselves to one another and asked about their backgrounds. Tumalind repeated that the slavers had considered her a dancer and Teh-pavk suggested she tell the Uhmteld this as soon as she could. The girl explained how she'd run away from home one day, trying to get out of some work duty

369

her father had imposed because she'd disobeyed her mother. She'd grown hot and had bathed in the local lake. It was there that she'd been captured by the slavers. And she'd been here ever since, of course.

'You must do exactly as the Uhmteld and the Uhmbard tell you, Tumalind. I made the mistake of lying on my side when the Uhmbard had told me to lie on my back. Once he'd frowked away my virginity, the Uhmteld brought me here and they held me over her chair whilst she used a broad leather strap on my backside. I couldn't sit for a sixday. Next time he called me, I made sure I did exactly as he said. He was a little more gentle when he frowked me that time.'

Another woman approached and asked if Tumalind had finished eating. She led her to the Uhmteld for her introduction to harem rules. Tumalind wondered when she'd get the chance to explain she was a dancer but the Uhmteld made it unnecessary.

'All girls who come here from other lands are told by the slavers that dancers are treated with respect. It's true. But most girls can't dance as the Uhmbard requires. Nevertheless, I'll give you a chance to prove yourself. You'll dance now for me and I'll decide whether you're good enough to entertain the Uhmbard and his guests. If not, you will probably find you're destined for the common men, who may consider your dancing good enough to spare you from sex, if that's your wish.'

The Uhmteld clapped her hands for silence. In the quiet, several women came forward with their instruments and waited to be asked to play. Tumalind, still tired from her journey, waited for the music to start so she might interpret it as she'd been shown by the slavers.

Teh-pavk had one more warning to impart. *'One other thing, Tumalind. The slavers will have told you to dance to the music as it sounds to you. But, whatever else you do, don't make your moves sexually explicit. The Uhmbard's a sophisticated man and looks for subtlety and grace rather than sexual excitement from his dancers. He gets all the sex he wants from his wives.'*

The music started.

Chapter 38

A DANCE FOR LIFE

*O*kkyntalah stood just inside the opening, hiding as best he could within the shadows as the man arrived outside, carrying his curved sword ready to attack. He pushed the unnamed woman through the door before him and she stumbled onto the bed. The man followed. Okkyntalah stepped out of the shadows and felled him with a swift punch to the back of his neck. As the man tried to rise, Okkyntalah knocked him down again and sat on him, ushering the woman out of the way. He held his blade against the man's throat.

'What do you mean by this?'

The man made no answer but spat toward the woman. 'You'll die for your trickery, woman.'

'She had no knowledge of what I might do in these circumstances. I ask again, what do you mean by coming here armed to kill me?'

'You're a stranger in this city. The woman's actions drew my suspicions. It was easy to find out from her that you were not one of us. What do you want here?'

'As to that, I'd hope for hospitality from the people of this city. But I see Ov-Bebna is, as I was warned, a city of cut-throats, thieves and bullies.' He turned to the woman. 'Did this man harm you?'

She displayed the marks; clear palm prints and a pair of stripes from a switch.

'So brave a warrior; look how he marks an unarmed, naked woman. Such a man of courage. On your feet, bowelcreep.'

The man rose slowly. Okkyntalah scanned him for other weapons and discovered a small knife sheathed at his belt. He noted that the woman no longer wore the belt he'd given her.

'Remove your belt. In fact, take off all your clothes.'

The man was sullen and refused to move until Okkyntalah's blade caused blood to leak from a small wound cut into his arm. He stripped quickly, dropping the coat of ribbons and the belt at his feet.

'On your knees.'

The man hesitated and Okkyntalah showed his intentions by making a cut and allowing blood to flow down the leg. The man dropped to his knees. Okkyntalah reversed his sword and knocked the man unconscious with a single blow from the hilt.

'What happened to the belt?'

The woman looked frightened and stood before him, trembling. 'He took it. I think he replaced his own with yours.' She nodded to the items on the bed.

Okkyntalah glanced and saw this was true. He retrieved the belt and slipped his own hunting knife back onto it beside the short curved blade of the other man's knife. The coat of linen strips was the only other item of clothing and Okkyntalah examined it. Stinking of the man's sweat, it would nevertheless have to do. He tested the strength of the fabric and found it surprisingly strong. Cutting two lengths, one from each side of the garment, he used these to bind the man hand and foot, tying the bonds tightly so he'd be unable to shuffle or use his hands or feet to escape.

'No food, then?'

The woman nodded and left the shelter. She returned in moments, carrying the food she'd gone for. The small wooden platter held some bread, fresh dates, grapes, a piece of white, soft cheese and a slice of some cold cooked meat. She also had a shank bone from a small creature, with plenty of meat attached. Shaulah set about this at once and Okkyntalah invited the woman to sit with him on the bed, after he'd rolled and shoved the now naked man into one corner, his face in against the wall.

She was reluctant to eat at first, until he fed her some small morsels, much to her surprise and delight. Once she understood he really did want her to eat with him, she did so with relish, occasionally placing small pieces of food into his mouth, as if this was some new game for her.

The food finished, he drank from his girba and offered it to her for refreshment. She took it gratefully and drank her fill before passing it back, gratitude and surprise mingling on her face.

'What will happen to you when this man wakes?'

'He will have me stoned to death.' She said this with such a matter of fact tone that Okkyntalah at first thought she was making a joke. But it was quickly obvious that she was absolutely serious.

'Is this place your home?'

'I have no home. Women sleep and live where the men allow them.'

'So, who does this place belong to?'

'It's a place for sex out of the sun. That's all.'

He gave this consideration. 'Are there many such places?'

'Many. You wish to have sex with me now?'

'I'd rather we were alone for that. Is there some place I can take this man where he won't be easily found?'

She nodded and moved back to the door. He followed her, leaving the man behind but calling Shaulah after him and taking his belongings, in case he was unable to return.

The coat of strips he donned before leaving, folding his tabard into his pack. At least he was less conspicuous in the local garb.

The woman took him through a narrow gap at the end of the alley, a few paces from the shack. The space they entered was no more than a void between the ends of the walls of three other properties, all backing onto each other without actually meeting. He inspected the area and discovered some rubble from a fallen wall and an old woven screen that one of the property owners had clearly tossed over their high wall as rubbish.

It took only a little time and effort to drag the unconscious man to the place. Okkyntalah sent the woman back to the shelter so she wouldn't witness the murder. It was clear she remained in danger whilst this man lived and the man had shown himself a bully. He felt he had no choice in this brutal city. The screen covered the body and would keep it concealed until the smell of decay led those nearby to discover its cause. By then, both he and the woman would be long gone.

She awaited him in the shack. The bed made tidy again following the short fight. The man's curved sword was still on the floor where it had fallen after Okkyntalah's initial attack. He retrieved it and examined the blade. It needed some work but was fundamentally sound. At least the smithies seemed to know what they were doing. He added it to the sheath on his belt and hoped he wouldn't look too well armed for the local population.

'You've been kind to me, sire. Allow me to serve you in any way you wish, or I will be dishonoured.'

He had no wish to take advantage of this poor woman, in spite of her availability and seeming desire. 'I have my own woman.'

'You think me unworthy. I will do whatever you require of me.'

'I think you're very attractive. But I'm married and love my wife.'

'Wife? You are like the Uhmbard, then?'

'I have only one wife. I gather he has quite a few.'

'Am I so repulsive you reject me?'

He could think of no way in which he could show her she was worthy. In this society, where women were worthless articles of flesh to be used and discarded, he could at least demonstrate that a man and woman could be together for mutual pleasure.

As they rested, side by side, Shaulah on guard at the entrance, she stared at him with wonder and he knew his magic had worked again. It puzzled him that other men failed to see the mutual benefit of such care and attention to women. It was a simple enough thing; to please as you were pleased. And it brought so much more to the act for both parties. Odd that so many men felt unable to first arouse and then satisfy the woman they lay with.

'I didn't know. They talk of such things in the women's places, where we gather for rest and comradeship, but they talk of it as a rumour, as a fairy tale. You are real and you are a man and you have shown me it's possible. Tell me what you need and I will provide. Let me help you in your task of recovering your wife. I can do no less for you.'

It wasn't the outcome he'd sought or expected but it was a great help. But, first, they must recover. He took her in his arms, embraced her and urged her to rest her head on his chest.

'Sleep and rest now. Evening will be soon enough for us to start my rescue bid.'

He felt her relax against him before he fell into a sleep brought on by weariness. In this city of brutality and cruelty, he placed his trust again in the alertness of his dog.

Tumalind danced to the music, weaving her movements into the threads of the melody and living through the notes as they filled the air about her. She imagined the music as a fluid that wrapped her body and let it take her where it would. It was easy in this first piece to sway and wave her arms, to bend her legs and arch her back, to move through the air like a wind-blown willow by the water.

The music died and she floated to the ground to lie prone and still, awaiting the decision.

The Uhmteld clapped once and a hand grasped Tumalind's arm to urge her to her feet. She faced the senior wife and stood with her eyes cast down.

'You have some talent. Let me see how you respond to something a little more explicit.'

Again the hand clap. New music started. This was unmistakably sensuous, even vulgar in places. Tumalind considered the act of love and wove it into her dance without any hint of crudity, letting her body describe the pleasure of loving and the wonder of giving to another the pleasure that she experienced with Okkyntalah. She hoped her interpretation, acted from the heart, would transcend the vulgar and obvious and turn the erotic dance into something far above the level of mere titillation, would give life to her own thoughts on the delight to be had in sharing bodies in the act of true love.

The music ended and silence fell as Tumalind rested in her final pose, her forward leg outstretched, her other folded beneath her and her arms resting forward to touch her ankle, with her head bowed between them. She remained thus, in spite of the discomfort of the hard floor beneath her.

'Rise, my child. You are, indeed, a dancer.'

The silence was broken then as the women applauded and called out their appreciation. A hand urged her back to her feet and Tumalind rose and bowed again before the Uhmteld.

374

Now came the most difficult part. The Uhmbard would want to break her virginity and then would discover that a man had been there before him.

She had no choice. There was, as far as she could see, no other way to prevent her being tossed out into the streets to fend for herself in a violent and abusive society for which she'd had no preparation. The man had, after all, captured her for his own ends, been unnecessarily harsh with her and, she was sure, raped many of the kidnapped girls, even if she herself had been spared that trial.

'May I speak plainly, Paltra?'

There was a gasp of surprise at this request and Tumalind realised she'd crossed some barrier and could expect some form of punishment for her boldness.

'You will address me, child, by my rightful title. I am the Uhmteld of Tohltaz, not some jumped-up noblewoman from your own backward lands. You will refer to me as Most Enlightened One, since that is my position in this court. Do you understand?'

'My apologies, Most Enlightened One, I meant no disrespect. I was not aware of your title as I haven't...'

'Enough. You have something you feel you must say to me, girl?'

Now she'd made the one woman who might help her angry. But there was no going back. In any case, she must make the accusation and hope for the outcome that Teh-pavk had suggested.

'Most Enlightened One I have to make a serious accusation against my captors. One of the men, K'ang Du-Saru by name, took me to a private place and, when we left that place I was no longer whole.'

'I understand your delicacy, my child. The man raped you and you are no longer virgin?'

'Most Enlightened One, I am no longer virgin. I believe that it is proper for me to make this clear before I am presented to the Uhmbard of Tohltaz in his great mightiness.'

It was the best she could come up with and caused a small outburst of nervous giggling but didn't incur the wrath of the senior woman.

'You were right to confess to this fault. It is well you did so. Had I taken you to His Almighty, Wise and Omnipotent Highness without this warning, not only would you have been executed in a most unpleasant manner, but I should have been made to look foolish before my master. I commend you for your honesty. Though you would normally be spared the discomfort for a day or two, in the light of your admission, it is necessary for your preparation, as a dancer, to be completed at once. Tomorrow, you will dance for the Uhmbard and he will decide whether your skill is sufficient to counteract your fault.'

Four of the women bore down on her and took her to the place she'd been plucked. There, the torture began again on the rest of her back surface. By the time they turned her to purge her front of the hairs the Uhmbard found so offensive, she was in tears. But the preparation continued relentlessly. Only one concession was allowed her, as a dancer: her pubic hair was not entirely removed but reduced to a small triangle pointing to the opening. Beads were woven into the hair, forming a decorative pointer.

The underarm hair was the second most painful and one of the women brought her a cup of a strong spirit to drink, the quick intoxication rendering the rest of the hair removal more bearable.

It was the middle of the night before they finished the process. She was again sponged with the burning fluid and then rubbed gently with scented oil that eased the discomfort so that she might sleep and be rested for her ordeal before the Uhmbard in the morning.

Okkyntalah awoke to near darkness. The woman still slept beside him and Shaulah lay asleep but still on guard across the entrance. He allowed himself the luxury of a slow awakening in this strange place. The camel he'd left tethered to the tree concerned him; he must try to get it better hidden.

He roused the woman softly, gently, teasing the hair from her swollen eye and kissing her cheek. 'Come, there are things I must do.'

She nodded and rose to her feet; a pretty woman, without the marks of the beating she'd received at the hands of some brute. He told her of the camel and his intentions.

'You've been good to me, sire. May I speak plain in return?'

'I'd prefer you to.'

'Then, I must tell you that I can't venture beyond the gate at night and that you may also be prevented, or at least, challenged.'

'In what way, challenged?'

'The guards may challenge you to wrestle.'

He considered this. He was fit and strong. He could probably win against most of the men he'd seen around the place so far.

'And you? What might happen to you?'

'If you lost, they'd use me, perhaps give me a beating. If you won, they'd let you go, of course, but on your own.'

'Which would mean leaving you behind to their mercies. I see. Is there another way out of the city? One that isn't watched?'

'You're a brave man, sire. I can take you to such a place. It's not easy and it is not safe. If we're caught, I'll be whipped and you'll be confined to the Pit.'

He was curious about the Pit; the word seemed to frighten her. But for the moment it was more important to visit the place she knew and decide whether the risk was worth the effort. 'Can we get back in the way we leave?'

'With difficulty, sire.'

'Show me.'

She walked him through narrow streets where no one but the occasional sad woman was to be seen. From time to time, they passed or heard sounds of merriment. The male voices sounded gleeful and often drunk even this early in the evening. The women he heard sounded frightened, or laughed with false merriment along with the men. She took him to a part of the city where many buildings were in need of repair, the streets rutted and pitted. Here, they met no one until a man leapt out at them, his arm raised in threat with what Okkyntalah took to be a sword in the darkness of the moonlight night. He drew his own weapon and killed the attacker with a single blow. The woman moaned. Okkyntalah stooped to see whether he'd killed the man and discovered the weapon he'd threatened with was no more than a stick.

'What's this?'

'Outcasts live here, sire. Men without status, some without parts. They're the only ones we don't feed or serve. The man you killed was known to me. He was not the worst of men. But he was sand blind and the Uhmbard had cut out his tongue for some crime years ago. I think he might be better off dead, sire.'

Okkyntalah wondered how his life had changed to this warrior who now killed without thought. When had that happened? He was a simple hunter. A man who lived for family, a man who cared for people. How had he become an executioner of other men? He had no answer and the woman clearly wanted to move on. Her stance and nervous movements made her fear of this place clear.

'Take me on.'

She moved ahead and led him down narrowing passages until they were obliged to walk in single file with the dog following. At last, she stopped and, in almost total darkness, pointed to a gap in the wall above her. It was just too high for him to reach unaided. Without a word, she knelt on all fours so he could step on her back.

'Stay, Shaulah.'

The dog sat. He climbed from the woman's back into the opening where the wall had been breached. From there, he reached down and pulled the woman up beside him. The space they occupied was small and held them close together as he looked out and down. There was no sign of life outside the wall and the drop was little further than the one inside. He helped her descend and then jumped silently after her, rolling in the sand to break his fall.

'Where's the gate?'

She pointed. Finding the camel took almost no time. It was where he'd tethered it.

The woman glanced all about her in the light cast by the waxing moon.

'What's scaring you?'

'Your beast belongs to the heathens and will bring you death if found. I'll be whipped if I'm discovered out here, sire. I'm surprised a man like you would risk that just to help a beast.'

'The camel bore me here in safety and will help me escape this place with my wife. It makes sense to care for it, don't you think?'

'I'm sorry, sire. I spoke from fear, no more. Will you take me with you, sire?' She gasped as if she hadn't meant to say that last out loud. 'Forgive me. I meant no...'

'Don't be frightened of me. If I can find a way to take you without endangering Tumalind, then I'll do it. Are there places we might find horses?'

She nodded.

'Guarded or easy to reach?'

'The stables are within the walls, not far from the gate. Women look after them all. There are many there. I don't know much about them, sire. Horses are valued. But the men, if you'll forgive my boldness, the men don't seem to care for them the way they should, I think, sire.'

He untied the camel and let it go. It was not worth the risk of a hue and cry and there were horses he could steal when they were ready to leave. Taking the woman's hand, he returned to the breach in the wall. It was too high for him to reach from her back. She knelt and he stepped onto her shoulders to pull himself up. He couldn't then reach her hands as she stretched up. He unfastened his belt and, lying across the breach, dropped the length until she could reach it. As she reached to climb up to him, there was the sound of alarm behind him and Shaulah growled.

'Wait there. I'll be back for you soon.'

He had to leave her to save his dog from this threat. Below, by the reflected light of the moon, he could see movement and heard Shaulah growling in a way that meant trouble. He dropped from the wall with the small curved knife in one hand and the sword unsheathed in the other. Two men. One limping on a wasted leg and the other unmanned. They were trying to catch the dog. Both started when he dropped out of the sky toward them. But they'd seen the dog and wouldn't give up their claim so easily. He didn't want to kill unarmed men, especially such sorry samples.

'The dog's mine. Try to steal her and I'll kill you. Go.'

The men looked at each other, made a signal they both understood, and closed on him together in the confined space. The first, with the game leg, folded as he plunged the curved blade of the knife into his chest. The other man saw his friend killed before his eyes and ran into the night. How long before he brought others?

Okkyntalah now had to reach the break in the wall without the woman's aid. He could find no purchase for his hands on the smooth surface and it was too high for him to find a handhold at the bottom of the breach. There was no alternative. He propped the dead man into a sitting position with his back against the wall and stepped onto his shoulders to climb into the space.

The woman was frantic below, weeping in the moonlight and terrified she'd been abandoned.

'Catch the end of the belt. And hurry. We may not have much time.'

She stopped crying and reached for the end of the leather, grasping it tightly with both hands. Okkyntalah heaved and raised her from the ground. 'You need to use your feet to help you climb.'

She scrabbled at the wall with her feet but found no purchase. Okkyntalah heaved with all his might and raised her to the bottom of the break. 'Grip the wall with one hand and let go the belt.'

She did as she was told and hung precariously as he bent to clasp her arms to haul her up. Behind him, Shaulah growled again, signalling the trouble he'd expected. But he must first get the woman safe on top of the wall. She helped as she could but the space was small and he grazed her hip against the ragged edge before she was in place.

'Stay there.'

He dropped again to the inner side. This time they were prepared for him. Three men crowding the small space. Such fools. They couldn't face him all at once in such a narrow place.

'Leave me be. I've no wish to kill you. But I will if you don't leave this place. Now.'

The man at the rear muttered something and withdrew.

'Go.'

The unmanned fellow seemed determined and urged his companion on with muttered curses. Neither man attacked, but they blocked the way. Okkyntalah raised the sword and thrust the blade toward them. The other brought his own blade up to meet it. But he was no swordsman and Okkyntalah easily parried the move, swiping the blade out of his hands and lunging forward in attack. The second man saw the danger and turned tail. The first man, now alone again, unarmed, fell to his knees and begged for mercy.

'Get out. Go!'

He crawled away on hands and knees into the deeper darkness beyond. But Okkyntalah wasn't convinced the thing had ended. Waiting long enough to be sure there was no immediate danger, he turned and urged the woman from the wall, telling her to lower herself down until he could hold her and take her to the ground.

'Toss down my belt and the other weapons first.'

She did as he suggested and then almost fell into his arms as she climbed down. For a moment they just held each other, sharing relief at their escape from different dangers. He replaced the belt and handed her the small curved knife.

'Use it if you have to. I'm not sure they'll just let us leave without a fight.'

She held it as though it was something evil she'd rather not touch.

'If you're worried about killing, just remember all the times men have abused and beaten you.'

She nodded slowly and he saw surprise and determination replace doubt.

'Good. Follow me.'

Chapter 39

DANCER FOR LIFE

Tumalind slept soundly, but morning found her feeling lethargic and groggy. She couldn't dance like this.

'You look dreadful. That'll be the Juuvu you drank last night. Come with me and have breakfast. A strong cup of kaffe will revive you for your dance.' Teh-pavk took her by the hand and led her to the tables at the far end of the room.

She'd slept on cushions on the floor, along with all the wives. Even the Uhmteld shared the space; her only privilege being an area marked as her own and floored with sumptuous cushions. All the other women slept wherever they happened to be when the lamps were extinguished. A number, she noted, seemed to spend the night in very close contact, and this surprised her until she considered the reality of the situation. Over four hundred women and only one man.

Breakfast brought her awake, especially the strong, dark kaffe; a drink she'd never tasted before. It was thick with honey that only partially hid the bitterness. But, whatever else was in that small cup, it banished her feeling of lethargy and left her feeling wide awake and full of energy. The fruit and bread, fresh juices, squeezed for them by women servants, satisfied her hunger.

Tumalind was taken before the Uhmteld in the middle of the day.

'Turn for me.'

She revolved in front of the woman, raising her arms above her head when asked and bending and stretching before her.

'Good. Go with Teh-blavv. She will apply the colours to you. Do as she says. I don't want to have to spank you before you see the Uhmbard. Hand marks on your skin will displease him and it's vital he be pleased with you if you're to gain your place as Dancer rather than be sent to work in the streets with the other unfortunates. Go now. And do as she instructs.'

Teh-blavv led her to one of the sunken pools first and joined her in the water, where they cleansed each other with soft sponges and scented lotions. The process was the most pleasant thing she'd experienced so far and she'd have happily spent the day in the refreshing water. But it was over too soon and Teh-blavv took her to a plinth that sat in a small alcove, daylight entering through high windows partially obscured by filigree woodwork.

'That's beautiful workmanship.'

Teh-blavv looked at it, as if for the first time. 'I suppose it is. It lets in the light but stops the guards outside from peering in at us.'

Tumalind lay as directed, cushions taking away the hardness of the stone beneath her. The girl instructed her to close her eyes and she felt Teh-blavv's fingers gentle on her eyelids, felt something soft smoothed over her face. Throughout the process, she was made to lie absolutely still and say nothing. Even when fingers strayed to her breasts and smoothed something on and around her nipples, she must remain still and keep her eyes closed.

'These painted pictures don't come off?'

Tumalind, conscious of her instruction to lie still and say nothing, didn't know how to respond to the question.

'Well, do they?'

She shrugged and decided it might be best to speak. 'They're called tattoos and the colours are in the skin; they won't come off, ever.'

She felt fingers touch the designs, tracing first the small butterfly and then the bird of paradise from its exuberant tail to the sharp beak that pecked at her entrance.

'They're beautiful. Did it hurt to have them made?'

'A little. But it's part of what we do on the island on Muhnilahm.'

There was a short silence and the fingers moved off her skin. A light tap on her thigh made her open her eyes.

'You may sit now.'

Six women surrounded her and she realised all had been involved in the preparation of her body for the ordeal to come.

'You're one of those Followers, then?' The woman who asked this said it with a tone of distaste, as though accusing her of something unpleasant.

'I'm a Follower of Ytraa, yes. Is that bad?'

The woman who'd asked the question shrugged. 'I've heard they eat their children; that's all.'

'Then you've heard a lie. We care very much for our children and raise them with love.' It came to her, apparently unbidden, that not all children were raised with love; some were abandoned to the Point because of faults in their appearance or abilities. Perhaps her island wasn't quite as perfect as it ought to be.

Teh-blavv guided her to a second alcove. Here, two tall windows, both masked with the filigree woodwork, stood either side of a tall shiner. It wasn't as good as the glass mirrors she'd seen in Litkala, but it gave a very good reflection. She was encouraged to inspect her body and face there.

Her eyes had been painted with blue paste on the lids so that when she closed one, she saw that it formed a sort of pool surrounded by a carpet of green that covered the area around each eye from just below the brow around and halfway down her cheek. Her mouth was an impossible red, the lips painted with something that made them shine with colour. A line of black descended along the bridge of her nose to the tip, where it parted and split into two lines that crossed each cheek and ended at the openings to her ears. Each of her ears was painted with yellow around the outer edge and small dots of blue and green covered the lobes. Her chin bore an intricate design in black and white, depicting what looked like a stylized beetle.

Her throat was marked with alternate stripes of blue and gold that led across her chest to her breasts, where they spiralled around, missing the butterfly, until they reached the nipples, now both golden. A shining gemstone of deep ruby colour twinkled in her navel and curved lines of coloured dots crossed the space from the stone across her belly and to the edge of the patch of beaded pubic hair. Her feet were criss-crossed with fine lines of purple and yellow, crossing and interweaving so that they appeared as delicate baskets enclosing her feet.

She could not see her back but the girl told her she was decorated with spiral devices in blue and gold on each buttock and a trio of lines in red, green and yellow that wove across each other in sensuous curves up the length of her back.

Teh-blavv examined her and seemed content. She led her back to the Uhmteld, who bade her stand still whilst she scrutinised her thoroughly.

'An excellent job, my children. I think we've done all we can to persuade the Uhmbard of her suitability. The rest, girl, is up to you. Perform well and impress the Uhmbard, and I will give you a Dancer name. Of course, if you fail, no name will be needed on the streets amongst the lesser men.

'I'll take you now to dance for the Uhmbard. You will say no words to him unless he asks you a direct question, which you will answer with truth only. You will remain on your belly until instructed otherwise. Once you have finished your demonstration, you will again lie flat on your belly and await further instructions. Do you understand?'

'Yes, Most Enlightened One.'

The Uhmteld led her from the women's quarters. They crossed a wide, walled square, where armed guards stood at each corner and along the length of the inner walls at intervals of about three paces. The men all applauded her appearance and made coarse remarks about her sexual attraction. But none moved from his post.

The corridor leading to the room where she would dance was also lined with armed men. These wore the same brief skirt and wide belt of their companions outside, but also bore tall conical helmets of shining brass on their heads. As she passed between their ranks, each man explored her with his eyes but remained upright.

'Dubbies like twin mounds of honeyed rice.'

'Fern inviting every prod in the world.'

'Tail begging for spanks.'

'Legs leading to pleasure without limit.'

These comments, and others of a cruder nature, assailed her as she passed their scrutiny on the way to the men's master. She felt more exposed and displayed than admired. These men would use her, given the chance, but none would share pleasure with her; they would take only what they wanted and leave her feeling abused.

At last the corridor ended and the final two guards stood in her way before the doors. They made her turn for them, made her bend and display in ways that left her feeling unclean and despoiled even though no one touched her. Laughing, they opened the door and announced her arrival. The Uhmteld said nothing during the whole journey and left her at the doors.

The Uhmbard was seated on a wide throne of soft leather, cushions beneath his limbs and a wife either side of him stroking his legs. This much Tumalind saw before she fell on her face to slither the rest of the way into the room.

She heard the single clap that signalled she'd reached the appointed place.

'Dance.'

The music started softly. She slowly rose, taking her time before she was on her feet and swaying rhythmically, as she allowed herself to be lost within the notes and melody of three instruments combining to make a complex tune. She danced as if for Okkyntalah, knowing this would allow her to move without inhibition but would prevent an open display of vulgarity, whilst being inviting and sensual.

One tune led into another and she danced without pause, breathing evenly to prevent the appearance of breathlessness as the music beat out faster and more provocatively. She moved and swayed, bent, skipped, spun and jumped and wondered if she would do this until she died from exhaustion. It seemed she'd danced forever when the music finally tailed into silence and she flowed gracefully back into a prone position, initially face up and with her fern on display to the Uhmbard. Slowly, she rolled onto her stomach, turning at the same time, so she would face him if he asked her to raise her head.

The silence that followed contained only sounds that reminded her of her father at home with her mother and she was sure one of the wives was serving the master. The act was brief and a clapped signal followed it.

'Stand, woman.'

She hoped the command was for her, rose swiftly with as much grace as she could, and stood with her feet a little apart, her hands in her hair but her face downcast so that she saw his feet but no more of him.

'You may gaze on me.'

She obeyed and saw a look in his eyes that she'd once surprised on Tryonta's face. It wasn't connected to love or even to desire especially; it was a look that spoke of the wish to possess her absolutely and without barriers. She forced her mouth into a smile of pleasure and hoped her eyes wouldn't give away her true feelings of contempt and disgust.

'Dancer, approach.'

She moved across the space with the grace she'd used to interpret the music, swaying and bending to an unheard melody that expressed everything that was woman to a man. At his feet, she stopped and again waited. He bade her revolve for him and she did until told to stop when she again faced him.

'You are blessed and may live as a Dancer. I will require you often, since you show an aptitude not displayed by many. For the moment, retire to the Dancer's quarters. Do not disappoint me, Dancer, when I call for you again.'

She assumed she was dismissed and slowly fell to the floor and onto her face.

'No. You leave as Dancer now. Entertain me so I wish I could pursue and enter you.'

The music started at once and she danced her way from throne to door, moving as provocatively as she was able. At the door, she turned to face him and made her body boldly available before she turned and knocked for the guards to free her from the presence. In the open doorway, she once more presented herself before she turned and skipped down the corridor and out of his sight. The guards now seemed full of respect for her; silent and admiring where they'd been coarse and prurient.

The Uhmteld awaited her return and beckoned her to stand again before her.

'You've done well, my child. I'm pleased with you and, in keeping with your new rank and position, I award you the Dancing name of Tah-Tumalind. A servant will take you to your new quarters. Be always ready to perform. The other Dancers will advise you. You have, of course, yet to face the ordeal of admission of your incomplete state. I advised the Uhmbard only that you were not available for penetration at this time, so that he would not have his pleasure in you spoiled by the truth. Of course, another wife must be found for the Moonday, now.'

The servant took her across the open courtyard again, this time to a low building with wide, deep openings unfettered by filigree woodwork masks and overlooking the square. It seemed that the privilege of being a Dancer would not, after all, free her from humiliation. The guards had unrestricted views of the interior. The Dancers were under constant watch. It would be difficult for anyone to rescue her from such a well-guarded place and her mood of hope dissipated as she considered the impossibility of escape from here.

Okkyntalah led the way through the narrow passages until Shaulah warned him, with a growl, of unseen danger ahead. He put his hand out behind him, to stop the woman moving, and sneaked a look around the corner. There were three of them waiting. All armed with one weapon or another. He slipped back into the shadows before they saw him.

'Is there any other way out of this place?'

'No, sire. And I know the city very well. We must go this way. Is there some problem?'

He considered his options. Waiting might simply bring more of these ruffians. It was either now, with a chance of success, or later with less hope.

'If anything should happen to me, see my dog is well cared for. Will you do that for me, please?'

He shrugged off his pack, the long bow and the quiver of arrows, to free him for the coming fight. It would be a coward who attacked such men from cover with a bow.

'Sire, I'd do anything for you. Anything at all.'

'Good. Remain here, with my dog, until I return. If I don't come back, take care as you leave this place.'

He was gone before she had time to respond; surprise his great advantage. And he was on the trio before they could react, his sword drawn in one hand and his knife ready in the other.

They stood amazed at his confrontation of them, unready to fight it seemed.

'I've no wish to kill you all. Stand aside and let me pass.'

He saw their covert signals and waited until one made a move. Killing without proper cause was foreign to his nature and he'd already had to murder one man in cold blood this day; he'd kill no more without good cause.

But they would fight. It went his way at first and he'd despatched two of his adversaries almost without battle. The unmanned fellow had fallen to a sword blow across his neck and the small man had taken the hunting knife into his heart without completing the strike he'd started. But the third man, big and strong, desperate for reasons Okkyntalah couldn't fathom, was a fighter. As they struggled with each other, the man called out and others gathered in the space until Okkyntalah was outmatched. He understood that there was some strange code of honour with these men. They did not wish to kill him, merely to defeat him for his things. But this had been forgotten in the bloodshed and now it was his surrender they required.

'You can't win against us all. We'll have to kill you. But if you put down your weapons we'll spare your life and you can join us here in health.'

386

That sounded hopeful. Were these men of honour? If he gave himself up to them would that also spare the woman and his dog?

'Take me to a place more open and unwalled, where I may see whether I should take my chances. Here, in this slum, I cannot move or breathe enough to make a proper stand.'

'You'll wrestle, stranger? Wrestle for your life?'

It was a challenge that the woman had said might be thrown at him. Behind the words were threats of death if he declined. He had to rely on instinct here, to have faith in the underlying honour that men showed for life. Here, in this city where women were abused and enslaved, men were mostly valued.

'I accept.'

They led him from the place, a buzz of excitement running through the gathering. And, as they moved away from where he'd left the woman and Shaulah, more men, some with women, joined the group that fast became a crowd.

In the large square he'd crossed in fear and silence with the woman, one of the group shouted out a message he didn't understand. But it was clear that here was where the wrestling match would happen. He had no knowledge of the rules of engagement and no clue as to his opponent.

The crowd parted and a line of men, followed by women carrying lighted torches, entered the central space. Okkyntalah, still armed, stood alone in an area made by the surrounding mob. At the head of the new group, a man more muscled than any he'd ever seen, bore down on him. Shorter, but far heavier than Okkyntalah, the man moved with an animal confidence in his strength and prowess. Without any orders, the women bearing torches arranged themselves in a circle around him and knelt, holding their lights high to illuminate the scene for all those watching.

'Put down your weapons, stranger. No one here will take them.'

The command came from a man in something Okkyntalah took to be a uniform. The man was some sort of official; a short skirt and wide belt complementing his curved sword worn on a leather sash that ran diagonally from shoulder to hip.

Okkyntalah turned the sword around and handed it to this man, hilt first. He took it and bowed, before Okkyntalah did the same with his hunting knife.

The muscular man stripped and took a stance, ready. Okkyntalah followed suit and waited for some explanation, some indication of what was expected of him.

The man in uniform raised a hand for silence and the crowd fell still, waiting.

'No gouging. No biting. The first to incapacitate will win.'

The crowd murmured their approval and the muscled man nodded. Okkyntalah, seeing no other way, also nodded.

'Begin.'

For a short while, he and the wrestler circled each other, sizing one another up and looking for potential spots of weakness. Okkyntalah wondered if blows would be exchanged or whether this was like the wrestling he'd engaged in on the island, where all depended on who could stay upright.

The wrestler moved fast and suddenly, catching him unawares as he plunged forward and engaged him in a hold that almost squeezed the air out of him. Okkyntalah brought his arms around and down at same time as he kicked the wrestler's feet away. The man not only fell heavily but had to let go of Okkyntalah to avoid more pain in the fall.

The crowd both jeered and cheered. Coin had been placed and bets made. There would be losers and winners apart from those who wrestled, and they brayed for success for their chosen. Okkyntalah heard the cries from the crowd, advising him to jump on the fallen wrestler. But that seemed a cowardly way to him and the man rose to his feet. He looked at Okkyntalah with a little more respect but also some puzzlement. Okkyntalah guessed, belatedly, that he had lost his advantage by being too concerned about the rules of fighting here.

The wrestler threw a punch, catching Okkyntalah in the midriff and winding him briefly. He moved away from the second blow but felt his feet swept from under him. The wrestler dived to pin him to the ground. Okkyntalah rolled out of the way and was back on his feet before the man could take advantage. He realised he must outwit this man if he was to win here. The wrestler's great weight gave him an advantage and he must use this to his own gain. Okkyntalah, suffering the first blow, hit back and then struck out with his foot as the man scrambled back upright. He connected with his opponent's thigh and made the man jump back, limping. The crowd jeered, though some cheered. The judgement as to fairness seemed inconclusive and Okkyntalah was unsure whether kicking was allowed.

The wrestler ran at him again but Okkyntalah was prepared this time. He waited till the last moment. Stepped aside. Put a foot out and, as the man tripped over, helped him on his way with the flat of his hand between his shoulder blades. The wrestler fell his length amid a great roar of cheering and some laughter. Perhaps the various responses had no connection to the rules and only indicated pleasure or concern about the money to be lost or gained.

Okkyntalah, understanding he now had the advantage, leapt on the wrestler. He was quicker than expected and rolled away before he made contact. He was on Okkyntalah like a stripecat. His hands found his throat and he began to squeeze. Regardless of rules, Okkyntalah realised he'd die in those hands if he didn't free himself. He kicked out behind him, engaged with the man's parts and felt the soft tissue squelch under his foot.

The stranglehold eased as the wrestler fought the pain, but he wouldn't let go. Okkyntalah kicked again. The hands released as the wrestler tried to keep his place above him. Freed from the throttling, Okkyntalah leapt upright and then launched himself feet first at the man as he was scrambling to rise. The wrestler's right arm gave way beneath him, just as Okkyntalah's feet landed on his shoulder. He fell and took the whole weight on his head. Okkyntalah heard the snapping bones even as he felt the resistance go beneath him. He rolled to absorb the momentum of the move and rose slowly to his feet.

The man was dead. His head lay at an impossible angle. Neck broken by the move Okkyntalah had made.

The silence of the crowd lasted only moments before pandemonium broke out. The official called out loudly, shouting for attention until the noise subsided.

'You must come with me, stranger. The Pit awaits.'

Several of the men formed a group around him to prevent any escape attempt. He was shepherded away, cries of anger and of triumph following him. Three of the women came with torches to illuminate the way. As they left the square, he saw the woman with his dog also leave. She carried his belongings and he wondered what would happen to them and her now.

They took him through the city to the gate. The soldiers on duty saluted the official in uniform and he explained his requirements to them. Okkyntalah was made to stand in the light of the torches as one of the guards from the gate went into their small guardhouse and returned carrying a reed wand. The official stood before Okkyntalah and placed a hand on his shoulder.

'You have been found guilty of murder by act of violent conduct in the commission of a wrestling bout. The sentence for this is twenty lashes and three consecutive periods in the Pit. Prepare for the lashes.'

He pushed Okkyntalah away and, unaware that one of the women had been made to kneel on all fours behind him, fell over her and lay sprawled on the ground. She remained in position and he was ordered to mount her as if they were dogs. In this position he was lashed twenty times on the buttocks. A painful but not damaging chastisement. He apologised to the woman beneath him and she whispered her surprised thanks for his concern.

The swift beating over, he was led to a space next to the gate, just within the walls and hard by the road that took traffic in and out of the city. A small square, with sides no longer than his legs, opened in the ground there, creating a black void. He was told to drop into the space. Hesitation in this, he understood, would look like cowardice and such a quality was publicly denounced in this place. He stepped out and dropped into the void.

389

It was deeper than he'd expected but his fall was cushioned by something that gave beneath him. He fell his length and his hands plunged into soft, foul material that stank of corruption. There was no light in the pit but that which filtered through the small square above him. He felt something run across his leg as he shifted to move and extract his hands from whatever he'd fallen onto. The creature, which he realised quickly was not alone, was a rhaat. And they were bold enough to approach and nose at him in the dark. He kicked out, discouraging them from whatever they intended.

The brightness of the flaming torches meant that it took him a few moments to adjust to the almost total darkness of the Pit. When he was finally able to discern something of his surroundings, he wished he'd remained unaware. The thing he'd fallen onto was undoubtedly a body, rotting and decomposing. The stench, already foul, became unbearable once he'd identified its source.

From above, sound slowly moved away, leaving him in silence as the crowd dispersed. He had no way of knowing how long he would be left here. Whether he would be fed or given water, or how he would eventually be given the means to return to the surface that seemed two manheights above his head. Alone amongst the charnel remains of some unfortunate who'd never been released, he tried to find a place to rest until greater light provided more clues about his surroundings.

Chapter 40

THE CAUSE BEGINS

Tumalind rested, her body thoroughly relaxed by the oiling and massage Tah-Vlatak had given her after she'd settled in her new room. The young woman had talked as she worked, explaining she'd been caught in the desert when a girl of only thirteen years and was now twenty-two. She'd been a Dancer all that time and was aware she had a position much better than the wives and far superior to the poor women on the streets of the city. But she still longed to return to her people, who she referred to as the K'ahll; a people who dwelt in tents and roamed the desert.

Fed, and provided with wine, Tumalind was confident she wouldn't be called to Dance again until the following day at the earliest. It seemed the Uhmbard chose not to work his Dancers too hard. In any case, there were nearly two dozen and he apparently enjoyed variety.

The cushions beneath her were soft and supporting. Evening light had displayed her to the men in the square outside but that was now in darkness and she knew of their presence only by an occasional noise or soft words that sometimes passed between those on duty. At any rate, Tah-Vlatak had assured her she was absolutely safe and secure in her quarters and needn't concern herself about the men at all.

'They're loyal. But that doesn't stop one or two Dancers taking a chance with them; then they're eager enough. Mind you, if they dare interfere with us against our will, they'll lose their means to do so in the future. And then be sent to the desert, tethered and spread-eagled with their eyelids cut off and honey smeared on their wounds to attract the fierce desert ants. They say it takes them two days of agony to die like that.'

Tumalind had said nothing, appalled at man's ability to create suffering for his fellows. The Followers had punishments she'd often seen as cruel but it seemed they were not alone in this and it saddened her to think such things were done in the world. That thought set her to thinking of her dishonesty about the slave trader. The Uhmteld had warned her that she must face the Uhmbard on the morning when the slave trader would be there to be judged. She'd have to accuse the man to his face and describe, in detail, exactly what he'd done to her. That, in itself, wasn't what she feared; she'd only to substitute her womanhood for her mouth and she could make the description well enough. But the lie about his penetrating her sat uneasily with her, even though she knew she'd had no real choice, other than to face a whipping and the prospect of a life spent on the streets of this vile place.

She needed to take her mind off such things if she was to take advantage of the wonderful massage and find sleep. She would talk to Ivdulon or Feldrark and see what plans they had. That would occupy her mind.

'How are you? Safe, at least, I hope?'

She explained her situation to Ivdulon and all that had happened since they'd last mindtalked. The wise woman explained that Feldrark had set a rescue mission in motion. It had taken a day in planning but the force of fifty armed and experienced soldiers had set off, sailing initially to the Bituhn Crofts, where they were expected to arrive that very night.

'What then?'

'They'll purchase more supplies and pack animals and set off for the desert. Has Okkyntalah reached you yet? One of my connections tells me he's in hot pursuit.'

That news was both encouraging and worrying. She'd seen how swift and cruel the system of justice could be here. If Okkyntalah should fall foul of their laws he could be executed before she ever saw him. The thought was too much for her after the days she had spent.

'I'm sorry, I've caused you to worry, Tumalind. Be courageous and positive. Your young man has shown himself to be resourceful and brave. And he's sensible, unlike most men, so he'll be careful how he goes about finding and rescuing you. If only he could mindtalk, I could guide him. Still, I'm sure he'll be fine. He's strong and able. Don't you worry about him. Just sit tight and wait for our soldiers to arrive. They'll get you out of there safe, I'm sure of it.'

It wasn't entirely the message she'd hoped for, but there was comfort as well as anxiety to be gained there. She'd remain positive for Okkyntalah, be brave and hopeful until there was no hope left to be had. But, in the meantime, the problem of the lie preyed on her mind. She explained to Ivdulon.

'Did you choose to be kidnapped and taken to a foreign place? Of course you didn't. Is it your fault their laws and customs are as they are? No. Tumalind, you're in a perilous position, in a place without support for the moment. You must use whatever tricks, lies, and methods are available to you. These men are wicked and cruel. You're a lone woman naked amongst lecherous wolves and serpents. The last thing you should be concerned about is telling a lie that will preserve your life.'

'But we're brought up to tell the truth, Ivdulon. I find it so difficult. And I'm accusing a man of something I know will end his life. It's as if I'm killing him myself.'

'You're far too good, Tumalind. Let me ask you again; did you choose to be where you are?'

'No. I was taken against my will.'

'Did you have any choice in what happened to you on the way?'

'Only in that I lied then that I was virgin, so they wouldn't rape me.'

'A justifiable and sensible precaution. But the men who took you broke so many laws that they placed themselves outside of the general law by their actions. It's they who've put themselves in the position they're now in, not you. And, at least, you're only accusing one of them of the crime, not all of them.'

'It doesn't feel right.'

'Of course it doesn't. But it's the only logical thing you can do. You're in an impossible position and this is the only way out for you. You have no choice, Tumalind. None at all. Unless you truly believe you deserve that most horrible living death they'll make you suffer if you admit the truth.'

'Thank you, Ivdulon. It helps.'

She lay under the soft warm air and thought of Ivdulon's words. But the idea of causing a man's death by lying still sat uneasily with her.

Okkyntalah rested against the sloping wall until dawn brought light enough to show him his surroundings in more detail. He wished then that the dark remained. The corpse he'd fallen on during his drop into the Pit was decomposing. Another, dry and almost reduced to bones, lay huddled in one corner, rhaats peeking out from the disturbed and chavelled bones. A third rested broken on the floor beside the skeletal one. This was a woman and had been dead only days if her condition was a guide. Already, she was putrefying, the whip marks on her back crawling with the maggots that explained the presence of so many flies in this cell.

He looked above and saw the sky brighten with coming day. The cell was constructed so that the walls dropped at an angle from the hole above and spread out to form the floor space he now occupied. It measured little more than two manlengths along each side. If he was to spend time in this place, he must do what he could to make space for his own comfort. Those who'd died here were beyond his help but he might make his own life a little more bearable by moving the remains until they occupied a small part, as far away from him as he could gather them.

The task was grisly, with the flesh already falling from the bones of the man he'd fallen on, pools of sticky liquid drying into pads of stinking jelly when he dragged the carcase up to join the skeleton. The woman's body was foul and she leaked fluids as he moved her and dragged her atop the man. He turned her swollen face away, so she could no longer stare at him with those accusing eyes.

That job done, he cracked free the thigh bone from the skeleton and set about killing the small horde of rhaats that feasted on the dead flesh and would attack him, given the

393

chance. It took more time and effort than he wanted but must be done if he was to escape the worst of the disease these beasts were known to carry. A bite might kill a man who wasn't strong.

By the time he'd finished, the sun was overhead and shining directly into the cell to make it unbearably hot. A small oven to cook him. Already he was thirsty and no sign had appeared that he'd be fed or given water here. But he knew that anxiety about an unknown future could quickly destroy him. His one hope for survival was to rest now. The flies bothered his hands, befouled as they were with the rotten flesh and coagulated blood of the dead, but they were happier to feast on those corpses than to bother the living who might fight back.

He curled on his side on the hard earth of the floor, keeping in the shade when possible, and spent the day waiting.

Night came and darkness slowly hid the horrors of the cell. But those accusing eyes still seemed to bore into his soul. Stars appeared and he lay down to watch them circle past in his small square that was all he had of the world. The Skyfire appeared at the edge of the black square and told him of passing time.

A figure moved into the space, silhouetted by the stars and brightness of the Skyfire. He recognised her at once. She whispered down at him and he made his voice soft in a reply that no one else should hear.

'Be ready to untie the cord quickly. I mustn't be found here. I'll come back when I can.'

She lowered down the pot and he untied the rope with fouled fingers, the stickiness making the task more difficult.

'Quickly, please!' Her urgency was driven by fear and he finished as quickly as he could in the darkness.

'Done. Go, with my thanks.'

She was gone, dragging the cord behind her, winding it even as she made her escape so close to the guardhouse.

There was water in a small bottle shaped container. He sipped, knowing this might be all he would have until released. There was a piece of bread. Some dates and figs and a leg of some game bird.

A veritable feast. He ate sparingly, taking all the bread before it could grow stale and hard and eating all the meat of the bird, knowing it would quickly spoil in the heat. The fruit he saved, in case he wasn't fed again. He completed his meal with another sip of water and dribbled a few drops on his fingers to take some of the fouling from them.

The woman had repaid his kindness. She wouldn't dare risk another visit. He would have to manage on what she'd left him. Turning his back to the horrors sharing his cell, he curled again and tried to sleep.

Tumalind stood patiently as Tah-Vlatak prepared her for the meeting with the Uhmbard. This time the decoration wasn't so ornate, as she would probably be expected only to attend and not to Dance. The woman talked as she completed all the necessary painting and applied colours to her face. She explained about life in the Dancers' quarters and described the usual day; time spent waiting to be called, time spent eating, drinking and keeping the body supple and well-honed with exercise for when Dancing was demanded.

The Uhmteld led her to the chamber. A different room from the one in which she'd Danced for him. In chains, the slave traders knelt on the floor, their bodies naked and their backs already scourged with stripes that bled. She turned away and dropped onto her face to slither across to the place she was commanded.

'Dance to the place. Always, in my presence, you will Dance.'

There was no music here, so she danced to a melody within her head; something bearing sadness and the serious nature of the occasion, with no hint of the sensual. When she reached the designated spot, she dropped to the floor and knelt with her face down.

'Point out the man who stole your virginity.'

She glanced upward and realised there were too few there. One was missing. K'ang Du-Saru wasn't there.

'The man who violated me is not here, Oh Almighty, Wise and Omnipotent Highness.'

'Not here?'

She was about to repeat that he was missing when one of the guards prodded the slave trader who was leader. He lifted his head a little and spoke, quietly at first.

'Speak up, man!'

'Almighty, Wise and Omnipotent Highness, the man you seek is dead. He was killed last night in a wrestling match with a stranger.'

'Excellent. I am saved the trouble of executing the loathsome dog. Have you discovered a replacement virgin for the one soiled by your man?'

'Almighty, Wise and Omnipotent Highness, I was collecting the new moonday virgin when your guards apprehended me and brought me here.'

'Hang these; it will set an example.' He spoke to the leader again. 'You will bring the new virgin to me at once.'

'At once, Almighty, Wise and Omnipotent Highness.'

'If she pleases me, I may spare you. Go now.'

The guards kicked and shoved the chained men out of the chamber. The Uhmbard turned back to Tumalind and beckoned her to him. She danced across the space, graceful and serious still.

'They deserve not your respect, Dancer. Show me your skill as you did yesterday. I wish to be pleasured after such corruption.'

Tumalind Danced. In the absence of music, initially, it was difficult to keep the movements going with only the remembered melody in her head. But the door opened and three women entered, two with instruments that immediately struck up the tune she had in her head, such was their skill. The third moved across the space in an unbroken series of cartwheels until she was before the Uhmbard, where she converted her movements so she could walk on her hands and then stand, on her hands, absolutely still in front of him. He clapped and she sat astride him. Tumalind watched her out of the corner of her eye and adjusted her own rhythms to those of the woman servicing the Uhmbard. Skilful and swift, she was done in moments and Tumalind was dismissed to Dance her way across the room and back to her quarters.

In the square, the other slavers were still chained. The guards were casually beating them, as if involved in some game, before they would be taken out and hung from a beam in the town square. K'eng Hin-Seru glared at her as she passed. His look of utter hatred quickly changed to agony as a guard whipped his already broken skin.

'How dare you gaze at the Dancer? I'll have your eyes out for that.'

She walked as quickly and as gracefully as she could from the scene and was glad that her room had no view of the beating, as long as she remained at the back.

A stranger had wrestled the slave trader and killed him. Was that stranger Okkyntalah? Was he here? Was he already trying to find her? Was he in trouble or was he safe? What would happen to him if he'd killed the man?

These questions occupied her thoughts as she tried to rest but it wasn't until Tah-Vlatak came in to give her some company that she found answers.

———

'Your compulsive truth-telling will be the death of you, Aklon.' Chellyth had no further need to shield him from the now dispersed crowd.

But there were a number for whom his announcement about Gadhallah had clearly been too much. The gathering had slowly formed into two distinct groups. The majority either fully accepting of his words or at least willing to give them some thought. The minority, a number a little short of two hundred, unwilling or unable to countenance what they saw as a wicked slander on a man they'd all but worshipped all their lives. To accept Aklon's words as the truth was to confess to having supported and admired a brutal, cowardly, child killer, and this was beyond them.

'If I fail to tell the truth, Chellyth, I am as bad as my father. He has known everything that I have described here, and more, all his adult life. But he chose to conceal the truth from the people, as did all the High Priests before him. His lust for power and position blinded him to reality. He rejected the history that failed to satisfy his own wishes and told only of those things that bolstered his own elevation. I will not follow in his footsteps. And I will see this foul sect of ours undone and replaced with something finer, more noble and more humane.'

'Passion was always your fault, Aklon. No wonder women adore you. What are we to do with the discontents? We can't let them infect the rest with doubt.'

'I will have no more bloodshed. It was to curb violence and death that I took on this task. They must make up their own minds. I cannot force them to believe. As time passes, they will come to see the truth because I will make it available to all when I return to the capital. I will take some of the Few to the pit of secrets and expose the truth to them so that they may spread the word first hand after witnessing the words.'

'You're a brave man, Aklon. But you're a fool if you think they'll give up their beliefs so easily. They've been steeped in these creeds, these tales and myths all their lives. The beliefs form their foundations. They'll not give them up just like that. Truth or no truth.'

'Nevertheless, it is what I must do. And I will use every tool I possess to succeed in this. I will not give up, Chellyth, simply because there are those too frightened, too stupid or too naive to see the truth when it is presented to them.'

Chellyth called Por-Kildu and he came willingly to stand beside her; the beauty beside the monster. Faithful to each other through all that came their way.

'Tell this wonderful fool that he'll cause civil war if he goes about telling folk the sort of thing he's spoken of here today.'

Por-Kildu took her hand in his and looked from his partner to his friend and back again. 'I love you both. I can't take sides here. In any case, my love, Aklon will do as he sees fit. We've accepted his decisions in the past. Look about you at the results of his wisdom and planning.' He indicated the wide valley with its settlement so much better than the place they'd left on the Point.

'And you, Aklon, hear Chellyth's words. She's wise and experienced in the ways of men. Look at what she's created from this pool of disparate peoples.'

Aklon looked across at the various groups going about their business in the new settlement. Their meeting had concluded that certain principles needed to be applied for his next move. He felt he had the information he needed to proceed. All he lacked, it seemed to him, was the determination to actually get out there and do the job. And that was a matter of will; something he'd been imposing on himself for years.

'I will set out tomorrow with a following of two hundred. Volunteers. I want people who have the wish to spread the word and to work at undoing all the evil my father and his like have done over the centuries. Will you call together all those who support the Cause for change, Chellyth?'

'You're ready, then, Aklon? You will take this road?'

'I am ready. I will take the only road I see open to me.'

She and Por-Kildu called some of the trusted deputies of the settlement to them and explained their need. The men and women went off into the various parts of the encampment and only a short time later around three hundred people had gathered. Aklon addressed them, explaining his expectations and intentions.

'I will place you in mixed groups of a dozen each. Large enough to protect one another but not so large as to present a problem for your hosts. Your first task is to visit the towns and villages, the outlying farms and settlements, to give word of the first lies and to warn of the building of the Skyfire. It is vital that you set the peoples' minds at rest in that regard. They have been told that the Skyfire will grow in size, brightness and power until it will be strong enough to burn those without faith. This is not true. The Skyfire is a wanderer in the vast void that lies above and all around this world. It is like the sun but not like it. It is an object that can cause no harm here on the world. I know this. I have seen the object itself and know that it is nothing more than a lump of matter from which a tail of light and bright dust trails, illuminated by the sun. I have seen this, I tell you.'

It was clear that most couldn't understand, let alone accept this description of an event that carried such enormous significance in their lives. It couldn't be prosaic and harmless.

'Very well. If you will not take my word for that aspect of it. Will you, at least accept it when I say that it will do no harm to any of us?'

'Because we're acting for Ytraa, you mean?'

It hurt him to agree with a half-truth but he saw there was no other way at the moment. Time enough for true education once the old superstitions and myths had been done away with.

'Exactly so, Delbon, exactly so. We do the work of Ytraa, as described by the Speakers of Ytraa, therefore we will not be harmed by Ytraa. But I want none of you threatening those who will not convert to our ways with harm from the Skyfire either. Do you understand?'

There was general murmuring at this but most seemed content to accept this message. Those who couldn't were dismissed, reducing the volunteers by a further fifty or so.

'The dissenters have gathered together and left the settlement, Chellyth.' The woman who brought this unwelcome news seemed almost fearful of telling it.

'I won't harm the messenger for the message. You've done well to tell me.'

The woman left again.

'It appears you may have opposition, Aklon, when you and the groups reach their destinations.'

'That was always expected, Chellyth.' He turned back to his volunteers. 'This news will make our task more difficult. But not impossible. We will simply have to work harder at convincing people. This is going to be a slow process, but I wish it to go ahead without bloodshed wherever that is possible.'

The talk went on and the various questions were answered, not always to everyone's conviction, so the volunteer group slowly diminished in size until there were two hundred and nine individuals, including Delbon and Phildrad. It took some time to select leaders for each separate group, mixing the genders and the skills so that each would be self-supporting and capable of finding their way, feeding and caring for themselves.

'If it comes to a situation where the choice is between fighting or fleeing, I want you always to choose the latter. We must not be seen as violent or threatening. We must be known to be tolerant, reasonable and open to compromise. A small step forward is better than no movement at all. Keep that ever in your minds.'

He chose some of the leaders of the groups as co-ordinators of larger sections so they could determine exactly which places each group would visit. Once all was settled, the first groups, those travelling the greatest distances, were armed and supplied with what they would need and set out before nightfall. The rest would follow in the morning.

Aklon had started the Cause. With the sending out of his people in this way, he'd begun something that would now be impossible to stop. Whether his plans would work, and how well; whether the result would be change that involved many or few was something he could not predict. But that change would occur was inevitable. He hoped to avoid civil war amongst the people and to eventually find a way to bring all Followers under the protection and rule of a more just and fair society devoid of superstition, threat and violent punishment. These were the qualities he asked his people to demonstrate and to speak of to the people they attempted to convert.

In the morning, he would set off for Chalamamnon and enact his scheme to enter the High Priest's house to put on display the contents of the pit of secrets. Whether he would have to harm Wendarah and her cronies to achieve this he had no idea. But he would do what must be done.

The Few had begun the Cause and the Cause must win in the end.

Chapter 41

THE PIT

*T*umalind, distracted and nervous after the news of a foreigner killing the slaver, was unsure that she wanted the company of Tah-Vlatak but the woman had arrived, bearing a tray with soft wine and ripe fruits.

'I know how difficult it can be, performing for the Uhmbard. He's so exacting. I struggle to find something new with each Dance. You're younger and won't have to worry about such things yet.'

'No. I suppose not.'

'Is everything well with you, Tah-Tumalind?'

The use of her formal name should have put her on her guard, but, more and more convinced that the man who'd killed the slaver was Okkyntalah, her mind was elsewhere. She had no idea why she should be so certain, but she couldn't escape the feeling.

'What do you know of the man who avenged me with the slaver, Vlatak?' Her use of the informal name should indicate that she was simply indulging in gossip.

'Only what I hear from others, who probably know less than they pretend, Tumalind. This place is full of gossip. And most of it's untrue, you know.'

'I just wondered, that's all. He's done me a real favour, hasn't he, whoever he is?'

'I suppose he has. Saved you having to face a trial with the slaver declaring you a liar and you having to defend your good name against a man. Yes, the young warrior's helped you no end. But, as to who he is, I don't know. They say he's tall and handsome and the women in the kitchens, in fact all the slaves, won't hear a bad word said against him. I even heard a really outlandish tale that they're willing to risk trouble by feeding his dog. Can't be true, of course. No woman with any sense would risk a whipping for the sake of a dog. But that's what they're saying.'

Tumalind was even more convinced now that it was Okkyntalah. 'It seems hard on him to be punished, don't you think? I mean, I assume it was a fair fight?'

'You're a funny one. Why trouble your head, Tumalind? He's a man, after all and we know what that means. Trouble and demands. He's no different from any other man, no matter that the kitchen maids are all torturing themselves with dreams of sharing his bed. Well, they can dream all they want. He's got three days in the Pit. He'll never come out. No one ever does; not after three days. Now, let's share this wine and fruit and talk of more important things.'

Tumalind understood it would be unwise to pursue the matter further. But it was

Okkyntalah, who'd come to rescue her and who now lay dying in a hole in the ground because he'd somehow become involved with one of the men who'd taken her. It was unbearable.

She sipped wine, nibbled a fig. Her silence and unwillingness to indulge in idle banter eventually persuaded Tah-Vlatak to leave her to herself in search of more interesting company.

'You need friends here, Tumalind. Don't forget that.'

'I'm sorry I'm such poor company. I think I'm still trying to come to terms with my new status here. Give me a day or two and I'll be my normal cheerful self, I promise, Vlatak.'

'Very well. I'll give you some time to mope and then come and cheer you up with some ribald tales after breakfast tomorrow. That sound all right?'

'Sounds wonderful. Thanks for understanding.'

The woman went, leaving a silence broken only by late afternoon sounds of crickets, occasional cries of hawks, and the soft sighing of the wind. A sudden cry from the courtyard caught her curiosity and she moved to the opening overlooking the square in time to see K'ang Fi-Tozu, still naked and striped from his beating, leading a tearful but beautiful girl towards the entrance that would take her to the Uhmbard's quarters. It looked as though the slaver had found a replacement virgin in time to save his life. Though where he could have come across such a maiden in this place was a puzzle.

Tumalind returned to her cushions on the far side of her chamber and relaxed as much as she could.

'Tumalind, I wish to introduce you to Nuldron, who's with the party coming to rescue you.'

'Ivdulon; thanks.'

'Hello?'

The voice in her head was new. A man, she guessed; though gender wasn't always clear in mindtalk. But the name sounded male and the picture of the voice in her mind seemed mannish.

'Hello, Nuldron. I'm Tumalind. Where are you?'

'We arrived at the Bituhn Crofts yesterday and the quartermaster is currently negotiating for supplies and pack animals as I speak. We're intending to move through one of the lesser passes to get to the flat plain of the desert as quickly as possible and then we'll be crossing the sand as fast as the animals can carry us. There's a woman in the mountains apparently, who's friendly and can mindtalk. She'll guide us to the various wells for water on our journey. We're hoping to arrive at the city within three or four days. So, hang on and keep yourself safe until then. I'll be always on hand for you. Ivdulon has maps and some *knowledge of the desert, so she'll also be in contact as and when we need her. I hope to be talking to you face to face in a very few days.'*

This was good news. But her concerns over Okkyntalah rather diminished her excitement and happiness at the prospect of rescue.

⟝──◆──⟞

Okkyntalah was fed and watered again by the unnamed woman in the dead of the night.

Dead.

That's what he would've been, he knew, had she not risked so much to bring him food and, especially, water. The temperature in the pit increased during the day until it was unbearable. He had no recourse other than rest and an attempt to sleep. Killing the rhaats and shifting the decomposing bodies had helped his situation, though it had done nothing to reduce the number of flies that plagued him. He was aware of his own stink, the foul stench of death that made the air too thick to breathe with comfort, the occasional fall of sand as some trader or curious soul moved close to the entrance in daylight. Once or twice, rocks had come down unexpectedly. One had hit his shoulder, causing a small wound and another had almost knocked him unconscious. There were only a few rocks scattered on the floor of the Pit and at least this suggested the habit of stoning captives was fairly unusual.

The day was long. Heat, the most oppressive and persistent element of his environment, was difficult to bear. The water she provided merely prolonged his suffering, it seemed.

Night approached with some relief, though he knew he must face another full day when dawn returned. Three periods, he hoped meant three days only. If the woman came again, he might at least exist until the time came for release.

And what then? Would further punishment follow the period of confinement? How would he retrieve his things and his dog? How long before he was fit enough to attempt a rescue of Tumalind. The thought of her, so close, wanting him and needing his help, kept him going through those harsh times that seemed to last forever in this Pit.

Darkness brought the reduction in heat that made it bearable. He lay and watched the stars roll overhead. The Skyfire appeared at one edge and he followed its slow progress across the gap, noting its brightness, its growing size. Did the prediction still apply? Should he continue to believe in the power of this message from the sky after what he'd learned from Ivdulon first hand, and later through Tumalind's mindtalk with the wise woman? She described the sign as no more significant than something she called a returning wanderer. There were many of these; some came often but were so small they were invisible without the aid of an observerscope. Others were very large and highly

403

visible, but appeared at such long intervals that men forgot about them between manifestations.

Ivdulon had made it clear that far from the Skyfire being a sign from Ytraa, Gadhallah had used the known regular appearance of this wanderer as a way to begin his creed of the Followers of Ytraa. His people had kept records of the night skies on wooden boards for many hundreds of cycles. Though this was all heresy, Okkyntalah could see sense and logic in it. It gave him little comfort to know his faith was founded on a lie, especially without some other set of beliefs on which he might rely. He'd never given much thought to his faith before he'd left the island and set off in search of his beloved. Nothing that had happened on that journey had increased his faith and much had made it seem irrelevant.

'Okkyntalah.'

The whisper was soft, the voice again full of fear. He looked up and welcomed the woman once more. She lowered her gifts, and then vanished into the blackness again before she could be caught by the guards in their gatehouse. If he escaped alive, he would find a way to thank this wonderful woman who kept his hope of life going.

There was a larger pot of water this time, but he took only a little at a time, knowing he had almost a full day before there could be any hope of escape. The food was better than before; though he realised that his hunger may make it seem that way. She'd included more meat and fruit and replaced the bread with a sweet, fruited cake that tasted so good he couldn't stop eating it once he'd started. After that, he had to take a little more water.

Restored a little, he fell into another troubled sleep.

Sunlight, heat and falling sand woke him. A rope descended into the Pit and hung there. No word was said and no one appeared at the opening.

He stood. Flexed his aching limbs. Tried to drive away the fatigue that heat, thirst and the hard floor brought. He took more water, since this seemed to be the end of his sentence in the Pit.

The rope was coarse and sticky with things he cared not to linger on for too long. But it was his escape. Or, at least, so it seemed. He tested and found it anchored, since it held fast when he put his full weight on it. There was no give at all, so no one held this rope; it was fastened to something solid and long enough only to fall to within half a manheight from the floor.

Weary, half-starved and uncertain, he must find the strength to climb if he was ever to get out. He understood now the decomposing bodies that were his company. These were those who'd failed to move when given the chance. Perhaps the opportunity lasted only a short time. He must try now, or perhaps lose his freedom.

Grabbing the rope with both hands, he hauled himself up until he could bend his legs enough to find purchase on the free end with his feet. This first stage was the most difficult. But determination, youth and strength, helped him drag his tired body and limbs up that far. He couldn't rest after the exertion, knowing his arms and legs wouldn't keep him up for long. He must keep moving. It was such a short distance to the top. Such a great, impossible height he must ascend.

The coarse rope bit into his flesh at hands and feet, scraped his skin where it passed along his torso and between his legs, as he embraced it in his efforts to rise from the growing heat of the Pit. He pulled with hands made quickly raw. Pushed with feet made sore. Up by degrees, the sunlight more powerful, the hole wider as he approached.

Up.

Stop.

Up.

Stop.

Up; the process taking so much time and effort. He reached a spot just below the opening and some careless, or vindictive, foot kicked sand into his open eyes and he nearly slipped down. Voices yelled encouragement of the bully. But another called with authority, demanding he be left alone.

Okkyntalah held on. Dry eyes smarting, almost blinded from the intrusion, he moved up.

The change in light told him his head rose above the surface. A short, sharp cry of encouragement made him look in that direction and he saw, through misted and burning eyes, a shape he guessed to be the woman who'd saved him with her food and water.

Now he must transfer his weight from rope to the sand that surrounded the edge of the opening. An enormous effort. Only one chance. The hand that left the rope first must find purchase on the surface. And he was all but blind. He gripped harder with feet that ached and screamed from pressure on sore skin. He released the rope with his left hand and sought the edge. For precious moments, he floundered as the rope spun. Disorientated him. He would fall. Fall back in. Never find the strength to repeat the climb.

Tumalind, still dazed by the early morning events, walked proud and tall through the streets, past staring eyes of men, past the gaze of envious women, under her canopy, borne by four of the palace guard.

'Come quickly, Tah-Tumalind, please.'

The entreaty from a serving girl had woken her. The speed of her preparation and the explanation tumbled out of the mouths of envious and respectful maids who painted and decorated her, had left her puzzled, hopeful and scared.

'The Uhmbard honours you with this privilege.'

She'd bowed before the Uhmteld and promised she would behave with dignity and obey the instructions to the letter.

'The Uhmbard wishes to show the people he is merciful and wise. You will witness. But must not make contact with the man. You must not even acknowledge his existence. You belong to the Uhmbard. His Almighty, Wise and Omnipotent Highness may present you in your glory for other men to devour with their eyes and to wonder at the majesty of the Uhmbard who has the power to own such a specimen of womanhood. But he will not permit you to see another man or another man to be acknowledged by any sign from you. You will maintain the proper pride and indifference of your position as Palace Dancer. You understand?'

She was minded to ask what would happen to her, and to the man, should she disobey this command. But she knew better than to ask a question to which the answer was already evident.

The man who'd killed her assailant was to be released early, in recognition that he'd removed an unpleasant duty from the Uhmbard. As recompense for her suffering of the assault, Tumalind would be permitted to witness the release of the stranger.

So, here she now was, walking at a stately pace, shaded by her canopy and guarded by four men, heading for the gate and the punishment place where she hoped and prayed Okkyntalah would emerge before her, free and unharmed. The Uhmteld had made it only too clear what was expected of her. She was merely to be present as he came from the Pit. It was enough. An honour she must accept with pleasure. She would smile but not look directly at any man as she paraded her beauty and grace through the city.

Word of the appearance of a Palace Dancer on the street had spread rapidly and she found the narrow ways lined with gawping men and women. Her eyes remained on the skyline ahead, her head ever raised above the level of the common people. She knew she must look proud, haughty, and indifferent to the suffering and inequality that surrounded her. But she also knew the price she would pay for failing to do exactly as she'd been told.

They reached the place and she stood under her canopy, her gaze straying to the appalling cavity that a guard identified as the opening to the Pit. She watched, without looking at the men who performed the task, as the rope was made rough with particles of rock dust, sharp and abrasive, stuck to it with a mix of dung and water, before it was dropped into the space. It seemed an age before any movement occurred.

So desperate was she that she almost called his name. But she was spared the need as the rope tightened at last. He'd grasped it and was ascending. Flies buzzed about the pit and some detached themselves from the swarm to come in her direction. The perfumes

406

and oils with which she'd been anointed seemed, however, to deter them from actually landing on her skin.

A movement caught her eyes and she watched a man approach the edge of the Pit. Most seemed content merely to wait for the stranger to emerge. But this figure, though she wouldn't look at him directly, she knew to be the chief slave trader. His gift of the replacement virgin had been accepted and the Uhmbard had released him, along with his clothes. She saw him kick sand into the opening, just as the hair of the man rising appeared in the gap. Some of the crowd made sounds of encouragement, though the women seemed to silently disapprove. A soldier from the gate told the slaver to leave and he moved away with a muttered curse.

One of the women approached closer than most and seemed concerned on a personal level. So much so, that Tumalind began to think that the man in the Pit was not Okkyntalah after all, but some man related to this woman with her bruised eye.

But the man emerged and she must see, before she had to look away in case he should look at her and she at him. That brief glimpse told her it was Okkyntalah. It was so hard not to watch him. Not to call his name. Not to let him know she was there and wanting so much to help.

By looking across the hole, she was able to witness the movement without appearing to look directly at the man emerging. Two of the palace guards watched her face for any sign of her glance at the man and she knew she must remain strong. She must appear detached, no matter how her heart was breaking as her husband, battered, bleeding and exhausted, dragged himself from the Pit.

There was a point when it seemed he would fall back in. A gasp came from some of the women watching, but none went to his aid. She wanted to yell at them to help him but she must not. At last, with what was clearly an enormous effort, he pulled his upper half onto the surface and rested for a moment, half in and half out of the opening. She willed him to make the final move that would see him safe on the sand.

The guards readied themselves for the return journey but she would not leave until it was certain he'd escaped completely. They waited, but their eyes kept watch on her face.

Okkyntalah finally lifted the rest of his body into the open. As he rolled over, he looked in her direction but made no sign of recognition and she wondered that she could appear so changed as to be unrecognisable to him. But then it was time for her to return to the Palace. As she turned, a voice called out and someone answered. Something in the words, though they'd been unclear, suggested Okkyntalah was the subject of debate. But she was already being escorted away from the scene and had no way of knowing what would happen to him now.

'These frowkin' flies are going to eat us alive!'

Chislanda gave him a sympathetic smile. The insects seemed to leave her alone, or perhaps her life in the city on stilts had given her some sort of immunity to the biting gnats. Whatever the reason, Aglydron was pleased she wasn't bothered by them. At least he was able to cover his torso with a tabard now they were out of Kah-Labaz. He missed the sight of the bared breasts of the women, though he knew it was blasphemous, no matter what their High Priest might have to say about it. The new virgins from the city beneath the smoking mountain retained their scandalous dress, if dress it could be called.

Hephrastihn, with her amazing green eyes and long blonde hair, was a sight to be appreciated. She had no inhibitions about displaying her body. Though he'd heard her say she liked the tabards and tunics and might try one or the other out. In spite of his expressed feelings about her near nakedness, he hoped she'd remain that way as long as possible.

'Pretty, isn't she, Aglydron?' Was that sarcasm in Chislanda's voice? Her smile was genuine enough.

Perhaps he was just sensitive because he knew his lust for the virgin was wrong. He placed an arm about her shoulders and gazed into her eyes. 'I still only want to join with you, though. Pretty as she is, I prefer you in my arms, Chislanda.'

She shook her head at him. 'You've grown soft, my love. This passion we share has made you less fixed in your ideas and more tolerant of others. It's very endearing.'

He smiled. Life had changed for him; of that there could be no doubt. He'd grown less pious, less demanding about the rites and rituals of the Followers. In fact, he'd even welcomed the new prayer positions, which were the custom in Kah-Labaz as well as Litkala. None of the pilgrims now adopted the old posture they'd used on the island and he felt that prayer sessions were the better for that.

Dagla Kaz was up ahead, leaning on the rail of the boat with his arm around the waist of the new priestess from the city. Kaz-Ca-Valorysta was openly wanton and wore only token cover. He'd expected Dagla Kaz to object but the High Priest had said nothing publicly and continued to be with the priestess as they journeyed from the lake and up river through this swamp so full of flying insects that seemed to want nothing less than to devour him.

Two days they'd been sailing. The word was that they would be through the swamp by early morning and it was true that the reeds seemed now confined to the northern bank of the river. The southern shore was starting to rise a little, with the suggestion of a wooded area at the top of the ridge. Grassland mostly, he looked at it with his farmer's eye and knew it would make wonderful grazing. He wondered why it remained so empty. Perhaps it was simply too far from civilisation.

They were making for Mehrrhyphrol at last. Once there, they would either continue on up the river, if possible, or take to their legs again. In that case, they would begin the long trek either through the Mountains of Geldakq or alongside that great range until they reached the pass at Aagtaz. Dagla Kaz had told them that he'd have to rely on their new guide from Kah-Labaz as far as the great city of Mehrrhyphrol, since Sondukal had declared he was no use as a guide beyond Kah-Labaz and had not come with them. There was talk of him exploring the wider region of the unknown.

'We'll discover which way we shall travel once we reach the great city.' Dagla Kaz had said. 'Until then, we simply have to spend our time on board this wonderful little vessel. The Skyfire grows daily more bright and large. Time is short and we must take the route that will allow us to arrive in Choshinahm soonest. Our route back, with the exchanged virgins and the Godwood, will be more hazardous and take longer than our journey to the Groves of Ytraa. I want us there as soon as can be. It may prove hard for us. But we have a duty to fulfil and I will see no one causing us delay. So, make sure you spend your time on the boat in useful activity. We'll miss the luxury of cabins for sleep and privacy once we're forced to move on foot again.'

It was true, for him at least, since the High Priest and a few of the other senior figures had cabins. The rest did not. But he and Chislanda had taken full advantage of their time alone in the city and, when they could find privacy, on the boat. It would be more difficult to join privately once on the road again. And, more importantly, the going would grow more difficult as the land rose and grew rougher and wilder. They'd passed the point now where any of the party, apart from their new guide, knew the region they travelled. It was rumoured that the city of Mehrrhyphrol was a place of great wickedness and violence. But they'd heard that of Litkala and it had proved false.

Kah-Labaz had revealed itself as a city less pious than some would prefer, but it had also proved to be a place of civilisation and good behaviour. And, at least, the inhabitants of those two cities were Followers. That could not be said of the people who inhabited the land they now sailed through. The local religion, although not definitely understood, was rumoured to be based on some very strange ideas. None of the Followers welcomed their arrival in the new city, but it was on their route and, in spite of the fear and disgust created by tales of strange practices, they must go there.

Chapter 42

GOSSIP

Okkyntalah woke to brightness, pain, noise and a hard surface only slightly softened by thin fabric. Every part of him hurt. He tried to focus but found his vision blurred and indistinct, so that he saw only shapes and colours. Moving forms were definitely women. One came towards him and bent down. A pale cloth covered his eyes and cool liquid took away some of the pain. He allowed trust in someone who was kind, and relaxed again.

He knew time had passed. There were new sensations. His head rested on something soft and warm. A hand stroked his chest, gently wandering across the skin, exploring and caressing with a tenderness that made him smile before he even opened his eyes.

She was there, her face looking down at his with her eye no longer swollen but still bruised, the mouth back to normal. She smiled down at him and moved her hand away from his skin, as if embarrassed to be discovered in so intimate an activity.

'Please. Don't stop. I was enjoying that.'

She smiled again and took up her soft caress again. His head was in her lap and her back against a wall. The light suggested evening would soon fall. The noise and activity he'd woken to at first was now mostly silence and calm. The shapes and colours were no longer what he saw; his sight had returned to normal. But his body hurt all over; skin sore, muscles aching, head throbbing. And he was hungry.

'Is there any food, please? And something to drink?'

She called to someone unseen. It was only moments before another woman came. She was older, limped, and seemed a little wary. He smiled up at her as she handed the bowl and earthenware cup to his nurse.

'Thank you.'

The older woman glanced with surprise at his helper, who nodded in acknowledgement. She gave a little bow and smiled before she left them, but she turned and stared twice more at him before she moved out of sight.

'You're an unusual...no, a unique man. No man here would ever thank a woman, or say "please" to her. Can I help you sit, so you can drink, sire?'

'Please.'

She helped him rise, her skin brushing against his with a gentle intimacy that made him aware of his real state.

'Thank you.'

411

She smiled at his little joke. The woman helped him drink the fresh water but stopped him when she felt he'd had enough, her hand a soft pressure on his and her eyes full of pleading. He understood her wishes and her concern and stopped gulping the liquid. It was sweet in his dry throat, cooling as it drained inside him.

He leant his back against the wall and she sat, cross-legged by his side, and fed him morsels of fruit from the bowl. Small bites that teased his hunger but wouldn't make him sick. He revelled in her care and attention, enjoying this service and devotion without fully understanding its cause. When the bowl was empty, she gave him more to drink. The pounding in his head began to subside and his body slowly felt the ease of food and fluid after the deprivation of the Pit.

He remembered something; something vague and troubling that he couldn't yet identify about his emergence into daylight.

'Someone kicked sand into my eyes.'

She nodded. 'K'ang Fi-Tozu was the leader of the slavers who brought in the new moonday virgin for the Uhmbard. But he was beaten by the palace guards because she'd been violated by one of his men; the very one you killed. That's why the Uhmbard let you out before your sentence was over. A reward for saving him the trouble of holding a trial, sire.'

This made little sense to Okkyntalah but he was glad his sentence had been reduced: he wasn't certain he'd have escaped if he'd had to spend another full day in that place. He pictured, again, his struggle to emerge. And then it came to him.

'I think there was a woman there, shaded under a sort of canopy. I couldn't make out what she looked like, but she seemed familiar.'

'The new Dancer. She's a wonder. The rumour is that she's the one who was supposed to be the new moonday virgin. It's very unusual, but that must be why she was allowed out of the Palace. She must've come to see you go free, so she'd know the man who killed her attacker had been amply rewarded. She caused quite a stir. The Uhmbard doesn't usually let us see his Dancers, of course, sire.'

There was something here that troubled him. Something that should make sense but failed to do so. But he was too tired now to think it through.

'Do you have a name? I need to call you something.'

'I explained before, but you must've forgotten. I'm a woman. I have no name. You should call me "woman" if you need to attract my attention, sire.'

'But if I use that word, and there are as many of you around as there were before, how will I know that you, and you alone, will come to me?'

'A woman will come. Won't that serve, sire?'

'I've just noticed you're ending every sentence with "sire". Why is that?'

She looked a little shamed and just a touch alarmed. 'I'd forgotten. You told me not to. I'm sorry if I offend, it's a hard habit to break, si...'

He smiled at her, took her hand. 'Call me Okkyntalah, please. And, since you won't give me a name to use for you, I'll have to think of one myself.' He looked at her, gestured she should stand and turn before him.

She did as he asked and stood, waiting until he signalled her to sit beside him again.

'Yes, "Dahrlyth" will suit you well. How do you like your name, Dahrlyth?'

She seemed both confused and overcome with a sort of joy at his suggestion. 'You would name me, really?'

'I do name you. I name you "Dahrlyth", which means "adored one", and I welcome you to my world. Now, of course, you must kiss me.'

She placed her mouth on his, holding the kiss with a fervour he hadn't expected, and demonstrating her passion.

Darkness surrounded them, and the silence of early evening was slowly invaded by the noise of men beginning their revels for the night. Male voices demanded, urged, commanded, scolded and joked with one another. Female voices acquiesced, cried out in pain, pleaded and fell into the laughter that illustrates surrender rather than joy. These all came in through the open space that was the window of the place where he lay with Dahrlyth. She snuggled close to him, her softness a comfort.

'That was both unexpected and rather splendid, Dahrlyth. Thank you.'

'Thank you...Okkyntalah. But I must ask you, if you'll permit, that you don't name me in the hearing of another man. He would definitely beat me and might end my life for bearing something only men may have.'

Okkyntalah sighed. This city was a vile place, full of evil. When he found Tumalind and escaped with her, he must find a way to take Dahrlyth with them. Tumalind would understand. Tumalind.

'It was Tumalind under the canopy. Is Tumalind the Uhmbard's new Dancer?'

Dahrlyth sat up at once, recognising his distress and confusion. 'The Uhmbard's wives and Dancers all bear names, of course. The word in the city is that the new Dancer is known as "Tah-Tumalind", I believe. She's known to you, Okkyntalah?'

'She's my wife. She's the woman I came here to rescue. And she didn't even talk to me!'

Dahrlyth held his hands in hers and bent forward, kissed his cheek. 'Please. I must tell you, for you're a stranger and won't know, but...'

Okkyntalah didn't hear her words. Angry, betrayed; at a loss to understand how Tumalind could leave him at the edge of the Pit after all they'd been through together, all that he'd gone through to reach her here in this vile and putrid place. She'd stood there, naked for all to see, and she hadn't even spoken to him. Well, if she was whoring with the so-called Uhmbard, he'd have his way with any women who came his way. He grasped Dahrlyth and caressed her, kissed her and, with her enthusiastic acquiescence, took her with a passion he'd always kept for Tumalind.

Aklon had selected Phildrad as his sole companion for the dangerous expedition to Chalamamnon: some of the groups would come after them in a few days. The man had proved himself a quick and able learner, ready to kill at need but retaining a proper respect for life, so that he spared lives when he could. He also had the advantage for Aklon that he rarely questioned his judgement but simply acted when told. For what lay ahead, Aklon needed instant, blind obedience.

Each of the parties had set out with at least two members of the original settlement with them. Clothing came from those left behind. A mark, something to identify them as the Few and promoters of the Cause was needed. Por-Kildu had come up with the simple idea of leaving the left side of the tabard unfastened. It was easily achieved, required no extra work or materials, and allowed the people to pass scrutiny without offending any rules, yet marked them out as subtly different.

Aklon and Phildrad had been last to leave, the others now well on their way to whatever villages and towns they'd selected. There was concern over the dissenters; a small number had been sufficiently aggrieved as to leave the settlement and had gone to find those other diehards who'd left earlier. Along with the earlier escapees, it made a band of soldiers some three hundred or so strong who would undoubtedly cause trouble.

'Perhaps we should've killed them.'

'No, Chellyth. There has been enough blood spilt. I will not use the tactics of my father or the Holy Ones in this fight. Let us show mercy and tolerance where they would show brutality and prejudice.'

But it was an undeniable fact that he now had the worry of a band of trained fighters acting against him. It would make the task of conversion so much more difficult.

'We huntin' Aklon? Only I could do wi' a bit to eat, like.' Phildrad's down to earth question brought him back to the present and he realised that the man's pragmatic attitude was another reason he'd chosen him as companion.

'We are. Let us tether the horses and then see what we can find in these damp and hostile hills, shall we?'

Later, cooking their snake over a fire that Phildrad had thought impossible in the rain-soaked jungle, Aklon smiled to himself.

'A dorltah for 'em, Aklon.'

'Oh. I was just recalling that almost every time I have dined in the jungle, it has been

414

one of our slippery little friends who has provided me with meat. Most easily missed and stood upon and most easily caught napping in the beam of sunlight. But I must confess, for all their faults, the humble snake provides a tasty meal.'

'Not with a woman, Aklon?'

'Sometimes I do other things. How are you, Ivdulon?'

'Well. I connect for a reason. It may be of use, but you'll have to be the judge of that. I've just completed some calculations concerning the moon and the sun and their relationship to the world. I can tell you that in three nights, beginning at around the middle hour, the moon will appear to grow dark and will, after a small time, glow with a blood red colour. It will stay that way for a short period before it reverts to its normal luminance.'

'And how sure are you that this will happen, Ivdulon?'

'Ah, you fear an announcement that fails to come true might damage your reputation as a prophet. Very wise. I can tell you only that, were I in your place, I'd make the announcement to all and sundry.'

'You are that certain?'

'I am.'

'Then, I thank you for another aid in my fight for credibility, Ivdulon. And, now, if you do not mind, I will break the connection. My companion is looking at me with the oddest expression.'

'A wise decision. Farewell.'

'Back, then?'

'Was I absent, Phildrad?'

'You looked like you wasn't 'ere, that's for sure. Mind, Chellyth an' Delbon both said they'd seen you go off like that, so I wan't too worried, like.'

'Phildrad, you are a good companion and a worthy deputy. Shall we sleep so that we may rise early and be on our way, do you think?'

'Want me to take first watch?'

'You think we need a watch?'

'No tellin' what them rebels might do, is there?'

'You have a point, Phildrad. By all means take the first watch. Wake me when the Skyfire is directly overhead, please.'

The time seemed to pass in an instant and Phildrad was shaking him awake from a dream that left him feeling a little disorientated. The horses were spooked, whinnying softly and stamping their feet, but not yet shying.

'There's summat shiftin' through the undergrowth. Over that way.'

He followed Phildrad's pointing finger in the glow of the campfire and allowed his ears to concentrate on the place; filtering out the noises of the shod horses' hooves. There

415

was movement amongst the plants there. A large creature. Ponderous and heavy. Either a longnose or, hopefully not, a terzet horn.

'I suggest we rebuild the fire and stay as quiet as possible. If it is a longnose it is unlikely to come near the flame. But a terzet horn may be too stupid to fear fire.'

They softly pushed more of their gathered dead wood into the embers, where one or two of the branches gave signs of their damp condition by smoking and hissing. But the blaze quickly grew brighter. The area illuminated by the fire spread to the edge of their clearing and a pair of small eyes stared out at them, a few handbreadths lower than a manheight.

'My guess is a terzet horn. Arm yourself with your sword and be ready to grasp a brand from the fire. If it charges, make for the trees at the far side of the clearing. They move quite quickly for such large beasts, but they are not able to turn very easily. We will go in opposite directions to confuse it. We may be forced to abandon the horses.'

'I know. Fought one o' the buggers back on mainland.'

Aklon tilted his head in question, but his companion said no more and simply did as he was bid. For a long time nothing happened. Even the horses grew bored and settled again. The eyes continued to stare at them and they held onto their weapons, ready to either escape or fight. In the end, the creature snorted and stamped its feet but turned away and they heard it crashing through the undergrowth away from them.

'Tell the tale, then, Phildrad.'

Phildrad conveyed the essence of the story of the rescue of Netrodyl near Qlentz but made no reference to the long scar that remained his reward for his bravery. Aklon had noticed it previously but was now certain of its origins and looked at his companion with even greater respect.

The remainder of the night was spent awake and listening in case it should return. They set off at first light, weary and unrested, leading their mounts in twos between the tree trunks.

When, at last, they were able to ride, they took advantage of full daylight and travelled swiftly, swapping horses half way to allow the beast of burden to run without extra weight as both of them urged their mounts on and held the reins of the free horse they trailed. Phildrad had used his time at the settlement well and now rode with some confidence.

They reached the outlying farm, from which they'd taken the horses, just before dusk and rode right up to the farmhouse. Aklon jumped from his mount and the door opened before he could knock. The farmer seemed surprised and a little fearful of his visitors.

'I return your horses, plus an additional beast for your trouble. My thanks for your help and my apologies for putting you to the trouble of loaning them to me.'

416

The farmer was nonplussed and surveyed the horses, scratching his head in wonder. 'Well, they said you was a brutal man, an' you proved 'em wrong in that. Now you've proved you're no thief neither. A man of 'is word is an 'onourable man in my eyes. I'd be happy to invite you take meat with me, Paltrohn.'

'I accept. Thank you. But please, call me Aklon. I so loath titles, you know?'

The farmer called for a lad, who took the horses to the stables and fed them. They sat around the long table in the farm kitchen, the rest of the family looking them over with awe and not a little fear. But it wasn't long before Aklon had put them at their ease with his courteous manner and his tales of comical incidents.

They slept in beds that night and Aklon wasn't surprised to find he was joined by the elder daughter, who asked Phildrad to give them privacy for a while. Her eyes had hardly left his face all evening and she'd laughed with delight at his stories. He delighted her further without laughter before she reluctantly left for her own room and Phildrad returned, eager for sleep.

'Sure we can trust these folk?'

'I have no doubt they are good people, Phildrad. You must learn when to trust and when to suspect.'

As he fell asleep, he hoped his trust hadn't been misplaced in this case. The mention of the price on his head had seemed a genuine warning at the dinner table. But was the farmer so grasping that he'd risk the welfare of his daughter in Aklon's bed merely for a small fortune? He thought not. His judgement was generally good in such matters. He fell asleep confident he'd wake a free man.

<hr />

Tumalind, desperate to know Okkyntalah's fate, quizzed the serving women who came to the Dancers' quarters to feed, bathe and tend them.

'What's this man to you, Tah-Tumalind? You're the Uhmbard's Dancer. That man can't have no meaning for you, can he?'

There was as much warning as curiosity in the question, but she had to know.

'Where I come from, it's the custom to care about what happens to someone, whoever it is, if they do you a service. That man killed the slaver who raped me. Surely it's only natural to want to know whether he suffered because of his actions?'

'You're not where you came from, Tah-Tumalind. Here, it's different. Here, we care nothing for men. They don't care nothing for us. But, you're still learning our ways, so I'll see what I can find out about the man. Will that be all now, Tah-Tumalind?'

The girl changed the cushions for fresh ones, swept invading sand from the bright, shiny floor, brought in fresh flowers from the garden in the centre of the square, and put new oil in the lamps in readiness for evening. She left and Tumalind rose from her cushions to stand at the opening to the square and gaze into the space and the sky beyond. She'd already grown used to the stares of the guards on duty so they no longer bothered her.

The floral display in the centre was being watered by other serving women, carrying great buckets of liquid from the washing pool so far away in the heat. One of them stumbled and spilt water on the sand before she reached the flowers. Tumalind had already witnessed the results of such a fall and turned away so she wouldn't have to watch the guards take advantage.

She felt forced back into her room against her will. Soon, one of the other Dancers would come and prepare her, in case she was wanted by the Uhmbard. They'd said she would have a sixday to get used to her new life and then she, too, would do some of the preparation of other Dancers, learning the crafts of body painting, making up faces, plucking out stray body hair, styling head hair and weaving beads into the pubic hair. It would be good to be doing something instead of idling her time, but there were parts of that duty she didn't relish.

She sought Nuldron and found him surprisingly close.

'We're crossing the sands on strange creatures we purchased in the small village just beyond the mountains. The villagers were happy to exchange the beasts, they call them desert ships, for our horses. They say they can go for days without need of water. But they're funny creatures, with great humps on their backs and large soft eyes...'

'Do they have broad feet and are the colour of sand?'

'How do you know?'

'They're called camels in Kabalyt. I like their soft eyes.'

'You surprise me each time I connect with you, Tumalind. How do I find you today?'

'Bored, and anxious about Okkyntalah. I saw him emerge from the Pit but he was clearly not at all well and I can't seem to find out anything else about him.'

'We should be at the city soon. Keep well and stay brave. We'll do all we can to rescue you and your Okkyntalah soon. Now, I must leave you for a while; we're at the final well and must draw water.'

News of their imminent arrival should make her happy, but Okkyntalah's fate played heavily on her mind and she couldn't settle until she had more news of him; until she had good news about him. Teh-pavk could mindtalk; perhaps she knew something of his fate?

'Teh-pavk, can you talk with me?'

'Not now. I'm being prepared, with the others, to service the Uhmbard. Looks as though the new moonday virgin wasn't very good at giving him what he wants. I heard he spanked her with his own hand and then frowked her roughly because she didn't understand what he wanted. I hope he isn't still mad. I don't want a spanking like that again. 'Bye.'

And she was gone before Tumalind could ask her anything. Teh-blavv bore all the signs, but she hadn't displayed any inclination to mindtalk. Tumalind knew the girl might be one of those with the gift but without knowledge of it. Would she scare the girl if she intruded into her mind? It didn't matter: she needed to know about Okkyntalah and the harem was the place where all the gossip happened. She reached out with her mind and found more dormant mindtalkers in the harem. These poor girls might think they were going mad if her voice suddenly intruded into their heads. But Teh-blavv should recognise her. She found the girl and entered, careful in case she caused her worry. With a few lessons from Ivdulon, she'd learned how to feel and see with the mind of those she connected to and she witnessed the sight that Teh-blavv could see.

A circle of harem women surrounded the Uhmteld. All were in the old prayer position used by Followers before Feldrark had suggested the upright stance. Only, here, they spread their legs wide and Tumalind suddenly saw the position for what it really was. That she'd displayed so openly as she grew up and worshiped Ytraa, shocked her. The pose was clearly sexually inviting to any man. How could she have not realised this? The answer came as quickly as the question: what she'd done almost from the day she could stand had become something so normal for her that she'd never questioned it. Only now, as she saw it from outside, and used for the purpose that the priests had clearly intended, did she see the reality. She didn't want to see this; the priming of women so that they'd be ready to receive the Uhmbard, might even display a desire they otherwise may not really feel. That women would behave this way with one another, and in public, both shocked and distressed her. She broke away.

It seemed her attempts to find out about Okkyntalah were doomed to failure for now. She'd have to await the return of the serving girl who'd promised to discover what she could for her. In the meantime, she had nothing to do and could only wait until another Dancer came to paint her body and prepare her for the Uhmbard, should he send for her.

Witnessing the women and what they'd been doing to each other, raised more questions about the faith she'd followed all her life. She began to analyse the rites and rituals, to examine every aspect of the Followers of Ytraa, recalling what Aklon-Dji had told her of the historic truth, and she knew that what they did in the name of their god had nothing to do with good and everything to do with evil. The discovery was almost overwhelming and she wept with shame, anger and resentment at the way she and all her fellow Followers had been so abused.

And then the Dancer came to prepare her and she dried her tears and thought about how the women were abused and tortured daily in this place. The realisation of the evil made her wonder if there was a place where decent folk could live their lives in good ways. Her mind took her back to Feldrark and Litkala; there, at least, there seemed to be awareness of the reality of their common faith. Once she was alone again, she must connect with Ivdulon and see what she might do to help in the great changes that the wise woman had hinted at when they'd last met in the flesh so many sixdays ago. For now, she must endure the small talk and gossip brought by the new Dancer who'd come to tend to her.

Gossip. Did that promise news of Okkyntalah after all?

Chapter 43

MESSAGES

*A*kkyntalah examined his attitude to Tumalind's neglect and indifference to his suffering. Had she not always cared for him, loved him with her heart and soul as well as her body? How could she abandon him; leave him to die for all she knew, ignore him completely at the very time he most needed her? There must be something else. Perhaps the Uhmbard, the ruler of this city, the man the rest of them spoke of with awe, perhaps he'd somehow seduced his wife and captured her heart. He knew women could be overcome by their experience with a man. His own life had shown him that a woman could be made to feel more for a man than she should. Look at how young Linlyss had desired him, how even the experienced and abused Myllthlan had treated him as someone special. And now Dahrlyth, abused, hurt and maltreated by all the men in this vile place, had risked her life to save him simply because he'd frowked her with consideration for her feelings and treated her with kindness.

Could it really be that simple? Could a woman be so ruled by her sexual experiences that she'd change her allegiance, even change her love? Perhaps Tumalind had loved him only because she'd had no other man. Maybe the Uhmbard was expert in loving women. It was rumoured he had over four hundred wives. With that sort of experience of women, it would be impossible not to understand their needs and wants. He must be the most expert lover in the world. How could he be otherwise? The simple usage of women for sex would soon pawl with so many to choose from. So, it would become a challenge to win the hearts of those he could use as he wished. It would be too easy, too unsatisfying for any man to simply use so many women. No. It wasn't possible. Any man faced with such choice must become expert in the treatment of women. Must learn how they can be turned from unwilling partners into lovers who desired and even loved him.

That was it. Tumalind had been frowked by a man with much more experience of women than he had himself. And she'd fallen for the ruler of this place and was now his entirely. There was no other explanation for the way she'd avoided him. It was true that he'd been almost blind when he emerged from the Pit. He couldn't tell her expression, couldn't see if she was even looking at him. But it had been her; of that there was no doubt. Standing openly naked in front of everyone, showing herself to all the men. She was like a prize cow displayed by a farmer. His Tumalind, a rare beauty exhibited to the lesser men to make them jealous, to make them realise what a potent and deserving man the Uhmbard was to satisfy and deserve such a woman as Tumalind.

It was possible she'd been placed in a position where she couldn't actually come and help him from the Pit itself. But nothing could have stopped her calling to him, letting him know she was there and that she knew he was there to rescue her. Nothing could prevent that sort of show, could it? No. She must've have been completely won over by the leader of the people here. How would she react when he went to rescue her? Would she even want to escape?

That last thought had him more anxious than any other. After all, no matter how she felt about the Uhmbard for the moment, he could win her back once she was away from the man. But would she let him take her? Would her infatuation for this man stop her going with her husband when he arrived inside the palace to take her home with him?

The long night passed in darkness and his hopes slowly died until he felt there was no point in even trying to recover her. The risk had always been great. To try it, knowing she would resist him, seemed pointless. He would be risking her life as well as his.

But he loved her so much. Could he let her go like this? Could he abandon her, as she had him? As dawn coloured the ceiling of his sleeping place with the coming day, he finally fell into exhausted sleep, dreaming troubled dreams of separation and loss from the only woman he'd ever truly loved.

◦ ─┼─◦─

Tumalind relaxed on her cushions, prepared for her next call, should it ever come. The midday meal would soon arrive and she might learn something of her love. The Dancer who'd prepared her knew nothing of Okkyntalah and dismissed her questions with flippant remarks to talk instead about the way one of the guards had propositioned her. Some guards were so overcome by the proximity of the Dancers they were guarding that they lusted over them until they went nearly mad with desire.

'We all know how easily a man can be controlled by sex, especially if the woman knows what she's doing. And which of us doesn't know, eh? We're born to take advantage of men's desire for us.' She'd bragged that she had personally driven more than one guard to his death, flaunting her body in her room, pretending to be practicing her art whilst the man outside was forced to watch her promise everything a man could want with her divine body.

But this new one was different. This one had been a little more subtle. For this one, she'd undone the beaded barrier and allowed access. No one knew officially, of course. But it was known to happen with the Dancers. Since the Uhmbard never used them for sex but only as stimulation for his acts with other women, there was less general concern about them being virgin, as long as he was never told.

'But we're not supposed to even look at other men. Or talk to them.'

'No one ever admits it, of course. And the Uhmbard and Uhmteld must never find

422

out. But it's important you know the real rules about Dancers. The one thing we must avoid at all costs is pregnancy. That's a death sentence, of course. And a very painful one. But Dancers can, and do, entertain specially selected men.'

'Isn't it dangerous? Why would you risk it?'

'Stops us going mad. I mean, Dancing in the most suggestive way and never being able to get any satisfaction? No. We need a man sometimes, to stop us going bad. Just make sure you entertain the right ones, and don't tease the wrong ones. Men always have precedence, and if one of them accuses you of frowking, you'll soon find yourself whipped and exiled to the sands to die.'

Swearing Tumalind to silence on the matter, the Dancer had left again, on her way to find a guard to entertain her. The whole incident unsettled Tumalind but explained the looks she'd seen in the eyes of certain guards. It actually made sense as well. Women made to present themselves as objects of ultimate sexual desire and not permitted to fulfil that want must be in danger of being driven wild by it over time.

But she wanted no other man than Okkyntalah and knew that would always be the case. She'd do everything in her power to get back with him, everything she could to be with him until one of them died.

The girl from the morning returned with platters of food and goblets of wine on wooden trays edged with gold. The luxuries of the palace life style hadn't really impinged on her and Tumalind remained unimpressed by the shows of wealth and ostentation that surrounded her in this place. Even the serving girls wore gilded nipples and bright jewels in their navels.

'I've heard some news of the man, Tah-Tumalind. Will you hear it?'

'Of course.'

'They say, or so I heard from a girl in the palace, that he was taken to one of the city kitchens by a woman. No one seems to know exactly why, except there's a rumour that the man's kind to women. Of course, that can't be true. But it's what they're saying. Anyway, whatever the real reason, he's being kept there. Men never go into such places. I mean, why would they? And they're sort of looking after him. He's only the second man to come out the Pit alive, you know? Most die down there from lack of water and food and because of the heat and rhaats. Every so often, they send a woman down there to clear out the corpses. Ugh. Horrible job. Can you imagine what it must be like down there with dead bodies rotting and all the rhaats eating them and the flies? Ugh. Makes you shudder just thinking about it, doesn't it?

'Sorry, Tah-Tumalind, have I upset you?'

Tumalind wiped away tears she'd tried so hard to hide. 'Take no notice of me. I get a bit sentimental sometimes. Silly, I know. I expect you'll think me really mad if I ask if

423

there's any way of getting a message to the man.'

'The Uhmbard would spank you so you couldn't sit for a portion if he heard. It's not worth the risk, Tah-Tumalind.'

'But it is possible?'

'I never leave the palace.'

'But others do. The girls who water the flower beds?'

'It's very risky, you know.'

'I only want someone to take my thanks for killing my attacker. Is that too much to ask?'

The girl considered. 'Don't see why you care, really. But if it'll make you happy, I'll see what I can manage. But I'm not promising. It's dangerous and there'll be more than one serving woman needed to send such a message. Tell me exactly what you want said to him and I'll do my best.'

Tumalind had to make her message both comprehensive and apparently neutral. She couldn't express her love for him or tell him openly that she awaited his arrival to recover her. But she wanted him to know how much she loved and missed him and that she was waiting for him to find and rescue her. She hoped the girl would take her message without altering her words, so Okkyntalah would understand exactly what she meant.

'At last! I thought we were never going to get away from those heathen flies.' Aglydron gazed out at the grasslands, the swamp now just a memory. Chislanda stood beside him at the rail, her hand on his arm as he held the smooth timber support.

'Your High Priest seems to know what he's doing, Paltrohn, don't you think?' The young man at the other side of Aglydron smiled and turned to nod toward Dagla Kaz.

'Oh, he's a wise and experienced man. He's led this pilgrimage over many lands and seas to reach this point. I, for one, find it hard to question a man of such rank and experience.'

The youngster extended his hand to make the gesture of greeting. 'I'm Gidwallehn. We never really had the chance to introduce ourselves in the city. I'm from Kah-Labaz, and I have to confess, I'm pleased to be away from the smoke and ash we live with much of the time. It's good to be out in the open and sailing like this. Bit of an adventure for me.'

'I'm Aglydron, from Muhnilahm; not Paltrohn at all. Is that why you're here? For adventure?'

The young man looked a little shame-faced. 'Partly, Aglydron. Mostly I'm along because the High Priest in the city called for volunteers. I do my duty when I can. But I also hope to find a good and faithful partner once we arrive in Choshinahm. Imagine the opportunities in such a place. If they're Followers, they'll still be the original ones, but without knowledge of Gadhallah's great pilgrimage. I can tell them what I know of that. And, if they aren't Followers, think of the chance to convert them and bring them back from their heathen ways. Either way, it'll be a wonderful opportunity to do good for Ytraa and the Followers, don't you think?'

'I can see you're a man after my own heart, Gidwallehn. I'm glad you introduced yourself. But, you know, your story of Gadhallah will be missing the end, since you settled at Kah-Labaz. You'll know nothing of the journey that took him to the true Homeland, the island of Muhnilahm.'

'No. Nothing. Nor of Litkala, of course.'

'Oh, Litkala; let that city's own tell their tale. But I can tell you all about the journey taken by the true Followers, you know. If you'd like that.'

The young man seemed keen to learn and Aglydron was in his element passing on knowledge he'd gained as a pupil of the Holy Ones. As they talked, he studied the young man and was intrigued by his eyes; the same colour as those of Dagla Kaz, and of Tumalind.

Where was Tumalind now? How was she? Had he really betrayed her by refusing to proclaim the truth about her father? It obviously must be the High Priest, but his pride had stopped him admitting it. Now she was gone and he might never see her again.

The session on history petered out but Aglydron felt an affinity with the young man, felt they had a common understanding.

'You know, of course, that Tumalind, the one who vanished in the night with her husband, was my daughter?'

Gidwallehn nodded, his face betraying his thoughts on that matter, so that Aglydron felt compelled to defend her.

'She was worried that man, Tryonta, wanted to join with her, even though she'd told him plainly that she didn't want that. Okkyntalah and her both wanted to be exclusive, you know?'

'Still, to go off like that. It caused no end of worry for Dagla Kaz. You could see how mad it made him.'

'Ah, well; that's another thing. Tumalind was more likely his daughter than mine. The eyes, you see. Exactly like his, and yours. My wife, Shoarhn, has light brown eyes and black hair. I can't see how we could've produced a girl with eyes like yours and hair the colour of burnished copper, can you?'

'Poetry, Aglydron? That's not like you.' Chislanda's open smile stopped him falling into his habit of serious denial.

'Oh, a man feels things for his daughter that he doesn't for other young women. I'm

425

proud of the way she turned out, I suppose. Even if she isn't my seed. I raised her, didn't I? And she grew into a kind, clever and faithful young woman. I just wish we could've sorted out this misunderstanding with Tryonta, that's all.'

'Not only Tryonta. The High Priest was also interested, Aglydron. She had to run away in case her own father joined with her, since she could hardly refuse Dagla Kaz, could she?'

Gidwallehn looked alarmed and distressed at this news. 'The High Priest really wanted to join with his own daughter?'

'Well, I don't think he acknowledges her that way. She's very like his other daughter. Jodisa and Tumalind could easily be sisters, so I expect Tumalind looks a lot like Jodisa's mother and they say Dagla Kaz misses that woman. Perhaps he was hoping to rediscover her in Tumalind?'

'I can't believe he'd want to join with her if he thought she was his own child, though.'

'As I say, I don't think he accepts that. But I can't help thinking his seed grew her and not mine.'

The young man looked across at the High Priest, studied him with serious concern, until Dagla Kaz, almost as if aware of the scrutiny, stared back at him. The youngster turned away at once. 'He doesn't know, does he?'

Aglydron heard these words and knew, from their tone and softness, that these were spoken thoughts and not intended for the ears of others. But that didn't stop him asking the inevitable question.

'What doesn't the High Priest know, Gidwallehn?'

The youth looked startled and chewed his bottom lip. 'Something a man like him should know, I think. Perhaps I should tell him.'

'If you have knowledge of value to the High Priest, you must tell him what you know. It's your duty.'

'It is. You're right, Aglydron. I shall, as soon as I have the opportunity.'

The early morning buzz and bustle soon woke Okkyntalah and he rose to watch the women at their tasks, as they prepared the kitchen to feed the many men who would soon require breakfast. They moved with a natural grace that he'd always admired. And they had a quiet efficiency that made them work well together. Oh, he was aware of their occasional quarrels and fights, but they seemed to lack the resentment he often witnessed when men fell out with one another. It had always fascinated him that they could find fault with one another and then behave as loving sisters. It was as if the thinking part and the feeling part weren't quite connected. He loved them for their capacity to love and accept love. How the men here could treat them so indifferently, so cruelly, was a mystery to him. Women were wonderful creatures who deserved all the affection and care a man could give them.

'A quound for them, Okkyntalah?'

He hadn't heard Dahrlyth approach with all the noise and talk around him. He looked up at her as he sat against the wall and nodded. 'I was just thinking how wonderful all women are, that's all.'

'All women?'

'Well, apart from one or two.'

She smiled. 'There's a message from the palace for you. Do you want some breakfast?'

'That's an odd message. Why would the palace…?'

She laughed. 'That's not the message. I was just asking. I'll send the girl who has the message to you.'

Okkyntalah grinned at her and told her what he'd like to eat and drink. She disappeared into the crowd and a short time later a younger woman appeared. Fearful and anxious, she approached without actually looking at him and stood a little distance off, waiting.

'You have a message for me, woman?' He tried to make the tone as gentle and soft as he could, anxious to put her at her ease without worrying her about his status.

'Sire. You're the man who was in the Pit, sire?'

'The very same. Who sends me a message from the palace?'

She looked around, as if terrified to be overheard. 'I must come close to speak it softly, sire.'

'You can come as close as you like. I won't eat you.'

She dropped to her knees and shuffled right up to him until she was able to lean over and whisper in his ear.

'I have to say it word for word. The message comes from the Dancer, Tah-Tumalind, and she says that you must be full as the waterfall, be silent as the pit of secrets and keep the night as your true friend. She also wishes you to know that she is grateful to you for killing the man who took her maidenhood. That is all. Do you have a reply for her, sire?'

Okkyntalah found the message puzzling. Clearly she'd used some sort of coded language, but it didn't seem to make sense. There was something wrong here, something he didn't know but felt was vital to his understanding.

'Can you tell me, is there any reason why the woman can't come and speak to me herself?'

'Oh, sire, she's a Dancer. You…forgive me; I think you're a stranger here?'

He nodded.

427

'You may not know, sire, that, as a Dancer for the Uhmbard, she cannot leave the palace and must not speak to any other man, on pain of death. Mustn't even glance at another man. Does that answer your question, sire?'

It explained a great deal and he felt relief surge through him. He wanted so much to tell his wife how much he loved her, how he would soon be there to take her back home. But it was obvious that he could only let her know in coded language. Secrecy was all, it seemed, in this.

'Tell Tah-Tumalind I make the night my friend, especially when the Skyfire burns directly overhead. Tell her healing is delayed but excitement will come soon.'

She repeated his message, a puzzled frown indicating that it made little sense to her. And then she was gone, vanishing into the crowd; his only contact with his beloved Tumalind.

Dahrlyth had been waiting a little way off and now came with a tray carrying his breakfast. Already he was feeling better than he had. The food, care and attention provided by this extraordinary woman helping him heal and renew his energy.

'I need my belongings. They are near?'

She nodded and rose at once to collect them and return them to him. He grasped her hand as she placed the items beside him on the floor, squeezed it gently. 'Come to me tonight, if you can.'

She nodded and returned to her labours, providing food for the other men who relied on this particular kitchen; one of many, she told him, in the city.

He ate and drank, and relaxed to gather his strength. Tomorrow he would see Tumalind again.

How could he have doubted her? How could he have suspected her of any form of betrayal? Now he knew, he understood the reasons for her silence and her apparent lack of concern. He would give himself this day and night. Tomorrow night he'd make the journey, risking all, to recover his beloved.

⁕

Time dragged so heavily. The message had been sent and she was desperate to have her reply. Though, judging by the way most things happened in this forsaken city, she might have to wait a long time and may never have a response. Her message may not even reach Okkyntalah. She must do something to keep her mind occupied. Perhaps a mindtalking session with Rrildyss to discover what was happening with her father? Yes, that would keep her occupied for a short while.

'Tah-Tumalind. The Uhmbard requires you to Dance. Please come with me.'

Tah-Vlatak had prepared her after breakfast and Tumalind followed the serving girl and was joined by Tah-Vlatak in the corridor. The older woman nodded at her and took her hand. 'We are to Dance together. We will be required to be as a man and a woman are together in this. Do not be afraid, do not show any form of disgust or revulsion in what we must do. We will not know who is to be the man, who the woman, until the Uhmbard tells us. If we fail to please him, we'll be spanked by the guards in the square before all the wives. I don't welcome such painful humiliation.'

'Neither do I, Tah-Vlatak. I'll be as professional and detached in this as I always try to be. But thank you for the warning.'

They entered the area where the Uhmbard sat on an upholstered couch with three wives attending him. He looked bored as they closed the doors behind them. He raised a languid arm and pointed at Tah-Vlatak. She nodded and mouthed to Tumalind that she would play the man in this.

Humiliating, repugnant and so difficult not to laugh at times, the two women did what was required of them, Dancing with as much eroticism as they could muster to arouse the jaded palate of the potentate. He responded well to their suggestions and, once he was entertained by the responsive wives, the pair of Dancers discretely left and retired to their own rooms. Tumalind wasn't surprised when one of the palace guards crossed the courtyard in her direction but was relieved when he moved from her room to the one next door, where Tah-Vlatak resided.

She rested awhile and then remembered her earlier decision. Her day's duties were done now; she was unlikely to be required again. She could relax. A serving girl brought her refreshments and, once she was alone again, she sent out her mind to find the High Priest from Litkala, discovering her resting on deck under a cloudless sky.

'You've been silent far too long, Tumalind. Where are you and how are you?'

'Ivdulon hasn't told you, then?'

It quickly became obvious that the High Priest had no knowledge of Tumalind's plight and they talked over her worries and concerns. Rrildyss could offer no advice, having no experience of the things Tumalind described to her.

Looking for a way to take her mind off her plight, Rrildyss described their voyage and the visit to the city; describing the clothes worn by those Followers and expressing her concerns for their near nakedness.

'It's as well you're not here, then, Rrildyss.' She went on to describe conditions for the women in general and for the wives and Dancers in particular.

The High Priest was horrified. But without the experience to advise her under these circumstances, she fell to gossip and then suggested Tumalind might like to introduce herself to their new mindtalker from Kah-Labaz. That this was her way of avoiding a conversation the High Priest found difficult was of no surprise to Tumalind, but she allowed the introductions and spent some time discussing matters with Gidwallehn.

'Aglydron tells me that the High Priest, Dagla Kaz, is probably your real father. Shall we connect with him and see what he has to say on the issue, Tumalind?'

'No! Sorry, I didn't mean to startle you with my insistence then. It's just that it's absolutely vital that Dagla Kaz remains unaware of mindtalk.'

'Oh? Why's that?'

'I can't tell you the whole reason, since I don't know it myself. Just that I know that the lives of many people would be placed at risk if he were made aware of his gift at this time. I ask you not to connect with him please, for the sake of all those people.'

'Seems a little odd to me. I'll have to give the matter some thought.'

'Perhaps a connection with his daughter, Jodisa, might help convince you. Shall I introduce you to her?'

'If you wish. Though I'll take some convincing about the High Priest.'

Tumalind connected with Jodisa and quickly explained her dilemma before introducing the two strangers. She left them to talk and visited Ivdulon, who was, as always, in her high tower, poring over maps and charts. She explained the problem with Gidwallehn and the wise woman tried to put her at her ease.

'I'll connect with him and make him understand. You set your mind at ease, you've problems enough of your own to deal with. But I understand that the rescue party will be with you tomorrow, if all goes well. Perhaps you should talk some more with Nuldron. There may be things you can impart that'll help them in their rescue bid.'

'As usual, you're full of sound advice, Ivdulon. I'll leave Gidwallehn to you, then.'

But she didn't connect with Nuldron straight away, since a serving girl had entered and was clearly waiting for her to acknowledge her presence. Perhaps she bore the message she hoped to receive from Okkyntalah.

Chapter 44

CAPTURE

Okkyntalah's night with Dahrlyth was more restful. She was content simply to lie with him. His knowledge that Tumalind awaited his arrival made him resist any other passion. They lay together, sleeping when they could and softly talking in the now deserted kitchen. All the other women had gone to their duties. The usual night sounds filled the air until, gradually, silence fell on the place and gave peace at last.

In the early hours, when all was quiet and no ears were near to hear, he woke her gently to question her on all she knew about the palace. She answered as she could but was anxious.

'May I ask you, Okkyntalah, something I wouldn't dare ask any other man?'

'Dahrlyth, ask me anything. Treat me as you would your sisters. To me, men and women are equal in every way.'

She gazed at him, eyes wide under the light of a moon almost full, framing them in brightness through the opening in the kitchen wall. 'You're an extraordinary man. In you I see why some women might fall in love with a man. Though there are no others like you in this place.'

'And your question, Dahrlyth?'

'Sorry. I wonder why you want to know about the palace. I fear you've some idea of taking back your wife from there. I must warn you that to try would mean both of you would die most horribly.'

'I've been in danger many times, Dahrlyth. I've faced odds many men would run from and yet I've come out victorious. But I don't believe that means the rescue will be easy. If I've learned one thing in life, it's that little that's worthwhile comes easy. You think I shouldn't risk my life, or Tumalind's, in this scheme, and I respect your concern. But I can't leave here without trying to rescue my wife. It's why I came. I love her. And I know, without doubt, she wants to take the risk, wants me to find her, rescue her, take her home. Then we can live normal lives, raise a family and be together for as long as the gods allow.'

'I'll miss you, Okkyntalah. I'll be saddened by your death.'

'I'm not going to die. Not here and now. I'm planning a long and fruitful life. When Tumalind and I leave here, would you like to come with us across the desert? Find a new life in the great city of Litkala, or maybe on our island home?'

She stared at him. 'You mean it. You're not playing with me, teasing me, as other

431

men would.'

'I might tease a woman in some ways, Dahrlyth, but never about something important. Will you come with us?'

'I will. And die for you, if need be.'

'Much better to live for me. But, if you're willing, you might help in my plan. Are we safe to go out now and take a good look at the palace?'

'I rarely tread the streets this late. But the men will all be sleeping and any woman awake won't question a man.'

They set off under a moon so bright it might almost be daylight. The streets were empty and silent. Soft, windblown sand covered every horizontal surface in this city and they made no sound. Night leant the streets a more comfortable temperature than did the midday sun. She took him by the quickest route, cutting corners, so that they soon arrived before the palace doors, closed but unguarded, at least on the outside.

Okkyntalah held her hand as they walked twice round the outside of the building. On the second circumnavigation, he stopped frequently, peering in through small windows to see what he could of the interior. The layout seemed relatively simple; an outer block of buildings that effectively made four walls of a square. He guessed that a second, smaller block lay within, separated by a wide corridor open to the sky. This much he could determine by the views he had through the small windows. Dahrlyth told him she believed there was another square in the very centre of the property and in the rooms overlooking this guarded place the Dancers lived.

'The wives live in part of the outer block, in a single room where over four hundred of them lounge in comfort, with many servants, they say.'

From the size of the palace grounds, Okkyntalah could believe that number of wives possible. 'Do you know which side of the square?'

She nodded and pointed to the east. 'The harem is guarded by many great strong men with no parts but they have eyes at the back of their heads as well as the front. They never sleep and will die before they see a wife of the Uhmbard's harmed.'

Okkyntalah smiled inwardly at these rumours. 'Other guards?'

'The courtyard inside is manned by hundreds of armed soldiers of the Uhmbard's personal bodyguard; all fierce warriors. It's said they line all four sides and carry swords that flame with poisonous fire.'

'Is there a place where I might see over the outside walls?'

She pointed north and led him to the place. The only building with more than one storey; a block three floors high, punctured by regular square holes. Okkyntalah walked all round the outside.

'What purpose does this serve?'

'It's a lookout over the desert to spot the movements of the K'ahll, a violent and evil people who eat their own children and kill strangers on sight.'

Okkyntalah made no comment about this particular myth but looked for a way into the building and discovered no door or window openings; only the square holes in the sides. He shrugged and climbed, using these as hand and footholds. Dahrlyth waited on the ground.

From the top, deserted but clearly in use during daylight hours, judging by the abandoned food and drinking vessels, he could see over the city in all directions. Though there was nothing beyond the walls and cultivated areas, apart from what appeared to be a small encampment to the south. He turned to the palace and discovered that his guess at the plan of the building was reasonably accurate. He could even see into the open courtyard and count the guards. Four against both visible sides. Had they spotted him and, if so, what they would make of it? He'd seen enough.

'Good. We must return and rest now. Tonight we make our escape.'

She held his hand as they returned and, when they lay down together, she trembled against him so that he comforted her within his embrace. At last she calmed and they slept. The day and coming night promised danger but also brought hope of freedom.

Tumalind, prepared for Dance, should the Uhmbard require her, lay bored and fitful on her cushions. Tah-Vlatak had been and gone and she was alone, left to her own devices and imaginings, wondering how long she must wait for this life to end and her old life to return. That Okkyntalah was set to try to rescue her, she was sure. That her warnings and worries would have no effect on his attempt, she had no doubt. But her mind kept returning to the dangers and risks involved. Nuldron hadn't been back in touch and she had no knowledge of how close was the rescue party from Litkala; only that it was moving closer. She must know.

'Tumalind, I've something for you. Whether you can make use of it, or whether it will serve only as a curiosity, I don't know. But let me tell you and you can decide for yourself.'

'Ivdulon! I was about to connect with Nuldron to discover how close they are.'

'My information will take only moments. It's this: the night after next, at around the mid hour, the moon will begin to be devoured by shadow. It'll glow blood red and stay that way for some short time, before the shadows slowly fall away and it returns to normal. That's it. I don't know whether you can make use of this, but you might. I'll leave you to connect with your rescuers.'

Ivdulon was gone as suddenly as she'd appeared. Tumalind wondered: could she make use of such information? Could she gain from knowing something would happen in the near future? She might at least gain respect from such a prediction. Though she hoped

433

she'd be gone from the city by the time this strange event occurred.

She'd consult Nuldron first, and then devote some thought to Ivdulon's news.

'We're within sight of the city walls. There's some debate about whether we should make ourselves known during daylight, or whether we should await darkness. I suggested I enter a trance to see if I could divine any information, since I can't reveal to most of those here the magic of mindtalk. They're unsure of my value in this regard, so if you could give me some useful information; something that could be proven correct by sending a couple spies to the city, I might be able to influence the decision in a positive manner.'

Tumalind told him about the arrangement of the bathing pool and the drinking water pool beside the track to the gates. She described the gates themselves in as much detail as she could recall and explained the manner of dress of men and women in the city.

'That should help. All women are naked? I knew them to be heathens, but that's a surprise. Give me a little time to enter a trance state and I'll let them have this information before I come back for more detailed descriptions of the palace and the route to it.'

He was gone and Tumalind was again alone. She was excited that her rescue was so close. Both Okkyntalah and the rescue party might appear at the same time. She must ensure the party knew about Okkyntalah's presence so he wasn't in danger if the two attempts coincided. The danger that she might be rescued by the party from Litkala and taken from the city before Okkyntalah was aware was a serious worry, but she understood she could only tell the larger party of this danger. Okkyntalah must remain ignorant.

To take her mind off that worry, she dwelt on Ivdulon's news. How to make use of it? What to do with it? How to explain her knowledge without putting herself in danger of having to confess to mindtalk with all the potential risks that would bring?

A dream. She'd let it be known she'd had a dream. These people were susceptible to forecasts that could be had from dreams. It might, if the rescue failed for some reason, place her at some advantage that may be of use in the future.

She left her chamber and sought out Tah-Vlatak, finding her gossiping with another three Dancers in the common room used for such gatherings. It was the first time she'd ventured here and they welcomed her as a sister.

Here, the cushions were piled high and men without parts stood one in two corners as guards. The central pool, level with the floor, was served by a tall fountain of clear water that tinkled as it fell to the surface. Two Dancers were relaxing in the cool water. Serving girls held platters of fresh fruit, wine and goat's cheese and she took a selection and went to sit with her companions just within the brightness of the sunlit opening onto the courtyard.

They talked of nothing. Events in the palace held little interest for Tumalind, yet she listened and paid attention in case she could learn something of value.

As a test, she put a question that had puzzled her since her arrival. 'Where are all the children? I mean, all these wives and all this sex. There must be lots of children…'

It was immediately obvious, by the looks of horror and fear they displayed that she'd said something very dangerous. She had to restore some normality. Pretend nothing had happened, since that was the way things were done in this strange place.

'Vlatak, I need to ask you something. I don't know how such things are managed here, but I've had a dream.'

The others were instantly calmed and feigned interest, willing her to continue.

'Tell me what you dreamt and I'll let you know what you should do.'

She thanked Vlatak and made up a tale in which she could involve Ivdulon's prophesy of the blood red moon.

'I believe there's a portent here, Tumalind. I think you'd better describe your dream to the Uhmteld.'

They went together and Tah-Vlatak led her into the harem, where the wives made space for them to pass through, their stares of respect making Tumalind blush a little. The Uhmteld was in audience with three senior wives but ended their consultation as soon as she was aware of the Dancers.

Vlatak curtsied and Tumalind followed suit. 'Most Enlightened One, Tah-Tumalind has dreamed a dream and I believe you would benefit from hearing it.'

The Uhmteld sat up straight and paid full attention. 'Tell me, child.'

Again Tumalind told her story. How the day had passed before her as three other Dancers had Danced before the Uhmbard, how the Uhmbard had shared pleasure with six of his wives and how the Dancers had rested afterwards, exhausted by their efforts. She told how she'd then passed through another day alone and had Danced a Dance of mystery and delight in the palace courtyard under the sun. The Uhmteld frowned at this unlikely event but bade her continue with her dream. Tumalind then told how the night had grown dark and the moon, almost full, had risen to reflect in the palace pools.

'Then shadows seemed to devour the moon until it became a blood red orb hanging darkly in the sky, full of foreboding and mystery. I watched, transfixed and afraid, sure that something terrible would happen. But the shadows drained away and the light was restored to its former glory, even increasing in brilliance as the redness left it.'

'This is a dream for the Uhmbard, my child. I'll send a messenger and see when he will hear it from your lips. Remain here. You're prepared for Dance? Of course. Good. I cannot tell the omens in such a dream but I'm certain there are things here to be learned. And there are wise men who interpret such things. Of course, what those may be and how the Uhmbard will react to your dream of foreboding is difficult to predict. But be prepared to be tested as the bearer of ill omen.'

※

Aklon woke too late to the disturbance to defend himself. The bindings were placed already around his legs as he lay helpless. It took only three strong men to secure his arms behind him and tie them too securely for him to escape. The farmer's daughter had returned in the early hours and spent the rest of the night with him, sending Phildrad to sleep in her bed.

She screamed and slipped from the bed, taking the bedcover for modesty, and giving him a look that said she'd had no part in this treachery.

'My dear girl, I never believed for one moment you were involved. Do not distress yourself. I take it my companion has been similarly betrayed and trussed?'

No one spoke for a moment, as the farmer entered the room, his face a mask of frustration. 'No. 'e 'asn't. Woke up afore I could take him, an' jumped right through the shutters like a rhaat startled out a fowl's coop.'

Aklon smiled. 'A good soldier, that. Now, to what do I owe this unfortunate turn of events, my good man?'

The farmer scratched his balding pate and surveyed him. 'Why, we may be just country folk, but there's a price on your 'ead.'

'Is it the price or your concern for justice that has me tied here?'

The farmer looked embarrassed. 'Look, Paltrohn, if it were jus' me I'd be 'appy to let you go on your way without another word. Onny, there's the women and children to be considered an' you're a danger to them, as I see it.'

'Yet your daughter was happy to entertain me. And you made no objection to that joining.'

'She were part of the plan to capture you, y'see? Though, tell the truth, she weren't never told.'

'So, not quite as concerned about the danger to your women as you claim?'

'Not like you're a danger to them directly, Paltrohn. No. You've already shown yoursen to be an honourable man, as far as the 'orses was concerned. So I can't see you bein' no danger to my womenfolk in that way. No. It's that you're renegade an' if I let yer go an' them at the top 'ears on it, we'll all be for a whippin' like.'

'I see. And I understand. So, what is your next move?'

The farmer looked at the three burly figures who'd trussed him up and then back at Aklon. 'Well, happen I best send word to capital an' tell 'em I've got you 'ere safe an' bound if they want to come an' collect you.'

'That seems sound. However, I have a small favour to ask. One that will involve you in little trouble at this stage and might entertain you with its results, should you go along

436

with what I have in mind. Will you hear me out?'

'They all say you're a dangerous and violent criminal who rapes and despoils women and children an' steals everything you can. You've already proved none o' that's true. Mayhap the rest needs some thinkin' on as well.'

'You are a wise man. May I know your name?'

'I'm Uebritihl, Paltrohn. An' I an' my forefathers 'ave farmed 'ere since the Followers landed on these shores.'

'A proud and worthy lineage, then, Uebritihl. I commend your labour, your management and your stewardship of the land. And I commend your wisdom also. I could spend a good deal of time in explaining why my father, Dagla Kaz, made me renegade but you are a man of wisdom and would need more proof than I can presently provide to back up my claims. I will say only that I am the victim in this; that I wished to spread truth to the people of this island and that my father, for reasons of his own, felt that such truths would be detrimental to his welfare and status. A feeling, I might add, that was wholly justified.'

The farmer absorbed the words, expressing some uncertainty in his face but saying nothing.

'So, as a demonstration that I am a man of my word and one of perhaps more power than you expect, I will merely make a prediction. If that prophesy fails to come about by a little after the mid-point of tomorrow night, then I will actively encourage you to send one of your men to the capital. In fact, I will willingly and voluntarily accompany one or more of your men on such a journey and, once at the destination, commend you and your men for their courage in capturing me and delivering me to the authorities. Does that all sound reasonable?'

'All you've said an' done so far 'as seemed reasonable, Paltrohn. I'm at a loss as to whether I should believe you or the authorities, like.'

'As I said, a wise man, Uebritihl. So. My forecast. At, or near the mid-point of tomorrow night, after the moon has undergone a swift transformation under the influence of shadows across its brilliant surface, I shall paint it blood red. For a brief period such colour will remain on the surface and I will then reverse the procedure and return the beautiful night lantern to its full glory.'

The farmer seemed interested. 'But I've seen the moon go red afore, Paltrohn. Not often, but a couple o' times in me life I seen it.'

'Perhaps. Indeed, I would be most disappointed if a man of your experience and wisdom had failed to witness such an event. However, have you known beforehand that such an omen would appear?'

'Well, if it comes to that, I 'ave to confess that I ain't. No. I don't rightly know no one as can tell when such a thing might be. An' didn't I 'ear that you predicted the true Skyfire would grow brighter than that false one and keep getting more bright each night?'

'I did make such prophesy. I am pleased that the news has spread out of Pampahn, where I first made the observation. So, are you prepared to believe the words of a man who has such an intimate knowledge and even some control of the night sky? And, if you have such trust, would you then be prepared to extend that belief a little further and acknowledge that my demonstrated truths may well indicate that my other truths are also worthy of notice? That perhaps, in fact, I should be allowed to remain a free man in order that I may spread such truth as I know to the rest of the Followers?'

'You use a mighty lot of words to say a few things. But you're in the right of it. I'll set you free once the moon glows blood red tomorrow night. An' if it don't, then I'll send you bound on your way with three o' me men armed to take you to the capital.'

'A generous and sensible man. Now, a word of warning. My companion, Phildrad, is quite likely to attempt a rescue. My band of followers is quite dedicated and most will not easily give up the fight. If I could persuade you to loosen my binding, to allow me the freedom to move a little and restore the blood to my dying extremities, I could perhaps persuade my colleague to return here and be bound with me until the events occur. Does that also sound reasonable?'

It took a little more persuasion, but eventually Aklon was bound less tightly and allowed to make his way into the farmyard, where he located Phildrad hiding in the bordering trees and signalled him to return.

The pair of them spent the rest of the day trussed, not too tightly, but securely, in the farmhouse, where they were fed and attended by the household women, the daughter of the night making a secret request of him to repeat his previous joining and smiling with delight when he agreed to this if he was released.

Phildrad was concerned. 'It's a risk, Aklon. S'pose this 'ere thing with the moon don't 'appen?'

'Then, my friend, you and I are in for a very uncomfortable journey to Choshinahm, at the conclusion of which, we will undoubtedly be slaughtered before we have any opportunity to prove our case to the authorities.'

The Uhmbard listened to the story of her dream with the air of one troubled but unwilling to admit to such emotion. Tumalind was allowed to speak from a kneeling position three paces before the enthroned potentate and she felt his eyes on her the whole time.

'Have you dreamt in such a fashion before, woman?'

'Almighty, Wise and Omnipotent Highness, I have not.'

438

'But you thought it necessary that I be troubled with this dream?'

'Almighty, Wise and Omnipotent Highness, I reported my dream to others and it was deemed worthy of your attention.'

'Was it? Dance for me whilst I attempt to divine the meaning of this dream of yours.'

He clapped his hands and one of his attendants brought in one of the ever present musicians, a girl who played the lyre as if it were an instrument from the gods, and another disappeared to return only moments later with a tall thin elderly man who had the blackest eyes Tumalind had ever seen. He took no notice of her, however, and knelt before the Uhmbard as the leader engaged him in deep conversation. Tumalind saw that, from time to time, the Uhmbard stared at her and the thin man was allowed to look also.

They continued to discuss her dream as she Danced.

At last they reached a conclusion. He had the music stop and, beckoned Tumalind to him. She moved as directed and lay on her belly in front of the two men.

'Rise to your feet.'

She moved upright as gracefully as she could and stood before him, her arms behind her and her face pointed to the floor.

'Why should you, a mere woman, be sent such an important omen?'

Asked a direct question, she understood a response was expected. 'I can't tell, Almighty, Wise and Omnipotent Highness.'

He drew in a deep breath and dismissed the thin man. 'I'm not convinced the gods would select a woman for such a task. Bend here.'

She took up the position he indicated and gritted her teeth as he spanked her soundly with both hands.

'You, Dancer, had better be right in this prediction. Should the moon fail to behave as you have forecast, I'll be forced into the necessity of ending your life. Since the loss of a Dancer would pain me greatly, I'd be obliged to ensure that the process of your dying was as protracted and painful as I could devise. I hope, for the sake of both of us, that your dream turns out to be true. In that event, I shall, of course, reward you with a gift appropriate to your station. Dance from my presence. And make it provocative.'

Tumalind did her best, under threat of death, to entertain the despot as she saw him take a wife, and slowly she left the chamber. Again, the question arose in her mind. Where are the children?

Her bottom smarted from the beating, but that was as nothing compared to the threat. A painful and lingering death would be her reward if she remained in captivity and Ivdulon's prediction proved false or unreliable.

439

Chapter 45

A RESCUE BID

Okkyntalah's initial fears, that the palace entrance would be locked and heavily guarded proved unfounded. Dahrlyth he'd hidden from view, opposite the entrance, where she could observe his movements. She was to run from her hiding place, bearing his belongings and bringing the dog when he returned with Tumalind. She'd gone into the small space reluctantly, but had agreed to his conditions for her rescue.

The single guard, no more than a token presence in this city where absolute rule had made the leader complacent, had looked at Okkyntalah with curiosity rather than alarm. He'd had no chance to voice concern before Okkyntalah had silenced him with his hunting knife.

He closed the door behind him. No one would be about so early, but he had to keep risk to a minimum on this near-suicidal mission.

First, he must find Tumalind and let her know he was here. The rest of the plan he'd make up as he went along. Dahrlyth had told him as much as she knew of the arrangements within the palace, but her previous information had proved less than reliable and he went warily forward. Two guards snored outside the door to the harem, swords in hands. The risk of them waking was too great and he made their sleep permanent; silent sweeps of his sword spilling blood without either of them uttering a sound.

In the courtyard, the guards had been reduced for the night. Two were sleeping, backs to the wall, their weapons slack in their laps. He surveyed the remaining three: he must disable them before he dare search for Tumalind.

The Dancers' chambers surrounded the square, their blank black windows and entrances open only to that space. Okkyntalah hid in the entrance of the corridor leading to one half of the palace. Diagonally opposite, across the open area, another dark oblong led to the other part of the palace. He needed to lure the nearest guard toward him and out of sight of the other two.

Tapping the hilt of his knife gently against the stone framework created more sound than he expected. But it had the effect. The nearest guard signalled his colleagues and made for the entrance. Okkyntalah hid in the shadows and waited. The guard stood, just within the doorway, trying to locate the rhythmic sound of Okkyntalah's gentle tapping. When it stopped, and Okkyntalah made a high-pitched, soft giggle, the guard strode without fear into the shadows. And breathed his last.

He dragged the man along the corridor and returned to the opening. He prayed for a kind trick of fate to help him dispense with the two guards still awake. For a time, a precious, anxious time, nothing happened and he was at a loss what to do. Would the same hoax work again?

He tried knocking, watching for their reactions. Both looked across at the opening, and he feared he might've bitten off more than he could chew. One clandestine murder in silence was simple: two must be altogether more complicated. The guards came together and spoke in soft voices, pointing and gesticulating toward the entrance. From what Okkyntalah knew of the city, from experience and conversations with Dahrlyth, he felt it unlikely the guards would be suspicious or wary. More probably, they'd expect the attentions of some woman, as had proved the downfall of his earlier victim.

They came toward the entrance as a pair. He must be swift. The first died easily. But the second reacted with a sword thrust and started a cry of alarm that Okkyntalah ended before it reached any real volume. Nevertheless, the call had been unmistakeably human, and concerned. Anyone close and awake must've heard. He stood in the shadows, controlling his breathing so he could hear any sound of approach. In the quadrangle, the sleeping guards made no move and nothing stirred from any room. Complacency certainly did rule here. Guards unprepared for attack, after years without trouble or conflict, were no real protection.

Once his heart stopped pounding, Okkyntalah moved into the square. The first chamber was dark; moonlight illuminating an oblique shape through the entrance but shedding little light into the room itself. He moved to the back and found a woman asleep in a curl on top of cushions. He made no sound but could tell, without moving closer, that this wasn't his beloved.

The next bedroom echoed with the snores of a man and the soft breathing of a woman. He left, knowing Tumalind would be alone. The third chamber revealed another lone woman, sleeping in abandonment and displaying bright beads as an invitation against the deeper darkness that lay there. Not Tumalind.

In the fourth, he found her, illuminated by the oblong of light from the window. One hand rested beneath her head, the other arm was flung out; a leg stretched long and straight, the other bent at the knee so the sole of her foot rested against her knee. For a moment he stood, captivated; loving her as she lay so vulnerable and relaxed. As he moved to place a hand over her mouth, she opened her eyes. Her lips parted, ready to cry out.

'Tumalind. It's me.' His whisper reached her in time and she relaxed. 'I knew you'd...'

He stopped her speaking with a finger to her lips and she understood at once. Rising, she took his hand and allowed him to lead her to the door. In the brightness of the quadrangle, three guards faced him, weapons drawn. He put Tumalind behind him and awaited their attack, as one raised the alarm with a loud cry.

As usual, the boat was tied up against the bank for the night. This time, they'd stopped on the eastern shore, its sloping banks more readily accessible than the steep rise of the west. Sleep had been a long time coming and Aglydron had only settled once he'd drowned his lust in Chislanda. Relaxed and satiated, he'd fallen asleep at the midpoint of the night.

He woke from a dream of luxury and enjoyment. Noise and activity came as he struggled to leave sleep. A hand clutched him and he opened his eyes in time to see Chislanda bundled away by two dark shapes bearing pointed sticks. Light, orange and yellow, flickered on the scene as he fought for full consciousness. Screams and calls of distress, indignation, pain and alarm assaulted his ears. And, at last, he was wide enough awake to act. Chislanda had vanished into darkness. He made to follow but stumbled and fell flat as something wrapped around his ankles and felled him. His legs were bound together and he could only drag his body forward with his hands.

The flickering light he now saw was the boat, flaming and crackling with heat as fire consumed it. Against the brightness of flames, he saw people moving; chaos. Men and women were fighting with each other. Shouts of protest, screams of fear and pain, yells of denial rent the air. He watched three women, each held by two men, carried into darkness. Then all resolved itself and he understood that a raiding party had attacked the camp and these men were taking the women.

He tried to move further but his bound legs prevented fast movement and he sat to see if he might undo them. In the light of the fire, he discovered a single length of rope with heavy stones attached to each end. He recognised it as a type of bolas, like that he used when hunting wild horses on the island. It took moments to unwind and give him freedom.

His first thought then was of his nakedness, from sleep. He ran back to the sleepsack and sought his tabard. As he was dressing, other men from the party came to discover his condition. All but one were naked and he suddenly recognised his piety as a poor response to the disaster.

'Are you hurt, Aglydron?' Tarruss towered over him.

'No. They've taken Chislanda. I have to …'

'No. All the women have been kidnapped. We need to know who's still alive and what our situation is.' Caarl stood beside Tarruss.

The men moved off toward the rest of the camp.

'I have to rescue Chislanda…'

'Stay. Go into the dark and you're a target for their arrows. We've already lost enough to that tactic. But they shoot only those who try to follow. Stay with us, or you'll be killed.'

The soldier's words made sense and he felt compelled to do as the senior officer demanded. But the thought of Chislanda at the mercy of unknown brigands was almost too much to bear. Though reluctant, he followed the others as they travelled the camp looking for injured and surviving members.

It soon became clear that not all the women had been taken. The ship's captain and two of her crew, Corphanda, Rrildyss Kaz, Dilanthas and Linlyss were still present. Of the men, two virgin gifts had been killed as they chased the raiders, Gidwallehn had an injury to his shoulder and Tryonta's left arm bled from a wound. A crew member had drowned as she leapt into the river to escape burning.

'It's not the way of the Vagboh to kill without need. They merely seek women, since their own too frequently die in childbirth.'

Dagla Kaz stared at Quyreena in the fading light of the flames. 'You know something of these thieves in the night?'

'Rumours, mostly. They live in the great forest, to the east. There's supposed to be a small town right in the centre of the trees. A fellow traveller once told me he'd been there; Pastroahn, he called it. Said it was one of the most civilised and unspoilt places he'd ever been. And this was a man who'd travelled the whole world.'

'Rumour only? Caarl, what do you advise?'

Aglydron was struck by how poor a leader Dagla Kaz had shown himself. He was fine when it came to ceremony and diplomacy. But any emergency seemed beyond the man.

'We can't follow them in the dark. I suggest we deal with the injured, gather around a single campfire, and set off at first light. A party of that size, with captives, will not move very fast and will leave an obvious trail.'

'As far as men's plans go, makes sense, I s'pose.'

'I'll thank you for your silence on this occasion, Corphanda. This is a matter for those with greater experience and knowledge than you possess.'

Aglydron saw her rankle but, to his surprise, she said no more.

'Has anyone else anything to contribute?'

Shock and despair had gathered after their loss and the whole party set about collecting scattered belongings around the campfire nearest the river. Corphanda tended the wounds. Rrildyss Kaz took herself off to the edge of the circle of firelight, apparently to pray. Aglydron thought this an admirable response from the High Priest of Litkala. He would do the same, once he'd played his part in collecting the stores and other items into a single place.

The remaining members of the party settled, this time with a couple of people on watch, and tried to sleep in readiness for the morning's chase.

'Do you know anything about this forest, Tarruss?'

The giant hunkered down and then lay on his sleepsack beside Aglydron. 'Only what we've heard tonight. Of course, we've no choice but to go after the women. I fear we may find ourselves in more trouble than we are already before we end this pilgrimage, though.'

With that bleak thought, Tarruss lay his head on a rolled tabard left behind by one of the women and fell into sleep. But sleep was a long time coming for Aglydron as he pictured Chislanda and her distress at being captured and removed from him.

✦

Tumalind faced down her terror and sought into the night. She found Nuldron. '*Are you close?*'

'*We're in the palace. I was about to ...*'

'*No time. Come straight through to the central courtyard. I'll guide you. We need help here, now.*'

She'd witnessed the trick played by Ivdulon; the wise woman had shown her how she could see through the eyes of another by concentrating through the connection. Tumalind guided the mindtalker through the corridor and, through his eyes, saw as more guards moved towards the quadrangle. Already there was fighting as the party with Nuldron attacked the gathering palace guards.

Okkyntalah had killed one of the sentries and was fighting two more. She led Nuldron within hearing distance of the courtyard before she broke contact to help her husband. With the dropped sword of the man he'd killed, Tumalind moved into the fight. Slicing inexpertly, she caught one of the guards along his back and opened flesh. It gave Okkyntalah the chance he needed and he finished the injured sentry off with another blow. The remaining guard was ready and determined, however. And, by now, the noise had woken those who'd been sleeping. Others, who'd lain with Dancers, were emerging with weapons drawn.

Okkyntalah was surround for a moment and his death seemed certain. But the rescue party swarmed through the opening and soon there were fights all over the quadrangle. In the moonlight, shadows acted as places where some could hide. Tumalind remained in the entrance to her room, where she'd see anyone who came her way. She gripped the curved sword she'd used to save Okkyntalah.

The fighters from Litkala were battle hardened from their engagement with the people of Mipahnhil. But the palace guards had never dealt with anything more threatening than naked unarmed women, or slave traders in need of execution. They were

445

no match and the rescue party soon had the upper hand in spite of the enemy's greater numbers.

The eunuchs joined the fray, leaving their charges unguarded, and dying because of this desertion. Soon the courtyard was a mass of fallen bodies, blood flowing through tiled channels that had previously been the route only for water used to cleanse the floor after executions.

The fighting ceased as abruptly as it had commenced. Only two of the rescue party had been killed; another three injured. The leader of the rescuers approached Tumalind, now with Okkyntalah at her side. The stench of death and gore was too much and she vomited but quickly recovered. The women screaming in the harem might wake the citizens. Tumalind became aware they might be in more danger from undisciplined but loyal menfolk of the town than they'd been from the guards.

'We have to take the Uhmbard. They'll never attack if he's in danger.'

'Where? Take us to him.'

She led them through the corridors and found the Uhmbard's chamber empty. In the harem, she discovered, in the silenced mass of women who cowed in fear as the rescue party entered, the Uhmteld, seated on her throne.

'Where's the Uhmbard?'

'You will refer to me as....'

Tumalind gripped her by the arm. 'I'll have you whipped and beaten until you talk. Tell me where he is.'

'I will not be...' She surveyed the armed men and women and understood. 'Come with me.'

The Uhmteld led them along another corridor to a chamber Tumalind hadn't previously visited. There, behind bodyguards and cowering with a dozen of his wives as further defence, the Uhmbard waited. The elite guards were fierce in their defence of their Uhmbard and none surrendered; all were swiftly killed, leaving only the terrified wives to shield him.

Tumalind asked the rest to leave her to this duty. She moved through the women, who did nothing to stop her or to defend their leader. Grasping his arm, she dragged him, protesting, into the open.

'Tell your people we'll kill you if they try to stop us leaving.'

He nodded.

The street outside the palace was thronged with armed men, many carrying torches, though the sky was already beginning to brighten. Women lined the thoroughfare, anxious as well as curious about the disturbance. Okkyntalah left the rescue party, with their captive, the coerced wives and their own dead and injured, and crossed the road.

446

'Dahrlyth, we're ready to leave.'

A gasp of amazement escaped the women nearby, as a woman emerged from a low doorway in one of the adobe buildings. Tumalind watched this unknown woman hand Okkyntalah his belongings and then kiss him passionately. She released herself, moved up to a man waiting in the street to defend his leader, and took the sword from his amazed hand. Waving it above her head, she called out to the other women to do likewise.

'Women of Ov-Bebna, we've been given hope. We've been slaves for too long to these unworthy men. Do we kill them here and now or do we teach them what it is to be slaves? Or do we better them and treat them as the equals that they never let us be?'

Learning that their Uhmbard was captive and had commanded that no attack should be made on the strangers, the men were taken by surprise and did nothing to prevent the women. Most seemed shocked and amazed, made immobile by a turn of events so unexpected. Their faces and gestures displayed utter confusion and indecision. But many of the women did exactly as Okkyntalah's woman suggested. One using her captured sword to kill the man she took it from.

Tumalind would wait to discover the nature of Okkyntalah's relationship with the woman he'd called on. For the moment, she'd been rescued and he was back with her. Nothing else mattered.

The problem, as the leader of the rescue party saw it, was domestic. He had a job do and he led his party from the tumult, the rabble of the town coming after them in a disorderly and confused manner now that the women had shown themselves capable of rebellion.

At the abandoned and deserted gate, Okkyntalah urged the column to halt, as other members of the rescue party came in sight, leading beasts of burden. He approached the party leader.

'We've no more use for the Uhmbard and Uhmteld. But I wouldn't see them free to take the lead again when this rebellion amongst the women is so new.'

'What would you do; kill the despot and his whore?'

'No. There's a better way.'

He led them to the opening in the ground where Tumalind had watched him struggle to escape only days previously. 'I spent almost three days in there and, but for the help of the woman I named back there, I would've died. They can call for help and maybe they'll be let out, but I doubt they'll have the power they once held after they've been in the Pit. Better that their own people decide their fate, I think.'

They forced the struggling Uhmbard first into the space and heard him cry out in alarm and terror. The Uhmteld needed no such force but sat on the edge of the Pit, turned and lowered herself in. The resultant cry suggested she landed on top of her husband. The citizens, men and women, gathered round, the men aghast at this treatment of their erstwhile God. Tumalind turned away, unwilling to watch, as two women crouched over the hole and took some revenge.

'This, then, people of Ov-Bebna, is the power of your so-called God. He's powerless to prevent the action of a few well-disciplined men and women. Your own women have taken up arms. I suggest you men, if that's what you are, learn quickly from these women, for they have the power now to do to you as you have done to them for so long. To the women I say only that you now have the upper hand. Be vigilant and careful but be merciful in treating these men who might yet become worthwhile creatures.'

Tumalind, impressed with her husband's skills and words, clung to Okkyntalah and looked at him with admiration.

He spoke with the leader of the recue party and decisions were quickly made.

The fallen of the rescue party they buried in a spot outside the gates that Dahrlyth selected. 'We will keep this place as sacred ground, in honour of those who rescued us.'

There were spare camels and horses to take those few who wished to leave the city with the recue party. Seven women chose to go. Tumalind was pleased to see the Dancer, Tah-Vlatak, and Teh-blavv, the wife who'd first helped her when she'd arrived.

But the woman called Dahrlyth elected to stay in the city and be part of the new group they would form to rule. She approached Tumalind and took Okkyntalah's hand in hers to pass into Tumalind's hand.

'Your husband loved me better than any man, but he never deserted you, I give him back to your care, Paltra. He's proved himself a worthy man and leaves me a better woman than he found me. Enjoy your life with Okkyntalah and may you be blessed with as many children as you wish to bring into this world.'

She then stretched up and kissed Okkyntalah with undisguised passion before she turned and walked back to her people. He watched her out of site and Tumalind knew that he cared deeply for this strange and courageous woman.

They left the city behind, Tumalind dressed again in a tabard and the other captive women covered, some for the first time in their lives. Okkyntalah rode beside her on his camel, a little ungainly. She smiled at him as she gripped the leather strap that gave her purchase and fell in with the rhythm of the beast of burden. Life was good again. She'd regained her freedom, and the man she loved above all else. And he'd rescued her, been true and brave, and recovered her against all odds. There would be time enough to learn about the woman, Dahrlyth, and more time to reward him for his courage. For now, she mouthed a kiss and smiled as he hung on to his mount and tried to master it.

The day grew hot and windless, sand surrounded them, as they set up camp a few leagues from the city. Their tents weren't like the one Okkyntalah had used on his rescue trip, but more substantial and less efficient at reducing heat.

Tumalind spent some time in conversation with the man called Nuldron and Okkyntalah wondered what she had in common with a stranger of his age. That mystery was quickly solved, as Nuldron and she met with the leader who then called the whole gathering into a meeting on the sands between the tents.

Nuldron, at a signal from the leader, gestured for silence and then spoke. 'I've a thing to tell you that a few already know and others will find difficult to believe. It's been kept secret from you all these years for very good reasons. Now, however, for those gathered here, it's more important that you learn our secret than that we keep it.

'Tumalind and I, and others I won't name, can communicate with each other over great distances. We engage in something called mindtalk, and can use this method anywhere and anytime.'

He held up his hand for silence at the noisy disbelief from those who'd never been in contact with a mindtalker. 'I can prove it, easily. Take me, or Tumalind, away from the gathering and then tell something secretly to the other. Whoever is not told will return and reveal the secret.'

A short discussion ensued as to whether this was necessary and it was deemed the best solution to the disbelief. It took only a little time before the disbelievers were convinced and the meeting could continue.

'Now, I need to tell you why I've revealed the secret here and now. Ivdulon, Feldrark and Rrildyss Kaz are all mindtalkers and we've been in conversation with them. Some of you are aware that our High Priestess is on a pilgrimage with the fool from Muhnilahm; a questionable journey to Choshinahm. But we're not gathered to discuss the merits or defects of that. Something has happened to them. The wild men of the Great Forest have taken most of the women. We know, from previous contact with these primitive men, that they won't harm them to begin with. But, after they've been with them for thirty days, all those women who haven't voluntarily done so will be forced to join with the tribal men. Some of those captured are Virgin Gifts and, for the greater good of the Followers of Ytraa, we can't allow them be violated.

'Feldrark has asked that those willing to volunteer should go to the rescue of the women and meet up with the remaining members of the pilgrimage. As the route there is to the north-east and the journey back to Litkala is due south, we need to decide, today, who is going where. I now leave the floor to our leader to determine how we should proceed. My job was merely to relate the circumstances.'

Nuldron joined the rest, as the troop leader took up position under a sun that grew more unbearable with each passing moment.

'You don't need to make up your minds now. We'll eat and sleep through the desert day. This evening, when we're ready to leave, you can choose. But I must tell you that I'll lead the group to the Great Forest. Someone else must take the return party to Litkala. That's all for now. Go to your tents for shade and food. And, I thank all who took part in the rescue of our respected and much valued lady, Tumalind.'

'Please. Let me add my personal thanks to all of you for your valiant action. Without your bravery, I might well have been forced to Dance forever for that vile despot, and Okkyntalah may have died in his courageous attempt to rescue me. Thank you all.'

Okkyntalah took her in his arms and held her, as the others cheered.

The soldiers called their approval. But there was much muttering as they gathered into groups to share tents. Okkyntalah and Tumalind shared with the rescued women. They sat on warm sand within the canvass space, shade a welcome break from oppressive heat, and waited for the army's cooks to bring food and water.

'Your man will want me to Dance for him, Tah-Tumalind?' Tah-Vlatak stripped away the tunic she'd been given and posed before him.

'And I should give him sex?' Teh-blavv prepared herself.

Okkyntalah wasn't sure where to look but Tumalind rescued him.

'No Dancing now, Vlatak, and the only sex he's having will be with me, as soon as we have some privacy.'

It was clear they had much to tell these women, much to help them understand their new positions in society. For the moment, food, rest, and the decision whether to go to Litkala was foremost in his mind. The women sat cross-legged on their discarded garments and looked up at him with something approaching worship. He knew both would have him in their beds if he wished it, but it was Tumalind he wanted, no other woman.

'Will you go to rescue the women, Okkyntalah?'

He shook his head, still amazed at how easily she read him. 'I should. But that means leaving you behind to make your way to Litkala with that group, or taking you back to the people we ran away from. I think it's up to you, my love.'

Chapter 46

THE CHASE BEGINS

Aglydron watched the sky darken. They'd walked through daylight and then under the brightness of a near full moon. Now, however, filled with foreboding, he cowered under outlying trees of this huge forest as the light failed, and the moon clouded ominous red. The Skyfire gave more light now than the fading orb, lending a strange illumination to the space between the trunks.

He had no one to lie with.

The party had stopped once it became impossible to follow the tracks. The day had seen swift walking over grasslands teeming with biting insect life and patched with herds of huge grazing creatures. Tarruss and Caarl had felled one with their bows and the company was now replete, with supplies of meat enough to last two or three days.

He understood what the wild men might do to Chislanda. Though the strange ship's captain seemed convinced the women wouldn't be harmed, he couldn't imagine they had been taken for any purpose but one. The thought of her subjected to such brutal abuse prayed on his mind and destroyed all hope of sleep.

Seven other women had been taken; five virgins, Myllthlan, and the priest from Kah-Labaz, Kaz-Ca-Valorysta. Why couldn't it have been Rrildyss Kaz and the ship's captain, with her odd preference for other women, instead of the two women he most loved in the world?

And, now, to add to his concerns, that ever-present, reliable night companion, the moon, dripped blood. A portent. It must be an omen. An evil one. Yet another attack on his faith. Must he be tested again for his loyalty to Ytraa and the Lord Gadhallah? So many tests, so many pitfalls since he'd stolen away from the island with Okkyntalah and Jodisa-Li.

How he longed to return to Morstahn and his farm. And, yes, at times like this, to the security and trust of his neglected wife. How did Shoarhn fare these days? How were the boys? His twins, who he'd so looked forward to raising to look after the farm and him when he grew too old to labour. Oh, he loved Chislanda and longed to be with her again, to find her safe and unmolested. And he felt a deep affection for that remarkable woman, that wonderful healer, that expert lover, Myllthlan. But, when the world was a threatening place, he'd find solace and security most easily and readily in the arms of his loving, giving wife. He should never have left her without explaining why and where he must go. She must think him dead, after all this time.

451

No. No. Of course not. What was he thinking? Tryonta and Kaz-Ca-Wendarah had taken back his message to her when they returned to the island. She'd know of his adventures, possibly of his attachment to Chislanda. He hoped, then, that she'd find some other, not the renegade, to be with in her life on the farm he'd worked so hard to build for his family. And he knew, without doubt, that if he were restored to Chislanda, it would be Chislanda and not Shoarhn to whom he'd cleave for the rest of his life. Where might that be?

'Not sleeping, Aglydron?'

He glanced up into the young face bent over his, her pale skin shimmering in the flickering light of the campfire. Linlyss, the cheeky virgin from Litkala studied him with what looked like pity. She deserved none of his care or concern. Strumpet and opportunist. He'd never liked her, ever since she'd declared her determination to have Okkyntalah take her virginity. Well, they'd put a stop to that. Feldrark's intervention had soon put her in her place. Virgin Gift she'd become and Virgin Gift she'd stay until they arrived at Choshinahm. Then she'd be wife to whichever Follower chose to take her on.

'I'd sleep better for your absence, girl.'

She blinked and looked almost as though she might cry. 'I don't understood why you 'ate me, Aglydron. I wish I knew 'ow I've upset you. I really do.'

And she was gone again into the night, leaving him feeling to blame for her sadness. Her wondering made him wonder, too. Why was he so against the girl? What had she really done to offend him? And he knew the answer: she'd preferred Okkyntalah. Jealousy: the crux of the matter. It was unworthy. He'd be a bigger man than that. Come morning, he'd seek her out and make an offer of friendship to the girl, who must be lonely, frightened and in need of comfort. He could do that, at least. And, in the act, perhaps appease the fate that had dipped the moon in blood.

He looked up and saw, to his surprise, the colour now fading again, the brightness slowly returning to that orb in the sky. It was a clear sign. He knew he'd been right to make his declaration of intent. Come morning, he'd befriend the girl and keep close to comfort her when she required it.

But he fell asleep dreaming of a house where Shoarhn, Chislanda and Myllthlan resided with him in harmony and Linlyss was nowhere to be seen.

As evening closed on them, the party made preparations for journeys they must separately make. They were divided into two groups. Most prepared to rescue the pilgrims. The rest were to cross the sands the way they'd come and return to Litkala.

Tumalind had made her choice, hard though it was. No matter what, she wouldn't again be separated from her husband. And he wouldn't abandon those poor virgins or the

452

special healer, Myllthlan, who he loved in a different way from his devotion to her. So, they would go to Kah-Labaz with the soldiers and she'd face again the difficulties of close contact with Dagla Kaz and Tryonta. Though, following her mindtalk with Feldrark, Ivdulon, Rrildyss Kaz and even Gidwallehn, she'd been assured that others would now protect her from any attack.

They were finishing packing the tents and supplies onto their separate beasts of burden when the moon began to fade. She knew the cause: Ivdulon had predicted what would happen and explained why this strange thing would be seen. But Tah-Vlatak and Teh-blavv had witnessed her telling her dream to the Uhmteld and were now in awe as they watched it come true. They came to her, from the group they'd joined to travel to the city of Litkala.

'You're more than you seem, Tah-Tumalind. I can't abandon a woman with such powers, a woman who saved me from a life I loathed, a woman who understands what I've been through. I must come with you.'

'Me too. You're more than a magician who talks with others many leagues away. Any woman who can tell the movement of the stars and moon and who understands such omens as this, must be blessed by all the gods. I shall stay with you.'

She tried to explain, even going so far as to enter Teh-blavv's mind and show her that she, too, possessed this gift. But the girl was far from gifted, and neither of them could be deflected now she'd displayed this borrowed power. No matter how she protested, they were determined to go with her.

This left the other party only as an escort for Nuldron and he professed a need for no more than a couple of companions. In the end, they decided he'd be accompanied by three soldiers; the other three women from Ov-Bebna, and the injured troops, with just three pack animals.

Okkyntalah, who'd been absent during the declaration made by the two women, persuaded them they would be better off in the city. 'The road we take is hard and difficult. There's more danger for two beautiful women and you may even cause problems for us when it comes to the fight. You're not soldiers, like these other women, and so fighters will have to be taken away from the real battle to keep you safe. It would be better for all if you were to go to Litkala with Nuldron. We'll join you there once we've rescued the others.'

So enamoured were they of Okkyntalah that they obeyed him without question and went, albeit reluctantly, with the small group heading for the city. Further beasts of burden were provided for them.

'Okkyntalah, I've always loved you. But each day you show me why in a different way. Thank you for that.'

He smiled at her. 'They were never a threat to you, Tumalind. But you'll be more relaxed without them along. And you've enough to worry about on this trip, without the added anxiety they'd bring you.'

By the time all was settled, the moon had again grown bright enough to illuminate the land and the two groups said their farewells and went their separate ways. Nuldron, off to the south, where he'd meet the boat awaiting his return and exchange the camels for horses again. And the large party, led by the troop leader, who heard of Okkyntalah's intervention and thanked him for the removal of the two Ov-Bebna women, off toward the city under the smoking mountain.

Tumalind was more relieved than she cared to admit to bid farewell to the two women from Ov-Bebna. Rivals for her husband's affections, they'd both tried already to seduce him. He loved women, and these two were very attractive. During the evening, as he'd gently removed the beads from her pubic hair, so they might join unimpeded, Tah-Vlatak had displayed her own beads in the most blatant invitation.

'Your gentle hands can undo them best, Paltrohn.'

Tumalind had firmly suggested that she, or Teh-blavv should do the duty. Reluctantly, the Dancer had agreed to let the harem wife perform the task. But they clearly had no concerns about faithfulness, nor any experience of such a quality.

Now, however, the city of Kah-Labaz beckoned. It would take two days of hard riding to reach and much might happen on the way. When they arrived, there'd be a ship to take them across Mhistahn to the Great Forest and difficult reunions with her father, Tryonta, and Dagla Kaz, with all that might entail.

Dahrlahg could be trouble. Something about the girl had worried Shoarhn ever since Irrildys had brought her to the house.

'She's unwed and her buck's away at the battles with the rebels; gone to get rid of that lot on the Point, apparently. But her mother, who I've known all my life, says she's a good and willing worker. Course, she'll have to live with you. Too far to travel every day. Any case, you'll want her milking morning and night, won't you?'

Shoarhn smiled at the way her new friend had taken over her life in this way, organising help just because she'd mentioned needing it with Aglydron away and the boys growing up fast. Quiet, steady and reliable, the girl was also stunningly pretty with her auburn hair, large dark eyes and a body to please most men. But, regardless of Shoarhn's anxiety, she seemed content to wait for her betrothed to return from his fighting on the Point. She planned then to go with him for their first joining on the Plains of Ytraa.

She shared the boys' room for the moment. They both thought she should move into

Tumalind's old room, since her daughter wouldn't need it, if and when she eventually came home.

Dahrlahg returned from the barn, pails of milk bending the yoke with their weight. She placed them on the floor and looked uncertainly at Shoarhn, who sighed.

'No, Dahrlahg. I don't want you to do more than you need, dear, but I have explained that the night milking goes for cheese. You'll have to take it back and place it in the churn ready, please. It's only the morning milk we sell. Right?'

'Forgot. Teck it back, then shall us?'

'Please. Pour every last drop into the churn, turn the handle one hundred times.'

The girl blushed and lowered her pretty face.

'Oh. That's why you brought it here. Too embarrassed to admit you can't count. No matter. Let me collect the twins and I'll show you. We'll practice counting on the way there. You can count your steps back.'

The girl had smiled then, her embarrassment cloaked by Shoarhn's kindness.

Now they were clearing up after the evening meal. The twins were abed and sleeping, and the rest of the night stretched ahead of them, seemingly one of many with little conversation with this taciturn and ill-educated young woman. How she longed for Aklon to show up and pleasure her with his body and mind.

A commotion outside the house made her poke her head out of the door to investigate. All the occupants of the house over the wide street were staring into the sky. Shoarhn followed their gaze and saw the moon turning red. She'd seen this before, as a young girl, and felt sure it meant nothing. Certainly, nothing untoward had occurred to her or her family the first time. Though the event was disturbing, because no one seemed able to explain it, she determined not to let it worry her.

Dahrlahg ventured out and immediately fell to her knees, threw off her tabard, and prayed in the old way. The girl simply followed the example of other people in the street. But Shoarhn wasn't inclined to join them in their devotions and their pleading to their god, a god in which her faith diminished daily since her association with Aklon. How she wished he'd come to her and make more of the Cause that had already begun with announcements from runners and his prediction about the growing of the true Skyfire. No doubt Aklon would use this bleeding of the moon and the superstitions it aroused.

She went back inside, leaving the others to their prayers.

A little after the midpoint of the night, Dahrlahg finally re-appeared; her knees, hands, elbows and forehead stained red after her prolonged contact with the dust in the street. But the moon shone as normal.

'E will come 'ome, won't 'e? Not be one of 'em killed by that renegade an' 'is people, will 'e?'

455

Shoarhn understood the problem she'd face if that were the case. To have her new helper on the wrong side would be a real worry. The sooner both men, her helper's betrothed and Aklon, returned, the better for all concerned.

'Is the lad very pious?'

'Pious?'

'Did he do more than the usual amount of praying and worship?'

'Not 'im. No. You'd 'ardly think 'e were a Follower, tell the truth. If I 'adn't stopped 'im, 'e'd have frowked me good an' proper long ago. It's onny me what's made 'im wait till the proper time, like.'

It was the longest speech she'd heard from the girl and one she'd most welcomed. If the lad wasn't pious, the chances were he'd have been one of those who'd joined the Few to help Aklon convert the rest of the island population. But she wished he'd come home and bring her lover with him soon. She missed the man so much that it hurt.

'But, when 'e does come 'ome, I'll be tellin' 'im he'll have to make his mind up. Either me and a Follower, or e'll go without from me.'

Not the news she wished for, then. Perhaps she could work to engage the girl in thought and get her to understand that the Lord Gadhallah was an evil man and the faith of the Followers of Ytraa a wicked distortion. Perhaps.

<hr>

Dagla Kaz stared anxiously across the campsite. How had this happened to him? Hadn't he done everything he could to appease his God? Hadn't he sacrificed his luxury, comfort and security to make this pilgrimage? Why did the whole mission have to be fraught with danger and disaster?

'Your god is puny and without the greed a man needs from a god. Worship money, man; it buys what you lack.'

The voices in his head were frequent now. They intruded at different times, saying things that seemed to fit with his thoughts or doubts. Sometimes it was unnerving, at others, it brought comfort. But it was no good dwelling on the unfairness of it all. That was futile and childish. He must accept that the fates had trouble in store for him. Perhaps that was the true meaning of the bloodied moon. Such portents were always a worry but coming at this time it was particularly concerning. Perhaps Ytraa was a real god after all and his activities had angered the deity.

He returned to his sleep sack alone, once the moon's increasing brightness signalled an end to the mysterious and portentous message. Alone. Those wild men had stolen not only his virgins, but his new partner. Kaz-Ca-Valorysta had already proved herself an adept for his entertainment. He missed her this night, when he sought comfort to take his mind off events that threatened to overwhelm the pilgrimage yet again.

When they reached the place these wild men lived, he'd see they paid dearly for their stealing, whether they'd harmed the women or not. Given the chance, he'd slow roast the lot of them over coals so they died agonising deaths for their wickedness.

And he? Would he spend eternity in the bowels of Mhortag for his irreverent behaviour? Would he be cast out, unwanted and unwelcomed by his God? What awaited him at the end of his life? Better to live as long as possible and repent and make restitution before he died. Better to put off the dreadful moment when that truth would be known.

Truth. That's what his renegade son worshipped, wasn't it? Did the traitor still live, or had the Holy Ones caught and tortured him to death, as his message through Tryonta had decreed? Why was Aklon so convinced he should tell the people the truth? What did he gain from such? It made no sense to dispense with a life of luxury and power simply to inform the people their religion was founded on lies and falsehood.

The true Skyfire appeared overhead as it passed from behind the branches and leaves of the tree under which his sleepsack lay. It shone down on him, mocking and bright. Announcing an event he now found impossible to define in simple terms, because he no longer knew whether the recorded tales were true or false. Could this celestial phenomena really burn up people on the world? Could it distinguish between the pious and good and the feckless and bad? And in which category would it place him?

The Skyfire burned bright and threatening above him, an ever-present reminder. He finally closed his tired eyes and fell into a troubled, dream-filled sleep.

The girl, at her father's insistence, had retied the bindings after she'd finished with him and left him alone in the small room. As the sky darkened and the moon appeared, he awaited, with some trepidation, the fulfilling of Ivdulon's prediction. If he'd misplaced his trust in her, he and Phildrad were as good as dead.

But, the event proved Ivdulon's forecast. The farmer released both he and Phildrad, his words of praise and wonder a testament to his willingness to be converted. The girl wanted him to stay, at least for one more night, though her hulking husband made it clear he'd be pleased to see the back of him. Aklon had, in the process of prediction, won over four more converts and another two were wavering. So, the incident had been a small success.

Now, he and Phildrad crossed the country on foot, making for the capital and the High Priest's house, where he would expose the truth for everyone to see. That done, the next port of call must be Morstahn and Shoarhn, to spend time with her and reassure her of his devotion and safety. It would be so good to renew their loving before making the rounds of the towns and villages to add his weight to the work started by the other

457

groups.

He wondered if one of the groups had yet reached Morstahn, and what Shoarhn and the others would make of it. He knew she'd be pleased the Cause was well and truly under way, but he was unsure how much trouble it might bring in these early stages. He wished to be involved everywhere at once, instead of this piecemeal approach and reliance on deputies, no matter how determined and devoted to the Cause they may be.

And the dissenters worried him. They were a large enough group to instigate real trouble, should they wish to. Made up mostly of disgruntled soldiers, they were disciplined and determined. The last thing he wanted was war between the people of the island, with Followers driven to attack the Few and all the carnage and heartbreak such conflict must inevitably bring.

'You're quiet.'

He turned to Phildrad, walking beside him in the moonlight. 'Thinking.'

'Took a risk, you did. Back there.'

'I have taken risks all my life, Phildrad. They are a necessary part of the progress I wish to see take over the island.'

'We could've both been trussed up like game fowl; tortured an' killed.'

'Perhaps. But we are free. My connection is reliable. I have every reason to trust her word.'

'She must be frowkin' clever if she can predict summat like what 'appened 'ere tonight, though.'

'Very. But I thought you had met her? In any case, it did not happen only here, Phildrad. That event happened all around the world. In some lands it will be seen as a portent of doom. In some it will be a sign the gods are angry and people will be sacrificed in blood on altars. In others it will be taken as a sign for good on the way and there will be celebration and rejoicing. Here, we know it is no more than an event amongst the stars, with no connection to our lives on this world.'

''Ow can you be so sure, Aklon?'

'I have studied such things in the past. There has only rarely been a correlation between a sky borne event and some happening on the world, and I believe these things can be put down to nothing more exciting than coincidence.'

'An' the Skyfire?'

'I thought you were already convinced of the significance of that, or, rather the insignificance, since it means nothing whatsoever and is merely a returning wandering star that trails a tail behind it. If you observe it closely, you can see that the light it emits is from the tail it carries.'

'But, what is it, then, if it's not a sign from God?'

'It is an unfathomable event occurring in the sky, Phildrad. A place we cannot reach and therefore a place about which we understand very little. But ignorance should never make us superstitious. It should merely encourage us to find out what we can. The Skyfire may be a spectacular display, but it is no more than that. And, perhaps that is what it is: the sky showing off its power and glory to us. Why should it not do so?'

They walked in silence for the next two leagues until they overlooked the city that was their destination.

'Down there, Phildrad, is the reality of our life here on this world. Down there is the corruption brought about by desire for power and control. Down there is the source of lies and laws made to make people fear those in authority. Down there reside the documents and proofs of those lies, also. That is why we now risk our lives. We must alert the people of this place to what has been told falsely to them for so many portions. They will rebel against the knowledge. They will hate the one who tells them they have done the will of liars and charlatans. They will want blood, perhaps, for all the indignity and pain they have been made to suffer for a god and a religion without worth or truth. I hope to redirect such bloodlust into better action, or, at least toward those who deserve the denunciation of the people.

'Tomorrow is our hardest day, Phildrad. Tomorrow we let them see for themselves the lies they have been told. Many will not thank us for our truths. Many will wish to live their lives unchanged, without the need for admission of fault and credulous acceptance. Many will blame us, as messengers, for what they must be made to accept as the truth. The task before us is a hard one. Are you ready to take that risk with me? Are you ready, Phildrad, to become the messenger of doom?'

'You always make things so invitin'. I 'ardly know how to accept such a generous offer to get meself killed, an' in a painful way, if I know this lot. Aye, I'm with you. Mad and dangerous as you are. At least I'm sure you'll tell 'em only the truth. An' what more could a dyin' man desire, eh?'

'You are a good man, Phildrad. I will do my best to deliver you whole and unharmed to your lovely wife once this is properly begun.'

They went to the old mine, this time without the need for a blindfold for Phildrad. The fire cooked meat gifted by the farmer to save them hunting on their journey. The wine had kept reasonably well in the cool of the underground shelter and the oil for the lamps served their needs. They rested on the small flat bed where he had last entertained Syylvah.

No sign of dawn infiltrated the cave, but he woke to emerge as the sun rose behind the hill they occupied. A great shadow still veiled the wide sea they faced beyond the city below.

459

The time for hiding, disguise and secrecy was done. They needed open display and the courage and will that went with it. Side by side, they strode down the road toward the house of Dagla Kaz, now occupied by Wendarah Kaz. Whether it was guarded or open they wouldn't discover until they reached it. But, whatever their greeting at the house of the High Priest, Aklon would meet any resistance. He would ensure those who were against him knew of the secrets that lurked in the underground chamber. The reign of Dagla Kaz, the Holy Ones, and the discredited religion of the Followers of Ytraa would end. Now had come the time for the rule of honesty, truth, love and honour, no matter what risks that might entail.

⊹ ⸺⊰⊱⸺

Here ends book two of A Seared Sky.

The adventure concludes in book three, Convergence.

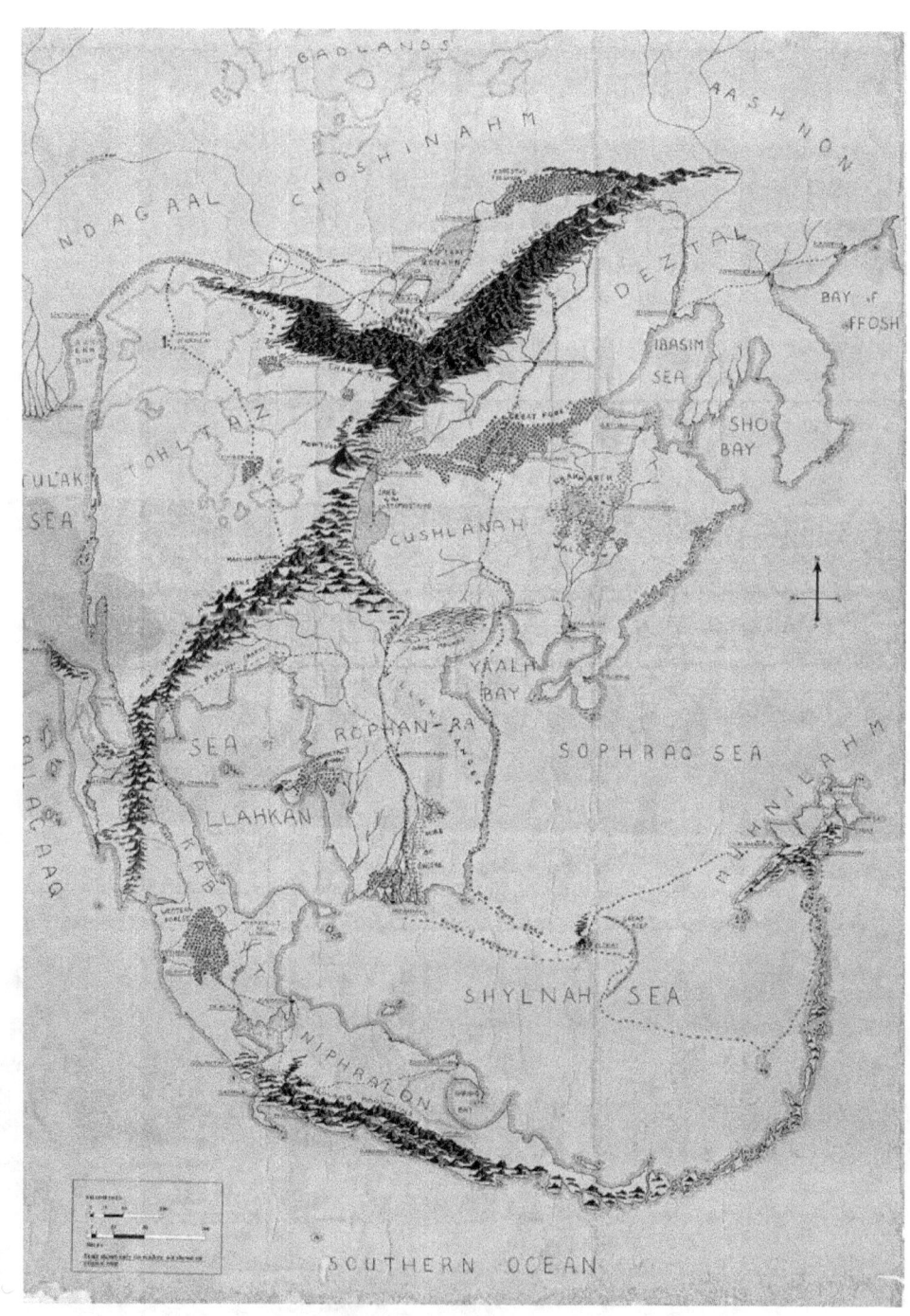

461

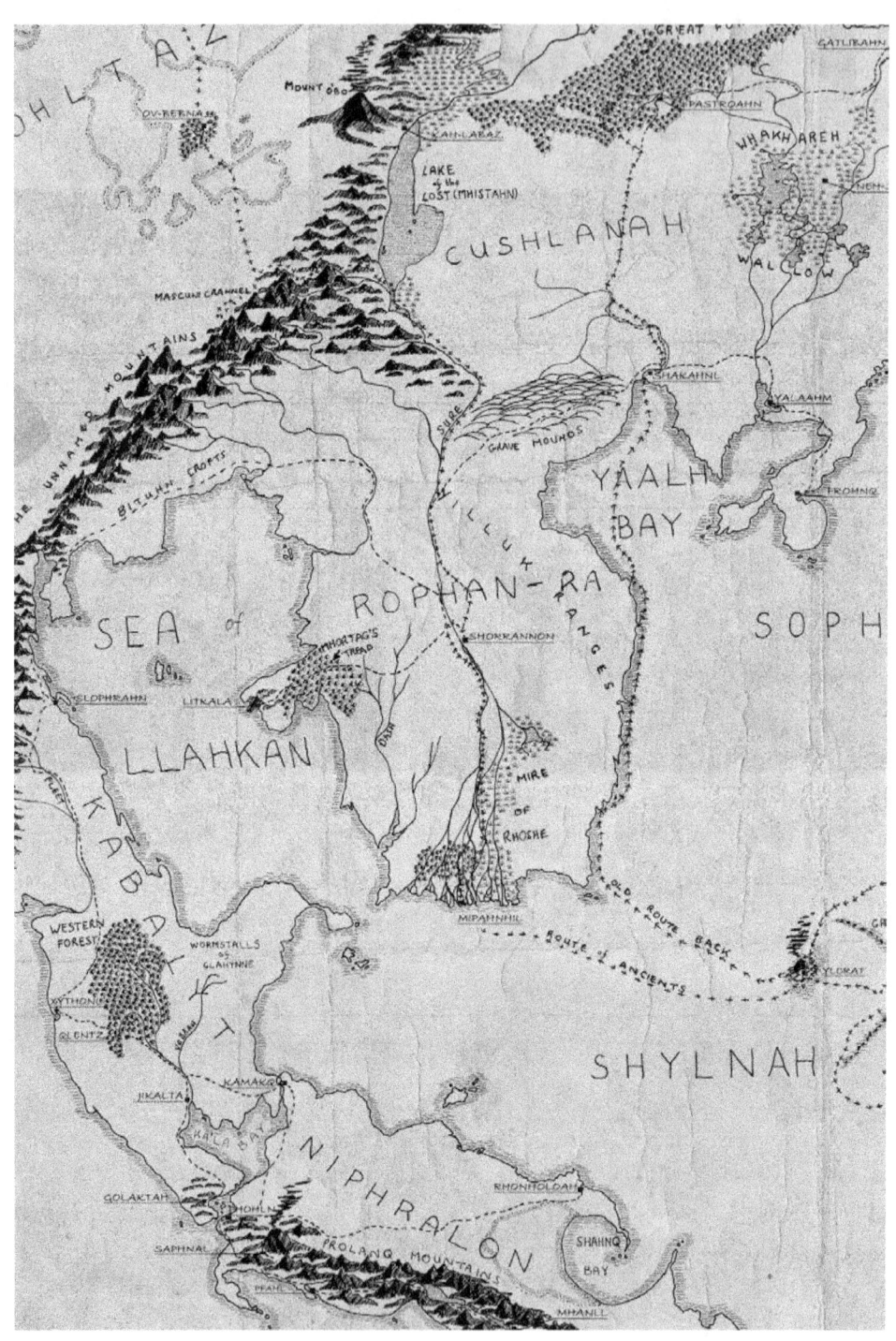

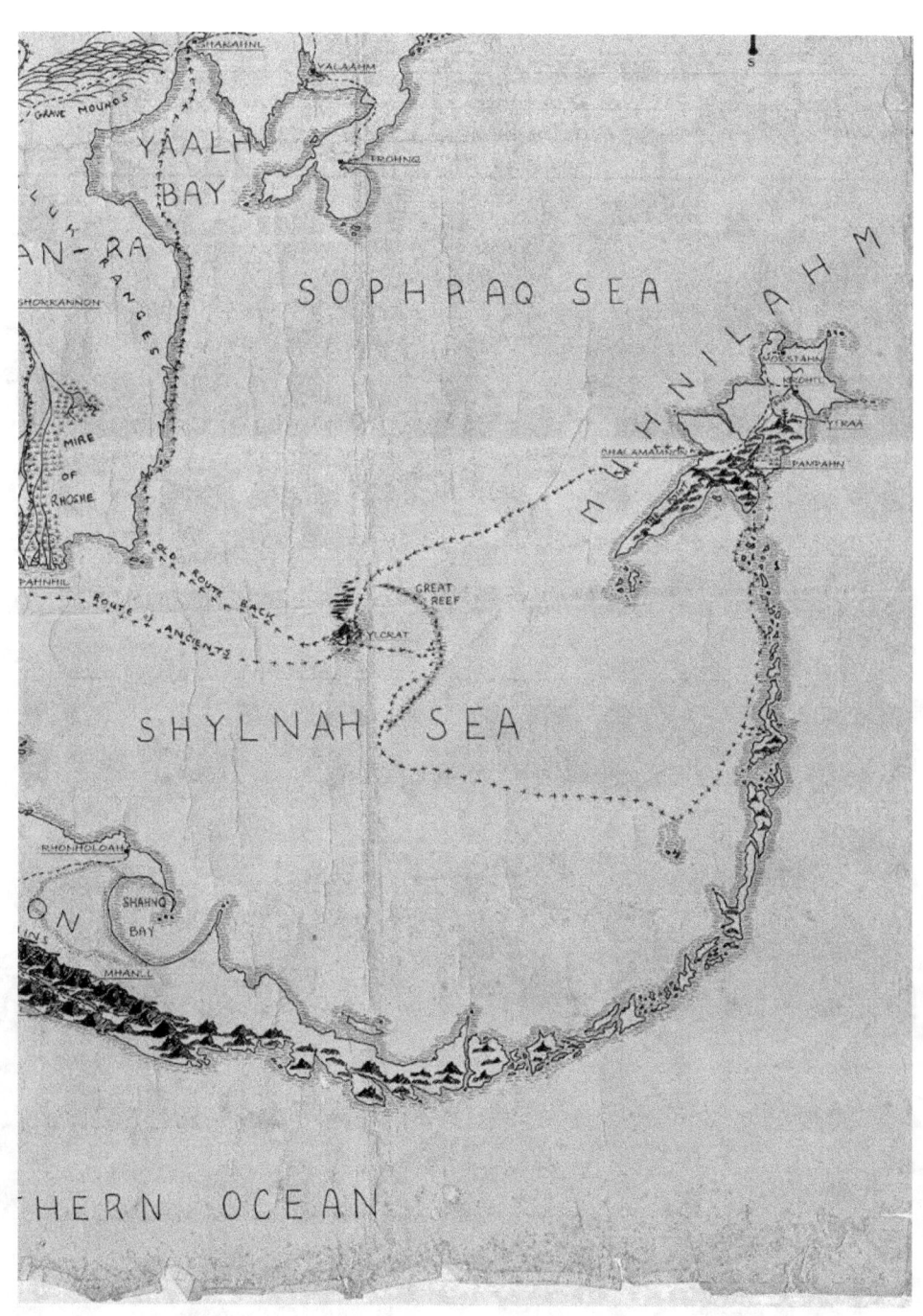

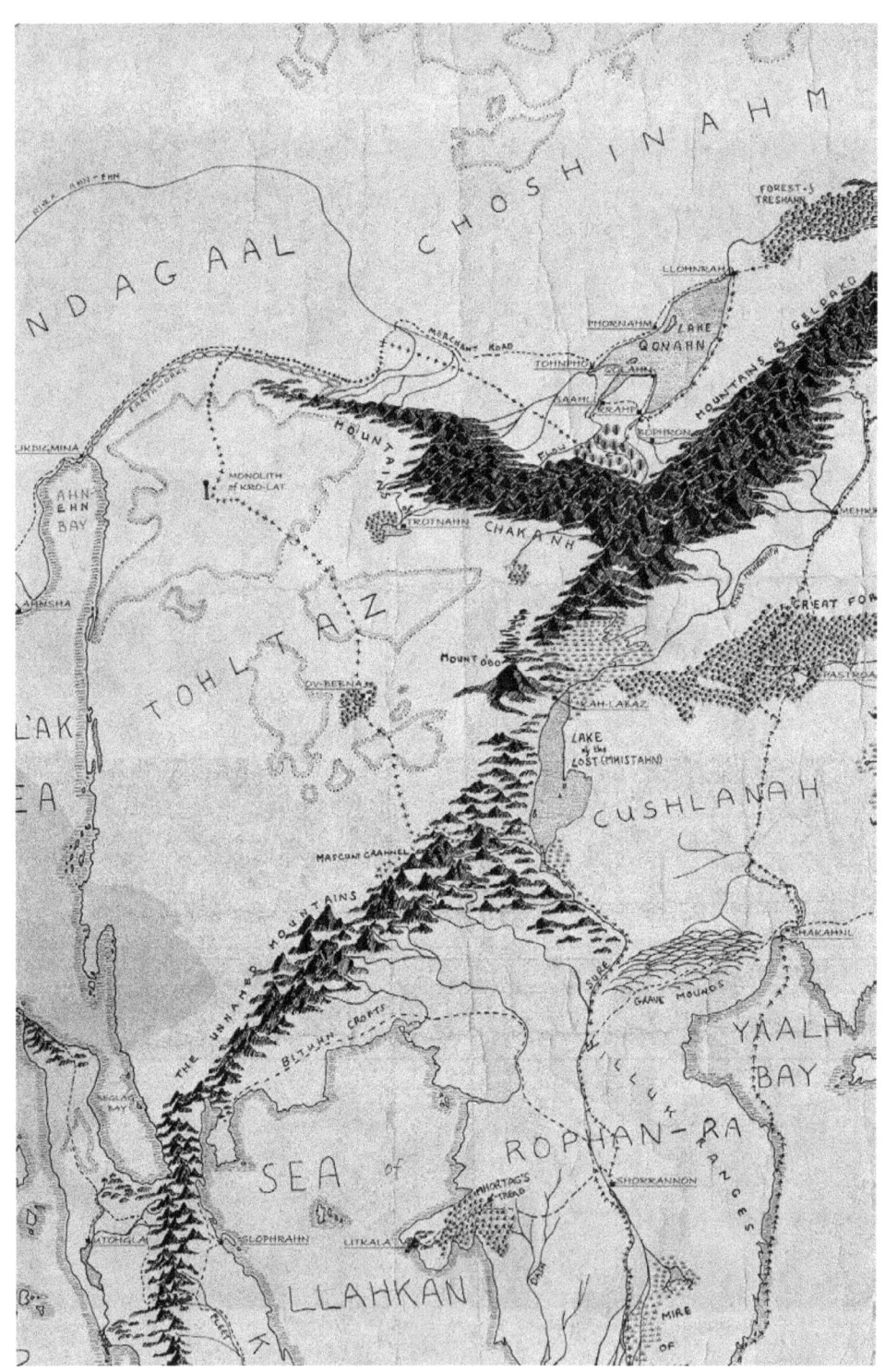

ABOUT THE AUTHOR

Stuart Aken is the author of other works of fiction. To explore these, please visit his blog at;

stuartaken.blogspot.com

Stuart loves to interact with his fans so please go and find him down on his various social media sites and say hi;

Tweet with him on Twitter
@StuartAken
Like his author page on Facebook
StuartAken
Join him on Goodreads
bit.ly/StuAkenGR
Pin with him on Pinterest
pinterest.com/stuartaken
Add him to your Google circles
bit.ly/StuAkenGPlus
Stumble with him on Stumbleupon
bit.ly/StumbleAken
And link with him on LinkedIn
bit.ly/StuAkenLinkedIn

If you've enjoyed this book, please tell your friends, and maybe find the time to place a brief review where others can discover what you think.

Characters in Alphabetical Order

Main players:

A'ahl is a young woman, held as consort by the village priest, Kaz-Ca-Wesdan. She is Caarl's wife and lives in Morstahn, Muhnilahm.

Aglydron is a pious Follower who chases the pilgrimage. He is Tumalind's father, Shoarhn's husband, and Chislanda's forced mate. He comes from Morstahn, Muhnilahm.

Aklon-Dji is Renegade and an outlaw with a price on his head. Leader of the Few, he is Dagla Kaz's disinherited son and Jodisa-Li's brother and was born in Chalamamnon, Muhnilahm.

Baklan is captain of the ship, Nupraxyss, and hails from Kabalyt. He was killed by the pirates in 'Joinings'.

Bardrohn is a whining volunteer Virgin Gift. He comes from Litkala, Rophan-Ra.

Byfthlyn is a volunteer Virgin Gift looking for adventure. He is from Kah-Labaz, Tohltaz.

Caarl is the senior soldier on the island of Muhnilahm and accompanies the pilgrims as expedition leader and guide. He is A'ahl's husband and lives in Morstahn, Muhnilahm.

Chellyth is a young woman who leads the criminals and outcasts living on The Point, Muhnilahm. She and her husband, Por-Kildu, are known as The One.

Chislanda is a bereaved mother from Mipahnhil, Rophan-Ra. Her husband is Doklas and she takes Aglydron as a mate.

Choryssa is a soldier from Krohtl, Muhnilahm. She is Delbon's partner when in town.

Corphanda, a tubby widow, looks after the female Virgin Gifts on the pilgrimage. She comes from Pampahn on Muhnilahm

Cymlihter is a dark haired slave to Kaz-Ca-Wesdan in Chalamamnon.

Dagla Kaz, the supreme ruler and High Priest of the Followers on the island of Muhnilahm, leads the pilgrims on their mission. He is father to Jodisa-Li, disinherits Aklon-Dji because of serious doctrinal and moral differences, and is based in Chalamamnon.

Dahrlahg is a rather dim young woman brought to help Shoarhn by Irrildys. She is Pentryil's betrothed, and lives in Morstahn, Muhnilahm.

Dahrlyth is a sex slave in Ov-Bebna, Tohltaz. She befriends and helps Okkyntalah.

467

Delbon is one of Aklon-Dji's trusted colleagues. His partner, Choryssa, is a soldier. He is a member of the Few and resident of Krohtl, Muhnilahm.

Dilanthas is a shy original Virgin Gift from Krohtl, Muhnilahm. She was one of the originals, Chosen to go on the pilgrimage.

Diryss, from Morstahn, becomes unwilling consort to village priest Kaz-Ca-Wesdan. He takes her to Chalamamnon, Muhnilahm.

Fehtohn is a vain young man and a volunteer Virgin Gift from Litkala, Rophan-Ra.

Feldrark is spiritual leader and Wharhll of Litkala, Rophan-Ra and married to Jodisa-Li. He is the only son of the Kiral and Kirallah.

Gidwallehn is a dutiful young man from Muhnilahm who volunteers as a Virgin Gift.

Hephrastihn is a nice girl from Kah-Labaz, Tohltaz, who volunteers to be a Virgin Gift.

Horsylth, a Palace servant in Litkala, Rophan-Ra, is a young woman with a fisherman for a partner.

Irrildys is an unhappy wife who seeks comfort from other men. She is Shoarhn's friend in Morstahn, Muhnilahm and one of the Few.

Ivdulon lives alone in a tower overlooking Litkala, Rophan-Ra. She is a wise woman, astronomer, inventor and mindtalker.

Jhonaht is the astronomer from Krohtl, Muhnilahm. He announced the arrival of the false Skyfire.

Jodisa-Li was heir apparent to Dagla Kaz, from Chalamamnon, Muhnilahm, until she met and married Feldrark. She is sister to Aklon-Dji.

K'ang Du-Saru is a highly muscular man who enjoys life as a Slaver. He is from Ov-Bebna, Tohltaz.

K'ang Fah-Tesi is a man who enjoys using women and acts as a Slaver from Ov-Bebna, Tohltaz.

K'ang Fi-Tozu, related to the Uhmbard, and put in charge of Slave trade in Ov-Bebna, Tohltaz. He is driven more by duty than ambition.

Kaz-Ca-Charrohn is the sexually demanding female Village Priest from Krohtl, Muhnilahm.

Kaz-Ca-Porlesah is the female Village Priest from Pampahn, Muhnilahm, who befriends Aklon-Dji.

Kaz-Ca-Uldrad becomes the male Village Priest in Morstahn, Muhnilahm, when his predecessor is promoted.

Kaz-Ca-Valorysta is a lower level Priest from Kah-Labaz, Tohltaz, who willingly becomes consort for Dagla Kaz, as she shares his peculiar sexual tastes.

Kaz-Ca-Wendarah is the ambitious female Village Priest from Chalamamnon, Muhnilahm, who becomes deputy for Dagla Kaz after returning from the pilgrimage.

Kaz-Ca-Wesdan is the predatory Village Priest from Morstahn, Muhnilahm. He acts as deputy High Priest in the absence of Dagla Kaz.

K'eng Hin-Seru is a cruel and petty man who is a Slaver from Ov-Bebna, Tohltaz.

K'eng Hok-Tusi is one of the male Slavers from Ov-Bebna, Tohltaz.

Lasdilyss, Phildrad's wife, is carer to his elderly parents in Pampahn, Muhnilahm, and a lover of Aklon-Dji.

Lethrymynyhl is a tall and willing volunteer female Virgin Gift from Kah-Labaz, Tohltaz.

Linlyss is a volunteer Virgin Gift from Litkala, Rophan-Ra. She is a gifted Lyre player who has designs on Okkyntalah.

Malarhah, a slave girl in Mipahnhil, Rophan-Ra, befriends Feldrark. She died in the fighting in 'Joinings'.

Myllthlan is a gifted Healer from the island of Ylcrat. She is loyal to Aglydron but loves Okkyntalah.

Netrodyl is a wayward, uneducated young woman who was rescued in a forest near Qlentz, Kabalyt.

Nuldron is an Engineer and mindtalker from Litkala, Rophan-Ra, who provides contact on a desert mission.

Okkyntalah is a brilliant hunter from Morstahn, Muhnilahm. He is Tumalind's betrothed and is loved by women.

Patradko Kaz is the male High Priest from Litkala, Rophan-Ra.

Patrilha is a soldier from Pampahn, Muhnilahm who meets Aklon-Dji at The Point.

Pedradol-Dji is the son of the High Priest at Kah-Labaz, Tohltaz. He volunteers as a Virgin Gift in hopes of impressing his father.

Pharah-Li, the spirited daughter of Rrildyss Kaz in Litkala, Rophan-Ra, has designs on Dagla Kaz.

Phildrad, a superb cook from Pampahn, Morstahn, is required to go on the pilgrimage. He is Lasdilyss' husband.

Por-Kildu is a much-scarred man who, with Chellyth, leads the criminals and deviants on The Point, Muhnilahm, as The One.

Porryh is an original Virgin Gift Chosen for the pilgrimage. She is troublesome and determined to change her status. She comes from Chalamamnon, Muhnilahm.

Quyreena is Captain of the ship, Mekoque. She belongs to a small cult that worships a female deity by living as lesbians. She originates from Ahnsha, Ndagaal.

Rehthlynn is a loyal subject from Litkala, Rophan-Ra. He takes on the role of guardian to the male Virgin Gifts.

Rrildyss Kaz is High Priest in Litkala, Rophan-Ra, a gossipy mindtalker and Pharah-Li's mother.

Shaulah is Okkyntalah's faithful hunting dog; a bitch.

Shoarhn is a farmer in Morstahn, Muhnilahm. She is Tumalind's mother, Aglydron's wife and Aklon's lover.

Sondukal is an experienced tracker and guide. He works from Litkala, Rophan-Ra, in the service of Feldrark.

Spiritman is a gifted Masseur in Litkala, Rophan-Ra, who is permitted to care for women as he lacks sexual parts.

Stellanyl is an attractive unattached young woman selected as Okkyntalah's sexual partner on the mission from Litkala, Rophan-Ra.

Syylvah, a nymphomaniac informant and member of the Few, who considers herself Aklon-Dji's lover, is married to the useless Wurrt in Chalamamnon, Muhnilahm.

Tah-Vlatak is a Dancer in Ov-Bebna, Tohltaz, where she entertains the Uhmbard. She befriends and guides Tumalind.

Tarruss, a gentle giant of a man, is taken on as guardian for the pilgrimage. He is a metalworker who comes from Krohtl, Muhnilahm.

Tasallyss is a Midwife in Morstahn, Muhnilahm, who attends A'ahl at the request of Shoarhn.

Teh-Blavv is a Harem wife of the Uhmbard's in Ov-Bebna, Tohltaz. She was born in Trotnahn and advises Tumalind.

Teh-Pavk is a Harem wife of the Uhmbard's in Ov-Bebna, Tohltaz. She is a mindtalker and helps Tumalind.

Tryonta acts as Dagla Kaz's trusted and feared henchman and comes from Chalamamnon, Muhnilahm.

Tumalind, an original Virgin Gift falsely Chosen to go on the pilgrimage, is Okkyntalah's betrothed and Shoarhn and Aglydron's daughter from Morstahn.

Uhstyhll is a male Virgin Gift from Muhnilahm, who volunteers for the pilgrimage as he has been branded a thief after stealing food in his early life.

Ven-Gadla is a helpful merchant from Kabalyt who provides transport.

Wakkyll is a volunteer Virgin Gift from Muhnilahm. His arrogance has prevented him finding a mate at home.

470

Xylthynn is a volunteer Virgin Gift from Litkala, Rophan-Ra. She is along on the mission in hopes of finding the right man, having failed to do so in the city.

Yatukon is the masked leader from Ylcrat. He is endowed with magical powers and subjugates the women of the island.

Yytlomohn is a volunteer Virgin Gift from Muhnilahm. She has escaped her controlling father who blamed her for the death of his wife in childbirth.

Zyreenha is a volunteer Virgin Gift from Litkala, Rophan-Ra. Her first betrothed died in an accident and she is seeking a new life away from that memory.

Mythical and Legendary Characters, and Titles in Use:

Dji: title of a recognised male heir to a High Priest.

Gadhallah: Revered Founder of the Followers, born in Choshinahm.

Galhta: title given the male leader of the people in Mipahnhil.

Holy Ones: a sect of extreme Followers who have powers over the general populace.

Kaz: title identifying the High Priest of the Followers.

Kaz-Ca: title of lower level priests to the Followers.

Kiral: title of the male civic leader in Litkala. Feldrark's father.

Kirallah: title of the female civic leader in Litkala. Feldrark's mother.

Krakgragog: the savage God of the Fire Mountain on Ylcrat.

Li: title of a recognised female heir to a High Priest.

Mhortag: the Devil, as accidentally created by Ytraa, according to Gadhallah.

Mythanpho: possibly legendary heroic figure and Vaarkil's wife on Lake Qonahn, Choshinahm.

Paltra: general title of respect for senior women.

Paltrohn: general title of respect for senior men.

Skyfire: the name given to a celestial sign (a comet) that presages doom for those who fail to Follow to the letter of the law.

Sonclusipah: Gadhallah's daughter and sole heir, born in Choshinahm.

Tryhnn: kindly Goddess of open water.

Ulkhon: the Sun God and reputedly Mythanpho's father.

Uhmbard Of Tohltaz: the leader-cum-God and harem owner in Ov-Bebna, Tohltaz.

Uhmteld Of Tohltaz: the senior wife to the Uhmbard in Ov-Bebna, Tohltaz.

Vaarkil: possibly legendary hero found in Lake Qonahn, Choshinahm. Offspring of Tryhnn and an unknown man. Mythanpho's husband.

Wharhll: title given to the spiritual leader in Litkala; traditionally male.

Yldohn   : deputy to Gadhallah and Zerryth's husband.

Ytraa: Supreme God of the Followers as determined by Gadhallah. This being is man, woman and God combined and is credited with creation of the world.

Zerryth: deputy to Gadhallah and Yldohn's wife.

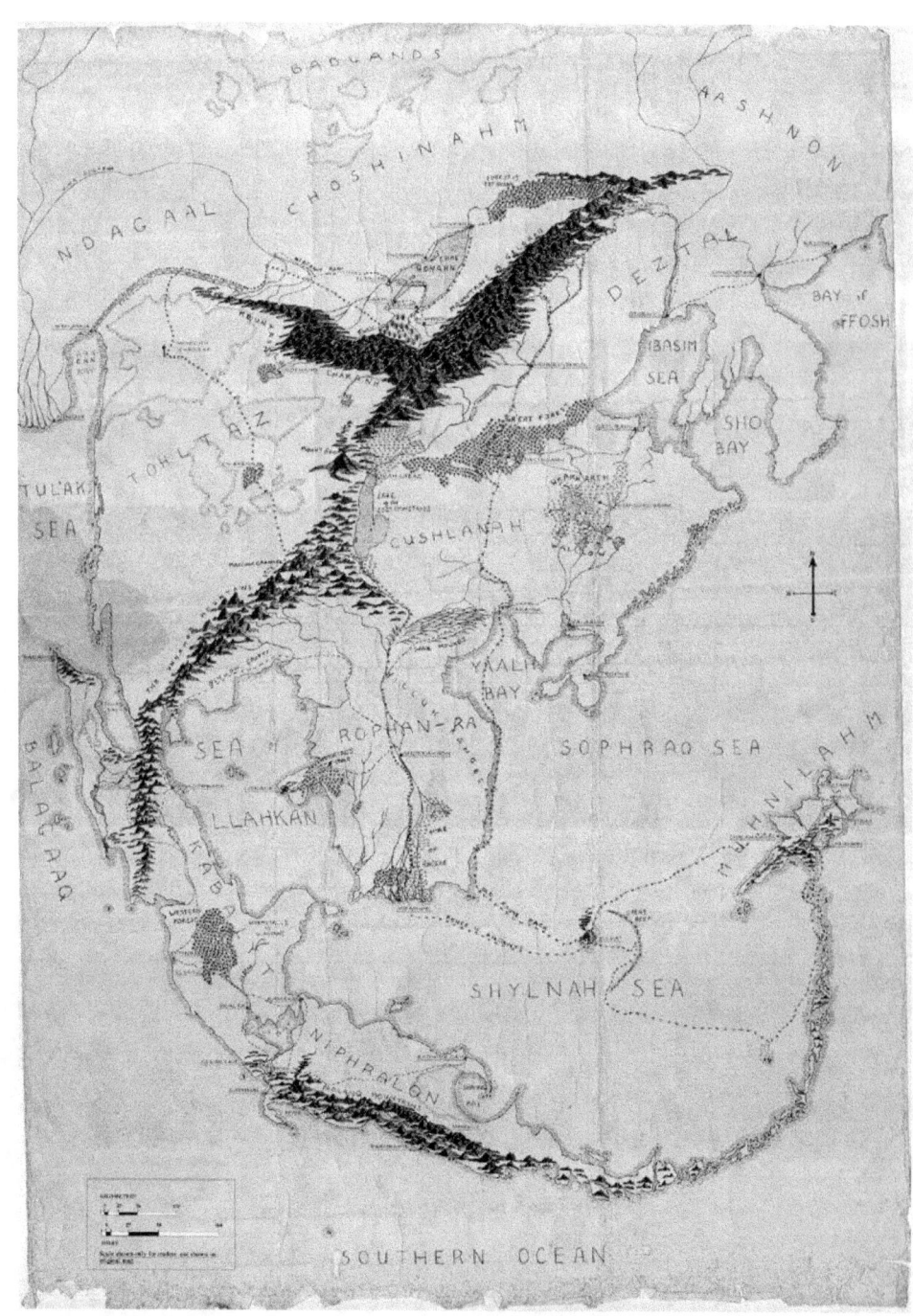

www.ingramcontent.com/pod-product-compliance
Lightning Source LLC
Chambersburg PA
CBHW081325020726

47506CB00006B/1187